THE DON FLOWS HOME

TO THE SEA

THE DON

Flows Home

to the SEA

By MIKHAIL SHOLOKHOV

TRANSLATED FROM THE RUSSIAN BY
STEPHEN GARRY

VINTAGE BOOKS
A Division of Random House
NEW YORK

CONTENTS

KEY TO
PRINCIPAL CHARACTERS

ANDREYANOV, Colonel. White officer; chief of staff to Gregor Melekhov.

ANIKUSHKA. A Cossack.

ASTAKHOV, STEPAN. A Cossack.

ASTAKHOVA, AKSINIA. Wife of Stepan.

BESKHLEBNOV, FILIP AGIEVICH. An old Cossack.

BOGATIRIEV, PIOTRA. Brigade commander in Don Cossack insurgent army.

CHUMAKOV. Squadron commander in Fomin's band.

FITZHELAUROV, General. Commander of White Volunteer Army forces.

FOMIN, YAKOV YEFIMOVICH. A Cossack commander, at first a red, then leader of a White bandit group.

GORCHAKOV, Captain. White officer, friend of Listnitsky.

GORCHAKOVA, OLGA NIKHOLAEVNA. Wife of Gorchakov.

KAPARIN, Captain. Red officer, afterwards Fomin's chief of staff.

KOPYLOV, MIKHAIL GREGOREVICH, Captain. Chief of staff to Gregor Melekhov.

KORSHUNOV, GRISHAKA. An old Cossack.

KORSHUNOV, MIRON GREGOREVICH. His son, father of Natalia Melekhova.

KORSHUNOVA, MARIA LUKINICHNA. Wife of Miron.

KORSHUNOV, DIMITRY MIRONOVICH (Mitka). Son of Miron and Maria Korshunov.

Principal Characters

KORSHUNOV, AGGRIPINA MIRONOVNA. Daughter of Miron and Maria.

KOSHELIOV, ALEKSANDR. A young Cossack, adherent of Fomin's.

KOSHEVOI, MIKHAIL (Mishka). A Red Cossack.

KOTLIAROV, IVAN ALEXIEVICH. A Red Cossack.

KUDYNOV. Commander of Don Cossack insurgent forces.

LISTNITSKY, NIKHOLAI ALEXIEVICH. A landowner.

LISTNITSKY, EUGENE NIKHOLAEVICH. Son of Nikholai Listnitsky, a White officer.

MELEKHOV, PANTALEIMON PROKOFFIEVICH. An elderly Cossack.

MELEKHOVA, ILINICHNA. Wife of Pantaleimon.

MELEKHOV, PIOTRA PANTALIEVICH. Pantaleimon's elder son; a Cossack officer.

MELEKHOV, GREGOR PANTALIEVICH (Grishka). Pantaleimon's younger son; a Cossack officer; commander of Cossack insurgent division.

MELEKHOVA, YEVDOKIA PANTALIEVNA (Dunia). Pantaleimon's daughter.

MELEKHOVA, DARIA. Wife of Piotra Melekhov.

MELEKHOVA, NATALIA. Wife of Gregor Melekhov.

MELEKHOV, MISHATKA. Son of Gregor and Natalia.

MELEKHOVA, POLYA (Poliushka). Daughter of Gregor and Natalia.

RYABCHIKOV, PLATON. Commander of Cossack insurgent regiment.

SEKRETOV, General. Commander of White Volunteer Army forces.

SHAMIL, MARTIN and ALEXEI. Cossacks, brothers.

STERLADNIKOV, VASSILY. Cossack, adherent of Fomin's.

STOCKMAN, OSIP DAVIDOVICH. A Communist organizer.

TOKIN, CHRISTONIA (Christan). An elderly Cossack.

YERMAKOV, KHARLAMPYI. Commander of Cossack insurgent regiment.

ZYKOV, PROKHOR. A Cossack; orderly to Gregor Melekhov.

Red Don or White

RED DON OR WHITE

Chapter 1

Long lines of trucks rolled from the Don through the Ukraine, carrying white flour, butter, eggs, and cattle to Germany. Each truck was guarded by a German soldier in a blue-grey tunic and peakless, round cap, his bayonet at the ready. The German yellow boots with iron-shod heels tramped over the Don tracks. The Bavarian cavalry led their horses down to drink in the Don. But on the Don-Ukrainian frontier the young mobilized Cossacks were fighting the Petlura regiments. Almost half the Twelfth Don Cossack Regiment was in action near Starobielsk, conquering a further piece of Ukrainian territory. To the north of the Don province the Bolsheviks were being driven back. Reorganized, and reinforced by officers from Novocherkass, the White Army was beginning to look like a real fighting force: the small detachments sent by the various districts were being amalgamated, the regular regiments were being reorganized and fitted out with their former equipment saved from the German war, the regiments were being formed into divisions, and the ensigns in charge at the staffs were being replaced by the original colonels, while even the commanding officers were gradually being changed.

By the end of the summer the army was crossing the Don frontiers and occupying the nearest villages of the Voronezh province.

3

For four days a squadron of Cossacks commanded by Piotra Melekhov had been marching northward through villages and districts. Somewhere to the right of them the Red Guards under Mironov were retreating towards the railway without risking a fight. During their march the Cossacks saw no sign of the enemy. They did not advance far at a time: without discussing the question, Piotra, and, for that matter, all the Cossacks, had decided that there was no point in hurrying to death.

On the fifth day they crossed the river Khoper. A swarm of midges hung like a muslin curtain over the meadowland; their fine, vibrating hum sounded incessantly. They crawled into the ears and eyes of the horses and the riders. The horses snorted and shook their heads, the Cossacks waved their arms and incessantly smoked home-grown tobacco.

Gregor was riding at the side of Christonia. They had kept together since the first day of their departure from Tatarsk. Anikushka, grown even fatter during the last few weeks and looking more like a woman than ever, had also attached himself to them.

The squadron numbered not quite a hundred. Piotra's assistant was Sergeant Major Latishev, who had married into a Tatarsk family. Gregor was in charge of a troop. His Cossacks were almost entirely drawn from the lower end of the village: Christonia, Anikushka, Prokhor Zykov, and a score of other, younger Cossacks. One of the other troops was commanded by Mitka Korshunov, who had been promoted to the rank of senior sergeant by General Alferov himself.

Piotra Melekhov and Latishev rode side by side. The Cossacks talked among themselves, occasionally breaking rank and riding five abreast. Some of them attentively surveyed the unfamiliar district, the meadowland, with pockmarks of ponds over it, the green barrier of willows and poplars in the distance. From their accoutrements it was evident that they were on a long expedition: their saddlebags were packed with clothing and equipment, and their greatcoats were carefully rolled and strapped at the backs of their saddles. Every strap of the horses' harnesses was well waxed, and everything was in good repair and drawn tight. A month previously they had been confident that there was not going to be a war, but now they rode with a humble realization that bloodshed could not be avoided.

They rode past a village with reed-thatched roofs to the huts. Anikushka pulled some home-made pastry from his trouser pocket, bit off half of it, and chewed away, his jaws working like a hare's.

"Hungry?" Christonia glanced at him.

"Why not? . . . My wife cooked this."

"You can guzzle!" Christonia said, and added in a complaining and indignant tone: "Chew away, you unclean spirit! Where does he shove it all?" He turned to Gregor. "It's horrible to look at him these days. He's not a big man, but he looks as though he's about to burst."

"Piotra Pantaleev, where are we going to spend the night?" Tomilin shouted.

Piotra waved his whip. "Maybe in the next village. Or maybe we'll push on to Kumilzhensk."

Merkulov smiled in his curly black beard and whispered to Tomilin:

"He's trying to get into Alferov's good books, the swine! He's in a hurry!"

They did halt in the next village for the night, and set out again at dawn for Kumilzhensk. But after riding some distance they were overtaken by a courier. Piotra opened the packet brought by the man, and sat swaying in his saddle as he read the letter, gripping the sheet of paper as tightly as though it were heavy. Gregor rode up to him.

"An order?" he asked.

"Aha!"

"What does it say?"

"I'm to hand over the squadron. All the men of my year of service are recalled and are to go to form the Twenty-eighth Regiment. The artillery-men and the machine-gunners also. It says: 'Put yourselves at the disposition of the commander of the Twenty-eighth Regiment. . . . To set out at once. . . .' At once!"

He turned to the squadron and shouted: "Forward!" The Cossacks rode on at a walking pace, glancing at one another and attentively watching Piotra, waiting for him to speak. On their arrival at Kumilzhensk he announced the terms of the order. The Cossacks of earlier enrolment bustled around preparing for their return journey. They decided to spend the night at Kumilzhensk and to break up and go their separate ways the next day at dawn. All day Piotra had been seeking an opportunity to have a talk with his brother, and now he went along to him in his quarters.

"Come out into the square," he invited Gregor.

Gregor silently followed him out. Mitka Korshunov came running after them, but Piotra coldly said:

"Clear off, Mitka! I want to have a talk with my brother."

Gregor glanced sidelong at Piotra and saw at once that he had something on his mind. He tried to turn the conversation into lighter channels:

"Isn't it strange! We've only ridden a hundred miles from home, and the people are quite different. They don't talk like us, and their buildings are not the same as ours. Look, there's a gate with a roof over it just like a shrine has. We don't have that. And look!" He pointed to a hut. "The ledge of that hut has got a covering to it also. So that the wood won't rot, I suppose?"

"Dry up!" Piotra scowled. "We're not out here to talk about that sort of thing."

"Well, what do you want to talk about?" Gregor asked, frowning impatiently.

"About everything." Piotra smiled guiltily and painfully and bit the ends of his whiskers. "The times are such, Grishka, that we may not see each other again. . . ."

The half-conscious hostility which Gregor had felt for his brother suddenly disappeared, swept away by Piotra's words and his miserable smile. The unhappy smile frozen on his lips, Piotra stared at his brother. With a movement of his mouth he suppressed the smile; his face hardened, and he said:

"Look how they've divided the people, the scum! Like a field with a plough, one on one side and another on the other. It's a devilish life and a terrible time. You, for instance, you're my blood brother, but I don't understand you, God's truth! I feel that you're going more and more away from me. That is true, isn't it? You know it is. I'm afraid you'll be going over to the Reds. You haven't found yourself yet, Grishka."

"And have you?" Gregor asked, staring as the sun set behind a chalky hill; all the western sky burned with the afterglow.

"Yes, I have. I've found my furrow. You won't turn me out of it. I shan't stumble like you, Gregor."

"Ho!" Gregor's lips curled in a smile.

"No, I won't!" Piotra angrily twirled his moustaches and blinked as though blinded. "You won't drag me into the Red noose. The Cossacks are against them, and so am I. I don't want to argue, and I won't! We don't go the same road."

"Drop this talk!" Gregor said wearily, and turned to go to his quarters. At the gate Piotra halted and asked:

"Tell me, I want to know. . . . Tell me, Gregor, you won't go over to them?"

"I don't know."

Gregor replied limply and reluctantly. Piotra sighed, but he did not question his brother further. He walked away disturbed and hollow-cheeked. To both him and Gregor it was painfully clear that the track which they had travelled together was lost in an impenetrable undergrowth of experience. Just as a path, beaten out by horse-hoofs, slips down a hillside, and at the very bottom abruptly ends in a thicket of bushes.

Next day Piotra led half the squadron back towards Vieshenska. The remaining youngsters set out under Gregor's command for Arzemovsk. From early morning the sun baked mercilessly. The steppe seethed in a brown haze. Behind them loomed the blue lines of hills, and sand stretched in a saffron flood. The sweating horses swung along at a walking pace. The Cossacks' faces browned and flushed beneath the sun. The saddle-peaks, stirrups, and snaffles were so hot that they could not be touched with the bare hand. There was no cool even in the forest: there also hung a steaming vapour and the strong scent of rain.

Gregor was troubled by a dull yearning. All day as he swayed in the saddle he thought disconnectedly of the future. Like the beads of a glass necklace Piotra's words tinkled in his ears. The bitter taste of wormwood burned his lips, the road smoked with the heat. Under the sun the golden-brown steppe extended full length, while arid breezes wandered over it and sent the dust flying.

Towards evening a translucent mist veiled the sun. The sky faded and greyed. In the west, clouds gathered mournfully, hanging almost motionless on the fine-spun thread of the horizon. Then, driven before the wind, they floated on menacingly, dragging their brown tails irritatingly low, their edges turning a sugary white.

The detachment crossed a rivulet and pressed into a poplar wood. Before the wind the leaves revealed their milky-blue under sides and murmured in deep tones. Somewhere beyond the river Khoper a slanting, sleety rain was scattered from the white fringes of the clouds, and the colourful hues of a rainbow appeared on its curtain.

They spent the night in a lonely little village. Gregor saw to his horse, then went out into the garden of his quarters. His host, an elderly, curly-haired Cossack, told him anxiously:

"You see that beehive? I bought the swarm the other day, and now for some reason all the young ones are dying off. Look, the bees are dragging them out." They halted by the log hive, and he pointed to the opening. With a low buzzing, the bees were bringing out the young ones' bodies and flying off with them.

The master regretfully screwed up his eyes and bitterly smacked his lips. He had a jerky walk and swung his arms violently and awkwardly. Gregor stared at him with a vague feeling of dislike.

Gregor sat down in the kitchen to drink tea sweetened with thick, sticky honey like gluc. The honey smelt sweetly of herbs and meadow flowers. The tea was poured out by the master's daughter, a tall, handsome soldier's wife. Her husband had retreated with the Reds, and so her father was conciliatory and peaceable. He did not appear to notice his daughter's swift glance under her lashes at Gregor. She stretched out her hand for the tea-pot, and Gregor saw the gleaming, curly black hair in her armpits. More than once his eyes met her groping, inquisitive glance, and he thought she flushed and smiled warmly as their eyes crossed.

"I'll make your bed up in the front room," she said after the tea, and went to fetch a pillow and rug. As she passed him she scorched him with an openly hungry glance. While puffing up the pillow she said hurriedly and quietly, as though the matter were of no import: "I sleep under the shed. It's stifling in the hut, and the fleas bite. . . ."

Gregor removed only his boots, and as soon as he heard the old Cossack snoring, he went to her under the shed. She made room for him at her side, drew the sheepskin over herself, and lay silent, touching Gregor with her legs. Her lips were dry and harsh, smelling of onions and an intangible freshness. Gregor lay in her slender, swarthy arms until dawn. All night she pressed him violently to herself, insatiably caressing him, with jest and laughter biting his lips till the blood came, and leaving on his neck, breast, and shoulders the blue marks of her biting kisses and the tiny traces of her fine teeth. After the third cock he tried to rise to go to the hut, but she held him back.

"Let me go, dear; let me go, my little berry!" he pleaded, smiling in his moustache and gently trying to release himself.

"Lie a little longer . . . lie down."

"But we'll be seen. It'll be light soon."

"Well, let them see us!"

"But how about your father?"

"He knows."

"What do you mean?" Gregor raised his brows in amazement.

"Why, you see . . . yesterday he told me that if the officer wanted to I was to sleep with him, for otherwise they'd take away the horse because of my husband, or something worse. . . . My husband's gone off with the Reds."

"So that's it!" Gregor smiled humourously, although in his soul he felt affronted.

She dissipated his unpleasant feelings. Amorously fondling the muscles of his arm, she shivered and said:

"My husband isn't like you. . . ."

"What is he like, then?" Gregor asked, staring with sobered eyes at the paling vault of heaven.

"He's no good . . . he's weak. . . ." She trustingly nestled against Gregor, and dry tears sounded in her voice. "I lived with him without any sweetness in my life. He s no good for a woman's need."

This unknown, childishly naïve soul opened simply to Gregor's eyes, as simply as a little dew-fed flower opens. Gregor was intoxicated, and his pity was aroused. He caressingly stroked the rumpled hair of his new-found friend and closed his weary eyes.

The fading light of the moon soaked through the reed roof of the shed. A falling star sped violently towards the horizon, leaving a dying phosphorescent train in the ashen sky. A duck quacked on the pond, and the drake called with an amorous hoarseness.

Gregor went off to the hut, lightly carrying his chilly body, flooded with a delicious ringing weariness. He fell asleep with the salty taste of her lips on his lips, carefully preserving in his memory the Cossack woman's yearning body and its scent—a complex scent of herb honey, sweat, and warmth.

He was awakened by his Cossacks two hours later. Prokhor Zykov saddled his horse and led it outside the gate. Gregor said good-bye to the master, whose eyes firmly met Gregor's hostile stare, and nodded to the daughter as she passed into the hut. She bent her head; a smile and the intangible bitterness of regret lurked in the corners of her fine lips.

He rode down the side street, staring back. The lane wound past the hut where he had spent the night, and he saw the woman he had warmed gazing after him across the fence, her palm shielding her eyes. With unexpected yearning Gregor looked back and tried to discern the expression on her face, to take in all her figure. But he could not. He saw only her head turning as her eyes followed him, as the head of a sunflower turns to follow the slow, semicircular march of the sun.

Chapter 2

In April 1918 there was a great cleavage in the Don province. The front-line Cossacks of the northern districts retired with the retreating detachments of Red Guards, while the Cossacks of the lower districts drove and pressed them towards the frontiers of the province, fighting at every step to free their native land.

Only in 1918 was this great cleavage accomplished. Yet it had had its beginnings hundreds of years previously, when the poorer Cossacks of the north, who had neither rich land nor vineyards nor valuable hunting and fishing grounds, broke away from Cherkass, from time to time made arbitrary descents upon the districts of Great Russia, and were the main stronghold of all rebels from the time of Stenka Razin onward. Even in later days, when the entire province, crushed by the czarist autocracy, was seething with unrest, it was the Cossacks of the upper districts who openly rose and, led by their atamans, shook the czarist system, fighting the

Imperial troops, plundering caravans on the Don, and raising the province to insurrection.

By the beginning of May 1918 two thirds of the Don province was clear of Bolsheviks. It became necessary to set up some form of local government, and May 11 was fixed as the date for the assembly of members of the Don Provisional Government and delegates from the districts and villages. At a meeting of the Vieshenska district Pantaleimon Melekhov was elected as a delegate. Together with Miron Korshunov he set out to drive to Millerovo at dawn of May 6, in order to reach Novocherkass betimes. Miron went with him to Millerovo to buy some paraffin, soap, and other things for domestic needs, and also to make a little money by purchasing some sieves for Mokhov's mill.

Miron Korshunov's raven horses easily drew along the light wagonette. The two men sat side by side in the colourful wicker basket. They reached the top of the hill above the village and began to talk. The Germans were stationed in Millerovo, and so Miron asked anxiously:

"Do you think the Germans will have a whack at us? They're an evil lot."

"No," Pantaleimon reassured him. "Matvei Kashulin was in Millerovo the other day, and he says they're afraid. They don't dare touch the Cossacks."

Miron laughed into his beard and played with his cherrywood knout. Evidently happier in mind, he turned the conversation to other matters.

"What government will you set up, do you think?" he asked.

"We'll have an ataman. One of ourselves. A Cossack!"

"God grant it! Choose a good one. Put the generals through their paces as a gypsy does a horse."

"We will. The Don is not yet poor in wise heads."

They lapsed into silence. A breeze chilled their backs. Behind them across the Don the flaming fire of the dawn was splendidly, silently burning the forests, the meadows, the lakes, and woodland glades. A sandy rise looked like yellow copper, and the stunted bushes reflected a dull bronze.

They arrived at Millerovo the next evening and spent the night with a Ukrainian acquaintance living by the elevator. After breakfast next morning Pantaleimon went to the railway station, while

Miron harnessed his horses and drove off to the shops. He safely passed the level crossing, and then for the first time in his life he saw Germans. Three Landsturmers were coming straight towards him. One of them, a short, thick-bearded man, waved his hand.

Anxiously chewing his lips, Miron pulled on the reins to stop his horses. The Germans came up to him. A tall, well-fed Prussian said with a smile:

"Look, there's a real live Cossack! He's even wearing Cossack clothes. I expect his son fought against us. Let's send him alive to Berlin. He'd make a queer exhibit."

"We want his horses; he can go to the devil!" one of the others replied. He cautiously passed round the horses' heads and approached the wagonette.

"Down you get, old man! We need your horses to take some flour from the mill to the station." He pointed to the mill and, with a gesture that left no doubt of his meaning, invited Miron to get down. His two comrades turned away and walked towards the mill, looking back and laughing. Miron went a greyish yellow, jumped nimbly out of the wagonette, and went to the horses' heads to lead them. But the German pursed his lips, seized Miron by the sleeve, and signed to him to turn back.

"Let go!" Miron pulled himself away and turned whiter. "You're not going to have my horses."

By Miron's tones the German guessed the nature of the reply. He bared his teeth, stared fixedly at the Cossack, and raised his voice authoritatively. He took hold of the strap of the rifle slung across his shoulder, but at that moment Miron remembered his youth. He gave the man a short arm jab with his fist on the cheekbone. The German fell headlong, and as he tried to get up Miron gave him another blow on the back of his head, glanced around him, and snatched up the man's rifle. He knew now that the man could not fire at him as he turned the horses round, and his only fear was lest he had been seen from the railway. Never before had the raven horses galloped at such a pace! Not even at a wedding had the wagonette wheels rattled so violently. "Lord, save me! Defend me, Lord! In the name of the Father!" Miron muttered as he incessantly used his whip. His inborn greed was almost his undoing: he wanted to drive to the Ukrainian to collect his things. But his prudence won, and he turned out of the town. He drove the eight miles to the first village swifter (as he afterwards put it) than the prophet ✦ Elijah in his chariot of fire. He turned into the yard of a Ukrainian acquaintance and, more dead than alive, told the man what had happened, imploring him to hide him and his horses.

"Hide me! I'll pay you whatever you like! Only save me from death and hide me somewhere. I'll send you a flock of sheep. I'll not regret half a score of my best sheep!" Miron pleaded and promised.

He remained with the Ukrainian until night was falling, then drove off again like a madman at a gallop, until the horses were covered with foam. Only when he had put a good distance between himself and Millerovo did he rein in the horses.

But he did not send the Ukrainian the promised sheep. That autumn he happened to call at the village and, catching the man's eyes fixed expectantly on him, he told him:

"Our sheep have all died off. . . . We're in a bad way as regards sheep, but I've brought you some pears from my own garden for old time's sake." He hoisted out of his wagon a sackful of pears damaged by the journey and, with eyes averted, remarked: "Our pears are good, very good. . . ." Then he hurriedly said good-bye.

While Miron was galloping out of Millerovo, Pantaleimon was at the railway station. A young German officer wrote out a pass for him, questioned him through an interpreter, and benevolently told him:

"You can have a pass, but remember that you need an intelligent government. Elect a president, a czar, or what you will, provided he has some statesmanship and carries out a loyal policy in regard to Germany."

Pantaleimon stared at him with unfriendly eyes, took his pass, and went to buy his ticket. Arrived at Novocherkass, he was amazed at the number of young officers in the town. They crowded the streets, were sitting in the restaurants, and flocked around the ataman's palace and the court of justice where the Council was to be held.

In the house set apart for the delegates Pantaleimon met several other Cossacks from his district. The delegates were mainly composed of Cossacks, there being only a few officers and rather more representatives of the provincial intelligentsia. The talk centred on the question of electing a provincial government, but only one thing emerged clearly: an ataman must be chosen. The names of several popular Cossack generals were being bandied about, and the merits of respective candidates discussed. But none appeared to be satisfactory.

One of the men taking part in the discussion, a lieutenant and district delegate, spoke with some heat:

"What do you mean, 'There isn't any suitable man'? How about General Krasnov?"

"What Krasnov?"

"Gentlemen, aren't you ashamed to ask? He's a famous general, commander of the third cavalry corps, intelligent, a Cavalier of St. George, and a highly talented regimental commander."

The lieutenant's fervent adulatory words provoked a delegate representing one of the active-service regiments to remark:

"And I tell you we know all about his talents! A fine general he is! He distinguished himself all right in the German war! He'd never have got beyond a brigadier if it hadn't been for the revolution."

"How dare you say that, when you don't know General Krasnov?" the lieutenant answered in icy tones. "And how dare you talk like that about a general who is universally respected? You appear to have forgotten that you're a rank-and-file Cossack."

The Cossack was overcome with confusion, and muttered:

"All I say, Your Excellency, is that I myself served under his command. On the Austrian front he ran our regiment up against the barbed wire. And so we don't think much of him. But, of course, he may be quite different!"

"What do you think they gave him the Cross of St. George for? You fool!" Pantaleimon hurled himself on the front-line man. "You've got into the habit of grumbling; everything's bad, you can't stand anything. If you'd talked a little less there wouldn't have been all the mess we're in now. You magpies!"

All the Cherkass district was solidly in favour of Krasnov. The old men liked him; many of them had served with him in the Japanese war. The officers were delighted with his past; he was a Guards officer and splendidly educated; he had been in the Imperial Palace and the Emperor's suite. The liberal intelligentsia were satisfied with the circumstance that he was not only a general, but also a writer whose stories of officers' life had appeared in various journals, so that although he was a military man he was cultured.

So when, on the third day of the Council, a tall general strode on to the platform, the hall broke into a thunder of handclaps and cheers. This general, youthfully handsome despite his years, posing in a picture-postcard attitude, his chest covered with crosses and medals, his face expressing his agitation, seemed to many of those present a first faint revival of the former Imperial might.

Pantaleimon's eyes watered, and he snuffled into his red handkerchief. "There's a general! You can see at once he's a man! Rather like the Emperor, and you could easily mistake him for the dead Alexander," he thought.

Krasnov made a brilliant, perfectly conceived speech. He talked movingly of Russia under the curse of the Bolsheviks, of its former might, and of the fate of the Don. He outlined the present situation, briefly touched on the German occupation, and aroused a tumult of approbation when he ended his peroration by referring to the possibility of an independent existence for the Don when the Bolsheviks had been defeated.

"The Military Council will govern the Don province. The Cossackry, liberated by the Revolution, will restore all the splendid ancient order of Cossack life, and we, like our forefathers in the days of old, will say in ringing, powerful voices: 'Your health, White Czar of Kremlin Moscow, from us, the Cossacks of the gentle Don.'"

He was elected military ataman that same evening. But he would not accept the position until the Council had conceded certain conditions. He demanded unlimited powers in his capacity as ataman, and agreement to certain fundamental laws. As the latter were merely the laws of the former Imperial régime, slightly modified to bring them into conformity with the new situation in the Don, the Council agreed, and agreed with gladness. Even the flag he proposed was reminiscent of former days: blue, red, and yellow stripes (to signify the Cossacks, foreign settlers, and Kalmyks). Only the governmental armorial bearings suffered a radical change as a concession to the national spirit. Instead of the rapacious double-headed eagle with outspread wings and unsheathed talons, they represented a naked Cossack with a fur cap on his head, armed with sword, rifle, and ammunition, riding a wine-barrel bareback.

The Council dispersed on May 18. The members went home satisfied, delighted with the choice of ataman and with the news from the front.

Deeply moved, possessed by a tremulous gladness, Pantaleimon Prokoffievich took the train back from Novocherkass. He was unshakably convinced that the ataman's power had passed into good hands, that the Bolsheviks would be quickly beaten and his sons would return to the farm. As he sat in the car with his elbows on the table, he could still hear the farewell strains of the Don hymn.

But the train had not travelled many miles from Novocherkass when through the window he saw the advance patrols of Bavarian cavalry. A group of horsemen was riding at the side of the railway track, coming towards the train. Leaning forward, his eyebrows knitted, Pantaleimon watched the hoofs of the horses triumphantly treading the Don earth. After they had passed he sat for a long time huddled in his seat, breathing heavily, his back to the window.

Chapter 3

Mikhail Koshevoi was driven by forced marches from Vieshenska to the front. He reached the district village of Fiedoseev, but there the district ataman kept him for a day, then sent him back to Vieshenska under escort.

"Why are you sending me back?" Mikhail asked the district secretary.

"We've received instructions from Vieshenska," the man replied reluctantly.

When he reached Vieshenska it transpired that his mother had crawled on her knees to the village assembly and had pleaded with the elders, who in the name of the community had sent a request that he should be made a drover on the district horse ranch. The district ataman shouted this information at Mishka, and angrily ended his harangue:

"We won't trust Bolsheviks with the defence of the Don! You

can go to the horse ranch, and afterwards we shall see. Look at me, you son of a swine! We had pity on your mother, or we'd have . . . Clear out!"

Mishka wandered down the street unescorted. Weary with his miles of tramping, his feet refused to obey him. He just managed to trudge to his village by nightfall, and the next day, wept over and caressed by his mother, he rode out to the horse ranch, carrying in his memory the picture of his mother's ageing face and the first strands of silver in her hair.

To the south of Kargin the virgin, never furrowed steppe stretched in a tract some twenty-five miles long and four broad. This piece of land of many thousands of acres had been set apart as a grazing ground for the district stallions. Every year on St. Yegor's day the drovers drove the stallions from their winter stables and brought them to the pasturage. A stable, and barracks for the drovers, overseer, and a veterinary surgeon, had been built with money assigned from the district exchequer. Each year the Cossacks of the Vieshenska district would bring out their mares, and the veterinary surgeon and the overseer would ascertain that each mare was of the requisite size. The healthy mares were gathered into droves of forty, and each stallion would lead its drove off into the steppe, guarded by a drover who jealously watched over his mares.

Mishka rode off to the ranch on the one horse belonging to his farm. By noonday, beyond the steaming haze rising above a dell, Mishka discerned the barracks and the grey weather-stained roof of the stables. Still farther, far to the east, he could see a brown patch of horses running down to a pond. A rider galloped—a toy man on a toy horse—at their side.

Mishka rode into the barrack yard, dismounted, tied the reins to the pillar of the porch, and went inside. In the spacious corridor he was met by one of the drovers, a thickset, freckled Cossack.

"Who do you want?" he asked in an unfriendly voice, scanning Mishka from head to foot.

"I want the overseer."

"He's not here. He's gone out. His assistant's here. Second door on the left. And what do you want him for? Where are you from?"

"I've come as a drover."

"Fine men they send out! . . ." the man went muttering towards the door. The rope of his lasso, thrown across his shoulder, dragged on the floor behind him. Opening the door and standing with his back to Mishka, he waved his whip and said more kindly: "Ours is heavy work, brother. Sometimes we spend a couple of days on end in the saddle."

Mishka stared at his rounded shoulders and bandy legs. In the light of the doorway every line of his awkward figure was silhouetted distinctly and sharply. His bow legs amused Mishka. "He looks as if he'd ridden forty years bareback on a barrel," he thought as he fumbled for the door latch.

The assistant overseer received the new drover calmly and cere-monially. Soon afterwards the overseer himself arrived. He was a healthy-looking Cossack, a former sergeant major of the Ataman regiment. He gave instructions for Mishka to be included on the ration roll and went out with him to the porch.

"Can you train horses?" he asked. "Have you ever broken in a horse?"

"I can't say I have," Mishka admitted frankly, and at once noticed a shade of dissatisfaction pass across the overseer's face. Scratching his back, the man stared fixedly at Mishka.

"Can you use a lasso?" he asked.

"I can."

"And you're decent to horses?"

"Yes."

"They're like human beings, only they're dumb. Be decent to them!" he ordered and, needlessly going into a fury, he shouted: "Look after them, and not with the whip!"

For a moment his face was thoughtful and animated, but the expression immediately passed, and a heavy crust of dull equanimity took its place.

"Married?"

"No."

"You're a fool! You ought to get married!" the overseer gladly pulled him up.

He stood silently staring for a moment into the far-flung breast of the steppe, then yawned and went into the barracks. During a month's service as drover Mishka heard not a word more from his lips.

All together there were fifty-five stallions on the ranch, and each drover had two or three droves to look after. Mishka was entrusted

with a large drove led by a powerful old stallion named Bakhar,
and a smaller drove of some twenty mares and a stallion nicknamed
Banal. The overseer sent for one of the most efficient and fearless
of the drovers, a man named Soldatov, and told him:

"Here's a new drover. Mikhail Koshevoi from Tatarsk village.
Show him Banal's and Bakhar's droves and give him a lasso. He'll
live in your hut. Show him where. Off with you!"

Soldatov silently lit a cigarette and nodded to Mishka:
"Come on."

In the porch he asked, pointing to Mishka's mare standing half
asleep in the sun:
"That your animal? In foal?"

"No."

"Put her to Bakhar. He's from the Imperial stud farm, a cross
with an English horse. Well, up you get!"

They rode off together. The horses waded up to their knees in
grass. Before them, wrapped in a tender blue haze, the steppe lay
majestically silent. The sun streamed down from the zenith beyond
a thread of opal clouds. A heavy, oppressive aroma arose from the
hot grass. To the right the pearly-white, smiling surface of a lake
gleamed in the mistily outlined depression of a dale. But all around,
as far as the eye could see, was green, illimitable space, quivering
streams of haze, the ancient steppe fettered in the noonday heat,
and on the horizon a magically, intangibly azure mound.

The two Cossacks rode along without talking. Mishka was experiencing a new feeling of quiet humility. The steppe oppressed
him with its silence, its all-wise majesty. Bent towards his horse's
mane, his companion dozed in his saddle, his freckled hands folded
over the saddle-bow as though he were about to receive the sacrament.

Mishka took over the two droves allotted to him and put his
things into the field hut. Three other drovers shared the hut with
him, Soldatov being their senior. He willingly introduced Mishka
to his duties, telling him the character and habits of the stallions,
and with a thin smile advising him:

"By rights you're supposed to do your work on your own horse,
but if you go on riding her day after day, you'll wear her out. Let
her join the drove, saddle someone else's, and change horses pretty
often."

Before Mishka's eyes he selected a mare from the drove and dextrously lassoed her. He saddled her with Mishka's saddle and led her up to him.

"Mount this one! You can see she's never been broken in, the devil! Up you get!" he shouted angrily, pulling strongly with his right hand on the reins, while his left pressed against the mare's belly. Handle them gently! And keep your eyes open for Bakhar. Don't ride too near him or he'll smash you," he added as he held the stirrup and fondly patted the mare's udder.

For a week Mishka rested, spending all day in the saddle. The steppe humbled him, authoritatively compelled him to live a primitive, vegetative existence. The drove would shift around not far off, and Mishka would sit dozing in the saddle or, throwing himself down on the grass, would thoughtlessly watch the white flocks of clouds wandering over the sky. At first this state of renunciation of the world delighted him. Life so remote from people even seemed pleasant. But towards the end of the first week, when he was accustomed to his new situation, a vague fear began to trouble him. "Over there people are settling their own and others' fates, and here I am minding mares. I must clear off or I shall dry up!" he thought. But a second, lazy whisper inside him said: "Let them fight; there they're dying, but here there is liberty, grass and sky. There men are angry, but here there is peace. Why worry over what others are doing?" Yet his thoughts began to prick his humble quietude, and this drove him to seek the company of others. He tried more frequently than at first to fall in with Soldatov and attempted to make his closer acquaintance.

Evidently Soldatov was never oppressed by his loneliness. He rarely spent the night in the hut, but was almost always with his droves. He lived an animal life. He was always planning new ways of preparing food, and could cook unusually well, as though he had done nothing else all his life. Once he saw Mishka plaiting a fish-line from horsehair, and asked him:

"What are you doing that for?"

"To catch fish."

"And where are the fish?"

"In the lake."

"What do you catch them with?"

"With bread and worms."

"You're not joking?"

"Have a bit!" Mishka pulled a piece of carp out of his trouser pocket and offered it to Soldatov.

Another time, as Mishka was following his drove, he came upon a bustard caught in a trap set by Soldatov. Near by stood a cleverly made imitation of a bustard, and the nets were artfully hidden in the grass. Soldatov cooked the bustard that same evening in a hole in the ground, first scattering burning coals over it. He invited Mishka to dine with him.

"How did you come to be here?" Mishka asked him.

"I'm an only son." Soldatov was silent for a moment, then he asked abruptly: "Listen! Is it true what the boys say, that you're one of the Reds?"

Not expecting such a question, Mishka was embarrassed.

"No—well—yes, I went over to them. . . . And I was caught."

"Why did you go over? What were you looking for?" Soldatov asked, chewing more slowly.

They were sitting around the fire above a dry ravine. The dung blocks smoked thickly, a little flame flickered up from the ashes. Behind them the night breathed off a dry heat and the scent of withered wormwood. The inky sky was streaked with falling stars.

Mishka stared cautiously at Soldatov's face lit up by the firelight, and replied:

"I wanted to fight for the people's rights."

"What rights? Tell me."

Soldatov's voice was low and stealthy. For a second Mishka hesitated; he thought his companion deliberately put a fresh block on the fire in order to conceal the expression on his face. Then he plucked up courage and said:

"Equality for everybody, that's what! There ought not to be lords and peasants. Understand?"

"Don't you think the Cadets will win?"

"No, I don't."

"So that's what you wanted. . . ." Soldatov changed his tone and jumped to his feet. "You son of a swine, you wanted to betray the Cossacks to the Jews?" he shouted piercingly and evilly. "You wanted to root us all up? Aha! So that the Jews could build their factories all over the steppe? So that they could drive us off our land?"

The astounded Mishka slowly rose to his feet. He thought Soldatov was about to strike him, and stepped back. Seeing that Mishka was retreating, the other swung his fist. But Mishka caught his arm in mid-air and, squeezing it at the wrist, promisingly advised him:

"You stop it or I'll mark you! What are you shouting for?"

They stood facing each other in the darkness. Trampled under their feet, the fire died out; only a dung block, kicked aside, smoked at the edges. With his left hand Soldatov seized the collar of Mishka's shirt, gathering it in his fist and raising it upward, seeking to release his right hand.

"Let go of my shirt!" Mishka panted, twisting his strong neck. "Let go, I tell you! I'll kill you, do you hear?"

"No. . . . I'll kill you . . . you wait!" Soldatov snorted.

Mishka released himself, threw the other back, and, feeling a horrible desire to strike, to kick him, to give his own hands free play, tremblingly readjusted his shirt.

Soldatov did not attempt to come at him. Grinding his teeth, he shouted between his curses:

"I'll tell. . . . I'll tell the overseer at once. You serpent! You reptile! Bolshevik!"

"If he tells—make up some lie—they'll put me in prison. They won't send me to the front, so I shan't be able to go over to the Reds. I'm done!" Mishka turned cold, and his thoughts, seeking a way out, cast about desperately like a fish in a little pool left by the abating flood water of a river. "I'll kill him! Choke him now! There's nothing else for it." And already his mind sought for an excuse: "I'll say he tried to kill me. And I caught him by the throat. . . . In the fight. . . ."

He strode towards Soldatov, and if the other had come to meet him at that moment, death and blood would have crossed swords above them. But Soldatov stood shouting curses, and Mishka halted, his legs trembling, the sweat pouring down his back.

"Wait. D'you hear? Soldatov, stop it! Don't shout! You started on me first. . . ." His jaws working, his eyes wandering distractedly, he began to plead abjectly: "I didn't strike you. And you seized hold of my shirt. What did I tell you anything for? If I offended you, forgive me . . . by God! Well?"

Soldatov gradually calmed down. After a while, turning away and pulling his hand out of Mishka's cold, sweaty hand, he said:

"You wave your tail like a snake! All right, I won't tell anybody. I'll have pity on your foolishness. But don't let me see any more of you, I can't stand the sight of you. You swine! You've sold yourself to the Jews, and I've got no pity on such as sell themselves for money."

Mishka smiled abjectly and miserably in the darkness, though Soldatov could not see his smile, as he could not see Mishka's tightly clenched fists.

They parted without another word. Koshevoi frenziedly whipped up his horse and galloped off in search of his drove. In the east, lightning was flickering and thunder rolling.

The storm passed over the steppe that same night. Towards midnight a wind sprang up and went raging over the ground, dragging a chilliness and a bitter dust after it like a curtain. The sky was overcast. The lightning scattered the piled masses of dark cloud, there was a long silence, and then in the distance a premonitory roll of thunder. A granular sowing of rain began to beat down the grass. By the gleam of a second flash of lightning Koshevoi saw the clouds heavily, menacingly black in the sky, and on the earth his horses gathered into a bunch. The thunder broke with a terrifying roar, and the rain suddenly poured down in torrents.

The steppe murmured vaguely, the wind tore the cap from Mishka's head and forced him to bend down over his saddle-bow. For a minute there was a rocking silence; then the incendiary lightning flamed again across the heaven, leaving a still more palpable darkness. The next thunderclap was so loud and rolling that Mishka's horse sat back on its haunches, then reared on its hind legs. The horses in the drove began to stamp their hoofs. Pulling on the reins with all his strength, Mishka shouted in the attempt to cheer them:

"Stop! Whoa!"

By the sugary-white zigzag of lightning that flickered through the clouds he saw the drove turn and gallop furiously towards him, their noses almost touching the ground. Their dilated nostrils drew in the air in great gasps, and their unshod hoofs drummed muffledly on the earth. Bakhar was in front, coming on at top speed. Koshevoi pulled his horse round and just succeeded in dodging the drove; they poured past and halted a little way off. Not realizing that, agitated and frightened by the thunder, they had galloped to him because of his shout, Mishka called again even more loudly:

"Stop! Now!"

Again in the darkness he heard the thunderous roar of hoofs galloping towards him. In his terror he struck his mare between the eyes with his whip, but he was too late: one of the frantic horses crashed against his animal's croup with its breast and he flew out of the saddle as though flung from a sling. He was saved from death by a miracle: the main body of the drove tore more to the right of him, and only one mare caught his right arm with her hoof. He rose and cautiously moved away, keeping as silent as possible. He heard the drove a little way off awaiting his cry, ready to dash again towards him at a furious gallop, and he heard the characteristic snort of the stallion.

He did not reach the hut until dawn.

Chapter 4

During the winter Eugene Listnitsky had been twice wounded, but each time the wound had been trivial, and he had returned to the struggle. But in May, while the Volunteer Army was resting in Novocherkass, he felt indisposed and obtained a fortnight's furlough. Although he greatly wanted to go home, he decided to stay in Novocherkass, in order not to lose time on long journeys. A comrade in his platoon, a Captain Gorchakov, took his furlough at the same time, and he proposed that Listnitsky should stay with him at his house in Novocherkass.

"I haven't any children, and my wife will be glad to see you. I've told her about you in my letters," he said.

At noon they drove to a little detached house huddled in one of the streets close to the railway station.

"There is my residence," Gorchakov said, hastening his steps. His

large black eyes moistened with happy agitation. He strode into
the house, filling the rooms with the pungent smell of the soldier.

"Where's Olga Nikholaevna?" he shouted to the maid who came
out from the kitchen. "In the garden? Come along, Listnitsky."

In the garden a spotted shade was lying under the apple trees,
and the air was scented with honey and hot earth. From a side-
walk a tall woman dressed in yellow came to meet them. She stood
for a moment with her palms pressed to her breast as though frightened, then ran towards them with her hand outstretched. She ran
so swiftly that Listnitsky saw only her knees beating against her
skirt, the pointed toes of her slippers, and a golden flood of hair
tossing turbulently around her head. Standing on tiptoe and flinging
her bar arms around her husband's neck, she kissed him on his
dusty cheeks, his nose, eyes, and lips. Listnitsky rubbed his pince-
nez, sniffed in the scent of the verbenas, and smiled a self-conscious,
constrained smile.

When her outburst of delight had subsided, Gorchakov carefully
but firmly released her fingers from his neck and, putting his arm
across her shoulders, turned her lightly round.

"Olga, this is my friend Listnitsky."

"Listnitsky? I'm very glad to meet you. My husband has told
me about you," she said, running her smiling eyes over him.

They went back together to the house. Gorchakov's hairy hand
with its ugly nails rested around his wife's slender waist. Listnitsky
glanced covertly at that hand and felt childishly unhappy, as though
he had been unjustly and seriously injured by someone. He stared
at the silky skin of her cheeks, at the rosy shell of her tiny ear, half-
hidden by a strand of rusty gold hair. His eyes slipped to the opening of her gown at her chest, and he saw a swelling milky-white
breast and a tiny brown nipple. Occasionally she turned her light
blue eyes to him, and their glance was kindly and friendly. But he
was pricked with an irritating pain when those same eyes, turned
to her husband's swarthy face, lit up with a very different light.

Only at dinner-time was Listnitsky able thoroughly to observe
his friend's wife. In her shapely figure and her face was that
fading, waning beauty which blooms in a woman who has seen her
thirtieth autumn. But in her humorous, rather chilly eyes and in
her movements she still retained an unexpended reserve of youth-
fulness. Her face with its soft, attractively irregular lines, was

perhaps quite ordinary. But one contrast struck the eyes at once: she had fine, dark red, parchingly hot lips, such as are found only among the swarthy women of the south, but her skin was translucently rosy and her eyebrows were fair. She laughed freely, but her smile seemed studied. Her low voice was toneless and lacking in light and shade. To Listnitsky, who for two months had seen no women except bedraggled nurses, she seemed exaggeratedly beautiful. He stared at her proudly carried head, at the heavy knot of hair, answered questions ineptly, and soon, pleading fatigue, retired to his room.

Sweet and yearning the days passed by. Afterwards Listnitsky turned them over reverently in his mind, torturing himself senselessly and stupidly, like a child. The Gorchakovs united in avoiding him. Under the pretext that repairs had to be done he was transferred from the room adjacent to their bedroom to one in a far corner of the house. He realized that he was a constraint to them, but he had no desire to go elsewhere. For days on end he lay under the apple trees, in a dusty orange coolness, reading the newspapers hurriedly printed on packing paper, or falling off into a heavy, unrefreshing sleep. His boredom was shared by a handsome pointer, who was silently jealous of his master's monopoly of his mistress, and transferred himself to Listnitsky, lying down at his side.

With a woman's instinct Olga realized the source of his mood. Restrained from the beginning, she grew even more restrained in her attitude towards him. Once, as they were returning one evening from the town garden, they were walking along side by side. (At the gate Gorchakov had been stopped by officer acquaintances.) Listnitsky took her under his arm and alarmed her by pressing her elbow strongly against his side.

"What are you staring at?" she asked with a smile.

He detected a low, playfully challenging note in her voice. Only then did he risk playing his card. He bowed his head and smilingly whispered:

> "Enthralled by a disturbing presence
> I gaze beyond the darkened veil
> To see a strand by magic enchanted
> And an enchanted dale."

She quietly released her hand and said in a merry tone:

"Eugene Nikholaevich—I—I cannot but notice your attitude to me. Aren't you ashamed? Wait, wait! I thought you would have been a little—different. Let us put an end to this. I am a poor subject for such experiments. So you feel like love-making? Don't spoil our friendly relations, and please drop your nonsense. Do you agree? Give me your hand."

Listnitsky feigned a noble indignation, but he could not sustain the role and, following her example, burst into laughter. After Gorchakov had caught up with them she grew even more animated and gay, but Eugene was silent, mentally jeering at himself.

Despite her intelligence she sincerely thought that after this they would become friends. Outwardly Listnitsky justified her confidence, but in his spirit he was almost coming to hate her, and after some days, catching himself in the tormenting task of finding repellent traits in her character and person, he realized that he was on the verge of a genuinely deep feeling.

The days of furlough seeped away, leaving their sediment in the consciousness of all three. The Volunteer Army, freshly complemented and rested, prepared to strike a blow, and marched to the Kuban, taking Gorchakov and Listnitsky with it.

Olga saw them off. A black silk gown emphasized her quiet beauty. She smiled with tear-stained eyes; her swollen lips gave her face an agitating, childish expression. So she remained in Listnitsky's memory. And he long and carefully retained the memory of her clear, unfading portrait, in his devotion endowing her with an intangible aureole.

In June the Volunteer Army was drawn into battle. In the very first struggle Gorchakov was struck by a piece of shell. He was dragged behind the lines and an hour later, as he lay bleeding on a cart, he told Listnitsky:

"I don't think I shall die. . . . They're going to operate on me at once. . . . They say they haven't any chloroform. It's not worth dying. What do you think? But in any case—in full possession of my senses and so on—Eugene, don't leave Olga. Neither I nor she has any relations. You are honest and decent. Marry her—or don't you want to?"

He stared at Eugene with entreaty and hatred in his eyes; his unshaven cheeks quivered. He pressed his blood- and mud-stained hand carefully against his chest and went on, licking the rosy sweat from his lips:

"Promise me? You won't abandon her? If the Russian soldiers don't beautify you as they have me! You promise? She's a fine woman." All his face twisted wryly. "A woman from Turgeniev's pages. There aren't any like her these days. You promise? Why are you silent?"

"I promise."

"Well, and now go to the devil! Good-bye. . . ."

He gave Listnitsky a tremulous handclasp, then, with an awkward, desperate movement, drew him to himself. Trembling with his effort, raising his wet head, he pressed his parched lips to Listnitsky's hand. Then he hastily covered his head with the edge of his greatcoat and turned away. Eugene caught a glimpse of the cold rigor on his lips and the moist grey tinge of his cheek.

He died two days later. The very next day Listnitsky was sent to the rear with a seriously wounded left arm and thigh.

A long and obstinate struggle was in progress. With his regiment Eugene had gone twice into the counter-attack. A third time the ranks of his battalion were called upon to advance. He ran stumbling through the uncut wheat, holding a spade above his head with his left hand, his rifle gripped in his right. A bullet sped with a ringing whistle past the blade of the spade, and he felt a prick of joy: "Missed." But the next moment his arm was flung aside by a short, terrifyingly strong blow. He dropped the spade and ran on with unprotected head for another fifty yards. He tried to carry his rifle at the trail, but could not raise his hand. The pain flowed sullenly into every joint. He lay down in a furrow, and cried out again and again, unable to restrain himself. Even as he lay, a bullet struck him in the thigh, and he slowly and painfully lost consciousness.

At the rear they amputated his shattered arm and drew fragments of bone out of his thigh. Two weeks he lay lacerated by despair, pain, and yearning. Then he was transferred to Novocherkass, and he spent another thirty exhausting days in the hospital. Occasionally Olga visited him. Her cheeks had taken on a greenish-yellow tinge. Her mourning deepened the yearning of her eyes. Listnitsky stared at her faded face and was silent, ashamedly, stealthily concealing his empty sleeve beneath the blanket. Almost unwillingly she asked him for details of her husband's death. Her eyes wandered over the beds, and she listened with apparent abstraction. When he left the hospital, Eugene went to call on her. She met him on the steps of the house, and turned away when, as he kissed her hand, his head bent low into the thick mass of her golden hair.

He was carefully shaven and wearing an elegant jacket, but his empty sleeve tormented him; the short, bound stump of arm stirred shudderingly within it. They went into the house. Without sitting down he began to speak:

"Before his death Boris asked me . . . made me promise not to leave you. . . ."

"I know. He told me in his last letter. . . ."

"His desire was that we should be together. Of course provided you agree, provided you will marry a disabled man. I ask you to believe . . . a speech about my feelings now would sound . . . but I sincerely desire your happiness."

His embarrassment and disconnected, agitated remarks moved her.

"I've thought about it. I am willing," she said.

"We'll go to my father's estate. We can settle the rest afterwards."

"Yes."

He respectfully touched her marble hand with his lips. When he raised his humble eyes he saw the shade of a smile slipping from her lips.

Love and an oppressive sensual desire attracted Listnitsky to Olga. He began to visit her daily. Worn out with the everyday struggle, his heart longed for fairyland. He deliberated with himself like the hero of a classical novel, patiently seeking exalted feelings which he had never felt, in the desire perhaps to conceal and adorn the nakedness of his simple physical attraction to her. Nevertheless with one wing the legendary touched reality: not only sexual attraction, but some other invisible thread bound him to this woman who had so fortuitously entered his life. He sadly analysed his own experiences, realizing only one thing with clarity: he, mutilated and knocked out of the ranks, continued as before to be authoritatively governed by an unbridled and savage instinct: "everything was lawful to him." Even during the mournful days when Olga was still carrying within her the bitterness of her heavy loss,

Eugene, afire with jealousy of the dead Boris, longed for her, longed frenziedly. His life foamed like a raging whirlpool. In those days men who had smelt power, who were blinded and deafened by all that was happening around them, lived passionately and avidly, only for the moment. Perhaps for that reason also Listnitsky hastened to tie the knot of his and Olga's lives, maybe sadly realizing the inevitable destruction of that for which he had faced death.

He wrote to inform his father that he was intending to marry and would be bringing his wife to Yagodnoe. He ended his letter with the mournfully ironic words: "I have done my bit. I could still with one hand exterminate the revolting scum, this accursed 'people' over whose fate the Russian intelligentsia have wept and slobbered for decades. But, truth to tell, it now seems savagely senseless to me. Krasnov will not be reconciled to Denikin, and inside both camps there is intriguing, plotting, infamy, and mischief-making. I'm coming home to embrace you with my one arm and to live with you, watching the struggle from outside. I am no longer a soldier, but a stump, physically and morally. I am tired: I capitulate. Undoubtedly this is partly due to my marriage and the desire to ensure myself a 'quiet harbourage.'"

A few days before they departed from Novocherkass Eugene transferred to Olga's house. After the night in which they came together she appeared to grow hollow-cheeked and to darken in her features. She yielded to his importunities, but seemed oppressed by the situation in which she found herself, and was wounded in her spirit. Eugene did not know, or wished not to know, that they had different measures for the love that bound them together, but the same measure for their hatred.

Before their departure for Yagodnoe, Listnitsky thought only reluctantly and disconnectedly of Aksinia. He protected himself from thought of her as a man shields himself from the sun with his hand. But willy-nilly memories of his association with her, which in the course of the years had developed into a vital union, began to disturb him more and more insistently. At one time he even thought it would not be necessary to break relations with her: "Olga would agree." But a sense of what was decent rose uppermost, and he decided that after his arrival he would talk to her and, if possible, break with her.

They arrived at Yagodnoe late on the fourth day after leaving Novocherkass. Eugene's old father met them about a mile from the estate. Eugene noticed how slowly his father removed his hat and lifted his leg across the seat of his light droshky.

"I have come to meet my dear guests. Let me have a look at you," the old man said, awkwardly embracing the bride and thrusting his greenish-grey moustache into her cheeks.

"Get in with us, Papa. Sit in my place, and I'll sit with the coachman," Eugene proposed.

The old man sat down at Olga's side, wiped his moustache with his handkerchief, and restrainedly examined his son. "Well, how are you?"

"I'm very glad to see you again, Papa."

"So you're maimed, you say?"

"It can't be helped."

His father gazed at him, endeavouring to conceal his commiseration beneath a harsh expression, and keeping his eyes away from the empty sleeve of the tunic.

"It's nothing. I've got used to it." Eugene shrugged his shoulders.

"Of course you get used to it," his father hastened to say, "so long as your head is whole. You've come back with honour. And you've even taken a beautiful prisoner."

Eugene was delighted with his father's refined, old-fashioned gallantry, and asked Olga with his eyes: "What do you think of him?" From her animated smile and her warm eyes he realized that she liked the old man.

Eugene sat with his back to the horses, smiling as he glanced at his father, at Olga, at the road slowly rising behind them, at the distant hilltop and horizon.

"What a lonely spot! And how quiet!" With a smile Olga watched the crows flying across the road, the clumps of wormwood and clover speeding past.

"They've come out to meet us." His father screwed up his eyes.

Eugene looked over his shoulder and, although still too far away to recognize anybody, felt that one of the women was Aksinia and flushed heavily. He expected her face to show signs of agitation when the droshky passed through the gates. His heart beating violently, he glanced to the right and noticed her.

But he was astonished to see her quietly gay and smiling. It was as though a burden had fallen from his shoulders, and he nodded to her.

"What a vicious beauty! Who is she? Challengingly beautiful, isn't she?" Olga indicated Aksinia with eyes that expressed her admiration.

But Eugene had recovered his composure. He calmly and coldly agreed:

"Yes, she's a beautiful woman. She's our maid."

Olga's presence set its impress on everybody at Yagodnoe. The old master, who previously had spent all day wandering about in his nightshirt and warm woollen pants, gave orders for his old coats and trousers to be brought out of the chests in which they had been packed in naphthalene. Formerly careless of his own person, he now shouted at Aksinia if there was the least crease in his linen, and made terrible faces when she gave him uncleaned boots of a morning. He freshened up, and pleasantly surprised Eugene by the smoothness of his shaven cheeks.

As though in presentiment of some evil, Aksinia tried to please the young mistress and was ingratiatingly humble and over-willing to serve her. Lukeria nearly jumped out of her skin to prepare good meals and excelled herself in inventing new and tasty sauces and gravies. Even old Sashka, greatly aged and feeble, was affected by the baneful influence of the changes occurring in Yagodnoe. His old master happened to meet him close to the steps, examined him from head to foot, and wagged his finger menacingly:

"What's all this, you son of a swine?" Old Listnitsky rolled his eyes ferociously. "What a state your trousers are in!"

"Well, what state?" old Sashka replied impudently, although he was a little confused by the unusual inspection and the master's trembling voice.

"A young woman in the house, and you trying to drive me into my grave, you scum? Why don't you button up your fly, you stinking goat?"

Old Sashka ran his dirty fingers down the long row of buttons as though playing an accordion. He was about to make some further impudent retort, but his master stamped his foot so hard that the sole of his old-fashioned pointed boot gaped away from the upper, and he snorted:

"Back to your stable! Quick march! I'll tell Lukeria to scrub you with boiling water. Get that dirt off you, you old hack!"

Eugene rested and went wandering off with a rifle to shoot partridges. He was oppressed by the problem of Aksinia. But one evening his father summoned him to his room; anxiously looking at the door and avoiding his son's eyes, he asked:

"I, you know—you must excuse me for interfering in your personal affairs. But I want to know what you propose to do about Aksinia."

Eugene betrayed himself by the haste with which he began to puff at his cigarette. He flushed and, feeling that he flushed, went still more red.

"I don't know. . . . I honestly don't know . . ." he admitted frankly.

The old man said weightily:

"But I know! Go and talk to her at once. Offer her money, hush money." He smiled. "Ask her to go away. We'll find someone else."

Eugene went immediately to the servants' quarters. He found Aksinia standing with her back to the door, mixing dough. He stared at the fluffy curls around her neck, and said:

"Aksinia, I want to speak to you for a minute."

She turned swiftly, endeavouring to give her face an expression of complaisance and tranquillity. But Eugene noticed her fingers trembling as she turned down her sleeves.

She threw a timorous glance at the cook and, unable to control her joy, followed Eugene with a happy, questioning smile.

On the steps outside he said to her:

"We'll go into the orchard. I want to talk to you."

"All right." She agreed gladly and humbly, thinking this meant the renewal of their former relationship. As they went Eugene asked in an undertone:

"Do you know why I have called you out?"

Smiling in the darkness, she caught at his arm; but he snatched it away, and she realized all. She halted.

"What is it you want, Eugene Nikholaevich? I'm not going any farther."

"Good, we can talk here! No one will hear us." Eugene hurried and was entangled in an invisible network of words. "You must understand. I can't be with you now as I was. I can't live with you, you understand? I'm married now, and as an honest man I can't do anything shameful. My conscience won't allow it," he said, tormentedly ashamed of his high-flown words.

Night had only just arrived from the darkened east. In the west a strip of sky was still livid with the sunset. In the threshing-floor men were threshing by lantern-light, taking advantage of the fine weather, and the machinery pulsated with life. The man incessantly feeding the threshing machine was crying hoarsely and happily: "More, more!" In the orchard was a deep silence and the scent of nettles, wheat, and dew.

Aksinia said nothing.

"What do you say? Why are you silent, Aksinia?"

"I've got nothing to say."

"I'll give you money. You must go away. I think you'll agree. It will be difficult for me to be always seeing you."

"In a week my month will be up. Can I finish out the time?"

"Of course, of course!"

Aksinia was silent for a moment. Then sideways, timidly, as though she had been beaten, she moved closer to Eugene, and said:

"Well—I'll go. You won't be sorry after? It was my need that made me so shameless. I was tortured with being alone. Don't condemn me, Eugene."

Her voice was ringing and dry. Eugene tried in vain to discover whether she were serious or joking in her remarks.

"What do you want?" He coughed irritatedly, and suddenly felt her again timidly feeling for his arm.

A few minutes later he emerged from behind a damp, scented currant bush. Before he reached the house he stooped and with his handkerchief rubbed his trouser knees, green with grass juice. As he went up the steps he looked back. Through the window of the servants' quarters he saw Aksinia with hands flung up behind her head, tidying her hair. A smile was playing on her lips.

Chapter 5

The feather-grass ripened. For unending miles the steppe was clothed in swaying silver. The wind strode springily over it, rustling and driving opal-grey waves now to the south, now to the west. Wherever the flowing breezes turned, the feather-grass bowed devoutly, and a darker track stretched over its grey expanse. The varicoloured grasses came to flower. The withered, joyless wormwood disappeared from the hill-crests. The brief nights decayed swiftly. At night the coal-black sky was sprinkled with innumerable stars, the moon—the Cossacks' "little sun"—darkened to its wane and gleamed pallidly, the spacious Milky Way mingled with other starry roads. The acrid air was close, the wind dry and scented with wormwood; the earth, also saturated with the bitterness of the almighty wormwood, yearned for cool. The proud starry ways, trodden by neither hoof nor foot, faded and hid themselves; the wheaten sprinkle of stars perished in the dry black skyey earth, which neither yielded sprout nor rejoiced in seedlings; the moon was an arid salt-marsh. The drought withered the grass of the steppe, and over it hovered the never ceasing silver struggle of the quails and the metallic ringing of the grasshoppers.

During the day-time the steppe was one sultry, oppressive, misty haze; in the faded, cloudless dove-blue of the sky hung the merciless sun and the brown steely arc of the kite's outspread wings. Dazzlingly, irresistibly the feather-grass stretched over the steppe, a smoking camel-brown hue; the kite careened and floated in the sky, and its enormous shadow slipped noiselessly over the grass.

Beloved steppe! A pungent wind ruffles the manes of the mares and the stallions. The thirsty horse's snort is salty with the wind and, scenting its saltily bitter breath, the horse chews its silky lips and neighs as it tastes the tang of the wind and the sun. Beloved steppe under the low-hanging Don heaven! Winding ravines, dry valleys, ruddy cliffs, expanse of feather-grass worked with the darker traces of horse-hoofs, mounds rising in a wise silence, preserving the former Cossack glory. Low I bow and filially kiss your fresh earth, I kiss the Don Cossack, unrusting, blood-soaked steppe.

The stallion had a small, lean, snake-like head. His ears were small and mobile. His chest muscles were magnificently developed. He had fine, strong legs, with irreproachable pasterns and hoofs turned like river pebbles. His hindquarters were limber and pendulous. He was a pure-blooded Don horse with not a drop of foreign blood in his veins, and his lineage was evident in all his characteristics.

While at drink one day he fought in defence of his mares with another, stronger and older stallion, and was badly kicked on his left foreleg, although the stallions are never shod when at pasture. The two horses reared, kicked with their forelegs, bit each other, and tore open the flesh.

The drover was not at hand; he was lying asleep in the steppe, his back turned to the sun. The other stallion sent Malbruck to earth, then chased him far away from his drove. Leaving him there streaming with blood, he took possession of both droves.

The wounded stallion was brought into the stables; the veterinary surgeon healed his damaged leg, and six days later Mishka Koshevoi, who had ridden in with a report, saw Malbruck, dominated by the mighty instinct to continue his stock, bite through his halter rope, gallop out of his stall, round up the hobbled mares grazing in the barrack yard, and drive them into the steppe, first at a trot, then hurrying them by biting at the laggers. The drovers and overseer ran out of the barracks, but they were too late.

"He's left us nothing to ride, damn him!" the overseer cursed, gazing after the horses outdistancing them, not without secret approval.

At noon Malbruck brought back his mares to drink. Drovers on foot separated him from the mares, and Mishka saddled him, rode him out into the steppe, and released him among his own original drove.

During two months' service as drover Mishka carefully studied the life of the horses at pasture and was filled with profound respect for their intelligence and their far from human nobility. He saw stallions riding mares, and this primeval act, accomplished in primitive conditions, was so naturally wise and simple that it involuntarily aroused comparison with human beings, by no means in the latter's favour. But there was much that was human in the horses' relationships. For instance, Mishka noticed that the ageing stallion Bakhar, who was unappeasably rough and evil in his conduct with his mares, singled out one four-year-old sorrel beauty, with a broad star on her forehead and burning eyes, for very different treatment. In her company he was nervous and agitatedly brusque, and always snuffed at her with a special, restrained, yet passionate snort. When at stand he was fond of laying his wicked head on the croup of his favourite mare and so dozing for hours. Mishka watched him, noticing the bunches of muscles limply playing beneath his fine skin, and it seemed to him that Bakhar loved that one mare with a hopelessly strong and sorrowful, old man's passion.

Mishka was diligent in his service. Evidently the report of his ardour came to the knowledge of the district ataman, for in the middle of August the overseer received instructions to send Koshevoi back to Vieshenska.

Mishka made ready in a trice, handed in his equipment, and set off for Vieshenska towards evening of the same day. He urged on his mare incessantly, and by sunset he had already passed Kargin. On the hills beyond, he overtook a wagonette going in the direction of Vieshenska. The Ukrainian driver was hastening his steaming, well-fed horses, and in the back of the light-springed wagonette half-lay an elegant-looking, broad-shouldered man in a coat of town cut and a grey felt hat thrust on the back of his head. For some time Mishka rode behind the wagonette, staring at the man's shoulders shaking as it jostled in the ruts, and at the white, dusty band of his collar. A yellow hand-bag and a sack covered with an overcoat lay at the traveller's feet. Mishka's nose caught the unfamiliar scent of a cigar. "Some official going to Vieshenska," he decided as he brought his mare level with the man. Glancing sidelong under the edge of the man's hat, his jaw dropped, and a shiver of great astonishment and fear ran down his back. The man who lay in the cart, impatiently chewing the black end of his cigar and screwing up his light-hued eyes, was Stepan Astakhov. Still not quite sure, Mishka took another glance at the strange, greatly changed face of his fellow-villager and now felt quite certain that it was Stepan. Sweating with agitation, he coughed:

"Excuse me, sir, but aren't you Astakhov?"

The man in the wagonette pushed back his hat, turned, and raised his eyes to Mishka.

"Yes, I'm Astakhov," he replied. "What of it? Are you—wait, aren't you Koshevoi?" He half-rose in the wagonette and, smiling only with his lips beneath his moustache, retaining an inaccessible harshness in all the rest of his face, he stretched out his hand gladly, a little discountenanced: "It is Koshevoi! Mikhail! I'm very glad. . . ."

"But how—? How are you here?" Mishka dropped the reins and threw out his hands in astonishment. "They said you'd been killed. But I see Astakhov all right!"

He broke into a smile and fidgeted in his saddle. Stepan's appearance and his clean, pure speech confused him. He changed his method of address, dropped his friendly forms of expression, and sadly felt that some invisible barrier separated them. They began to talk. The horses moved at a walking pace. The sunset was flowering gloriously in the west, the clouds went sailing over the azure heaven into the night. A quail called piercingly in the millet at the roadside, but a dusty silence was settling over the steppe as it passed from the bustle and turmoil of the day into the evening stillness. In the distance the shrine at the crossroads to Tatarsk and Vieshenska was silhouetted against the lilac sky.

"Where've you come from, Stepan Andreich?" Mishka asked pleasantly.

"From Germany. I've come back to my own land, as you see."

"But our Cossacks said you'd been killed before their very eyes."

Stepan replied restrainedly, deliberately, as though burdened by the questions:

"I was wounded in two places. As for the Cossacks . . . what of them? They left me there. . . . I was taken prisoner. . . . The Germans healed my wounds and sent me to work. . . ."

"But we never had a letter from you in the village. . . ."

"I had no one to write to." Stepan threw away the end of his cigar and immediately lit another.

"But how about your wife? She's alive and well."

"I wasn't living with her. I thought everybody knew that."

His voice sounded dry, and there was not a warm note in it. The mention of his wife did not seem to disturb him.

The driver cheerlessly waved his whip, the tired horses pulled unwillingly at the traces. The wagonette bounced over the ruts, and Stepan ended the talk by turning his head away, after asking:

"Going to the village?"

"No, I'm off to the district ataman."

At the crossroads Mishka turned to the right and rose in his stirrups:

"So long for the present, Stepan Andreich!"

Stepan touched the edge of his dusty hat with his fingers and replied coldly, enunciating every word as though he were a foreigner: "Good health to you!"

Chapter 6

The Reds concentrated their forces, clenching their fist for a counterblow. The Cossacks were suffering from a severe shortage of munitions and developed their offensive only feebly, making no attempt to cross the boundaries of the province. Successes shifted from one side to the other. In August there was a relative cessation of activities, and the Cossacks who returned home for a brief furlough talked of an armistice in the autumn.

Meantime in the rear the grain was being harvested in the districts and the villages. The lack of workers made itself felt. The old men and the women could not manage the harvesting, and in addition they were continually hindered by requisitions of wagons and horses to carry military stores and provisions to the front. Almost every day five or six wagons were mobilized in Tatarsk, sent to Vieshenska to load army stores, and then on to the Cossack forces.

The return of Stepan Astakhov excited all the village. In every hut and every threshing-floor it was the sole topic of conversation. A Cossack believed to have been buried long since, a man remembered only by the old women, and that with a muttered "Peace to his ashes!" had come home. If that wasn't a miracle . . . !

Stepan halted at Anikushka's gate and carried his things into the hut. While Anikushka's wife was getting him something to eat he went along to his own hut. With the firm tread of the master he strode up and down the moonlit yard, walked under the roofs of the half-demolished sheds, examined the hut, shook the fences. The fried eggs had long since grown cold on Anikushka's table, but Stepan still went on with his examination of his grass-grown home, cracking his fingers and muttering to himself.

The same evening the Cossacks visited him to look at him and question him about his life as a prisoner. Anikushka's front room was packed with women and lads who stood in a solid wall, their mouths gaping as they listened to Stepan's stories. He talked reluctantly; not once was his ageing face lit up with a smile. It was evident that life had completely changed him.

Next morning Pantaleimon Melekhov called while Stepan was still asleep. The old man coughed into his hand and waited outside until he woke up. From the room came the damp, mouldering smell of the earthen floor, of unfamiliar, chokingly strong tobacco, and that intangible scent which clings for so long to a man who has been on the road.

Stepan was awake now, that was clear. There was the sound of a match being struck to light a cigar.

"May I come in?" Pantaleimon asked, and, as though about to present himself before a superior officer, carefully arranged the folds of the new shirt which Ilinichna had insisted on his wearing for the occasion.

"Come in!"

Stepan was dressing, puffing at a cigar and screwing up his eyes to keep out the smoke. Pantaleimon stepped a little nervously across the threshold and, astonished by Stepan's changed features and the metal buckles of his silk braces, halted and stretched out his black palm.

"Good morning, neighbour."

"Good morning."

Stepan drew the braces over his powerful shoulders and with dignity put his hand into the old man's hairy palm. They hurriedly ran their eyes over each other. In Stepan's eyes flickered sparks of hostility; in Melekhov's slanting, dilated pupils were respect and a light, ironic astonishment.

"You're older, Stepan; you're older, my boy."

"Yes, I've grown older."

"We'd said our prayers for the dead over you, just as we did for my Grishka . . ." the old man began, and broke off in vexation.

This wasn't the time to recall that! He tried to correct his mistake. "Praise to God, you've come back alive and well! God be praised! We'd said our prayers for Grishka, too, but like Lazarus he rose and walked. He's got two little ones now, and his wife Natalia, praise be, has got better. She's a fine woman. . . . Well, and how are you?"

"Will you come and visit your neighbours? Come along, do us that honour. We'll have a talk."

Stepan refused, but Pantaleimon was importunate and began to take offence, so that at last he consented. He washed, combed back his close-cut hair, and smiled when the old man asked: "What have you done with your forelock—worn it out?" Confidently setting his hat on his head, he led the way into the yard.

Pantaleimon was ingratiatingly amiable, so much so that Stepan involuntarily thought: "Trying to make up for the old wrong. . . ."

Obeying the silent command of her husband's eyes, Ilinichna bustled about the kitchen, sent Natalia and Dunia scurrying, and herself laid the table. The women occasionally cast inquisitive glances at Stepan sitting beneath the ikons, their eyes groping at his coat, his collar, the silver watch-chain, his unusual way of doing his hair, and exchanging badly concealed, astonished smiles. Daria came in with flushed face from the yard, confusedly smiling and wiping the fine line of her lips with the corner of her apron. She screwed up her eyes.

"Why, neighbour, I didn't know you. You don't look like a Cossack," she exclaimed.

In order not to waste time Pantaleimon set a bottle of home-made vodka on the table, pulled out the rag stopper, sniffed at the bitter-sweet aroma, and praised its quality.

"Try it! I make it myself," he said.

Stepan was reluctant to drink, but after a glassful he began swiftly to get drunk and more communicative.

"You ought to get married now, neighbour," Pantaleimon remarked.

"And what shall I do with my old wife?"

"Well, what of her? Do you think she won't have worn after all this time? A wife's like a mare: she keeps her teeth so long as you ride her. We'll find you a young one."

"Life these days is too mixed up. . . . It's not the time for weddings. I've got ten days' furlough, and then I'm to go to Vieshenska, and on to the front, I expect," Stepan replied, losing his foreign style of speech as he grew more intoxicated.

He left soon afterwards, accompanied by Daria's admiring stare and leaving argument and discussion behind him.

"How he's educated himself, the son of a bitch! How he talked! Like an excise officer or someone of the nobility. When I went in to him he was standing pulling silk bands with buckles over his shoulders. God's truth! His back and chest were harnessed up like a horse. What's it all for? He's just like an educated man now!" Pantaleimon declared admiringly, obviously flattered by the circumstance that Stepan had accepted his hospitality and overlooked the old wrong.

On putting two and two together it was concluded that when Stepan had finished his service he would live in the village and would restore his hut and farm. He had casually mentioned that he had means, and this evoked Pantaleimon's sombre speculation and involuntary respect.

"He's got money, that's clear!" Pantaleimon said after Stepan had gone. "Other Cossacks come back from being prisoners dressed in no more than their skins, but he's come back clothed in silk. He must have killed someone or stolen the money."

Stepan spent the first few days of his return quietly in Anikushka's hut, rarely showing himself in the street. The neighbours watched him, set guard over his every movement, and even tried to cross-examine Anikushka's wife as to what he intended to do. But she shut her lips tightly and pleaded ignorance. Rumours spread thickly through the village when she hired a horse and wagonette from the Melekhovs and early on the Saturday morning drove off no one knew whither. Only Pantaleimon scented what was afoot. "She's going for Aksinia"; he winked to Ilinichna as he harnessed the lame mare into the wagonette. He was not mistaken. Stepan had ordered the woman to go to Yagodnoe and "ask Aksinia whether she will return to her husband, forgetting all the past wrongs."

That day Stepan completely lost his restraint and composure. He wandered all day about the village, sitting a long time on the porch of Mokhov's house, telling Mokhov stories of his life in Germany and his way home through France and across the sea. All the time he talked or listened to Mokhov's complaints he was anxiously studying his watch.

Anikushka's wife returned from Yagodnoe as dusk was falling. As she prepared a meal in the summer kitchen, she told how Aksinia had been startled by the unexpected news, had asked many questions, but had flatly refused to return.

"She has no need to come back, she's living like a lady. She's grown smooth and her face is white. She never sees hard work, and what more does she want? You wouldn't believe the way she's dressed up! Today's a work day, but she was dressed in a skirt as clean as snow, and her arms were spotlessly clean," Anikushka's wife told him, swallowing her jealous sighs.

Stepan's cheeks flushed, and angrily yearning little fires blazed up and died away in his downcast eyes. Restraining the trembling of his hand, he took a spoonful of sour milk out of his basin. He questioned her with intentional deliberation.

"She praised her life, you say?"

"And why not? Nobody would be against living like that."

"But did she ask about me?"

"Why not? I tell you she turned white when I told her you had come back."

After his evening meal Stepan went out into the grass-grown yard. The brief August shadows came and faded quickly. In the humid cool of the night the drums of the winnowing machines and the harsh voices sounded obtrusively. Under the yellow, spotted moon the village people were fussily active, winnowing the piles of grain threshed during the day and carrying it to their granaries. The burning, pungent scent of newly threshed wheat and a chaffy dust enveloped the village. Somewhere near the square a motor thresher was chugging, dogs were barking. The sound of singing came from distant threshing-floors. A fresh dampness rose from the Don. Stepan leaned against the fence and stared at the flowing stirrup of the Don visible across the street, at the fiery, winding wall of water trampled by the moon. Little curly ripples wound downstream. On the farther side of the river the poplars were drowsily resting. Stepan was quietly but irresistibly overcome with yearning.

At dawn rain was falling, but after sunrise the clouds dispersed, and some two hours later only the clumps of half-dry mud clinging to the cart-wheels recalled the wet weather. In the morning Stepan rode to Yagodnoe. Agitatedly tethering his horse at the gate, with a clumsy attempt at gaiety he went in. The spacious, grass-grown yard was deserted. Chickens were rummaging in the dung by the stables. A cock as black as a rook was stalking about by the fallen fence. The fat borzois lay in the shade by the coach-house. Six speckled black young pigs had overthrown their mother and, kicking away with their legs, were sucking at her. The dew sparkled on the shady side of the iron roof of the house.

Attentively staring around him, Stepan entered the servants' quarters, and asked the corpulent cook:

"Can I see Aksinia?"

"And who are you?" Lukeria asked, wiping her sweaty, freckled face with her apron.

"That's nothing to do with you. Where is Aksinia?"

"With the master. Wait!"

Stepan sat down, putting his hat on his knees with a gesture of terrible weariness. The cook bustled about the kitchen without paying any more attention to him. The sour smell of curds and fermentation filled the room. The flies settled in a black sprinkle over the stove, the walls, and the floury table. Stepan waited, listening tensely. The familiar sound of Aksinia's walk sent him starting up from the bench. He rose, letting his hat fall from his knees.

Aksinia entered, carrying a pile of plates. As she noticed Stepan, her face turned deathly pale and the corners of her lips quivered. She halted, helplessly pressing the plates against her breast, not removing her startled eyes from Stepan's face. Then somehow she broke away from where she was standing, went swiftly to the table, and put down the plates.

"Good morning," she said.

Stepan breathed slowly, deeply, as though in sleep; a tense smile forced his lips apart. Silently leaning forward, he stretched out his hand to Aksinia.

"Come into my room," she invited him with a gesture.

Stepan picked up his hat as though it were heavy. The blood rushed to his head and veiled his eyes. As soon as they had entered her room and sat down on opposite sides of the table, Aksinia, licking her dry lips, asked with a groan:

"Where have you come from?"

Indefinitely and unnaturally gay, Stepan drunkenly waved his hand. The same smile of gladness and pain still clung to his lips.

"From prison in Germany. . . . I've come to see you, Aksinia. . . ."

He fidgeted awkwardly, jumped up, pulled a small packet out of his pocket, hurriedly tore the rag off it with uncontrollably trembling fingers, and drew out a lady's silver wrist-watch set with a cheap blue stone. He stretched it out to her in his sweaty palm, but she did not remove her eyes from his unfamiliar face with its distorted, humble smile.

"Take it, I've kept it for you. . . . We've lived together. . . ."

"What do I want with it? Wait!" she whispered through numb lips.

"Take it. . . . Don't be offended. We must drop our old silliness."

Keeping him off with her hand, she rose and went across to the stove.

"They said you were dead. . . ."

"And would you have been glad?"

She did not reply, but more calmly examined her husband from head to foot, needlessly adjusting the folds of her carefully ironed skirt. With arms behind her she said:

"Did you send Anikushka's wife to me? She told me you had sent for me to come back to you—to live."

"Will you come?" Stepan interrupted her.

"No!" Aksinia's voice sounded curt. "No, I won't come."

"Why not?"

"I've got out of the habit . . . and besides, it's rather late—too late."

"But I want to restore my farm. All the way back from Germany I thought of it, and while I was living there I never stopped thinking of it. What will you do, Aksinia? Has Gregor left you, or have you found another? I've heard some story about you and the master's son here. . . . Is it true?"

Aksinia's cheeks burned, and tears of shame started from under her eyelids.

"It's true enough. I'm living with him."

"Don't think I'm reproaching you." Stepan took alarm. "I was going to say that maybe you haven't yet decided on your life. He won't want you for long, he's just playing with you. You've got wrinkles under your eyes. He'll turn you out as soon as he's had enough of you. And then where will you go? Haven't you had enough of living in serfdom? Think it over. . . . I've brought money back with me, and when the war ends we'll live well. I thought we'd come together. . . . And I want to forget the past."

"But what were you thinking of, dear old friend Stepan?" she asked merrily through her tears, with a little shiver. Breaking away from the stove, she came right up to the table. "What were you thinking of when you ground my young life into the dust? You drove me into Grishka's arms. You dried up my heart. Do you remember what you did with me?"

"I didn't come here to settle accounts. You—how do you know, maybe I've been quite ill over this." Stepan stared at his arms flung over the table and spoke slowly, as though rooting the words out of his mouth. "I was always thinking about you. The blood clotted in my heart. . . . You never left my thoughts day or night. . . . I lived there with a widow, a German. . . . I lived well, but I left her. . . . I was drawn home. . . ."

"And you feel like a quiet life?" Aksinia demanded, her nostrils quivering passionately. "You want to get on with your farming? You'd like to have children, I suppose, and a wife to wash for you, to feed you?" She smiled unpleasantly and darkly. "No, not for me, Christ save me! I'm old. . . . You can see my wrinkles. And I've forgotten how to bear children. I'm a paramour, and paramours mustn't have children. Is it such a one you want?"

"You've grown bitter. . . ."

"Such as I am, I am."

"So you say no?"

"I say no, I won't go! No!"

"Well, good-bye." Stepan rose, uncertainly turned over the wrist-watch in his hand, and laid it down again on the table. "Think it over and let me know," he added.

Aksinia saw him to the gate. She stood staring after him as the dust was cast up by the wagon-wheels and enveloped his broad shoulders. She struggled with unhappy tears, but sobbed a little as she thought sorrowfully of what had not happened, weeping over her life once more thrown to the wind. When, after learning that Eugene had no more need of her, she had heard of her husband's return, she had resolved to go to him, to gather up again the fragments of the happiness which had not been hers. And with that intention she had waited for Stepan. But when she saw him abased and humiliated she had darkened with pride, and her pride, the pride which would not allow her to remain rejected in Yagodnoe, had arisen all-powerfully within her. Her evil, uncontrollable will had determined her words and behaviour. She had remembered her former shame, had remembered all she had suffered from this man, at his great iron hands. And, herself wishing otherwise, horrified in her soul at what she was saying, she had panted out the stinging words: "No, I won't go! No!"

Once more she stared after the retreating wagon. Stepan waved his whip and disappeared beyond the lilac of the low, roadside wormwood.

The next day Aksinia received her wages. She collected her possessions and, as she said good-bye to Eugene, burst into weeping.

"Don't think badly of me, Eugene Nikholaevich."

"Why, of course not, my dear. . . . Thank you for everything." His voice sounded artificially cheerful in his endeavour to hide his embarrassment.

She departed. She arrived at Tatarsk early in the evening. Stepan met her at the gate.

"So you've come?" he asked with a smile. "For good? May I hope that you won't ever go away again?"

"I shan't go," she answered simply, her heart constricting as she looked around the half-demolished hut and the yard, vigorously overgrown with weeds and scrub.

Chapter 7

After advancing for many days, the Vieshenska regiment at last came into conflict with the retreating Red Guards. One noonday the squadron under Gregor Melekhov's command occupied a small village nestling in a dense green of gardens. Gregor dismounted his Cossacks in the shade of willows growing close to a stream which had cut a shallow channel through the village. Somewhere near at hand springs were burbling though the black, clinging earth. The water was ice-cold, and the Cossacks drank it greedily, scooping it up in their caps, afterwards clapping them on their sweaty heads with grunts of satisfaction. The sun shone straight down on the village. Sprinkled with the venomously sultry rays, the grasses and the willow leaves hung limply; but there was cool in the shade by the side of the stream. The burdocks were brilliantly green, the duck-weed gleamed with a virgin smile in the little creeks, beyond a bend ducks were splashing and flapping their wings in the water. The horses snorted and dragged towards the water, pulling the reins from their riders' hands and wading into the middle of the stream. As they stirred up the mud, they sought with their lips for fresher water. The sultry breeze sent the drops spraying from their mouths. A sulphurous smell arose from the clayey earth, and a bitter-sweet scent from the stream-washed, mouldering roots of the willows.

The Cossacks had just lain down to talk and smoke among the burdocks when their advance patrol returned. At the words "The Reds," the men at once started to their feet. They tightened the horses' saddle-girths and went once more to the stream to drink and fill their flasks, each man thinking: "Maybe this is the last time I shall drink such water, as fresh as children's tears."

The road led them across the stream. They halted on the farther side. Beyond the village, about a mile away an enemy patrol of eight horsemen was cautiously moving over the grey wormwooded and sandy rise in the direction of the village.

"We'll take them prisoner. All right?" Mitka Korshunov suggested to Gregor.

With half a troop he rode out of the village to outflank the patrol; but the Red Guards discovered the Cossacks in time and turned back.

When the two other squadrons composing the Vieshenska Regiment arrived an hour later, they advanced again. The patrols brought back the information that the Reds, numbering approximately a thousand, were coming to meet them. The squadrons of the Vieshenska Regiment had lost contact with the 33rd Bukanovsky Regiment on their right; nevertheless it was decided to engage the enemy. They rode to the top of the rise and dismounted, the horses being led off into a spacious hollow dropping down to the village. Somewhere to the right the patrols were already in action, and they could hear the rattle of hand machine-guns.

The thin line of the Reds appeared soon afterwards. Gregor stationed the men of his squadron at the top of the hill. The Cossacks lay along the crest, which was overgrown with scrub. From under a stunted crab-apple tree Gregor gazed through his field-glasses at the distant lines of the enemy. He could clearly see the first two lines, and behind them a further column of soldiers deploying into line among the brown ungathered shocks of cut grain.

He and the rest of the Cossacks were astonished to see a horseman, evidently the commander, riding on a high-standing white horse in front of the first line. There were two more in front of the second line. The third line was led by an officer; beside him fluttered a banner, a tiny crimson patch of blood against the dirty yellow background of the field.

"Their commanders go in front! That's heroic of them!" Mitka Korshunov laughed with sarcastic admiration.

Almost all the Cossacks raised themselves from the ground to look. Palms were set to brows. The talk died away. And a severe majestic silence, the harbinger of death, lay gently and softly, like the shadow of a cloud, over the steppe and the valley.

Gregor looked back. Dust was billowing beyond the ashy grey island of willows down by the village: it was the second squadron riding to outflank the enemy. For a while the progress of the movement was hidden by a valley, but then some four miles away the squadron rode in extended order up a slope, and Gregor mentally estimated the time and place at which it would be in line with the enemy flank.

He went back to his men. The Cossacks' faces, livid and shining with heat and dust, turned towards him. The men lay down, exchanging glances. At the command "Ready!" there was a rapacious rattle of bolts. From above them Gregor could see only outflung legs, the tops of caps, and backs in dusty shirts, the outlines of shoulder-blades wet with sweat. The Cossacks crawled from spot to spot in search of cover or better vantage points. Some attempted to dig hollows in the earth with their swords.

Meantime the wind brought the indistinct strains of singing to the hillside. The lines of Red Guards wound along unevenly, and their voices came faintly, lost in the sultry, spacious steppe. Gregor felt his heart beating violently and spasmodically. He had heard that groaning refrain before! He had heard the sailors singing it at Gluboka, devoutly removing their caps, their eyes gleaming passionately. A sudden mournful anxiety grew within him.

"What are they roaring?" an elderly Cossack asked, turning his head cautiously.

"Gregor, you've been among them," said Andrei Kashulin, impudently glancing up at Gregor, standing close by him. "You know what they're singing, don't you? I expect you've sung the song yourself."

". . . Own the earth . . ." the words came clearly at that moment crossing the intervening space, then the silence again descended over the steppe. The Cossacks were amused, and someone in the middle of the line burst into laughter.

"Do you hear that? They want to own the earth!" Mitka Korshunov sneered, and cursed foully. "Gregor Pantaleev! Shall I send that one on horseback off his horse?"

He fired without waiting for permission. The bullet disturbed the rider, and he dismounted, handed his horse to a soldier, and marched on foot in front of his men, his bare sword gleaming.

The Cossacks began to fire, and the Reds lay down. Gregor ordered the machine-gunners to open fire. After a couple of rounds the first line of Reds rose and advanced at a run for some thirty yards, then again lay down. Through his field-glasses Gregor could see them working with their trenching tools, digging themselves in. A bluish dust hung above them, and little mounds like mole-hills grew in front of the line. An irregular volley came from the mole-hills. The battle threatened to be protracted. In less than an hour the Cossacks had losses: one of the first troop was mortally wounded, three others crawled back to the horses in the hollow. The second squadron appeared on the enemy's flank and galloped into the attack. It was repulsed with machine-gun fire, and the Cossacks galloped back in panic, scattering and riding in bunches. The squadron was reassembled, and silently advanced again. And again the squall of machine-gun fire drove them back like leaves before the wind.

But the attack had shaken the morale of the Red Guards. The first two lines were flung into confusion and began to retreat.

Without ceasing fire Gregor brought his squadron to its feet. The Cossacks began to advance, not stopping to lie down. The first irresolution passed, and they were emboldened by the sight of a battery galloping into position. The first gun was posted and opened fire. Gregor sent a man to order the Cossacks in the hollow to bring up the horses. He prepared for the attack. By the crab-apple tree whence he had watched the opening of the battle a third gun was posted. An observer and a senior officer were standing about half a mile away from the battery, gazing through field-glasses at the retreating lines of Reds. Telephonists were running with a wire to connect the battery with the observation post.

There was a howling, shattering roar, and Gregor watched for the shell to fall. The first shrapnel covered the rows of ungathered wheat, and a white, cottony clump of smoke hung against the blue background. The four guns in rotation sent shells into the rows of cut wheat, but, contrary to Gregor's expectation, the gunfire caused no perceptible confusion in the ranks of the Reds. They continued to retreat unhurriedly, organizedly, and disappeared into a valley. Realizing the senselessness of attack, Gregor none the less decided to discuss the matter with the commander of the battery, whose appearance inspired him with confidence. He awkwardly went up to the officer and, touching the end of his moustache with his left hand, gave him a friendly smile.

"I thought of leading my men into the attack," he said.

'How can you attack?" The captain shook his head violently, wiping the sweat away from his brow with the back of his hand. "You can see how steadily they're retreating, the swine! They won't yield. And it would be absurd to think they would: all their commanding officers, men raised from the ranks, are in those sections. An old comrade of mine is there."

"How do you know?" Gregor asked distrustfully.

"From deserters. Cease fire!" he ordered his men, and, as though to justify the command, explained to Gregor: "Our fire is not achieving anything, and we're short of shells. You're Melekhov, aren't you? My name's Poltavtsev." He thrust his great sweaty hand into Gregor's and drew some cigarettes out of his pocket. "Have a smoke?" He offered Gregor one.

With a muffled thunder the drivers galloped up with the limbers from the hollow. Gregor mounted his horse and led his squadron after the retreating Reds. The enemy occupied the next village, but yielded it without a struggle. The battery and the three squadrons of the Vieshenska Regiment scattered through the village. The terrified inhabitants would not show their heads outside their huts. The Cossacks swarmed through the yards in search of food. Gregor dismounted outside a hut standing a little apart, led his horse into the yard, and tied it up by the porch. He found the master of the house, a tall, elderly Cossack, lying on the bed, groaning and tossing his disproportionately small head on the dirty pillow.

"Are you ill?" Gregor smiled at the man.

"Yes, I'm ill."

But the man was only feigning illness and, judging by the uneasy shifting of his eyes, he guessed that Gregor did not believe him.

"Will you give my Cossacks some food?" Gregor demanded imperatively.

"How many are there?"

"Five."

"Well, bring them in. Whatever God has sent us we'll give them."

After eating with his Cossacks, Gregor went into the street. The battery was drawn up in full fighting order by the well. The horses were eating barley from baskets. The drivers and gunners were sheltering from the sun in the cool of the ammunition boxes or were sitting and lying around the guns. One gunner was stretched out fast asleep, his legs crossed, his shoulders twitching. Probably he had lain down in the shade, but the sun had shifted and was now scorching his uncovered curly hair, in which wisps of hay were mingled.

The officers and commander of the battery were sitting and smoking on the ground, their backs against the wall of the well. Not far from them a group of Cossacks sprawled in a six-pointed star over the burnt weeds, drinking sour milk from a pitcher and occasionally spitting out grains of barley which had found their way into the milk.

The sun streamed down mercilessly. The village streets were almost deserted. Cossacks were sleeping under the granaries and the roofs of the sheds and in the yellow shade of the burdocks by the fences. The horses standing saddled by the palisades were exhausted and drowsy with the sultry heat. A Cossack rode past, lazily raising his whip to the level of his horse's back. Then again the village lay like a forgotten steppe track, and the guns and the worn-out, sleeping men seemed fortuitous and unnecessary.

Bored with nothing to do, Gregor was about to turn back into the hut; but three Cossack horsemen from another squadron rode down the street, driving before them a small group of Red Guard prisoners. The artillery-men stirred and sat up, brushing the dust from their coats and trousers. The officers rose to their feet. Sleepy Cossacks came running out of the neighbouring yards.

The prisoners—eight sweating, dusty youngsters—approached. They were surrounded by a dense crowd.

"Where did you catch them?" the battery commander asked, examining the prisoners with cold curiosity. With a touch of braggadocio in his voice one of the escort replied:

"We found them in the sunflowers by the village. They were hiding like quails from a kite. We saw them from our horses and rounded them up. We killed one. . . ."

The Red Guards fearfully herded together. Evidently they were afraid they would be summarily executed. Their eyes ran helplessly over the faces of the Cossacks. Only one, apparently older than the rest, his face brown with sunburn, in a greasy tunic and puttees worn to shreds, contemptuously stared across their heads with his black eyes and pressed his lips together. He was thickset and broad-shouldered; on his black hair, as coarse as a horse's mane, was a cap evidently preserved from the days of the German war. He stood at ease, his thick black fingers with dried blood on the nails fumbling at his unbuttoned shirt collar and his hairy Adam's apple. He seemed to be perfectly calm, but one leg a little behind the other, monstrously thick in the puttee wound to the knee, was quivering. The other men were pale and without outstanding characteristics. He alone struck the eye by the sturdy breadth of his shoulders and his energetic, Tatar face. Perhaps that explained why the battery commander turned to him with the question:

"Who are you?"

A light came into the man's tiny eyes, like fragments of anthracite, and almost imperceptibly, yet neatly, he drew himself up.

"A Red Guard. Russian."

"Where were you born?"

"Penza province."

"A volunteer, you snake?"

"Not at all. I was a senior non-commissioned officer in the old army, found myself in the Red Guards in 1917, and have remained in them ever since. . . ."

One of the escort intervened. "He fired at us, the swine!" he informed the officer.

"Fired?" The captain frowned sourly and, catching the gaze of Gregor standing opposite him, he indicated the prisoner with his eyes. "What a—! Shot at the Cossacks, did you? And didn't it occur to you that you might be caught? Supposing we settle accounts with you here and now?"

"I was going to shoot myself." The man's broken lips bristled into a deprecating smile.

"And why didn't you?"

"I had used all my bullets. . . ."

"Ah!" The captain's eyes were cold, but he stared at the soldier with undisguised satisfaction. "And you, you sons of bitches, where are you from?" he demanded in a very different tone, running his eyes over the others.

"We were from Saratov, Your Excellency . . . from Baleshov," a tall, long-necked youth whined, blinking and scratching his head.

Gregor curiously examined the youngsters with their simple peasant faces and their obvious appearance of infantry conscripts. Only the one black-haired man aroused a feeling of hostility in him. He turned to him half in anger:

"Why did you admit just now that you fired at the Cossacks? I suppose you were in charge of a Red company, weren't you? A commander? And a Communist? You'd used all your bullets, you say? Well, supposing we sabre you on the spot? What then?"

The nostrils of his shattered nose quivering, the Red Guard said still more boldly:

"I didn't tell you out of dare-devilry. Why should I try to hide it? If I fired at them I ought to admit it. That's what I say. As for the rest— Sabre me if you want to. I don't expect any mercy from you." He smiled again. "That's what you're Cossacks for."

An approving smile ran round the ring. Humbled by the soldier's deliberate tone, Gregor turned away. He saw the prisoners go over to the well to drink. A company of Cossack skirmishers marched in column formation round the corner.

Later, when the regiment reached a period of incessant fighting and the front stretched in a winding line, Gregor was continually falling in with the enemy. When in immediate proximity to them, he always felt the same keen feeling of tremendous, insatiable curiosity about the Bolsheviks, about these Russian soldiers with whom for some reason it was necessary to do battle. It was as though the naïvely boyish feeling which he had experienced in the first days of the German war, when he had seen the Austro-Hungarian troops for the first time, had remained with him for ever. "What sort of men are they?" There might never have been a period in his life when he had fought with the Reds against the Chornetsov detachment at Gluboka. But at that time he had clearly known the features of his enemies: the majority of them were Don officers, Cossacks. Now it was a question of Russian soldiers, different men altogether, of those who in all their millions supported the Soviet government and were fighting, as he thought, to seize the Cossack lands and possessions.

Once more in the course of a battle he came almost face to face with Red Guards. As he was riding with a troop patrol along the bottom of a ravine, he suddenly heard curses in Russian and the sound of footsteps. Several Red Guards, a Chinese among them, came running over the crest and, dumbfounded at the sight of the Cossacks, froze stock-still for a moment.

"Cossacks!" one of them shouted in a terrified voice, falling to the earth.

The Chinese fired a shot, then in a harsh, sobbing stutter shouted as one of the Cossacks fell:

"Comrades! Up with the Maxim! At the Cossacks!"

Mitka Korshunov sent the Chinese down with a shot from his revolver and, swinging his horse round, was the first to gallop back along the side of the ravine. The others galloped after him, attempting to pass one another. Behind them sounded the baritone voice of the machine-gun. The bullets shrilled through the leaves of the brambles and hawthorns growing over the slopes and tore up the stony bottom of the ravine.

Little by little Gregor began to be steeped in hatred for the Bolsheviks. They had burst into his life as enemies, they had taken him away from the land! He noticed that the other Cossacks were dominated by the same feeling. It seemed to them all that it was only because the Bolsheviks had invaded the Don province that there was

any war at all. As each man looked at the ungathered swaths of
wheat, at the uncut grain trodden underfoot by his horse, he remembered his own land over which his women were toiling beyond
their strength, and his heart was consumed with fury. Sometimes
Gregor thought that his enemies, the Tambov, Ryazan, and Saratov
peasants, must be moved by the same passionate feeling for the
land. "We're fighting about it as if it was a woman," he thought.

Fewer prisoners were taken. More frequently summary execution
was meted out on the spot. A wave of looting swept over the front:
the Cossacks pillaged the families of Red Guards and those suspected
of Bolshevik sympathies; they stripped the prisoners naked. They
took everything, from horses and wagons to quite unnecessary articles. Cossacks and officers all stole. The baggage trains were piled
high with trophies: clothes, samovars, sewing-machines, harness,
anything that had the least value. From the baggage trains the articles flowed homeward in a steady stream. Relatives arrived at the
front, willingly bringing ammunition and provisions and piling their
wagons with plunder. The cavalry regiments—and they were in the
majority—were especially unbridled. The infantry had nothing in
which to put loot except their packs, but a horseman could fill his
saddlebags, could load up his saddle and strap bundles behind it
until his horse looked more like a pack-mule than an army charger.
Pillage in war-time had always been a prime factor in the Cossacks'
behaviour. Gregor was well aware of that, both by the stories of past
wars and from his own experience. Even in the days of the German
war, when his regiment had been wandering through Prussia, the
brigade commander, an estimable and honest general, had pointed
with his whip to a little town lying under the hills and had told the
regiment:

"Take it! For two hours the town is at your disposition. But after
two hours the first man caught looting will be put against a wall!"

Gregor had never been able to behave like the other Cossacks:
he took only food for his horse and himself, refusing to touch anything else and loathing pillage. He was especially repelled when
his own Cossacks looted. He kept a tight hand over the squadron.
If any of his men took anything, it was in secret and very rarely. He
gave no orders for prisoners to be stripped and exterminated. His
unusual softness of heart caused discontent among his Cossacks and
the regimental command, and he was summoned to give an explana-

tion of his conduct to the divisional staff. One of the members of
the staff roared at him roughly:

"Ensign, what are you spoiling your squadron for? What's all this
liberalism of yours? Preparing a soft bed for yourself against a possible change in the situation? Playing with both sides for old times'
sake? Now, no arguing! Don't you know your discipline? What?
Replace you? We will! I'll give orders for you to hand over the
squadron this very day, and no grumbling from you, brother!"

He was reduced to the rank of a troop commander. His regiment
captured a village, and with his troop he occupied the hut assigned
to him. It appeared that the owner had retreated with the Reds,
and his elderly wife and daughter, a girl in her teens, waited on them
submissively. Gregor went into the best room and looked around:
the owners had evidently lived well, for the floor was painted, they
had Viennese chairs, a mirror, the usual photographs on the walls
and a fulsomely worded school certificate in a black frame. Gregor
hung his wet raincoat to dry on the stove and rolled a cigarette.
Prokhor Zykov entered, put his rifle down against the bed, and informed him unconcernedly:

"Wagons have arrived from Tatarsk, and your father with them,
Gregor Pantalievich!"

"Any more tales like that?"

"It's true; there are six wagons from our village."

Gregor put on his greatcoat and went out. He found his father
leading his horse through the gate of the yard. Daria, wrapped in a
home-made coat, was sitting in the wagon, holding the reins. A moist
smile and laughing eyes gleamed at Gregor from beneath the cowl
of her coat.

"What brought you here?" Gregor shouted, smiling to his father.

"Ah, son, it's good to see you alive. We're visiting you as uninvited guests. . . ."

Gregor embraced his father's broad shoulders and began to unfasten the traces from the wagon. As they unharnessed the horses
they exchanged fragmentary remarks. "We've brought you ammunition for you to go on fighting with," his father told him. Daria took
some fodder for the horses out of the wagon.

"And why have you come, too?" Gregor asked her.

"I came with Father. He hasn't been well. Mother was afraid
something might happen and he be alone in strange parts."

Pantaleimon flung a bundle of green hay to the horses, then went over to Gregor and asked in a hoarse whisper, his black, bloodshot eyes dilated anxiously:

"Well, how is it going?"

"Oh, all right. We keep on fighting."

"I heard a story that the Cossacks won't march beyond the province boundaries. Is that true?"

"Only talk," Gregor replied evasively.

"What do you mean by it, my lad?" the old man said in an unfriendly and anxious tone. "You can't go on like that. We old men hope. . . . Except for you, who is going to defend our father Don? If you don't want to fight, which God forbid . . . your men told me. . . . They're spreading rumours, the sons of bitches."

They went into the hut, and the Cossacks gathered to hear the news of the village. After a whispered consultation with the mistress of the hut, Daria untied a bag of food and began to prepare the evening meal.

"I hear you've been reduced from squadron commander," Pantaleimon asked.

"I'm a troop commander now." Gregor's unconcerned reply irritated the old man. Frowns appeared on his brow. He limped to the table, hurriedly muttered a prayer, wiped a spoon with the edge of his coat, then asked in an affronted tone:

"And what's that for? Didn't you please your superior officers?"

Gregor felt disinclined to talk about the matter in front of the Cossacks, and he shrugged his shoulders with annoyance.

"They appointed a new commander, one with education," he said.

"But serve him all the same, my son! Them and their education! You got a real education during the German war, more than any of their bespectacled officers." The old man was obviously indignant. But Gregor frowned and glanced sidelong at the Cossacks to see whether they were smiling.

He felt no resentment at his reduction in rank. He had gladly handed over the squadron, realizing that he would no longer be responsible for the lives of the men from his own village. None the less his self-esteem had been wounded, and his father's remarks involuntarily caused him annoyance.

The mistress of the hut went into the kitchen and, reading approval in the face of his fellow-villager Bogatiriev, who had also arrived with the transport, Pantaleimon returned to the topic disturbing him.

"So it's true that you don't want to go farther than the boundary?" he asked, addressing himself generally to the Cossacks in the room.

His sheepish, kindly eyes blinking, Prokhor Zykov was silent, quietly smiling. Mitka Korshunov, who was squatting near the stove, finished his cigarette. Three other Cossacks were sitting or lying on benches, but nobody replied to the question. Bogatiriev waved his hand bitterly.

"They don't seem to trouble much about these things," he said in his deep bass voice.

"And why should we go farther?" one of the Cossacks asked lazily. "Why should we? My wife's dead and left me with orphan children, and am I to throw away my life for nothing?"

"We'll drive them out of the Cossack lands, and then back home for us!" another Cossack resolutely supported him.

Mitka Korshunov smiled only with his eyes and twisted his thin moustache.

"I could go on fighting for five years! I like it!" he declared.

At that moment there was a shout outside in the yard:

"Turn out! To horse!"

"There, now you see!" the first Cossack to speak exclaimed in despair. "Here we are not yet dry from the rain, and they're shouting: 'Turn out!' That means up into position again. And you talk about boundaries. What boundaries are there? We ought to be going home. We must try to make peace, and you talk . . ."

The alarm proved to be unfounded. Gregor angrily led his horse back into the yard, needlessly kicking it in the groin and snorting:

"Walk straight, you devil!"

"What was the alarm for?" Pantaleimon, who was smoking at the door, asked the Cossacks as they entered.

"Alarm! . . . They mistook a herd of cows for the Reds!"

Gregor removed his coat and sat down at the table. The other Cossacks threw their swords, rifles, and cartridge-belts on the benches. When the others had lain down to sleep, Pantaleimon called Gregor into the yard. They sat down on the steps.

"I want to talk to you," the old man touched Gregor's knees and whispered. "I went to see Piotra a week ago. I did well there, son. Piotra's got a fine eye for the farm. He gave me clothing, a horse, sugar . . . a fine horse."

"Wait!" Gregor interrupted harshly, burning as he guessed the drift of the old man's remarks. "You haven't come here for that?"

"And why not?"

"What do you mean: 'Why not'?"

"Other men take things, Gregor."

"Other men! Take things!" Gregor repeated furiously, at a loss for words. "Haven't they got enough of their own? You're swine! Men were shot for that sort of thing in the German war. . . ."

"Don't you carry on like that!" his father coldly stopped him. "I'm not asking you. I don't want anything. I'm alive today, but tomorrow I'll be stretching out my legs. You think of yourself. Tell me, what will you find at home when you come back? One small wagonette, and that . . . And why shouldn't you take from those who've gone over to Reds? It's a sin not to take from them. Every bit and stick would be of use at home. . . ."

"No more of that, or I'll pack you off quick! I've given Cossacks a good hiding for that, and here is my father come to plunder the people!" Gregor quivered and panted.

"And that's why they've reduced you from squadron commander," his father sneered.

"Yes, and I'll give up the troop, too."

They were silent for a moment. As he lit a cigarette, by the light of the match Gregor momentarily saw his father's embarrassed and affronted face. Only now did he realize the reason for his father's arrival. "And that's why he's brought Daria, the old devil! To look after the loot!"

"Stepan Astakhov's turned up. Have you heard?" Pantaleimon calmly announced.

"What?" Gregor let the cigarette drop from his hand.

"It appears he was taken prisoner and not killed after all. He's come back with clothes and possessions to him, believe it or not! He brought it in two wagons!" the old man lied, bragging as though Stepan were a relative. "He fetched Aksinia back from Yagodnoe, and then went off to the army. They've given him a good job; he's a storekeeper at Kazanska or somewhere."

"How are your grandchildren?" Gregor turned the conversation in another direction.

"Oho, they're fine, son! You should send them a present."

"Send them presents from the front!" Gregor sighed mournfully, but his thoughts were with Aksinia and Stepan.

"You haven't a spare rifle, have you?"

"What do you want it for?"

"For home. To keep away the animals and strangers. Just in case, I've got a whole box of cartridges. I took it when I was carting ammunition."

"Take a rifle out of the wagon. We've got plenty of that kind of present," Gregor smiled gloomily. "Well, now go to sleep. I've got to make a round of the pickets."

Next morning part of the regiment, Gregor's squadron among them, was shifted from the village. Gregor departed confident that he had upset his father, and that the old man would go back with empty hands. But after seeing the Cossacks off, Pantaleimon went as though he were the master into the granary, took horse-collars and harness down from the pegs, and carried them to his wagon. The mistress of the hut followed him, weeping and shouting and clinging to his shoulder:

"My father! My dear man! Aren't you afraid of a sin? What are you hurting orphans for? Give me back the collars. Give me them for the love of God!"

"Now, now; you leave God out of it!" Pantaleimon pushed her off. "I expect your husband would take things from us. I know your commissars! What's yours is mine, so shut up!"

Then, watched in sympathetic silence by the other carters, he broke the locks on the chests and selected new trousers and coats, held them up to the light, felt them in his black hands, and tied them up in a bundle.

He and Daria set off on the homeward journey about noon. The wagon was piled high, and Daria sat with compressed lips on top of the bundles. Behind her towered a boiler which Pantaleimon had torn out of its place in the bath-house. He could hardly carry it to the wagon, and when Daria said reproachfully: "You wouldn't leave a thing, Father!" he angrily told her:

"Shut up, you squawker! Leave them that boiler? You're as fine a housewife as Gregor, you slut! I've taken a fancy to that boiler. You keep your mouth shut."

As, streaming with tears, the woman shut the gate behind him, he said benevolently:

"Good-bye, woman. Don't be angry. You'll soon get some more."

Chapter 8

A chain of days, link forged within link. Marches, battles, rests. Heat and rain. The mingled scent of horse's sweat and the hot leather of the saddle. Blood that under the continual strain is turned to a boiling stream in the veins. Through lack of sleep a head heavier than a six-inch shell. Gregor longed for rest, for sleep. And afterwards to walk along the soft furrow left by the plough-share, whistling to the bullocks; to hear the trumpet call of the cranes, to remove the flying silver gossamer from the cheeks, and to drink and drink of the autumnal scent raised from the earth by the plough.

But instead, grain slashed by the blades of roads. Along the roads crowds of prisoners, unclothed and cadaverous, black with dust. Squadrons trampling the roads, threshing the grain with iron horse-shoes. In the villages, requisitions on the families of the retreating Reds, whippings for their wives and mothers.

Emasculated by boredom the days dragged on. They faded from the memory, and not one incident, even those of importance, left any trace behind. The day-to-day life of the war seemed even more dreary than that of the German campaigns, maybe because every-thing was known in advance. All those who had participated in the previous war were contemptuous of the present struggle: its dimensions, its forces, its losses were all on a petty scale by com-parison with the German war. Only death, just as in the fields of Prussia, rose in all its sombre height, terrifying and compelling an animal self-preservation.

"Call this a war? It's only an imitation. In the German war,

when the Germans fired one of their guns whole regiments would
be torn up by the roots, and now we talk of losses if a couple of
men are wounded in one company." So the front-line men thought.
But even this playing at war irritated them. Dissatisfaction, weariness, anger accumulated. In Gregor's squadron the Cossacks said
with growing insistence: "We'll drive the Reds out of the province
and finish. We won't go farther. Let Russia manage her own
affairs, and we'll manage ours. We don't want to force our system
on them."

All autumn a sluggish struggle went on. The main strategic
centre was Tsaritsyn, and both Reds and Whites flung their finest
forces in that direction. In consequence neither side had any strong
preponderance on the northern front. The Cossacks had large
forces of cavalry and, exploiting this advantage, they carried on
co-ordinated operations, flanking movements, and attacks on the
enemy's rear. But the Cossacks gained the ascendancy only when
they were opposed by morally unstable divisions consisting of
newly mobilized Red Army men drawn mainly from the area immediately behind the front. The Saratov and Tambov men surrendered in thousands; but as soon as the Red command flung a
workers' regiment or a sailor detachment into action the situation
was changed, and the initiative passed from hand to hand, only victories of local significance being won by each side.

While taking part in the war, Gregor tranquilly watched its
course. He was convinced that by winter there would be no front.
He knew that the Cossacks were pacifically inclined and that there
could be no talk of a protracted struggle. Newspapers rarely
reached the front. When one arrived, Gregor would pick up the
yellow sheet of printed packing paper and would grind his teeth
as he ran his eyes down the military communiqués. The Cossacks
around him would roar with amusement as he read aloud the bold,
artificially cheerful lines:

"September 27: A struggle with varying success on the Filimonov
sector. During the night of the 26th the brilliant Vieshenska Regiment drove the enemy out of one village and, following up the
success, entered Lukianovsk. Trophies and large numbers of prisoners were captured. The Red detachments are retreating in disorder. The Cossacks are in splendid spirits. The Don Cossacks are
panting for fresh victories!"

"How many prisoners did we take? Large numbers? Ha-ha! The sons of bitches! We took exactly thirty-two. And they say . . ." Mitka rocked with laughter, pressing his hands to his sides, all the enormous gap of his mouth stretched wide open.

The Cossacks did not believe the reports of the Cadets' successes in Siberia and the Kuban. The newspapers lied shamelessly and without restraint. One Cossack of Gregor's troop read an article on the Czechoslovakian rising and declared in Gregor's hearing:

"The Reds will smash the Czechs, and then they'll turn all their army against us and squeeze us until we're a jelly."

"Don't try to frighten us! You've gone rotten with all this idiotic talk," said Prokhor Zykov.

But as he rolled himself a cigarette Gregor mentally decided with quiet malevolence: "He's right."

That evening he sat a long time huddled over the table, his shirt collar unbuttoned. There was a harsh expression on his sunburnt face, with its cheekbones covered with an unhealthy fullness of flesh. He thoughtfully twisted the end of his sunbleached moustache and stared fixedly with eyes grown cold and evil during these past few years. He sat thinking tensely, with unusual difficulty, and, as he lay down to sleep, remarked as though replying to a general query:

"There's nowhere to retreat to."

It was evident that Gregor's star still burned with a quiet, flickering gleam. Evidently the time had not yet arrived for it to break away and fly off, burning the sky with its cold, dying light. During the autumn three horses were killed beneath him, and his jacket was holed in five places. Death seemed to be playing with him, wrapping him in its black wing. One day a bullet pierced through the copper hilt of his sword, and the sword-knot fell at his horse's feet as though bitten off.

"Someone's praying hard for you, Gregor," Mitka Korshunov said to him, and was astonished at Gregor's cheerless smile.

The front passed beyond the railway line. Every day great reels of barbed wire were brought up by the transport wagons. Every day the telegraph sped the words along the front: "Any day now the Allied Armies will arrive. It is necessary to consolidate the position on the boundaries of the province until the arrival of rein-forcements and to resist the pressure of the Reds at all costs."

The mobilized inhabitants of the district ploughed up the earth, digging trenches and protecting them with barbed-wire entangle-ments. But at night, when the Cossacks abandoned the trenches and went into the villages to warm themselves, Red Guard advance parties approached the Cossack trenches, threw down the defences, and fastened printed appeals to the Cossacks to the rusty points of the barbed wire. The Cossacks read them greedily, as though they were letters from home. It was clear that in such conditions to carry on the war was senseless. Frosts set in, alternating with thaws and tremendous falls of snow. The trenches were filled with snow. It was difficult to lie down for even an hour in them. The Cos-sacks froze, their feet and hands suffered from frost-bite. In the infantry and Cossack skirmishing detachments many were now without boots; others had gone to the front as though going out into their farmyard, dressed in shoes and light summer trousers. They had no faith in the Allies. "They ride on beetles," one of Gregor's troop bitterly remarked one day.

From the end of November the Reds took the offensive. They stubbornly forced the Cossack divisions back to the railway line. After a long struggle, on December 29 the Red cavalry threw back the Cossack 33rd Regiment; but in the section held by the Vie-shenska Regiment they met with a desperate resistance. From behind the snowy selvages of yard fences the regimental machine-gunners welcomed the enemy infantry with a hail of bullets. The machine-gun on the right flank spread a rain of death, while on the left flank certain squadrons were thrown into a flanking manœuvre.

Towards evening the feebly advancing Red Army forces were replaced by a detachment of sailors newly arrived at the front. They poured into the attack against the machine-guns, not lying down and not shouting.

Gregor fired incessantly, until the barrel of his rifle was red-hot and burned his hands. He cooled the rifle, then again thrust in cartridges, aiming with screwed-up eyes at the distant little black figures.

The sailors smashed through the Cossack defence. Taking to their horses, the squadrons galloped away through the village and up the rise beyond. Gregor glanced back and involuntarily dropped his reins. From the hillside he could see the far-stretching, mournful snowy steppe, with little mounds of snow-covered bushes, and lilac evening shadows lying along the sides of the hollows. For the length of a mile over the steppe lay the bodies of sailors shot down by the machine-gun fire. In their sailor jackets and leather jerkins they looked like crows settled on the field.

In the evening the disintegrated squadrons, having lost contact with the regiments on either side of them, halted for the night in two villages situated on a little stream, a tributary of the river Buzuluk. All night transport wagons were dragging through the village where Gregor's squadron was quartered. A battery halted for a long time in the street. Gunners and staff orderlies wandered into Gregor's hut to warm themselves. At midnight three of the battery command burst into the hut, awakening the owners and the Cossacks. Their gun had stuck fast in the stream not far from the village, and they had decided to leave it there for the night and to drag it out with bullocks in the morning. Gregor awoke and stared at the gunners cleaning the sticky mud from their boots, undressing, and hanging up their leg-rags to dry. A little later an artillery officer, splashed with mud to his ears, came in. He asked permission to stop there for the night, drew off his greatcoat, and with an unconcerned air spread the mud spots over his face with the sleeve of his tunic.

"We've lost one gun," he said, staring at Gregor with eyes as humble as a weary horse's. "They got our range after we had fired twice. Our gun was in a yard, it couldn't have been better hidden . . ." to every phrase he quite unconsciously attached some unprintable oath. "Are you of the Vieshenska Regiment? Will you have some tea? Woman, how about a samovar, eh?"

The officer proved to be a garrulous, boring companion. He drank tea unwearyingly. Within half an hour Gregor knew that he was born in Platovsky district, had been in the German war, and had been twice unsuccessfully married.

"It's 'Amen' to the Don army now," he said, wiping the sweat from his lips with his tongue. "The war's nearly over. Tomorrow the front will break up, and in a fortnight we shall be back at Novocherkass. We wanted to take Russia by storm with barefoot Cossacks! Aren't we idiots? And the commanding officers are all scoundrels. You're a Cossack, aren't you? Yes? And they wanted you to pull the chestnuts out of the fire for them. But behind the front they're handing themselves out laurels and porridge."

He blinked his light-tinted eyes, all his body lying over the table, the corners of his mouth moodily and involuntarily drooping, while his face still retained the expression of a humble, worn-out horse. Gregor sleepily watched the heavy movements of his fleshy shoulders and arms, the red tongue flickering in and out of his mouth. He wanted to sleep, inwardly raged against this obtrusive, doltish officer, and was half sick with the smell of the man's sweaty feet.

In the morning Gregor awoke with an irritating feeling that something had been left unsettled. The development he had expected even in the autumn startled him none the less by the abruptness of its coming. He had overlooked the rise of discontent with the war, which at first had rippled through the squadrons and regiments in little streams, but then had imperceptibly run together to form a mighty flood. And now he could see only that flood, violently, avidly washing away the front.

All the next day the regiment was retreating. Transport wagons galloped along the roads. From somewhere to the right, beyond the grey clouds veiling the horizon, came the thunder of gunfire. The squadrons splashed over the melted road, the horses churned up the wet snow with their hoofs. Orderlies galloped along at the edge of the road. Silent crows stalked awkwardly, like dismounted cavalry-men, about the wayside, importantly watching the retreating columns of Cossack squadrons, skirmishers, and lines of wagons as though reviewing a parade.

Gregor realized that nobody could halt the springs of the retreat now. The same night, filled with the joy of determination, he deserted from his regiment.

"Where are you off to, Gregor?" Mitka Korshunov asked, watching with a smile as Gregor put on his greatcoat and fastened his sword-belt and revolver holster.

"What do you want to know for?"

"I'm just curious."

Gregor's face worked, but he replied merrily, with a wink:

"To the land ol 'mind your own business.' Understand?" He went out.

His horse stood saddled. Until sunrise he galloped over the frozen field by-ways. "I'll stay at home, and I'll hear as they go by and can rejoin the regiment," he thought casually of those with whom he had been fighting side by side only the previous day. By evening of the following day he was leading his horse, worn out and emaciated with the two-hundred-mile ride, into his father's yard.

Chapter 9

A week later the front had completely dissolved. The first to leave the front open was the 28th Regiment, in which Piotra Melekhov was serving. After secret negotiations with the command of the enemy opposite them, the Cossacks resolved to retire and to let the Red Army pass without hindrance through the territory of the upper Don region. Yakov Fomin, a narrow-minded and short-sighted Cossack, was a leader of the insurgent regiment; but in reality Fomin was only a dummy, and behind him a group of Bolshevik-minded Cossacks directed the movement.

After a stormy meeting in which the officers, fearing a bullet in the back, reluctantly urged the necessity of continuing the struggle, while the Cossacks vigorously, insistently, and unorganizedly shouted that the war was unnecessary and that peace should be made with the Bolsheviks, the regiment began to retreat. At the end of the first day's march the commander and the majority of the officers abandoned the regiment and attached themselves to another brigade.

Following the example of the 28th Regiment, the 36th Regiment also abandoned its positions. It arrived at Kazanska in its full complement, including its officers. Surrounded by horsemen, the commander rode up to the house where the district commandant was quartered, dismounted, and entered with a swash-buckling air, playing with his whip.

"Who is the commandant here?" he demanded.

"I am his assistant," Stepan Astakhov rose and said with dignity. "Shut the door."

"I'm the commander of the 36th Regiment. My name's Naumov . . . I have the honour . . . I have got to equip my men with new clothes and boots. They are ragged and barefoot. Do you hear?"

"The commandant is not here, and without his authority I cannot hand out a single pair of boots from the stores."

"What?"

"That's what!"

"You—whom are you talking to? I'll arrest you, damn you! At him, lads! Where is the key to the stores, you rear rat?" The officer banged on the table with his whip and, paling with frenzy, thrust his fur cap back on his head. "Give me the key, and no arguing!"

Within half an hour bundles of fur jackets, felt boots, leather boots were flying through the stores door on to the snow, and bags of sugar were passing from hand to hand. A noisy and merry babel of voices arose on the square.

Meantime the 28th Regiment, with its new commander, Sergeant Fomin, had retreated as far as Vieshenska district. Twenty miles behind them came the divisions of Red Guards, pouring through the seventy-mile gap in the northern front. For a whole week there was an unusual quiet in the north. There was no sound of gunfire, the machine-guns were silent. Disheartened by the defection of the 28th Regiment, the Cossacks of the lower Don district were retreating without fighting. The Reds advanced cautiously, slowly, their advance patrols carefully reconnoitring the villages lying ahead of them.

During those days of disintegration the hostility which, even during the Imperialist war, had divided the Cossacks from their officers by an invisible furrow developed to unprecedented dimensions. At the end of 1917, when the Cossack regiments had been slowly flowing back to the Don, instances of murder and betrayal of the officers were rare. But a year later they had become an almost everyday incident. The Cossacks compelled their officers to imitate the Red Army commanders and to go in front when advancing, then quietly shot them in the back. With his crafty, quick-witted mind Piotra Melekhov had long before this realized that to argue with the Cossacks was to invite death for himself, and from the earliest days of the revolt he had carefully worked to break down the barriers separating him, an officer, from the rank and file. Like them he talked on convenient occasions of the uselessness of the war, speaking insincerely and with great difficulty, but not being found out. He began to paint himself in Bolshevik colours and, as soon as he saw that Yakov Fomin was coming to the leadership of the regiment, began deliberately to worm his way into his good graces. Like the rest, Piotra was not slow to curse the officers and to spare the prisoners, although in his heart he was filled with hatred and his hands trembled with the desire to strike and kill them. Thus he managed to win the Cossacks' confidence, and to change his features before their very eyes.

When the commander of the regiment led off the other officers, Piotra remained behind. Peaceable and quiet, always keeping himself in the background, restrained in all his behaviour, he arrived with the regiment at Vieshenska. But after spending two days there, he could hold out no longer and, without reporting to the staff or to Fomin, he fled home.

That day a meeting had been going on since early morning in Vieshenska market square outside the old church. The regiment was waiting for the arrival of delegates from the Red Army. The Cossacks wandered in droves over the square, dressed in greatcoats, short fur jackets, and coats fashioned from overcoats, or in woollen padded coats. It was impossible to believe that this enormous nondescript mob was the 28th Regiment. Piotra wandered despondently from one group to another, studying the Cossacks. At the front he had not been struck by the style of their dress; for that matter, he had not previously seen the entire regiment in one compact mass. Now, hatefully biting the ends of his moustache, he stared at their heads with their strange assortment of fur caps, hats, and cowls, he looked at their bodies and saw as rich a variety of felt boots, leg-boots and leg-rags wound above short boots taken from Red Guards. "Ragged bums! Damned lot of peasants! Degenerates!" he muttered to himself in impotent anger.

Not one of Vieshenska's inhabitants was to be seen on the streets. The entire place was in expectant hiding. The white breast of the snow-swept Don showed through the gaps of the cross-alleys, with the forest beyond looming black as though etched in India ink. Around the grey stone pile of the church the women come from the villages to visit their husbands were huddled like a flock of sheep.

Piotra, dressed in a fur-lined jacket with an enormous pocket on the chest, and wearing that accursed officer's astrakhan cockade of which he recently had been so proud, continually felt sidelong, cold glances fixed on him. They deepened his already anxious, distracted mood. He stood listening for a while to a Red Army man in a greatcoat of good quality and a new fur cap, who was standing on a barrel in the middle of the square. With his fur-gloved hand the man adjusted the scarf about his neck and looked around him.

"Comrade Cossacks . . ." the low, chilly voice entered Piotra's ears.

Piotra looked about him and noticed that the Cossacks, troubled by the unusual word "comrade," were staring at one another agitatedly. The Red Army man talked for a long time about the Soviet government, the Red Army, and relations with the Cossacks. He was continually being interrupted by shouts:

"Comrade, what do you mean by 'commune'?"

"And what is the Communist Party?"

The speaker pressed his hand against his chest and patiently explained:

"Comrades! The Communist Party is a voluntary affair. The party is joined of their own free will by those who want to struggle for the great task of liberating the workers and peasants from the oppression of the capitalists and landowners."

Almost immediately there was a shout from someone else:

"Explain to us about Communists and commissars."

Hardly had the man finished his explanation when a further shout arose:

"We don't understand what you're talking about. We're ignorant people here. Use simpler words."

When the Red Army man had finished, Yakov Fomin made a long and boring speech. As he listened Piotra recalled the first time he had seen Fomin in the army, when Daria had visited him at the station on the way to Petrograd. Before his eyes appeared the stern, moistly gleaming eyes of the deserter from the ataman regiment, the greatcoat with the number "52" on the shoulder-straps, and the man's bearish walk. "Couldn't stand any more, brother!" Piotra remembered the words. "A deserter, a fool like Christonia; and now he's the commander of the regiment, and I'm left out in the cold," Piotra thought, his eyes glittering bitterly.

He turned and walked swiftly towards his quarters. He saddled his horse, listening as the Cossacks riding away from Vieshenska fired their rifles, in accordance with immemorial custom announcing the return of service-men to their villages.

Chapter 10

The terrifying still, short days seemed longer than those of harvest-time. The villages lay like the untrodden, virgin steppe. It was as though all the Donside districts had died, as though a pestilence had laid waste the district settlements. And it was as though clouds had covered all the Don region with their black, opaque wings, spreading silently and terribly, until a wind should send the poplars bending to the earth, a dry, crashing peal of thunder should burst and march to crush and shatter the white forest beyond the Don, to send the savage stones leaping from the chalky hills, and roar with the destructive voice of thunder. . . .

Since morning a mist had enveloped Tatarsk and the steppe. A roaring in the hills presaged a frost. By noonday the sun had peeled out of the clinging mist, but it grew no lighter. The mist aimlessly wandered over the heights of the Donside hills, huddled into the cliffs, and perished there, settling a white dust over the mossy slopes of chalk and on the bare snowy ridges.

In the evening the red-hot shield of the moon arose from beyond the roots of the naked forest. It mistily sowed the bloody seeds of war and incendiary fire over the silent villages. And in its miserable, faded light an inarticulate alarm was born in the hearts of men. The animals fidgeted anxiously; the horses and bullocks could not sleep and wandered about the yards until dawn. The dogs howled balefully, and the cocks began to crow one against another long before midnight. Their stirrups and weapons clattering, an invis-ible mounted army might have been marching down the left bank of the Don, through the dark forest and the grey mist.

Almost all the Tatarsk Cossacks who had been on the northern front had returned to the village, abandoning their regiments as they slowly retreated towards the Don. Some came back to un-

saddle their cavalry mount for many days and to await the arrival
of the Reds, thrusting their military equipment into a rick of straw
or under the eaves of a shed. But others only led their horses into
the yard, spent the night with their wives, and next morning, re-
plenishing their stock of provisions, rode off again along the steppe
tracks, looking back for the last time from the hilltop down on the
white, dead sweep of the Don, and on their native village, left
maybe for ever.

Who goes to meet death? Who can guess the end of the human
road? With difficulty the horses moved away from the village.
With difficulty the Cossacks tore sorrow for their dear ones out of
their chilling hearts. And over that road many returned in thought
to their homes; along it many heavy thoughts were pondered. And
maybe tears as salt as blood slipped over the saddle, down from
the stirrup to the hoof-marked road.

The night after Piotra arrived from Vieshenska there was a family
council in the Melekhov hut.

"Well, what's this?" Pantaleimon asked as soon as Piotra crossed
the threshold. "Had enough of fighting? Come back without your
officer's epaulets? Well, go and shake hands with your brother and
mother. Cheer them up. Your wife's almost dead with longing for
you. Bravo, bravo, Piotra! Gregor! What are you lying on the
stove like a marmot for? Come on down."

Gregor let his bare legs hang and, smilingly scratching his hairy
chest, watched as his brother unfastened his sword-belt with fingers stiff with cold and fumbled with the knots of his cowl-strings.
Daria smiled speechlessly into her husband's eyes and unbuttoned
his sheepskin jacket, carefully avoiding his right side, where a
hand-grenade was fastened to the belt close to the revolver holster.

Brushing her brother's moustache with a kiss as she passed,
Dunia ran out to see to his horse. Ilinichna wiped her lips with her
apron and prepared to kiss her "firstborn." Natalia bustled about
at the stove, her children clinging to her skirt. Everybody waited
for Piotra to speak. But he merely threw a hoarse "Good health!"
to them from the threshold and removed his outer clothes in silence,
spending much time brushing his boots with a millet-straw broom.
Then, straightening up, his lips suddenly trembled, he distractedly
leaned against the head of the bed, and all saw the tears shining
on his frozen, darkened cheeks.

"Here, soldier! What's the matter?" his father asked, concealing his alarm beneath a jest.

"We're finished, Father!" Piotra's mouth writhed, his bleached eyebrows quivered, and, hiding his eyes, he blew his nose into his dirty palm.

Gregor knocked away the cat rubbing itself against him, and with a groan jumped down from the stove. His mother burst into sobs and kissed Piotra's lousy head, but immediately tore herself away from him.

"My dear! My poor boy, shall I get some sour milk for you? Go and sit down, your soup's getting cold. You're hungry, I'm sure."

At the table, dangling his nephew on his knees, Piotra cheered up. Mastering his agitation, he told of the withdrawal of the 28th Regiment from the front, the flight of the officers, of Fomin, and the last meeting he had attended in Vieshenska.

"What do you think about it all?" Gregor asked, his hand resting on his daughter's head.

"There's nothing to think about. I'll spend tomorrow at home and ride off when night comes. Get me some victuals ready, Mother," he turned to her.

"You're clearing out, that means?" Pantaleimon thrust his fingers into his tobacco-pouch and remained standing with a pinch of tobacco between them, awaiting Piotra's reply.

Piotra rose, crossed himself, and stared at him harshly and bitterly.

"Christ save me, I've had enough! Clearing out, you say! And what else? Why should I stay behind? To have the red-bellies cut my block off? Maybe you're thinking of staying here, but I'm not! They'll have no mercy on officers."

"And what of your home? So you're deserting it?"

Piotra merely shrugged his shoulders at his father's question. But Daria at once gave tongue.

"You're going off, and we've got to remain? That's fine, I must say! We'll stay behind to watch over your interests! And lose our lives because of you, maybe! You be damned! I'm not staying!"

Even Natalia intervened in the discussion. Outshouting Daria's ringing recitative, she exclaimed:

"If the village is touched we won't stay. We'll go on foot."

"You fools! Stupid bitches!" Pantaleimon roared in a frenzy, rolling his eyes and involuntarily looking for his stick. "Shut your
mouths, you she-devils! This is a man's business, and you're poking
your noses in. Well, and supposing we do leave everything and go
where our feet take us? What shall we do with the cattle? Put
them in our pockets? And the hut, too?"

"You're touched, my girls!" Ilinichna spiritedly supported her
husband. "You haven't had to work to build up the farm, and it's
easy for you to leave it. But I and the old man have toiled day and
night, and we're not going to clear out!" She pressed her lips together and sighed. "You go, but I'm not moving from here. Better
to be killed on your own threshold than to die under a stranger's
whip."

For a minute there was a general silence. Then Dunia, who was
knitting a stocking, raised her head from her work and said in a
whisper:

"We can drive the cattle with us. . . . We needn't stay behind
because of the cattle."

Again the old man flamed up. Like a stallion kept long in the
stables he stamped his feet, all but falling as he stumbled over a
kid lying by the stove. Halting in front of Dunia, he roared:

"We'll drive them! . . . And the old cow? What of her? Where
will you drive her to? May your sins choke you! You foster-child!
You nitwit! Coddled her and coddled her, and then we have to
listen to that! And the sheep? What will you do with the lambs?
You daughter of a bitch! Better hold your tongue!"

Gregor glanced sidelong at Piotra and as in the old days saw in
his brother's eyes a mischievous, quizzical, and simultaneously respectful smile and noticed the familiar twitch of his wheat-coloured
moustache. Piotra swiftly winked; his body shook with restrained
laughter. Joyously Gregor realized his own desire for laughter, so
unfamiliar of recent years, and he openly laughed deeply and thunderously.

"Well there! Praise be! . . . We've been talking . . ." The old
man gave him an angry look and sat down with his face turned to
the frosted window.

Only at midnight did they come to the general agreement that
the three Cossacks were to clear out of Tatarsk, while the women
were to remain behind to watch over the hut and the farm.

Ilinichna lit the stove long before sunrise, and by morning she had baked bread and dried two bags of rusks. The old man had his breakfast by the stove, and at dawn went out to collect the cattle and to get the sledge ready for departure. He stood a long time in the granary, his hand thrust into the full corn-bin, letting the grains of wheat trickle through his fingers. He went out as though he were leaving a corpse, removing his cap and shutting the door quietly behind him.

He was still bustling around the sledge under the shed when Anikushka appeared in the street, driving his cow down to drink. The two men greeted each other.

"Going to clear out, Anikushka?" Pantaleimon asked.

"I clear out? Belt a naked man! What I have is inside me!"

"Any news?"

"A great deal, Prokofich!"

"What?" Pantaleimon grew anxious and thrust his axe into the side of the sledge.

"The Reds will be here soon. They're getting near Vieshenska. A man from Bolshoi Gromok saw them and said they're killing people as they come. There are Jews and Chinese among them."

"Killing people?"

"As soon as smell them!" Anikushka cursed and moved on, talking as he walked: "The women of the villages are making vodka and giving it to them to drink, so that they won't harm them; and then they get drunk, go on and capture the next village, and run amuck."

The old man looked around the shed, noting every post and wattle set up by his own hands. Then he went to the threshing-floor to get hay for the journey. He took down an iron hook and, still not realizing the inevitability of departure, began to drag out the poorer hay (he always kept the better for use during the spring ploughing). But he changed his mind and, angry with himself, went to another rick. It did not occur to him that within a few hours he would be leaving the yard and the village and driving somewhere to the south and maybe would never return. He pulled down some hay, and again, out of habit, turned to rake up the scattered wisps. But he drew his hand back as though the rake were hot and, wiping his sweaty brow, said aloud:

"What should I look after it for now? All the same, it'll be flung under their horses' feet; they'll eat it or burn it." His old legs dragging, his back bowed, he grated his teeth and picked up the fork of hay.

He did not go into the hut, but shouted through the open door:

"Get ready! I'll be harnessing the horses in a minute. We'd better not be late in starting."

He put the body harness over the horses, dropped a sack of oats into the back of the sledge, and, astonished that his sons had not yet come out to saddle their horses, went into the hut.

In the kitchen a strange sight met his eyes: Piotra was furiously untying the bundles prepared for their departure and throwing trousers, tunics, and women's holiday ornaments on the floor.

"What's all this?" the old man asked in utter amazement, even removing his cap.

"It's them!" Piotra pointed his finger across his shoulder at the women. "They're grumbling! They never go anywhere! If one's going, all ought to go or none at all! They're saying the Reds may force them, and we're going away to save the property. And if they kill them they'll die and be done with it!"

"Take your things off, Father!" Gregor smilingly removed his own greatcoat and cap, while weeping Natalia caught at his hand and kissed it from behind and Dunia joyously clapped her hands.

The old man put on his cap, but took it off again at once and, walking across to the ikons, crossed himself with a great sweeping gesture. He bowed thrice, then rose from his knees and looked around.

"Well, if that's the case, we stay! Queen of Heaven, cover and defend us! I'll go and unharness the horses."

Anikushka happened to drop in and was astonished to see all the Melekhov family with laughing, cheerful faces.

"What's the matter?" he asked.

"Our Cossacks aren't going away," Daria replied for them all.

"Well, now! Thought better of it?"

"Thought better of it!" Gregor reluctantly laid bare his teeth and winked. "No point in going out to look for death! It'll find us here."

"If the officers aren't going, then God has commanded us also what to do," Anikushka exclaimed, and he clattered out of the hut as though wearing horseshoes.

Chapter 11

The decision to remain behind after all brought Pantaleimon renewed strength and a sense of proportion. In the evening he went out to see to the cattle and unhesitatingly chose hay from the poorer rick. In the darkening yard he examined the cow carefully from all sides and satisfiedly thought: "She's getting very fat. Has the Lord blessed her with twins?" A few minutes later he was grumbling at Dunia because she had spilt chaff about and had not broken the ice in the trough. He asked Aksinia, who had run out to close the shutters of their hut, whether Stepan was thinking of clearing out. Wrapping herself in her kerchief, Aksinia answered in a singsong voice:

"No, no. Where could he go to? He's lying on the stove with some sort of fever. His head's burning. He's fallen sick and he can't go away."

"And we aren't going either. The devil knows whether it's for better or worse."

Night fell. Beyond the Don, beyond the grey gulf of forest, the pole-star glowed in the greenish depths of the heavens. In the east the sky was enveloped in purple. The sunset burned in the west. The hump of the moon emerged from the spreading horns of the poplars. The shadows deepened against the snowdrifts. It was so quiet that Pantaleimon could hear someone breaking the ice in the ice-hole by the Don.

The lamp was lit in the hut. Natalia slipped between the light and the window. Pantaleimon was drawn towards the warmth. He found all the household gathered inside. Dunia had just returned from a visit to Christonia's wife. She emptied the cup of leaven she had borrowed and, afraid of being interrupted, hurriedly told the latest news.

In the best room Gregor greased his rifle, revolver, and sword, wrapped his field-glasses in canvas, and then called Piotra.

"Have you collected your arms?" he asked. "We must hide them."

"But supposing we want to defend ourselves?"

"It would be wiser to be quiet," Gregor laughed. "If they find them they'll hang us by our trousers at the gate."

They went into the yard. For some inscrutable reason they hid their weapons separately. But Gregor had thrust his new black revolver under the pillow of his bed.

They had hardly finished supper and were getting ready for bed when the dog chained in the yard began to bark hoarsely, pulling on its chain and choking itself in the collar. The old man went out to see what was the matter and returned with someone wearing his cowl well down over his eyes. The man, who was in full military uniform, entered, crossing himself. A cloud of steam came from his frosted moustache.

"Don't you know me?" he asked.

"Why, it's Cousin Makar!" Daria exclaimed.

Only then did Piotra and the others recognize their distant relative Makar Nogaitsev, a Cossack of Singin village, well known throughout the district for his good voice and his drunken bouts.

"What's brought you here?" Piotra smiled, without moving from where he was standing.

Nogaitsev pulled an icicle from his moustache and threw it down by the door, stamped his feet in his great felt boots, and unhurriedly began to remove his outdoor clothes.

"It's unpleasant clearing out by myself, so I thought I'd come and call for you. I heard both the brothers were at home; so I told my wife I'd go and collect the Melekhovs, and then the party would be merrier."

He unshouldered his rifle and set it down at the stove alongside the forked oven-poles, raising a laugh from the women. He thrust his pack under the oven, but carefully laid his sword and whip on the bed. As usual, his breath smelt of home-made vodka, and his eyes had a drunken look in them.

"Are all the Cossacks clearing out of Singin?" Gregor asked, holding out his tobacco-pouch. The guest pushed his hand away.

"No, thanks. I don't smoke. The Cossacks? Some have cleared off, and others are looking for somewhere to hide themselves. Are you going off?"

"Our Cossacks aren't going away. Don't you try to get them to," Ilinichna said in alarm.

"You're not staying behind, surely? I can't believe it. Cousin

Gregor, is that true? You're asking for trouble, brothers."

"What is to be . . ." Piotra sighed, and, suddenly flushing, he asked: "Gregor, what do you think? You haven't changed your mind? Shall we go?"

"Not now." A wreath of tobacco-smoke enveloped Gregor and hung about his curly head.

"Shall Father see to your horse?" Piotra asked Makar inconsequently.

The long silence was disturbed only by the sound of the distaff droning as Dunia span. Nogaitsev sat on till dawn, trying to persuade the brothers to ride with him beyond the Donietz River. During the night Piotra ran out twice to saddle his horse, but each time, driven back by Daria's menacing eyes, went to unsaddle it again.

Daylight came, and the guest made ready to depart. When he was fully dressed he stood with his hand on the latch, coughed meaningly, and said with a hidden menace in his voice:

"Maybe your way is the better, but you may change your minds after. If we ever come back we shall remember those who opened the gate for the Reds to enter the Don and stayed behind to serve them. . . ."

Snow had been falling heavily since early morning. Going out into the yard, on the farther side of the Don Gregor saw a black crowd of people pouring towards the crossing. Horses harnessed in eights were dragging something, and he could hear talk, neighing, and curses. The grey figures of men and horses emerged through the falling snow as though through a mist. By the way the horses were harnessed up Gregor guessed it was a battery. "Surely not the Reds?" His heart beat violently at the possibility, but on second thoughts he was reassured.

The scattered crowd drew near the village. But at the crossing of the river one wheel of the foremost gun broke through the ice at the edge. The wind carried the shouts of the drivers, the scrunch of the breaking ice, and the hurried, slipping stamp of the horses' hoofs to Gregor's ears. He went into the cattle-yard at the back of the hut and cautiously peered out. By their appearance he could now see they were Cossacks. A few minutes later an elderly bombardier rode through the Melekhov gate on a high, broad-backed horse. He dismounted at the steps, tied the reins to the balustrade, and entered the hut.

"Who's the master here?" he asked after greeting the household.

"I am," Pantaleimon replied, anxiously awaiting the question: "And why are your Cossacks at home?" But the bombardier wiped his whiskers free of snow and pleaded:

"For the love of Christ, help us to get our cannon out. It's gone into the river up to its axles right by the bank. Have you any bullocks? What is this village? We've got lost owing to the snow. And the Reds are right on our tails."

"I don't know. . . ." The old man hesitated.

"What don't you know? You're fine Cossacks! We want men to give a hand."

"I'm unwell," Pantaleimon lied.

The bombardier looked from one to another like a wolf, not turning his neck. His voice seemed to take on a more youthful and healthy tone:

"Aren't you Cossacks? So you can let military property be lost? I'm left instead of the commander of the battery, the officers have all fled, for more than a week I've hardly been off my horse, I'm frozen, I've lost the toes of one foot through frost-bite, but I won't desert my battery. And you— If you won't help us I'll call my Cossacks and we'll—" Angrily yet tearfully he shouted: "We'll make you, you sons of bitches! Bolsheviks! We'll harness you up, old man, if that's what you want. Go and call some more men, and if they won't come, by God, we'll blow your village off the earth. . . ."

He spoke like a man not quite confident of his own strength. Gregor felt sorry for him. He seized his sword and said harshly, without looking at the excited bombardier:

"Don't shout so much! We'll help you out, and then go your way in peace."

A large crowd was soon found ready to help. With the aid of the battery command Anikushka, Tomilin, Christonia, the Melekhovs, and a dozen women laid down wattle fences, lifted the field-gun and the ammunition chests, and helped the horses get under way. The frozen wheels could not turn on their axles, but slid over the snow. The exhausted horses had difficulty in taking the least rise; the drivers, half-demented, went on foot. The bombardier removed his cap and bowed, thanked those who had lent a hand, and, turning in his saddle, quietly ordered the battery to follow him.

Gregor stared after him with a mingled gaze of respect and distrustful surprise. Piotra approached, chewing his moustache, and, as though replying to Gregor's unspoken thought, remarked:

"Now if they were all like that! That's the way to defend the gentle Don!"

"Talking about that bombardier?" Christonia asked. "Look how he drags those guns about! I didn't want to help, but I got frightened. But tell me, what good are those guns to the fool? He's like a dangerous pig tied to a log. It's hard and no use to him, but he goes on dragging it about."

Silently smiling, the Cossacks went their ways.

Far beyond the Don—it was now past dinner-time—a machine-gun muffledly stuttered out a couple of rounds, then was silent.

Half an hour later Gregor, who had spent all day at the window in the best room, stepped back, and his face turned an ashy pallor.

"Here they come," he said.

Ilinichna groaned and threw herself towards the window. Eight horsemen were galloping along the road. They reached the Melekhov's yard, stared at the crossing over the Don, and turned back. Their well-fed horses waved their docked tails and threw up clumps of snow with their hoofs.

Terrible as was this first moment of the arrival of the enemy troops, the risible Dunia could not restrain herself even then. When the patrol turned back, she snorted into her apron and ran into the kitchen. Natalia met her with a frightened stare.

"What's the matter?" she asked.

"Oh, Natalia—my dear—how they ride their horses! One man was wriggling backwards and forwards, backwards and forwards in the saddle . . . and his arms and elbows were knocking against his sides."

So well did she imitate the Red Army men rolling in their saddles that Natalia ran, suppressing her laughter, to the bed and threw herself face downward on the pillow, to avoid drawing down her mother-in-law's wrath upon her. Daria's eyebrows quivered with her nervous laughter, and she remarked between her outbursts:

"I'm afraid they'll wear holes in their trousers. Call themselves horsemen! . . ."

Even Piotra, who came gloomily in from the best room, was cheered for a moment by their merriment.

"It's strange to watch the way they ride," he said. "But they don't mind. If they break one horse's back they'll just take another! The peasants!" He waved his hand in a gesture of ineffable contempt.

An hour later Tatarsk was filled with the sound of tramping feet, strange speech, and barking dogs. An infantry regiment with machine-guns on sledges, transport wagons, and a field kitchen crossed the Don and poured into the village. The soldiers streamed down the streets, breaking into groups and entering the yards. Five of them came through the Melekhov gate, led by a thickset, elderly, clean-shaven man with flat broad nostrils, evidently an old active-service man. He halted at the steps for a moment, watching the dog barking and choking on its chain, then removed his rifle from his shoulder. The shot brought a white mist of snow down from the roof of the hut. Adjusting the tight collar of his shirt, through the window Gregor saw the dog rolling in the bloodstained snow, in its death-throes biting its wounded side and the iron chain. He saw the women's white faces, the vacant eyes of the mother. Hatless, he strode towards the porch.

"Stop!" his father shouted after him in a strange voice.

Gregor threw the front door open. "What did you shoot the dog for? It wasn't hurting you!" he demanded, standing on the threshold.

The broad nostrils of the Red Army man drew in deep gasps, the corners of his thin lips curled downward. He looked round and threw his rifle into the ready position.

"What's that to do with you? You think it a pity? I'll put a bullet into you without any pity. Would you like me to?"

"Now, now, drop it, Alexandr," a tall, red-haired Red Guard approached and said with a laugh. "Good afternoon, master! Ever seen Reds before? We want quarters. Did he shoot your dog? Quite unnecessary! Comrades, in you go!"

Gregor was the last to pass into the hut. He found the Red Army men cheerfully greeting its inhabitants, removing their packs and their Japanese leather cartridge-belts, and throwing greatcoats, padded coats, and caps on the bed. The kitchen was at once filled with the evil-smelling, spiritous scent of soldiers, of human sweat, tobacco, cheap soap, gun-grease, and long journeys.

The man called Alexandr sat down at the table, lit a cigarette, and, as though continuing a conversation, asked Gregor:

"Have you been with the Whites?"

"Yes."

"There. . . . I can tell an owl at once, by its flight, and you by your snot. A White! An officer too, I suppose? Gold epaulets?" He sent the smoke in two columns out of his nostrils, turned cold, unsmiling eyes on Gregor standing at the door, and tapped his cigarette with tobacco-stained, swollen nails.

"You've been an officer, haven't you? Admit it! I can see it by the way you hold yourself. I was in the German war myself."

"Yes, I was an officer." Gregor smiled forcedly. Catching Natalia's terrified, imploring gaze fixed on him, he frowned and his eyebrows quivered. He was vexed at his own smile.

"Pity! It appears I shouldn't have shot the dog!" The man threw the end of his cigarette at Gregor's feet and winked to his comrades.

And again, despite his will, Gregor felt his lips twisting into a deprecatory, pleading smile, and he blushed with shame at his involuntary, uncontrollable manifestation of weakness. "Like a well-schooled dog before its master!" the thought burned into his mind, and for a moment he saw the dead dog's lips as they had used to writhe when he, the master, approached it, and its fluffy red tail wagging as it lay on its back.

In the same unusual voice Pantaleimon asked: "Perhaps you would like some supper?"

Without waiting for an answer Ilinichna went towards the stove. The forked pole trembled in her hands, and she could hardly lift the pot of cabbage soup out of the oven with it. Her eyes downcast, Daria set the table. The Red Army men sat down without crossing themselves. The old man watched them in fear and secret disgust. At last he could restrain himself no longer, and had to ask:

"So you don't pray to God?"

Only the faintest semblance of a smile flickered over Alexandr's lips. Amid a roar of laughter from the others he replied:

"I wouldn't advise you to either, old man! We've sent our gods to the devil long since." He frowned. "There isn't any God, but fools don't believe that and go on praying to these bits of wood."

"Yes, yes. . . . Educated people have, of course . . ." Pantaleimon hastened anxiously to agree.

Daria had set out a spoon for each man, but Alexandr thrust his away and asked:

"Haven't you got any not made of wood? We don't want to catch any diseases. You don't call this a spoon, do you?"

Daria flared up. "You ought to carry your own if you don't like ours," she exclaimed.

"You keep your mouth shut, young woman! You haven't got any others? Then give me a clean towel and I'll wipe this one."

Ilinichna brought the soup to the table in a bowl, and he asked her:

"You try it first, mother!"

"Why should I try it? Do you think it's too salt?" the old woman asked in alarm.

"Taste it when you're told; taste it! You may have put some powder or other into it for your guests. . . ."

"Take and try a spoonful! Now!" Pantaleimon ordered sternly, and bit his lip. Then he brought an alder stump which he used as a stool when mending boots, pushed it under the window, and sat on it embracing an old boot. He took no more part in the conversation.

Piotra remained in the best room and did not show himself. Natalia also went and sat there with the children. Dunia stood huddled against the stove, knitting a stocking, but after one of the Red Army men had called her "young lady" and invited her to sup with them, she went out. The conversation died away. After eating, the guests lit cigarettes.

"May we smoke?" one of them asked.

Gregor refused the cigarette offered to him. He was inwardly trembling; his heart choked as he looked at the man who had shot the dog, and he maintained a challenging and insolent attitude to him. Evidently the man was looking for trouble, for he tried continually to draw Gregor into the conversation.

"What regiment did you serve in, Your Excellency?" he asked.
"In several."

"How many of our people have you killed?"

"There's no counting in war-time. You needn't think, comrade, that I was born an officer. I earned my commission during the German war. They gave it to me for my war services. . . . ."

"I'm no comrade to officers. We put your sort up against a wall. I've aimed at more than one, myself."

"What I say is this, comrade: you're not behaving decently, acting as if you'd taken the village by storm. We ourselves deserted from the front and let you through, but you come as if you were entering a defeated country. Anyone can shoot a dog, and it's not clever to kill unarmed people or to be insulting, either. . . ."

"Don't you tell me what I'm to do! We know you . . . 'deserted from the front'! If we hadn't defeated you, you wouldn't have deserted. And I can talk to you how I like!"

"Shut up, Alexandr! We've had enough of your voice!" the red-haired man told him.

But Alexandr went right up to Gregor, dilating his nostrils and breathing heavily.

"Better not upset me, officer, or it'll be the worse for you!"

"I'm not upsetting you!"

"Yes, you are!"

Opening the door of the front room a little, Natalia called to Gregor. He walked round the man standing in front of him and swayed in the doorway as if drunk. Piotra welcomed him with a baleful, groaning whisper:

"What are you playing at? What did you answer him back for? You'll ruin yourself and us! Sit down!" He thrust Gregor forcibly on to a chest and went into the kitchen. Gregor sat gasping in great mouthfuls of air; the heavy flush left his cheeks, and his eyes faintly glittered.

"Gregor! Dearest! Don't get drawn into a quarrel!" Natalia pleaded, trembling and putting her hands over the mouths of the children, who were on the point of bellowing.

"Why didn't I clear out?" Gregor asked, looking mournfully at Natalia. "You needn't worry, I won't. But shut up! I can't stand any more."

Later three more Red Army soldiers arrived. One, in a high

black fur cap, evidently a commander, asked:

"How many are quartered here?"

"Seven men," the red-haired man answered for them all.

"We're putting a machine-gun outpost here. You'll have to make room for them."

The three men went out. Immediately afterwards the gate creaked and two wagons drove into the yard. One of the machine-guns was dragged into the porch. Someone struck a match and cursed furiously in the darkness. The machine-gunners smoked under the shed, pulled down hay, and lit fires in the threshing-floor. But none of the hut's inhabitants went out to them.

"Someone ought to go and see to the horses," Ilinichna whispered as she passed Pantaleimon. But he only shrugged his shoulders and made no attempt to stir. All night doors were banging. The Red Army men made their beds on the floor in the front room. Gregor brought and spread rugs for them and put down his sheepskin coat as a pillow for their heads.

"I've been in the army myself and I know," he smiled pacifically at the man who regarded him as his enemy. But Alexandr's broad nostrils dilated, and his eyes watched Gregor uncompromisingly.

Gregor and Natalia lay down on the bed in the same room. The Red Army men put their rifles by their heads and huddled together on the rugs. Natalia wanted to put out the lamp, but they asked menacingly:

"Who asked you to put the lamp out? Don't dare to touch it! Turn down the wick, and the light should last all night."

Natalia put the children to bed at her feet, and lay against the wall without undressing. Gregor silently stretched himself out beside her.

"If you'd cleared off," he thought, grinding his teeth, "if you'd gone off they'd have had Natalia spread out on this bed now and be taking their joy of her as the men did Frania in Poland."

One of the Red Guards began to tell a story, but a familiar voice interrupted him, making challenging pauses in the semi-darkness:

"Ah, it's a miserable life without women! But the master's an officer! He wouldn't give his wife up to us ordinary snotty-nosed folk. Do you hear, master?"

The menacing voice of the red-haired man interrupted him:

"Now, Alexandr, I've had enough of trying to tell you. In every billet it's the same; you make a scene, behave like a hooligan, and bring discredit on the Red Army banner. It isn't good enough! I'm going straight to the commissar or the company commander. Do you hear? He'll have something to say to you!"

There was a dead silence, which was broken by the sound of the red-haired man drawing on his boots and snorting angrily. After a minute or two he went out, slamming the door behind him.

Natalia could not restrain herself any longer and broke into a noisy whimper. With one shaking hand Gregor stroked her head, her sweaty brow and wet face. With the other hand he mechanically buttoned and unbuttoned her blouse.

"Quiet, quiet!" he whispered almost inaudibly to her. At that moment he knew beyond all doubt that he was ready for any trial and humiliation in order to save his own life and those of his dear ones.

A match was struck and revealed Alexandr sitting up and sucking at a cigarette. He grumbled in an undertone and began to dress.

Gregor, impatiently straining his ears, in his soul boundlessly grateful to the red-haired man, trembled joyously when he heard steps under the window and an indignant voice: "And all the time he's trying to make trouble . . . comrade commissar."

Steps sounded on the porch, and the door creaked as it was opened. Someone's voice ordered in a youthful tone of command:

"Alexandr Tiurnikov, dress yourself and come out at once. You'll spend the night with me, and in the morning we'll try you for conduct unworthy of a Red Army soldier."

Gregor's eyes met the stern gaze of a man in a black leather jerkin standing beside the red-haired man. He was obviously young, and youthfully severe. His lips were compressed with unnecessary firmness.

"So you've had a troublesome guest, comrade?" he asked Gregor, smiling faintly. "Well, now you can sleep; tomorrow we'll quiet him down. Good night. Come on, Tiurnikov!"

They went out, and Gregor gave a sigh of relief. In the morning, when the red-haired man had paid for the night's quarters and provisions, he deliberately lingered behind and remarked:

"Well, masters, don't be angry with us. That Alexandr of ours is a little touched in the head. Last year some officers in Lugansk (he's a native of Lugansk) shot his mother and sister before his eyes. And that's why he's like that. Well, thank you. Good-bye. Why, I'd almost forgotten the children!" To the twins' inexpressible delight he pulled two dirty grey pieces of sugar out of his pack and thrust them into their hands.

Pantaleimon gazed at his grandchildren and, deeply moved, exclaimed:

"There's a present for you! We haven't seen sugar for eighteen months or more. God be with you, comrade! Bow to your uncle, children. Thank him, Polia! What are you standing dumb for?"

The Red Army man went out, and the old man turned angrily to Natalia:

"Don't you know how to behave? You should have given him a doughnut for his journey. We ought to repay the good man somehow."

"Run after him!" Gregor ordered her.

Flinging her kerchief over her head, Natalia ran and overtook the man at the wicket gate. Reddening with confusion, she thrust a doughnut into the deep pocket of his greatcoat.

At noonday a Red cavalry regiment passed at a forced march through the village, seizing the cavalry horses of some of the Cossacks as they went. From far beyond the hill came the sound of gunfire.

As evening came on, Piotra and Gregor went out into the yard more than once. They could hear the roar of field-guns and the quiet rattle of machine-guns somewhere far beyond the Don.

"They're putting up a good fight over there!" Piotra remarked, brushing the snow from his knees and fur cap. Then he added inconsequently:

"They'll take our horses. They could see at once that your horse is a cavalry mount. They'll take it for sure."

But the old man had already realized this. At nightfall Gregor went to lead the two horses down to the river to drink. As he brought them out of the stable, he noticed that they were both limping on their forelegs. He went to fetch his brother.

"The horses are maimed," he told him. "Yours on the right and mine on the left foreleg. And not a sign of a cut anywhere."

The horses stood without stirring on the shadowed snow, under the dim evening stars. Piotra lit a lantern, but his father came out from the threshing-floor and stopped him.

"What's the lantern for?"

"The horses have gone lame, Father."

"And that's no pity, is it? Or do you want some peasant to saddle them and ride them off?"

"Well, isn't it bad, then?"

"I did it. I took a hammer and drove a nail into their legs below the gristle, and now they'll limp until the Reds have gone."

Piotra shook his head and chewed his moustache, but the old man's remedy saved the horses. That night the village was again alive with soldiers. Cavalry galloped along the streets, and batteries dragged past to be ranged in the square. Christonia came along to the Melekhovs', squatted down and lit a cigarette.

"Isn't anyone quartered on you?" he asked.

"God has spared us so far. There were some here, and all the hut was filled with their peasant stink. That's why we call them 'stinking Russians,' I suppose. The name fits them," Ilinichna muttered discontentedly.

"They've visited me," Christonia's voice sank to a whisper, and his enormous palm wiped a little tear from his eyes. But he shook his head, groaned, and seemed ashamed of his tears.

"Why, Christonia, what's the matter?" Piotra laughingly asked, for the first time in his life seeing Christonia in tears.

"They've taken my horse. . . . I went through the German war on him. We suffered together. . . . He was like a man, and had more sense than a man. He used to saddle himself. 'Saddle!' I'd say to him, but he wouldn't take any notice. 'What,' I'd say, 'have I got to spend all my life saddling you? Get on with it yourself.' And he'd get the saddle on to his back. . . ." His voice passed into a swift, whistling whisper as he ended: "I'm afraid to look into the stable now. The yard's dead. . . ."

Gregor pricked up his ears. Outside the window there was the scrunch of snow and the clatter of swords.

"They're coming to us. Perhaps someone told them . . ." Pantaleimon fidgeted with his hands, not knowing what to do with them.

"Master! Hey, come outside!" a voice shouted.

Piotra threw his sheepskin coat across his shoulders and went out.

"Where are your horses? Bring them out!" he was ordered by the leader of three horsemen.

"I don't mind, but they're lame, comrades."

"Where are they lame? You bring them out! Don't be afraid, we won't take them if they are."

Piotra led the horses out one after the other.

"You've got a third in there. Why haven't you brought it out too?" one of the men asked, shining the lantern into the stable.

"She's a mare and in foal. And she's old, a hundred years old."

"Hey, bring saddles. Wait, you're right, they are lame. By Christ, where are you leading those cripples to? Take them back!" the man holding the lantern roared furiously. Piotra pulled on the halter ropes and turned his face with its twitching lips away from the light.

"Where are your saddles?"

"The comrades took them away this morning."

"You're lying, Cossack! Who took them?"

"God's truth. . . . God strike me, they took them. A cavalry regiment passed through the village and took them. The saddles, and two collars as well."

The three horsemen rode away cursing. Smelling of horses' sweat and urine, Piotra went into the hut. His firm lips quivered as he clapped Christonia on the shoulder and bragged:

"That's the way to do it. We lamed our horses, but they'd already taken the saddles. . . . Ah, you dolt!"

Ilinichna put out the lamp and went in the darkness to make the beds. "We'll sit in the dark, or the light may bring us some unwelcome visitors," she remarked.

That night there was merrymaking at Anikushka's. The Red Guards quartered on him asked him to invite his Cossack neighbours in for a spree. Anikushka called for the Melekhovs.

"They're Reds?" he asked. "Well, what if they are Reds? They've been baptized, haven't they? They're Russian like us. By God, believe it or not, I'm sorry for them. There's a Jew among them, but he's a man, too. We killed off the Jews in Poland, I know. But this one gave me a glass of vodka. I like the Jews. Come on, Gregor. Piotra!"

At first Gregor refused to go, but his father advised him:

"Go along, or they may say we think them lower than ourselves. Go on, don't bring up their past sins against them."

Piotra and Gregor went with Anikushka into the yard. The warm night promised fair weather. In the air was a scent of ashes and burning dung-fuel. The three Cossacks stood for a moment in silence, then went on. At the wicket gate Daria overtook them. Her arched, pencilled eyebrows gleamed a velvety black in the dim light of the moon.

"They're making my wife drunk," Anikushka muttered. "But they won't get what they want. I've got eyes. . . ." Tipsy with home-made vodka, he went reeling against the fence and stumbled off the path into a snowdrift. The blue, granular snow scrunched like sugar beneath their feet. The wind sent it whirling up from the ground; it flew rapaciously at the white clouds and the passive earth, covering the village, the tracks, the steppe, and all human and animal traces.

In Anikushka's hut the air was so thick that it was impossible to breathe. Sharp black tongues of soot were winding up from the lamp, and nothing could be seen through the haze of tobacco-smoke. Open jugs were standing on the table, the entire hut stank of liquor. The tablecloth was like a dirty rag. His long legs flung out in front of him, a Red Army accordion-player was working the bellows of his instrument vigorously. Red Army men were sitting on the benches with women neighbours of Anikushka. Anikushka's own wife was being caressed by a healthy-looking old fellow in padded khaki trousers, and boots loaded with enormous spurs that might have been taken from a museum. His cap was thrust on the back of his head, and his brown face was sweating. One moist hand was pressing the woman's back. She was already fuddled, and although she would have moved away if she could, she was without strength. She caught her husband's look and took no notice of the other women's smirks, but she was not strong enough to remove the powerful arm from her back. She sat laughing drunkenly and feebly.

In the middle of the room a cavalry troop commander wearing breeches and chrome-yellow boots was dancing and writhing like a green devil. Gregor stared from the threshold at the boots and breeches and thought: "Taken off an officer!" He raised his eyes to the man's face: it was darkly swarthy, streaming with sweat, the large round ears protruded, the lips were thick and pendulous. "A Jew, but smart on his feet," Gregor thought. They poured out home-made vodka for him and Piotra. Gregor was careful how he drank, but Piotra quickly got drunk. And within an hour he was doing the "Cossack" dance on the earthen floor, tearing up the dust with his heels, and hoarsely asking the accordion-player to go faster. Gregor sat by the table cracking pumpkin seeds. Beside him was a machine-gunner, a native of Siberia.

"We've smashed Kolchak," he told Gregor. "Now we'll deal with your Krasnov as he deserves, and that will be the lot! And you can turn to your ploughing, sow the land, and make it bear fruit. The earth's like a woman; it won't yield, you have to take what you want. And anyone who gets in the way we'll kill! We don't want your land. We only want to divide it up equally among everybody."

Gregor assented, but all the while he was quietly studying the Red Army men. There seemed to be no cause for anxiety. They were all watching Piotra, smiling approvingly as he displayed his skill in the dance. Someone's voice exclaimed rapturously: "There's a devil! That's fine!" But Gregor happened to catch the eyes of a curly-haired Red soldier fixed attentively on him and, put on his guard, he drank no more.

The accordion-player struck up a polka. The Red Army men took their Cossack women by the arm. Swaying tipsily, one of them invited a young wife, a neighbour of Christonia's, to be his partner; but she refused and, picking up her skirt, ran across to Gregor.

"Come and dance," she asked him.

"I don't want to."

"Come on, Gregor, my azure flower!"

"Don't be a fool! I won't!"

She dragged at him by the sleeve, forcedly laughing. He frowned and resisted, but, noticing her wink, he yielded. After a couple of rounds she took advantage of a lull in the dance to put her head on Gregor's shoulder and whisper almost inaudibly:

"They're planning to kill you. . . . Someone told them you're an officer. Get out of here."

Then she added aloud: "Oh, my head's swimming."

Gregor took her to a seat, then strode swiftly across to the table and drank a cup of vodka. He turned to ask Daria:

"Piotra drunk?"

"Almost."

"Get him home!"

Daria led Piotra out, with masculine strength resisting his pushing and stumbling. Gregor followed them.

"Hey, where are you off to? No, don't go!" Anikushka ran after Gregor, but he gave him such a glance that Anikushka unlinked his arm and staggered off.

At the threshold Gregor waved his cap. "Honest company!" he muttered.

The curly-haired Red Guard adjusted his belt and followed Gregor. On the steps, breathing in his face, the man whispered:

"Where are you going?" He seized the sleeve of Gregor's great-coat.

"Home!" Gregor replied without stopping, dragging the man after him. With joyous excitement he resolved: "You don't take me alive!"

Breathing heavily, holding Gregor's elbow with his left hand, the Red Guard walked at his side. They halted at the wicket gate. Gregor heard the door scrape behind them, and at the same moment he noticed the Red Guard's right hand pawing at his side and heard his fingernails scratch the holster of his revolver. For one second Gregor saw the man's hostile eyes fixed on his face. He turned and seized the hand tearing upon the holster flap. Gripping it by the wrist, with terrible strength he drew the man's arm over his right shoulder, stooped, and with all his old skill flung the heavy body across his back and dragged the hand downward. He heard the crunching sound of the elbow joint cracking. The man's head slipped downward, touched the snow, and was buried in a drift.

Bending low behind the fences, Gregor ran along a side lane towards the Don. He ran springily, making for the point where the road dropped down to the bank. "So long as there isn't an outpost there . . ." he thought. He halted for a moment. Behind him all Anikushka's yard lay open to view. He heard a shot. The bullet whistled rapaciously past him. More shots. "Under the hill, across the Don," he decided. When he was in the middle of the crossing a bullet whistled close to him and buried itself in the ice, sending fragments flying. From the farther side of the river he looked back. The shots were still sounding like a drover's whip. He felt no warmth of gladness at his escape, but was oppressed with a feeling of indifference to all that happened. "They might have been hunting an animal," he thought mechanically as he halted again. "They won't search for me. They'll be afraid to come into the forest. I gave his arm something to remember me by. The scum, he thought he could take a Cossack with bare hands."

He made his way towards the winter ricks, but apprehensively avoided them and like a hare wound a long entanglement of tracks. He decided to spend the night in an abandoned rick of dry bulrushes. He dug into the top. A mink slipped away from his feet. He burrowed up to his head in the rotten-smelling bulrushes and rested, shivering. His mind was without thought or plan. The merest suggestion of an idea flickered through his head: "Saddle the horse tomorrow and get through the front to my own side?" But he could find no answer in himself and lay quietly.

Towards morning he began to freeze. He looked out: above him the early morning light was glimmering joyously, and in the deep abysm of the blue-black heaven, as though in the shallows of the Don, a bottom seemed to appear: an early, smoky azure in the zenith, and a fading sprinkle of stars around the edges.

Chapter 12

The front passed on beyond Tatarsk. The noise of war died away. On the last day troops were quartered in the village the machine-gunners of a cavalry regiment set Mokhov's phonograph on a broad sledge and galloped their horses up and down the streets. The phonograph wheezed and grumbled, the horses' hoofs sent the snow flying into its broad horn. The machine-gunners hurriedly cleaned the horn and turned the crank as confidently as they handled their machine-gun. Like a grey flock of sparrows the village urchins poured after them, clinging to the sledge and shout-

ing: "Daddy, play the thing that whistles! More, Daddy!" Two
supremely fortunate lads were seated on a machine-gunner's knees,
and when he was not turning the phonograph crank he was carefully and firmly wiping the younger boy's streaming nose.

Afterwards, as the sounds of struggle faded, transport wagons
dragged slowly through Tatarsk, serving the Red Army on the
southern front with provisions and munitions.

On the third day messengers went from hut to hut calling on the
Cossacks to attend a village assembly.

"We're going to elect Krasnov ataman!" one jesting Cossack remarked to Pantaleimon.

"Shall we be allowed to elect an ataman, or will they appoint
one from above?" Pantaleimon inquired.

"We shall see!"

Gregor and Piotra went to the assembly. The younger Cossacks
were present to a man. The old men stayed away; only Avdeich
the Braggart had gathered a little circle of Cossacks around him
and was telling how a Red commissar had spent the night with him
and had invited him to accept an important position.

The Cossacks gathered in little groups in the square. Gregor had
not seen his old friend Mishka Koshevoi since the spring mobilization and, noticing him, he went up, shook his hand, and asked with
a smile:

"Hallo, Mishka, where did you disappear to? Under whose flag
have you been serving?"

"Oho! First I was working as a drover, then they drafted me into
a disciplinary company on the Kolchak front," Mishka replied. "I
got away and came home to join the Reds at the front, but they
watched me closer than a mother keeps an eye on an untried
daughter. Then the other day Ivan Alexievich came up to me all
dressed in uniform and says: 'Get your rifle ready and come on!' I
had only just come home, and I asked him: 'Surely you're not clearing out?' He shrugged his shoulders and said: 'I hear they're going
to send us an ataman,' said good-bye, and went. I thought he really
had cleared out. But the next day a Red regiment marches into the
village and I see him with them. Why, there he is now! Ivan
Alexievich!" he shouted across the square.

Ivan came up, the mill-hand David with him. He squeezed
Gregor's hand in his own oily fingers and clicked his tongue:

"How is it you stayed behind, Gregor?"

"And how about you?"

"Well, it's different in my case."

"Thinking of my commission?" Gregor asked. "I risked it and stayed on here. I was all but killed yesterday. The Reds chased me and began to shoot at me, and I was sorry I hadn't cleared out. But now I'm not sorry."

"What was it all about?"

"I was at Anikushka's, and someone told them I was an officer. I fled across to the other side of the Don, after giving one of them something to remember me by. In return they went to our hut and took everything—trousers, coats, and all. I'm left with what I stand up in."

"We should have cleared off to the Reds when we had the chance." Ivan Alexievich smiled sourly and began to smoke.

The meeting began. It was opened by an ensign from Vieshenska, one of Fomin's men:

"Comrade Cossacks! The Soviet government has taken root in our district. Now we must set up an administration, elect an executive committee, a chairman, and a vice-chairman. That's the first question. And then I've brought an order from the regional Soviet that all firearms and other weapons are to be surrendered."

"Fine!" someone at the back said venomously. There was a long silence.

"There's no call for that sort of remark, comrades." The ensign drew himself up and set his fur cap down on the table. "Of course the weapons must be given up, as you don't want them for your home needs. If anyone wants to help in the defence of the Soviets he will be given weapons. All rifles must be brought in within three days. And now we'll hold the election."

"They gave us our weapons; what are they wanting to lay their hands on them for now?" The speaker had not finished his remark when all eyes were turned on him. It was Zakhar Koroliov.

"And what do you want to keep them for?" Christonia asked simply.

"I don't want them. But when we let the Red Army into our province, there was no agreement that they should disarm us."

"That's true. And we've kept our swords in good order at our own cost."

"I came back with my rifle from the German war, and now have I got to give it up? They want to pillage us. What can we do without our arms? Without them I'm like a woman with a torn skirt: I'm naked."

Mishka Koshevoi demanded to be heard, and shouted:

"Enough of this, comrades! I'm surprised to hear you talking like that! Is there a state of war in this district or isn't there? And if there is, there's no point in talking over the matter. Hand them over! Didn't we make the Ukrainians do the same when we occupied their villages?"

The ensign stared at his fur cap and said emphatically:

"Anyone who doesn't give up his arms within three days will be handed over to a revolutionary court and shot as a counter-revolutionary."

After a momentary silence Tomilin coughed and called out:

"Let's get on with the election."

Some dozen names all together were put forward. One of the youngsters called out: "Avdeich," but the joke fell flat. The name of Ivan Alexievich was the first to be put to the vote, and he was elected unanimously.

As the Melekhov brothers and Christonia were returning to their huts after the meeting, they met Anikushka on the road. Under his arm he was carrying his rifle and cartridges wrapped up in one of his wife's aprons. When he saw the Cossacks he was taken aback and disappeared into a side turning. Piotra looked at Gregor, Gregor at Christonia, and with one accord they all smiled.

Chapter 13

An easterly wind raged over the steppe. The snow had levelled out the hollows and depressions. Neither roads nor tracks were visible. In all directions stretched the bare, white, wind-swept plain. The steppe was dead. Occasionally a crow, as ancient as the steppe itself,

flew high over the snow, calling as it flew. The wind carried its cry
far across the steppe, and long and mournfully it sounded, like a
bass string accidentally plucked in the nocturnal silence.

But beneath the snow the steppe was still alive. Where the
ploughed land lay in frozen waves of silver snow, where the earth
had been wrapped in dead ripples since the autumn, there, gripping
the soil with greedy, living roots, lay the winter rye under the frosts.
Silkily green, all in tears of frozen dew, it feebly pressed against the
crumbling black earth, feeding on its vital black blood and waiting
for spring, for the sun, in order to rise, to break through the fine,
diamond-studded snowy crust, and to spring up a vigorous green in
May. And it would rise in its time. The quails would struggle in it,
the April skylark would sing above it. The sun would shine on it and
the wind send it swaying, until the ripe full ears were laid low by the
scythe of the master and humbly cast their grain down on the
threshing-floor.

All the Don district was living a secret, crushed existence. Dreary
days had arrived. A sombre rumour crawled from the upper reaches
of the Don, down its tributaries, along the Chira, the Khoper, the
Yelanka, along the large and small rivers sprinkled with Cossack
villages. It was said that the front, which had rolled on and come to
a halt at the Donietz River, was in the terrible grip of extraordinary
commissions and tribunals. It was said that any day they would arrive in the Cossack districts, that they had already appeared in
Migulin and Kazanska districts and were holding brief and illegal
trials of the Cossacks who had served with the Whites. Seemingly
the fact that the upper Don Cossacks had themselves deserted from
the front was not accepted in their defence, and the court procedure
was terrifyingly simple: an accusation, a couple of questions, sentence—and then machine-gun death. It was said that already in
Kazanska and Shumilinsk many a Cossack head was rolling neglected in the brushwood. The front-line men only laughed. "Lies!
Officers' stories! The Cadets have always tried to frighten us with
similar yarns," they jested.

In Tatarsk the Cossacks gathered of an evening in the side lanes,
sharing the news, then going to drink home-made vodka, wandering
from hut to hut. Quietly and bitterly the village lived. At Shrove-
tide only one wedding sent the sleigh-bells ringing: Mishka Koshevoi

gave his sister in marriage. And of this wedding the neighbours talked with spiteful sneers:

"Fine time to get married, this is! A case of had to, I expect!"

The day following the elections the village was disarmed hut by hut. The warm porches and corridors of Mokhov's house, now occupied by the Revolutionary Committee, were piled with weapons. Piotra Melekhov handed in his and Gregor's rifles, two revolvers, and a sword, but he gave up only those weapons they had brought back from the German war, and kept their officers' revolvers. Piotra returned home with a feeling of relief. He found Gregor in the porch, his sleeves turned up to his elbows, taking the rusty parts of two rifles to pieces and cleaning them with paraffin.

"Where the devil have you got them from?" Piotra's moustache drooped in his astonishment.

"Father brought them back when he visited me at Filonovo." Gregor's eyes glittered and he roared with laughter, smacking his sides with his paraffin-stained hands. As unexpectedly his laugh died away, and he showed his teeth wolfishly:

"Rifles? That's nothing. Do you know?" his voice dropped to a whisper, although there was no stranger in the hut. "Do you know, today Father told me he's got a machine-gun." Gregor's lips again parted in a smile.

"You're lying! Where did he get it? What's it for?"

"He says some transport Cossacks gave it to him for some sour milk, but I think he's lying, the old devil! He stole it, I expect. He's like a beetle: he drags away everything he can carry off. He whispered to me: 'I've got a machine-gun buried in the threshing-floor. The spring would have made fine hooks, but I didn't touch it.' 'What did you want the gun for?' I asked him. 'I took a fancy to the spring,' he answered. 'I thought it might be useful for something.'"

Piotra was furious and wanted to go and talk to his father about it. But Gregor dissuaded him:

"Wait a bit! Help me clean these and put them together. What will you say to him?"

Piotra snorted as he cleaned the rifle-bolt, but after a moment he said thoughtfully:

"Maybe he's right. It might come in useful. Let it lie there."

That day Ivan Tomilin called to pass on the rumour that shootings were going on in Kazanska. They sat smoking and talking around the stove. During the conversation Piotra sat with knitted brows, thinking hard. When Tomilin had gone he remarked:

"I'll drive to Rubiezhin and see Yakov Fomin. I hear he's back home. They say he's organizing the regional Revolutionary Committee. I'll go and ask him to step in if anything should happen."

While Pantaleimon was harnessing the mare to the sledge, Daria wrapped herself in a new sheepskin and whispered to Ilinichna. The two women went together into the granary and brought back a bundle.

"What's that?" the old man asked.

Piotra was silent, but Ilinichna hurriedly whispered:

"I've got some butter saved up here which I'd kept in case we needed it. But this isn't the time to think of butter, so I've given it to Daria. Let her take a present to Fomin, and maybe he'll listen to Piotra." She burst into tears. "They've served and earned their way to officers, and now others are staring at their epaulets. . . ."

"Stop your whining!" Pantaleimon angrily threw the whip into the bottom of the sledge and went across to Piotra.

"Take some wheat for him too," he said.

"What the devil should he want wheat for?" Piotra burst out. "It would be better if you went to Anikushka and bought some vodka for him; but wheat—"

Pantaleimon at once went off, returning a few minutes later with a great jug of vodka under his arm. As he set it down he remarked approvingly:

"It's good vodka, as good as that of czarist days."

"He's been tasting it, the old hound!" Ilinichna went for him. But apparently the old man did not hear her, for he limped youthfully into the hut, wiping his lips with his sleeve and screwing up his eyes satisfiedly.

In addition to the vodka Piotra took a piece of pre-war Cheviot tweed, a pair of boots, and a pound of expensive tea as presents for his former fellow-soldier who had now grown so powerful. All these things and much else had been his share of the booty when the 28th Regiment had captured the railway station at Lesk and had looted the wagons and warehouses. He had sent them back by his father when the old man visited the front. When Pantaleimon returned home Daria had aroused the envy of Natalia and Dunia by adorning herself in underlinen never seen before in the village. It was made of the finest foreign linen, whiter than snow, and every little article was embroidered with arms and initials. The lace of her knickers was finer than the foam on the Don.

The first night after Piotra's return from Vieshenska she had gone to bed in her knickers. Before putting out the light Piotra had smiled condescendingly:

"So you've got hold of some men's pants to wear?" he remarked.

"It's warmer and nicer in them," Daria replied dreamily. "What makes you think they're men's? They'd be longer if they were, and besides, what do men want lace for?"

"I expect lords wear lace on their pants. But I don't care. Wear them if you want to," Piotra replied sleepily, scratching himself.

But when he lay down at his wife's side the next night, he drew away in alarm, staring with involuntary respect and uneasiness at the lace, afraid to touch it and feeling that Daria was alienated from him. On the third night he grew angry and demanded in a tone that brooked no refusal:

"Take your trousers off and chuck them to the devil! They're not fit for women to wear, and they're not women's clothes. You're lying there like a lady. You're not the same woman in them."

Next morning he rose before Daria and, coughing and frowning, tried the knickers on himself. He stared long and doubtfully at the silk ties, at the lace and his own legs, bare and hairy below the knees. Turning round, he happened to catch a glimpse of himself in the mirror, with the knickers puckered in elegant folds at the back, and spat and cursed as he crawled like a bear out of the garment. His great toe caught in the lace, he all but fell over on to the chest and, now really furious, tore off the ties and escaped into freedom. Daria sleepily asked: "What are you doing?" But Piotra maintained an injured silence, merely snorting and spitting. The same morning she took the knickers and with a sigh packed them away in the chest. Already she had many articles packed away for which none of the women could find any use. But she had made use of the skirts: although they were extraordinarily short the clever Daria wore them so that the underskirt hung below her own long skirt and showed the lace for a good inch. Then she would go out to display herself, sweeping the earthen floor with Dutch lace.

As she drove with her husband to visit Fomin, Daria was clothed finely and richly. Lace was showing under her sheepskin greatcoat, and her woolly coat was good and new, so Fomin's wife, who had crawled out of the mud into princedom, would realize that Daria was not an ordinary Cossack woman, but was at any rate an officer's wife.

Piotra waved his whip and smacked his lips. The pot-bellied old mare set off at a trot along the Donside road. They arrived at Rubiezhin about dinner-time and found Fomin really at home. He made Piotra welcome, seated him at his table, and smiled into his ruddy whiskers when his father brought the jug out of Piotra's sledge.

"Well, friend, why haven't we seen you before?" Fomin said in his slow, pleasant bass voice, glancing sidelong at Daria with widely set, amorous eyes and twisting his moustache with dignity.

"Why, you know, Yakov Yefimich, the regiments retreated. It's a serious time."

"You're right, it is! You should have brought us some pickled cucumbers and cabbage, or some dried fish. . . ."

The tiny hut was heated to suffocation. After a drink Piotra turned to his business.

"There's a lot of talk in the villages that the Cheka has arrived and is laying hands on the Cossacks," he remarked.

"A Red Army Tribunal has arrived in Vieshenska. But what of it? What are you bothered about it for?"

"You know, Yakov Yefimich, I'm regarded as an officer. And everybody can see it for himself."

"Well, what then?" Fomin felt that he was master of the situation. His slight intoxication made him self-confident and arrogant. He stroked his moustache and stared at Piotra fixedly and authoritatively.

Piotra played up to him and became humble and servile in his attitude, though adopting a slightly more familiar tone:

"You and I have served together. You can't say anything bad about me. Was I ever against you? Never! God strike me, but I was always on the side of the Cossacks!"

"We know. Don't you fear, Piotra Pantalievich! We know them all through and through. They won't touch you. But there are some we shall touch! There are lots of serpents left behind hiding their weapons. . . . You've given yours up? Eh?"

The transition from Fomin's slow speech to his pressing inquiry was so swift that for a moment Piotra lost control of himself, and the blood flooded to his face.

"You've given them up? Well, what are you waiting for?" Fomin insisted, leaning across the table.

"Of course we have, Yakov Yefimich. Don't you think . . . with open heart. . . ."

"With open heart! We know your open hearts! I'm a local man, you know!" Fomin drunkenly winked. "Shake hands with a rich Cossack with one hand, and hold a knife in the other. . . . The dogs! There aren't any open hearts here. I've seen through many people in my time. The traitors! But don't you fear, they won't touch you. My word is gold!"

Piotra left for home early in the evening, in high spirits and with renewed hope.

After seeing Piotra off, Pantaleimon went to visit old Korshunov. He had called on him just before the arrival of the Reds, but Luki-nichna had been getting Mitka ready for flight, and the hut had been in a state of confusion. Feeling that he was in the way, Pantaleimon had returned home. But now he thought he would go and find out whether all was well with them and sit and talk about the times that had come upon them.

In the yard he met Grishka, very infirm and with several teeth gone. It was Sunday, and the old man was going off to vespers. Pantaleimon was taken aback when he saw him, for all the crosses and medals he had won during the Turkish war were visible and shining beneath his sheepskin, little red shoulder-knots gleamed challengingly from the standing collar of his old-time tunic, his ancient striped trousers were carefully tucked into white socks, and on his head was a military cap sporting a cockade.

"Why, grand-dad! Are you in your senses? What are you wearing your crosses and a cockade for in such times?"

"Eh?" The old man put his hand to his ear.

"Take that cockade off, I say. Take off those crosses. They'll arrest you if you turn out like that. It can't be done under the Soviet government, their laws don't allow it."

"I served my White Czar in faith and truth, my lad. And this government is not of God. I don't recognize it as a government. I took my oath to Czar Alexander, and not to peasants!" The old man chewed his pale lips and pointed with his stick to the hut. "You want Miron? He's at home. But Mitka had to clear out. Queen of Heaven, watch over him! Your boys have stayed behind, haven't they? What fine Cossacks they've turned out to be! They took their oath, but now the army is in need, they remain by their wives. Is Natalia well?"

"Yes. But take your crosses off! God, you've gone balmy, grand-dad!"

"God be with you! You're young to teach me!" The old man came straight at Pantaleimon, and, hopelessly shaking his head, Melekhov stepped aside into the snow to let him pass.

"Did you see our old warrior?" Miron Gregorievich rose to meet Pantaleimon. "There's a fine way to bring trouble down on our heads! He fastened on his medals, put his cap on, and went! He's become quite a child, he doesn't understand a thing."

"Let him comfort himself as he can; it won't be for long!" Luki-nichna sat down with the Cossacks, bitterly complaining. "Well, how are you all? We heard Grishka had been chased by the anarchists. They've taken four of our horses and left only the mare and a year-ling. They've robbed us of everything."

Miron screwed up his eyes as though taking aim at someone and spoke with a new tone of authority. "And what's the cause of our life being ruined?" he demanded. "Who has done it? It's all this devilish government. Is it sensible to make everybody equal? You can drag the soul out of me, but I'd never agree to it. I've had to work hard all my life, and then they want to make me equal with those who've never lifted a finger to raise themselves out of their need. No, we'll wait a little longer! This government will cut the veins of the good farmer! And then why should we work, and whom should we work for? The front lies along the Donietz. But is it likely to stop there? I'm telling those I can rely on that we ought to sup-port our Cossacks who are beyond the Donietz. . . ."

"But how?" Pantaleimon cautiously asked, for some reason drop-ping his voice to a whisper.

"How? Why, by kicking out this government! Yes, and kicking them so hard that they'll find themselves back in Tambov province.

Let them share their equality with the peasants there. I'll give all that I own down to the last thread to destroy these enemies. Now is the time; otherwise it will be too late. Only we must take them by surprise! The regiments have gone on, and there are only the village chairmen left behind. It would be a simple matter to get rid of them!"

Pantaleimon rose to his feet. Carefully weighing his words, he anxiously advised Miron:

"Make sure you don't slip! Or you'll be laying up trouble for yourself. Once let the Cossacks waver and the devil knows where they'll get to. You can't talk to everybody about such matters these days. I can't understand the younger Cossacks at all. Some have cleared out, and others have stayed behind. It's a hard life. And it's not life, but darkness."

"Don't you have any doubt!" Miron smiled condescendingly. "I'm not talking in the dark. People are like sheep: where the ram goes, the whole flock follows. And so we must show them the road. We must open their eyes to this government. Where there are no clouds there's no thunder. I tell the Cossacks straight: they must rise in revolt. I hear they've given orders to hang all the Cossacks. And how are we to take that?"

Pantaleimon went home still more distracted, thoroughly in the grip of anxiety and yearning. Now he felt how completely foreign, hostile elements had begun to take charge of life. The future was hidden in mist. The past glimmered through the dusks of experience. Here was Miron Korshunov, at one time the richest Cossack in all the district. And now the last three years had worn down his power. His workers had all gone, he was sowing far less, and he had had to sell his bullocks and horses for ridiculous prices paid in falling currency. Only the hut with its carved balcony and faded cornices remained to tell the tale of his former glories. And in Miron Gregorievich himself two elements were struggling for mastery: his fiery blood revolted, drove him to work, forced him to sow his land, to build sheds, to repair his farm implements, and to grow rich. But more and more frequently he was oppressed by the thought: What was the good of getting rich? It would all fall to the ground. And indifference tinted everything with its deathly hue. His terrible hands did not seize the hammer or hand-saw as in past days, but lay idly on his knees. Old age had come upon him prematurely.

Even the earth grew repellent to him: in the spring he turned to it as to an unloved wife, out of habit, from a sense of duty. He increased his possessions without rejoicing and lost them without his former bitter regret. When the Reds had taken his horses he had not even shown himself, yet two years previously for a trifle of flax trodden by bullocks he had all but impaled his wife on a pitchfork.

Pantaleimon limped home and lay down on the bed. He felt a sucking pain in the pit of his stomach, and a yawning nausea rose in his throat. After supper he asked his wife to get him some salted watermelon. Then he was attacked by a shivering fit and could hardly make his way across the room to the stove. Towards morning he was tossing in delirium, feverish with typhus. His lips cracked, his face turned yellow, and the whites of his eyes were darkened with a blue tinge. Old woman Drozdikha came and let his blood, drawing two soup-plates of the thick black liquid from his veins. But he did not return to consciousness: his face went still whiter, and his mouth gaped as he gasped heavily for air.

Chapter 14

On February 6 Ivan Alexievich was summoned to Vieshenska to see the chairman of the district Revolutionary Committee. He was due to return to Tatarsk the same evening, and Mishka Koshevoi sat waiting for him in Mokhov's empty house, behind the great writing-table in the old owner's former office. On the window-sill (there was only one chair in the room) a militia-man from Vieshenska, named Olshanov, was reclining, smoking silently and spitting with great dexterity across the room. Outside the windows the sunset sky was fading into a starry night. Mishka was writing a protocol authorizing a search of Stepan Astakhov's hut, occasionally glancing up at the frosted window.

Someone passed along the veranda into the porch, his felt boots quietly scrunching.

"Here he is!" Mishka stood up. But there were unfamiliar steps in the corridor, an unfamiliar cough, and Gregor Melekhov entered, red with the frost, icicles clinging to his brows and whiskers.

"Hello! Come in!" Mishka greeted him.

"I've come to have a talk and to ask you not to send us on transport work. Our horses are lame," Gregor said.

"But what about your bullocks?" Mishka gave him a sidelong glance.

"You can't use bullocks for transport!"

There was the sound of feet scraping on the frost-bound boards as someone strode up the steps, and the next moment Ivan Alexievich ran into the room.

"I'm frozen, frozen, boys!" he cried. "Hello, Gregor! What are you wandering about at night for? The devil made this cloak; the wind comes through it as if it was a sieve."

As he removed his cloak he went on, his eyes gleaming: "Well, I've seen the chairman. I went into his office and he shook hands and said: 'Sit down, comrade!' A district chairman, mark you! And what was it like in the old days? He'd have been a major-general, and you'd have had to stand in front of him as if you were on parade. That's the government we've got now—everybody's equal."

Gregor could not understand the reason for Ivan's animated, happy face and exultant words, and he asked:

"What is it you're so glad about, Ivan Alexievich?"

"What about?" Ivan's dimpled chin trembled. "He saw that I was a man, and so why shouldn't I be glad? He gave me his hand as an equal and told me to sit down. . . ."

"Even the generals go about in shirts made of sacking these days." Gregor stroked his whiskers. "I saw one officer wearing epaulets drawn with pencil. And they give the Cossacks their hands too. . . ."

"The generals did it because they had to, but these do it by nature. See the difference?"

"There isn't any difference." Gregor shook his head.

"And do you think the government is just the same? What did you fight for? For the generals? And you say it's all the same!"

"I fought for myself, not for the generals. If I'm to tell the truth, neither these nor those are to my liking."

"Who is, then?"

"Why, no one."

Olshanov, the militia-man, spat right across the room and smiled sympathetically. Evidently there was no one to his liking either.

"I don't think you used to hold those views," Mishka remarked with the deliberate intention of wounding Gregor. But Gregor showed no sign that the shot had gone home.

"You and I thought the same once . . ." he replied.

Ivan Alexievich had been anxious to get rid of Gregor in order to tell Mishka about his journey and talk with the district chairman, but the conversation began to trouble him. Under the influence of what he had seen and heard at Vieshenska he threw himself into the argument.

"You came along here to pull our legs!" he said. "Gregor, you don't know yourself what you want."

"You're right, I don't," Gregor willingly agreed.

"What have you got against this government?"

"And what are you standing up for it for? Since when have you been so Red?"

"We're not going to talk about that. We'll talk about what is now. And don't say too much about the government, because I'm village chairman, and it isn't wise for me to argue with you here."

"Let's drop it, then. I came here about transport requisitions. As for your government, say what you like, it's a filthy government. And you praise it like a mother her child: 'It's a snotty little brat, but it's ours!' Tell me straight out, and we'll leave it at that: What benefit is it to us Cossacks?"

"Which Cossacks? There are all sorts of Cossacks."

"All that there are."

"Liberty, equality. . . . Wait. . . ."

"That's what they said in 1917, but now they must think of something better!" Gregor interrupted him. "Are they giving us the land? Or liberty? Are they making everyone equal? We've got enough land to choke ourselves with already. And we don't want any more liberty. We used to elect our own atamans, but now they're set over us. This government will bring the Cossacks nothing but ruin. It's a peasants' government, and we don't need it. And we don't need the generals either. The Communists and the generals are all alike: they're all yokes on our necks."

"The rich Cossacks don't need it, but how about the others? You

fool! There are three rich Cossacks in the village, and how many
poor? And what will you do with the labourers? No, we can't take
your view of it. Let the rich Cossacks give up a bit out of their own
mouths and give it to the poor. And if they won't, we'll take it, with
their flesh as well! We've had enough of their lording it over us!
They stole the land."

"Not stole it, but conquered it. Our forefathers poured out their
blood for it, and perhaps that's why the earth is so black."

"That doesn't make any difference; they must share it with those
who need it. But you—you're like the weathercock on a roof. You
turn with the wind. Such men as you make life hard."

"You needn't swear at me! I came along out of my old friendship,
to tell you what was boiling inside me. You say 'equality.' That's
how the Bolsheviks have taken in the ignorant people. They talk
fine words, but they drive a man on like fish into a net. And where
is this 'equality' of yours? Take the Red Army. They passed through
the village, the troop officers in chrome leather boots, and 'Ivan' in
leg-rags. I saw commissars all dressed in leather: trousers and
coat and everything. And others didn't have enough leather to
make a pair of shoes. We've had a year now of the Soviet government, and they're well in the saddle. But where is their equality?
At the front we used to say the officers and men would be paid the
same. But no matter how bad the lord is, the lout become a lord is
ten times worse. The old officers were bad enough, but when a
Cossack gets to be an officer, you may as well lie down and die, you
couldn't have worse. He's had the same education as any other
Cossack, he's learned to twist the bullocks' tails, but now look at him!
He's got on in the world and he's drunk with his authority, and he's
ready to flay anyone else alive in order to keep his seat."

"Your words are counter-revolutionary," Ivan Alexievich coldly
replied, without raising his eyes to Gregor's face. "You won't turn
me into your furrow, and I don't want to break you. It's long since I
saw you last and I won't hide that you've changed. You are an enemy
of the Soviet government."

"I didn't expect that from you. So if I think about the government,
that's counter-revolutionary, is it?"

Ivan borrowed Olshanov's tobacco-pouch, then said more mildly:

"How am I to make you see it? Men get there with their own
minds and hearts. I can't manage it with words, owing to your ig-

norance and my own lack of education. I myself have to grope my way to many things. . . ."

"I've had enough of this talk!" Mishka shouted furiously.

They all left the house together. Gregor was silent. As they parted, Ivan Alexievich said:

"You'd better keep such thoughts to yourself. Otherwise, although I know you, I shall find ways of stopping you. You're not going to make the Cossacks waver, they're wavering enough already. And don't you stand in our road. We'll tread over you. Good-bye."

Gregor walked away feeling that he had burned his boats. That which previously had been uncertain had now become abundantly clear. He had only been saying aloud what he had been thinking for many days. And, because he stood at the parting of the ways, struggling between two elements and rejecting them both, a deep, never silenced exasperation had been born in him.

Mishka and Ivan went off together. Ivan began to tell of his meeting with the district chairman, but when he spoke, the colour and significance of it all had faded. He tried to recover his previous buoyant mood, but could not: something stood athwart the road, preventing him from living joyously and breathing in the fresh, frosty air. Gregor and his talk were the obstacle. As he recalled the discussion he said with hatred in his voice:

"Such men as Gregor only get between your legs. The scum! He never reaches the shore and floats along like cow-dung. If he comes again, I'll give him one! And if he starts agitating, we'll find a quiet little seat for him. What do you think? How are things going, Mishka?"

Mishka turned to him, a smile flickering over his girlish lips. "What a rotten thing politics is, by the devil! You can talk about whatever else you like, but you won't ever cause so much bad blood. Here's Gregor: we've been friends ever since we went to school together, we ran after the girls together, he was like my own brother to me, and now we begin to talk and I get so wild that my heart comes near to bursting, as though it was a watermelon. It was as though he was taking something from me, robbing me! And I could have killed him as we talked. There are no brothers or cousins in this war. You just draw a line and follow it." Mishka's voice trembled with his unbearable sense of injury. "Not over any girl he'd won from me did I ever get so angry as over his words. That shows you how far we've got!"

The snow melted as it fell. At noonday the snowdrifts in the cliffs came sliding down with a dull, heavy rumble. The boles of the oaks were laid bare of snow; little drops sprinkled from the branches and pierced through the snow to the very earth. Already the intoxicating vegetative scent of spring was rising, and the orchards were perfumed with cherries. Holes appeared in the icy sheet of the Don, the ice retreated from the banks, and clear green water flooded over the edges of the water holes.

A transport carrying munitions to the Donietz front was to change its sledges at Tatarsk. The Red Army men accompanying it proved to be spirited lads. Their commander remained in the Revolutionary Committee to watch over Ivan Alexievich, remarking: "I'll stay with you, or you'll be clearing off before we know where you are." The others went to collect sledges. Forty-seven two-horse sledges were required.

Yemelian, Mokhov's former coachman, went along to the Melekhovs' hut and saw Piotra.

"Harness up your horses to carry munitions to Bokovaya," he said.

Without turning a hair, Piotra snorted:

"The horses are lame, and yesterday I carried wounded to Vieshenska with the mare."

Yemelian said no more, but turned and ran to the stable. Piotra ran after him, shouting:

"Do you hear? Wait a minute. . . ."

"Stop playing the fool!" Yemelian gazed sternly at Piotra and added: "I don't want to look at your horses. I expect you've made them lame yourself. You can't pull the wool over my eyes. I've seen as many horses in my time as you've seen horse-dung. Harness them up; horses or bullocks, it's all the same to me."

Gregor went with the transport. Before his departure he ran into the kitchen, kissed his children, and hurriedly told them:

"I'll bring you back something nice, only you behave yourselves and listen to what your mother says." But to Piotra he added: "Don't worry about me. I shan't go far. If they want us to go farther than Bokovaya I shall leave the bullocks behind and come back. But I may not return to the village. I'm thinking of going to our aunt at Singin. I don't like hanging about here." He smiled. "Well, goodbye."

"The Reds are fighting so that they can have a better life, but we've already fought for our better life," Gregor thought as he reclined in the sledge, behind the slow, measured movement of the bullocks. "There's no one truth in this life. Whoever masters the other gets the fire for himself. And I foolishly sought for the truth, made myself ill over it, and went from one to the other. In the old days the Tatars tried to seize the Don lands and to make us slaves. And now it's Russia. There can be no peace with them! They are foreign to me and to all the Cossacks. We deserted from the front, and now everybody's thinking like me . . . but it's too late."

Occasionally shouting lazily at the bullocks, he dozed, huddled against the ammunition cases. He smoked a cigarette, then thrust his nose into the hay. It smelled of dry clover and the sweet haze of July days. He dropped off to sleep. In his sleep he dreamed that he was walking with Aksinia through high-standing corn. In her arms she was carefully carrying a child and her eyes were fixed watchfully on Gregor. Gregor could hear the beating of his own heart, the singing rustle of the ears; he saw the brilliant edging of grass along the field boundaries, the poignant blue of the sky. He loved Aksinia again with all his old, exhausting love; he felt that he loved her with all his body, with every beat of his heart. But at the same time he realized that this was not reality, that the colours before his eyes were the deathly tints of dreamland. Yet he rejoiced in his dream and accepted it as life. Aksinia was the same as she had been five years before, save that she was more restrained and cold. . . .

A jostle of the sledge awoke him, and the sound of voices sobered him. He glanced up and saw that they were passing a long line of transport sledges moving in the opposite direction.

"What is your load, friends?" Bodovskov, driving in front of Gregor, hoarsely asked.

The sledge-runner squeaked, the bullocks' cloven hoofs scrunched in the snow. There was a long silence before anyone would answer. At last one of the drivers said:

"Corpses. Died of typhus. . . ."

Gregor looked up. Bodies covered with tarpaulins lay stretched out on the passing sledges. The rail of his own sledge struck against a hand poking from under the tarpaulin, and the human flesh gave out a dull iron ring. Gregor turned unconcernedly away.

The cloying, calling scent of the clover again induced sleep, gently recalled the half-forgotten past, and renewed in him the feeling of

his former happiness. He felt a rending yet delicious pain as he
threw himself back in the sledge, his cheek touching the yellow stalks
of the clover. But his heart beat violently, and sleep was a long time
coming.

Chapter 15

A small group of men gathered around Tatarsk Revolutionary Committee. There were David, Timofei, Mokhov's former coachman
Yemelian, and the freckled cobbler Filka. Ivan Alexievich had to
rely on this group for support in his everyday activities, for he realized that an invisible wall was more and more cutting him off from
the rest of the village. The Cossacks ceased to come to meetings, or
when they did, it was only after David and the others had run several
times from hut to hut. Then they came, but silently agreed to everything proposed. At such times the younger Cossacks were always
in a large majority. But even among these there were no sympathizers. Stony faces, distrustful looks, lowering glances met Ivan's
eyes as he carried on the meeting. His heart turned cold within him,
his eyes acquired a yearning look, his voice grew weak and lacking
in confidence. One day freckled Filka blurted out:

"We've got cut off from the village, Comrade Ivan. The people
have become devils. Yesterday I went to get sledges to carry
wounded Red Army men to Vieshenska, but nobody would go."

"But how they're drinking!" Yemelian exclaimed. "In every hut
vodka's being made."

Mishka Koshevoi frowned and kept his thoughts to himself, but
as they were going home in the evening he asked Ivan Alexievich:

"Let me have a rifle."

"What for?"

"I don't like going about with empty hands. Or haven't you noticed anything? I think we must arrest someone. . . . We must
arrest Gregor Melekhov, old Boldirev, Matvei Kashulin, and Miron
Korshunov. They're whispering to the Cossacks, the snakes. They're

waiting for the return of their own men from the Donietz."

Ivan Alexievich sadly waved his hand. "If we begin to arrest so many, we must take them all. There are some who are sympathetic to us, but they keep their eyes fixed on Korshunov. They're afraid his Mitka will come back from the Donietz and tear their guts out."

Life took charge of affairs for Ivan. The next day an express messenger from Vieshenska brought an instruction to enforce a levy upon the richest families. The sum of forty thousand rubles was to be obtained from the village. The Revolutionary Committee allocated the amount to be raised by each family. By the following day two sacks of money, some eighteen thousand rubles in all, had been collected. Ivan Alexievich wrote to the District Committee. In reply three militia-men were sent back with the order: "Those who have not paid their levy are to be arrested and sent under escort to Vieshenska." Four old men were at once arrested and temporarily imprisoned in Mokhov's cellar, where he had formerly kept his winter apples.

The village resembled an agitated beehive. Korshunov flatly refused to pay. None the less the time had come when he must render account for his former prosperous days. An investigator, a young Vieshenska Cossack who had served in the 28th Regiment, and another man arrived in the village. They showed Ivan the mandate of the Revolutionary Tribunal and were closeted with him in his office. The investigator's comrade, an elderly, clean-shaven man, said seriously:

"Disturbances are occurring in the district. The White Guards who have remained behind are raising their heads and are beginning to oppress the toiling Cossacks. We must remove all those most hostile to us: the officers, priests, gendarmes, all who have actively fought against us. We'll draw up a list. Give the investigator every assistance. He knows some already."

Ivan stared at the man's clean-shaven face and ran over the names of family after family. He mentioned Piotra Melekhov also, but the investigator shook his head:

"He's one of us. Fomin asked that he shouldn't be touched. He's friendly to the Bolsheviks. I served with him in the 28th."

A few hours later the arrested Cossacks were sitting guarded by the militia-men in Mokhov's spacious yard, waiting for their families to send them provisions, clothing, and other necessary articles. Miron

Gregorievich, dressed in entirely new clothes as though preparing
to meet his death, was sitting at the end, next to old Bogatiriev and
Matvei Kashulin. Avdeich the Braggart was vaguely wandering
about the yard, aimlessly staring into the well or picking up a chain,
then wandering back from porch to wicket gate, rubbing his sweaty,
livid face with his sleeve. The others sat in silence, with bowed
heads, drawing designs on the snow with their sticks. Their women
ran tearfully about the yard with sacks and bundles. Lukinichna
wept as she buttoned the sheepskin jacket around her old man and
tied up his collar with a large white kerchief. As she stared into his
faded eyes she said:

"Don't you grieve, Miron! Maybe it will all turn out all right.
Lord!" Her mouth lengthened into a tearful grimace, but she pursed
up her lips and whispered: "I'll come and visit you and bring you
some mushrooms. You know you like them."

At the gate a militia-man shouted:

"The sledges have arrived. Put your things on them and come on!
The women must stand back; it's no use their crying now."

For the first time in her life Lukinichna kissed Miron's hairy hand,
then she tore herself away. The bullock-sledges slowly crawled
across the square towards the Don. The seven prisoners and two
militia-men followed them on foot. Avdeich dropped behind to tie
up his shoe and ran youthfully to overtake them. Matvei Kashulin
and his son walked side by side. Maidannikov and Koroliov were
smoking. Miron Korshunov held on to the sledge. Behind all the
rest came old Bogatiriev with a heavy, majestic stride. The contrary
wind blew back the ends of his white, patriarchal beard, and the
scarf flung over his shoulder fluttered as though in farewell.

On that same cloudy February day another unusual event occurred in Tatarsk. Of recent days the village inhabitants had grown
accustomed to the arrival of officials from the district. So no one paid
any attention to the two-horse sleigh which crossed the square with
someone seated at the driver's side. The sleigh stopped outside
Mokhov's house and the man got down, proving to be elderly, and
unhurried in his movements. He adjusted his long cavalry coat,
raised the ear-flaps of his Red cavalry fur cap from his ears, and,
holding the wooden case of his Mauser, went slowly up the steps.

In the Revolutionary Committee room were Ivan Alexievich and two militia-men. The newcomer entered without knocking, stroked his short, iron-grey beard, and said inquiringly:

"I want the chairman."

Ivan turned dilated eyes on the speaker and wanted to jump out of his seat. But he could not. He only worked his mouth like a fish and scraped the arms of his chair with his fingers. From under the Cossack cavalry cap Stockman was gazing at him. For a moment his eyes were screwed up, fixed on Ivan without a sign of recognition; then they lit up and a line of tiny furrows ran from their corners towards the temples. He strode across to Ivan, embraced and kissed him, brushing his face with his damp beard, and exclaimed:

"I knew it! If, I thought, Ivan's still alive, I shall find him chairman in Tatarsk!"

"Osip Davidovich, pinch me! Pinch me, swine that I am! I can't believe my eyes!" Ivan almost wept.

"It's true enough!" Stockman replied, gently releasing his hand from Ivan's. "Well, haven't you got anything to sit on?"

"Here, take this chair. But where have you sprung from? Tell me."

"I'm with the Political Section of the Red Army. I see you still can't believe that I'm genuine! Strange lad! But it's all very simple, brother. After they took me away from here, I was sent into exile, and there the Revolution found me. I and another comrade organized a Red Guard and we helped to fight Kolchak. It was a gay time, my boy! Now we've driven him beyond the Urals. And here I am on your front. The Political Section of the Eighth Army sent me here to work in your district, as I'd lived here and knew the conditions, so to speak. I arrived at Vieshenska, had a talk with the people on the Revolutionary Committee, and decided to come to Tatarsk first of all. I thought I'd come and stay here, work and help you organize things, and then go on elsewhere. You see, I haven't forgotten our old friendship. But we can come back to that later; now let's talk about yourself, about the situation here. Tell me all about everybody. Who's working with you? Who's still alive? Comrades" (he turned to the militia-men), "leave me and the chairman alone for an hour or so. Pfooh, the devil! As I drove into the village it smelt so much of the old days. . . . Yes, time stood still then, but now—Well, begin."

Some three hours later Mishka Koshevoi and Ivan conducted Stockman to his old quarters with squinting Lukeria. They strode along the brown track of the road, Mishka frequently seizing Stockman by the sleeve as though afraid he would disappear before his eyes or prove to be a phantom. After tea made from a decoction of cherry leaves Stockman lay down on the stove. He lay listening to the confused stories told by Mishka and Ivan, asking questions, biting his cigarette-holder, and just before dawn dozed off, dropping his cigarette on his dirty flannel shirt. Ivan went on talking for some ten minutes more, but when Stockman answered a question with a snore he quietly tiptoed out of the room, almost tearfully livid in the attempt to stop his coughing.

"Feel better?" Mishka asked with a quiet laugh, as they went down the steps.

Olshanov, who had accompanied the prisoners to Vieshenska, returned at midnight. He knocked and knocked at the window of the little room where Ivan Alexievich was asleep and at last awoke him.

"What do you want?" Ivan asked, his face puffy with sleep. "Brought letters back, or what?"

Olshanov played with his whip. "They've shot the Cossacks," he said.

"You're lying, you serpent!"

"They examined them as soon as they arrived and led them into a pine wood before it was dark. I saw it myself."

Fumbling with his felt boots and clothes, Ivan dressed hurriedly and ran to Stockman.

"We sent some prisoners to Vieshenska today and they've shot them!" he exclaimed. "I thought they would just keep them in prison, but this is different. This way we'll never do anything. The people will turn from us, Osip Davidovich. Why did they kill them? What will happen now?"

He expected Stockman to be as agitated and indignant as himself at what had occurred, but as he slowly drew on his shirt Stockman answered:

"Now, stop shouting! You'll wake Lukeria up!" He dressed, lit a cigarette, asked once more the reasons that had led to the arrests, then coldly said: "You must get this into your head, and get it well in!

The front is a hundred and twenty miles away from here. The main body of the Cossacks is hostile to us. And that's because your kulak Cossacks, your atamans and other heads, enjoy a tremendous influence with the toiling Cossacks. Why do they? Well, you ought to be able to answer that yourself. The Cossacks are a special military caste. Czarism developed in them this love for the authorities and for the 'father commanders.' And it was these same 'father commanders' who ordered the Cossacks to smash the workers' strike. They made fools of the Cossacks for three hundred years. Well, now! There's a very great difference between the kulak of, say, Ryazan province and the Don Cossack kulak. The Ryazan kulak has been squeezed; he's helpless and only potentially dangerous. But the Don kulak is an armed kulak. He's a dangerous and poisonous snake. He won't only spread lying tales about us, as Korshunov and the others did according to your own words, but he'll try to attack us openly. Of course he will! He'll take a rifle and shoot us. He'll kill you. And he'll try to get the other Cossacks, the Cossack who is not too badly off and even the poor Cossack, to follow him. Well, what was the situation here? They were accused of activities against us? All right! Few words, and to the wall with them! And there's nothing to dribble with sorrow about—'he was a good sort,' and all that. . . ."

"I'm not sorry, don't think that." Ivan Alexievich waved his hand. "But I'm afraid it'll set the others against us."

So far Stockman had retained some semblance of calm. But now he exploded, violently seized Ivan by the collar of his shirt, and, drawing him close to himself, did not so much say as roar the words:

"They won't be set against us if we instil our class truth into them. The toiling Cossack has only us to look to as his comrades, and not the kulaks. Oh, my God, you— The kulaks live on their labour and get fat on it, don't they? Oh, I see I'll have to take you in hand! A worker like you, and you dribble like one of the intelligentsia. . . . Just like some lousy little Social-Revolutionary! Ah, Ivan!" He released his collar, smiled faintly, shook his head, and ended more calmly:

"If we don't seize the most active enemies in the district, there'll be a rising. If we isolate them in time, there won't be a rising. It isn't necessary to shoot them all; we must destroy only the leaders and send the others into the heart of Russia. But you can't stand on ceremony with your enemies. You 'can't make a revolution with the gloves on,' as Lenin said. Was it necessary to shoot these men in this case? I think it was. Maybe not all, but certainly Korshunov. That's clear. And there's Gregor Melekhov: he's got away for the time being. We should have caught him in the act. He is more dangerous than all the others taken together. That talk he had with you was the talk of a man who will be an enemy tomorrow. And what we're going through here is nothing. On the fronts the finest sons of the working class are perishing, and in their thousands. We must be sorry for them, and not for those who are killing them or waiting for the opportunity to strike us in the back. And now you see daylight, don't you, Ivan?"

Chapter 16

Piotra had just entered the kitchen after collecting the cattle. Immediately behind him the latch of the outer door rattled, and Lukinichna, wrapped in a black shawl, crossed the threshold. Taking little steps, without a word of greeting, she tottered towards Natalia and fell to her knees in front of her.

"Mamma! My dear! What's the matter?" Natalia cried in an unrecognizable voice, stooping to raise her mother's heavy body.

Instead of replying Lukinichna beat her head against the earthen floor and intoned in a dull, broken voice:

"Beloved mine! For whom have you abandoned me?"

The two women broke into such a wail of sorrow, to which the children added their whining tones, that Piotra seized his tobacco-pouch from the stove ledge and rushed out into the porch. He guessed at once what had happened, and stood smoking on the steps. The howling voices died away in the kitchen, and he returned, an unpleasantly cold shiver running down his back. With her face buried in her wet handkerchief, Lukinichna was reciting:

"They've shot our Miron Gregorievich! My eagle is gone from life. . . . We're left orphans. . . . The chickens will peck at us now." Her voice rose to a howl: "His dear eyes are closed. No more will they see the light of day."

Daria sprinkled the swooning Natalia with water. Ilinichna wiped her cheeks with her apron. From the front room where Pantaleimon was lying ill came the sound of coughing and a grating groan.

"For the love of Christ!" Lukinichna seized Piotra's hand and pressed it frantically to her breast. "For the love of God, drive to Vieshenska and bring him back even though he is dead. Bring him back. Oh, merciful Queen of Heaven! Oh, I don't want him to rot there without decent burial."

"What are you thinking of?" Piotra stepped away from her as though she was plague-stricken. "A fine job I'd have to find him! My own life is worth more to me than that!"

"Don't refuse me, Piotra! For the love of Christ . . . the love of Christ. . . ."

Piotra chewed at his moustache and at last agreed to go. He decided to drive to a Cossack acquaintance of his father's at Vieshenska and enlist his help in the attempt to obtain Miron's body. He drove off at night. The village huts were bright with light, and every kitchen was discussing the executions. He stopped at the hut of his father's old regimental comrade and asked for his help. The Cossack willingly agreed, remarking:

"I know where they're buried. They're not deep. The only difficulty will be to find him. He's not the only one. Yesterday they shot a dozen. I make only one condition: afterwards you'll pay for a bottle of vodka. Agreed?"

At midnight, equipped with spades and a builder's stretcher, they passed through the cemetery to the pines where the sentences had been carried out. A fine snow was falling. Piotra strained his ears to every sound, inwardly cursing the expedition, Lukinichna, and even the dead Miron. The Cossack stopped close by a sandy ridge. "Somewhere around here they ought to be," he remarked.

They went on another hundred paces. A pack of dogs fled away with yelps and growls. Piotra threw down the stretcher and hoarsely whispered:

"I'm going back! Let him go to the devil! How are we to find him among all the others? The unclean spirit himself asked me to do this!"

"What are you afraid of? Come on!" the Cossack laughed at him.

They went on and came to a spot where the snow was heavily trodden and mingled with sand, close to an old willow bush. They began to dig.

Piotra recognized Miron by his red beard. He pulled the body out by the belt and tumbled it on to the stretcher. The Cossack lifted the handles of the stretcher, discontentedly grumbling.

"We should have driven with a sledge as far as the pines. We're fools! He's a good hundred and eighty pounds. And it's not easy going over the snow."

Piotra separated the legs projecting beyond the end of the stretcher and gripped the handles.

Until early morning they sat drinking in the Cossack's hut. Miron Gregorievich, wrapped in a rug, waited outside in the sledge. Piotra had left the horse harnessed to the sledge, and the animal stood the whole time pulling hard on its halter rope, snorting and pricking up its ears. It scented the corpse and would not go near the hay in the sledge.

Dawn was greying when Piotra arrived at Tatarsk. He had taken the meadow road and had driven the horse without respite. Behind him Miron's head beat a tattoo on the bottom of the sledge, and Piotra stopped twice to thrust some damp meadow hay under it. He drove the body straight home. Miron's favourite daughter, Aggripina, opened the gate for the dead master and fled back from the sledge into the snowdrift at the side. Piotra flung the body like a sack of flour over his shoulder and carried it into the kitchen, carefully setting it down on the table, on which a linen sheet had been spread. Then Lukinichna, streaming with tears, crawled to her husband's feet:

"I thought you would be coming back home on your own feet, dear master, but they've had to carry you." Her whispers and sobs, strangely like chuckles of laughter, were hardly audible. Piotra led old Grishaka by the arm into the room. The old man was shaking all over. But he walked strongly to the table and stood at the head.

"Well, Miron! So this is how we meet again, little son!" He crossed himself and kissed the icy, muddy brow. "Miron . . . and I shan't be long." The old man's voice rose to a groaning howl. With a strong, youthful movement he raised the dead hand to his lips, then dropped down by the table.

A spasm of rage clutched Piotra by the throat. He quietly went out into the yard, to his horse fastened up by the chicken-house.

Chapter 17

Early in March Ivan Alexievich summoned a village assembly in
Tatarsk. An unusually large crowd attended, perhaps because Stockman had proposed that the Revolutionary Committee should call a
meeting and distribute the property of those fled to the Whites
among the poorer Cossacks. The meeting was preceded by a stormy
encounter between Stockman and a district official who had come
from Vieshenska armed with authority to take away some confiscated clothing. Stockman explained to him that at the moment the
Revolutionary Committee could not hand over the clothing as only
the previous day it had been issued to a transport of wounded Red
Army men. The young official stormed at Stockman, sharply raising
his voice.

"Who gave you permission to hand over this clothing?" he demanded.

"We didn't ask anyone's permission."

"But what right had you to embezzle national property?"

"Don't shout, comrade, and don't talk nonsense. No one has em-
bezzled anything. We handed sheepskins to the drivers on a signed
undertaking from them that after they'd carried their wounded to a
certain point they would bring the clothing back. The soldiers were
half-naked, and if we'd let them go off as they were we'd have been
sending them to their deaths. What else could I do? Especially as
the clothing was lying unused in the cellar."

Stockman spoke quietly, restraining his irritation, and the conversation might have ended peacefully. But the youngster resolutely
declared in a steely voice:

"Who are you? Chairman of the Revolutionary Committee? I arrest you! Hand over your work to your assistant. I'll send you at
once to Vieshenska. I expect you've stolen half the property here,
but I . . ."

"Are you a Communist?" Stockman demanded, turning deathly
pale.

"That's not your business! Militia-man! Take this man at once

and hand him over at Vieshenska. Give him into the charge of the
district militia and get a receipt for him." Measuring Stockman with
a glance, he added:

"And we'll talk to you there! You'll dance to my tune, you dic-
tator!"

"Comrade, are you mad? Don't you know . . ."

"No talk! Silence!"

With a slow, terrible movement Stockman reached out for his
Mauser hanging on the wall. Fear danced in the youngster's eyes.
With astounding speed he pushed the door open with his back and
fell down the steps, his spine knocking against each stair. He flung
himself into his sleigh and urged his driver on with digs in the back
all the way across the square, looking behind him continually to see
whether he were being pursued.

A roar of laughter shook the windows of the Revolutionary Committee. David rolled in convulsions over the table. But Stockman's
eyelid twitched nervously as he muttered:

"The scum! The miserable scum!"

He went with Mishka and Ivan to the assembly. The square was
filled. Ivan's heart beat unpleasantly as he thought: "There's something in the wind. All the village has turned up." But his anxieties
were dissipated when, removing his cap, he went to the middle of
the ring. The Cossacks willingly yielded before him. Their faces
were respectful; some had smiling eyes. Stockman looked around
the ring of Cossacks. He wanted to dispel the tense atmosphere and
to draw them into conversation. Following Ivan's example he removed his fur cap and cried:

"Comrade Cossacks! It's six weeks now since the Soviet régime
was set up among you. But we, the Revolutionary Committee, still
notice that you are distrustful of us, and even hostile. You don't attend the meetings, rumours are going round among you, stupid
stories of mass shootings, of oppressions which the Soviet government is putting upon you. It's time we talked to one another more
frankly and came close to one another. You yourselves chose your
Revolutionary Committee, Ivan Kotliarov and Koshevoi are your
own Cossacks, and there should be no keeping things back among
you. To begin with, I declare here and now that the stories of mass
shootings spread by our enemies are nothing more nor less than
slanders. The object in spreading those slanders is clear: they want

to sow antagonism between the Cossacks and the Soviet régime, to drive you again into the arms of the Whites."

"You say there are no shootings? Then where have our seven men gone?" someone shouted from the back of the crowd.

"I did not say, comrade, that there have been no shootings whatever. We have shot and we shall continue to shoot the enemies of the Soviet régime, all who think of fastening a landowner's régime upon us. We didn't overthrow the Czar, we didn't put an end to the war with Germany, we didn't liberate the people for that. What did the war with Germany give you? Thousands of dead Cossacks, orphans, widows, ruin. . . ."

"That's true!"

"And we want to stop all wars," Stockman continued. "We stand for the brotherhood of the peoples. But under the czarist régime your hands were used to conquer the land for the landowners and capitalists and to enrich those same landowners and manufacturers. There's Listnitsky, who lived near here. His grandfather received ten thousand acres of land for his services in the 1812 war. But what did your grandfathers receive? They lost their heads on the German soil. They poured out their blood over it."

There was a roar of assent from the meeting. Stockman wiped the sweat from his shining brow and shouted:

"We shall destroy all those who raise their hands against the workers' and peasants' government. Your Cossacks who were shot by the command of the Revolutionary Tribunal were our enemies. You all know that. But with you, with the toilers, with those who are sympathetic to us, we shall go hand in hand, or like bullocks at ploughing, shoulder to shoulder. Together we shall plough the earth for a new life and we shall harrow it so as to remove the old weeds, our enemies, from the soil. So that they don't get their roots in it again and don't choke the growth of the new life."

From the restrained murmur and the animated faces Stockman realized that he had touched the Cossacks' hearts with his speech. He was not mistaken. They began to speak out what was in their minds:

"Osip Davidovich! We know you well, you lived among us once, you're like one of us. Explain to us, don't be afraid. This government of yours, what does it want from us? Of course we're for it, our sons deserted from the front; but we're ignorant people, and we can't make it all out." Old Gryaznov spoke long and only half-intelligibly, walking backward and forward, and evidently afraid to say too much. But armless Alexei Shamil was not afraid.

"Can I speak?" he cried.

"Come on, then," Ivan replied.

"Comrade Stockman, first tell us: can I say what I like?"

"Yes."

"And you won't arrest me?"

Stockman smiled and silently waved his hand. Alexei's brother Martin pulled on his sleeve from behind and whispered anxiously:

"Stop it, you fool! Stop it or they'll be marking you down! You'll be put on the list, Alexei!"

But Alexei pulled himself away and turned with his face to the meeting, his cheek twitching:

"Cossacks! I shall speak, and you judge whether I speak right or not." He turned about on his heels in military fashion and gazed at Stockman. "This is what I understand. If I'm right, all right; if I'm wrong, then say so straight out. And I shall say what all of us Cossacks are thinking, and why we feel we are injured by the Communists. You said you're not against the working Cossacks. You're against the rich, and you're brothers with the poor. Well, tell the truth: did they shoot our village Cossacks or not? I won't say anything about Korshunov: he was ataman, and all his life he'd ridden on other Cossacks' backs. But what was Avdeich the Braggart shot for? And Matvei Kashulin? Bogatiriev, Maidannikov, and Koroliov? They were just like us, ignorant and all mixed up. They'd learned to hold plough-handles and not books. And if they said something bad, was it necessary to put them up against a wall for that?" He took a breath, and stepped forward. "You've arrested those who talked like fools and you've punished them, but you don't touch the merchants. With their money the merchants bought up our lives. And we haven't anything to buy them back again with; we spend our lives digging up the ground, but fortune passes us by. You've shot some of them maybe, but they would have driven their last bullock out of their yards to save their skins. Yet you've never demanded a contribution from them. And we all know what's happening in Vieshenska. There the merchants and priests are all alive and whole. And in Kargin, too. We hear what's happening all around us. Good report stands still, but evil report flies all over the world."

There was a confused roar of "That's right," and the crowd drowned his words. But he waited until the noise died away and, taking no notice of Stockman's upraised hand, continued to shout:

"And we realize that maybe the Soviet government is good, but the Communists who have got the jobs are trying to drown us in a spoonful of water. They're giving it to us for 1905, we've heard the Red soldiers say that. And we say among ourselves that the Communists want to destroy us, to take us prisoners. They want the Cossack spirit to die out of the Don! That's what I say. I'm like a drunken man: I say at once whatever comes into my head. And we're all drunk with this good living, with the shame which has come upon us and upon the Communists."

Alexei pushed back into the crowd of Cossacks, and there was a long silence. Stockman began to speak, but he was interrupted by shouts from the back:

"He's right! They're insulting the Cossacks. You know what songs are being sung in the villages now? Not everybody is ready to speak out his mind, but they'll sing it!" The crowd rocked with cross-talk.

Stockman violently crumpled his cap in his hand and, drawing out of his pocket the list Koshevoi had written, he shouted:

"No, it's not true! Those who're for the Revolution have nothing to take offence about. This is what your fellow-villagers, the enemies of the Soviet régime, were shot for. Listen!" He began to read aloud slowly and distinctly:

"List of enemies of the Soviet régime, arrested and handed over to the investigation commission of the Revolutionary Tribunal.

"Korshunov, Miron Gregorievich, former ataman, rich through exploiting other men's labour. Senilin, Ivan Avdeich, made propaganda for the overthrow of the Soviet government. Kashulin, Matvei Ivanovich, did the same. Maidannikov, Siemion Gavrilov, put on epaulets and shouted in the streets against the Soviet government. Melekhov, Pantaleimon Prokoffievich, was member of the Military Council. Melekhov, Gregor Pantalievich, is a lieutenant hostile to the Soviet government, and dangerous. Kashulin, Andrei son of Matvei, took part in the execution of the Podtielkov Red Cossacks. Bodovskov, Fiodot Nikiforov, did the same. Bogatiriev, Arkhip Matveev, was a churchwarden, against the government, and incited the people against the Revolution. Koroliov, Zakhar Leontveev, refused to surrender his arms and is unreliable."

Against the names of the two Melekhovs and Bodovskov were notes which Stockman read: "These enemies of the Soviet government cannot be arrested as two of them are away, mobilized for transport purposes, and Pantaleimon Melekhov is ill with typhus. The two men away will be arrested and sent to Vieshenska immediately they return, the third when he is able to stand."

The meeting was silent for a moment. Then there was an outcry: "It isn't true." "It's a lie that they spoke against the Soviets!" "Is this the kind of thing you arrest men for?" "Because they looked at your teeth?"

Stockman spoke again. They seemed to be listening to him attentively, and there were even occasional shouts of approval. But when at the end he raised the question of distributing the property of those who had fled to the Whites, there was silence.

"What's the matter with all of you?" Ivan Alexievich asked in vexation.

The meeting began to break up like scattered grapeshot. One of the poorest of the villagers stepped irresolutely forward, then hesitated and fell back again.

"The owners will come back, and then what? . . ."

Stockman attempted to persuade them not to break up, but Koshevoi, as white as chalk, whispered to Ivan Alexievich:

"I said they wouldn't touch it. It would be better to burn it all rather than give it to them now. . . ."

Thoughtfully smacking his whip against his trouser-leg, his head bowed, Koshevoi slowly went up the steps of Mokhov's house. In the corridor some saddles lay on the floor. Evidently someone had arrived recently: a yellow, dung-coloured clump of snow impressed by a boot still clung to one of the stirrups, a little pool of water was forming under it. Koshevoi raised his eyes from the saddles and the floor of the terrace to the carving of the balustrade, then he glanced at the steaming windows. But nothing that he saw made any impression on his mind. Mishka's simple heart was boiling with pity and hatred for Gregor Melekhov.

A heavy scent of tobacco and horses' equipment pervaded the anteroom of the Revolutionary Committee. One of the women servants left behind when the Mokhovs had fled beyond the Donietz was lighting the stove. In a farther room the militia-men were laughing noisily. "A funny lot! Found something to laugh about!" Mishka thought indignantly as he strode past and entered the committee room.

Ivan Alexievich was sitting behind the writing-table. His black fur cap was pushed back on his head, and his sweaty face was tired and furrowed. Stockman was sitting at his side on the window-ledge. He welcomed Mishka with a smile and invited him to sit down by him. Koshevoi sat down, throwing out his feet.

"I heard yesterday from a safe source that Gregor Melekhov's come home," he said. "But I haven't been around to him yet."

"What do you propose to do about it?" Stockman rolled a cigarette and glanced expectantly at Ivan Alexievich.

"Put him in the cellar, or what?" Ivan replied irresolutely.

"You're the chairman of the Revolutionary Committee—watch out!" Stockman smiled and evasively shrugged his shoulders. He could smile with such mockery that it burned deeper than a whiplash. Through his teeth Ivan sharply said:

"I as chairman would be ready to arrest both Gregor and his brother and send them to Vieshenska."

"There's no point in arresting the brother. Fomin's on his side, and you know how well he speaks of Piotra. But Gregor must be arrested today, and at once! We'll send him to Vieshenska tomorrow, and dispatch material concerning him by a mounted militia-man to the chairman of the Revolutionary Tribunal today," Stockman replied.

"Better arrest Gregor in the evening, don't you think, Osip Davido-vich?" Ivan suggested. "There'd be less talk then."

"Well, that's a silly objection," Stockman answered.

Ivan turned to Koshevoi. "Mikhail, take two men and go and arrest him at once. Keep him separate. Understand?"

Koshevoi slipped off the window-ledge and went to the militia-men. Stockman began to stride up and down the room. After a moment or two he stopped at the table and asked:

"Have you sent off the last consignment of arms collected?"

"No, they're going today."

Stockman frowned but, raising his brows, he asked quickly:

"What did the Melekhovs hand over?"

Ivan Alexievich knitted his brows in the effort to recollect, and said at last with a smile:

"They handed over two rifles and two revolvers. Do you think that's all they've got?"

"Do you?"

"Oho! I've found someone more stupid than myself!"

"I think so too!" Stockman bit his lips. "If I were in your shoes I'd make a careful search of their place after the arrest. Give orders to the commandant for it to be done. It's one thing to think, but another to act."

Koshevoi returned half an hour later. He ran sharply along the veranda, flung the doors open violently, and, halting on the threshold to take breath, shouted:

"By all the devils!"

"What's up?" Stockman strode swiftly across to him, his eyes dilated terribly. Whether at the quiet tones of Stockman's voice or for some other reason, Koshevoi went into a rage and roared:

"Stop making those eyes! They say Gregor's ridden off to his aunt at Singin. And what could I do? But where were you? Who opened the door for him? You've let him slip through your hands. You needn't shout at me, I'm only a sheep, it's my job to go and arrest him. But what were you thinking of?" He leaned against the stove and laughed at Stockman coming straight at him: "No farther, David Osipovich! No farther, or by God I'll strike you!"

Stockman stopped right in front of him and cracked his fingers. Staring into Mishka's smiling eyes, he said through his teeth:

"Do you know the road to Singin?"

"I do."

"Then why did you come back here? And you say you fought the Germans!" He frowned with deliberate contempt.

The steppe lay beneath a blue, smoky haze. The livid moon rose beyond the Donside hills, shining wanly and not obscuring the phosphorescent light of the stars.

Six horsemen were galloping along the road to Singin. Stockman rode at Mishka's side. With untroubled mien he was telling Mishka of some humorous incident, and Mishka bent over his saddle-bow and smiled with a childlike smile, panting and trying to peer beneath the cowl into Stockman's stern face.

At Singin a diligent search yielded no results whatever.

PART II

The Cossacks Rise

THE COSSACKS RISE

Chapter 1

On his arrival with the transport at Bokovskaya, Gregor was compelled to drive on a further stage. He returned only after ten days. Two days before his arrival in Tatarsk his father was arrested. Old Pantaleimon had only just risen from his sick-bed. He was still more gaunt and grey. His hair lay as though moth-eaten on his forehead, his beard was thin and edged with grey.

The militia-men carried him off after giving him ten minutes to get his things together. He was put down in Mokhov's cellar until he could be sent to Vieshenska. With him in arrest were nine other elders and one honorary judge.

Piotra communicated the news to Gregor before his brother had ridden into the yard, and advised him:

"You turn round and go back, brother! They've been asking when you'll be home. Go and get warm and see your children, then clear off to Ribny village, where you can hide and wait your time. If they ask me I'll tell them you've gone to your aunt at Singin. They've put seven of ours up against the wall, have you heard? So long as Father doesn't go the same way! But as for you . . ."

Gregor sat for half an hour in the kitchen, then, saddling his horse, galloped through the night to Ribny. A distant relative and trustworthy Cossack hid him in his shed among the dung-fuel bricks. There he lay for two days, coming out only at night.

Chapter 2

On March 10, two days after his return from Singin, Mishka Koshevoi went to Vieshenska to find out when there would be a meeting of the Communist group. He, Ivan Alexievich, David, Yemelian, and Filka had all decided to join the party. He carried with him the last consignment of weapons handed over by the Cossacks, a machine-gun discovered in the school-yard, and a letter from Stockman to the chairman of the district Revolutionary Committee.

He found Vieshenska in a state of aimless confusion. Men were running anxiously about, mounted couriers were arriving and departing, the streets were noticeably empty. Not realizing the cause of all the hurry-scurry, Mishka was astonished. The vice-chairman of the committee abstractedly thrust Stockman's letter into his pocket and, when Mishka asked whether there would be any answer, snorted harshly:

"Go to the devil! I haven't time for you now."

Mishka turned into the Revolutionary Tribunal to have a smoke with some acquaintances and asked them:

"What's all the fuss about?"

One of them reluctantly replied:

"There's trouble in Kazanska. The Whites have broken through, or the Cossacks have revolted, or something. Fighting was going on there yesterday, by all accounts. Telephonic communication has been cut off."

"You should send a mounted courier there."

"We have, but he hasn't come back. And today we sent a company to Yelansk. There's trouble there too."

They sat smoking at the window. A fine snow was sifting past the panes of the merchant's house in which the Revolutionary Tribunal was quartered.

Suddenly shots rang out somewhere outside the village, close to the clump of pines. Mishka turned pale and threw down his cigarette. Everybody ran into the yard. The shots were now sounding loud and heavy, and bullets were beginning to patter against the sheds and the gate. A Red Army soldier was wounded as he stood in the yard. The remnants of the military company were drawn up hurriedly in front of the Revolutionary Committee, and the commander led them at a run towards the slope leading down to the Don. A panic set in. People ran to and fro across the square. A riderless horse galloped past.

In his consternation Mishka himself never remembered how he came to be in the square. He saw Fomin burst like a whirlwind from behind the church, a machine-gun harnessed up to his horse. The wheels failed to take the corner, and the gun turned over and dragged along, swinging from side to side. Fomin, bending low over the saddle, disappeared under the hill, leaving a silvery trail of snow-dust behind him.

"To the horses," was Mishka's first thought. He ran down the side roads, bending double, not stopping once to take breath. He found Yemelian harnessing the horses, fumbling terror-stricken at the traces to fasten them to the singletrees.

"What's happening, Mikhail? What's up?" he stammered, his teeth chattering.

In their hurry they could not find the reins, and when they did find them the collar-thongs had come untied. The yard where they had halted looked out into the steppe. Mishka stared towards the pines, but no line of infantry appeared in that direction, there was no avalanche of cavalry. Firing was going on somewhere in the distance, the streets were deserted, the place wore its customary dreary look. Yet something terrible was happening: the revolt had come in very truth.

All the time Yemelian was busy with the horses, Mishka did not remove his gaze from the steppe. He saw a man run from beyond the shrine, past the bridge where in the previous December the wireless station had been burned down. The man was running at full speed, bent forward, his arms pressed against his breast. By his coat Mishka recognized him as the Tribunal investigator Gromov. Then from behind a fence galloped a horseman. And Mishka recognized him also: it was a Vieshenska Cossack named Chernichkin, a young, active White Guard. As he ran, Gromov looked back once, twice, and pulled his revolver out of his pocket. There was the sound of a shot, then a second. Gromov ran to the top of a sandy hillock and fired. Chernichkin jumped out of the saddle as his horse was moving, unslung his rifle from his shoulder, and lay down behind a snowdrift. After his first shot Gromov crawled sideways, clinging to the brushwood with his left hand. He circled the hillock and lay face-downward on the snow. "Dead!" Mishka turned cold. Even as he sat in the sledge galloping out of the gate, he saw Chernichkin run to the body and slash with his sword at the black coat huddled over the snow.

It was foolhardy to attempt to cross the Don at the usual crossing-place, for horses and men would prove an excellent mark against the white stretch of the river. So Yemelian turned across the lake into the wood. As they crossed the lake the horses' hoofs left little pools of water on the half-melting ice, and the runners made deep furrows. They galloped madly back to Tatarsk. But at the crossing below the village Yemelian pulled on the reins and turned his wind-reddened face to Mishka:

"What's the best thing to do? Supposing there's been trouble of the same sort in our own village?"

Mishka's eyes looked distressed. He stared at the village. Two horsemen were galloping along the street nearest the river, and he thought he recognized them as militia-men.

"Drive into the village. There's nowhere else we can go to," he said resolutely.

Very reluctantly Yemelian whipped up the horses. They crossed the river and drove up the slope on the farther side. Antip, son of Avdeich the Braggart, and two other older men from the upper end of the village came running towards them.

"Oh, Mishka!" Seeing a rifle in Antip's hands, Yemelian pulled on the reins and turned the horses sharply round.

"Stop!" came the command.

There was a shot. Yemelian fell, still clutching the reins in his hand. The horses galloped into a fence. Mishka jumped out of the sledge. Running towards him, his feet slipping, Antip swayed, halted, and threw the rifle to his shoulder. As Mishka fell against the fence, he saw the white teeth of a three-pronged fork held in the hands of one of the men.

He felt a burning pain in his shoulder and fell without a cry, covering his face with his hands. A man, breathing heavily, bent over him and thrust at him with the fork.

"Get up, damn you!"

The rest Mishka remembered only as though in a dream. Antip threw himself on him and seized him by the chest, weeping: "He betrayed my father to his death. Let me have him, good people! Let me have my heart's desire of him!" He was dragged off. A little crowd gathered. Someone's reasoning voice sounded coldly: "Let the lad be! Are you Christians, or what? Let him be, Antip! You won't bring your father back to life, and you'll be the cause of a man perishing. Go home, brothers! They're sharing out sugar at the warehouse, go along and get your share."

When Mishka recovered consciousness in the evening, he was lying under the same fence. His side, pierced by the fork, burned and ached. But the prongs, passing through his sheepskin and sweater, had only penetrated the flesh for a couple of inches. He scrambled to his feet and listened. Evidently the insurgents had patrols guarding the village. Occasionally there was the sound of a shot, which set the dogs barking. He took the cattle-path by the Don, came to the top of the cliff, and crawled along by the fences, his hands grabbling in the snow, starting up and falling again. He did not know where he was and crawled at random. His body was trembling with the cold, his hands were frozen. The cold drove him through someone's wicket gate. He opened the brier-grown gate and went into the back yard. He saw a shed to the left and made towards it. But he at once heard steps and a cough. Someone entered the shed, his felt boots scrunching. "They'll kill me at once," Mishka thought indifferently, as though of a third person. The man stood in the twilight of the doorway.

"Who's there?" The voice was weak and sounded frightened. Mishka passed along the partition wall.

"Who is it?" the man asked in a louder and more anxious tone. Mishka recognized the voice of Stepan Astakhov and came out.

"Stepan, it's me! Koshevoi! Save me, for the love of God! You needn't tell anyone, need you? Help me!"

"So it's you!" Stepan, just risen from his bed after typhus, said in a feeble voice. His mouth smiled broadly but uncertainly. "Well, spend the night there, but clear out tomorrow. But how did you get there?"

Mishka groped for his hand and shook it, then thrust himself into a pile of chaff. As soon as dusk fell the next evening, resolving on a desperate step he cautiously made his way home and knocked at the window. His mother opened the door, and burst into tears at the sight of him. Her hands clutched and clawed at his neck, and her head rolled on his chest.

"Go away, for the love of Christ go away, Mishka! The Cossacks were here this morning. They searched the whole yard for you. Antip Avdeich struck me with his whip. 'You're hiding your son. I'm sorry I didn't kill him at once,' he said."

Mishka had no idea where to find his friends. From his mother's brief story he gathered that all the Donside villages had risen, that Stockman, Ivan Alexievich, David, and the militia-men had fled, and Filka and Timofei had been killed in the square at noon of the previous day.

"Now go away. They'll find you here." His mother wept, but her voice was firm. For the first time for many days Mishka cried, sobbing like a child and bubbling at the lips. Then he took the old mare and led her into the yard. Her foal followed her. His mother helped him to climb into the saddle, and crossed herself. The mare went unwillingly, whinnying to her foal. Each time she called, Mishka's heart leaped into his mouth.

But he escaped safely from the village and trotted along the Hetman's highroad to the east, in a northerly direction. The night was dark and friendly to refugees. His mare whinnied frequently, afraid of losing her foal. Mishka grated his teeth, and stopped again and again to listen whether he could hear the heavy beat of horse-hoofs before or behind him. But a magical silence lay all around. All he could hear was the foal taking advantage of the halt to suck at its mother, its little hind legs thrust deep into the snow.

Worn out, he rode at dawn into a village of the Ust-Khopersk district. He was stopped by an outpost of a Red regiment, and two of the Red Guards conducted him to the staff headquarters. A staff officer questioned him long and distrustfully, trying to make him contradict himself. Mishka grew tired of answering such stupid questions as: "Who was chairman of your Revolutionary Committee?" and "Why haven't you any documents?"

"Don't try to tie me up, comrade," he protested. "The Cossacks didn't tie me up like this." He pulled up his shirt and showed his side and belly pierced by the fork. He was trying to think of something with which to impress the officer, but at that moment Stockman entered.

"You prodigal! You little devil!" Stockman shouted, putting his arm round Mishka's back. "What are you cross-examining him for, comrade?" He turned to the officer. "He's one of our own boys. Why didn't you send for me or Kotliarov, and then there wouldn't have been any need for questions. Come on, Mikhail. But how did you escape? Tell me, how did you escape? We'd struck you off the list of the living. We thought you'd died the death of a hero."

Mishka remembered how he had been taken prisoner, his failure to defend himself, his rifle left in the sledge, and flushed painfully.

Chapter 3

The shed stank strongly of rotten straw, dry dung, and wisps of hay. In the day-time a grey light filtered through the roof. At night there was the squeaking of mice, and silence.

The mistress of the hut surreptitiously brought Gregor food once a day, in the evening. A pitcher of water stood buried in the dung-fuel bricks. Life wouldn't have been too bad, but he had smoked all his tobacco. He was tormented by his situation during the first day and, unable to hold out without something to smoke, in the morning he crawled over the earthen floor and collected some dry horse-dung in his hands. He rubbed it in his palms and made it into cigarettes. In the evening the master sent him withered leaves torn from a copy of the Gospels, a box of sulphur matches, and a handful of dry clover and roots. Gregor was overjoyed, smoked until he was nearly sick, and had his first sound sleep on the dung bricks.

Next morning he was awakened by his Cossack friend running into the shed and shouting sharply:

"You asleep? Get up! The Don has broken its ice!" And he laughed heartily.

Gregor jumped to the floor, bringing the dung bricks rumbling down behind him.

"What's happened?" he demanded.

"The Yelanska and Vieshenska Cossacks have risen on this side. Fomin and all the government at Vieshenska have fled to Tokin. They say that Kazanska, Sumilinsk, and Migulinsk districts have also risen."

The bunches of veins swelled on Gregor's brow and neck, his eyes spirted little green sparks. He could not conceal his joy: his voice trembled, his black fingers fidgeted with the fastenings of his greatcoat.

"And here in your village? Has anything happened here?" he asked.

"I've heard nothing. I saw the chairman just now and he laughed. 'I don't care what God we pray to, so long as there is a God,' he said. But you can come out of your hole."

They went into the hut. Gregor walked with great strides, and the Cossack hurried at his side, telling him the news:

"In Yelanska district Krasnoyarsk was the first to rise. Two days ago a score of the Yelanska Communists went to arrest some Cossacks. The Krasnoyarsk men heard of it, got together, and decided: 'How long are we going to stand this? They're taking our fathers, they'll be taking us next. Saddle horses and we'll go and get the arrested men free.' Some fifteen fine lads were collected. They had only a couple of rifles, some swords and pikes. They found the Communists resting in a yard at Melnikov, and poured into the attack on their horses. But it was surrounded by a stone wall, and they were beaten off. The Communists killed one of them, peace to his soul. But from that moment the end of the Soviet régime was near, damn it!"

Gregor greedily ate the remains of his breakfast and went with his friend into the street. The Cossacks were standing about in little groups at the corners as though the day was a holiday. They went up to one group. The Cossacks raised their hands to their caps in greeting and replied restrainedly, staring expectantly and curiously at Gregor's unfamiliar figure.

"He's one of us. Don't be afraid. You've heard of the Melekhovs of Tatarsk? This is Pantaleimon's son Gregor. He came to me to save himself being shot," the master said proudly.

They began to talk, but just as one of the Cossacks was telling how the Reds had been driven out of Vieshenska two horsemen appeared at the end of the street. They galloped along, stopping by each group of Cossacks, turning their horses and shouting something, waving their arms. Gregor waited eagerly for their approach.

"They're not any of our villagers. They're messengers from somewhere," one of the Cossacks remarked as he stared.

The two men rode up to the group. One of them, an old man with sheepskin flung wide open, his face red and sweating, his grey hair hanging over his forehead, youthfully reined in his horse and stretched out his right hand:

"Cossacks, why are you standing at the street corners like women?" he cried. Tears broke his voice, his livid cheeks quivered with his agitation. "What are you standing for, sons of the Don? They're shooting your fathers and grandfathers. They're taking away your possessions. The Jewish commissars are jeering at our faith, and you're chewing sunflower seeds and playing cards. You're waiting till the Russian noose tightens round our throats. All Yelansk district from small to great has risen. They've driven the Reds out of Vieshenska, and you— Have you got peasants' kvass instead of Cossack blood in your veins? Rise! Get your arms! Krivsky village has sent us to raise your village. To horse, Cossacks, before it's too late!" He fixed his frenzied eyes on the face of one elderly acquaintance and shouted with great scorn: "What are you standing there for, Siemion Christoforovich? The Reds cut down your son at Filonovo, and you're saving yourself on the stove!"

Gregor did not stay to hear more. He ran towards the yard. Tearing his nails till they bled, he dug his saddle out of the dung blocks, saddled his horse, brought it at a run out of the chaff-shed, and flew through the gate as though possessed.

"I'm off! God be with you!" he managed to shout to his friend and, bending over the saddle-bow right against his horse's neck, lashing the animal with his whip, he put it into a gallop. The snowy dust settled again behind him, his legs rubbed against the saddle, the stirrups clattered loosely against his boots. He felt such a tremendous, ferocious gladness, such an influx of strength and resolution, that, despite himself, a whistling rattle burst from his throat. His imprisoned, secret feelings were released within him. Now it seemed at last that his road henceforth was clear, as clear as a moonlit track.

During the exhausting days when he had been hiding like an animal in the dung blocks and starting at every sound and voice outside, he had weighed and decided everything. It was as though those days of search for the truth, those hesitations, those transitions and painful inward struggles, had never been. Like the shadow of a cloud they had passed, and now his searchings seemed aimless and empty. What had there been to think about? Why had his spirit tossed like a hunted wolf in search of a way of escape, of a resolution of the contradictions? Life seemed absurdly, wisely simple. Now he believed that there never had been any truth beneath whose wing all might shelter; now he thought that each had his own truth, his own furrow. For a piece of bread, for a strip of earth, for the right to live, men always had fought and would fight so long as the sun shone on them, so long as their blood flowed warmly through their veins. Those who wanted to deprive him of his life, of his right to live, must be fought, and fought resolutely, with no wavering, but steeled with hatred. His feelings must not be bridled, must be given rein.

The path of the Cossacks had crossed the path of the landless peasantry of Russia, the path of the factory people. Fight them! Wrest from them the heavy Don earth, washed with Cossack blood. Drive them as once the Tatars had been driven beyond the bounds of the province. Strike Moscow, fasten a shameful peace on them! There is no passing on the causeway: someone must push aside someone. So they had tried their hand? So they had released the Red regiments on the Cossack lands? Then to sword!

Flaming with a blind hatred, Gregor galloped until his horse carried him across the white-maned pall of the Don. For one moment a doubt assailed him: "It's rich against poor, and not Cossack against Russian. . . . Mishka Koshevoi and Ivan Alexievich are Cossacks too, and they're Red through and through." But he angrily shook off the thought.

Tatarsk appeared in the distance. He pulled on the reins. His horse, foaming like soap, dropped into an easy trot. At his own gate he urged it on again; its breast flung open the wicket gate, and it galloped into the yard.

Chapter 4

By the day of Gregor's arrival in Tatarsk two companies of Cossacks had already been assembled. A village assembly had decided to mobilize all men capable of bearing arms, from sixteen to sixty. Many felt the hopelessness of the position: in the north was the Voronezh province held by the Bolsheviks, and the Khopersk district sympathetic to the Reds; in the south was the front, which might turn back and crush the insurgents under its avalanche. Certain more cautious Cossacks did not want to take up arms, but they were compelled. Stepan Astakhov flatly refused to go and fight.

"I'm not going," he declared when Gregor, Christonia, and Anikushka went to see him in the morning. "Take my horse, do what you like with me, but I don't want to take up a rifle."

"What do you mean, you don't want to?" Gregor demanded, his nostrils quivering.

"I don't want to, and that's all."

"And if the Reds take the village, what will you do? Will you clear out or stay behind?"

Stepan turned his eyes from Gregor to Aksinia and replied after a pause:

"We shall see."

"If that's the case, get outside! Take him, Christonia! We'll put you up against a wall at once!" Trying to avoid looking at Aksinia, huddled up against the stove, Gregor pulled Stepan by his sleeve. "Come on!"

"Gregor, don't be a fool! Let go!" Stepan turned pale and feebly resisted. Christonia seized him from behind around the waist, muttering:

"If that's your spirit, then come on!"

"Brothers!"

"We're no brothers of yours! Come on, I tell you!"

"Let me go; I'll join the company. I'm weak after typhus."

Gregor smiled wryly and let go of Stepan's sleeve. "Go and get a rifle," he said. "You should have joined long since."

He went out without a word of farewell. But even after what had happened Christonia had no compunction in asking Stepan for some tobacco and sat talking as though nothing had occurred between them.

Towards evening two sledgeloads of arms were brought from Vieshenska, including eighty-four rifles and more than a hundred swords. Many Cossacks turned out hidden weapons. The village mustered two hundred and eleven Cossacks, of which one hundred and fifty were horsed, while the others marched on foot.

The insurgents were still without a unified organization. The villages were acting unco-ordinately, independently forming squadrons, electing commanders from the most militant of the Cossacks, taking into account not rank but services. They undertook no offensive operations, and only made contact with the neighbouring villages and sent out mounted patrols.

Before Gregor's arrival his brother Piotra had been chosen as commander of the mounted squadron in Tatarsk, while Latishev took command of the infantry. The artillery-men, with Ivan Tomilin at their head, had gone off to a near-by village where the Reds had left a damaged field-gun, and were trying to repair it. The firearms brought from Vieshenska were distributed among the Cossacks. Pantaleimon, released with the others from Mokhov's cellar, dug up his machine-gun. But there were no cartridge-belts, and the squadron would not accept the gun as part of their equipment.

The next evening news came that a punitive division of Red soldiers, numbering some three hundred, with seven field-guns and twelve machine-guns were advancing from Kargin to suppress the rising. Piotra resolved to send out a strong patrol and also informed Vieshenska. The patrol of thirty-two men under Gregor's command left in the twilight. They galloped out of the village, maintaining the same pace almost as far as Tokin. Some two miles this side of the village, close to a shallow gully, Gregor dismounted his Cossacks and distributed them in the gully. The horses were led off into a dell, where deep snow was lying. He sent three Cossacks—Anikushka, Martin Shamil, and Prokhor Zykov—on to the village. They set out at a walking pace. Night had fallen. Low clouds rolled over the steppe. The Cossacks sat silently in the gully. Gregor watched the silhouettes of the three horsemen until they dropped over the hill and blended with the black outline of the road. Now their horses were no longer visible, only their heads could be seen. Then they disappeared completely. A moment or two later a machine-gun be-

gan to stutter on the other side of the hill. Then another, evidently a
hand machine-gun, broke out in a higher tone. The hand-gun lapsed
into silence and after a brief pause the first gun hurriedly finished
another belt. A hail of bullets swept through the dusk high above
the gully. The three Cossacks came galloping back at full speed.

"We ran into an outpost," Prokhor Zykov shouted when still some
way off.

Gregor gave orders for the horses to be held in readiness, then
jumped out of the gully and, taking no notice of the bullets burying
themselves with a whistle in the snow, went to meet the Cossacks.

"Did you see anything?" he demanded.

"We could hear them moving about. There must be a lot of them,
judging by the voices," Anikushka pantingly told him.

While Gregor was questioning them, eight Cossacks ran down
from the gully to where the horses were stationed, mounted their
horses, and galloped off in the direction of home.

"We'll shoot them tomorrow," Gregor said quietly as he listened to
the sound of the retreating hoofs.

The Cossacks left in his command sat on for another hour, preserving a strict silence and straining their ears. At last someone caught
the sound of horses' hoofs.

"They're coming from Tokin direction," he declared.

"A patrol?"

"It can't be."

They whispered to one another and poked their heads over the top
of the gully, vainly trying to distinguish something in the impenetrable darkness. Fiodot Bodovskov's Kalmyk eyes were the first to
discern the approaching riders. "Here they come," he said confidently, unslinging his rifle. Some ten horsemen were riding quietly
and in broken rank along the road. Half a length in front of the
others was a stately, warmly clad figure. Staring up at them against
the dark background of the sky, Gregor could distinctly see the line
of the horses' bodies, the outlines of their riders, and even the flat
fur cap of the leader. The horsemen were only some thirty yards
away, and it seemed that they must surely hear the Cossacks' hoarse
breathing and the heavy beat of their hearts.

Gregor had already issued orders for fire to be held until he gave
the command. He was waiting confidently and calculatingly for the
right moment. He had already decided on his plan: he would chal-

lenge the riders and would open fire when they reined together in confusion.

Quietly the snow scrunched on the road. Little yellow sparks occasionally flew up from the horses' hoofs as their shoes slipped on a bare stone.

"Who goes there?" Gregor lightly jumped over the edge of the gully and stood up. His Cossacks poured after him. But Gregor was unprepared for what followed.

"Whom do you want?" the leading rider asked in a hoarse voice that betrayed no sign of fear or surprise. The man turned his horse in Gregor's direction.

"Who are you?" Gregor shouted sternly, not stirring from the spot and half raising his revolver.

The man replied loudly and angrily:

"Who's daring to shout like that? I'm the commander of the punitive expedition and am empowered by the staff of the Eighth Red Army to suppress the revolt. Who is your commander? Let him come here."

"I'm the commander."

"You? Ah. . . ."

Gregor saw a black mass in the rider's uplifted hand, and dropped to the ground, shouting: "Fire!" A flat-headed bullet from the man's Browning flew over his head. A deafening roar of shouts broke out from both parties. Bodovskov ran and clung to the reins of the Red commander's horse. Stretching across him, Gregor struck with the flat of his sword at the man's head and brought him tumbling from the saddle. The engagement was over in a couple of minutes. Three Red Army men galloped off, two were killed, and the remainder disarmed.

Gregor curtly cross-examined the Red commander, thrusting the barrel of his revolver into the man's mouth:

"What's your name, you serpent?"

"Likhachev."

"What were you hoping to do, riding with only nine men as bodyguard? Did you think the Cossacks would fall on their knees before you and ask forgiveness?"

"Kill me!"

"All in good time!" Gregor consoled him. "Where are your documents?"

"In my pack. Take them, you bandit . . . swine!"

Paying no attention to Likhachev's curses, Gregor himself searched him, pulled a second Browning out of the pocket of his sheepskin jacket, and removed his Mauser and field-pack. In a side-pocket he found a cigarette-case and a small notebook of papers.

Likhachev cursed and groaned incessantly. Gregor's blow had struck his head and slipped to his right shoulder.

"Take off your jacket, commissar!" Gregor commanded. "You're sleek, you've grown fat on Cossack bread, and I don't think you'll freeze."

The prisoners' hands were bound behind them with bridles and straps, and they were seated on their horses. The party spent the night in Bazki, not far from Vieshenska. Likhachev tossed about on the floor by the stove, groaning and grinding his teeth. Gregor washed and bound up his shoulder. But he refused to answer the man's questions. He sat at the table studying the captured documents, the lists of Vieshenska counter-revolutionaries supplied by the Revolutionary Tribunal, the notebook, letters, and marks on the map. Occasionally he stared at Likhachev, exchanging glances as though crossing swords. The Cossacks remained awake all night, going out from time to time to see to their horses, or lying and talking and smoking in the porch.

Just before dawn Gregor dozed off, but quickly awoke and raised his head from the table. He saw Likhachev seated on the straw untying the bandage with his teeth and tearing away the compress. He glanced up at Gregor with harsh, bloodshot eyes. His teeth were bared tormentedly, and his eyes gleamed with such deathly agony that Gregor's drowsiness passed as though removed by an invisible hand.

"What are you doing?" he demanded.

"What the hell is it to do with you? I want to die," Likhachev roared, paling and dropping his head on the straw. During the night he had drunk half a bucket of water and had not once closed his eyes. In the morning Gregor sent him by sledge to Vieshenska, together with the captured documents and a brief report.

Escorted by two mounted Cossacks, the sledge rattled up to the red brick building of the Executive Committee in Vieshenska. Likhachev half lay in the back. He rose, with one hand holding the blood-soaked bandage. The Cossacks dismounted and conducted him into the house.

Some fifty Cossacks were crowded in the room occupied by the provisional commander of the united insurgent forces. Likhachev stumbled to the table where Suyarov, the commander, a little Cossack with no outstanding characteristics, except perhaps the derisive slits of his yellow eyes, was sitting. He glanced at Likhachev and asked:

"So you're Likhachev, my lad?"

"Yes. There are my documents." The Red commander threw his notebook on to the table and stared obstinately and sternly at Suyarov. "I regret that I have failed to execute my instructions to crush you like snakes. But Soviet Russia will deal with you as you deserve! Please shoot me at once!"

"No, Comrade Likhachev. We've ourselves revolted against shootings. We're not like you, we don't shoot people. We'll heal your wound, and you may yet be of service to us," Suyarov replied, his eyes gleaming mildly. He turned to the crowd. "Outside, all of you! Hurry up!"

Only the commanders of five companies were left in the room. They sat down at the table. Someone pushed a stool across to Likhachev with his foot, but he refused to sit down. He leaned against the wall, staring over their heads out of the window.

"Well now, Likhachev," Suyarov began, after exchanging glances with the company commanders. "Tell us how many there are in your detachment."

"I won't."

"You won't? Well, it doesn't matter. We shall get it from your papers. And if not, we'll examine your Red Guard. One other thing we ask you: write to your detachment to come on to Vieshenska. We've got nothing to fight with you about. We're not against the Soviet government, but against the Communists and Jews. We'll disarm your men and send them home. And we'll let you go free. In a word, write that we're toilers too and that they needn't be afraid of us, we're not against the Soviets. . . ."

Likhachev spat right on Suyarov's little grey beard. He wiped his beard with his sleeve and went red in the face. One of the commanders smiled, but no one rose to defend the honour of their leader.

"So you're insulting us, Comrade Likhachev?" Suyarov spoke with obvious insincerity. "The atamans and officers used to insult us and spit on us, and you, a Communist, also spit! Yet you all say you're on the side of the people. Well, tomorrow we'll send you to Kazanska."

"Won't you think it over?" one of the company commanders asked sternly.

Likhachev adjusted the coat across his shoulders and turned to the guard at the door.

Yet they did not shoot him. The insurgents were struggling to resist "shootings and pillagings." The next day he was driven to Kazanska. He walked in front of his mounted guard, lightly stepping over the snow, his eyebrows knitted. But in the forest, as he passed a deathly white birch he smiled vividly, stopped, stretched out his sound arm, and tore off a twig. On it little buds were already swelling with the sweet March juices, and the vernal aroma of life was coming from them. Likhachev thrust the buds into his mouth and chewed them, gazing with misty eyes at the trees fresh with the young spring, and smiling at the corners of his lips.

He died with the black petals of the buds on his lips. Five miles from Vieshenska, in the sandy dunes, the guards bestially cut him down. While he was still alive they thrust their sword-points into his eyes, cut off his arms, his ears, his nose, slashed a cross over his face. They unbuttoned his trousers and outraged, defiled, his great handsome, masculine body. They outraged the bleeding stump, then one of them stepped on his quivering chest and with one stroke sent the head rolling from the body.

Chapter 5

From beyond the Don, from the upper reaches, from all districts came reports of the extensive scope of the rising. Seven districts had revolted and had hastily assembled companies, three other districts were openly ready to come over. Vieshenska became the centre of the revolt. After long argument and discussion it was decided to retain the previous form of government. The Cossacks commanding most respect, chiefly younger men, were elected to the regional Executive Committee. Danilov, a former artillery officer, was elected chairman, Soviets were formed in the districts and villages, and, strange to relate, even the once reviled word "comrade" remained in everyday intercourse. The slogan was raised: "For the Soviet régime, but against the communes, shootings, and pillaging." Instead of the white cockade or ribbon round the cap, the insurgents wore a white and a red ribbon crossed.

The officers elected to lead the rising came straight from the Cossack ranks. But they could only confirm that which the companies had already accomplished. As organizers and leaders their hands were tied, nor were they strong enough to direct such chaff or to keep pace with the swift movement of events.

A Red cavalry regiment was dispatched against the rising and, gathering the Bolsheviks of Ust-Khopersk, Yelansk, and part of the Vieshenska districts as it marched, it fought its way through village after village, moving over the steppe westward along the Don. On March 18 a Cossack galloped into Tatarsk with an urgent appeal for help to be sent to the Yelanska insurgents. They had retreated without resisting, for they had no rifles or ammunition. The Reds had swept them with machine-gun bullets; two batteries had opened fire on them. In such circumstances it was hopeless to wait for instructions from the district centre. So Piotra Melekhov decided to advance against the Reds with his two squadrons.

He took over command of the four squadrons assembled by neighbouring villages, and in the morning led his Cossacks out of Tatarsk, sending patrols on ahead. Some six miles outside the village, at the spot where Gregor and his wife Natalia had ploughed and had been overtaken by the first snow of winter, the spot where he had first confessed to her that he did not love her, the cavalry dismounted and spread into a line, the horses being led off under cover. Below them they could see the Reds marching in three lines out of a spacious valley. The enemy were still some two miles away, and the Cossacks unhurriedly made ready for the battle.

Piotra trotted up on his well-fed, steaming horse to where Gregor was in charge of a half-squadron. He was cheerful and animated. "Brothers, don't waste your bullets. Fire when I give the command. Gregor, lead your half-squadron some fifty yards more to the left. Hurry!" He gave a few final orders, then raised his field-glasses to his eyes. "Why, they're setting up a battery on Matveev mound," he exclaimed.

"I saw that some time ago; you don't need glasses to see it," Gregor remarked. He took the field-glasses from his brother's hand and gazed.

"Piotra, come over here," he asked, stepping a little away from the line of men. Piotra followed him. Frowning with obvious discontent, Gregor said:

"I don't like this position. We ought to get away from these gullies. They may attack us on the flank, and then where should we be? What do you think?"

"What's the matter with you?" Piotra angrily waved his hand. "How can they attack us on the flank? I'm holding one company in reserve, and in the worst case the gullies will be of value to us. They're no danger."

"You watch out, my boy!" Gregor warned him. After casting another swift glance around the position, he went back to his Cossacks.

Despite strict orders to the contrary, the Tatarsk infantry, "dancers" as the horsemen jestingly called them, had gathered into little groups, dividing up bullets, smoking, and laughing. Christonia's fur cap rose a head above the rest, and Pantaleimon Melekhov's red three-cornered cap was clearly visible. The majority of them were old men and youngsters. The Yelansk men were drawn up about half a mile or so away. There were six hundred men in their four companies, but almost two hundred of them had been told off to mind horses.

The talk died down as soon as the field-guns of the battery behind the mound began to fire. The heavy, booming sound hung long over the steppe. The first shell was badly aimed and fell nearly half a mile short of the Cossack lines. The black smoke of the explosion crumbled and clung to the bushes. Machine-guns began to cough from the Red lines. The frost muffled the fullness of their sound, and they knocked like a night-watchman's hammer. The Cossacks lay down in the snow, behind the bushes, and among the brushy, headless sunflower stalks.

"That smoke's pretty black. It looks as though they're using German shells," Prokhor Zykov shouted across to Gregor.

A red-bearded company commander from Rubiezhin village came running to Piotra. "I've got an idea, Comrade Melekhov," he said. "Send one of the squadrons down to the Don and let them pass along the bank to the village and strike the Reds from the rear. They're sure to have left their baggage sledges undefended. And it'll put them in a panic."

Piotra approved of the "idea." He strode across to Gregor, explained what was proposed, and curtly ordered him:

"You withdraw your half-squadron and strike at their tail."

Gregor withdrew his Cossacks, mounted them in a gully, and led them at a swift trot towards the village.

The Cossacks in position fired two rounds and then were silent. The Red line lay down. One of the bullets from their machine-guns struck Martin Shamil's horse, and it tore itself out of the hand of the Cossack guarding it, galloped frantically through the line of Rubiezhin Cossacks, and sped down the hill towards the Reds. A stream of machine-guns swept across it, and the animal's hind quarters leaped high into the air before it crashed to the snow.

Piotra gave orders to fire at the machine-gunners. One little Cossack famous for his marksmanship picked off three gunners, and the Maxim was put out of action. But reserve gunners quickly took their places, and the gun was soon sowing its seed of death once more. The Cossacks buried themselves deeper and deeper in the snow, until they reached the bare earth. Evidently the Red batteries were short of ammunition, for after some thirty rounds they ceased fire. Piotra impatiently glanced back to the top of the hill and sent two couriers into the village with orders for all the adult population to come out, armed with forks, scythes, and axes. He hoped that their appearance on the hill would impress the Reds with an exaggerated idea of the Cossacks' strength.

In response to the command crowds of people soon appeared on the brow of the hill and poured down the slope. The Cossacks greeted them with jests:

"Look at those black stones rolling down!"

"All the village has turned out, women and all."

"Pity the Red batteries have stopped firing," remarked armless Alexei. "If they were to send one shell among that lot they'd be running back to the village with wet skirts." Apparently he seriously regretted that the Reds did not fire a single shell at the women.

The crowd drew up in two long, irregular lines and halted. Piotra ordered them to keep well behind the Cossack lines. But their very appearance must have impressed the Reds, for they began to retreat, dropping down to the bottom of the valley. After a brief conference with his company commanders Piotra laid bare his right flank by withdrawing two lines of Yelansk men, ordering them to ride to the north to support Gregor's attack. In full view of the Reds the squadrons formed and rode down towards the Don.

The Cossacks renewed their fire on the retreating enemy. Meantime several of the more desperate women and a swarm of lads had penetrated into the ranks of the fighting line. Daria was among them. She went up to Piotra and asked:

"Piotra, let me have a shot at the Reds. I know how to handle a rifle." She took Piotra's carbine and, kneeling down, confidently set the barrel against her shoulder and fired a couple of shots.

The "reserves" on the hillside began to stamp their feet and jump to keep themselves warm, and the two lines shook as though swayed by the wind. The women's cheeks and lips went blue; the frost quickly penetrated beneath the broad hems of their skirts. Many of them, old Grishaka among them, had had to be helped by the arm up the hill. Yet they kept up an excited conversation as they told of the exploits of former wars and battles, and of the misery of the present war, in which brother was fighting brother, father against son, and the cannon fired from so far away that they could not be seen with the naked eye. . . .

With his half-squadron Gregor struck at the baggage sledges, killed eight Red Guards, and captured four sledges laden with ammunition and two saddle-horses. He lost one horse, and one Cossack suffered the merest scratch.

But while Gregor was retreating along the Don with the captured sledges, completely unmolested and rejoicing at his success, the struggle had come to an end on the hill above Tatarsk. Before the beginning of the battle a squadron of Red cavalry had set out on a seven-mile march to outflank the Cossacks and, suddenly appearing around the hill, they fell upon the men minding the horses. A panic set in, and the Cossacks fled with the horses out of the gully. Some of them succeeded in leading the mounts back to the lines, but most of

them were cut down by the Red cavalry or ran in confusion to escape. The infantry were unable to fire for fear of hitting their own
men, and they poured down into the gully like peas out of a sack,
taking to disorderly flight. Those of the Cossack cavalry who succeeded in catching horses (and they were the majority) vied with
one another in a headlong race back to the village.

As soon as Piotra heard the shout and realized what had happened, he commanded:

"To horse! Latishev, take the infantry across the gully!"

But he failed to reach his own horse. The youngster who had
charge of it came galloping towards him, leading his and Fiodot
Bodovskov's mounts. But a Red Army man behind him pounded and
slashed at his shoulder. Fortunately a rifle was hanging at the lad's
back, and instead of cutting him down, the sword slipped against the
rifle-barrel and flew out of the man's hand. But the youngster's horse
turned aside and galloped off, and Piotra's and Fiodot's horses followed it. Piotra groaned and stood for a moment, white-faced, the
sweat pouring down his cheeks. He looked back. Some dozen Cossacks were running towards him.

"We're lost!" Bodovskov shouted, his face distorted with terror.

"Down into the gully, Cossacks! Brothers, into the gully!" Piotra
mastered himself, led them at a run to the edge, and rolled helter-
skelter down the steep slope. At the bottom he jumped up and shook
himself like a dog, with all his body at once. Ten Cossacks tumbled
down behind him.

At the top, shots were still ringing out, shouts and the trample of
hoofs were to be heard. In the gully bottom the Cossacks brushed
the snow and sand from their caps or rubbed sore spots. Martin
Shamil set to work to free his rifle-barrel of snow. Only young
Manitskov, the son of the former ataman, trembled with fear, and
tears ran down his cheeks.

"What are we to do?" he howled. "Piotra, tell us! Death is right
ahead of us! Where shall we go? They'll kill us!"

Fiodot Bodovskov turned and ran along the bottom of the gully
towards the Don. The others followed him like sheep. Piotra
brought them to a halt:

"Stop! Don't run away! I'll shoot!"

He led them under the overhanging brow of the cliff and pro-

posed, stammering but endeavouring to maintain at least a semblance of calm:

"You can't get out at the bottom. They're sure to be chasing our
men. We must hide in the gully. Some of us on the other side. . . .
We must hold this spot. We can stand a siege here!"

"We're lost! Fathers! Brothers! Let me get out of here! I don't
want . . . I don't want to die!" The younger Manitskov burst into
a weeping wail. Bodovskov's Kalmyk eyes flashed, and he smashed
his fist into the lad's face, bringing the blood streaming from his nose
and sending his body crashing against the wall of the cliff. But the
boy ceased to whine.

"How can we fire at them?" Martin Shamil asked, seizing Piotra
by the arm. "We haven't any bullets. And they'll bomb us out with
hand-grenades."

"Well, what else are we to do?" Piotra turned suddenly blue, and
his lips foamed. "Lie down! Am I commander or not? I'll kill you!"
He waved his revolver over their heads.

His whistling whisper seemed to put new life into them. Bodovskov, Martin Shamil, and two other Cossacks ran to the other side
of the gully and lay down under the cliff; the others remained with
Piotra. In springtime the rushing flood of hill water sends the stones
rolling down and washes away the bottom of the gully, eating into
the layers of red clay and cutting holes and passages in the walls of
the cliff. And in these holes the Cossacks hid themselves.

Above them they heard the sound of running feet, and snow and
sand sprinkled down into the gully.

"There they are!" Piotra muttered.

No one approached close to the edge, but the Cossacks heard the
sound of voices and someone shouting at a horse.

"Talking over how to get at us," Piotra thought, and again the
sweat poured down his back and over his chest and face.

There was a shout from above them. "Hey, you, come on out!
We'll kill you in any case!"

Snow fell thickly in a milky-white stream into the gully. Evidently
someone was coming close to the edge. Another voice remarked
confidently:

"They jumped down there; here are their footmarks. And I saw
them myself."

"Piotra Melekhov, come out of there!"

For a moment Piotra was gripped with a blind joy. "Who is there among the Reds who knows me? They must be our own Cossacks, they've driven them off," he thought. But next moment the same voice made him shiver.

"It's Mikhail Koshevoi speaking. We call on you to surrender. In any case you won't get out."

Piotra wiped his damp brow, and streaks of bloody sweat were left on his palm. A strange feeling of equanimity, almost of oblivion, crept over him. And very distant seemed Antip's shout:

"We'll come out if you'll let us go. If not we shall shoot!"

"We'll let you go," the reply came from above, after a momentary silence.

With a terrible effort Piotra shook off his lethargy. He thought he had detected a sneer in the words "let you go." He hoarsely shouted: "Back!" But no one listened to him.

He was the last to emerge. Within him, like a babe below a woman's heart, life was stirring powerfully. Dominated by the instinct for self-preservation, he removed the bullets from his rifle magazine before he climbed up the steep wall. His eyes were muddy, his heart filled all his breast. He was choking like a child in heavy sleep. He tore his collar open. His eyes were filled with sweat, his hands slipped over the cold slope of the cliff. Panting, he clambered to the spot where they were standing, threw his rifle down at his feet, and raised his hands above his head. The Cossacks who had come out before him were huddled close together. Mishka Koshevoi stepped out of the group of Red foot and horse soldiers and strode towards them. He went up to Piotra and, standing right in front of him, his eyes fixed on the ground, asked quietly:

"Had enough of fighting?" He waited a moment for an answer, then, staring at Piotra's feet, asked in the same tone: "You were in command of them, weren't you?"

Piotra's lips quivered. With a gesture of terrible weariness, with great difficulty he raised his hand to his wet brow. Mishka's long eyelashes flickered, his swollen upper lip curled upward. His body was shaken with such a violent shudder that it seemed he would not be able to keep his feet. But he at once raised his eyes to Piotra's, gazed straight into his pupils, piercing them with a strangely alien gaze, and muttered hurriedly:

"Undress!"

Piotra quickly threw off his sheepskin jacket, carefully rolled it up, and laid it on the snow. He removed his cap, his belt, his khaki shirt, and, sitting on the edge of his jacket, began to pull off his boots, momentarily turning paler.

"Don't take off your shirt," Mishka whispered and, shuddering, abruptly shouted:

"Quicker, you . . ."

Ivan Alexievich dismounted and came across to them, gritting his teeth and fearful of bursting into tears.

Hardly moving his lips, Piotra called to him: "Cousin!" Ivan stood watching silently as the snow melted beneath Piotra's bare feet. "Cousin Ivan, you were the godfather of my child. . . . Cousin, don't shoot me," Piotra pleaded. Seeing Mishka had already raised his revolver to the level of his chest, he dilated his eyes as though guarding against a dazzling flash, hurriedly set his fingers ready to cross himself, and buried his head on his breast.

He did not hear the shot; he fell headlong, as though struck violently from behind.

Koshevoi's outstretched hand seized him above the heart and squeezed the blood from him. With his last earthly effort Piotra threw open the collar of his shirt and lay bare the bullet hole beneath his left nipple. At first the blood oozed slowly from the wound; then, finding vent, it spirted up in a thick dark stream.

At dusk a reconnaissance party sent out from Tatarsk returned with the news that they had found no trace of the Reds, but that Piotra Melekhov and ten other Cossacks were lying dead on the steppe.

Gregor arranged for sledges to bring in the bodies; then, driven out of his own home by the women's lamentations over the dead Piotra and the dull misery in Daria's voice, he went to spend the night with Christonia. Until dawn he sat by the stove in Christonia's hut, smoking cigarette after cigarette and carrying on an aimless conversation with the drowsy Christonia, as though afraid of being left face to face with his own thoughts, with his yearning for his brother.

Day broke. A thaw set in early in the morning. By ten o'clock puddles were appearing in the dung-littered road. A cock crowed as if it were springtime, and a hen clucked away as at sultry noontide.

On the sunny side of the yards the cattle huddled and rubbed against the fences. The melting snow smelled damp and rotten. A tiny yellow-breasted tomtit was swinging and chattering on a bare bough of the apple tree standing by Christonia's gate. As Gregor stood at the gate awaiting the arrival of the sledges, he involuntarily translated the tomtit's chatter into the language of his childhood. "Sharpen plough, sharpen plough!" the tit called joyously this melting morning. But if it were to turn frosty Gregor knew that its voice would change, and the tit would hurriedly counsel: "Put on your boots! Put on your boots!"

He turned his eyes from the road to the swaying tit. "Sharpen plough! Sharpen plough!" it chattered blithely. As he listened Gregor recalled how when they were children he and Piotra had driven the turkeys out to feed in the steppe, and Piotra had cleverly imitated the turkey's gobble and had translated it into child-talk. Gregor had laughed happily and asked his brother to talk again like a turkey.

At the end of the street a sledge appeared, a Cossack walking beside it. Then a second and a third came into sight. Gregor brushed away his tear and the quiet smile aroused by the uninvited memory and hurriedly went towards his own gate. His mother was half-crazed with grief, and at that first terrible moment he wanted to keep her away from the sledge carrying Piotra's body. It was Alexei Shamil striding along bareheaded beside the first sledge. With the stump of his left arm he was pressing his cap to his breast, in his right hand he was holding the reins. Gregor glanced into the sledge: Martin Shamil was lying face upward on the straw, his face and tunic stained with congealed blood. Manitskov was in the second sledge, his gashed face thrust into the straw, his head huddled on his shoulders, the cranium slashed away by a clean and dextrous stroke. Gregor glanced into the third sledge, but he was unable to recognize the dead body. He seized the bridle of the fourth horse and led it into his yard. Behind it ran the neighbours, women and children. The crowd gathered around the steps.

"There lies our dear Piotra Pantaleev! He's gone from us!" someone quietly said.

Stepan Astakhov came bareheaded through the gate. Grishaka and three other old men appeared from somewhere. Gregor glanced around distractedly.

"Help me carry him into the hut," he asked.

The driver was about to pick up Piotra by his feet, but the crowd silently and respectfully opened a path for Ilinichna as she came down the steps. She stared at the sledge. A deathly pallor hung on her brow and covered her cheeks, her nose, creeping down to her chin. Pantaleimon, silently trembling, held her under the arm. Dunia was the first to lift up her voice. Then Daria, dishevelled, her face swollen with weeping, ran down the steps and threw herself into the sledge:

"Piotra, my dear, dear Piotra! Stand up! Stand up!"

Gregor's eyes were sombre. "Go away, Daria!" he shouted savagely, uncontrollably, and violently pushed her off. She fell into a snowdrift. Gregor swiftly raised Piotra under the arms, the driver held his bare feet. But Daria crawled on all fours after them up the steps, kissing, clutching at her husband's inflexible, frozen hands. Feeling that in another moment he would completely lose control of himself, Gregor thrust her off with his foot. Dunia forcibly tore away Daria's hands and pressed her swooning head against her breast.

The kitchen was desolately silent. Terribly small, as though he had shrunk, Piotra lay on the floor. His nose was pinched, his flaxen whiskers had darkened, but all his face had drawn taut and grown finer. His bare, hairy feet emerged from his trouser-legs. He was slowly melting, and under him was a little pool of rosy water. The more the frozen body thawed, the stronger became the salty scent of blood and the cloyingly sweet smell of decay.

Under the shed Pantaleimon was making a coffin. The women were still occupied with Daria, who had not recovered consciousness. From time to time a piercing, hysterical shriek came from her room, followed by the lower tones of Auntie Vasilisa, who had run to "share" the Melekhovs' grief. Gregor sat on a bench staring at his brother's yellowing face, at his hand with its round blue nails. A terrible chill of alienation already severed him from Piotra. He was no longer his brother, but a transient guest who had now to depart.

He lay with his cheek unconcernedly pressed against the earthen floor, a tranquil, mysterious little smile frozen under his moustache. And tomorrow his wife and mother would be making him ready for his last journey.

"Better that you should have died somewhere in Prussia than here under your mother's eyes," Gregor slowly, reproachfully told him. Glancing at the body, he turned suddenly pale. Over Piotra's cheek a tear was slipping. Gregor jumped across to him, but, gazing more attentively, he sighed with relief. It was not a dead tear, but a drop melting out of Piotra's hair that had fallen on to his brow and was slowly trickling down the cheek.

In the evening his mother heated three pitchers of warm water for him, and his wife prepared clean linen, his best trousers, and his uniform tunic. Gregor and Pantaleimon washed the body that no longer belonged to Piotra, that felt no shame for its nakedness. Then they dressed him in his Sunday best and laid him out on the table. Daria came. Into his broad, icy hands, which only yesterday had embraced her, she put the candle that had lighted them both as they had walked behind the priest around the church lectern on their wedding day. Cossack Piotra Melekhov was ready to be conducted to that place whence there is no returning to native habitations.

Chapter 6

By order of Kudynov, commander of the combined insurgent forces, Gregor Melekhov was appointed commander of the Vieshenska regiment, consisting of ten squadrons of Cossacks. The staff at Vieshenska gave him instructions to march in the direction of Kargin district, to shatter Likhachev's detachment at any cost, and to drive it beyond the bounds of the region.

The day he took command of the regiment, he reviewed his Cossacks as they rode out of Vieshenska. He sat bowed in his saddle, his horse reined in tightly at the roadside, while past him in column formation rode squadrons drawn from the Donside villages: Bazka, Bielogorka, Olshanska, Merkulov, Gromkov, Siemenovsky, Ribinsk, Vodchinsk, Liebazhi and Yerik. With one gloved hand he stroked his moustache as he inspected each squadron with grim, watchful eyes. Rings of tobacco-smoke floated and dissolved above the ranks, and steam rose from the horses.

When the regiment was some three miles outside Vieshenska a patrol returned to report that the Reds were retreating in the direction of Chukarin. Gregor dispatched three squadrons to outflank the enemy detachment, and with the remainder rode so hard on their heels that the Reds began to abandon their baggage train and ammunition chests. As the Likhachev battery was driving out of Chukarin it lost some of its guns in a little stream. The drivers cut the traces and galloped off. The Cossacks rode twelve miles beyond Chukarin towards Kargin without encountering opposition, and they began to talk of reaching Novocherkass.

Gregor was delighted with the captured battery. "They didn't even stop to spike the guns," he thought contemptuously. With the help of bullocks, the Cossacks hauled the battery out of the stream, gunners were at once forthcoming from the various squadrons, double sets of horses, six pairs to each gun, were harnessed to the limbers, and a half-squadron was assigned as guard.

The Cossacks took Kargin at dusk. Part of the Likhachev detachment together with the remaining three field-guns and nine machine-guns were captured. The others managed to escape northward.

Rain fell all night, and in the morning the gullies and ravines were running with water, the roads became almost impassable, the horses floundered in the melting snow and mud, the men dropped with weariness. Two squadrons sent to pursue the retreating enemy captured some thirty of the Reds in the morning and brought them back to Kargin.

Gregor had established his headquarters in the large house of a local merchant. The prisoners were driven into the yard. The commander of the two squadrons reported to Gregor:

"Twenty-seven Reds taken. What's to be done with them?"

Gregor seized him by the top button of his greatcoat and bent close to his ear. Little sparks glittered in his eyes, but beneath his whiskers his lips were smiling with a wolfish smile.

"Send them under escort to Vieshenska. You understand? But they are not to get farther than the other side of that rise." He waved his whip in the direction of the sandy slope rising above Kargin.

"That's the first step towards settling accounts for Piotra," he thought.

Out of Kargin Gregor led thirty-five hundred swordsmen. The Vieshenska general staff and the Executive Committee sent urgent commands and instructions after him, ordering him to march on and forbidding the killing of prisoners. One of the members of the committee wrote to him privately in a flowery epistle:

HIGHLY RESPECTED COMRADE MELEKHOV:

Rumours are coming to our ears that you are ruthlessly executing the Red Army prisoners. We hear that among the prisoners was a woman Communist, who might have been very useful to us in learning the strength of the enemy. Dear comrade, repeal your order, which is dangerous to us. The Cossacks are murmuring at such ruthlessness and are afraid that the Reds will kill their prisoners too and destroy our villages. You are marching on with your companies like Taras Bulba in the historical novel of the writer Pushkin, putting everything to fire and sword and upsetting the Cossacks. Please do not condemn the prisoners to death, but send them to us. In that will be our strength. With all good wishes for your health. We send you hearty greeting and await your further success.

For three days success attended Gregor. He captured Bukovsky by storm and led his troops on towards Krasnokutsk. A small detachment barring the way was taken prisoner, but he did not give orders for the prisoners to be killed; he sent them back to Vieshenska. Afraid of this sudden threat to their rear, the command of the Red front on the Donietz River dispatched several regiments and batteries to deal with the rising. The Red reinforcements came into conflict with Gregor's regiments close to Christyakov. The struggle lasted for three hours; then, afraid of being surrounded, Gregor withdrew his forces towards Krasnokutsk. But the next morning his regiments were attacked by a force of Red Cossacks from Khopersk, and Don Cossacks were once more sabring one another in great style. Gregor himself lost his horse and was wounded in the cheek. He withdrew his regiments from the engagement and retreated to Bukovsky.

The same evening, wishing to obtain more information about the enemy, he questioned a prisoner, a Cossack from Khopersk district. The man replied willingly, but with a forced and crooked smile.

"What reserves of ammunition have your forces got?" Gregor demanded.

"The devil knows how much!"

"And guns?"

"Eight at least."

"Where was your regiment raised?"

"From the Kamensky villages."

"What did the Cossacks say when they were mobilized?"

"They didn't want to go."

"Did you know why we have risen?"

"How should we know?"

"Then why didn't you want to go?"

"Well, aren't you Cossacks like us? Haven't we had enough war already?"

"Would you be willing to serve with us?"

"As you will. But I don't want to. . . ."

Gregor stared with knitted brows after the man as he was led out of the room, then summoned his orderly, Prokhor Zykov. He went across to the window and, standing with his back to Prokhor, calmly ordered him:

"Tell the boys to take that man I've just been examining and lead him quietly into the garden. I won't take Red Cossacks prisoners!" He turned and gazed out of the window.

Prokhor went out. For a minute or two Gregor stood idly snapping the twigs of a geranium on the window-ledge. Then he turned and went swiftly out on the steps. He saw Prokhor Zykov talking quietly to a group of Cossacks sitting in the sun under the granary wall.

"Let the prisoner go! Write him out a pass!" he called to Prokhor without looking at the Cossacks.

He returned to the room, halted before an old mirror, and stretched out his arms in astonishment, at a loss to know why he had gone out and given this order for the prisoner to be released. He was a little irritated with himself for his sudden tender-heartedness, yet he was glad. It was all the more strange since only the previous day he had told the Cossacks: "The peasant is an enemy, but a Cossack who helps the Reds is doubly an enemy. There must be as short shrift for a Cossack as for a spy: against the wall and through the heavenly gates for him!"

He went out into the yard. The sun was shining warmly. The sky was as distant as in midsummer and of a midsummer azure, with little white clouds floating over it from the south. At a corner he assembled all the squadron commanders to hold a council of war. Some thirty men gathered and seated themselves on a fallen fence. Someone's tobacco-pouch was passed from hand to hand.

"What plans shall we make?" Gregor opened the council. "How are we to deal with these regiments that have driven us back, and what road shall we take?"

"How many are there against us? Did you find out from the prisoner?" one of the squadron commanders asked after a pause.

Gregor specified the regiments and hurriedly estimated the probable number enrolled in them. The commanders sat silent, none of them willing to speak without careful consideration. One openly told Gregor so.

"Wait a bit, Melekhov! Let's think. We mustn't make any mistake here."

After a while they began to express their opinions. The majority of them declared themselves against going far even if they were successful, but wanted to maintain a purely defensive struggle. But one of them hotly supported the order of the Vieshenska staff to march on.

"There's no point in our marking time here," he argued. "Let Melekhov lead us to the Donietz. We're only a handful, and behind them are all Russia. How can we stand still? They'll drive us back, and then we're done for. We must break through. We haven't got much ammunition, but we'll capture more. We must make a raid."

"And what about our people? The women, the old men and children?"

"Let them stay behind."

"You think you're clever, but you're a fool!"

Hitherto the commanders had only whispered their fears concerning the spring ploughing, and what would happen to their farms if they tried to break through. But now all the men from Chirik began to bawl at the top of their voices. The conference at once began to sound like a village assembly. One elderly Cossack outshouted the rest:

"We won't leave our yards! I shall be the first to lead my company back to its village. If we must fight, let it be around our huts and not to save others' lives."

Gregor waited until silence fell, then gave his decisive vote:

"We shall hold the front here. If the Krasnokutsk Cossacks join us, we'll defend them too. There's nowhere we can go to. The council is ended. To your squadrons! We shall be going out to our positions at once."

As, half an hour later, he watched the dense lines of horsemen winding endlessly along the streets, Gregor felt a sharp, proud joy. But together with his self-satisfied joy anxiety and a caustic bitterness stirred within him: Could he lead them as they needed to be led? Would he have the intelligence to direct the activities of thousands of Cossacks? Not one squadron, but an entire division was now at his disposition. And was he, a poorly educated Cossack, to hold sway over thousands of lives and bear Christian responsibility for them? "But most of all," he thought, "who am I leading them against? Against the people! Who is right? Lord, what a life!"

Grinding his teeth, he rode along beside the closed ranks of the squadrons. The intoxicating strength of power faded from his eyes, and the anxiety and bitterness remained, bowing his shoulders with their unbearable weight.

Chapter 7

Spring opened the veins of the rivers. More sappy grew the days, more turbulent the green hill torrents. The sun grew perceptibly redder, the impotent yellow hue faded from it. The spokes of the sunrays became velvety and hot. At noontide the ploughed land steamed and the pitted, scaly snow glittered unbearably. Saturated with moisture, the air was heavy and scented.

The sun warmed Gregor's back. It warmed all the men of the

regiments. The saddle seats were pleasantly warm. The brown Cossack cheeks were moistened by a rough, stinging wind. Occasionally it brought a breath of cold from a snowy slope. But the warmth was overcoming the winter. The horses danced and pranced in the grip of the spring, the moulting hair sprinkled from them, and their sweat pricked more strongly in the nostrils. The Cossacks had already tied up their horses' bushy tails. Already the cowls of camel-hair hung unwanted on the riders' backs, under the fur caps their brows were wet, and it was hot in their sheepskin jackets and padded coats.

Gregor led the regiments along a summer track. Squadrons of Reds were visible in the distance beyond a windmill. The struggle began close to the village of Sviridov.

Gregor was not yet able to direct a battle from outside the ranks of the fighters, as a divisional commander should. He himself led the Vieshenska Cossacks into the struggle, throwing them into the most dangerous spots. The battle developed without any unified direction. Each regiment ignored any agreement they had previously reached, and acted without regard to the course of the general situation.

There was no front in the usual sense of the word. And so it was possible to resort to extensive manoeuvring. An abundance of cavalry, which was the predominating force in Gregor's division, was an important asset. Gregor decided to exploit this advantage to the full and to carry on the war by "Cossack" methods: attacks on the flanks, sorties to the enemy's rear, threats to the baggage trains, and alarming and demoralizing the Reds with night raids.

But near Sviridov he resolved on a different plan. He himself led the squadrons at a fast trot into the attack, leaving one squadron dismounted and lying in ambush in the orchards on the outskirts of the village. Opposed to him were more than two squadrons of Red cavalry. They were not Khopersk Cossacks, for through his field-glasses he could see the docked tails of their horses, and the Don Cossacks never marred the beauty of their horses by docking their tails.

From the top of a rise he examined the locality through his glasses. From the saddle the land always seemed more spacious, and he felt more sure of himself when the toes of his boots were resting in the stirrups. A good mile separated him from the lines of Reds preparing to attack. He hurriedly drew up his regiments according to the old military plan, setting those armed with lances in the leading rank. He galloped to the front, turned his horse sideways to the Cossacks, and drew his sword:

"At an easy trot, forward!"

During the very first minute of the advance Gregor's horse put its hoof into a marmot-hole hidden under the snow, and it stumbled beneath him. He paled with anger and struck it violently with the flat of his sword. The horse was a good one, a fiery army mount borrowed from a Vieshenska Cossack, but he felt distrustful of it. He knew that a couple of days was not long enough for the horse to become accustomed to him. Nor had he had time to learn its character and tricks. He was afraid his new mount would not understand his use of the reins, nor obey his command almost before he spoke, as his own horse, killed at Christyakov, had understood and obeyed. The blow from the sword excited the animal, and it broke into a gallop, taking no heed of the reins. Gregor turned cold and even lost a little of his self-control. But as it dropped into a long, swinging canter, yielding more and more to the hardly perceptible movement of his hands directing its course, he grew more confident and cool. He dropped his eyes for a moment from the advancing ranks of the enemy and glanced over his horse's neck. Its red ears were pressed evilly against its head, its outstretched neck was quivering rhythmically. Gregor straightened up in the saddle, greedily gulped in the air, and thrust his boots far into the stirrups. He looked back. How many times had he seen behind him that thundering avalanche of horses and riders! And each time his heart had been gripped with fear of the impending clash, and he had felt an inexplicable feeling of savage agitation. From the moment when he put his horse into motion to the moment when he was approaching the enemy, there was always an intangible second of inward transformation. Reason, coolness, calculation—all abandoned him in that terrible instant, and one bestial instinct masterfully and indivisibly entered upon the government of his will. Yet anyone watching him at the moment of attack would have thought that his movements were directed by a cold, unemotional reason, so assured, controlled, and calculating did he seem.

The distance between the two forces decreased with consoling swiftness. Gregor picked out one rider galloping some three lengths in advance of his squadron. The great dark bay horse under him was moving with a short, wolfish stride. The man was waving an officer's sword in the air; his silver scabbard swung and knocked against his stirrup and gleamed fierily in the sun. A moment later Gregor was able to recognize the man as a Kargin Communist, who had been among the first to return, a young, twenty-five-year-old lad, from the German war in 1917. He had brought back with him Bolshevik convictions and a hard energy born of life at the front. He had remained a Bolshevik, had served in the Red Army, and before the rising broke out had returned from his regiment to organize the Soviet régime in his district. Now, confidently guiding his horse, picturesquely brandishing a sword which was of no value except on the parade ground, he was galloping straight towards Gregor.

Gregor bared his teeth and raised the reins. The horse obediently increased its speed.

Gregor had a trick of his own which he habitually employed in an attack. In childhood he had been left-handed. Even if he picked up his spoon with his right hand he would at once pass it into his left. His father had beaten him cruelly again and again to knock the habit out of him, and even the other boys had called him "Lefty Gregor." The beatings and cursings must have had their effect upon him, for when he was about ten years of age he had lost the trick of using only his left hand. But he had retained his left-handed dexterity and could do everything with it as well as with his right. When attacking, he always made use of his skill with the left hand, with invariable success. He would guide his horse against the selected enemy horseman, moving over to the left as usual in order to strike with the right hand, while his enemy did the same. When perhaps some twenty yards separated them and the other man was already leaning slightly to one side with sword ready to strike, Gregor would swing his horse sharply to the right, at the same time transferring his sword to his left hand. Being placed at a disadvantage by the necessity of striking at him across his own horse's head, the enemy would be nonplussed and disconcerted. And Gregor would bring his sword down with terrible force on the helpless man.

As a switch cut expertly slantwise from a bush drops without a tremor, without changing its position, and falls point downward into the sand beside the bush from which the Cossack sword has cut it, so the handsome Siemiglazov fell from his rearing horse and quietly slipped out of the saddle, his palms pressed against his sabred breast. Gregor at once straightened up in the saddle and stood in the stirrups. A second man came blindly at him, unable to rein in his horse. Beyond the animal's foaming muzzle Gregor was not yet able to see the rider, but he could see the curved blade of the man's sword. He pulled with all his strength on the reins and accepted and replied to the blow, gathering the reins in his right hand and cutting at the clean-shaven crimson neck.

He was the first to fight his way through and gallop clear of the mingled crowd of Cossacks and Reds. Looking back, he saw a seething mass of cavalry. He thrust his sword into its scabbard, pulled out his pistol, and sent his horse galloping off at full speed. The Cossacks streamed after him in a scattered line. At his side a sergeant in a fox-skin cap and sheepskin jacket was galloping. The man's ear and cheek had been slashed to the very chin, and his breast looked as though a basket of ripe cherries had been crushed against it. His teeth were bared and bloody.

The Red Army men, wavering and already half in flight, turned their horses, encouraged to take up the pursuit of the retreating Cossacks. One lagging Cossack was swept from his horse as though by the wind and trampled into the snow by the horses' hoofs. Now the village, the black mass of orchards, the shrine on the hillside, the broad street were at hand. Not more than two hundred yards away was the fence of the enclosure where the Cossack company lay in ambush. In full gallop Gregor shouted to the Cossack cavalry behind him:

"Open rank!"

The solid stream of Cossack squadrons split into two streams like the current of a river against a boulder. The avalanche of Red Army cavalry was laid bare. A volley rang out from the company concealed behind the fence; then a second; a third. A horse went down headlong with its Red Army rider, another crumpled at the knees and buried its head in the snow. Three or four other Reds were bowled out of their saddles. Before the Red cavalry could rein in their horses and turn round, the Cossacks had discharged all the contents of their rifle magazines and were silent. Hardly had Gregor succeeded in roaring: "Squadrons . . ." when the thousand horses' hoofs swung sharply round in the snow and the Cossacks were in pursuit.

But they followed the Reds reluctantly. Their horses were tired, and after a mile the Cossacks turned back. They undressed the dead Red Army men and unsaddled their horses. Armless Alexei Shamil himself killed off three wounded Reds, standing them with their faces to the fence and cutting them down one after another. When he had finished, the Cossacks, cigarettes in their mouths, crowded around the bodies. All three bore the same mark: their trunks were cloven from clavicle to waist.

"I've turned three into six," Alexei boasted, his eye and cheek twitching. The other Cossacks fawningly treated him to tobacco, staring with undisguised respect at his small fist and the swelling chest muscles visible through his open jacket.

The sweating horses stood trembling by the fence, with greatcoats flung over their backs. The Cossacks tightened the saddle-girths and stood in turn for water at the well. Many had to drag their wearied horses by the reins.

Gregor rode forward with Prokhor and five Cossacks. His eyes were as though a bandage had fallen from them. Again, as before the attack, he saw the sun shining over the earth, and the melting snow lying under the straw ricks; he heard the merry chatter of the sparrows in the village, caught the finest scents of the spring standing at the threshold. Life had returned to him not faded, not grown old with the blood so recently shed, but still more enticing with its meagre and illusory joys. The remnants of snow left on the black ground of the melting earth always seemed delusively whiter and brighter.

Chapter 8

Like flood water the rising swelled and spread, inundating all the Donside districts and the steppe to the east of the Don for three hundred miles around. Twenty-five thousand Cossacks took to horse. Ten thousand infantry were supplied by the villages of the upper Don region.

The war was waged in unprecedented conditions. Along the Donietz the Don White Army was holding the front, covering Novocherkass and preparing for a decisive struggle. And in the rear of the Eighth and Ninth Red Armies opposing the White forces a rising was storming, infinitely complicating the already difficult task of mastering the Don area.

The insurgent Cossacks suffered from a shortage of military equipment. At first there was an insufficiency of rifles, later of bullets. They had to be won at the cost of blood, through attacks or night raids. And they were won. In April 1919 the insurgents were completely equipped with rifles and had eight batteries and a hundred and fifty machine-guns.

At the beginning of the rising there were five million blank cartridges in the warehouse at Vieshenska. The regional Soviet mobilized all the finest blacksmiths, locksmiths, and gunsmiths, and a workshop for the casting of bullets was organized. But there was no lead, and nothing from which to cast the bullets. Then, at the call of the regional Soviet, all the villages began to collect their reserves of lead and copper. All the leaden parts in the steam mills were requisitioned, and a brief appeal was carried to the villages by mounted couriers:

Your husbands, sons, and brothers have nothing to shoot from their rifles. They are firing only with what they can win from the accursed enemy. Hand over all you have suitable for casting bullets. Take the leaden sieves from the winnowing machines.

Within a week not one winnowing machine throughout the entire district was left with a sieve. The women carried everything of use and of no use into the village Soviets; the lads of the villages where battles had occurred dug the shot out of the walls and rummaged in the ground in search of pieces of shell. But even in this activity there was not complete unity: certain of the poorer women who did not wish to deprive themselves of their last household utensils were arrested and sent to Vieshenska for being "sympathetic to the Reds." In Tatarsk the rich old Cossacks beat one younger Cossack, returned from his regiment, until the blood came, because he uttered aloud the one incautious remark: "Let the rich spoil their winnowing machines. Maybe they've got reason to fear the Reds more than ruin."

The stocks of lead were melted down in the Vieshenska workshop, but the finished bullets lacked nickel casings, and they also melted. When the rifles were fired the leaden bullets flew half melted from

the barrel and were effective only over a distance of three hundred yards. Nevertheless, the wounds inflicted by them were terrible.

The thirty-five thousand insurgents were divided into five divisions and a sixth special brigade. Gregor Melekhov was put in command of the first division, which lay along the river Chira. His section of the front bore the brunt of the attack of Red detachments
brought back from the main Donietz line, but he succeeded not
only in repulsing the pressure of the enemy, but in assisting the less
reliable second division with cavalry and infantry reinforcements.

The rising failed to spread northward as far as the Khopersk and
Ust-Miedviedietz districts, although they were in a ferment and messengers came from them asking for forces to be flung in the direction
of the Buzuluk and the upper reaches of the Khoper in order to raise
the Cossacks. The Cossack command could not resolve on an advance beyond the limits of the upper Don region, knowing that the
great mass of the Khopersk Cossacks supported the Soviet régime
and would not take up arms against it. Nor did the messengers in-
spire confidence, for they had to admit that the Cossacks discontented with the Reds did not number so very many, that the officers
left behind in quiet corners of the districts were all in hiding, the
front-line men were either at home or already in the Red forces, and
the old men had neither strength nor their former prestige in the
districts.

In the Ukrainian districts to the south the Reds had mobilized the
young men, and they were fighting very willingly against the insurgents.

Thus the rising was confined within the borders of the upper Don
region. And it grew clearer with every day and to every participant
from the command downwards that they would not be able to defend their hearts and homes for long. Sooner or later the Red Army
would turn back from the Donietz front and crush them.

On March 31 Gregor Melekhov was recalled to Vieshenska for a
conference with the supreme command. He handed over command
of his division to his assistant Ryabchikov and set off with his orderly
early in the morning. He arrived at the staff headquarters at the
very moment when Kudynov, the commander, was questioning a

messenger from Khopersk district. Kudynov was sitting huddled in a chair behind his table, twisting the end of his belt in his hands.

"And what do you yourself think about it?" he demanded.

"Well, of course—" The Cossack hesitated. "What can I say? I think like the rest. And you know what the people are like. They're afraid; they want to rise, but they're afraid."

"They want to, but they're afraid!" Kudynov shouted angrily, turning pale and fidgeting in his chair as though the seat were hot. "You're like a lot of girls! You want to, and you don't want to, and your mamma won't let you! Well, go back to your district and tell your elders that we shan't send a single troop into it so long as you don't begin yourselves. You can hang your Reds one by one!"

A stocky, black-whiskered man in a sheepskin jacket entered the room without knocking. He greeted Kudynov with a nod and sat down at the table, resting his cheek on his palm. Gregor, who knew all the staff by sight, did not recognize him and stared at the fine outlines of the face, the swarthy but not sunburnt complexion, the soft whiteness of his hands.

Indicating the newcomer with his eyes, Kudynov said to Gregor:

"Melekhov, this is Comrade Georgidze. He's—" He paused, twisted the Caucasian silver buckle on his belt, and turned to the messenger: "Well, you can go. We've got work on hand. Go back home and tell whoever sent you what I've said."

The Cossack rose from his chair. The flaming ruddy-brown fox-skin of his cap almost touched the ceiling. "I'm sorry if that's the case," he said, taking his cap off. "But you needn't shout at me, Your Excellency. I've brought you the message of our elders and I shall tell them your answer. But you needn't shout. First the Whites shouted at us, then the Reds; and now you're starting. Ah, our life is hard, hard these days." He furiously clapped his fur cap back on his head, bundled himself out into the corridor, and closed the door quietly behind him. But once he was outside, his anger got the better of him, and he slammed the outer door so violently that the plaster fell from the ceiling.

"The people are a fine lot, these days!" Kudynov remarked with a smile when the man had gone. "In the spring of 1917 I was driving to the district centre, and it was ploughing-time, just about Easter. The free Cossacks were ploughing and had gone quite mad with their freedom, and they were ploughing all over the road as though they hadn't enough land already. I called to one Cossack who was ploughing up the road, and he came over to me. 'Hey, you, what are you ploughing up the road for?' I asked him. He got alarmed and replied: 'I won't do it any more, I'll smooth it down again.' I frightened two or three more in the same way. But a little farther on I found the road ploughed up again and saw the man who had done it with his plough. I called to him: 'Hey, come here!' He came up to me. 'Who the hell gave you the right to plough up the road?' I shouted. He stared at me (a strong-looking little Cossack he was too) and his eyes glittered. Then he turned without a word and ran to his bullocks. He picks up an iron bar and runs back, seizes the side of my tarantass, and puts his foot on the step. 'Who are you?' he shouts, 'and how long will you go on sucking our blood? For two pins I'd make a hole in your head for you.' And he raises the bar. I said to him: 'Now, Ivan, I was only joking.' But he replies: 'I'm not Ivan now, but Ivan Osipovich, and if you can't talk to me properly, I'll smash your face in!' And so with this Cossack just now: he whines and bows and snivels, and then at the end he shows his real character. The people are puffed up with pride."

"It's the blackguard in them that's come to the top, and not pride. Blackguardism has acquired the status of legality," the Caucasian officer said and, without waiting to be contradicted, closed the subject: "Please let us begin the conference. I should like to get back to my regiment today."

Kudynov turned to Gregor. "You stay here," he said. "We'll confer together. You know the proverb: 'Two heads are better than one.' By a stroke of luck for us Comrade Georgidze happened to be left behind in Vieshenska district, and he'll be able to help us. He's a lieutenant-colonel and he's been through a staff training college."

"How did you manage to get left behind in Vieshenska?" Gregor asked Georgidze, for some unaccountable reason turning inwardly cold and cautious.

"I came down with typhus. I was left behind in Dudorovsky when the retreat began on the northern front."

"What regiment were you in?"

"I wasn't in the front line. I was attached to the staff."

Gregor wanted to question him further, but the frowning expression on the Caucasian's face made him feel the unwisdom of continuing the examination, and he broke off in the middle of a sentence.

A minute or two later the chief of staff, Safonov, and the commanders of the Fourth Cossack Division and the sixth special brigade entered, and the conference began. Kudynov briefly informed them of the situation at the front. The Caucasian was the first to speak. He slowly opened up a map on the table and spoke fluently and confidently.

"To begin with, I think it absolutely necessary to throw certain reserves of the Third and Fourth Division into the sector held by Melekhov's division and the special brigade. According to the information we have and from examination of the prisoners, it's absolutely clear that the Red command is preparing a serious attack on this particular sector. We've learned that they're sending two cavalry regiments, five special detachments, three batteries, and machine-guns to correspond. At a rough estimate this adds fifty-five hundred men to their forces. In that case they will undoubtedly have the numerical superiority, not to mention their ascendancy in equipment."

The yellow sun streamed into the room from the south. A blue cloud of tobacco-smoke hung motionless under the ceiling, and somewhere in it a fly, poisoned by the smoke, buzzed desperately. Sleepy after two nights of vigil, Gregor drowsily stared out of the window. His eyelids felt as heavy as lead, and the warmth of the overheated room combined with his weariness to drug his will and his consciousness. Outside the window the low spring breezes were dancing, the last snow was glittering rosily on the hillsides, and the poplars beyond the Don were swaying so strongly in the wind that as he watched them he thought he could hear their incessant bass whispering.

The Caucasian's clear and insistent voice aroused his attention. He forced himself to listen, and imperceptibly his drowsiness passed.

"The weakened activity of the enemy on the front held by the first division, and his determined efforts to advance on the Migulinsk-Mieshkov line warn us to be on our guard. I suggest . . ." he stumbled over the word "comrades" and, fiercely gesticulating, raised his voice. "I suggest that Kudynov and Safonov are committing a serious error in taking the Red manœuvres at their face value and proposing that the sector held by Melekhov should be weakened. It is the A B C of strategy to draw off your enemy's strength in order to fling your own forces against the weakened sector. . . ."

"But Melekhov doesn't need the reserve regiments," Kudynov interrupted.

"On the contrary! We must have reserves to our hand in order to close the gap in the event of their breaking through."

"It appears Kudynov has no intention of asking me whether I shall hand over my reserves or not," Gregor remarked with rising anger. "But I shan't give them up; not a single squadron!"

"Why, brother, that's—" Safonov began, smiling and stroking his whiskers.

" 'Brother's' got nothing to do with it. I won't hand them over, and that's all I've got to say. I'm responsible for my sector and for my men," Gregor retorted.

The dispute thus suddenly arisen was ended by Georgidze. With his red pencil he pointed out the threatened part of the front on the map. And when the heads bent close together over it, it was clear to them all that any attack being prepared by the Red command was indeed only possible on the southern sector, as it was closest to the Don and most advantageous in regard to communications.

The conference was over within an hour. The moody Kondrat Miedviediev, commander of the fourth division, who had been silent throughout the discussion, said at the end, distrustfully looking around him:

"We can send reserves to Melekhov's support. We've got men to spare. But one thing is bothering me. Supposing they attack us on all sectors at once, then what shall we do? They'll drive us into a bunch and we shall be in a serious position, like snakes caught on a little island."

"Snakes can swim, but we've got nowhere we can swim to," one of the others laughed.

"We've thought of that," Kudynov said thoughtfully. "But if that situation arises we must leave behind all those unable to bear arms, leave our families too, and fight our way through to the Donietz. We're not a small force, there are thirty thousand of us."

"And the Cadets will take us! They've got scores to settle with the upper Don Cossacks!"

"The hen is sitting, but where are the eggs? There's no point in talking like that!" Gregor put on his cap and went out. As he closed the door he heard Georgidze reply:

"The Vieshenska Cossacks and the insurgent forces will redeem their guilt to the Don and to Russia if they fight manfully against the Bolsheviks. . . ."

"So he says, but he's smiling to himself, the serpent!" Gregor thought. Again, as at the first moment of his meeting with this officer, he felt an inward anxiety and causeless anger.

At the gate he was overtaken by Kudynov. They walked along together for a minute or two without speaking. The wind was ruffling the puddles on the dung-littered square. Evening was drawing on. Round and heavy white clouds were slowly floating like swans from the south. Vital and scented was the moist smell of the melted earth. Under the fences the grass was showing green, and now Gregor could indeed hear the groaning sough of the poplars beyond the Don.

"The ice will be breaking soon," Kudynov remarked.

"Yes."

"Damn it . . . we shall die without even the luxury of a smoke. A tumbler of self-sown tobacco costs forty Kerensky rubles now."

"Tell me!" Gregor turned as he walked and sharply demanded: "That officer from the Circassians, what is he doing here?"

"You mean Georgidze? He's chief of the operations department. He's a brainy devil! It's he who draws up all the plans. He beats the whole lot of us at strategy."

"Is he always stationed in Vieshenska?"

"No. We've assigned him to the baggage train of the Chernovsky regiment."

"Then how does he manage to keep in touch with events?"

"He's always riding into Vieshenska. Almost every day."

"Why don't you keep him here?" Gregor asked, endeavouring to get to the bottom of the matter.

Kudynov coughed and covered his mouth with his hand. He answered reluctantly:

"It's not advisable in front of the Cossacks. You know what they're like. They'd say: 'The officers have got into the saddle again and are making us take their line.' "

"Are there any more like him in our forces?"

"Two or three in Kazanska. But don't you fret yourself. I know what you're thinking. But, my boy, there's nowhere we can go to except to the Cadets. Isn't that so? Or are you thinking of setting

up your own little republic of ten districts? No, we'll have to go
with hanging heads to Krasnov. 'Don't condemn us, Piotra Mikho-
laeivich Krasnov,' we must say, 'we went a little wrong in deserting
the front.' "

"Went wrong?" Gregor interrupted.

"Well, didn't we?" Kudynov answered in sincere surprise.

"I've got the idea. . . ." Gregor flushed and smiled forcedly. "I
think we went wrong when we began the rising."

Kudynov was silent, staring curiously at Gregor.

They parted at a crossroad beyond the square. Kudynov went on
to his quarters, and Gregor returned to the staff and told his orderly
to bring the horses. As, slowly disengaging the reins, he rode off, he
was still trying to understand the reason for his feeling of hostility
to the Caucasian. Abruptly his mind cleared as he thought: "What
if the Cadets have purposely left these clever officers with us in
order to stir up revolt in the rear of the Reds and to guide us along
their own way?" His memory brought evidence to the support of
this conclusion. "He wouldn't say what regiment he was from. He
said he was attached to the staff, but no staff passed this way. And
what devil carried him to Dudorovsky, into that lonely little village?
Oh, it's clear we've got ourselves into a fine mess! The educated
people have tied us up! The lords have got us into their net. They've
hobbled our lives and are using us to do their work. You can't trust
anyone in the least thing. . . ."

Once they had crossed the Don, he put his horse into its fastest
canter. Behind him his orderly, a good soldier and brave Cossack,
creaked in his saddle. Such were the men Gregor selected to follow
him through fire and water; with such men, tried in the German
war, he surrounded himself. The orderly, formerly a scout, was
silent all the way, smoking even in the wind and while cantering.
As they dropped down into a village he advised Gregor:

"If there isn't any need for hurry, let's spend the night on the
road. The horses are tired out, and it will rest them."

They halted for the night in a village. After the freezing wind of
the steppe the crumbling hut built of wattles was homely, comfortable, and warm. The earthen floor stank saltily of calf and goat
piddle, and the stove smelt of soggy burnt bread baked on cabbage

leaves. Gregor replied reluctantly to the old Cossack woman's questionings. She had seen three sons as well as her husband join the rising. She had a deep, masculine voice, and almost her first words were to tell Gregor roughly:

"You may be an officer and commander of the Cossack fools, but you've got no power over me, an old woman, old enough to be your mother. Talk to me, won't you? You sit yawning and yawning; I suppose you don't want to talk to a woman! I've sent three sons to your war, and the old man too for his sins. You command my sons, but I gave birth to them, suckled them, brought them up, carried them in my skirt. And it wasn't easy, either. Don't turn your nose up, but tell me: will there be peace soon?"

"Soon. . . . You ought to be in bed, old lady."

"Soon! But how soon? Don't you try to put me to bed; I'm the mistress here, not you. I've got to go out to see to the goats and lambs. We bring them in out of the yard at night; they're still young. Will there be peace by Easter?"

"When we drive out the Reds we'll make peace with them."

"You don't mean to say!" The old woman dropped her hands, with swollen wrists and fingers crooked with work and rheumatism, on to her bony knees and bitterly chewed her withered brown lips. "Have they given in, then? What are you fighting them for? The people have gone stark staring mad. You think it a game to shoot with your firearms and to look handsome on your horses, but what of us mothers? It's our sons that are being killed, isn't it?"

"And aren't we our mothers' sons, you bitch?" Gregor's orderly said angrily, completely losing his temper with the old woman's talk. "They're killing us, and you talk of our 'looking handsome on our horses.' You've lived till you're grey-haired, but you go on babbling away and won't let anyone sleep."

"Sleep, sleep, you plaguy fool! What have you put your spoke in for? You sit there as silent as a well, and then suddenly break out like that!" the old woman retorted.

"There'll be no sleep for us with her tongue, Gregor Pantalievich," the orderly groaned in despair. Lighting a cigarette, he struck the flint so hard that a pyrotechnic display of sparks flew from it. "You're as nagging as an aching tooth, woman. I should think your old man would be only too glad if a bullet does get him. 'Glory be,' he'll say, 'I'm free of the old woman!' "

Gregor compelled them to make peace. As he dropped off to sleep on the floor, he heard the door slam, and his legs felt a cold draught. Then a lamb bleated sharply right by his ear. The tiny hoofs of the goats clattered over the floor, and his nostrils caught the fresh and joyous smell of sheep's milk, the frost, and the scent of the cattle-yard.

He woke up about midnight and lay with open eyes. In the stove the coals were gleaming rustily beneath the opal ash. The lambs lay huddled together around the stove, and in the pleasant midnight silence he could hear them sleepily grinding their teeth and occasionally snorting. A distant full moon stared through the window. In its yellow square of light a restless little black kid was kicking and jumping about the floor, raising a pearly dust. The hut was illumined by a yellowish-blue light almost as bright as day. A piece of looking-glass sparkled on the shelf of the stove, and in one corner the silver frame of an ikon gleamed darkly and faintly. Gregor's thoughts turned again to the conference in Vieshenska, the messenger from the Khopersk district, and the Caucasian lieutenant-colonel. At the memory of him his original unpleasant, oppressed anxiety returned. The kid walked over his sheepskin and stared long and stupidly at his belly, then, growing bold, parted its legs. A fine stream fell on the outstretched palm of the orderly sleeping at Gregor's side. The man groaned, awoke, rubbed his hand on his trousers, and shook his head bitterly.

"He's wet me, damn him! Get away!" He struck the animal on the head. Bleating piercingly, the kid jumped off the sheepskin, then went to Gregor and licked his hand with its rough little tongue.

Chapter 9

After their flight from Tatarsk, Stockman, Koshevoi, Ivan Alexievich, and several Cossacks who had been serving as militia-men attached themselves to the Red 4th, Zaamursky Regiment. But late in March, hearing that in Ust-Khopersk a company was being formed of Communists and Soviet workers who had fled before the insurgents, Stockman, Ivan, and Mishka went to join it. They hired a sledge and were driven by a Cossack Old Believer with such a childishly rosy and clean face emerging from his great beard that even Stockman's lips twisted into a smile as he looked at him.

Mishka hummed a song to himself all the way, Ivan Alexievich sat in the back of the sledge with his rifle on his knee, and Stockman fell into conversation with their driver.

"There's nothing wrong with your health, comrade!" he remarked. The old man, overflowing with health and strength, smiled warmly. "No, God be praised! And why should there be? I've never smoked, I drink water instead of vodka, and I eat good wheat bread. So why should I ever be ill?"

"And have you been in the army?"

"For a little while. The Cadets took me."

"Why didn't you go with them to the Donietz?"

"You ask strange questions, comrade." He dropped the woven horsehair reins, removed his glove and wiped his mouth, frowning as though offended. "Why should I have gone there? I wouldn't have served with them if they hadn't made me. Your government is just, though you've gone a little wrong."

"How?" Stockman rolled a cigarette and lit it, but still had to wait for an answer.

"What are you burning that weed for?" the Cossack said at last. "Look how the spring is coming all around, and you soil it with your stinking smoke. I'll tell you how you've gone wrong. You've squeezed the Cossacks, oppressed them. There are a lot of fools among you, otherwise you wouldn't have suffered."

"How have we oppressed them?"

"You know as well as I do. . . . You've shot people. Today it's one man's turn, tomorrow another's. And who's going to wait for his turn to come? Even a bullock will shake its head if you go to cut its throat. There's Bukanovsky village over there, for instance. You see the church, where I'm pointing with my whip? Well, there was a commissar there. Did he deal justly with the people? I'll tell you. He rounded up old men out of the village, took them into the brushwood, parted their souls from their bodies, and wouldn't even let their families bury them. And all their crime was that at some time or other they had been elected honorary judges. And do you know

what sort of judges they were? One of them could only just sign his
name, another stuck his fingers in the inkpot or made a cross. Their
only crime was that they had long beards and forgot to button up
their flies because they were so old. They were just like children.
And this commissar settled other men's lives as if he was God. One
day an old man was going across the square with a bridle to get his
mare, and some urchins called after him as a joke: 'Here, the commissar's calling for you.' The old man crossed himself with his
heretical cross (they're all New Believers there) and took his cap
off before ever he went into the house. He went in all shaking, and
asked: 'Did you want me?' And the commissar says: 'No, nobody
wanted you, but as you've come, you'll get the same as the others.
Take him outside, comrades!' Well, naturally they took him and
put him up against a wall. His old woman waited and waited, but
he never came back. He'd gone. This commissar sees another old
man from a different village in the street, and calls to him: 'Where
are you from? What's your name?' Then he snorts: 'You've got a
beard like a fox's tail. You're too much like the dead Czar Nikholai.
We'll make soap of you. Take him away!' he orders his men. They
shot him only because he'd got a long beard and happened to be
seen by the commissar at a bad moment. And isn't that doing shame
to the people?"

Mishka had stopped humming as soon as the man began his story,
and at the end he said angrily:

"Your lies aren't very good ones, daddy!"

"You tell better ones! Before you say it's lies find out the truth.
Then you can talk!"

"And do you know all this for certain?"

"The people were all talking about it."

"The people! The people say you can milk chickens, but they
haven't any teats. You've been listening to lies, and your tongue
wags like a woman's."

"The old men were peaceable."

"Peaceable!" Mishka jeered. "Your peaceable old men probably
helped to stir up the rising, your judges may have had machine-
guns buried in their yards, and you say they were shot for their
beards or for a joke. Why didn't they shoot you? Your beard's as
long as an old goat's."

"I sell my goods at the price I've paid for them. Who knows, the people may have been lying; they may have done some harm to the new government," the old man muttered disconcertedly. He jumped out of the basket sledge and strode along in the melting snow at the roadside. The sun shone graciously over the steppe. The gleaming azure sky held the distant interlacing of hills and valleys in a mighty embrace. The scented breath of the approaching spring was faintly perceptible in the rustling breeze. To the east, beyond the white zigzag of the Donside hills, through a lilac haze arose the summit of the hill above Ust-Khopersk. Fringing the horizon, the white fleecy clouds stretched over the earth in a great billowing pall.

"My grandfather," the old man began again, "he's still alive, and a hundred and eight years old, they say; and his grandfather told him that during his lifetime, that is my great-great-grandfather's, a prince was sent by Czar Peter into our upper Don (Dlinnorukov or Dolgorukov his name was). And this prince came down from Voronezh with soldiers and destroyed the Cossack settlements because they didn't want to accept Patriarch Nikhon's accursed faith and serve the Czar. They caught the Cossacks, slit their noses, and hanged some of them and sent them floating on barges down the Don."

"What are you telling us all this for?" Mishka asked sternly.

"Why, I expect even if he was Prince Dlinnorukov, the Czar never gave him any such rights; and the commissar in Bukanovsky was like that too. 'I'll give you something to remember me by for ages,' he shouted in the assembly at Bukanovsky. But was he given any such right by the Soviet government? That's the point. He never had any orders to do such things."

On Stockman's temples the skin gathered into puckers. "I've listened to you," he said. "Now you listen to me."

"Maybe in my ignorance I've said something which wasn't true. If so, you must excuse me," the man muttered.

"Wait, wait! What you said about the commissar certainly didn't sound like the truth. But I'll find out. And if it was so, if he did treat the Cossacks like that, we shan't ask him what he thinks of it! But when the front reached your village did the Red soldiers shoot a comrade of their regiment because he'd stolen from some Cossack woman? That's what I heard in your village."

"That's true. He robbed a woman of a chest. That's right, it did happen. And it's true they shot him. We argued afterwards where he ought to be buried. Some said in the cemetery, but others said he would desecrate the spot, and so he was buried by the threshing-floor where they had shot him."

"So there was such a case?" Stockman swiftly rolled a cigarette.

"Yes, yes; I don't deny it," the man willingly agreed.

"Then don't you think we shall punish the commissar if we find he was guilty of what you said?"

"But, dear comrade! Maybe there's no one over him. That other man was a soldier. But a commissar. . . ."

"The inquiry will be all the more strict! Understand? The Soviet government settles only with its enemies, and we shall ruthlessly punish any representatives of our government who unjustly oppress the toiling people."

The silence of the March noonday steppe, broken only by the whistle of the sledge runners and the sound of the horses' hoofs, was suddenly shattered by the roar of cannon. The battery at Krutovsky village had renewed its bombardment of the left bank of the Don.

The conversation in the sledge died away. They turned on to the Hetman's highroad, and the spacious lands beyond the Don, speckled with patches of snow melting on the yellow sands, with capes and blue-grey sweeps of willow and pine woods, came into view. At Ust-Khopersk the driver reined in his horses outside the house of the Revolutionary Committee. Stockman rummaged in his pocket, pulled out a Kerensky forty-ruble note, and handed it to the driver. The man broke into a smile, revealing his yellow teeth under his damp whiskers, and hesitated in embarrassment:

"Why, comrade, for the love of Christ! It wasn't worth all that!"

"Take it for your horses' labour. And don't you have any doubts of the government. Remember, we stand for the government of the workers and peasants. It's our enemies that have driven you on to the rising: the kulaks, the atamans and officers. They are the main cause of the rising. And if any of our men have unjustly offended a toiling Cossack who is sympathetic to us and helping the Revolution, we shall find ways of settling with him."

"You know the saying, comrade: 'God's high in heaven, and it's far to the Czar.' It's a long way to your Czar too. 'Don't struggle with the strong, don't go to judgment with the rich.' And you're strong and rich. You're throwing your forty rubles away; five would have been a good price. But thank you all the same."

"He gave you that for your talk." Mishka Koshevoi smiled and smacked his trouser-legs. "Yes, and for that fine beard of yours. Do you know whom you have been driving, you old blockhead? A Red general!"

"Ho!"

"Yes, you can 'Ho!' You're like all the rest, damn you! Give you little, and you'd go crying round the district: 'I drove comrades and they gave me only five rubles!' You'd have felt sore about it for twelve months after. And when we give you more, you roar to heaven: 'How rich they are! Threw away forty rubles! He couldn't count his money, he had so much!' Well, good-bye, longbeard!"

A Red Guard came galloping out of the yard where the Moscow regimental staff was quartered. "Where's that sledge from?" he shouted, reining in his horse.

"What do you want to know for?" Stockman asked.

"We want ammunition carried to Krutovsky."

"Well, you can't have this sledge, comrade!"

"And who are you?" The Red Guard, a handsome youngster, rode up to Stockman.

"We're from the Zaamursky regiment. Don't requisition this sledge."

"All right, he can go. Drive off, old man!"

On inquiry, Stockman learned that a partisan company was being organized not in Ust-Khopersk, but in Bukanovsky. It was being recruited by the same commissar of whom the Old Believer had spoken on the road. The Communists and Soviet workers from Yelansk, Bukanovsky, and other districts, supplemented by Red Army men, had come together to form quite an imposing fighting unit of two hundred bayonets with several dozen swords and a mounted patrol. The company was temporarily at Bukanovsky, and together with a company of the Moscow regiment was holding up the insurgents attempting to advance from the upper reaches of the rivers Yelansk and Zimovna.

After a talk with the chief of staff of the Moscow regiment, Stockman decided to remain in Ust-Khopersk and join the second battalion of the regiment. He had a long talk with the political commissar.

"You see, comrade," the yellow-faced commissar said unhurriedly, "the situation here's rather complicated. My lads are mostly Moscow and Ryazan men, with a few from Nizhnii-Novgorod. They're hefty fellows, chiefly workers. You stay with us, there's plenty of work for you to do. We must work among the population and educate them. You know what the Cossacks are like. You've got to keep a sharp ear open."

"You needn't tell me that!" Stockman replied, smiling at the man's patronizing tones. "But tell me, who is this commissar in Bukanovsky?"

The man stroked the grey brush of his short moustache and replied languidly, raising his bluish, transparent eyelids:

"He's a good fellow, but he doesn't properly understand the political situation. He's evacuating all the male population of the district into the heart of Russia now."

Next morning the second battalion was called to arms, and within the hour it was marching in column formation towards Krutovsky village. A mounted patrol was sent from Krutovsky across the Don, and the column followed it. The ice of the river was pitted with spongy blue holes. Behind them the battery on the hill was firing in the direction of the poplar clumps visible beyond Yelansk village. The battalion was under orders to pass the village of Yelansk, which had been evacuated by the Cossacks, and to march on through the district, joining forces with the first battalion advancing from Bukanovsky. The shells flew high over the heads of the column, and their explosions shook the ground a little distance ahead. Behind the column the ice of the Don was cracking and breaking. Ivan Alexievich, marching in the same rank as Stockman and Mishka, glanced back.

"The water's coming down, it looks like," he remarked.

"Stupid business to cross the Don at such a time. Look, the ice is breaking," Mishka snorted, stumbling as he marched over the ploughed land.

Stockman gazed at the backs of the men marching in front of him, at the rhythmic swaying of the rifle-barrels with their smoky-blue bayonets. Looking around him, he observed the calm and serious faces of the soldiers, the swinging movement of the grey caps with their five-pointed stars, the grey greatcoats going yellow with age. He heard the heavy tread of the many feet, and his nose caught the smell of damp boots, tobacco, and leather straps. He half closed his eyes and, feeling a great influx of warmth towards all these fellows whom yesterday he had not even met, he wondered: "It's good to feel it, but why have they suddenly become so near and dear to me? There's the common idea moving us, of course; but there's more in it than that. There's the common task, and perhaps the nearness of danger and death." His eyes smiled. "Surely not because of the nearness of death?"

He stared with almost a fatherly feeling at the broad back of the man marching in front of him, at the strip of clean red neck showing between the collar and the cap, then turned his eyes to his neighbour. The man was clean-shaven, with swarthy, blood-red cheeks and a fine, firm mouth. He was tall but well-built and marched almost without swinging his arm. A painful frown furrowed his forehead. Stockman drew him into conversation.

"Been in the army long, comrade?" he asked.

The man's light-brown eyes ran over Stockman coldly and interrogatively. "Since 1915," he replied through his teeth.

The restrained answer did not freeze Stockman off. "Where are you from?" he asked.

"I'm from Moscow."

"A worker?"

"Aha!"

Stockman glanced at the man's hands and noticed marks betraying an iron-worker.

"A metal-worker?"

The brown eyes again passed over Stockman's face. "I'm a metal-turner. Were you too?" And the stern eyes gleamed warmly.

"I was a locksmith. But why do you keep your eyes screwed up?"

"My boots are rubbing. They've gone hard with the wet."

"It isn't because you're afraid?" Stockman smiled inscrutably.

"Afraid of what?"

"Well, we're going into battle. . . ."

"I'm a Communist."

"And aren't Communists afraid of death?" Mishka joined in the conversation.

After a moment's reflection the man replied:

"You're still fresh to such matters, that's clear, brother. I mustn't be afraid. I've given myself orders. Understand? I know what we're fighting for and whom we're fighting, and I know we shall win. And that's all that matters." Smiling at some memory and glancing at Stockman, he related: "Last year I was in a detachment in the Ukraine. We were being pressed hard all the time. We had to leave our wounded behind. We received orders that someone was to break through the White lines at night and get to their rear to blow up a bridge over a river, so as to stop an armoured train from passing. Volunteers were called for. But there weren't any. The Communists among us—there were only a few—suggested we should cast dice to see who should go. But I thought it over and volunteered. I took a slow fuse and matches, said good-bye to my comrades, and went. The night was dark and misty. After going two hundred yards I crawled through uncut rye and then along a gully. As I crawled out of the gully I remember a bird went fluttering up right under my nose. I crawled past the White Guard some twenty yards away and got to the bridge. A machine-gun detachment was defending it. I lay there a couple of hours, waiting for the right moment, then set the train and began to strike the matches in the open. But they were damp with the dew and wouldn't burn, for they'd been in my breast pocket and I'd had to crawl on my belly. Then I did get frightened. Dawn would be breaking soon, and my hand trembled and the sweat poured into my eyes. 'It's all up,' I thought. 'No explosion, but a shooting party,' I thought. I tried and tried and finally got a match to light and set fire to the fuse. I hid myself among a pile of sleepers on the embankment. When the explosion came, there was a fine to-do: two machine-guns began to rattle away, and horsemen galloped right past me. But they'd have had a job to find me at night. I got away from the sleepers into the corn. And only then—do you know, all the strength went out of my hands and legs, and I couldn't move. I lay down. I'd made my way to the bridge bravely, easily. But it was another thing to get back! I was like a bit of chewed rag. Of course I got back at last. And the next morning I was telling the boys about my bad luck with the matches, and one of them asked: 'But what about your cigarette-lighter? Had you lost it?' I felt in my pocket, and there it had been all the time. I fished it out and it worked first time!"

Scattering snow over Ivan Alexievich as he marched silently along on the outside file, a couple of sledges with machine-guns galloped past. One of the gunners fell out of the second sledge, and a roar of laughter went up from the Red Army men as the driver cursed and pulled up his horses violently for the gunner to jump back into the sledge.

Chapter 10

The First Division of the insurgent forces made Kargin the centre of their resistance to the Reds. Gregor Melekhov fully realized the strategic value of the position around Kargin and resolved not to yield it in any circumstances. Hills stretched along the left bank of the river Chira, and from their commanding heights the Cossacks could defend their lines splendidly. Below, on the farther side of the Chira, lay Kargin, and beyond it the steppe stretched for many miles to the south, intersected here and there with ravines and gullies. Gregor himself selected the position for his three-gun battery, not far from a mound covered with oaks which dominated the district and constituted a magnificent observation point.

Every day saw a battle around Kargin. The Reds usually attacked from two directions: from the steppe on the south and along the Chira from the east. The Cossack lines stretched some two hundred yards beyond the little town. The fire of the Reds almost always forced them to retreat through Kargin and up the steep bottoms of narrow gullies into the hills. But the Reds were not strong enough to drive them farther. Their advance was greatly hampered by the lack of cavalry, which could have outflanked the Cossacks and forced them into further retreat, and the infantry, irresolutely marking time outside the town, would have been set free for further operations. The infantry could not be employed for such a manœuvre, for at any moment the Cossack cavalry could have swooped down on the marching soldiers and broken them up.

The insurgents also had the advantage of knowing the district perfectly, and they lost no opportunity of dispatching cavalry unperceived along the ravines to attack the enemy flank and rear, continually threatening the Reds and paralysing their further movement.

Gregor drew up a plan to shatter the enemy. The Cossacks were to retreat, make a feint, and draw the Reds into Kargin, while a cavalry regiment executed a flanking movement through the valleys to attack them from the rear. The plan was worked out to the last detail. At a conference on the previous evening the commanders of the various detachments received exact instructions. Everything was as simple as A B C. After carefully checking every possibility, everything that might unexpectedly hinder the realization of the plan, Gregor drank two glasses of home-made vodka and, without undressing, threw himself on his bed, covered his head with his greatcoat, and slept like the dead.

The Reds occupied Kargin next morning. Part of the Cossack infantry fled through the streets into the hills in order to draw them on. The Red soldiers slowly spread through the little town.

Standing on a mound close to a battery, Gregor watched the Red infantry occupy Kargin and gather near the river Chira. It had been agreed that at the first shot from the battery the two companies of Cossacks lying in the orchards under the hills should pass to the attack, while the flanking regiment was to attack from the rear. The commander of the battery wanted to fire his first shell at a machine-gun sledge swiftly galloping down into Kargin, but at that moment the observer reported that a force of Reds was advancing from the east over a bridge some three miles away.

"Fire at them with the mortar-gun," Gregor advised, not removing his eyes from his field-glasses.

The gunner swiftly sighted the gun, and the mortar roared heavily, ploughing up the ground behind it in its recoil. The very first shell hit the end of the bridge just as the second gun of a Red battery was driving on to it. The shell swept the horses away, and they learned afterwards that of the team of six only one was left unscathed. Through his glasses Gregor saw a yellow-grey column of smoke arise in front of the gun; the horses reared as they were enveloped in the smoke, and the men fell and fled. A mounted soldier near the limber was lifted together with his horse, and they were carried bodily off the bridge, falling on to the ice.

The gunners had not expected to achieve such a success with the first shot. For a moment there was silence around the Cossack mortar, and only the observer shouted something and waved his arms as he stood on the mound a little way off.

At the same moment a faint "Hurrah!" rose from the dense undergrowth of the cherry orchards and gardens below. There was the crack of rifle-shots. Throwing caution to the winds, Gregor ran up the mound. The Reds were fleeing through the streets; he heard a disorganized roar of voices, sharp shouts of commands, the rattle of shots. One of the Red machine-gun sledges began to gallop up a slope, but almost at once, not far from the cemetery, it turned sharply and opened fire over the heads of the Reds at the Cossacks pouring out of the orchards.

In vain did Gregor scan the horizon for signs of the Cossack cavalry. They were still not to be seen. The Reds on the left flank were running towards the bridge connecting Kargin with the adjacent village of Arkhipov, while their right flank was still pouring down through Kargin, dropping under the fire of the Cossacks who held the two streets close to the river Chira.

At last the first squadron of cavalry appeared round the hills, then the second, the third, the fourth. They deployed into line and swept sharply to the left to cut off the fleeing crowds of Red soldiers. Crushing his gloves in his hand, Gregor impatiently followed the course of the struggle. The Cossack cavalry swiftly approached the main road, and the Reds turned and fled back in ones and twos and little groups towards the village of Arkhipov. There they met the fire of the Cossack infantry and turned once more and ran back to the road. The Cossack cavalry wheeled round to face Kargin and swept the Reds away like leaves before the wind. Close to a bridge some thirty of the enemy were cut off without hope of escape, and they began to defend themselves. They had a machine-gun and large reserves of belts. Hardly had the Cossack infantry emerged from the orchards when the machine-gun began to work at a feverish speed, and the Cossacks dropped, crawling under the shelter of sheds and stone fences. From Gregor's post of observation he saw his Cossacks dragging a machine-gun through Kargin. By one of the yards on the outskirts they hesitated, then ran inside it. A few minutes later their machine-gun began to stutter from the roof of the granary. Through his glasses Gregor saw the gunners grouped with outflung legs behind the shield; one was lying on the roof, another was clambering up a ladder with ammunition belts wound round him.

The Cossack battery opened fire in support of the infantry, concentrating its aim on the groups of Reds. Within fifteen minutes the Red machine-gun by the bridge suddenly lapsed into silence, a faint "Hurrah" arose, and the figures of mounted Cossacks appeared and disappeared among the bare trunks of the willows.

It was all over.

By Gregor's order the inhabitants of Kargin and Arkhipov dragged the hundred and forty-seven dead Red Army soldiers into a shallow trench which was dug just outside the village. The Cossacks captured six two-wheeled ammunition carts with horses, a damaged machine-gun, and forty-two baggage-wagons with stores. The Cossacks lost four dead, and fifteen were wounded.

After the battle there was a week's respite from fighting on the Kargin front. The Red command threw forces against the Second insurgent Division and, forcing it back, soon captured a number of villages in the Migulinsk district. Every morning the sound of distant gunfire was to be heard in Kargin, but reports on the course of the struggle arrived only tardily, and they failed to give any clear idea of the situation.

During those days, in an attempt to rid himself of the sombre thoughts possessing him, Gregor took to drinking heavily. The insurgents were suffering a severe shortage of flour, and frequently the Cossacks had to eat boiled wheat, as the mills could not cope with the armies' needs. But as there were enormous stocks of grain, there was no shortage of home-made vodka, and it was poured out in a steady stream. Instances of men going drunk into battle were frequent. On one occasion an entire squadron of Cossack cavalry rode half-drunk into the attack, galloped straight up against a machine-gun, and was almost completely wiped out. Gregor was kept amply supplied with vodka, for his orderly, Prokhor Zykov, distinguished himself in capturing the liquor. After the battle of Kargin, at Gregor's request, he brought in three pitchers of vodka and called for singers, and Gregor, feeling a joyous freedom from restraint and seeking oblivion from his thoughts, drank with the Cossacks until daybreak. Next evening he again called for singers and again delighted in the roar of voices and human merrymaking, all that created the illusion of real enjoyment and veiled the unpleasant reality.

The craving for drink quickly developed into a habit with him. As he sat at the table in the morning, he already felt an invincible desire for vodka. He drank much, but never too much. He always remained steady on his feet. Even when the others were drunkenly sleeping under the tables and on the floor, covering themselves with their greatcoats, he still seemed to be sober, though his face was pale and his eyes fixed and he frequently pressed his hands to his head.

After four days of incessant carousing he began to show signs of its effects: he went baggy and blue beneath the eyes, and his glance was senselessly stern. On the fifth day Prokhor Zykov suggested with a promising smile:

"Come with me this evening to a fine woman I know at Likhovidov. She's handsome. But you mustn't be bored at first. I know she's as sweet as a watermelon, though I haven't tried her. But she's sharp, the devil, and wild. You won't get what you want from her the first time you ask. But you won't find a better hand at making vodka. She's got the finest vodka in all the Chira villages. Her husband's retreated beyond the Donietz, and she thinks he must be dead."

They rode to Likhovidov that evening. Gregor was accompanied by two of his commanders, Ryabchikov and Yermakov, by armless Alexei Shamil, and the commander of the Third Division, Miedviediev, who was on a visit to the First Division. Prokhor Zykov rode in front. Arrived in the village, he turned down a side street and opened a little gate leading into a threshing-floor. For some five minutes they followed him past straw and hay ricks, then through a bare cherry orchard. The golden chalice of the crescent moon stood in the dark-blue heaven, the stars twinkled, and a magical silence lay all around, save for the howl of a distant dog and the sound of their horses' hoofs. A yellow point of light glimmered against the dark background of the sky, and the silhouette of a large, reed-roofed hut appeared. Bending from his saddle, Prokhor opened a creaking wicket gate. At the steps Gregor jumped from his horse, wound the reins around the balustrade, and entered the porch. Groping for the door latch, he opened the door and passed into a spacious kitchen. A young, stocky, but well-built Cossack woman with swarthy face and black, well-shaped brows was standing with her back to the stove, knitting a stocking. On the stove a girl perhaps nine years old was sleeping with one arm flung out.

Without removing his outdoor clothes Gregor sat down at the table. "Have you got any vodka?" he asked.

"Don't you think you might say good-evening first?" the woman replied, not glancing at Gregor and not stopping her knitting.

"Good evening, if you feel like that. Have you got any vodka?"

She raised her eyebrows, smiled at him with her black eyes, and listened to the sound of steps in the porch.

"I've got some vodka. But there are a lot of you come to spend the night, aren't there?"

"Yes. A whole division."

The other Cossacks crowded through the doorway. One of them rattled out a rapid dance rhythm with a couple of wooden spoons. They piled their greatcoats in a heap on the bed and laid their weapons on the benches. Prokhor hurried to help the woman set the table. Armless Alexei went into the cellar to get some pickled cabbage, fell down the steps, and came up carrying the fragments of the broken plate and a pile of wet cabbage in his greatcoat.

By midnight they had drunk two pails of vodka and had eaten incalculable quantities of cabbage. Then they decided to kill a sheep. Prokhor groped for one in the sheep-pen, and with one stroke of his sword Yermakov cut off his head. The woman lit the fire and set a pot of mutton on to cook. Once more the sound of the wooden spoons rattling out a dance rhythm was heard, and Ryabchikov danced around, kicking out his legs, smacking his shanks with his hands, and singing in a sharp but pleasant tenor voice.

"I smell blood!" Yermakov suddenly roared, testing his sword-blade on the window-frame. Gregor, who liked Yermakov for his exceptional bravery and Cossack frenzy, restrained him, knocking on the table with his copper mug.

"Kharlampy, don't be a fool!" he shouted.

Yermakov obediently thrust his sword back into its scabbard and thirstily seized a glass of vodka.

"With such comrades death has no terrors!" armless Alexei said, sitting down at Gregor's side. "Gregor Pantalievich, you're the pride of our hearth! You're the only man in all the world we swear by!

Shall we have another drink together?"

Only when dawn was at hand did Gregor begin to feel that he was getting drunk. As though they were a long way off, he heard the other men speaking. He heavily opened his bloodshot eyes and, with an intense exercise of will-power, kept his senses.

"The gold epaulets are ruling us again! They've got the government into their hands," Yermakov roared, embracing Gregor.

"What epaulets?" Gregor asked, pushing his hands away.

"In Vieshenska. Do you mean to say you haven't heard? A Caucasian prince is in control there! A colonel. I'll kill him! Melekhov! I lay my life at your feet: don't desert us! The Cossacks are murmuring. Lead us to Vieshenska and we'll kill them all and burn the place down. We'll kill Kudynov, the colonel, everybody! We've got enough men to settle with them. Let's fight both the Reds and the Cadets. That's what I want!"

"We'll kill the colonel. He stayed behind on purpose! Kharlampy, we must bow our knees to the Soviet government. We are in the wrong." Gregor suddenly recovered his senses for a minute or two and smiled wryly: "I'm only joking. Drink up, Yermakov."

"What are you joking about, Melekhov? Don't joke, this is a serious matter," Miedviediev said sternly. "We want to overthrow our government. We'll send them all packing and put you in their place. I've talked with the Cossacks, and they've agreed. We'll tell Kudynov and his band: 'Clear out! We don't like you!' If they go, well and good. But if not, we'll send a regiment to Vieshenska and sweep them away, damn them!"

"No more of that talk!" Gregor roared furiously.

Miedviediev shrugged his shoulders, left the table, and ceased to drink. Ryabchikov struck up a song. The shadows outside were turning lilac when the woman led Gregor into the front room.

"You've given him enough to drink! Now stop it, you devils! Can't you see he's good for nothing?" she said to the others, holding up Gregor with one hand, with the other pushing away Yermakov, who was following them with a mug of vodka.

"Don't you lie down with him now; you won't get anything out of it." Yermakov winked, swaying and spilling the vodka from the mug.

"That's nothing to do with you. You're not my father," she retorted.

She pushed Gregor into the room, put him on the bed, and, with loathing and pity in her eyes, sat watching his deathly pale face with its unwinking, staring gaze. She fingered and stroked his hair until he fell asleep. Then she made her own bed on the stove at her daughter's side; but Shamil would not let her sleep. With his head on his arms he snorted like a startled horse, then suddenly awoke and hoarsely roared a snatch of song. Once more he dropped his head on his arms, slept for a few minutes, then again burst into song.

When Gregor awoke next morning, he recollected Yermakov and Miedviediev's words. He had not been completely fuddled with drink, and without much difficulty he recalled their talk about over-throwing the government, seeing at once that the drinking bout at Likhovidov had been organized with the deliberate object of win-ning his support for the plan. The Leftward-minded Cossacks, who were secretly dreaming of complete separation from the rest of the Don province and of forming their own miniature Soviet gov-ernment without the Communists, were intriguing against Kudy-nov, who had openly expressed his desire to retreat to the Donietz and join forces with the White Army. They did not realize all the disastrous results of strife inside the insurgents' camp, when at any moment the Red forces might sweep them away together with their dissensions. "A child's game," Gregor thought as he lightly jumped off the bed. When he was dressed he called Yermakov and Mied-viediev into the room and closed the door fast behind them.

"Now listen, brothers!" he said. "Get yesterday's talk right out of your heads, and no grumbling, or it will be the worse for you. It isn't a question of who's in command. It's not a question of Kudynov or someone else, but of the fact that we're in a ring, we're like a barrel in its hoops. If not today, then tomorrow the hoops will crush us. We must march our regiments not towards Vieshenska, but on Migulinsk, on Krasnokutsk," he said emphatically, not turning his eyes from Miedviediev's moody, passionate face. "You think it over and realize that if we begin to get rid of our commanders and to organize mutinies, we're done for. We must go over either to the Whites or to the Reds. There's no middle way: one or the other will crush us."

"You won't go and tell others about our talk!" Yermakov asked as he turned away.

"It will go no farther, but only on condition that you stop agitating among the Cossacks. What about Kudynov and his shadows? They've not got half the power that I have so long as I'm in command of a division. They're a poor lot, I know, and they'll deliver us into the hands of the Cadets if we let them. But where are we to go to, anyway? There's not a single road open to us; all the arteries are cut."

"That's true!" Miedviediev agreed, and for the first time since he had entered the room he raised his eyes to Gregor's face.

Two more days Gregor spent drinking in the villages lying around Kargin, passing an empty life in drunken carousals. The smell of vodka even saturated his saddle. Women and girls who had lost their virgin flower passed through his hands, sharing with him their transient amours. But each morning, satiated with the amorous fevers of the latest delight, Gregor soberly and tranquilly thought: "I've lived and experienced everything in my day. I've loved women and girls, I've trodden the steppe, I've rejoiced in fatherhood, and I've killed men, have gone myself to face death, and delighted in the blue sky. What new thing can life show me? Nothing! And I can die! It won't be so terrible. I can play at war without risk. I'm not rich, and my loss won't be great."

A flood of memories poured through his mind as he lay at the latest woman's side. Old friends, old faces, former voices, scraps of conversation, laughter. His memory turned to contemplation of the beloved steppe, and suddenly, blindingly, it opened its expanse before him. He saw the summer cartroad, a bullock-wagon with his father sitting on the cross-tree, the ploughed land and the golden brush of harvested grain, a black sprinkle of ravens on the road. As his mind wandered among memories of the irrevocable past, it stumbled against Aksinia. "My love, my unforgettable love!" he thought, and contemptuously shifted away from the woman sleeping at his side. Sighing, he impatiently awaited the dawn, and hardly had the sun begun to tinge the east with hues of raspberry and gold when he jumped up, washed, and went to his horse.

Chapter 11

Like an all-consuming steppe fire the rising spread. But a steel ring of fronts surrounded the insubordinate districts. The shadow of destiny lay like a brand on men. The Cossacks were playing with death, and for many of them the coin to which they had called "Heads!" came down "Tails." The youngsters lived and loved violently, the older men drank vodka until they fell under their seats, played at cards for money and bullets (bullets being worth more than money), rode home for furloughs so that, if only for a minute, they might set down their rifles and pick up the axe, might rest among their dear ones, might mend the fence or get the harrow or horse-collar ready for the spring labour. Many who thus tasted the life of peace returned drunk to their regiments, and before they were sober again, they went into the attack and marched straight up against the machine-guns. Or, aflame with frenzy, not feeling the horses under them, they went savagely out on night raids, captured prisoners, and ruthlessly, with elemental savagery, worked their will on them, finishing them off with their swords.

The spring of 1919 was brilliant with unprecedented beauty. The April days were fine and as translucent as glass. Over the inaccessible, azure sweep of heaven the flocks of wild geese and copper-tongued cranes floated, floated, overtaking the clouds, flying ever to the north. On the pallid green pall of the steppe close to the lakes the settled swans sparkled like scattered pearls. The birds sang and called continually in the water-meadows along the rivers. Over the flooded pools the geese called, preparing for flight, and the osiers whistled incessantly with the amorous ecstasies of the drakes. The willows were green with catkins, the poplars blossomed with sticky, scented buds. The green-flushed steppe was drenched with inexpressible charm, flooded with the ancient scent of the bare black earth and the ever young grass.

The insurgents' war was peculiar in the respect that each Cossack was close to his native village. They grew tired of going on outpost duty and secret raids, tired of making their way over hills and down valleys on patrol duties, and they obtained permission from their

most beautiful time of nature —
most death as well

company commander, rode home, and sent their withered, aged fathers or their adolescent sons out in their places. The squadrons always had a full complement of fighters, yet it was a continually changing complement. But some of the Cossacks were more cunning. As soon as sun was setting they would gallop away from their squadron's night quarters, would cover some twenty or thirty miles, and were home soon after nightfall. They would spend the night with their wife or lover, would saddle their horses when the second cock crew, and before the Milky Way had faded in the sky they were back with their squadron.

Many of them could find no pleasure in war just outside their native yards. "There's no point in dying," more than one said after frequent partings from his wife. The command was particularly afraid of mass desertion setting in when the spring field labour was due to begin. Kudynov made a special visit to each of the divisions, and with unwonted severity declared:

"Better that the winds should roam over our empty fields, better that we should not cast the grain over our earth! But I will not allow any Cossack to be given furlough. Anyone caught at home without leave will be cut down and shot."

Gregor took an active part in one battle below Klimovsky. Towards noon of the April day cross-fire broke out around the yards at the end of the village, and a few minutes later the Red lines were advancing towards the village. On the left flank sailors—the crew of some vessel in the Baltic fleet—moved deliberately. With a fearless attack they drove the Cossack squadrons out of the village and pushed them back along a valley.

When the Reds began to get the upper hand Gregor, who was watching the struggle from a hill, waved his glove to Prokhor Zykov to bring him his horse. He jumped into his saddle and at a swift trot rode down to a valley where he had stationed a squadron of cavalry in reserve. Through the orchards and over the fences he made his way to the squadron and found the Cossacks dismounted and at ease. When still a little way off, he drew his sword and shouted: "To horse!" In a moment the two hundred Cossacks had mounted. The squadron commander rode forward to meet Gregor.

"Are we to attack?" he asked.

"Yes, and high time too!" Gregor's eyes flashed. "I'll lead the squadron myself." He turned to the men:

"In troop formation as far as the other end of the village, forward!"

Beyond the village he ordered the squadron to form up in readiness to attack, tried whether his sword would slip easily from his scabbard, and, riding some fifty yards in front of the squadron, led it at a gallop towards Klimovka. At the top of the rise overlooking Klimovka he reined in his horse for a moment and studied the position. Below him the horse and foot Red soldiers were galloping and running in retreat. Gregor half turned towards his squadron.

"Draw swords! Into the attack! Brothers, follow me!" he shouted, drawing his sword and crying: "Hurrah!" He set his horse at a gallop towards the village. The tightly drawn reins quivered in his left hand, the sword raised above his head whistled through the wind.

An enormous white cloud obscured the sun for a minute or two and, overtaking Gregor, a grey shadow slipped with apparent deliberation over the rise. He turned his eyes for a moment from the huts of Klimovka to the bright yellow joyous light fleeing somewhere before him. An inexplicable and unconscious desire to overtake the light speeding over the ground took possession of him. He struck his horse and put it into its fastest gallop, and after a few moments' desperate riding the horse's outstretched head was lit up with a network of sunlight, and its ruddy hair suddenly gleamed brilliantly golden. At that very moment a shot rang out from the street in front; the wind brought the sound of the explosion to his ears. Another second, and then, through the thunder of his horse's hoofs, through the whistle of bullets and the roaring of the wind past his ears, he ceased to hear the thunder of the squadron galloping behind him. It was as though the heavy roar of the mass of horses had fallen away from his ears, as though he were outdistancing it. The rattle of rifles sounded like dry brushwood on a camp-fire; the bullets whistled past. In perplexity and alarm he looked round, and anger and bewilderment distorted his face. The squadron had turned their horses and were galloping back, were abandoning him. A little way behind him the commander was rising in his stirrups, awkwardly waving his sword and weeping and shouting in a hoarse, broken voice. Only two Cossacks were following Gregor, while Prokhor Zykov had turned his horse and was galloping up to the squadron commander. The others were scattered and galloping back, thrusting their swords into their scabbards and plying their whips.

For a brief second Gregor reined in his horse, trying to discover what had happened behind him, why the squadron had suddenly taken to flight before a man had fallen. And in that moment he resolved: he would not turn, would not flee, but would ride on. He saw seven Red sailors bustling around a machine-gun on a cart behind a fence some two hundred yards in front of him. The Reds were attempting to swing the machine-gun round to train on the Cossacks, but apparently in the narrow alley they could not manage it. The rifle bullets shrieked more fiercely about his ears. He turned his horse to come down into the alley from behind, across a fallen fence. He looked back from the fence to the gun, and now saw the sailors quite close to him, hurriedly unharnessing the horses. Two were cutting the traces, a third was bent over the machine-gun, the others were kneeling and firing at him from their rifles. As he galloped towards them he could see their fingers feverishly working the triggers and heard the shots right against him. They were reloading the magazines, bringing the butts to their shoulders, and firing so swiftly that Gregor, streaming with sweat, felt joyously certain that they would not hit him.

The fence crashed beneath his horse's hoofs and was left behind him. He raised his sword and fixed his eyes on the foremost sailor. One more spasm of fear scorched him like lightning: "They'll be firing at point-blank range . . . right at the horse's chest. . . . He'll throw me . . . and then I'm done!" Two shots right at him, a shout: "Take him alive!" Before him he saw the ribbons of a sailor's cap, with the tarnished gold of a ship's name on it. Gripping the stirrups with his feet, Gregor felt his sword sink into the sailor's soft body. The second sailor managed to send a bullet through the flesh of Gregor's left shoulder before he fell beneath Prokhor's sword, his head cloven in two. At the sound of a rifle magazine Gregor turned: the little black eye of a rifle-barrel was staring at him from behind the machine-gun. He dodged the bullet which whistled past his head, flinging himself sideways with such force that the saddle shifted and the snorting, terrified horse swayed, then jumped across the centre pole of the cart and cut down the man, before he had time to reload his rifle.

In the flash of a moment he had sabred four sailors and, not listening to Zykov's shouts, would have galloped in pursuit after a fifth running round the corner of the alley. But the squadron commander galloped in front of him and seized his horse by the snaffles:

"Where are you going? They'll kill you! They've got another machine-gun behind the shed there."

Two more Cossacks and Prokhor, who had dismounted, ran to him and pulled him forcibly from his horse. He struggled in their hands, shouting:

"Let me go, you snakes! I'll kill them—all of them."

"Gregor Pantalievich! Comrade Melekhov! Come to your senses!" Prokhor pleaded with him.

"Let me go, brothers!" he asked in a different, fading voice. They released him. The squadron commander whispered to Prokhor:

"Put him on his horse and lead him back. I think he's ill."

He was about to go to his own horse, but Gregor threw his cap to the ground and stood swaying. Suddenly grating his teeth, his face contorted terribly, he groaned and began to tear open the fastenings of his greatcoat. As the squadron commander stepped back towards him, he fell where he stood, headlong, his bare chest against the snow. Weeping, and shaking with his weeping, he began to mouth like a dog at the snow under the fence. Then, in a moment of horrible clarity of mind, he tried to get up. But he could not and, turning his tear-stained, distorted face to the Cossacks standing around him, he shouted in a broken, savage voice:

"Whom have I killed?"

For the first time in his life he writhed in a fit, shouting and spitting out foam from his lips:

"Brothers, there's no forgiveness for me. . . . Kill me. . . . Cut me down, for the love of God! Death . . . put me to death. . . ."

The commander and a troop officer ran to him and threw themselves on him, tearing off his sword-belt and field-pack, closing his mouth, and holding down his legs. But he struggled under their weight for a long time, scattering the snow with his convulsively kicking legs and beating his head against the bare, hoof-marked earth—the earth on which he had been born and had lived, taking full measure from life, rich both in bitterness and in petty joys.

The grass grows on the earth, indifferently accepting the sun and the rain, feeding on its life-giving juices, humbly bowing beneath the destructive breath of the storm. And then, scattering its seeds to the wind, it dies as indifferently, with the rustle of its withering blades welcoming the radiant death of the autumnal sun.

The following day Gregor handed over the command of the division to one of his regimental commanders and, accompanied by Prokhor Zykov, rode off to Vieshenska. Beyond Kargin they saw a large flock of wild geese settled on a pond lying in a deep valley. Prokhor pointed to them with his whip and laughed:

"It would be fine to shoot a goose, Gregor Pantalievich. And then to have a drink of vodka."

"We'll ride closer, and I'll try my hand at a shot," Gregor said.

They dropped down into the valley. Prokhor halted with the horses on the brow of the hill while Gregor removed his greatcoat, set the safety catch on his rifle, and crawled down a narrow gully overgrown with last year's scrub. He crawled for a long time, hardly raising his head—crawled as though reconnoitring an enemy outpost, as he had when he had captured the German sentry on the Stokhod River. His faded khaki shirt blended with the green-brown hue of the ground, the gully concealed him from the sharp eyes of the sentry gander standing on one leg at the waterside. He crawled until he could get a good shot, then raised himself a little. The gander turned its grey, snaky neck and watched him anxiously. On the water the geese were floating, diving, and paddling. The quiet sound of their chatter and the splash of water came to his ears. "I can take aim through the fixed sight," he thought, his heart beating as he lifted the rifle to his shoulder and fired at the gander.

As soon as he had fired the shot he jumped to his feet, deafened by the beating of wings and the clutter of the geese. The gander at which he had aimed flew up, but vainly tried to gain height. The others rose in a dense cloud above the pond. He fired twice more at the cloud of birds, watching whether any fell, then turned and despondently went back to Prokhor.

"Look! Look!" Prokhor shouted to him, jumping into his saddle and standing upright on his horse, pointing with his whip to the geese distancing in the blue expanse.

Gregor turned and trembled with gladness, with the agitation of the successful hunter. One goose had dropped behind the flock and was swiftly sinking, its wings flapping slowly and intermittently.

Rising on tiptoe and putting his hand to his eyes, Gregor watched it. Suddenly the bird dropped like a stone, the sweep of its wings gleaming a dazzling white in the sunlight.

Prokhor rode up to Gregor and threw him his horse's reins, and they both galloped along the slope. They found the goose lying with outstretched neck, its wings fluttering as though trying to embrace the unkind earth. Gregor bent down from his saddle and picked up the prize. Prokhor tied it to his saddle-bow, and they rode on.

At Vieshenska Gregor halted at the hut of an old Cossack acquaintance, asked him to cook the goose at once, and sent Prokhor off for vodka. He made no attempt to report to the staff. They sat drinking until late in the afternoon. During the conversation the old Cossack poured a stream of complaints into Gregor's ears.

"The officers here are carrying on in a fine way, Gregor Pantalievich," he began.

"What officers?" Gregor asked.

"Our own officers—Kudynov and the others."

"What are they doing?"

"They're squeezing all the foreigners. They're arresting the families of those who've gone off with the Reds—arresting women, children, and old men. They've taken a relation of mine because of his son. But what's the point of that? Supposing you'd gone off with the Cadets to the Donietz, and the Reds had arrested your father, Pantaleimon, that wouldn't have been fair, would it?"

"Of course not."

"But our own government is arresting them. When the Reds came here they did wrong to no one, but these have gone mad, there's no holding them in."

Swaying a little, Gregor rose and reached for his greatcoat hanging on the bedpost. He was only slightly drunk.

"Prokhor!" he shouted. "My sword and pistol!"

"Where are you going, Gregor Pantalievich?"

"That's not your business. Do as you're told."

Gregor belted on his sword and revolver, fastened and belted his greatcoat, and went straight to the prison on the square. The sentry on duty at the gate barred his way and asked for his pass.

"Stand aside, I tell you!"

"I can't let anyone in without a pass."

Before Gregor had succeeded in pulling his sword half out of its scabbard, the sentry had fled through the door. With hand still on his sword-hilt, Gregor followed him into the corridor.

"I want the commander of the prison," he shouted. His face was pale, his brows knitted. Some limping little Cossack came running to him, a clerk peeped out of the office. A moment later the commander appeared, sleepy and angry.

"You know that without a pass . . ." he thundered, but, recognizing Gregor and staring into his face, he stammered:

"So it's you . . . Comrade Melekhov? What do you want?"

"The keys to the cells."

"To the cells?"

"Well, have I got to say it a dozen times? Give me the keys, you cur!" Gregor strode towards the man, and he fell back. But he replied firmly enough:

"I won't give you the keys. I have no right."

"Right!" Gregor grated his teeth and drew his sword. In his hand it described a whistling circle under the low ceiling of the corridor. The clerk and the warder flew like frightened sparrows, and the commander pressed against the wall, his face whiter than the whitewash, and hissed through his teeth:

"There they are . . . but I shall make a complaint."

"I'll give you good cause for complaint! You're too used to the rear. Brave fellows, arresting women and old men! I'll shake up the lot of you! Ride off to the front, you serpent, or I'll cut you down where you stand." Gregor thrust his sword into its scabbard and struck the terrified commander with his fist, driving him with his knee and fist towards the outer door and roaring:

"To the front! Go on! Go on! Damn you . . . you rear lice!"

He thrust the man outside and, hearing an uproar in the inner yard of the prison, ran that way. At the entrance to the kitchen stood three warders. One of them held a rusty Japanese rifle and was shouting hurriedly:

"An attack is being made on the prison. We must drive him off. That's the old law."

Gregor pulled out his pistol, and the warders ran headlong into the kitchen.

"Come out, all of you. And go home!" Gregor roared, throwing open the doors of the crowded cells. He released all the prisoners, some hundred persons all together, forcibly dragged out those who were afraid to go, drove them into the street, and locked up the empty cells.

A crowd began to gather outside the prison gates. The released prisoners poured into the square and hurried home. The Cossacks of the guard ran out of the staff headquarters across the square to the prison, Kudynov accompanying them.

Gregor was the last to leave the empty prison. As he passed through the crowd he swore at the inquisitive women, and with hunched shoulders walked slowly to meet Kudynov. The Cossack guard running across the square recognized and greeted him. He shouted to them:

"Go back to your quarters, boys! What are you running for? Quick march!"

"We heard there was a mutiny in the prison, Comrade Melekhov."

"It's a false alarm," he replied.

The Cossacks turned and went back, laughing and talking. Kudynov hurriedly approached Gregor, stroking his long hair as he came.

"Hello, Melekhov! What's up?" he exclaimed.

"Your health, Kudynov! I've just broken into your prison."

"On what grounds? What game are you playing?"

"I've let them all out. What are you staring at? On what grounds have you been arresting women and old men? What game are you playing?"

"Don't you dare to take your own line. You're behaving high-handedly."

"I'll behave high-handedly with your body! I'll bring my regiment straight back from Kargin, and then you'll see a high hand!" Gregor suddenly seized Kudynov by his Caucasian leather belt and, stuttering with cold fury, whispered:

"If you'd like me to, I'll open the front at once. If you want it I'll part your soul from your body on the spot." He ground his teeth and released his hold of the quietly smiling Kudynov. Adjusting his belt, Kudynov took Gregor by the arm.

"Come along to my room. What are you boiling over like that for? You should see what you look like—a very devil! We've been wanting to see you here. As for the prison, that's nothing. You've let them out, but there's no harm done by that. I'll tell the lads to be less obstreperous in arresting the women whose husbands are with the Reds. But why are you undermining our authority here? Ah, Gregor, you're a headstrong lad. You could have come to us and said: 'The prisoners ought to be released,' and so on. We'd have looked through the lists and set some of them free. But you let them all go. It's a good job we keep the important criminals separate, for if you'd released them . . ." He clapped Gregor on the shoulder and laughed.

Gregor pulled his arm out of Kudynov's grip and halted outside the staff headquarters.

"You've all grown very brave here, behind our backs. Filled the prison with people! You might show your abilities out there at the front."

"I've shown them no worse than you in my time. And I would now. Come and take my place, and I'll take over your division."

"No, thank you."

"Ah, that's just it."

"But we're wasting a lot of time talking about nothing. I'm going home to get a rest. I've been unwell. And I've been wounded in the shoulder."

"What have you been unwell with?"

"Yearning." Gregor smiled wryly.

"No, but joking apart, what's the matter with you? We've got a doctor prisoner here; he was with the sailors at Shumilinsk. He might have a look at you."

"He can go to the devil!"

"Well then, go home and rest. Whom have you put in charge of the division?"

"Ryabchikov."

"But wait a moment. What's the hurry? Tell me what's been happening at the front. We heard yesterday that single-handed you'd been killing sailors without number at Klimovsky. Is that true?"

"Good-bye!" Gregor strode away, but when a little way off, he turned round and shouted: "If I hear that you've started arresting again . . ."

The day was declining. A chilly wind crept up from the Don. A flock of teal flew over Gregor's head with a whistle of wings. As he was entering the yard where the horses were stabled, the sound of gunfire came to his ears from the upper reaches of the river.

Chapter 12

In Tatarsk Gregor found life empty and dreary without the other Cossacks. Rarely were any of them able to get back to the village on furlough. Only once, at Eastertime, half the Tatarsk infantry company turned up in the village. They spent a day there, changed their clothes, collected dripping, dry toast, and other eatables, and then crossed the Don like a crowd of pilgrims, but with rifles instead of staves, and marched off in the direction of Yelanska district. From the hill above Tatarsk their wives, mothers, and sisters watched them depart. The women howled with weeping, wiping their eyes with the ends of their kerchiefs and shawls and blowing their noses into the hems of their skirts. Along the farther bank of the Don, over the sandy dunes marched the Cossacks: Christonia, Anikushka, Pantaleimon Prokoffievich, Stepan Astakhov, and others. The linen bags containing their victuals hung from their fixed bayonets, their mournful songs were carried away by the wind, and they talked languidly among themselves. Most of them marched dispiritedly, but they were clean and their stomachs were full. Before the holiday their wives and mothers had heated water and washed away the dirt ground into their bodies and had combed the blood-swollen lice out of their heads. Among them were boys of sixteen and seventeen, freshly mobilized into the ranks of the insurgents, throwing out their legs bravely over the warm sand, for some unaccountable reason talking and singing gaily. For them war was a novelty, like a new game. During their first days of fighting they would raise their heads from the harsh earth to listen to the bullets whistling over their heads. "Greenhorns" the front-line Cossacks contemptuously called them as they taught them to dig trenches, to shoot, to carry their equipment on the march, and even the art of delousing themselves and of wrapping their feet in rags so that they should not get tired so quickly in their heavy boots. But meantime the lad would stare out on the world around him with astonished, birdlike eyes, raising his head and gazing out of his trench, afire with curiosity, trying to see the Reds while the Reds' bullets whistled past him. If death was his portion, the sixteen-year-old "soldier" would stretch himself out and lie like a great child with boyishly round arms, and he would be carried back to his native village to be buried in the grave where his for-bears were rotting. His mother would meet him, wringing her hands and crying aloud over the dead, tearing the grey hair from her head. And when the body was buried and the clay on the mound was drying, the aged, bowed mother would carry her unquenchable sorrow to the church, there to "remember" her dead son.

But if the bullet had not inflicted a mortal wound, then only would the lad begin to realize the merciless nature of war. His lips would tremble and writhe. The "soldier" would cry out in a childish voice: "Oh, Mother, Mother!" and little tears would roll from his eyes. The ambulance cart would shake him up over the trackless fields, the company medical officer would wash the wound and laughingly comfort him as if he were a child: "Now, Vania, don't behave like a cry-baby!" But the "soldier" Vania would weep, would ask to go home, call for his mother. If he recovered and returned to his company, then indeed he was beginning to have a thorough understanding of war. Another week or two of battles, of bayonet-fighting, and then see him stand in front of a captive Red soldier and, with feet set wide apart, spitting like any brutal sergeant-major, hear him hiss through his teeth:

"Well, peasant, so you're caught, you bastard! So you wanted the land? Wanted equality? I expect you're a Communak. Tell us, you snake!" In his anxiety to show his daring and "Cossack" frenzy he would raise his rifle and club the man who had come to his death on the Don lands, fighting for the Soviet government, for Communism, for the abolition of war from the earth.

And somewhere in Moscow or Vyatka province, in some lonely village of the enormous Soviet Republic, a mother would receive the report that her son had "fallen in the struggle against the White Guards for the emancipation of the toiling people from the yoke of the landowners and capitalists." She would read it again and again, tears running down her cheeks. Her motherly heart would be consumed with a burning grief, and every day until she died she would remember him whom she had carried in her womb, whom she had borne in blood and woman's agony, him who had fallen under an enemy's hand somewhere in the unknown Don region.

The half-company of Tatarsk infantry marched over the sandy

dunes, through the ruddy willows. The youngsters marched gaily, thoughtlessly; the older men with sighs, with secret, hidden tears. It was time to plough, to harrow, to sow; the earth called them, called incessantly day and night, and they had to go and fight, to perish in strange villages from enforced inactivity, from fear, need, and yearning. The soldier remembered his tiny husbandry, his implements and livestock. Everything was in need of a man's hand, everything wept without the master's overseeing. What could a woman do? The earth would dry out, the seed would not sprout, there was the danger of famine next year.

So the older men marched silently over the sand. They grew animated only when one of the youngsters sent a bullet after a hare. For such a waste of a good bullet the elder men decided to punish the offender. Their anger was poured out on him.

"Forty strokes for him," Pantaleimon suggested.

"Too many. He won't reach the front after that."

"Sixteen," Christonia roared.

On sixteen they decided. They stretched the offender out on the sand and drew down his trousers. With his clasp-knife Christonia cut switches covered with fluffy yellow catkins from the pussy-willows, and Anikushka laid on. The others sat around, smoking. Then they marched on again. Behind them dragged the sufferer, wiping away his tears and holding his trousers clear of his flesh.

As soon as they had reached the end of the sandy waste and came out on black earth, passing ploughed land, each of the Cossacks bent down, picked up a clod of the dry, sun-baked earth in his hand, crumbled it between his palms, and sighed:

"The earth is ready."

"Three days more and it won't be possible to sow."

"It's a little early on this side of the Don."

"Yes, it's early all right. Look, you can see the snow still lying on the hills."

They halted for the midday rest. Pantaleimon Prokoffievich treated the punished lad to some sour milk. He had carried it in a linen bag tied to his rifle-barrel, and water had leaked from the bag all along the road. As he offered the milk he said:

"Don't you be angry with your elders, you young fool. They've whipped you, but there's no woe in that."

"If they'd laid the blows on you, Daddy Pantaleimon, you'd be talking in a different tone."

"I've had much worse than that, my lad. My father once struck me on the back with a cart shaft."

"A cart shaft?"

"I said a cart shaft, didn't I? Eat up that milk! What are you gaping at me like that for? They didn't give you enough this morning."

The morning after Gregor's arrival in Tatarsk he went with Natalia to visit old Grishaka and his mother-in-law. Lukinichna greeted them with tears:

"Grisha, my son! We shall be lost without our Miron, peace to his soul. Who will work our fields for us? The granaries are filled with seed, but there's no one to sow it. We're left orphans, nobody wants us, we're strangers to everybody, unwanted. . . . Look how our farm is going to rack and ruin. Not a hand is raised to repair it."

In very deed the farm was rapidly decaying. The fences around the yards were overthrown, the mud wall of the shed had been eaten away by the spring water and was crumbling, the threshing-floor was unfenced, the yard littered and dirty, rusty and broken farm machinery lay by the shed. Everywhere were the signs of desolation and decay.

"Things have gone to pieces quickly without the master," Gregor thought unconcernedly as he went round the farmyard. He returned to the hut and found Natalia whispering to her mother. But as he appeared she lapsed into silence and broke into a wheedling smile.

"Mamma's just been asking, Gregor . . ." she said. "You were going out to the fields tomorrow. You might sow an acre or so for her."

"But what do you want anything sown for?" he asked. "Your bins are crammed with wheat."

Lukinichna clapped her hands. "But, Grisha, what about the earth?" she asked. "Our dead Miron ploughed up a lot of land."

"Well, what of it? It'll lie, won't it? If we're alive this autumn we'll sow it."

But Lukinichna stuck to her guns, grew cross with him, and at last pursed up her trembling lips:

"Very well, if you haven't got time. . . . But there's no one to help us."

"Oh, all right! I'm going tomorrow to sow for ourselves, and I'll sow a couple of acres for you. That should be enough. Grishaka's alive and well, isn't he?"

"Thank you, thank you." Lukinichna brightened up at once. "I'll tell Aggripina to bring the seed along to you today. Grand-dad? The Lord hasn't yet taken him to Himself. He's alive, but he's gone a little funny in his head. He sits at home all the time and reads the Holy Scriptures all night. Sometimes he talks and talks, but it's all meaningless, church language. You might go and see him; he's in his room."

"I looked in just now," Natalia said, a tear rolling down her cheek. But she added with a smile: "He said to me: 'You saucy baggage, why don't you ever come and see me? I shall be dead soon, my dear. I'll put in a word to God for you and my little grandchildren. I'm pining for the earth, Natalia. The earth is calling me. It's high time!' "

Gregor went in to see the old man. The smell of incense, of must and decay, the smell of an aged, slovenly man filled his nostrils. Grishaka was still wearing his old grey tunic, his trousers were in good order, his woollen socks darned. Since Natalia's marriage the care of the old man had passed to his second granddaughter, Aggripina, and she looked after him with the same love and attention that Natalia had formerly shown. He was holding a Bible on his knees. He looked up at Gregor from under his spectacles, opened his mouth, and showed his teeth in a smile.

"Still whole, then, soldier?" he said. "So the Lord has defended you from the bullets. Well, praise be! Sit down."

"So you're still well, Grand-dad?"

"Eh?"

"I say you're still well?"

"You're a queer lad, a queer lad. How can I be well at my age? I'm nearly a hundred now. Yes, nearly a hundred. And it seems only yesterday that I was walking with red hair, young and well. And as if I'd woke up today to find myself all decay. Life's flown by like a summer's day. My coffin's been lying in the shed these many years, but it seems the Lord's forgotten me. Sometimes I pray: 'Lord, turn Your merciful glance on me, Your Grishaka.' "

"You'll live a long time yet, old man. Your mouth is full of teeth."

"Teeth! You're a queer lad!" Grishaka grew cross. "You won't keep your soul in with your teeth when it makes ready to leave the body. So you're still fighting?"

"Yes, still fighting."

"That's what I said. But what are you fighting about? You don't know, yourselves. But it's all working out according to the divine command. Our earth is doomed to death. We've gone contrary to God, the people have risen against the authorities. And all government is from God. Even if it's the government of Antichrist, it's God-given all the same. I told Miron: 'Miron, don't make the Cossacks rise, don't talk against the government, don't drive the people on to sin.' But he said: 'No, Father, I can't stand it. We must rise, we must destroy this government; it's ruining us. We used to live like men, but now we're a lot of old men.' But he'd forgotten that 'they who take the sword shall perish by the sword.' And it's true. The people say you've been made a general and command a division, Grishka. Is that right?"

"Yes."

"But where are your epaulets?"

"We don't have them now."

"Don't have them now! What sort of general are you, then? In the old days it was a treat to look at the generals: they were well fed, big-bellied, and looked important. But you now—look at you! Your greatcoat's all muddy, you've got no epaulets, no white cords across your chest. You're nothing but lice, eaten up with lice."

Gregor burst into a roar of laughter. But Grishaka continued bitterly:

"Don't you laugh, you scum! You're leading men to their death, you've raised them against the government. It's a great sin you've committed; all the same, they'll destroy you, and us with you. God will show you His will. The Bible tells us all about these troublous times of ours. Listen and I'll read you the testimony of the prophet Jeremiah."

The old man turned over the yellow pages of his Bible with his yellow fingers and began to read, slowly enunciating each syllable:

" 'Declare ye among the nations, and publish, and set up a standard; publish, and conceal not; say, Babylon is taken, Bel is confounded, Merodach is broken in pieces; her idols are confounded, her images are broken in pieces.

" 'For out of the north there cometh up a nation against her, which shall make her land desolate, and none shall dwell therein; they shall remove, they shall depart, both man and beast.'

"Do you understand, Grisha? From the north they are coming and binding us Babylonians and removing us. Listen to this:

" 'In those days, and in that time, saith the Lord, the children of Israel shall come, they and the children of Judah together, going and weeping; they shall go and seek the Lord their God.

" 'My people hath been lost sheep; their shepherds have caused them to go astray, they have turned them away on the mountains: they have gone from mountain to hill, they have forgotten their resting-place.' "

"But what are you getting at? How are we to take all that?" Gregor asked, only half understanding the archaic language.

"This, you scum, that you troublers of the people run to the hills. And then you're not shepherds to the Cossacks, but worse than the silly sheep themselves. You don't understand what you are doing. Listen to this: 'All that found them have devoured them.' There it is! Aren't the lice devouring us now?"

"There's no getting away from the lice!" Gregor admitted.

"So it fits perfectly. And it goes on: 'And their adversaries said: We offend not, because they have sinned against the Lord, the habitation of justice, even the Lord, the hope of their fathers.

" 'Remove out of the midst of Babylon, and go forth out of the land of the Chaldeans, and be as the he-goats before the flocks.

" 'For, lo, I will raise and cause to come up against Babylon an assembly of great nations from the north country; and they shall set themselves in array against her; from thence she shall be taken; their arrows shall be as of a mighty expert man; none shall return in vain.

" 'And Chaldea shall be a spoil; all that spoil her shall be satisfied, saith the Lord. Because ye were glad, because ye rejoiced, O ye destroyers of mine heritage. . . .' "

"Daddy Grishaka! You might explain it all to me in simple language. I don't understand it at all," Gregor interrupted. But the old man chewed his lips, stared at him with an absent gaze, and replied:

"I'll be finished in a minute. Listen! '. . . because ye are grown fat as the heifer at grass, and bellow as bulls. Your mother shall be sore confounded; she that bare you shall be ashamed: behold, the hindermost of the nations shall be a wilderness, a dry land, and a desert. Because of the wrath of the Lord it shall not be inhabited, but it shall be wholly desolate; everyone that goeth by Babylon shall be astonished, and hiss at all her plagues.' "

"What does it all mean?" Gregor pleaded again, beginning to feel a little irritated.

The old man did not reply, but closed the Bible and lay down on the stove. "And everybody's like that," Gregor thought as he went out of the room. "When they're young, they have a good time, drink their vodka, and sin like the rest. But when they're old, the more they raged in their youth, the more they seek to save themselves from God. Here's Grishaka with teeth like a wolf's. They say that when he used to come home from service all the women in the village wept because of him, all fell before him. And now . . . If I live to old age I shan't be like that. I'm no Bible-thumper."

As he and Natalia returned home from their visit Gregor pondered on his talk with the old man, and the mysterious, incomprehensible "prophesyings" of the Bible. Natalia also walked along without speaking. She had been unusually cold to her husband on his arrival this time, and evidently stories of his conduct with the women of Kargin district had reached her ears. On the evening of his return she had made his bed for him in the best room, but had herself slept on the chest, covering herself with a sheepskin. She uttered not a word of reproach and asked him no questions. And Gregor had not said anything that night, deciding that it was better for the time being not to ask her why she was so unusually chilly in her welcome.

They walked silently along the deserted street, feeling more alien to each other than ever before. From the south a warm, gracious wind was blowing, and white clouds were gathered in the west. Distant thunder rolled faintly, and the village was scented with the blessed, vital perfume of opening buds and the moist black earth. White-maned waves coursed over the blue sweep of the Don. The lower edge of the ploughed land lying in a velvety black pall along the slope of the hill was steaming, and wisps of mist went floating over the Donside hills. A skylark was singing drunkenly right over the road, and marmots were whistling. Above all this earth, breathing with great fruitfulness and an abundance of life-giving forces, hung a proud and lofty sun.

In the middle of the village, close to a little bridge over a gully burbling with flood water, Natalia halted. She bent as if to tie up her shoelace, but in reality to hide her face from Gregor, and asked him:

"Why don't you speak?"

"Well, what is there to talk about?"

"There's plenty to talk about. You might tell me how you tippled in Kargin, and how you ran after whores. . . ."

"But you know already. . . ." He pulled out his tobacco-pouch and began to roll a cigarette. He puffed at it once or twice, then asked in his turn:

"So you've heard about it? Who told you?"

"As I can talk about it, of course I know. All the village knows, so there's plenty to hear it from."

"Well, if you know, what is there to tell you?"

He walked on with great strides. The sound of his footfalls and Natalia's more frequent steps rang out clearly in the transparent spring silence. She walked on for a moment without speaking, wiping away her tears. Then, choking down her sobs and clutching his arm, she asked:

"So you're starting your old tricks?"

"Shut up, Natalia!"

"You accursed, never satisfied hound! What are you torturing me again for?"

"You should listen less to other people's lies."

"But you've just admitted it yourself."

"It's clear they've told you more lies than truth. I am a little to blame. . . . Life itself is to blame, Natalia. All the time you're living on the edge of death, and sometimes you crawl across the furrow. . . ."

"How about your children? Aren't you ashamed to look them in the face?"

"Ha! Ashamed!" Gregor bared his teeth in a smile and added: "I've forgotten how to be ashamed. How can you feel shame when all your life's messed up? There you are killing people. You don't know what all the mess is about. . . . But how am I to tell you? You'll never understand. It's only your woman's cruelty that's speaking in you, and you'll never believe that my heart is gnawing me. . . . And I turned to vodka. The other day I went off into a fit. . . . For a moment my heart stopped beating and my body turned cold. . . ." His face darkened and the words came with difficulty. "It's hard for me, and anything to forget it: vodka or women. Wait! Let me finish. Something here is sucking and sucking at me, drawing all the time. Life's taken a false turn, and maybe I'm at fault in that too. . . . We ought to make our peace with the Reds and attack the Cadets. But how? Who will bring us into touch with the Soviets? How are we to strike an account for our common injuries? Half the Cossacks are beyond the Donietz, and those who're left behind have gone mad. . . . Everything is mixed up in my head, Natalia. Your grand-dad, Grishaka, read the Bible to me and said we hadn't done right, we shouldn't have risen. He cursed your father."

"Grand-dad's not right in the head. It's your affair now."

"That's the only way you can judge. You can't get to see anyone else's point of view."

"Oh, you needn't try to talk me over. You've done me wrong, and you've admitted it. But now you're trying to put everything on to the war. You're all of you the same. It's no little sorrow I've had through you, you devil. It's a pity I didn't finish myself off that time. . . ."

"There's no point in our talking any more about it. If it's hard for you, cry; tears always ease a woman's pain. But I can't be a comforter to you now. I've dabbled so much in men's blood that I've got no pity left for anyone. The war's dried it all out of me. I've grown hard. . . . Look into my soul and you'll find a blackness like an empty well. . . ."

They had almost reached the hut when a stinging slanting rain began to fall. It laid the dust on the roads, rattled on the roofs, and was refreshingly cool. Gregor unfastened his greatcoat and covered the weeping Natalia with it, putting his arm around her. So they went into the yard, pressed close together, covered by one greatcoat.

In the evening he got the plough and the sower ready in the yard. Siemion the smith's fifteen-year-old son, who had learned his

father's trade and was the only smith left in Tatarsk, fastened the
share to the old plough. The bullocks had come well through the
winter, for the hay left them by Pantaleimon had been ample for
their needs.

Next morning Gregor made ready to drive out into the steppe.
Ilinichna and Dunia had been up betimes to light the fire and prepare food by dawn. He thought to spend five days at work, sowing
for themselves and his mother-in-law, ploughing four acres for
melons and sunflowers. Then he would recall his father from the
infantry company to finish the sowing.

The lilac smoke ascended in a spiral from the chimney. Dunia
ran about the yard collecting brushwood for the fire. Gregor stared
at her shapely waist, at the swelling breasts, and thought sadly and
vexedly: "How the time has slipped by! It flies past like a mettle-
some horse. It was only the other day that Dunia was a snivelling
girl, with her pigtails dancing over her back as she ran, and now
she's ready for a husband. And I'm going grey-haired. Old Grishaka
was right: 'life has passed like a summer's day.' And such a little
while is man allotted to live, yet we must shorten it still more."

Daria came up to him. She had recovered very quickly from the
loss of Piotra. For a little while she had mourned, going yellow
with grief and seeming to age. But as soon as the spring breezes
began to blow and the sun to warm the earth, her grief had passed
with the melting snows. The blush was reddening her cheeks again,
her eyes glittered, and her former easy, swinging walk had returned.
Her old habits had returned also: she was painting her eyebrows
again, her cheeks shone with cream, she had recovered her love of
joking, of teasing Natalia, and her lips were parted in a smile.
Triumphant life had recovered command.

She came up to Gregor, smiling. The scent of cucumber cream
came from her face.

"Can I give you a hand, Gregor?" she asked.

"What with?"

"Ah, Grishka, why have you grown so stern with me, a widow?
You never even smile."

"You might go and give Natalia a hand. There's Misha all dirty
with running through the mud."

"And is that my job? You to give them birth, and I to wash them for you? No, thank you. Your Natalia's as fruitful as a rabbit. She'll be giving you ten more before she's finished. And I'd get tired with washing them all."

"Enough, enough! Off with you!"

"Gregor Pantalievich, you're the only Cossack left in the village at the moment. Don't drive me away; let me look at your attractive black whiskers from a distance at least."

Gregor laughed and tossed his hair back from his forehead. "I don't know how Piotra managed to live with you. . . ."

"You needn't be afraid," she replied and, glancing at him with her consuming, half-closed eyes, with feigned alarm she looked behind her at the hut. "Supposing Natalia was to come out now! How jealous she is of you! I took one little peep at you today, and her face completely changed. The young women were saying to me yesterday: 'What sort of law is this? There are no Cossacks left in the village, and Gregor's returned and won't leave his wife's side. How are we to live? Even if he is wounded, even if there's only half of him left, we'd be glad to have our pleasure of that half. Tell him not to go into the village at night or we'll catch him and he'll suffer for it.' I told them: 'No, my girls; our Gregor only plays about in other villages, but when he's at home he clings to Natalia's petticoat and won't leave her.'"

"You are a bitch!" Gregor remarked, laughing with amusement.

"I am what I am. But your lawfully wedded Natalia, the unde-filed, she gave you a good talking-to yesterday, and you won't be going beyond the law!"

"Don't meddle in other people's affairs, Daria!"

"I'm not. I only meant to say that your Natalia's a fool. Her husband comes home, and she goes for him, weeps, and lies down on the chest like a penny piece of gingerbread. I wouldn't deny myself a Cossack if I got the chance; I'd put even a brave fellow like you to fear. . . ." She grated her teeth, laughed aloud, and went off to the hut, looking back and laughing at the embarrassed Gregor.

"You were happy in dying when you did, brother Piotra," Gregor thought. "That Daria's not a woman but a she-devil, she'd have been the cause of his death in any case sooner or later."

Chapter 13

The last lights had been extinguished in Bakhmutkin village. A fine frost was sheeting the puddles with a thin shroud of ice. Somewhere in the fields beyond the village belated cranes had settled, and the north-east wind brought their quiet, weary chatter to the ears of the inhabitants, emphasizing the placid silence of the April night. In a yard a cow lowed, then was quiet. Snipes called yearningly as they flew through the darkness, and there was a whistling of innumerable wings from a flight of ducks hastening to the free expanse of the flooded Don.

On the outskirts of the village there was a sudden outbreak of human voices, the snort of horses, and the scrunch of frozen mud under their hoofs. A patrol of the two squadrons of the sixth special brigade quartered in the village rode into the main street. With talk and song they scattered among the yards, tying their horses to overturned sledges and putting down fodder for them.

The sound of their voices floated out to the Cossacks posted on guard beyond the windmill. It was dreary lying at night on the cold, frozen earth. No smoking or talking for the guard, nor even the attempt to warm themselves by clapping their hands together. They lay among the stalks of last year's sunflowers, staring into the yawning darkness of the steppe, listening with ears set to the earth. Ten paces away nothing was visible, and the April night was so rich in rustles and suspicious noises that any one of them might be caused by a Red Army soldier crawling towards them. With his glove one young Cossack wiped away a tear caused by straining his eyes in the darkness. He thought he heard the sound of a broken twig and a smothered panting a little way off. He jogged his neighbour with his elbow. The rustle of the brushwood and the heavy breathing grew more distinct and unexpectedly sounded right above the youngster. He rose on his elbow and, staring through the undergrowth, with difficulty made out the form of a great hedgehog which was hurrying along with nose to the ground on the track of a mouse. Suddenly it felt the presence of an enemy close to it, raised its head, and saw the man staring at it. The Cossack sighed with relief; "The devil! How it frightened me!" The hedgehog tucked in its head and for a moment became a prickly ball, then slowly unrolled and crawled away, knocking against the sunflower stalks. Again the silence descended.

In the village the second cock crowed. The sky cleared of clouds, and the first stars peered down through the thin veil of mist. Then the wind swept the mist away, and the sky gazed down on the earth with innumerable golden eyes.

Just then the young Cossack heard the distinct sound of a horse's hoofs and a jingle of metal in front of him, then, a moment later, the creaking of a saddle. The other Cossacks heard it also, and fingers were lightly set to rifle triggers. The silhouette of the rider emerged as though cut out against the background of the sky. He was riding at a walking pace in the direction of the village.

"Halt! Who goes there?"

The Cossacks jumped up, ready to open fire. The horseman halted and raised his hands above his head.

"Don't fire, comrades!" he cried.

"What's the password?" the officer in charge of the outpost shouted.

"Comrades—"

"What's the password? Troop . . ."

"Stop! I'm alone. I surrender."

"Wait a bit, brothers; don't fire! We'll take him alive."

The troop commander ran to the rider. The man swung his leg over the saddle and dismounted.

"Who are you? A Red? Yes, brothers, there's the star on his hat. You're finished. . . ."

"Conduct me to your commander," the horseman calmly replied. "I have to take a communication of great importance to him. I am Voronovsky, commander of the Serdobsky regiment, and I have come to negotiate with him."

"An officer! Kill him, brothers!"

"Comrades, kill me by all means, but first let me tell your commander what I have come for. I repeat that it is highly important. Take my weapons if you're afraid I shall run away." He began to unfasten his sword-belt.

The troop commander took his revolver and sword. "Search him!" he ordered, seating himself on the officer's horse.

After the search the troop commander and another Cossack drove the prisoner towards the village. He went on foot, the Cossack escort at his side and the troop commander riding his horse behind him. He stopped frequently to light cigarettes, and the scent of the good tobacco aroused his escort's cupidity.

"Give me one!" the Cossack asked.

The officer handed him his full cigarette-case. The Cossack took out a cigarette and thrust the case into his own pocket. The Red commander said nothing, but as they were leading him into the village, he asked:

"Where are you taking me?"

"You'll know soon enough!"

"But tell me!"

"To the company commander."

"Will you lead me to your brigade commander, Bogatiriev?"

"There isn't any such man here."

"There is. I know he arrived with his staff in Bakhmutkin yesterday."

"We don't know anything about that."

"Oh, enough of this, comrade! I know it, and you don't! It isn't a military secret, especially when it's known to your enemies!"

"Go on, go on!"

"I'm going on. So you'll lead me to Bogatiriev?"

"Silence! We're not allowed to talk to prisoners."

"But you are allowed to take my cigarette-case!"

"Get on and keep your tongue still or I'll put my bayonet through you."

They found the company commander asleep. He sat up rubbing his eyes and yawning, unable at first to take in what the troop commander was telling him. At last he said:

"Who do you say you are? The commander of the Serdobsky regiment? You're not lying? Where are your documents?"

A few minutes later he conducted the Red commander to the quarters of the brigade commander, Bogatiriev. As soon as he heard who had been captured, Bogatiriev jumped up as though possessed. He hurriedly buttoned up his trousers, lit a lamp, and asked the officer to sit down.

"How were you—how was it you were captured?" he asked.

"I came voluntarily. I want to talk to you alone. Order the others to go out."

Bogatiriev waved his hand, and the company commander and the gaping master of the house left the room. His face expressive of his curiosity, Bogatiriev sat down at a table. The officer Voronovsky smiled under his black moustache.

"Allow me first to say a word or two about myself," he said, "then I will tell you the mission on which I am come. I am a noble by birth, and was a staff captain in the Czar's service. During the German war I served at the front. In 1918 I was mobilized by decree of the Soviet government and am now in command of the Red Serdobsky regiment. For some time I have been waiting for an opportunity to come over to your—to the side of those fighting the Bolsheviks."

"You waited a long time, captain!"

"I know; but I wanted to wipe out my guilt to Russia by not only coming over myself, but bringing the Red soldiers under me as well (or rather, the most reliable of them), who had been deceived by the Communists and dragged into this fratricidal war."

Glancing at Bogatiriev and noticing his unbelieving smile, Voronovsky started like a girl and hurriedly continued:

"Naturally, you must feel a certain amount of distrust in me and my words. I should feel the same in your place. Let me prove to you by irrefutable facts . . ." He threw back his greatcoat and drew a penknife from his pocket, ripped the hem of his greatcoat with it, and drew out some yellow documents and a tiny photograph. Bogatiriev carefully examined the documents. One of them certified that the bearer was Lieutenant Voronovsky of the 117th Liubomirsky Regiment and was signed and sealed by the chief surgeon of a field hospital. The other documents and the photograph conclusively proved the truth of Voronovsky's statement.

"Well, and what next?" Bogatiriev asked.

"I have come to inform you that I and my assistant, the former Lieutenant Volkov, have been working among the Red Army men under our command, and the entire complement of the Serdobsky regiment, with the exception of course of the Communists, is ready at any moment to come over to your side. The men consist almost entirely of peasants from Saratov and Samara provinces. They are prepared to fight the Bolsheviks. We only need to come to an agreement with you on the conditions for the surrender of the regiment. At the present moment the regiment is stationed at Ust-Khopersk. It numbers about twelve hundred bayonets, and there are thirty-eight in the Communist nucleus, plus some thirty men who have formed a platoon of local Communists. We shall seize the battery attached to the regiment, but probably the battery complement will have to be wiped out, as the majority of them are Communists. My Red Army men are in a ferment because of the food requisitions which are taking place in their districts. We have utilized this circumstance to bring them over to the side of the Cossacks. But they are afraid that if they surrender they may be subjected to violence. And so, although it is a detail, I must come to an understanding with you on this point."

"What violence can there be?"

"Well, murder or pillaging. . . ."

"No, we shall not allow that."

"One other point: the soldiers insist that the Serdobsky regiment is to be maintained as a whole and is to be allowed to fight the Bolsheviks as a separate military unit side by side with you."

"It is not in my power to decide on that point."

"I understand. You must communicate with your higher command and will let us know?"

"Yes. I must inform the staff at Vieshenska."

"Excuse me, but I have very little time, and if my return is delayed my absence may be noticed by the regimental commissar. I think we shall be able to come to agreement on the terms of the surrender. Let me know the decision of your command as soon as possible. The regiment may be transferred to the Donietz front, or reinforcements may arrive, and then . . ."

"I shall send a courier to Vieshenska at once."

"One other thing. Order your Cossacks to return me my arms. They not only disarmed me"—he broke off and smiled with embarrassment—"but they took my cigarette-case! That of course is a detail, but it is of value to me as a family heirloom. . . ."

"Everything shall be returned to you. How are we to inform you of Vieshenska's answer?"

"In two days a woman will come to Bakhmutkin from Ust-Khopersk. The password—well let it be 'Union.' You can inform her.

Of course, under the conditions I have stated. . . ."

Within half an hour a Cossack courier was galloping to Vieshen-ska.

The next day Kudynov's personal orderly arrived in Bakhmutkin. He rode up to the brigade commander's quarters and, entering the hut without stopping to tie up his horse, handed Bogatiriev a packet marked: "Urgent and secret." Bogatiriev hurriedly tore open the envelope and read the letter, written in Kudynov's sprawling writing:

"The news is encouraging. I empower you to conduct negotiations with the Serdobsky regiment and at any cost to get them to surrender. I suggest we concede their requests and promise that we shall receive the regiment in its entirety and shall not even disarm them, on the indispensable condition that they capture and hand over the commissar of the regiment and the Communists, especially our own Vieshenska, Yelanska, and Ust-Khopersk Communists. Also the battery, baggage train, and regimental equipment must be captured. Hurry the matter as much as you can. When the regiment is ready to come over, bring up as large a force as possible, quietly surround them, and at once disarm them. If they try to resist, kill them to the very last man. Act cautiously but resolutely. As soon as they are disarmed, drive the entire regiment to Vieshenska along the right bank of the Don, so that they are far from the front and have to march through the open steppe. Then they will not be able to escape. We shall distribute them in twos and threes among different companies and shall see how they fight the Reds. Afterwards, if we succeed in uniting with our men on the Donietz, they can do as they like with them—if they hang them, to the last man, I shan't object. I rejoice in your success. Keep me informed by courier daily.

Kudynov"

In a postscript was written:

"If the Serdobsky regiment hands over our local Communists, drive them under a strong escort to Vieshenska through the Donside villages. Choose the most reliable Cossacks for the escort (the fiery and the older men), and tell them to inform the villagers in advance of their coming. There's no point in our soiling our hands with

*them; the women will settle them with pikes if the escort does the
job properly. That will be the wisest policy for us. If we were to
shoot them and the Reds heard of it, they might shoot their prisoners. And it's simpler to let the people loose on them, to unleash
the people's anger like a bloodhound. Lynching, and no questions
asked, or answers received!"*

Chapter 14

Late in April the 1st Moscow Regiment was seriously defeated in
a battle with the insurgents. Not knowing the locality, the Red
lines fought their way into Antonovsky village, only to find themselves floundering in a sea of mud. While, driven on by the stubborn orders of their commanding officer, they were struggling to
make their way through, two companies of mounted Cossacks en-
circled them and, after losing almost a third of its complement,
the regiment had to retire.

During the battle Ivan Alexievich was wounded in the foot.
Mishka Koshevoi carried him out of the fight and compelled the
driver of an ammunition wagon to give him a lift.

The regiment was driven back as far as Yelanska village. The
defeat had disastrous results on the entire advance of the Red
detachments in the area. A general retreat set in, and the 1st Moscow Regiment, finding itself cut off by the breaking of the ice at
the mouth of the Khoper River, crossed the Don to the right bank
and halted at Ust-Khopersk, there to await reinforcements. Shortly
after their arrival they were joined by the Serdobsky regiment. The
Serdobsky men were very different from those of the 1st Moscow
Regiment. The workers of Moscow, Tula, and Nizhnii-Novgorod,
who formed the main and militant body of the Moscow regiment,
fought fiercely, stubbornly, frequently engaging in hand-to-hand
struggles with the enemy, and continually losing men killed and
wounded. Even after their defeat in Antonovsky village they had
retired without losing one ammunition wagon. But the men of the

Serdobsky regiment had been hurriedly enrolled at Serdobsk, in Saratov province, and consisted chiefly of elderly peasants, most of them illiterate and many of them drawn from rich families. The men in command were mainly former Imperial Army officers, the Red commissar was spineless and had no authority over the soldiers, and the commanding officer Voronovsky and others were carrying on a secret agitation to demoralize their men and to persuade them to surrender the regiment to the Cossacks.

On the arrival of the Serdobsky regiment Stockman, Ivan, and Mishka were transferred to the new regiment and were quartered in the same hut as three Serdobsky men. Stockman anxiously noted the sullen spirit of his new companions and, after one sharp conflict with them, he came to the conclusion that a serious danger threatened the regiment. Two Serdobsky men entered the hut one evening and, without a word of greeting to Stockman or Ivan, remarked:

"We've had enough of fighting. They're seizing our families' grain at home, and here we have to fight for we don't know what."

"So you don't know what you're fighting for?" Stockman queried.

"No, we don't! The Cossacks are farmers just like us. And we know why they rebelled. Oh, yes, we know!"

Stockman's customary restraint failed him for once. "And do you know what language you are talking now, you swine?" he exclaimed. "White Guards' language!"

"Not so much of your 'swine,' or we'll give you one! Did you hear him, boys?"

"Quieter, quieter, long-beard! We've seen the likes of you before," a second intervened. "Do you think that because you're a Communist you can seize us by the throat? You look out or we'll plug you full of holes." He came across to Stockman.

"You're talking like counter-revolutionaries. We shall try you as traitors to the Soviet régime," Stockman panted, pushing the man off.

"You won't send all the regiment to the Tribunal," one of the Serdobsky men replied. "The Communists get sugar and cigarettes, and we get nothing."

"That's a lie!" Ivan Alexievich shouted, raising himself on the bed. "We get the same as you."

Without another word Stockman put on his greatcoat and went

out. They made no attempt to stop him, but jeered as he went. He found the commissar of the regiment in the staff headquarters. Calling him into another room, he informed him of his quarrel with the Serdobsky men and proposed their arrest. The commissar listened to him, scratching his beard and irresolutely adjusting his horn-rimmed spectacles.

"We'll call a meeting of the Communist nucleus tomorrow to discuss the position. But I don't think it's possible to arrest them in the present situation."

"Why not?" Stockman asked sharply.

"Well, you know, Comrade Stockman—I've noticed myself that there's something wrong in the regiment. Probably there's some form of counter-revolutionary organization at work, only I can't discover it. But the majority of the regiment is under its influence. They're peasant elements, and what are you to do? I've informed the divisional staff of the state of things and have suggested that they should withdraw the regiment and re-form it."

"But if you noticed the attitude of the majority, why didn't you inform the Political Department long since?"

"I tell you I have. But they're slow in replying. As soon as the regiment's withdrawn we shall punish severely all those who have violated discipline." He added with a frown: "I have my suspicions of Voronovsky and the chief of staff, Volkov. After the meeting of the nucleus tomorrow I shall ride to Ust-Miedviedietz to discuss the position with the Political Department. We must take urgent steps to localize the danger."

"But why not call a meeting of the nucleus at once? Time won't wait for us, comrade!"

"I know that, but it isn't possible at the moment. The majority of the Communists are on outpost duty. I insisted on that, as I thought it risky to trust any non-party elements in such a situation. And, besides, the battery, which is manned chiefly by Communists, will only arrive tonight. I summoned it here in connection with this trouble in the regiment. . . ."

Stockman returned from the staff to his hut and told Ivan and Mishka the outlines of his talk with the commissar. After the others had gone to bed he sat up writing a detailed statement of the position in the regiment, and at midnight awoke Mishka. Giving him the letter he had written, he said:

"Get a horse from somewhere at once and ride to Ust-Miedviedietz with this letter. At all costs, even of your own life, you must hand it in at the Political Department of the Fourteenth Division. How long will it take you to get there? Where will you find a horse?"

As he drew on his boots Mishka replied:

"I'll steal a horse from the mounted patrol, and I shall be at Ust-Miedviedietz in two hours at the most. The horses are a poor lot or I'd do it in less. I know which horse to take." He took the letter and slipped it into the pocket of his greatcoat.

"Why put it there?" Stockman asked in surprise.

"I can get at it easier if I'm caught," Mishka replied.

"Yes, but—" Stockman doubtfully began.

"If they catch me I can get at it and eat it."

"Brave lad!" Stockman smiled faintly and, as though overcome by a mournful presentiment, he put his arms around Mishka and embraced him, kissing him with cold, quivering lips. "Off with you!" he said.

Mishka went out, successfully untied one of the best horses of the patrol, and rode cautiously through the village and past the outpost, his forefinger against the trigger of his rifle. Only when he came out on the highroad did he sling the rifle across his shoulder and set to work to extract the last ounce of speed from his little Saratov horse.

At dawn a fine rain began to fall. The wind howled, and heavy storm-clouds drove up from the east. As soon as morning came, the Serdobsky men quartered with Stockman rose and went out. Half an hour later a Yelanska Communist named Tolkachev, attached, like Stockman and Ivan, to the Serdobsky regiment, flung open the door of the hut and panted:

"Stockman, Koshevoi, are you here? Come out!"

"What's the matter? Come in here!" Stockman called, picking up and hurriedly putting on his greatcoat.

"There's trouble in the regiment," Tolkachev muttered as he followed Stockman. "The infantry attempted to disarm the battery as it drove up just now. They started shooting, but the gunners drove off the attack, removed the gunlocks, and crossed by boat to the other side of the river. There's a meeting going on by the church now. . . . All the regiment. . . ."

"Get dressed! Quickly!" Stockman ordered Ivan Alexievich. He seized Tolkachev by his sleeve. "Where's the commissar? Where are the rest of the Communists?" he demanded.

"I don't know. Some of them have fled, but I came along to you. The telegraph office has been occupied, and no one is allowed in. We must clear out. But how?" The man dropped helplessly on a bed, his hands between his knees.

At that moment there was the sound of steps in the porch, and six Serdobsky men ran into the hut. Their faces were flushed and harsh with evil determination.

"All Communists to the meeting! Hurry up!" they shouted.

Stockman exchanged a glance with Ivan and compressed his lips. "We're coming," he replied.

"Leave your arms behind. You're not going into a battle," one of the men suggested. But Stockman slung his rifle across his shoulder as though he had not heard, and was the first to go out.

Eleven hundred throats were roaring in the square. Stockman went towards the crowd, his eyes seeking for members of the regimental command. Past him went the commissar, his arms held by two Red Army men, while another thrust him on from behind. His face deathly pale, the commissar pushed through the crowd. A minute or two later Stockman saw him mount a table in the middle of the mob. Stockman looked round: behind him was Ivan Alexievich, at his side were the men who had come to fetch him to the meeting.

"Comrades of the Red Army!" The commissar's words sounded faintly amid the roar of voices. "To hold meetings at such a time as this, when the enemy is so near . . . comrades . . ."

He was not allowed to continue. Around the table the grey Red Army caps shook as though rocked in the wind, fists were stretched out towards him, and shouts arose:

"So we're comrades now!"

"Pull the leather-jacket down!"

"Kill him! Bayonet him! We've had enough of his commissaring."

Stockman saw a huge, elderly Red Army man clamber on to the table and seize the commissar's little beard. The table rocked, and the man and the commissar tumbled together into the outstretched hands of those pressing around. A grey mass of greatcoats seethed where the table had stood, and the commissar's desperate shout was lost in the solid thunder of voices.

Stockman at once began to push his way to the centre of the crowd, thrusting the men ruthlessly aside. No one tried to stop him, but fists and rifle-butts urged him on; the rifle was torn from his back, his Cossack cap from his head.

At the overturned table his way was barred by a troop officer. "Where are you shoving to?" the man roared.

"I want to speak! Let a rank-and-file soldier say a word!" Stockman cried hoarsely, setting the table on its legs. Some of the men around him even assisted him to clamber on to the table. But the tumult in the square did not die away, and Stockman shouted at the top of his voice:

"Silence!"

After a moment the noise died down a little, and he cried in a voice quivering with emotion:

"Comrades of the Red Army! Shame on you! You're betraying the people's government at the most serious moment possible. You're wavering just when it is necessary with a firm hand to strike the enemy to his heart. You're holding meetings when the land of the Soviets is struggling for existence in an iron ring of enemies. You're on the verge of downright treachery. And why? You have been betrayed to the Cossack generals by your own treacherous commanders. These former officers have abused the trust of the Soviet government and, exploiting your ignorance, are planning to surrender the regiment to the Cossacks. Come to your senses! With your hands they want to assist to strangle the workers' and peasants' government."

The commander of the second company, a former officer, was about to throw his rifle to his shoulder, but Stockman caught his movement and cried:

"Don't you dare! You'll have plenty of time for that! I demand that you listen to a soldier Communist. We Communists have given all our lives, all our blood, drop by drop in the service of the working class and the oppressed peasants. We are used to looking death right in the eyes. You can kill me. . . ."

"We've heard enough!" "Let him finish!" Conflicting shouts arose.

". . . kill me, but I repeat: Come to your senses. Now is not the time to hold meetings, you ought to be marching against the Whites."

He swept his eyes over the half-silenced crowd of soldiers and noticed Voronovsky, the commander of the regiment, standing a little way off, smiling forcedly and whispering to a Red Army soldier at his side.

"Your regimental commander . . ." Stockman shouted, stretching out his hand and pointing to Voronovsky. But the officer put his hand to his mouth and whispered something to the man standing beside him, and before Stockman could finish his sentence a shot rang out in the humid air of the rainy April day. Stockman clutched at his breast and fell to his knees, his bare, iron-grey head was lost to sight. But he jumped to his feet again and stood swaying.

"Osip Davidovich!" Ivan groaned as he saw Stockman rise. He started to fight his way towards him, but the men around him seized him by the arm, and muttered:

"Shut up! Give up your rifle, you swine!"

They disarmed him, went through his pockets, and led him off the square. The other Communists were at once hunted down and disarmed also. In a side street close to a merchant's house there were five or six shots as they killed a Communist machine-gunner who refused to surrender his gun.

Meantime Stockman, choking violently, his face white as chalk, his lips frothing with rosy blood, stood swaying on the table. With the last effort of his will, the last remnants of his strength, he managed to shout:

"They have tricked you. The traitors—they're earning their own pardon and new officers' positions. . . . But Communism will live. . . . Comrades—come to—your senses. . . ."

Again the soldier standing beside Voronovsky threw his rifle to his shoulder. The second bullet sent Stockman down headlong from the table under the soldiers' feet. A Serdobsky soldier jumped on to the table and roared:

"We've heard a lot of fine promises, comrades, but they've all been empty talk and threats. And now this fine orator is dying the death of a dog. Death to the Communists, to the enemies of the toiling peasantry! I say that our eyes are opened, and we know who are our enemies. What was it they told us in our villages? They said there would be equality, the brotherhood of the peoples. That's what the Communists told us. And what have we got in reality? Cannibalism, brothers! My father sent me a letter with the marks of his tears on it, and said they were robbing and stealing in broad daylight.

They've taken all the grain from my father, and their decree hands it over to the toiling peasantry. And if the poor peasants are going to get fat on what they take away from my people, then I ask you, what is that but robbery and cannibalism on the part of the Communists? Kill them with fire and blood!"

The speaker was not allowed to finish his speech: from the west two squadrons of Cossack cavalry rode at a trot into the village, down the southern slope of the Donside hills marched Cossack infantry, and Bogatiriev, the commander of the special brigade, rode into the square with his staff and half a squadron for escort.

The Serdobsky regiment began hurriedly to line up in double file. Hardly had Bogatiriev's group appeared in the distance when their commander, Voronovsky, cried in such a tone of stern command as the Red Army men had never heard before:

"Regiment! At—tention!"

As soon as the insurgent squadrons entered Ust-Khopersk and surrounded the Serdobsky regiment, the brigade commander Bogatiriev went off with Voronovsky to hold a conference. It was held close to the square, in one of the merchants' houses, and was quite brief. Without putting down his whip Bogatiriev greeted Voronovsky and said:

"Everything's gone fine! It will be put to your account. But why weren't you able to save the guns?"

"An accident, a pure accident, commander," Voronovsky replied. "The artillery-men were Communists almost to a man, and they put up a desperate resistance when we tried to disarm them. They killed two of our men and fled with the locks."

"A pity!" Bogatiriev threw his cap on the table and, wiping his sweating face with a dirty handkerchief, smiled grimly. "Well, everything's fine! You go and talk to your soldiers. . . . Tell them they're all to give up their arms."

Jarred by the commanding tones of the Cossack officer, Voronovsky stammered:

"All their arms?"

"I'm not going to say everything twice. I've said 'all,' and I mean 'all.' "

"But we agreed that the regiment was not to be disarmed. Of

course I understand that the machine-guns, and hand-grenades . . .
all that sort of equipment we must surrender unconditionally. But
as for the Red Army men's equipment . . ."

"There is no Red Army now!" Bogatiriev evilly writhed his lip,
and struck his leg with his whip. "They're not Red Army men now,
but soldiers who will defend the Don lands. . . . And if they won't,
we'll find ways of making them. We're not going to play at funerals.
You've done injury to our land, and now you want to put forward
conditions. There can be no conditions between us. Understand?"

Volkov, the chief of staff of the Serdobsky regiment, took umbrage
at Bogatiriev's words. Running his fingers over the buttons of his
black satin shirt collar, he demanded sharply:

"So you regard us as prisoners? Is that the position?"

"I didn't say that, and there's no point in your plaguing me with
your guesses," Bogatiriev interrupted him, by his manner openly
proclaiming that the two officers were completely at his mercy.

There was silence in the room for a moment. A muffled roar came
from the square. Voronovsky strode up and down the room biting
his nails, then buttoned up his tunic and turned to Bogatiriev:

"Your tone is insulting to us and unworthy of you, a Russian officer.
I say that straight to your face. And we shall know, since you have
challenged us . . . we shall know how to act. Captain Volkov, I
order you to go to the square and tell the officers that in no circumstances are they to give up their arms to the Cossacks. Command
the regiment to stand to arms; I shall have finished my talk in a moment with this—gentleman Bogatiriev and will come to the square."

Bogatiriev's face was distorted with anger, and he opened his
mouth to speak. But, realizing that he had already said too much, he
stopped and at once changed his tone. Clapping his cap on his head,
and still playing with his whip, he said in a voice unexpectedly mild
and courteous:

"Gentlemen, you have misunderstood me. Of course I have not
received any special education, I haven't passed through a Junkers'
academy, and maybe I didn't explain myself properly. But we're
all on the same side. There ought to be no feeling of injury between
us. I only said that your Red Army men must be disarmed at once,
especially those who are not to be trusted by us or by you. That's all
I said."

"In that case you should have spoken more clearly, commander.

You must agree that your challenging tones, all your behaviour . . ."
Voronovsky shrugged his shoulders and continued more pacifically,
but with a hint of dissatisfaction still in his tone: "We ourselves were
of the opinion that the wavering and unreliable elements must be
disarmed and handed over for your disposition. . . ."

"Yes, that's what I said."

"Well, then, I say we were resolved to disarm them ourselves; but
as for our militant group, we shall retain it as a unit. We shall retain
it at all costs. We shall take command of it and shall honourably
clear ourselves of the shame of having been in the ranks of the Red
Army. That possibility you must allow us."

"How many bayonets will your group number?"

"About two hundred."

"Well, all right," Bogatiriev reluctantly agreed. An awkward silence followed. It was broken by Volkov.

"Am I to go?" he asked.

"Yes," Voronovsky replied. "Go and order those whom we had
listed to be disarmed."

Meantime the insurgent Cossacks had already begun an energetic
disarming of the regiment, without waiting for the results of the conference. Avid Cossack hands and eyes searched the regimental baggage-wagons, seizing not only ammunition, but well-made boots,
puttees, blankets, trousers, and food. At this experience of Cossack
justice, some twenty Serdobsky men attempted to resist. With his
rifle-butt one of them struck a Cossack busily searching him and
shouted: "Thief! What are you taking my tobacco-pouch for? Give
it back!"

He was restrained by his comrades. But an excited shout arose:
"Comrades, to arms!"

"They've tricked us."

"Don't give up your rifles!"

Hand-to-hand fighting broke out, and the resisting Red Army men
were driven up against a wall, where the insurgent cavalry cut them
down in a couple of minutes.

With Volkov's arrival in the square the disarming proceeded still
more rapidly. The Serdobsky men were drawn up in ranks and piled
their rifles and hand-grenades, cartridge-belts, the field-telephone
equipment, boxes of cartridges and machine-gun belts on the
ground.

Bogatiriev trotted on to the square. Riding his horse along in front of the Serdobsky men, threateningly raising his whip above his head, he shouted:

"Listen to me! From today on you'll fight the accursed Communists and their soldiers. Those who go with us will be pardoned, but those who try to get out of it will receive that reward!" He pointed with his whip to the men, already stripped to their underclothes, lying in a formless white heap under the wall.

A quiet murmur ran through the ranks of the Red Army men, but not one raised his voice aloud in protest, not one broke from the ranks. The mounted and foot Cossacks surrounded the square in a solid ring, and close to the church palisade the Serdobsky machine-guns had been trained on the Serdobsky ranks, Cossack machine-gunners standing behind them ready to open fire.

Within an hour Voronovsky and Volkov had picked out the reliable men from the rest of the regiment. The newly formed detachment was given the name of the "First Special Insurgent Battalion," and it went out the same day into the front line. The others, numbering some eight hundred, were convoyed by forced marches along the banks of the Don to Vieshenska. Three Cossack squadrons, equipped with the Serdobsky machine-guns, escorted them. Before his departure from Ust-Khopersk Bogatiriev called one of the insurgent squadron commanders to him and instructed him:

"Guard the Communists as you would a gunpowder magazine. Tomorrow morning drive them on the road to Vieshenska under a reliable convoy. And send couriers to the villages today to inform the people who are coming. They'll pass their own judgment on them."

Chapter 15

Gregor Melekhov spent five days in Tatarsk and sowed several acres of grain for his own and his mother-in-law's family. Then, as soon as his father returned exhausted and lousy from his regiment, he made ready to go back to his division. Kudynov had secretly informed him of the negotiations being conducted with the command of the

Serdobsky regiment and had asked him to return to the front as soon as possible.

At noon of the day on which Gregor planned to leave Tatarsk for Kargin, he led his horse down to the Don to drink. As he dropped down to the water, which had flooded to the very edges of the orchards, he saw Aksinia. It seemed to him that she was deliberately dallying with the drawing of water, filling her pails slowly, as though waiting for him to come down. None the less, overwhelmed by a flood of memories, he hastened his steps.

She turned as she heard footsteps, and her face assumed an expression of surprise. But her joy at the meeting and her old pain mastered her. She smiled such a miserable, distracted smile, so unbecoming to her proud face, that Gregor's heart was shaken with pity and love. Stung with yearning, humbled by memory, he halted his horse and said:

"Good morning, Aksinia dear."

"Good morning."

"It's a long time since we last spoke to each other."

"Yes, a long time."

"I'd forgotten the very sound of your voice. . . ."

"You forget quickly."

"Is it so quickly?"

Gregor held back the horse pressing against him. Aksinia bowed her head and tried to fish out her pail with the end of the yoke, but could not get it hooked into the handle. For a minute they stood there in silence. A wild duck flew over their heads with a whistle of wings. Insatiably licking the chalky soil, the waves beat against the bank. On the farther side the white-breasted billows were coursing through the flooded forest. Gregor turned his eyes from Aksinia to the opposite side of the river. The poplars stood with pale grey trunks in the water, rocking their naked boughs, and the willows, adorned with virgin catkins, were hanging over the river like fine green clouds. With a hint of vexation and bitterness in his voice, Gregor asked:

"Well—haven't you and I anything to talk about? Why are you silent?"

But Aksinia had regained her self-command and, without the quiver of a muscle in her face, she replied:

"It's clear we've said all we had to say. . . ."

"Truly?"

"And so it ought to be. A tree only blossoms once a year."

"And you think ours has already blossomed?"

"Do you think not?"

"It's strange, somehow. . . ." Gregor let his horse go to the water and, glancing at Aksinia, smiled sadly: "But I can't tear you out of my heart anyhow, Aksinia. Here I've got children growing up, and I'm myself half grey, and how many years lie like an abyss between us! But I still think of you. In my sleep I see you and I love you still. And sometimes as I'm thinking of you I begin to recall how we lived at Listnitsky's. How we loved each other! . . . Sometimes as I look back on my life it seems like an empty pocket turned inside out. . . ."

"I too. . . . But I must go . . . we're standing talking. . . ." She resolutely lifted the pails, put her sunburnt hands on the yoke, and was about to climb the slope. But suddenly she turned her face towards Gregor, and her cheeks flushed faintly with a fine, youthful blush:

"It was just here, right by this spot, that our love began, Gregor. Do you remember? The day the Cossacks went off to the training camp it was," she said, smiling, a cheerful note sounding in her voice.

"I remember it all!"

Gregor led his horse back into the yard and to the manger. Pantaleimon, who had remained at home to see Gregor depart, came out from the shed and asked:

"Well, will you be off soon? Shall I give a feed to your horse?"

"Off to where?" Gregor glanced abstractedly at his father.

"Why, to Kargin."

"I'm not going today."

"What's that?"

"I've changed my mind." Gregor licked his dry lips and turned his eyes to the sky. "Clouds are coming up and it looks like rain. There's no point in my getting wet through."

"That's true," the old man agreed, but he did not believe Gregor, for only a few minutes previously he had been in the cattle-yard at the back of the hut and had seen him talking to Aksinia. "Up to the old tricks," he thought anxiously. "I hope he won't be getting Natalia upset again. Damn him, surely it wasn't me who gave birth to such a hound!" He stared after his son's retreating back and, rummaging in his memory, recalling his own early manhood, he decided: "It's me, the devil! Only he's beaten his old father at it. I could kill him rather than have him turning Aksinia's head again and bringing trouble into the family! But how to kill him?"

Formerly, if he had caught Gregor talking to Aksinia, he would not have hesitated to strike him across the back with whatever came to hand. But now he said nothing and did not even reveal that he knew the true cause of Gregor's sudden change of mind. For Gregor was no longer "Grishka," a wild young Cossack, but a divisional commander, a general with thousands of Cossacks under him, even though he did not wear epaulets. And how could he, Pantaleimon, who had never been higher than a sergeant, raise his hand against a general, though he was his own son? His sense of discipline would not allow him even to consider it, and so he felt that his hands were tied, and he was alienated from Gregor. Even while ploughing the day before, when Gregor had shouted sternly to him: "What are you standing gaping there for? Get hold of that plough!" he had submitted and had not uttered a word in answer.

"Frightened of the rain!" he muttered. When there was not a sign of rain, when only one little cloud was scudding along over the sky! Should he tell Natalia? Feeling relief at the thought, Pantaleimon started to go into the hut. But he thought better of it and turned back to his task, afraid of the quarrel that would ensue.

As soon as Aksinia reached home and emptied her buckets she went to the mirror and stood staring anxiously at her ageing but still beautiful face. It still retained its depraved and seductive charm, but the autumn of life was beginning to cast fugitive hues over her cheeks, her eyelids were yellowing, rare strands of grey were entwined in her hair, her eyes were dimmed with mournful weariness. She stood staring at the reflection, then turned and threw herself on the bed, weeping such copious, sweet, and alleviating tears as she had not known for many days.

She lay on the bed until evening, then arose, washed, combed her hair, and with feverish haste, like a girl about to be presented to a prospective bridegroom, began to dress. She put on a clean shift, a woollen, claret-coloured skirt, threw a handkerchief over her head, glanced at herself in the mirror, and went out.

The shadows hovered dove-grey over Tatarsk. A pale, impotent moon was rising beyond the Donside poplars, and a rippling ribbon of moonlight lay across the water. The herds were still returning from the steppe, and the cows were lowing as they wandered into their yards. She did not stop to milk her own cow, but drove the calf out of the stable and let it go to its mother. Then she went to the Melekhovs' fence and found Daria, just finished milking the cow, turning with the pail in her hand to go towards the hut. Aksinia called across the fence:

"Daria!"

"Who's that?"

"It's me, Aksinia! Come into my hut for a minute."

"What do you want me for?"

"I want you badly. Come in, for the love of Christ."

"I'll strain this milk, and then I'll come."

"I'll be waiting for you in the yard."

A few minutes later Daria came out and found Aksinia waiting for her by the Astakhovs' wicket gate. She was surprised to see her attired in her holiday clothes.

"You've dressed quickly, neighbour!"

"I haven't much to do now Stepan's away. There's only one cow. . . ."

"What did you want me for?"

"Come into the hut for a little while." Aksinia's voice trembled. Guessing the reason for the talk, Daria silently followed her into the kitchen. As soon as she entered, Aksinia, without lighting a light, went straight to her chest, rummaged in it, and then, clutching Daria's hand in her own dry and burning hands, hurriedly slipped a ring on her finger.

"What's this? Not a ring, surely? You're not giving it to me?" Daria exclaimed.

"Yes, it's gold. You keep it."

"Well, thank you. What do you want me to do for it?"

"Ask your Gregor—to come to me."

"The old game again?" Daria smiled inscrutably.

"No, no! Oh, what are you thinking?" Aksinia took alarm, and tears started to her eyes. "I want to talk to him about Stepan. He may be able to get him furlough."

"But why didn't you come and see us? You could talk with him there if you have business with him," Daria sneered.

"No, no! Natalia might think. . . . It's awkward. . . ."

"All right, I'll tell him. I don't care what he does."

Gregor was finishing his supper; he had put down his spoon and was wiping his moustache with his hand. Feeling someone's foot touching his beneath the table, he looked up and saw Daria winking at him almost imperceptibly.

"If she's after getting me to take Piotra's place and says anything to me about it I'll kill her. I'll take her into the threshing-floor, tie her skirt above her head, and rip her up like a bitch!" he thought disconnectedly. But, rising from the table, he lit a cigarette and unhurriedly went out to the porch. Daria came out almost immediately after him. As she passed him in the porch, pressing close to him she whispered:

"Oh, you swine! Go along—she wants you."

"Who?" Gregor breathed the question.

"She!"

An hour later, when Natalia and the children were asleep, Gregor, his greatcoat fastened close around him, emerged with Aksinia from the gate of the Astakhovs' yard. They stood silent a moment in the dark side street and went as silently into the steppe, which beckoned with its stillness, its darkness, and the intoxicating perfume of the young grass. Wrapping her in the edge of his greatcoat, Gregor pressed Aksinia to him and felt her trembling, while her heart beat violently and spasmodically beneath her jacket.

Chapter 16

Before his departure next day, Gregor had a brief scene with Natalia. She called him aside and asked him in a whisper:

"Where did you go last night? Why were you so late home?"

"Was it so late?"

"Well, wasn't it? I woke up and heard the first cock crowing, and still you hadn't returned. . . ."

"Kudynov was here. I had to see him to talk over military questions. They're not for your woman's mind."

"But why didn't he come here to spend the night?"

"He was in a hurry to get to Vieshenska."

"Where did he stop?"

"At the Abonshchikovs'. It seems he's a distant relation of theirs."

Natalia asked no further questions. She seemed half convinced, but her eyes did not reveal her true thoughts, and Gregor could not be sure whether she believed him or not.

He ate a hurried breakfast, while Pantaleimon went out to saddle his horse. Crossing him and kissing him, Ilinichna whispered:

"Don't forget God, don't forget God, little son. We heard you'd cut down some sailors—Lord! Gregor, think what you're doing! Look what fine children you've got, and perhaps those you killed had children too. When you were a lad you were so gentle, but now all your kindness of heart has gone and you're become a wolf. Listen to what your mother says, Gregor. Your life isn't charmed, and an evil sword will find your neck. . . ."

Gregor smiled cheerlessly, kissed his mother's dry hand, and went to Natalia. She embraced him coldly and turned away. But he saw no tears, only bitterness and hidden anger in her eyes. He said goodbye to his children and went out.

As he put his foot into the stirrup and held on to the horse's shaggy mane, he was thinking: "Well, life has taken a new turn, but my heart is still cold and empty. . . . It's clear Aksinia can't fill that emptiness now. . . ."

Without a look back to his family gathered about the gate, he rode at a walking pace along the street. As he went past the Astakhovs' hut he glanced sidelong at the windows and saw Aksinia at the last window of the front room. She smiled and waved an embroidered handkerchief to him, then abruptly crumpled it in her hand and pressed it to her lips and to her eyes, darkened with the past sleepless night.

He rode at a swift cavalry trot up the hill. At the top he saw two horsemen and a wagon slowly moving along the field track towards him. He recognized the riders as Antip Brekhovich and another young Cossack from the farther end of the village. "Bringing home dead Cossacks," he guessed, as he saw the bullock-wagon. As he approached the Cossacks he asked:

"Whom are you bringing home?"

"Alexei Shamil, Ivan Tomilin, and Yakov Podkova."

"Dead?"

"Killed!"

"When?"

"Yesterday, at sundown."

"Is the battery safe?"

"Yes. The Reds surprised some of our battery men in their quarters."

Gregor removed his cap and slipped from his horse. The driver halted the bullocks. The dead Cossacks lay side by side in the bottom of the wagon, Alexei Shamil in the middle. His old blue shirt was flung open, the empty sleeve was put under his cloven head, and the stump of his arm, wrapped in a dirty rag, was pressed against his breast. In the dead grin of his toothless mouth a savage frenzy was frozen stiff; but the glassy eyes stared with calm and seemingly sorrowful pensiveness at the blue sky, at the cloud floating over the steppe.

Tomilin's face was unrecognizable. Indeed, there was no face, but a red shapeless mass, split slantwise by a sabre-stroke. Yakov Podkova was a saffron yellow, and his head had been almost completely severed from the neck. The white bone of the sabred clavicle stuck out of the unbuttoned collar of his shirt, and across his brow ran a black bullet-wound. Evidently one of the Red Army men had had pity on the dying Cossack's death-throes and had shot him almost at point-blank range, for his face was burnt and spotted with black traces of gunpowder.

"Well, brothers, let's remember our dead friends and smoke to the peace of their souls," Gregor proposed. Drawing aside, he loosened his horse's saddle-girths, dropped the bit from its mouth, tied the reins to its left foreleg, and let it graze on the silky, arrowing growth of green. Antip and the other Cossack willingly dismounted, hobbled their horses, and let them graze. The Cossacks lay down and smoked. Glancing at the shaggy bullocks straining after the grass, Gregor asked:

"But how did Shamil come to his death?"

"It was his own fault."

"How?"

"Well, it was like this. Yesterday at noon we went out on patrol duty. There were fourteen of us, and Shamil among us. He rode along merrily, so he could have had no boding. He waved his stump about, dropped his reins on his saddle-bow, and remarked: 'When is our Gregor Pantalievich going to come back? I'd like to have another drink and sing with him.' He was singing all the way. We didn't see a sign of the Reds anywhere, and at last the sergeant said we could dismount and rest ourselves and our horses. So we dismounted and lay on the grass in a gully, with a sentry on the hill. I saw Alexei loosening the saddle-girths of his horse, and I said to him: 'Alexei, you'd better not loosen those girths, in case we have to clear off in a hurry. And then how could you manage to tighten them again with your one hand?' But he snarled: 'I'll manage quicker than you. Don't try to teach me, you baby.' And he unfastened the girths and dropped the bit from his horse's mouth. We lay there smoking and talking and snoozing. But our sentry also dozed, lying under a bush. Suddenly I heard the snort of a horse some distance off. I didn't want to stir, but I got up all the same and went to the top of the hill. And there were the Reds riding straight towards us. I rushed down into the gully and shouted: 'The Reds are coming! To horse!' They wouldn't believe me at first, but they heard their commander shouting an order. Our sergeant drew his sword and wanted us to attack, but there were only fourteen of us and half a squadron of them, with a machine-gun too. We galloped off, and they couldn't use their machine-gun because of our position, so they began to fire with their rifles. But our horses were better than theirs, and we got well away, then dropped off our horses and began to fire back at them. Only then did I notice Shamil wasn't with us. When we rushed to mount he ran to his horse, got his sound hand to the saddle-bow and one foot in the stirrup, but as he tried to mount, the saddle slipped under the horse's belly. Somehow the horse got away from him and came galloping after us with the saddle swinging under it, and Shamil was left alone with the Reds. And that's how Alexei asked for death. If he hadn't loosened the girths he'd still be alive. They slashed him about so much that the blood poured out of him till you'd have thought a bullock had been slaughtered there. When we'd driven off the Reds we went past the gully and picked him up."

"Well, shall we be getting on?" the driver asked impatiently.

Gregor said good-bye to the Cossacks and went to the wagon to take a last farewell of his dead fellow-villagers. Only then did he notice that all three were barefoot, while three pairs of boots were placed at their feet.

"Who took their boots off?" he demanded.

"Our Cossacks did that, Gregor Pantalievich. They all had good boots, and the company thought it better to take them off and give them to those who had old ones. So we took them off and put three pairs of old ones in their places."

Gregor put his horse into a trot and kept up a steady pace almost all the way to Kargin. A gentle breeze ruffled the animal's mane. The long brown marmots ran across the road, warningly whistling. Their sharp, anxious whistle was in strange harmony with the profound silence which dominated the steppe. Male bustards flew low over the rises at the roadside. One, sparkling like snow in the sunlight, its wings flapping swiftly, mounted into the zenith as though swimming in the azure expanse, its neck stretched out in its precipitant flight. It flew off about two hundred yards and then sank, its wings fluttering still more swiftly. Close to the earth, against the green background of the grasses, its wings fluttered for the last time before it disappeared, engulfed in the sea of green.

The challenging, passionate call of the male bustards was to be heard on all sides. In one spot, some few paces off the road, Gregor saw a perfect circle of earth over three feet in diameter which had been beaten out by bustards fighting for a female. Not a blade of grass was to be seen in the circle, only a grey cloud of dust scarred with the traces of the birds' feet, and single stalks of wormwood and scrub, to which feathers were clinging. Not far from the spot a grey female bustard started from her nest and, not daring to take to wing, ran hurriedly on her little twinkling legs, her back hunched like an old woman's, into the grass and disappeared.

Fructified by the spring, an invisible, almighty, and palpitant life was unfolding in the steppe. The grass was growing luxuriantly; in their secret steppe lairs birds and animals were mating; the ploughed lands wore a fine brush of innumerable young shoots. Only the last year's scrub was huddling drearily along the slopes of the mounds standing sentinel over the steppe, seeking salvation from death by bowing close to the earth. But the fresh, vital breeze ruthlessly broke it from its withered roots and chased it off, driving it hither and thither over the living steppe.

Gregor arrived at Kargin late in the afternoon. He took over the divisional command next morning and, despite the last instructions sent from the staff at Vieshenska, after consultation with his chief of staff he resolved on an offensive. The regiments were experiencing a severe shortage of ammunition. It was necessary to obtain it by an attack, capturing it from the Reds, and this was the prime cause for Gregor's decision.

Towards evening one foot and three mounted regiments were drawn into Kargin. Of the twenty-two machine-guns in the division it was decided to take only six, as there were no cartridge-belts for the others. The Cossack forces began their offensive the next morning. Gregor himself took command of the 3rd cavalry Regiment, sent mounted patrols ahead, and led the regiment swiftly towards the south, where, according to reports, two Red Army regiments were concentrated in readiness for an attack on the Cossacks.

Some two miles outside Kargin he was overtaken by a courier bringing a letter from Kudynov. The letter read:

"The second Serdobsky regiment has surrendered to us. All the soldiers have been disarmed; twenty of them, who resisted, have been killed. Four field-guns were surrendered (the accursed gunners fled with the locks), more than 200 shells and nine machine-guns. We shall distribute the Red soldiers among the companies and make them fight their own people. One thing I'd almost forgotten. Two of your Communist fellow-villagers, Ivan Kotliarov and Mishka Koshevoi, as well as many Yelanska Communists, were captured. They're being driven along the road to Vieshenska. How are things going with you? If you are in need of cartridges, send word by the courier and we'll send 500.

Kudynov"

Gregor read the letter hastily, but when he came to the report of Ivan's and Mishka's capture he shouted for his orderly. Prokhor Zykov galloped up at once but, noticing the expression on Gregor's face, in his alarm he even saluted:

"Ryabchikov! Where's Ryabchikov?" Gregor shouted at him.

"At the end of the column."

"Ride and fetch him here at once."

Zykov galloped off, and a minute or two later Ryabchikov trotted up to Gregor.

"A letter from Vieshenska?" he asked, as he noticed the courier at Gregor's side.

"Yes," Gregor replied. "Take over command of the regiment and the division. I'm off."

"Well, all right. But what's the hurry? What does the letter say? Who wrote? Kudynov?"

"The Serdobsky regiment has surrendered at Ust-Khopersk."

"Fine! So we still live! Going at once?"

"At once."

"Well, God be with you! When you return you'll find us well advanced."

Gregor furiously whipped up his horse. "I must see Mishka and Ivan alive. . . . I must find out who killed Piotra. . . . I must save Ivan and Mishka from death . . . must save them. . . . There's blood between us, but after all there's our old friendship," he was thinking as he galloped down the hill.

Chapter 17

The morning after the surrender of the Serdobsky regiment the twenty-five captured Communists marched out of Ust-Khopersk, guarded by a strong convoy. There could be no thought of flight. Ivan Alexievich, limping in the middle of the prisoners, hatefully and yearningly stared at the faces of the Cossack escort and thought: "This is the end. Unless we get a trial, we're done for."

Among the Cossacks elderly bearded men predominated. They were commanded by an aged Old Believer, a former sergeant in the Ataman regiment. As soon as the prisoners left Ust-Khopersk he gave orders that they were not to talk or smoke, nor to ask questions.

"Say your prayers, you servants of Antichrist," he shouted at them, raising his pistol. "You're going to your death, and you shouldn't sin in your last hours. You devilish whoremongers, you've forgotten the Lord. You sold yourselves to the unclean One. You branded yourselves with the enemy's brand."

There were only two Communists of the Serdobsky regiment

among the prisoners; the remainder, with the exception of Ivan, were Russians from the Yelanska district, tall, healthy lads who had joined the Communist Party when the Soviet troops arrived in the area, and had served as militia-men, or chairmen of village revolutionary committees, and had fled to Ust-Khopersk to join the Red Army when the revolt broke out. In peace-time almost all of them had been craftsmen: carpenters, coopers, masons, bakers, shoemakers, and tailors. Not one of them seemed to be more than thirty-five, the youngest some twenty years. Strong, sturdy, with great hands gnarled with physical labour, their outward appearance was in sharp distinction from the hunchbacked old Cossacks of the convoy.

"Will they try us? What do you think?" one of the Yelanska Communists walking at Ivan's side asked him.

"I doubt it. . . ."

"They'll kill us?"

"I expect so."

"But they don't shoot their prisoners. The Cossacks said so. Don't you remember?"

Ivan Alexievich was silent, but a spark of hope was kindled within him. "That's true," he thought. "They won't dare to shoot us. Their slogan was: 'Down with the Commune, with pillaging and shooting.' They've not gone further than imprisoning, so the rumour goes. A whipping, and then prison. Well, that's nothing to be frightened of. We'll stay in prison until winter, and then there'll be a new rising in the Don, our people will drive out the Whites and release us."

The hope kindled like a spark, and it faded like a spark. "No, they'll kill us. They're as savage as devils. Farewell, life! Ah, we didn't take the right road! We should have fought them and had no pity on them. We shouldn't have spared them, but cut them down to the roots." He clenched his fists and shrugged his shoulders in impotent frenzy, and immediately stumbled, sent almost to the ground by a blow on his head from behind.

"What are you clenching your fists for, you swine?" the sergeant in charge of the convoy thundered at him, riding at him with his horse. He struck Ivan with his whip, raising a weal right across his face from the temple to the chin.

"Whom are you beating? Hit me, daddy! He's wounded, what are you striking him for?" one of the Yelanska men asked with quivering voice and an entreating smile. He stepped out of the crowd and put himself in front of Ivan.

"There'll be enough for you too! Beat them up, Cossacks! Beat the Communists!" the sergeant roared.

His whip-lash came down so hard on the man's thin shirt that the shreds of material shrivelled like leaves in a fire, and the blood poured from the cut, wetting the shirt. Panting with anger, the sergeant drove the prisoners on with his horse and began to ply his whip ruthlessly.

Again the lash descended on Ivan. Livid fires burned in his eyes, the earth swayed under his feet, and the green forest on the opposite bank of the river seemed to rock. He seized the stirrup and attempted to drag the sergeant out of his saddle, but a blow with the flat of a sword sent him headlong to the bitterly dusty ground, and the scorching blood poured out of his nose and ears.

Driving them into a herd as though they were sheep, the escort beat them long and harshly. Lying on the ground, Ivan, as though in a dream, heard shouts, the hollow tramp of feet around him, the frenzied snorting of the horses. A clot of warm horse's sweat fell on his bare head, and somewhere, very close, right above him, sounded a terrible, spasmodic sobbing and a shout:

"Swine! God damn you! Beating defenceless men! You . . ."

A horse trod on Ivan's wounded leg, and the blunt points of the shoe pressed into the flesh of his calf. A moment later a wet, heavy body, smelling of sweat and the salty scent of blood, crumbled down at his side, and Ivan heard the blood gurgling from the man's throat like liquid out of a bottle.

When the Cossacks had finished beating them up, they drove them down to the river and made them wash their wounds. Standing knee-deep in the water, Ivan washed his burning abrasions and bruises and, cupping his hands, eagerly drank the water, afraid he would not be allowed sufficient time to quench his insatiable thirst.

As they approached the first village, one of the Cossacks rode off in advance. And hardly had the prisoners passed the first yard when a crowd, armed with forks, hoes, pikes, and crowbars, poured towards them. As soon as they saw the Cossacks and women, Ivan and the others realized that this was to be the manner of their death.

"Let's say good-bye to one another, comrades!" one of the Communists exclaimed.

After his wash in the Don, Ivan Alexievich had grown stronger in spirit, and when he saw the Cossacks and women running towards him, he hurriedly took farewell of the comrades close to him and said in an undertone:

"Well, brothers, we knew how to fight; now we must know how to die proudly. One thing we must remember to our last breath: one thought remains our comfort. They may stick us with their pikes, but they won't kill the Soviet régime with a pike. Communists! Brothers! Die bravely, so that our enemies cannot laugh at us!"

After that first beating all that happened seemed to be incidents in an oppressive dream. Twenty miles they were driven through village after village, greeted at each by crowds of tormentors. The old men, women, and elder children beat them, spat in their blood-stained and swollen faces, threw stones and clods of hard earth, cast dust and ashes into their eyes. The women were especially brutal, resorting to the most cruel and ingenious tortures. Towards the end the twenty-five men were almost unrecognizable as human beings, so monstrously disfigured were their bodies and faces, so covered were they with caking blue-black blood mingled with mud.

At first each of the twenty-five sought to get as far as possible from their escort, so as to avoid the blows. Each tried to push into the middle, and in consequence they huddled into a solid mass of bodies. But the Cossacks continually separated them and compelled them to march in more open order. They lost all hope of the least protection from the beatings and struggled along in a disorderly mob, having only the one tormenting desire: to force themselves on and not to fall. For if they had fallen they could not have risen again. At first each had covered his face with his hands, had impotently raised his palms to his eyes when the iron prongs of the forks or the blunt ends of the pikes had appeared before him. But at the last they were possessed by complete indifference to everything. At first they had raised prayers for mercy, mingled with groans and curses and a desperate, animal roar born of unbearable pain. But by midday they went silently. Only one of them, a Yelanska man, the youngest of them all, a wag and the regiment favourite, groaned whenever a blow fell on his head. He shambled along with all his body quivering as though in a fever, dragging a leg smashed by a pole.

At one village one of the prisoners could bear no more. He cried out in a dreary, childish voice, tore open the collar of his shirt, and showed the Cossacks a little tarnished cross hanging from a string around his neck.

"Comrades, I only joined the party recently. . . . Have mercy! I believe in God. I've got two little children. . . . Have pity! You've got children too."

"What comrades are we of yours? Hold your tongue!" a hook-nosed old man told him. "So you've come to your senses now, have you? But when you shot our Cossacks, put them up against a wall, you didn't think of God then." Without waiting for a reply he swung his pike and struck at the man's head.

Nothing that his eyes saw and his ears heard made any impression on Ivan Alexievich or arrested his attention even for a moment. His heart was like a stone, and only once did it awaken. At noon, accompanied by curses and blows, they entered a village and struggled along the street. Suddenly, glancing to one side, Ivan noticed a child some seven years old clinging to its mother's skirt, tears streaming down its face, and screaming:

"Mummy! Don't beat him! Oh, don't beat him. · . . I'm sorry . . . I'm afraid. . . . He's all blood."

The woman, who was aiming a pike at one of the prisoners, suddenly cried out, dropped her weapon, and, seizing the boy by the hand, fled into a side alley. Touched by the childish tears and troubled pity, tears welled into Ivan's eyes and streamed down his cheeks. He sobbed as he remembered his own little son and his wife, and out of the sudden memory was born the impatient wish that he might not die in their sight. . . . Better earlier. . . .

They struggled along, hardly dragging their legs, swaying with weariness. Beyond the village there was a well in the steppe, and they asked the sergeant in charge for permission to drink.

"There's no point in your drinking. We're late already. Get on!" the sergeant shouted.

But one of the convoy spoke up on their behalf:

"Don't be so hard, Akim Sazonovich! They're men like us."

"How are they men? Communists aren't men. And don't try to teach me! Am I in charge or are you?"

"There are too many commanders like you. Come on, boys, and have a drink," the old Cossack said. He dismounted and drew up a pitcher of water from the well. The prisoners at once surrounded him, their fading eyes lit up, and twenty-five pairs of hands were stretched out to seize the pitcher. The old man hesitated, not knowing whom to allow to drink first. After an interminable second he poured the water into the sunken drinking-trough and stepped aside, crying:

"Here, are you a lot of cattle? Take your turn!"

The water ran over the slimy green, rotten bottom of the trough. The prisoners flung themselves towards it. His brows knitted with compassion, the old man drew up eleven pitchers of water one after another and filled the trough.

Ivan went on his knees to drink. When he had quenched his thirst he raised his head and, with extraordinary, almost blinding clarity, his eyes saw the frosty white pall of chalky dust on the Donside road, the blue of the farther hills, and above them, above the swiftly flowing, white-maned Don, in the inaccessible azure vault of the sky, a little cloud. Winged on by the wind, it floated with a sparkling white sail towards the north, its opal shadow reflected in a distant bend of the river.

The prisoners arrived at Tatarsk about five o'clock. The brief spring twilight was close at hand; the sun was sinking, its edge touching the border of the grey cloud-masses in the west.

The Tatarsk Cossack infantry company was sitting and standing in the shade of the great village granary. They were being transferred to the right bank of the Don to assist the Yelanska companies, who were having difficulty in withstanding the pressure of the Reds, and on their way to their new position the entire company had turned aside into the village to see their families and to replenish their stores of food.

They were to have continued their march at once, but they heard that Communist prisoners were being driven to Vieshenska, that Mishka Koshevoi and Ivan Alexievich were among them, and that they would soon be arriving in Tatarsk. So they decided to delay their departure. The Cossacks whose relations had been killed with Piotra Melekhov in the battle outside Tatarsk were particularly insistent on waiting to see the prisoners.

They stood talking languidly among themselves, their rifles piled against the granary wall, smoking, chewing sunflower seeds, and surrounded by women, old men, and children. All the village was in the street, and lads were posted on the roofs of the huts to watch for the coming of the prisoners.

At last a boyish voice cried:

"Here they come!"

The soldiers hurriedly rose, the people surged and roared, there was the sound of scampering feet as the lads ran to meet the prisoners.

"Our enemies are coming!" one of the old men said.

"Kill the devils! They killed our men!" another exclaimed. "We'll settle with Mishka Koshevoi and his friend."

Daria Melekhov was standing at the side of Anikushka's wife. She was the first to recognize Ivan Alexievich among the herd of prisoners as they approached.

"We've brought you one of your villagers. Paint yourselves in his blood, the son of a bitch! Give me a Christian kiss!" the sergeant roared above the howl of shouts, women's shrieks, and weeping. He stretched out his hand and pointed at Ivan.

"But where's the other? Where's Mishka Koshevoi?" Antip Brekhovich made his way through the crowd, unslinging his rifle as he went.

"There's only one of your men, there weren't any others! But one will be enough for you to tear to pieces!" the sergeant replied, wiping the sweat from his face with a red handkerchief.

The women's whistling and shrieking increased until it could rise no higher. Daria pushed her way towards the convoy and saw Ivan Alexievich, his face blue-black with bruises and blood, standing a few paces in front of her. The skin of his brow fluttered in shreds, and on the mass of mingled blood and hair on his scalp lay a pair of woolen gloves, which he had put there to protect the open wounds from the burning sun and the flies. The gloves had stuck to the wound, and so they remained on his head.

He looked around with a hunted expression, seeking for, yet afraid of finding his wife or his little son among the crowd. He turned to ask someone, anyone, to lead them away if they should happen to be present. He realized that he would get no farther than Tatarsk, that here he would die; and he did not want his family to see his death. Standing with huddled shoulders, he slowly and laboriously turned his head, his eyes wandering over the familiar faces of his fellow-villagers. In not one face did he discern a trace of compassion or sympathy; all, both Cossacks and women, glowered at him evilly.

Daria planted herself in front of him. Panting with hatred, with pain, with the exhausting presentiment of something terrible which must be accomplished here, on this spot, she stared into his face and could not tell whether he saw and recognized her or not.

With the same anxious, agitated expression Ivan continually shifted the stare of his one eye (the other was closed by a bruise) around the crowd. Suddenly his gaze rested on Daria, and he stumbled uncertainly forward, as though heavily intoxicated. His head was swimming with his terrible loss of blood, he was on the point of swooning. But the transitional state in which everything seems unreal and the light is darkening in the eyes troubled him, and with a supreme exertion of his will he kept on his feet. A distant semblance of a smile hovered on his lips. And this ghost of a smile disturbed Daria and made her heart beat fast and heavily, as though it were in her throat.

Panting violently, her face turning paler and paler, she went right up to Ivan Alexievich.

"Well, how are you, cousin?" she asked. The ringing, passionate timbre of her voice and the unusual intonation of her words hushed the roar of the crowd. In the silence his toneless but firm reply was clearly audible:

"And how are you, Cousin Daria?"

"Tell your own cousin how you killed—" Daria choked and clutched at her breast, momentarily unable to go on. Her whisper as she continued was heard on the very edge of the crowd: "—your own cousin, my husband."

"No, cousin, I didn't kill him."

"Then who was it sent him out of this world?" Daria raised her voice. "Who was it? Well, tell me."

"The Zaamursky regiment. . . ."

"It was you! You killed him. . . . The Cossacks said they saw you on the hill. You were riding a white horse. Do you deny that, you cur?"

"I was in that battle. . . ." Ivan's left hand slowly rose to his head and fumbled with the gloves stuck to the wound. His voice had a perceptible note of doubt as he continued: "I was in that battle, but it wasn't I who killed your husband, it was Mikhail Koshevoi. He shot him. The blood of Cousin Piotra is not on my hands."

"Then which of our villagers did you kill, you enemy? Whose children did you leave orphans in this world?" Jakov Podkova's widow screamed piercingly from the crowd. Women began to sob hysterically, intensifying the already strained atmosphere.

Afterwards Daria said she could not remember how and whence the cavalry carbine came into her hands. Someone must have given it to her. But when the women's voices arose she felt a strange object in her hands and, without looking at it, she felt that it was a rifle. At first she seized it by the barrel in order to strike Ivan with the butt. But the gun-sight stuck painfully into her palm and she shifted her fingers, turned the rifle over, then threw it to her shoulder and even took aim at Ivan's left breast.

She saw the Cossacks behind him run aside, laying bare the wall of the granary. She heard frightened shouts: "You're mad! Will you kill your own kinsman? Wait, don't shoot!" Urged on by the bestial expectation of the crowd, by the desire to avenge her husband's death, and in part by the vainglory of suddenly revealing herself as different from the other women, of realizing that the Cossacks were staring at her in amazement and even fear as they awaited her next step, driven at a frightful speed towards a deed predetermined in the depths of her consciousness, yet not desired in her heart of hearts, she hesitated, cautiously groping at the trigger. Then suddenly, unexpectedly even to herself, she strongly pressed it back.

The recoil of the rifle threw her almost off her feet, the sound deafened her. But through the slits of her screwed-up eyes she saw Ivan's face change abruptly, terribly, and irrevocably, saw him throw out and then fold his hands as though about to dive from a great height into water, and then fall headlong, his head jerking at a feverish speed, his body quivering, the fingers of his outflung hands clawing the ground.

Still not clearly realizing what she had done, Daria threw down the rifle, turned her back on the fallen man, and, with a gesture unnatural in its ordinary simplicity, adjusted her kerchief and tucked her straying hair beneath it.

"And he's still stirring!" one of the Cossacks said as with extraordinary deference he stepped aside to let her pass.

Not understanding what was said nor of whom it was said, she looked round and heard a deep, monotonous, protracted groan that seemed to come not from a man's throat but from his very heart. The groan passed into a death-rattle. Only then did she realize that it was Ivan Alexievich who had groaned, who had received death at her hand.

Swiftly and lightly she strode past the granary in the direction of the square. Only a few eyes turned to follow her, for the crowd's attention had passed to Antip Brekhovich. As though on the parade ground he ran swiftly on his toes towards Ivan Alexievich, for some reason hiding a bayonet behind his back. With deliberate and calculated movements he squatted on his heels, directed the point of the bayonet into Ivan's breast, and quietly said:

"Well, now die, Kotliarov!" With all his strength he pressed on the bayonet-handle.

Painful and slow was Ivan's death. Unwilling was life to abandon his healthy, muscular body. Even after the third blow of the bayonet he still gaped and a drearily hoarse "Ah-ah-ah!" came from between his bloodstained teeth.

"Hey, get away to the devil!" the convoy sergeant said, thrusting Antip off. The sergeant raised his revolver and took businesslike aim at Ivan.

His shot acted as the signal for the Cossacks to fling themselves on the prisoners. The hunted men broke and scattered in confusion. The dry and curt sound of rifle-shots mingled with the shouts. . . .

Gregor Melekhov galloped into Tatarsk less than an hour later. He had ridden his own horse to death, and as he was crossing the steppe from Ust-Khopersk it had dropped on the road. Dragging the saddle to the nearest village, he had borrowed a miserable nag. But he arrived too late. The Tatarsk infantry company had already disappeared beyond the hill on its way to the bounds of the Ust-Khopersk district, and the village was quiet and deserted. Night was spreading its sombre pall over the surrounding hills.

Gregor rode into his yard, dismounted, and entered the hut. There was no light in the kitchen. In the heavy shadows the mosquitoes were buzzing; the ikons in the corner glimmered faintly. Drinking in the familiar, disturbing scent of his home, Gregor called:

"Anyone at home? Mother? Dunia?"

"Gregor, is that you?" Dunia's voice came from the front room.

He heard the slapping of bare feet, and his sister's white figure, hurriedly fastening the belt of her underskirt, appeared in the doorway.

"Why have you gone to bed so early?" he asked her. "Where's Mother?"

"There's been—" Dunia lapsed into silence, and Gregor heard her breathing hurriedly and agitatedly.

"What's the matter? How long is it since the prisoners were here?"

"They've killed them."

"What?"

"The Cossacks killed them. Oh, Grisha! Our Daria, the accursed carrion—" indignant tears sounded in Dunia's voice "—she killed Ivan Alexievich herself . . . shot him. . . ."

"What are you babbling?" Gregor shouted, fearfully seizing his sister by the collar of her shirt. The tears glittered in Dunia's eyes, and by the terror frozen in their pupils he realized that his ears had not deceived him.

"And Mishka Koshevoi? Stockman?"

"They weren't among the prisoners."

Briefly, brokenly she told him of the execution of the Red prisoners and of Daria's deed.

"Mamma was afraid to stay the night in the same hut with her, so she went to sleep with neighbours," she finished. "And Daria came home drunk—drunk as a beast. She's asleep now."

"Where?"

"In the granary."

Gregor turned and went out, strode across the yard, and threw open the granary door. Her skirt shamelessly pulled up around her, Daria was sleeping on the floor. Her slender arms were flung out, her right cheek glistened with spittle, the smell of home-made vodka came strongly from her open mouth. She lay breathing heavily and stertorously, her head tucked in awkwardly, her left cheek pressed against the floor.

Never before had Gregor felt such a savage desire to use his sabre. For several seconds he stood over Daria, groaning and swaying, grinding his teeth, staring with invincible loathing and contempt at the body lying beneath him. Then he took a step forward and set the iron-shod heel of his boot on her face, pressing with all the weight of his body on his heel. As he felt the nose cracking and the cheek slipping beneath his boot, he roared hoarsely:

"You poisonous reptile!"

Daria groaned drunkenly and muttered something. Gregor clutched his head between his hands and ran out into the yard.

He rode back to the front the same night, not stopping even to see his mother.

Chapter 18

About noon one day early in May an aeroplane appeared above the village of Singin in Vieshenska district. Their attention attracted by the deep roar of the engines, the children, women, and old men ran out of their huts, craning their necks, setting their palms to their eyes, and staring as the aeroplane circled in the misty sky above them. The roar of the engine sounded louder and heavier as the machine slowly descended, seeking a smooth area on which to alight in the pasture-land outside the village.

"They'll be dropping bombs in a minute! Look out!" some fertile-brained old grand-dad shouted in terror. The crowd gathered at the street corner scattered like water-drops. The women dragged off their howling children, the old men jumped across the fences and fled into the orchards. Only one old woman was left at the corner. She would have run too, but either her legs failed her in her terror or she stumbled over a cat, for she fell. And where she fell she remained lying, shamelessly kicking out her fat legs and quietly calling:

"Oh, save me! Oh, death, death!"

Nobody returned to save the old woman. Roaring frightfully, the aeroplane passed right over the granary, and for a second the shadow of its wings blotted out the daylight from the mortally terri-fied old woman's eyes. At that moment, half dead with fear, hear-ing and feeling nothing either around her or beneath her, she wet herself like a child. Naturally she was too far gone to notice that the aeroplane had landed in the pasture-lands, and that two men in black leather jerkins emerged from the cockpit. They turned irresolutely towards the village, looking cautiously about them.

But her husband, who had hidden himself in the orchard, was a brave old fellow; although his heart was pumping away like that of a sparrow in the hand, he was bold enough to watch what happened. And it was he who recognized one of the two men as an officer, Piotra Bogatiriev, the son of a regimental comrade of his. Piotra, who was first cousin to Gregor Bogatiriev, the commander of the insurgent special brigade, had retreated with the Whites to the Donietz. But there was no doubt that it was he.

The old man stared inquisitively for a moment, sitting up like a hare, with arms hanging. Finally convinced that it was Piotra Bogatiriev slowly coming towards him, he rose to his feet and tried whether they would hold him up. His legs held him up splendidly and only trembled a little, so the old man slowly emerged from the orchard.

He did not go to his old wife, still lying in the dust, but walked straight towards Piotra and his companion, removing his Cossack cap as he went. Piotra Bogatiriev recognized him, and welcomed him with a wave of the hand and a smile.

"Tell me, is it really you, Piotra Bogatiriev?" the old man asked.

"Yes, it's me, grand-dad!"

"So the Lord has granted me in my old age to see a flying-machine! It surely did frighten us."

"There aren't any Reds in the district, are there, daddy?"

"No, my boy. They've been driven somewhere beyond the Chira into the Ukrainian districts."

"And have our Singin Cossacks risen too?"

"They rose all right, but many of them have been brought back."

"How?"

"I mean they've been killed."

"Ah! And my family, my father—are they well?"

"All alive and well. But have you come from the Donietz? You didn't see my son Tikhon there, did you?"

"Yes, and I've brought you a greeting from him. Well, daddy, guard our machine so that the boys don't get playing about with it. I'm going home." He turned to the other man. "Come along."

Piotra and his companion went off into the village. And from the orchards, from sheds, cellars, and every conceivable nook and

cranny the terrified people emerged. They surrounded the aeroplane, which still breathed out a smell of gasoline and oil. Its wings
had been shot through in many places with bullets and shrapnel. It
stood silent and hot like a hard-driven horse.

The old man who had been the first to recognize Piotra Bogatiriev
ran to the alley where his wife had fallen, in order to rejoice her
with news of their son. But she was not to be seen. She had picked
herself up and run into the hut to change into her best clothes. The
old man went into the hut, found her, and shouted:

"Piotra Bogatiriev's come home. He's brought us a greeting from
Tikhon." Then, noticing that his old wife was changing her clothes,
and not knowing the reason, his wrath boiled up and he roared at
her: "What are you dressing yourself up for, you old crone? Nobody's going to look at you, you withered devil!"

The elders of the village quickly assembled in the hut of Piotra
Bogatiriev's father. Each of them removed his cap at the threshold,
crossed himself before the ikons, and sat down briskly on the bench,
leaning on his staff. Between sips at a glass of cold milk Piotra Bogatiriev told how he had flown to the district on the instructions of the
Don government at Novocherkass, in order to establish contact with
the insurgent Cossacks and to assist them in their struggle against
the Reds by supplying ammunition and officers by aeroplane. He
informed them that before long the Donietz army would begin an
offensive along its entire front and would join forces with the insurgents' army. He reproved the old men for not having a better influence over the young Cossacks who had abandoned the front and had
let the Reds set foot on the Don land, and ended:

"But since you've thought better of it and driven the Soviet government out of the district, the Don government will pardon you
everything."

"But even now, Piotra Gregorievich, we've got a Soviet government, only without the Communists," one of the old men told him
irresolutely. "Our flag isn't the three-coloured one, but red and
white."

"And our youngsters, the swine, still call one another 'comrade'
when they meet," another added.

Piotra Bogatiriev smiled in his moustache and, screwing up his
blue eyes humorously, replied:

"Your Soviet government is like ice in spring. Let the sun warm it a little and it'll melt away. But we'll settle with those who organized the desertion from the front as soon as we return from the Donietz."

"That's right, cut them down, the devils! Death to all of them to the last man!" the old men roared in delighted approval.

Towards evening the commander of the insurgents, Kudynov, and his chief of staff, Safonov, who had been informed by courier of the aeroplane's arrival, galloped into Singin in a tarantass drawn by a troika of horses. Rejoiced beyond measure by the news, they ran into Bogatiriev's hut without stopping to remove the mud from their boots.

At a secret conference of the supreme command of the insurgent forces, held after Kudynov's return to Vieshenska, it was decided to ask the Don government for assistance. Kudynov was instructed to write a letter declaring the insurgents' repentance and regret for having entered into negotiations with the Reds and abandoning the front at the end of 1918. In his letter Kudynov promised that the fight against the Bolsheviks would be carried on vigorously to a victorious conclusion and asked for staff officers and cartridges to be sent by aeroplane across the front.

Piotra Bogatiriev remained behind with the insurgents, and the pilot carried Kudynov's letter back to Novocherkass. Thenceforth close contact was established between the Don government and the insurgent forces. Almost daily aeroplanes flew from beyond the Donietz, bringing officers, cartridges, and small quantities of shells for light field-guns. The pilots also brought letters from the upper Don Cossacks who had retreated with the Don army, and carried back answers from their families.

Guided by the situation on the Donietz front and by his own strategic necessities, the commander of the Don White Army, General Sidorin, sent Kudynov plans of operations, instructions, reports, and information of the Red Army divisions being transferred to the insurgent front. Kudynov informed only a chosen few about his correspondence with Sidorin, keeping it a close secret from all others.

PART III

Retreat and Advance

RETREAT AND ADVANCE

Chapter 1

By May 1919 the Soviet government was beginning to realize that the rebellion in the Don province was serious and called for drastic suppression, and the Red forces opposing the insurgents were considerably increased. Now for the first time Gregor Melekhov and his division felt all the might of a formidable attack, and they were compelled to retreat northward towards the Don, yielding village after village. Gregor put up a stubborn resistance around Kargin, but, under the pressure of the enemy's superior strength, he was forced not only to surrender Kargin but to ask Kudynov for reinforcements. In response to his appeal Miedviediev, the commander of the Third Division, transferred eight cavalry squadrons to his command. Gregor was surprised to see how well these squadrons were equipped. All had ample reserves of cartridges, all were in new clothing and good boots taken from Red Army prisoners. Despite the heat many of them were wearing leather jerkins, and almost every man had a pistol or field-glasses. With the aid of these reinforcements the advance of the Red Army was arrested for a time. Gregor decided to take advantage of the opportunity and, in answer to Kudynov's incessant requests, to ride into Vieshenska for a conference.

He arrived at Vieshenska early in the morning. The Don flood water was beginning to abate, the air was filled with the cloyingly sweet, glutinous scent of the poplars. Along the river the sappy dark-green leaves of the oaks were rustling dreamily. The bared earthy rises were steaming, and a slender, prickly green was showing on them. The hollows still gleamed with stagnant water, and above it gnats were swarming.

Gregor found Kudynov sitting with a serious and preoccupied face, intent on a strange task. As Gregor quietly entered he did not look up, but continued to pull the legs off a large, horribly green fly. He pulled off a leg, then closed his great dry palm around the fly and set it to his ear, listening concentratedly to the excited buzzing of the imprisoned insect.

Suddenly noticing Gregor, with a gesture of revulsion and irritation he threw the fly under the table, wiped his palm on his trousers, and wearily leaned against the shiny back of his chair.

"Sit down, Gregor Pantalievich," he said.

"How are you, chief?" Gregor inquired.

"Well; as well as can be expected. How are things going with you? So they're driving you back?"

"All along the line."

"Did you hold them at the Chira?"

"Not for long. But Miedviediev's reinforcements saved the situation."

"This is the position, Melekhov." Kudynov took the grey leather of his Caucasian belt in his hands and, staring with studied attention at the tarnished silver of the buckle, he sighed. "So far as we can see, our affairs will get still worse before they're better. Something is happening on the Donietz. Either our friends there are breaking through the Red front and pushing them back on to us, or else the Reds have realized that we're the cause of all their present troubles and are trying to close us in a vise."

"And what news is there from the Cadets? What reports did they send by the last aeroplane?"

"Nothing special. They don't tell you or me their plans, brother! They're trying to break through the Red front and come to our help. They've promised us assistance, but it doesn't always come. It's not an easy matter to break through a front, and you and I know what strength the Reds have got on the Donietz. We are living in the dark, and we can't see farther than the ends of our noses."

"Well, what did you want to talk to me about? How about this conference you called me in for?" Gregor asked, yawning with boredom. He was not particularly concerned for the result of the rising. It no longer seemed to trouble him. Like a horse dragging a roller around a threshing-floor, his thoughts had circled day after day around the one problem until at last he had mentally shrugged his shoulders: "There'll be no making peace with the Soviets now, that's certain. We've shed too much of their blood. But we let them come into the Don province, and although the Cadet government is saying smooth words to us now, they'll be making our fur fly later on. Damn it, whichever way it ends it'll be well ended."

Still not looking Gregor in the eyes, Kudynov unfolded a map and remarked:

"We've had a conference here in your absence and have decided. . . ."

"Whom did you have the conference with? With the prince?" Gregor interrupted him, recalling the council of war that had taken place in this same room in the winter, with the Caucasian general present.

Kudynov frowned and his face darkened. "He's no longer here," he replied.

"How is that?" Gregor asked with sudden interest.

"Haven't I ever told you? Comrade Georgidze was killed."

"How can you call him 'comrade.' He was a comrade only so long as he was wearing a sheepskin jacket. But if we'd joined forces with the Cadets—which God forbid—and he'd been still alive, he'd have been greasing his moustache the very same day, and he wouldn't have offered you his hand, but his little finger! Like that!" Gregor stuck out his dirty, swarthy finger and laughed, baring his teeth.

Kudynov still frowned, and open dissatisfaction, irritation, and restrained annoyance were expressed in his glance and his voice.

"There's nothing to laugh about," he snarled. "Don't laugh at another man's death."

Gregor smilingly replied: "I've no pity to spare for that white-faced and white-handed colonel. . . ."

"Well, he's been killed."

"In a battle?"

"It's difficult to tell. . . . It's a strange story, and the truth isn't easy to get at. On my orders he was attached to the transport. It

appears he didn't get on well with the Cossacks. There was a fight
going on close to Dudorevka, and the transport with which he was
riding was about two miles behind the firing line. He was sitting on
a wagon, and a stray bullet hit him and bowled him into the sand.
So the Cossacks said. They left him unburied . . . the Cossacks
must have killed him, the swine!"

"And they did well to kill him!"

"Enough of that talk; it will get you into trouble."

"Don't get angry. I was joking."

"Another time keep your stupid jokes to yourself. So according to
you the officers ought to be killed! 'Down with the epaulets' again?
Isn't it time you found some sense, Gregor?"

"Get on with your story."

"There's no more to tell. I guessed the Cossacks had killed him,
and went out and had a heart-to-heart talk with them. They denied
that they'd killed him, but I could see by their eyes that they were
lying. But what are you to do with them? You could piss in front
of them and they'd swear it was God's own dew falling." Kudynov
crushed the belt in his hands and flushed. "They killed the one man
who knew the art of war, and now without him I feel as though I'd
lost my right hand. Who will draw up plans for us now? We can
talk away here, but as soon as it's a question of strategy we're out of
our depth. I'm thankful Piotra Bogatiriev arrived, or I'd have had no
one to exchange a word with. And now I'm come to the real point:
If our people don't break through the front on the Donietz we shan't
be able to hold out. So we've decided, as I've already said, to throw
the whole army of thirty thousand into an attempt to break through.
If you're beaten back, then retreat to the Don. We'll clear the right
bank from Ust-Khopersk to Kazanska, dig trenches, and defend
ourselves. . . ."

He was interrupted by a sharp knock on the door. "Come in," he
shouted.

The commander of the sixth special brigade, Gregor Bogatiriev,
entered. His strong red face was glistening with sweat, his faded
auburn eyebrows were knitted angrily. Without removing his cap
he sat down at the table.

"What have you come for?" Kudynov asked, staring at Bogatiriev
with a restrained smile.

"Give us cartridges!" Bogatiriev demanded.

"We've given you some. How many more do you want? Do you think I've got a cartridge factory here?"

"And what did you give us? One cartridge for each man! They're firing at us with their machine-guns, and all we can do is bow our backs and hide ourselves. Do you call that war?"

"Wait a bit, Bogatiriev, we're discussing important matters," Kudynov said. As Bogatiriev rose to go out, he added: "But don't go. We've no secrets from you." He turned to Gregor. "Well, then, Melekhov, if we can't hold out even on this side, then we'll try to break through. We'll leave all who're not in the army, leave all our baggage, put the infantry on wagons, take three batteries with us, and march to the Donietz. We want to put you at the head. You won't object?"

"It's all one to me. But how about our families? Our girls, our wives, the old men will all be lost."

"What is to be— Better they should go under than that we all should."

Bogatiriev smiled and shook his head. "And by next year how many peasants will our women have given birth to?" he remarked. "You won't be able to count them. The Reds are hungry for women now. The other day we retreated from a village, and everybody cleared out with us, only one young wife staying behind. In the morning we saw her crawling towards us like a crab. The comrades had abused her until she could no longer stand on her feet."

Kudynov's mouth drooped at the corners. Gregor turned to go out. But before going he asked Kudynov:

"In the event of my bringing the whole division to Bazki, will there be anything for us to cross the river to Vieshenska on?"

"What an idea! The cavalry can swim their horses across the Don, surely? Who ever heard of cavalry being carried across a river?"

"But I haven't many Donside men, you know that. And the Cossacks from the Chira are not good at swimming. They've spent all their lives in the steppe, and where can they swim there?"

"They'll manage on their horses. They had to do it at manœuvres and in the German war."

"I'm talking about the infantry."

"There's the ferry. And we'll get boats ready, don't be afraid."

"The people will be coming, too."

"I know."

"You provide means of crossing for everybody, or I'll wring the soul out of you when I arrive. It won't be any joke if the people get left on the wrong side of the river."

"All right, I'll see to it, I'll see to it."

"And what about the guns?"

"Blow up the mortars, but bring the field-guns here. We'll get boats ready big enough to bring the batteries over to this side."

Since the battle in which he had killed the sailors Gregor had lived continually in a state of cold, numb indifference. He went about with head hanging despondently, without a smile. For a whole day pain and sorrow for the dead Ivan Alexievich had troubled him; then that, too, had passed. The only thing left to him in life (or so it seemed to him) was his passion for Aksinia, which had returned with new and unbearable strength. She alone beckoned him to herself, as a distant, flickering camp-fire in the steppe beckons a traveller through the freezing, dark, autumnal night.

Now as he returned from staff headquarters he thought of Aksinia: "We're going to try to break through, but what about her?" Without hesitation he decided: "Natalia will stay behind with the children, with Mother, but I'll take Aksinia with me. I'll get her a horse and she can ride with my staff."

He crossed the Don to Bazki, entered his quarters, tore a page from his notebook, and wrote:

"Aksinia, we may have to retreat to the left side of the Don. If so, leave everything and ride to Vieshenska. Look for me there; you will go with me."

He folded the note and sealed it with gum, gave it to Prokhor Zykov, and, flushing, concealing his embarrassment under unnecessary sternness, told him:

"Ride to Tatarsk and give this note to Aksinia Astakhova. See that no one of my people notices you give it to her. Better take it at night. I don't need an answer. And afterwards you can have two days' furlough. Off with you!"

Prokhor turned to go for his horse, but Gregor called him back:

"Go to my hut and tell my mother, or Natalia, that they'd better send clothing and anything else of value over to this side of the Don. They can bury the grain, but the cattle had better be driven across to this side."

Chapter 2

During the early days of June the insurgent forces began to retire along the whole of the front. They retreated fighting, contesting every inch of ground. Before them the inhabitants of the villages fled in panic towards the Don. The old men and the women harnessed up all the draught animals in their possession, and loaded their wagons with chests, utensils and implements, grain and children. The village herds were broken up and the owners drove their cows and sheep along the roadside. Enormous trains of refugees rolled down to the Donside villages before the army. The women, dusty, and black with sunburn, drove the cattle; the horsemen rode at the roadside. The creaking of wheels, snorting of horses and sheep, lowing of cows, crying of children, groans of the typhus sufferers also carried away in the flight, shattered the inviolate silence of the villages and the cherry orchards. So unusual was this myriad-toned, blended roar that the dogs went hoarse with barking, gave up flinging themselves at every passer-by, and no longer accompanied the wagons on their way for a good mile, as in normal times.

On the morning of June 4 the sky was covered with a tenuous mist. Not a single cloud was visible over all its expanse, save where to the south, just before sunrise, a tiny, blindingly rosy little cloud appeared. The side of it turned towards the east seemed to be streaming with blood. The sun rose above the sandy breakers of the left bank of the river, and the cloud disappeared from sight.

By noonday it was extraordinarily hot for early June. The air steamed as though before rain. From early dawn the refugee wagons had been dragging along the right bank of the Don towards Vieshenska. The sound of cart-wheels, of snorting horses, bellowing bullocks, and human voices floated across the river.

Prokhor Zykov handed Gregor's note to Aksinia, told Ilinichna Gregor's oral instructions, spent two days at home, and left for Vieshenska on the 4th of June. He expected to find his company in Bazki. But the heavy gunfire in the distance seemed to be coming from somewhere beyond the river Chira. Prokhor felt no strong desire to ride to where a battle was raging, and he resolved to make his way to Bazki and wait there for Gregor and the First Division to arrive.

He rode unhurriedly, almost at a walking pace, along the Hetman's highway to Gromok. He overtook the staff of a recently formed Ust-Khopersk regiment and attached himself to it. The staff was travelling on light, springed droshkies and a couple of wagonettes. On one of the wagonettes were documents and telephone apparatus; on the other a wounded elderly Cossack and another hooknosed man, terribly emaciated, his head covered with an officer's grey karakul fur cap. Evidently he was just recovering from typhus. He lay with a greatcoat covering him to his chin, yet he was asking someone to wrap his feet in something warm, and raged and cursed as he rubbed the sweat from his forehead with his bony hand.

"You swine! The wind's getting under my feet! Polikarp, cover me with a rug. I must needs come down just when I was needed. . . ." His eyes wandered absently around him.

The man he had called Polikarp dismounted and hurried to the wagonette. He said:

"Why, as it is, you're so hot you'll catch a chill, Samoilo Ivanovich."

"Cover me up, I tell you!"

Polikarp obediently carried out the order and dropped back.

"Who is he?" Prokhor asked him, with his eyes indicating the sick man.

"An officer from Ust-Miedviedietz. He was attached to our staff," the Cossack replied.

A swarm of refugees from Ust-Khopersk villages was retreating with the staff. Prokhor called to one old Cossack who was seated on a wagon piled high with various domestic treasures:

"Hey, where the devil do you think you're going?"

"We're going to Vieshenska," the man replied.

"Did they send for you to go to Vieshenska?"

"No one sent for us, but who wants to meet his death? When fear looks in your eyes you'll ride fast enough."

"I asked you why you are going to Vieshenska," Prokhor demanded. "You could have crossed the Don at Yelanska and stayed there in the steppe on the other side for weeks. No, you must go to Vieshenska! But you don't know why! And what have you got all those for?" Prokhor irritably pointed his whip at the bundles on the wagon.

"We've got our clothing, and horse-collars, flour, and suchlike that we need on the farm. We couldn't leave them behind. We'd have come back to find our hut bare. My boy, when you've got your things together with tears and sweat it isn't easy to leave them behind. If it had been possible I'd have packed up my hut, too, so that the Reds shouldn't get it, the cholera seize them!"

"But that great trough there, what are you dragging that with you for? And those chairs? The Reds wouldn't want them!"

"We couldn't leave them behind. They'd have broken them up or burned them. No, they won't get rich at my expense. I cleaned the hut right out!" The old man waved his whip at the wearily plodding horses, turned and pointed with the stock at a bullock-wagon behind him, and added:

"You see that girl wrapped up there, driving the bullocks? She's my daughter. She's got a pig with a litter of little ones in that wagon. The pig had them during the night as she lay in the wagon. Can you hear the little ones squealing? No, the Reds won't get very fat at my expense, the plague take them!"

"Keep clear of me when you get to the ferry, grand-dad!" Prokhor remarked, "or you and your pigs and all your possessions will go overboard into the Don."

"What for?" the old man asked in blank amazement.

"Because people are dying, and losing everything, and you, you old devil, are dragging everything with you like a spider," the usually peaceable Prokhor shouted. "I don't like dung-eaters like you." He touched up his horse and trotted on. Behind him the thin piercing scream of a little pig suddenly rose above the other sounds.

"What the devil is that?" the officer lying in the wagonette shouted, frowning and all but weeping. "Where has that pig come from? Polikarp! . . ."

"It's a pig fallen from a wagon, and the wheel went over its leg," Polikarp informed him.

"Tell the owner of the pig to cut its throat. Tell him there are sick men here. . . . That's hard enough, and then we have that scream! Hurry up!"

Prokhor, who had drawn level with the wagonette, saw the officer listening with knitted brows to the scream and vainly trying to cover his ears with his grey cap. Polikarp rode up again.

"He doesn't want to kill it, Samoilo Ivanovich. He says it'll get better, and if not they'll kill it this evening."

The officer went pale, struggled to raise himself, and sat up, dangling his legs over the side of the wagonette.

"Where's my revolver? Stop the horse! Where's the owner of that pig? I'll show him! Which wagon is he on?" he exclaimed. And the thrifty old Cossack was compelled to cut the pig's throat.

Prokhor rode off laughing and soon overtook a new long line of Ust-Khopersk wagons. There were not less than two hundred of them, and with their horsemen, cattle, and sheep they stretched for nearly a mile along the road. "There'll be a fine scene at the ferry!" Prokhor thought.

From the head of the line a woman riding a handsome dark bay horse galloped to meet him. As she came up to him she reined in her horse. She was seated in a richly ornamented saddle, the girths and seat gleamed with good, almost unscratched leather, the snaffles and metal parts glittered with silver. The woman sat the saddle intelligently and easily, she held the reins correctly in her strong, swarthy hand, but it was evident that the well-grown, military mount was contemptuous of his mistress. He rolled his eyes, arched his neck, and, laying bare the yellow line of teeth, tried to bite the woman's knee showing beneath her skirt.

She was wrapped to her eyes with a clean blue kerchief. Removing it from her lips, she asked Prokhor:

"Daddy, you haven't passed wagons with wounded on them, have you?"

"I've passed lots of wagons, but what of it?"

"Why, I can't find my husband," the woman slowly replied. "He was wounded in the leg, and he's being brought from Ust-Khopersk by a field hospital. But it seems the wound has festered and he told me to bring him his horse. This is the horse." The woman patted the animal's neck. "I saddled the horse and rode to Ust-Khopersk, but I couldn't find the hospital. And I've ridden and ridden, but I can't find him."

Admiring the Cossack woman's full, handsome face, Prokhor listened contentedly to the soft timbre of her low contralto voice and exclaimed:

"Why, woman, what do you want to look for your husband for? Let him go with the field hospital! Anyone would marry such a beauty as you with a horse like that for dowry. I'd risk it myself!"

The woman smiled reluctantly and bent to draw the edge of her skirt over her knee. "Tell me without any of your jokes, have you passed a field hospital?" she demanded.

"You'll find sick and wounded in that group there," Prokhor answered with a sigh, pointing at the line of wagons some distance behind.

The woman waved her whip, sharply turned her horse, and cantered off.

The wagons moved along slowly. The bullocks lazily waved their tails, driving off the buzzing horse-flies. It was so hot, so stifling and sultry was the air with its menace of thunder, that the young leaves of the sunflowers growing by the wayside were wilting.

Once more Prokhor rode alongside a string of wagons. He was astonished at the large number of young Cossacks with them—men who must either have been separated or else have deserted from their companies, had joined their families, and were riding with them to the river crossing. Some of them had tied their army horses behind the wagons and were lying talking with their wives or nursing children; others rode on horseback, fully armed with swords and rifles. "They've left their detachments and are fleeing," Prokhor decided as he stared at them.

The bullocks moved slowly, sullenly. From their protruding tongues strings of spittle hung down to the very dust. The wagons drawn by horses moved at the same pace, making no attempt to pass. The entire band was travelling at not more than three or four miles an hour. But suddenly there was the sound of gunfire in the distance to the south, and the cavalcade immediately came to life. The wagons drawn by one or two horses turned out of the line, the horses were put into a trot, knouts began to whistle, shouts arose. The willow switches hissed over the bullocks' backs, the wheels clattered faster. In their alarm all accelerated their pace. Heavy clouds of dust rose in dense billows from the road and floated back, settling on the stalks of grain and grasses.

Prokhor's own little horse had been dragging towards the grass, putting its nose down and tearing up bunches of clover, rape, and field-mustard. But when the gunfire broke out, Prokhor dug his heels into its flanks, and, as though understanding that now was not the moment for feeding, the animal willingly broke into a jog-trot.

The cannonade grew in intensity. The sharp crack of rifle-shots mingled with its shattering octave to send a rolling, thunderous roar through the sultry air.

"Lord Jesus!" A young woman riding on a wagon crossed herself, tore her brown nipple, glistening with milk, from her infant's mouth, and thrust her swollen, yellow breast into her shirt.

"Is that our men firing, or who, soldier?" an old man striding along by his bullocks shouted to Prokhor.

"It's the Reds, daddy. Our guns haven't got any shells."

"Queen of Heaven, save them!" The man let the reins fall from his hand, removed his old Cossack cap, and crossed himself as he walked, turning his face to the east.

In the south an oily black cloud ascended from behind a rise. It extended over all the horizon, and the sky was hidden behind its misty pall.

"Look, there's a big fire back there!" someone shouted.

"What can it be?" "Where is it burning?" voices asked above the rattle of the cart-wheels.

"It's along the Chira River."

"It's the Reds burning the villages along the Chira."

"God forbid! . . ."

"Look what a great cloud of smoke there is! That's more than one village on fire."

"Ivan, tell them in front to hurry up!"

The pall of black smoke extended over more and more of the sky. The roar of gunfire grew steadily louder. Within half an hour the southerly wind brought to the Hetman's highway the pungent and alarming scent of villages burning along the Chira, some twenty miles away.

In one spot the road to Gromok passed by an enclosure fenced with grey locks of stone, then turned sharply towards the Don, dropping into a shallow gully across which a log bridge was thrown. In dry weather the bottom of the gully gleamed yellow with sand and colourful pebbles, but after a summer rain the muddy floods of rainwater sped furiously down the hill, and a stream ran along the gully, washing and rolling over the stones, roaring down to the Don. On such days the bridge was submerged, but not for long. The transient hill water, which at its height would break down walls and root up fences with their posts, quickly abated, and the pebbles gleamed freshly again on the bottom of the gully.

The sides of the gully were densely grown with willows and poplars. In their shade it was cool even on the hottest days of the summer. Rejoicing in the cool, an outpost of Vieshenska militia numbering eleven men was stationed by the bridge, with instructions to arrest all Cossacks of military age attempting to make their way to Vieshenska. Until the first refugee wagons appeared in the distance, the men lay under the bridge, playing cards, smoking, some of them undressing and freeing their shirts and pants of the insatiable soldiers' lice. Two of them obtained permission from their officer and went off to bathe in the Don.

But their rest was of short duration, for refugees were soon pouring down to the bridge in an unbroken flood, and the drowsy, shady little spot grew suddenly populous, noisy, and hot, as though the sultriness of the steppe had come down from the Donside hills together with the wagons.

The commander of the outpost, a tall, lean, non-commissioned officer, stood at the bridge with his hand on the holster of his revolver. He let a good score of wagons pass without hindrance, but then, noticing a young Cossack, perhaps twenty-five years old, driving along in the line, he curtly ordered him:

"Stop!"

The Cossack frowned and pulled on the reins.

"What's your regiment?" the commander demanded, going up to the wagon.

"What's that to you?"

"What's your regiment, I asked you. Well?"

"I'm from a Rubiezhin company. And who are you?"

"Get down!"

"Who are you, I want to know."

"Get down, I tell you"; the commander went red to the ears. He unbuttoned the flap of his holster, drew out his revolver, and passed it into his left hand. The young Cossack thrust the reins into his wife's hands and jumped down from the wagon.

"Why aren't you with your regiment? Where are you driving to?" the commander questioned him.

"I've been ill. I'm going to Bazki now with my family."

"Have you got any document showing you had sick-leave?"

"Where could I get any document? The company was without a doctor."

"So you hadn't one! Karpenko!" He called one of his men. "Take this man along to the school."

"Who the devil are you?" the Cossack demanded.

"We'll show you who we are!"

"I've got to return to my company. You've got no right to stop me."

"We'll send you ourselves. Have you got any weapons?"

"A rifle."

"Get it out quick or I'll drill a hole in you. A young Cossack like you, and hiding behind your wife's petticoats! Have we got to defend you?" As the commander turned away he contemptuously called over his shoulder:

"Skunk!"

The Cossack fished his rifle from under a rug. Then, unwilling to kiss his wife in the sight of others, he took her by the hand, muttered something to her, and followed his escort to the school.

Once more the wagons crowded into the narrow street rolled thunderously over the bridge.

In an hour the outpost had arrested some fifty deserters. Some of them tried to resist, especially one elderly, long-moustached, fierce-looking little Cossack. When the commander ordered him to get down from his wagon he struck his horses with his whip. Two of the militia-men seized the animals by the bridles and brought them to a halt on the farther side of the bridge. Without stopping to think twice, the Cossack snatched up a rifle from under a tarpaulin and threw it to his shoulder.

"Out of the way," he shouted, "or I'll kill you, curse you!"

"Get down, get down!" the militia-man told him. "We've been ordered to shoot anyone who doesn't obey. We'll have you covered in a moment."

"You peasants! Yesterday you were killing the Reds, and today you're taking aim at Cossacks. . . . Stinking skins! Get away or I'll fire. . . ."

One of the militia-men jumped on to a front wheel of the wagon and, after a brief struggle, wrested the rifle out of the man's hand. The Cossack bent down like a cat, slipped his hand under the tarpaulin, pulled a sabre out of its scabbard, and, kneeling, reached across the side of the wagon, just missing the head of the militia-man as he sprang away.

"Timofei, drop it! Timofei! Oh! Don't do that. . . . Don't resist, they'll kill you!" his weeping wife cried to the infuriated Cossack.

But he rose to his full height in the wagon and swung his steely-blue, gleaming sabre around his head, keeping the militia-men away and cursing evilly. "Stand back or I'll cut you down!" he roared, his face quivering with anger, his eyes going bloodshot.

With difficulty they disarmed him, threw him down, and bound him. When they searched the wagon they found a simple explanation of his stubborn resistance, for in it they came upon a large pitcher of strong home-made vodka.

Meantime the narrow road was dammed with wagons and animals. So closely packed were the vehicles that the bullocks and horses had to be unharnessed and the wagons were dragged by hand down to the bridge. Frenzied with horse-flies, the evilly snorting horses and bullocks snapped the shafts and struggled across to the fences, paying no heed to their masters' orders. Curses, the whistling of whips, women's lamentations sounded a long time by the bridge. The wagons at the rear, where there was room to move, turned back and climbed up to the highway again, to make their way down to the Don at Bazki.

The arrested deserters were sent under escort to Bazki, but as they were all armed the escort could not control them. As soon as they had crossed the bridge a struggle broke out between the escort and the prisoners. After a little while the escort returned to the outpost, and the deserters marched themselves off in military order to Vieshenska.

Prokhor arrived at Bazki opposite Vieshenska early in the evening. Thousands of refugee wagons blocked all the streets and side lanes and lined the bank of the Don for nearly two miles. Over a thousand people were scattered through the woods waiting to be carried to the farther side. Batteries, regimental staffs, and military equipment were being transported by ferry across the river. The infantry were carried in row-boats, dozens of which were dotted over the Don. A seething mass of human beings was crowded around the landing-stage.

The first detachments of the cavalry covering the retreat began to arrive at midnight and were to cross as soon as dawn came. But there was no news of the cavalry of the First Division, and Prokhor decided to wait in Bazki for his squadron. He left his saddled horse tied to a refugee wagon and went off to look for acquaintances among the crowd.

In the distance he noticed Aksinia Astakhova going down to the river, a small bundle pressed against her breast, her warm jacket flung across her shoulders. Her striking beauty attracted the attention of some infantry-men at the river-side, and they called out to her and burst into a lewd and juicy roar of laughter. One tall, flaxen-haired Cossack ventured to put his arms around her from behind and pressed his lips against her swarthy neck. But she pushed the man off roughly, saying something and baring her teeth. The group of soldiers roared and the Cossack removed his cap, hoarsely pleading: "Just one little kiss!"

Aksinia hastened her steps and strode on, a contemptuous smile flickering over her lips. Prokhor did not call to her, but looked for other fellow-villagers among the crowd. As he slowly passed through the throng he heard drunken voices and laughter, and the next moment he came upon three old men sitting on a horse-cloth under a wagon. One of them had a pitcher of home-made vodka between his legs. The merrymaking old lads took turns at drinking the vodka from a copper mug made from a shell-case and chewing at some dried fish. The strong smell of the liquor and the salty odour of the fish brought hungry Prokhor to a halt.

"Soldier, come and have a drink with us!" one of the men invited him. Nothing loath, Prokhor sat down, crossed himself, and smilingly accepted a mug of the liquor from the hospitable old man.

"Drink while you're still alive! Here, take a bite at this bream. You needn't wait to be asked, youngster," another of the group said. "The old men are the wise men. You boys have still got to learn from us how to live and how to drink vodka."

Prokhor willingly pressed his lips thirstily against the brim of
the mug and, without pausing for breath, drank its contents to the
bottom.

"All my living is gone! So why shouldn't I drink?" bellowed the
owner of the vodka, a fleshy and healthy old fellow. "I've brought
two hundred poods of grain with me, but I've had to leave a thousand behind. I've driven five pairs of bullocks as far as this place,
but I've got to leave them behind too, now, because I can't get
them across the river. All that I've scraped together will be lost.
So sing up! Come on, friends!" His face turned livid and his eyes
filled with tears.

"Don't shout, Trofim Ivanich! If our lives are spared we shall get
rich again," one of the others argued with him.

"Why mustn't I shout?" The old Cossack raised his voice still
higher, and his face was stained with tears. "My grain will all be
lost. My bullocks will die. The Reds will burn down my hut. My
son was killed last autumn. So how can I help shouting? Who did
I get my farm and possessions together for? In the old days I'd
have ten shirts rot with sweat on my back during the summer, and
now I'm left naked and barefoot. Drink up!"

During their talk Prokhor ate a whole bream, drank seven mugs
of vodka, and became so drunk that when he wanted to leave them
he had great difficulty in getting on to his feet.

"Soldier, I'll give you some grain for your horse if you want it,"
the owner of the vodka offered.

"I'll take a sackful," Prokhor muttered, indifferent to all around
him.

The old man poured out a sackful of first-quality oats and helped
him to hoist it on to his shoulders. "But bring the sack back. Don't
forget, for the love of Christ!" he asked Prokhor, embracing him
and weeping maudlin tears.

"I won't bring it back. I say I won't, and I mean I won't." Prokhor obstinately, senselessly refused.

He reeled away from the wagon. The sack on his back drove
him on as it swung. To Prokhor it seemed as though he were walking over earth slippery with frost, for his feet went slipping and
quivering like those of an unshod horse stepping on ice. After a
few uncertain paces he halted, trying to remember whether he had
been wearing a cap or not. A horse tied to a wagon smelt the oats,

pulled towards the sack, and bit at the corner. The grain ran with a swish through the hole. Finding his burden lighter, Prokhor set off again.

He might have succeeded in carrying the rest of the oats to his horse, but a large bull which he was passing suddenly lashed out at him with his hoofs. The bull had been tormented by gnats and horse-flies and driven to a frenzy by the heat and continual standing and would not let anyone approach him. Prokhor, who was not the first victim of the bull's frenzy that day, went flying, struck his head against the hub of a wheel, and fell asleep at once.

He awoke about midnight. Above him leaden-grey clouds were flying westward through the sky. A young moon peered momentarily through a rift, then the sky was enveloped with clouds and the wind seemed to turn colder. Cavalry was passing quite close to the wagon by which Prokhor was lying. The earth groaned under the trample of innumerable iron-shod hoofs. Sensing the imminence of rain, the animals snorted. Sword-scabbards rattled against stirrups, the rusty glow of cigarettes shone out for a moment. The smell of horses' sweat and the acrid scent of leather equipment came to Prokhor's nostrils. Avidly dilating his nostrils at the familiar smell, he raised his heavy head.

"What regiment are you, brothers?" he asked.

"Cavalry," a voice jestingly replied through the darkness.

"Yes; but I asked what regiment?"

"Petliura's," the same voice answered.

"You swine!" Prokhor cursed and waited for a moment or two, then repeated his question:

"What regiment are you, comrades?"

"Bokovsky," came the answer.

Prokhor tried to get to his feet, but the blood rushed to his head and nausea rose in his throat. He lay down and went off to sleep again. Towards morning a raw chilliness came up from the river.

"He's not dead," he heard a voice above him through his sleep.

"He's warm . . . and drunk!" another man replied right by Prokhor's ear.

"Drag him out of the way! He's dropped down like a carcass. Give him a taste of your lance!" the first voice said.

With the shaft of his lance the second man gave the half-conscious Prokhor a painful jab in the ribs, and a pair of hands seized his legs and dragged him to one side.

"Unharness those wagons! A fine time to sleep! Here are the Reds right on our tails, and they're sleeping as if they were at home! Push the wagons out of the way, the battery will be passing in a minute. Hurry! Blocking up the road! . . . What a lot!" an authoritative voice thundered.

The refugees sleeping on and under the wagons began to stir. Prokhor jumped to his feet. He had neither rifle nor sword, and he had lost his right boot since his drunken bout of the previous evening. He was about to search in bewilderment for his things under a wagon, but drivers and gunners from an approaching battery ruthlessly turned the wagon over, together with the chests in it, and in a moment had opened a road for their guns.

The drivers ran to their horses. The broad leather traces quivered and tautened. The great wheels of the field-guns groaned along the ruts. The hub of an ammunition wagon caught in a wagon-shaft and snapped it.

"You're deserting the front! Fine soldiers you are, damn you!" the old man who had been so hospitable to Prokhor shouted from the wagon. The battery team went by in silence, hurrying to get across the river. In the early twilight Prokhor sought long for his rifle and horse. But he found neither. Down by the river he took off his other boot and threw it into the water; then he wet his head again and again in the endeavour to ease the unbearable pain that gripped it in iron bands.

The cavalry began to cross the river at sunrise. The Cossacks drove their horses down to the Don above the point where it turned at a right angle westward. The horses herded together and were unwilling to enter the bitterly cold water; the Cossacks shouted and drove them on with their whips. One raven horse with a broad star on its forehead began to swim, and the others followed it, snorting as they made the water seethe around them. The Cossacks followed them on six barges, a man standing on the prow of each barge with a rope lasso ready for any emergency.

"Don't get in front of them! Drive them across the current. Don't let it carry them away," the squadron commander shouted, making his whip whistle in his hand before he brought it down against the leg of his muddy boot.

The swift current began to sweep the horses downstream. The

raven horse easily outdistanced the others and was the first to emerge on the sandy shore of the left bank. At that moment the sun peered above the bushy branches of a poplar, a rosy shaft of light fell on the raven horse, and its hair, gleaming with the damp, flashed into a dazzling sombre flame.

The horses all reached the farther bank without accident. Cossacks were already waiting for them there, sorting out the mounts as they landed and bridling them. On the other side men began to send the saddles by boat across the river.

After inquiring about his own squadron Prokhor returned to the refugee wagons. Everywhere the pungent smoke of camp-fires made of brushwood, dismantled fences, and dried dung was rising in the breeze. The women were getting breakfast. During the night several thousand more refugees had arrived from the steppe districts on the right bank of the Don. Around the fires arose a hum of voices. Prokhor caught snatches of conversation:

"When shall we get a chance to cross?"

"If it's God's will that we're not to get across, I'll pour my grain into the Don rather than let the Reds get it."

"What we've lived to see—Lord! . . ."

"The Reds have been ordered to kill all the Cossacks from the age of six to the very oldest. . . ."

By a gaily decorated wagon a grey-haired old man, a village ataman by his looks and authoritative bearing, was haranguing:

"I said to him: 'So the people have got to die on the bank of the river? When shall we be able to cross to the other side? The Reds will cut us down to the roots.' And His Excellency said: 'Don't be afraid, daddy! We shall hold and defend our positions until all the people have crossed. We won't let our wives, children, and fathers suffer.' "

The crowd of women and old men surrounding him was listening with the greatest attention. A general medley of shouts arose from them when the old man paused for breath:

"Then why has the battery gone across?"

"And the cavalry have arrived."

"They say Gregor Melekhov's left the front undefended."

"Who will defend us now? The soldiers have gone in front, and left the people behind."

"It's every man saving his own skin."

"We must send elders to the Reds with bread and salt. Maybe they'll have mercy and not punish us."

A horseman turned the corner into the street. His rifle was hanging at his saddle-bow, a lance was swinging at his side.

"Why, that's my Mishka!" an elderly woman cried in delight. She ran to meet the rider, pushing between horses and wagons and jumping over shafts. The rider was seized by the stirrups and brought to a halt. He raised a grey sealed packet above his head and shouted:

"A dispatch for the chief of staff! Let me pass!"

"Mishka, my little son!" the elderly woman called agitatedly, the streaky grey strands of her hair falling over her radiant face. Pressing all her body against the horse's side, with a trembling smile she asked:

"Did you come through our village?"

"Yes. The Reds are in it now. . . ."

"Our hut—"

"Our hut is left, but Fiodot's has been burned down. Our shed caught, too, but the Reds put it out themselves. Fiodot's wife fled and told us their officer said not one of the poor Cossacks' huts was to be burned, but all those of the bourgeoisie."

"Well, the Lord be praised! Christ save them!" The woman crossed herself.

A stern old man intervened indignantly:

"What are you saying, woman? They've burned down your neighbour's hut and you're crying: 'The Lord be praised!' "

"My neighbour can quickly build a new hut, but what could I do if ours was to be burned down?" the woman swiftly retorted. "Fiodot's got a pitcher of gold buried, but I've had to work all my life for others."

"Let me go, Mother!" The rider leaned down from his saddle. "I've got to hurry with this packet."

The woman turned and walked along at the horse's side for a moment, then ran back to the wagon, while the courier shouted:

"Make way! I've got a packet for the commander-in-chief. Make way!"

The horse pranced and side-stepped, the people reluctantly

opened a road, and the rider went with apparent deliberation. But he soon disappeared behind the wagons, behind the backs of the bullocks and horses, and only the lance swung above the enormous crowd as he made his way to the river.

Chapter 3

In the course of the next day the entire insurgent force and the refugees also were transferred to the other side of the river. The last to cross was the Vieshenska regiment of Gregor Melekhov's First Division. Until evening Gregor with twelve picked squadrons withstood the pressure of the Reds, and about five o'clock, on receiving word from Kudynov that the army and the refugees had all crossed, he gave the order to retreat.

In accordance with the insurgents' plans the companies drawn from the Donside villages were to hold the river-bank, each opposite its own village. Where there were extensive gaps between the villages, the staff assigned companies drawn from the Cossacks of the steppe districts, the remainder of these being held behind the line as a reserve. Thus along the left bank of the Don the insurgent front stretched for nearly a hundred miles, from the farthest villages of the Kazanska district to the mouth of the Khoper.

Towards noon reports began to come in from the various companies, the majority announcing that they were already occupying their respective positions. As soon as they arrived they hurriedly prepared for a trench war, hastily digging trenches, cutting down and sawing poplars, willows, and oaks, constructing blindages and machine-gun nests. All the empty sacks were commandeered from the refugees, filled with sand, and arranged as breastworks in front of the long line of trenches.

By evening the digging of trenches was everywhere completed. Behind Vieshenska the first and third batteries were masked in pine plantations. For the eight guns there were all together only five shells. Cartridges were also well-nigh exhausted. Kudynov dispatched urgent couriers with instructions strictly prohibiting all rifle-fire and ordering that each company was to select its one or two finest marksmen and to supply them with adequate quantities of bullets, so that they could pick off the Red machine-gunners and any others who might show themselves in the streets of the right-bank villages. All other Cossacks were only to be permitted to fire if the Reds attempted to cross the river.

That night all fires and lights were prohibited in Vieshenska and the meadows surrounding it. All the Donside swam in a lilac mist. The first Red patrols appeared on the farther slopes early the next morning. Soon they were appearing and disappearing on all the hills of the right bank from Ust-Khopersk to Kazanska. Then the patrols vanished, and until noonday a heavy, deathly silence reigned. But the livid, sombre columns of village fires still rose in the south. The clouds, dispersed by the wind, began to gather again, and pallid day-lightning flickered over their ground. A roll of thunder shook the hanging cloud-masses, and a lashing rain began to fall. The wind sent it running in dancing waves over the chalky spurs of the Donside hills, over the sunflowers wilting with the heat, over the droughty grain. The rain revived the young, dusty leaves, the spring shoots gleamed juicily, the round sunflowers lifted their blackening heads again, and the honey scent of the ripening melons arose from the gardens. The thirsty earth steamed.

In the afternoon the Red patrols again made their appearance on the sentinel mounds that stretch in a chain along the right bank of the Don as far as the Sea of Azov. They rode cautiously down into the villages. After them the infantry poured down the slopes. Behind the sentinel mounds, whence the sentries of the Polovtsians and the nomad bands had formerly watched for the approach of the enemy, Red batteries were set up.

A battery opened fire on Vieshenska. The first shell burst in the square, and afterwards the little grey clumps of smoke from the explosion of shells and the milky-white caps of shrapnel covered the place. Then three more batteries opened fire at Vieshenska and the Cossack trenches along the Donside. Machine-guns began to rattle. Transport-wagons rolled up to the mounds, and trenches were dug along the slopes of the hills.

Now the thunder of cannon was to be heard along the entire front. From the dominating hills the Red batteries raked the oppo-

site bank until late in the evening. The trench-scarred fields held
by the insurgents were silent all along the line. The Cossack cavalry
horses had been concealed in secret river fastnesses impenetrably
overgrown with reeds, sedges, and rushes, where they would not
be troubled by the heat. The trees and the lofty osiers hid them
perfectly from the eyes of the Red observers.

Not a soul was to be seen on the green expanses of meadow, save
occasionally the tiny figures of refugees hurrying farther away from
the Don. The Red machine-gunners sent a few shots after them,
and at the heavy whistle of the bullets the terrified refugees flung
themselves to the ground. They lay among the thick grass until
dusk, and only then ran off to the forests, without a backward look
hurrying to the north, into the wooded wildernesses hospitably
beckoning with their dense growth of alders and birches.

For two days Vieshenska was subjected to a continuous and
intensive artillery bombardment. The inhabitants did not come
out of their cellars. Only at night did life appear in the shell-holed
streets. The insurgents' general staff came to the opinion that so
heavy a bombardment was the prelude to an attempt to cross the
river, and they were apprehensive that the Reds would cross opposite Vieshenska with the object of capturing the place and driving
a wedge through the long line of the front, splitting it in two, and
then by flank attacks crushing the rising completely. On Kudynov's
order more than twenty machine-guns supplied with plentiful reserves of belts were concentrated in Vieshenska. The battery commanders were ordered to fire their remaining shells only if the Reds
were to attempt to cross. The ferry and all the row-boats were
brought into a backwater above Vieshenska, and there were guarded
by a strong force.

To Gregor Melekhov the fears of the staff command seemed to
have no justification. At a general council of war he expressed his
opinion forcibly.

"Do you think there's any possibility of their crossing at Vieshenska?" he demanded. "Look: on this side the bank is as bare
as a tambourine, sandy and smooth, and by the Don itself there
isn't a tree or a bush. On such a bare shore machine-guns would
sweep them all off down to the last man. No, they won't try to
take Vieshenska. They're much more likely to attempt to cross
either where the river's shallow, where there are fords across sand

ɓanks, or else where there's woodland and undergrowth. We must keep a special guard over such spots, especially at night, and must concentrate our reserves there, warning the Cossacks not to make a sound or smell to show where they are."

"You say they won't try to take Vieshenska? Then why are they bombarding it as they are?" one of the others asked.

"Go and ask them!" Gregor replied. "Are they only firing at Vieshenska? How about Kazanska and Yerinska? They've got rather more shells than we have. Our own damned artillery has got five shells, and those five have got oak cases!"

Kudynov burst into a roar of laughter. "He's hit the bull's-eye," he remarked.

"There's no point in that sort of criticism now," the commander of the third battery said angrily. "We must discuss the situation seriously. . . ."

Kudynov frowned and played with his belt. "Melekhov's right in laughing at your artillery," he declared. "You were told again and again not to waste your shells, but to keep them for serious times. But no, you fired at everything that came in sight, even at their wagons, and you've got no right to take offence at criticism. Your position is as laughable as Melekhov says."

Gregor's arguments convinced Kudynov, and he resolutely supported the proposal to set a strong guard over all places suitable for crossing and to concentrate reserve forces close at hand.

Gregor's expectation that the Reds would not attempt to cross opposite Vieshenska but would choose a more suitable spot seemed to have confirmation the very next day. In the morning the commander of the company stationed opposite Gromok reported that all night they had heard sounds of activity coming from the other side of the river. Boards had been brought into Gromok on innumerable wagons, and immediately afterwards the noise of saws, the knocking of hammers and axes, had reached the Cossacks' ears across the river. It was evident that the Reds were making something. At first it was supposed that they were building a pontoon bridge, and two daring Cossacks went some half-mile farther up the river, undressed, and, covering their heads with bushes, quietly floated downstream with the current. They passed very close to the bank and heard Red army men talking in a machine-gun emplacement; but there was nothing in the water, and it was clear the Reds were not building a bridge.

As soon as the report arrived of the Reds' preparations Gregor saddled his horse and rode to the spot. He took a circuitous route for the major part of the road, but for the last two miles he decided to ride at a gallop across the open meadow, risking the possibility that the Reds would open fire upon him. He selected a green spur of willows jutting from the Donside woodland on the farther side of the meadow, then raised his whip. The blow fell on the horse's croup, and the animal set back its ears and flew like a bird towards the willows. But Gregor had not ridden a hundred yards through the meadow when a machine-gun began to rattle from the farther side of the river. The bullets whistled past him like marmots. "They've seen me, the devils!" he thought, shaking out the reins and bending low, his cheek touching the horse's mane. As though he had guessed Gregor's intention the Red gunner aimed lower, and the bullets hopped and skipped under his horse's front hoofs, sending the mud spirting up from the earth, still damp with the spring flood water.

Gregor rose in his stirrups and almost lay along the horse's outstretched neck. The green spur of willows rushed towards him with extraordinary speed. When he had covered half the distance, a field-gun thundered from the opposite hill. The roar of the explosion made Gregor rock in the saddle. The groaning whistle of the shrapnel had hardly died out of his ears, the reeds pressed down by the violent disturbance of the air had not risen again, when the gun thundered a second time. The grinding, oppressing roar seemed to reach its utmost height of intensity, then suddenly stopped for the hundredth of a second. And in that hundredth of a second a black cloud arose before his eyes, the earth trembled with the shattering blow, and the horse's forelegs fell somewhere into space. . . .

Gregor tumbled headlong, striking so forcibly against the ground that his trousers burst at the knees, and the straps broke. The mighty billow of air disturbed by the explosion threw him some distance from his horse. After falling he crawled a few paces over the grass, his cheek to the ground.

Dazed by the fall, he rose to his feet. From above him clods and sprinkles of earth and grass fell in a black rain. His horse was lying some twenty paces from the shell crater. Its head was motionless, but its hind legs, its sweaty croup, and its tail were quivering with a fine, convulsive shiver.

The machine-gun had lapsed into silence. For some five minutes there was not a sound except from the blue kingfishers calling warningly in the reeds. Struggling against his dizziness, Gregor went to his horse. His legs shook and were terribly heavy and felt as though he had been sitting in an awkward position for a long time. He removed the saddle from the horse, but hardly had he passed into the shell-scarred reeds of the nearest thicket when the machine-gun again began to stutter. But he could not hear the flight of the bullets, so evidently they were firing at a new target. He safely reached the company commander's dug-out an hour later.

"They've stopped hammering now," the man reported. "They'll begin again tonight. You might send us some cartridges, we've only got a couple per man."

"Cartridges will be brought this evening. Don't stop watching the other bank for one moment."

"We're watching all right! We're thinking of calling for volunteers to swim across tonight and find out what they're making."

"Why didn't you send someone last night?" Gregor demanded.

"We did send two men, but they were afraid to go into the village. They swam past close to the bank, but they wouldn't go any nearer. And whom will you get to go now? It's a risky business: run into one of their outposts and you'd be done for. The Cossacks aren't so very venturesome when they're close to their own villages. During the German war they were as risky as devils in order to win crosses, but now you have to plead with them to go on sentry duty. And the women are giving us trouble, too. They've come and found their husbands, and they spent last night here in the trenches. And you can't drive them out. I started to chase them off yesterday, and the Cossacks threatened me. 'You behave a bit quieter or we'll quickly settle with you!' they told me."

From the commander's dug-out Gregor went into the trenches. They zigzagged through the forest some fifty yards from the bank of the Don. A growth of acacias and young poplars concealed the yellow mound of the breastworks from the eyes of the enemy. Communication trenches connected the front line with the blindages where the Cossacks rested. Outside the dug-outs were grey heaps of dried fish-skins, mutton bones, sunflower seeds, melon-skins, and other remnants of food, and on the branches newly washed socks, linen drawers, leg-rags, women's shifts and skirts were hanging. From the first of the dug-outs a young, sleepy-eyed woman thrust her lank-haired head. She rubbed her eyes and looked around unconcernedly, then disappeared like a marmot into the black gap of the opening.

From the next dug-out the sound of quiet singing was coming. A muffled but high clear soprano voice was mingled with those of the men. Outside the entrance to the third an elderly, neatly dressed woman was sitting with the grizzled head of a sleeping Cossack resting in her lap. While he was comfortably dozing she was nimbly searching through his hair and killing the black head-lice on a wooden comb, or driving off the flies that settled on her "old man's" face. But for the angry rattle of a machine-gun on the farther side of the Don and the muffled explosion of shells coming from upstream one would have thought a band of woodchoppers was resting in the forest, so peaceable was the appearance of the insurgent company.

Never before during five years of war had Gregor seen such an extraordinary front line. Unable to restrain his smiles he strode past the dug-outs, continually coming on women attending to their husbands' needs, mending clothes, washing their linen, preparing food, and cleaning utensils.

"You're pretty comfortable here, aren't you?" Gregor said to the company commander as they returned to the dug-out.

The man took offence at the remark. "We mustn't grumble," he replied.

"A bit too comfortable!" Gregor frowned. "Get the women out of here at once. Is this place your own yard or a village market? The Reds will be crossing the river and you won't even hear them! Drive the women all out as soon as it's dusk. I'll be coming again tomorrow, and if I see any skirts around I'll knock your head off first of all."

"You're quite right," the man willingly agreed. "I'm against the women being here myself, but what are you to do with the Cossacks? Discipline's gone to pieces. The women wanted to see their husbands. We've been three months fighting now. . . ." He sud-

denly turned red and sat down on his pallet in order to hide a
woman's apron and, turning away from Gregor, glanced out of the
corners of his eyes to where the smiling black eyes of his own wife
were peeping round a sacking curtain which screened one corner
of the dug-out.

Chapter 4

On her arrival in Vieshenska, Aksinia went to stay with an aunt
living on the outskirts not far from the new church. She spent all
the first day looking for Gregor, but he had not arrived in Vieshenska. The whole of the following day bullets were whistling and
shells bursting in the streets, and she could not pluck up sufficient
resolution to leave the hut.

"He told me to come to Vieshenska, promised we'd be together,
and now he's flying the devil knows where!" she thought angrily,
biting her lips as she lay on a chest in the best room. Her old aunt
sat at the window knitting a stocking and crossing herself after
each shot.

"Oh, Lord Jesus! It's terrible, terrible! And what are they fighting for? What are they eating one another for?" she whimpered,
as the window-glass scattered with a jangle over the floor of the
hut.

"Aunty! Come away from the window; you may be hit," Aksinia
asked her. The old woman stared absurdly at her under her spectacles and replied in an annoyed tone:

"Aksinia, you're a fool! Am I an enemy of theirs? Why should
they fire at me?"

"You may get killed by accident. They can't see where their
bullets are going."

"Well, so then they'll kill me! So they don't see who they're
shooting at, eh? They're shooting at the Cossacks; the Cossacks
are their enemies. I'm old and a widow; what should they want
to shoot me for? I expect they know who they're aiming at with
their rifles and cannons."

At noon of that day Gregor galloped down the street, bending close over his horse's neck. Aksinia saw him from the window and ran out on to the porch, crying: "Grishka!" But Gregor had already disappeared round the corner, leaving the dust to settle gently on the road. It was useless to run after him. She stood on the steps weeping angry tears.

"That wasn't Stepan galloped by. What did you run out for as if you were mad?" her aunt asked her.

"It was one of our villagers," Aksinia replied through her tears.

"But what are you crying for?" the inquisitive old woman questioned her.

"What do you want to know for? It's not your business."

'Oh, so it's not my business! Then it was a lover of yours galloped past. You wouldn't have cried out like that for nothing. I've not lived all these years to no purpose."

Towards evening Prokhor Zykov entered the hut. Aksinia was in the best room at the time, and at the sound of Prokhor's voice she ran out, gladly crying: "Prokhor!"

"Well, girl, you've given me a fine hunt," he remarked. "I've worn out all my legs looking for you. He's as mad as can be! Firing going on everywhere, and everybody buried alive, and all he says is: 'Find her or you'll be finding a grave!'"

Aksinia seized Prokhor by the shirt sleeve and drew him into the porch. "Where is he, damn him?" she demanded.

"Hm! Where isn't he? He came back from the front line on his own feet. They'd killed the horse under him. He came back as ill-tempered as a bitch on a chain. 'Found her?' he asked. 'Where am I to find her?' I answered. 'I can't give birth to her.' And he said: 'A woman can't be lost like a needle!' The way he roared at me! He's a wolf in man's form. But come on!"

In a minute Aksinia had tied up her little bundle and hurriedly said good-bye to her aunt.

"Stepan sent for you?" the old woman asked.

"Yes, Aunty."

"Well, give him my love and tell him to drop in and see me."

Aksinia ran out of the hut without listening to her aunt's parting remarks. She hurried along the street so fast that she began to pant and turned pale. At last Prokhor had even to ask her to go more slowly.

"Listen to me!" he said. "I used to run after the girls myself when I was a youngster, but I was never in such a hurry as you are. Can't you wait? Is there a fire, or what?"

In the kitchen of a hut with fast-closed shutters a candle was burning smokily. Gregor was sitting at the table. He had just finished cleaning his rifle and was rubbing the barrel of his pistol when the door scraped and Aksinia stood on the threshold. Her pale, narrow brow was damp with sweat, and her dilated, angry eyes burned with such frantic passion in her white face that Gregor's heart quivered joyously as he looked at her.

"You send for me to come here—and then you yourself vanish," she said, panting heavily. For her at that moment, as once long since, in the first days of their passion, nothing existed except Gregor. Once more the whole world died when Gregor was absent and was reborn when he was near her. Heedless of Prokhor she threw herself towards him, caught up by a savage rapture, and kissed her lover's scrubby cheeks, printing tiny kisses on his nose, his brow, his eyes, his lips, whispering incoherently, weeping, and sobbing:

"I wore myself out. . . . I'm quite ill, Grishka dearest, my blood, my life!"

"Well, now! You see now . . . but wait. . . . Aksinia, stop it!" Gregor muttered in his embarrassment, turning his face and avoiding Prokhor's eyes. He seated her on the bench, removed the shawl from her head, and stroked her dishevelled hair.

"You are a—" he began.

"Yes, I know I am. But you—"

"No, by God, you—you're diseased with love!"

She put her arms round his shoulders, laughed through her tears, and whispered hurriedly:

"Well, how could you! You called me. I came on foot, left everything, and then you weren't here. You galloped past and I ran out and shouted after you, but you'd already turned the corner. They might have killed you, and then I shouldn't have had a last sight of you."

She whispered to him tenderly, sweetly, womanly, all the time foolishly stroking his bowed shoulders, incessantly staring into his eyes with her own humble eyes. Something in her gaze was so pitifully exhausted, yet so mortally harsh, like the eyes of a hunted animal, that it was painful and awkward for Gregor to look at her. He dropped his lashes over his eyes, smiled forcedly, and was silent, while the blush deepened and deepened on her cheeks and her pupils were veiled with a smoky blue haze.

Prokhor went out without a word of farewell. In the porch he spat and trod out the spittle with his foot.

"Infatuation, and nothing more!" he decided harshly as he went down the steps and demonstratively slammed the gate behind him.

For two days they lived as in a dream, confusing day and night, oblivious of all around them. Occasionally Gregor awoke after a brief, stupefying sleep and saw Aksinia's attentive eyes fixed on him in the twilight as though she were learning his features by heart. She lay as usual resting on her elbow, her palm supporting her cheek, and gazed almost unwinkingly.

"What are you staring at?" Gregor asked.

"I want to look my fill of you. They'll kill you; my heart tells me so."

"Well, if it tells you that, stare on!" Gregor smiled.

On the third day he went out for the first time since her arrival. Kudynov had sent messenger after messenger asking him to come to the staff for a conference, but he had sent them back with the message that the conference could be held without him. Prokhor had obtained a fresh mount for him from the staff and had ridden by night to the trenches and brought back his saddle. Now, seeing Gregor preparing to go out, Aksinia asked in alarm:

"Where are you going?"

"I want to ride to Tatarsk to see how our people are defending the village and to find out where my family is," he replied.

"Longing for your children?" With a shiver she wrapped her swarthy shoulders in a shawl.

"Yes."

"Gregor, don't go, will you?" she pleaded, and her eyes glittered. "Is your family more dear to you than I am? Is it? You're drawn this way and that. Do you think we'll all live together in harmony with Natalia? Is that the way you take me to yourself? Well, go, then! But don't come back to me! I won't have you back! I don't want to be treated like that. I don't!"

Gregor silently went out into the yard and mounted his horse. He reached his village meadowland early in the evening. The road ran through the Virgin Glade, where every year on St. Peter's Day the Cossacks drank vodka after allotting the meadowland. He passed Alexei's Thicket, running like a headland out into the meadows. Long years ago in this thicket wolves had attacked a cow belonging to a Tatarsk Cossack named Alexei. Alexei was dead long since; even his memory was worn away as the inscription wears off a tombstone, his surname was forgotten by his neighbours and kinsmen; but the thicket named after him still stretched its dark-green crowns of oaks and elms to heaven. Here the Tatarsk Cossacks were wont to cut down trees for fashioning domestic articles, but each spring vital young shoots arose around the old stumps, there would be a year or two of imperceptible growth, and once more Alexei's Thicket would be spreading its green branches and in autumn would be attired in a golden mantle of frost-nipped oak leaves.

Gregor rode under the cool shade of the branches along last year's road, now overgrown. He passed through the Virgin Glade and made his way up to the Black Cliff, his mind intoxicated with memories. In his boyhood, close to three poplars, he had often hunted wild young ducklings; by the Round Pond he had sat fishing with a line from dawn to dusk. A little farther on stood a single old cranberry bush. It was visible from the Melekhov yard, and every autumn Gregor had stood on the porch of the hut and delighted in the sight of the bush. From a distance it looked as though consumed by a crimson flame. His dead brother Piotra had been very fond of pies made with the bitter cranberries.

With a quiet melancholy in his heart Gregor looked around the well-known spots. His horse went at a walking pace, lazily driving the gadflies and mosquitoes off with its tail. The grasses gently bowed beneath the breeze, and the meadowland rippled with speckled shadows.

He rode to the trenches occupied by the Tatarsk infantry company and sent for his father. Summoned by Christonia, old Pantaleimon came hurriedly limping along.

"Well, greetings, chief!" the old man called to him as he came up.

"Hello, Father!"

"Come to visit us?"

"I had to. Well, how are our people? Where's Mother and Natalia?"

Pantaleimon waved his hand and frowned. Tears slipped over his dark-brown cheek.

"Why, what's the matter? What's happened?" Gregor asked sharply and anxiously.

"They haven't crossed the river. . . ."

"Why not?"

"Natalia has been lying in bed these two days—typhus it looks like. And the old woman wouldn't leave her behind. But don't be alarmed, my son; they're all right."

"And the children? Misha? Polya?"

"They're there too. But Dunia came across. She was afraid to stay behind—a single girl, you know. She's only just gone off with Anikushka's wife. I've already been home twice. I crossed the river quietly by night in a boat and visited them. Natalia's very bad, but the children are well, praise be! Natalia's unconscious; she was so hot the blood had caked on her lips."

"Why didn't you bring her over to this side?" Gregor exclaimed angrily.

The old man grew annoyed, and resentment and reproach sounded in his quivering voice as he answered:

"And what were you doing? Couldn't you have come here to get them?"

"I've got a division under me. I had to see to the crossing of my division," Gregor fiercely protested.

"We've heard of your goings-on in Vieshenska. You left your family and didn't trouble. . . . Ah, Gregor, if you're not ready to think of your own people, you should think more of God. I didn't cross the river here, or do you think I wouldn't have brought them? My platoon was in Yelanska, and by the time we reached here the Reds had entered Tatarsk."

"What I was doing in Vieshenska is nothing to do with you! And don't you . . ." Gregor's voice was hoarse and muffled.

"I didn't mean anything!" The old man took alarm, and stared dissatisfiedly at the Cossacks crowded a little way off. "But talk more quietly, they can hear you over there." He dropped his own voice to a whisper. "You're not a little child, you ought to know better. But don't worry about your family. Natalia will get well again, God willing, and the Reds aren't troubling them. They killed our calf, but that's nothing. They've been merciful and won't harm our folk. They took a lot of grain. But you can't have war without losses."

"Perhaps we could get them across now?"

"I don't think so. And where could we take Natalia to, sick as she is? It would be too risky. They're all right there. The old woman's looking after everything, and I'm not so anxious now as I was. But there were fires in the village."

"Who started them?"

"The square's been burned out and all the big merchants' houses. Korshunov's place was burned to the ground. Lukinichna got away, but old Grishaka remained behind to look after the farm. Your mother said he told her: 'I'll never leave my yard and the Antichrists won't come near me; they're afraid of the sign of the cross.' You know he'd begun to go a little soft. But the Reds weren't afraid of his cross; the hut and the farm buildings were all burned down and there's not a word of what happened to Grishaka. But it was time for him to die. He'd handed his farm over to his son twenty years back, and still went on living. It's your friend who's burning up the village, curse him!"

"Whom do you mean?"

"Mishka Koshevoi, God damn him!"

"It can't be him!"

"It's him all right; God's truth! He visited our hut and asked after you. He told your mother that when the Reds cross to the other side, her Gregor would be the first for the rope. 'He'll be hanging on the highest oak. I won't soil my sword with him,' he said. He asked after me too. 'If I catch old Pantaleimon,' he said, 'I won't kill him off at once, but I'll lay on the whip till his soul can get out through the cuts.' That's the devil he's turned out to be! He goes through the village setting fire to the merchants' and priests' houses and saying: 'In revenge for Ivan Alexievich and Stockman I'll burn down all Vieshenska district.'"

For another half-hour Gregor remained talking with his father, then went to his horse. The old man had made no further reference to Aksinia, but even so Gregor was oppressed. "Everybody must have heard, since Father knows," he thought. "Who told them? Who else except Prokhor has seen us together? Surely Stepan doesn't know too?" He ground his teeth in shame and annoyance with himself.

He treated Christonia and his other fellow-villagers to tobacco and talked with them for a few minutes. Just as he was about to mount his horse he saw Stepan Astakhov coming up. Stepan approached unhurriedly and exchanged greetings, but did not give him his hand.

Gregor stared at him anxiously and inquisitively. "Does he know?" he wondered. But Stepan's handsome face was untroubled and even cheerful, and Gregor sighed with relief.

Chapter 5

Gregor spent the next two days visiting the section of the front held by his First Division. He returned to find that the general staff command had transferred its headquarters to the village of Chorny, some way off from Vieshenska, and after resting his horse he rode to the village.

Kudynov greeted him gaily, staring at him with a challenging smile on his lips. "Well, Gregor Pantalievich, what have you seen?" he asked. "Tell us the news."

"I've seen Cossacks and I've seen the Reds across the river," Gregor replied.

"You've seen a good deal! We've had three aeroplanes here bringing cartridges and letters."

"And what did your friend General Sidorin write?" Gregor inquired.

"My cousin, you mean!" Kudynov continued the conversation in the same bantering tone. "He asks us to hold on with all our strength and not let the Reds cross. And he writes that the Don army is about to start a decisive offensive."

"He writes fair words!" Gregor sneered.

Kudynov suddenly turned serious. "They're going to break through. I'm telling only you and that in the strictest secrecy.

Within a week they'll have broken through the Red Army front. We must hold on!"

"We are holding on!"

"The Reds are preparing to cross the river at Gromok. They're still hammering away there. But where have you been? You haven't been lying low in Vieshenska all this time, have you? The day before yesterday I was searching all through the place for you, and one of my messengers came back and said you weren't in your quarters, but that a handsome woman had come out with tears in her eyes and said you'd ridden off. I couldn't help wondering whether you'd been amusing yourself with a girl and were hiding from us."

Gregor frowned; he did not take kindly to Kudynov's little joke. "You should listen less to lies and should choose messengers with shorter tongues!" he replied curtly. "If you send men with tongues too long for them, I'll shorten them with my sword."

Kudynov burst into a roar of laughter and clapped Gregor on the back. "Can't you stand a joke?" he demanded. "But I've got more serious business to talk over with you. We want to send a couple of cavalry squadrons across the river somewhere this side of Kazanska to make an attack on the Reds. Perhaps they could even cross at Gromok and put them in a panic. What do you think?"

After a moment's silence Gregor replied:

"It's not a bad idea."

"And would you lead the squadrons yourself?" Kudynov asked.

"Why me?"

"We want a fighting commander for the job, that's why. We want someone with plenty of spirit, for it's no joke of a task. The crossing could be so badly bungled that not a man would return."

Flattered by Kudynov's words, without further thought Gregor agreed to take command. "I'll go of course," he replied.

"These are the lines we've been planning and thinking along." Kudynov spoke animatedly, rising from his stool and striding up and down the creaking floorboards of the room. "It won't be necessary for the force to go far to the rear of the enemy, but they should ride along the Don and shake them up a bit in two or three villages so that they feel sick, win some cartridges and shells, capture some prisoners, and then return by the same road. It would all have to be done at night, so as to be back at the fording place by dawn.

Don't you think so? Well, think it over, and tomorrow choose the Cossacks you want to take, and set off. We agreed that except for you there's no one here to do the job. And if you succeed, the Don army won't forget it. As soon as we unite with our friends I shall write a report to General Sidorin himself. I'll set out all your services and you'll be raised in rank." He suddenly broke off as he noticed Gregor's face, hitherto calm, turn dark and distorted with rage.

"I'll show you. . . ." Gregor swiftly folded his arms behind his back and rose from his stool. "You think I'd go for the sake of rank? You think you can hire me? Promising me a higher position? I—"

"Wait a bit."

"I spit on your rank!"

"Wait! You've got me all wrong!"

"I've got you all right!" Gregor choked and sat down again on the stool. "You find somebody else; I'm not going to lead any Cossacks across the Don!"

"You're all worked up over nothing."

"I won't take the command. There's nothing more to be said."

"Well, I'm not going to force you or to plead with you. If you want to, you can; if you don't, it's as you wish. Our situation at the moment is very serious, and that's why we decided not to let them go on with their preparations for crossing if we could help it. I was joking about the rise in rank. You never can take a joke. I was joking about the women, and you flared up just the same. I know you're half a Bolshevik and don't like the officers. And you took it all so seriously! I was only teasing you, just to see you flare up." Kudynov laughed so naturally that for a moment Gregor was troubled by the thought that perhaps after all he had been joking.

"All the same, I refuse to undertake the command," he said obstinately. "I've changed my mind."

Kudynov played unconcernedly with the end of his belt. After a long silence he remarked:

"Well, whether you've changed your mind or whether you're frightened, it doesn't matter. What does matter is that you're spoiling our plans. But of course we shall find someone else to send. Judge for yourself how serious our position is. Kondrat Miedviediev has sent me a new proclamation today. He's directing their army against us himself; he's at Boguchar at present and will be on us today or tomorrow. Here, read it for yourself or you won't believe me." He pulled a yellowing sheet of paper with brown stains of blood on it out of his field wallet and handed it to Gregor. "They found it on some commissar, a Latvian. The serpent resisted to the last cartridge and then threw himself with fixed bayonet on an entire troop of Cossacks. Kondrat himself sent the man down. They've got brave men among them too with their ideas. They found this circular instruction on him."

Gregor took the yellowing sheet and read:

"To be read out before all companies, squadrons, batteries, and commands.

"The end of the shameful Don revolt!

"The last hour has struck. All the necessary preparations have been made. Sufficient forces have been concentrated to shatter the traitors. The hour has struck for settlement of accounts with the Cains who for over two months have been striking in the backs of our active armies on the southern front. With hatred and revulsion all the workers and peasants of Russia have watched these Cossack bands who under a delusive Red flag are assisting the Black Hundred landowners, Denikin and Kolchak.

"Soldiers, commanders, commissars of the Punitive Expedition, the preparatory work is completed. Now, at the signal—forward!

"The nests of the dishonourable traitors and betrayers must be destroyed; the Cains must be exterminated. No mercy on those districts which offer resistance! Mercy only to those who voluntarily lay down their arms and come over to our side! Against the assistants of Kolchak and Denikin—lead, steel, and fire! Comrade soldiers, Soviet Russia relies on you. In a few days you must cleanse the Don from the black stain of treachery. The last hour has struck!

"All, as one man, forward!

"Chairman of the Republic Revolutionary Military Council,
"People's Commissar for Military and Naval Affairs.

"Boguchar, May 25, 1919"

Chapter 6

After delivering Stockman's letter to the Political Section of the Fourteenth Division, Mishka Koshevoi was attached to the 294th Taganrog Regiment, which, together with other detachments of the Thirty-third Kuban Division, had been flung into the Don province to suppress the Cossack revolt. Mishka took part in the struggle to capture Kargin and a number of villages lying along the river Chira. From the day he learned of Stockman's murder and heard the rumour that Ivan Alexievich and the Yelanska Communists had been killed Mishka was possessed by a burning hatred for the Cossacks. He no longer thought, no longer listened to the voice of mercy in his heart when an insurgent Cossack fell into his hands. With blue eyes as cold as ice he would demand of the prisoner: "Have you fought against the Soviet government?" and would ruthlessly cut the man down without waiting for an answer. Not only did he kill his prisoners, but he set the "crimson cock" of an incendiary torch under the eaves of the huts in villages abandoned by the insurgents, and when the fear-demented cows and bullocks broke down the fences and galloped bellowing into the street, he shot them down.

He waged an irreconcilable, relentless war on the Cossack plenitude, on the Cossack perfidy, on all the inviolate and stagnant manner of life which had remained undisturbed for centuries under the roofs of the huts. Stockman's and Ivan's deaths were as fuel to his hatred, and the words of the proclamation: "The nests of the dishonourable traitors must be destroyed, the Cains must be exterminated," clearly formulated his blind feelings. The same day that the proclamation was read to his company he and three other comrades burned down a hundred and fifty huts in Kargin alone. He found some paraffin in a merchant's warehouse and went round the square with a box of matches clutched in his hand. He left behind him a trail of pungent smoke and flame enveloping the priests' and merchants' houses and the huts of the richer Cossacks, the habitations of those "whose slanders had driven on the ignorant Cossack masses to revolt."

The cavalry was always the first to enter the deserted villages, and before the infantry arrived Koshevoi had already fired the richest huts. He desired at all costs to get to Tatarsk to avenge on his fellow-villagers the deaths of Ivan and the Yelanska Communists. He would burn down half the village! He had already mentally drawn up a list of those huts that must be burned down if he did reach Tatarsk. And if his regiment did not happen to pass that way he was resolved to slip off at night without permission.

Other motives besides his desire for revenge were responsible for his anxiety to visit Tatarsk again. During the past two years he had been seeing Dunia Melekhova whenever he was in the village, and they had developed still undeclared feelings of love for each other.

Dunia had made him a tobacco-pouch and had given him a pair of goat's-hair gloves, and he kept an embroidered handkerchief of hers jealously guarded in his breast pocket. Whenever he drew it out he agitatedly recalled a hoar-frosted poplar standing by a well, a fine snow sprinkling from the sombre sky, and Dunia's trembling lips and the crystal glitter of the snow lurking on her eyelashes.

He made diligent preparations for his visit home. He took a colourful rug from the wall of a merchant's house in Kargin and fastened it under his horse-cloth. He found almost new striped trousers in a Cossack's chest, tore up half a dozen women's shawls for three changes of leg-rags, and slipped a pair of woollen gloves into his pack to put on just before he rode down into Tatarsk. From time immemorial it had been the custom for a soldier returning home to be dressed in his finest. And Mishka, still enslaved by the Cossack tradition, devoutly made ready to observe the old custom.

His horse was a fine dark sorrel which he had captured from a Cossack during an attack. His saddle was not too good; the leather was scratched and torn, the metal parts were rusty. The bit and snaffles were in like state, and he had to do something to improve their looks. Fortunately he had a happy inspiration: in one village he found a nickel-plated iron bedstead standing outside a merchant's house, and on the four bedposts were polished metal knobs that brilliantly reflected the sun. It was an easy matter to remove them and to fasten them by silken cords, two to the rings of the bit and two to the bridle-strap across the horse's forehead. The knobs gleamed like the white noonday sun on his horse's head, glittering so unbearably that the animal was dazzled and stumbled as it went. But although its sight suffered and its eyes watered, Mishka did not remove the knobs.

The regiment marched along the Don bank towards Vieshenska. So without much difficulty Mishka obtained permission from his patrol commander to visit his people for the day. Not only did he obtain permission, but the officer asked him if he had a girl, and, on Mishka saying he had, the man asked:

"Have you got a watch and chain?"

"No, comrade," Mishka answered.

"That's bad!" the commander remarked. He had been through the German war and knew what a disgrace it was to return to his native town without trophies. So he removed a watch and a massive chain from his own chest and handed them to Mishka, saying:

"You're a good fighter! Here, wear these while you're at home and dazzle the girls' eyes with them. I've been young myself, and I understand. Tell anyone who asks you that the chain is of new American gold."

Mishka put on the watch and chain, shaved himself by the light of the camp-fire, saddled his horse, and rode off. At dawn he trotted into Tatarsk.

The village seemed no different: the little belfry of the brick church still raised its tarnished gilt cross to heaven, the priests' and merchants' houses still surrounded the square, and the poplar still whispered the same language above the Koshevois' tumbledown hut. Only the profound stillness which entangled the streets like a spider's web was striking by its abnormality. The shutters of the huts were fast closed; here and there the doors were fastened with padlocks, but the majority were flung wide open. It was as though a pestilence had strode with heavy feet through the village, depopulating huts and streets, filling the habitations with emptiness and desolation. No sound was there of human voice, of a lowing cow, of a crowing cock. Only the sparrows chattered animatedly under the eaves of the sheds and on the brushwood.

Mishka rode straight to his own hut. None of his family came out to meet him. The door leading into the porch was wide open, and by the threshold old leg-rags, a bandage dark with blood, chickens' feathers and heads smothered with flies and already putrefying were lying. Evidently some days previously Red Army men had eaten a meal in the hut: the shards of broken pots, chicken bones picked

"Alive and well?"

"Alive, but don't ask whether I'm well."

"Where are your Cossacks?" he asked as he dismounted and went across to her.

"The other side of the Don. . . ."

"Waiting for the Cadets to arrive?"

"Mine's a woman's job. . . . I know nothing about such things. . . ."

"And is Dunia at home?"

"She's gone across the Don too."

"They carried her there!" Mishka's voice quivered with his anger. "I tell you, aunty, your son Gregor's turned out to be the most bitter enemy of the Soviet government. When we get to the other side his neck will be the first to feel the rope. But Pantaleimon Prokoffievich needn't have run away. He's old and lame, he should have stayed at home."

"To wait for his death?" Ilinichna asked harshly, and began again to gather the chips into her apron.

"Death's a long way off from him. We might have given him a taste of the lash, but we wouldn't have troubled to kill him. But I haven't come to talk about that." He adjusted the watch-chain across his chest. "I've come to visit Dunia Pantalievna; I'm awfully sorry she's gone across the Don too, but I tell you as her mother: I've long been wanting her, but we haven't much time to be worried about girls just now; we're fighting the counter-revolution and we shall finish it off without mercy. As soon as we're finished with it and a Soviet government is set up everywhere, then I shall be sending to you for the hand of your Dunia."

"This isn't the time to talk about such things."

"Yes it is!" Mishka scowled. "It's not the time to get engaged, but we can talk about the matter. I can't pick and choose my time. To-day I'm here, and tomorrow I may be sent across the Don. That's why I'm warning you. You're not to give Dunia's hand to anyone else, or it'll be the worse for you. If a letter comes from my regiment saying I've been killed, you can do what you like. But you can't now, because we love each other. I haven't brought her any presents, but if there's anything you'd like from any of the bourgeois merchants' houses, just say so and I'll go at once and bring it here. . . ."

"God forbid! I've never touched other people's goods yet."

clean, fruit-skins, and torn newspapers were scattered over the floor. Mishka passed into the front room. There everything was as in the old days. But he noticed that one half of the trapdoor leading to the cellar where the watermelons were stored in autumn seemed to have been lifted a little.

He went across to the trapdoor. "Surely Mother expected me? She may have hidden something in the cellar for me," he thought. Drawing his sword, with its point he raised the door. A smell of dampness and decay arose from the cellar. He went down on his knees and, peering into the darkness, at last discerned a half-bottle of vodka, a frying-pan with fried eggs in it, a piece of bread half eaten by mice, and a pot covered with a wooden mug, all standing on a spread tablecloth. So his old mother had been expecting him! She had prepared for him as for a welcome guest. His heart trembled with love and gladness as he lowered himself into the cellar. He found a canvas bag tied to a floor joist. He took it down and found in it his underlinen, old but beautifully mended, cleaned and ironed.

The mice had spoilt all the food, and only the milk and the vodka were left untouched. He drank the vodka, ate the solidified, ice-cold milk, took the linen, and clambered out.

His mother had probably fled beyond the Don. "She was afraid to stay, and it was well she didn't, for the Cossacks would have killed her," he thought. "As it is, I expect they ill-treated her because of me." He went out and untied his horse, but decided not to go straight to the Melekhovs' hut. It stood right above the Don, and a good marksman might easily pick him off from across the river. He resolved to go to the Korshunovs' hut and to return to the square at dusk, firing Mokhov's and the other merchants' and priests' houses under the cover of darkness.

He rode along behind the yards to the Korshunovs' spacious yard, rode in through the gate, tied up his horse, and was about to enter the hut when old Grishaka came out on the steps. His white head was shaking, his faded eyes were screwed up blindly. His worn old Cossack tunic with the red spots on its greasy collar was carefully buttoned, but his trousers were falling down, and the old man had to hold them up with his hands.

"How are you, grand-dad?" Mishka called as he stood by the steps waving his whip. The old man made no reply. Anger and dislike were mingled in his stern glance.

"How are you?" Mishka raised his voice.

"Praise be!" Grishaka answered reluctantly. He continued to stare at Mishka with the same angry attention.

"Why didn't you retreat across the Don, Daddy Grishaka?" Mishka asked.

"Who are you?" the old man demanded.

"Mishka Koshevoi."

"The one that used to work for us?"

"That's right. But why didn't you go across the Don?"

"I didn't want to, and I wouldn't. But what is it to you? Have you given yourself to the service of the Antichrists? Wearing a Red star on your cap? You son of a bitch, so you're fighting against our Cossacks? Against your own fellow-villagers?" With uncertain tread he tottered down the steps.

"I'm fighting against them," Mishka answered. "And if I see any of them I'll show them!"

"Ah, what does the Holy Book say? 'With what measure ye measure it shall be meted out unto you.' "

"You needn't quote the sacred writings at me, old man! I haven't come here for that. Get away from the hut at once!" Mishka said harshly.

"What for?"

"Never mind what for! Get out, I tell you!"

"I won't leave my own hut. I know what you're going to do. You're the servant of the Antichrists, you've got their brand on your cap. As the Scriptures foretold, so has it come to pass: 'Son shall rise against father, and brother against brother. . . .' "

"Don't try to get me mixed up. There's no question of brothers here, but of simple arithmetic. My father worked for you to the very day of his death, and before the war I worked for you, strained my guts out labouring for you, and now the time's come to settle accounts. Clear out of the hut, I'm going to set it afire. You've lived all your life in a good house, but now you can live as we've had to live, in straw huts. Understand, old man?"

"Yes, I understand. It's come to that, too. In the book of the prophet Isaiah it is written: 'Their slain shall be cast out, and their stink shall come up out of their carcasses, and the mountains shall be melted with their blood.' "

"I haven't time to argue the Scriptures with you!" Mishka said in a cold fury. "Will you clear out?"

"No, you enemy."

"It's through such as you that there's all this trouble and war going on. It's the likes of you who're troubling the people, raising them against the Revolution," Mishka said as he hurriedly unslung his rifle.

At the shot Grishaka fell headlong, but as he lay he muttered intelligibly:

"Not my will—but Thine be done. Lord, take Thy slave. . . ." He groaned, and the blood spirted out between his white whiskers.

"You ought to have gone long before this, you old devil!" Mishka said as he fastidiously avoided the old man's body and ran up the steps.

The dry leaves and twigs carried into the porch by the wind burst into a rosy flame; the board partitions separating the pantry from the porch quickly caught fire. The smoke rose to the roof and curled into the rooms. Koshevoi went out. By the time he had set fire to the shed and the granary the flames in the hut had broken into the open, licking the pine boards of the window-shutters, stretching their fingers up to the roof.

Until dusk Mishka slept in the neighbouring orchard under the shade of thorn-bushes. His hobbled horse grazed lazily close by. As evening drew on, the horse was troubled with thirst and neighed and awoke its master. Mishka rose, watered the animal at the well in the orchard, saddled it, and rode into the street. The smoke was still rising from the charred implements in the Korshunovs' yard; only the high stone foundations and the half-ruined stove raising a sooty chimney to the sky were left of the hut.

Mishka rode straight to the Melekhovs' yard. As he went through the wicket gate he found Ilinichna heaping chips into an apron.

"Hello, aunty!" he graciously called to her. In her terror at the sight of him she could utter not a word in reply, but dropped her hands, letting the chips pour out of the apron.

"How are you, aunty?"

"Praise be! . . . Praise be!" Ilinichna answered irresolutely.

"Well, as you like. Give a deep bow for me to Dunia if you see her before me. And now good-bye, aunty. Don't forget what I've said."

Ilinichna went into the hut without replying, and Mishka mounted his horse and rode off to the square.

He found it swarming with Red Army soldiers who had come down from the hills into the village for the night. Their animated voices sounded in the streets. Three of them going with a portable machine-gun down to an outpost on the river held up Mishka and examined his documents. Outside Siemion Chugun's hut he came across four more. Two of them were wheeling oats in a wheelbarrow, and two more were helping Siemion's wife to carry a sewing-machine and a sack of flour. The woman recognized Mishka and greeted him.

"What's that you've got there?" Mishka asked.

"We're taking these things along to this working woman's hut. We're giving her the bourgeois machine and the flour," one of the Red Army men boldly replied.

Mishka set fire to seven houses belonging to the merchant Mokhov and other merchants, the priests, and three rich Cossacks, all of whom had fled beyond the Donietz. Only then did he leave the village. He rode up the hill and turned his horse. Below him in Tatarsk the ruddy flames were rising with great tails of sparks against the black sky. The reflection of the conflagration flickered on the swift waters of the Don and, driven by the wind, the flames sank and bent to the west, avidly consuming the buildings.

A light breeze was blowing from the eastern steppes. It fanned the flames and carried fiery black particles through the air to settle far from the square.

Chapter 7

Surrounded on all sides, the insurgents continued to repel the attacks of the punitive Red forces. In the south, on the left bank of the Don, two insurgent divisions remained stubbornly in their trenches and would not allow the enemy to cross, although along the whole length of the front innumerable Red Army batteries were directing an almost incessant, ruthless gunfire against them. The three other divisions defended the insurgent territory from the west, north, and east, suffering terrible losses, especially on the north-eastern sector, but making no attempt to retreat and holding out steadfastly along the boundaries of the Khopersk region.

The company of Tatarsk Cossacks holding the river-bank opposite their own village caused the Red forces some alarm: growing bored with enforced inactivity, under the cover of night the Cossacks noiselessly crossed on barges to the right bank of the Don, caught a Red Army outpost by surprise, killed four men, and captured a machine-gun. Next day the Reds brought up a battery from below Vieshenska, and it opened a vigorous fire on the Cossack trenches. The moment the shrapnel began to rattle through the trees, the company hurriedly abandoned its trenches and fell back from the river into the heart of the forest. A day later the battery was withdrawn, and the Tatarsk Cossacks reoccupied their positions. The company suffered some losses from the gunfire: two youngsters belonging to recent reinforcements were killed by fragments of shrapnel, and the company commander's orderly, who had arrived from Vieshenska only just before, was wounded.

After this a comparative lull set in and life in the trenches took its normal course. The Cossacks were frequently visited by their women, who brought bread and home-made vodka at night, though they had no need of provisions: they slaughtered two stray calves, and in addition they went fishing in the ponds every day. Christonia was regarded as the chief of the fisheries' department. He used a seventy-foot dragnet left on the bank by some refugee, and when fishing he regularly used the net in the deepest part of the ponds, boasting that there was not a pond in all the river-side meadows which he would not wade across.

On the whole the company lived together amicably. There was an abundance of food and all the Cossacks were cheerful, with the exception of Stepan Astakhov.

Possibly he had heard from the other Cossacks, or maybe his heart had warned him, that Aksinia was seeing Gregor at Vieshenska; at any rate he suddenly began to pine, swore without cause at the troop commander, and flatly refused to do picket duty.

He lay all day on a sledge-rug marked with a black brand, sighing and avidly smoking self-sown tobacco. Then he happened to overhear that the company commander was sending Anikushka to Vieshenska for cartridges, and crawled out of his dug-out for the first time in two days. His streaming eyes, swollen with lack of sleep, were dazzled by the light as he gazed distrustfully at the tousled, blindingly brilliant foliage of the swaying trees, the white-maned, wind-driven clouds, and listened to the murmuring of the forest. Then he strode along past the dug-outs to look for Anikushka.

He would not talk to him in front of the other Cossacks, but called him apart and asked:

"Find Aksinia in Vieshenska and tell her from me that she's to come and see me. Tell her I'm all lousy, my shirts and leg-rags are going unwashed, and also tell her—" Stepan was silent for a moment, hiding an embarrassed smile behind his moustache, then ended: "Tell her I'm wanting her badly and that I'm hoping to see her soon."

Anikushka arrived at Vieshenska at night and found Aksinia's quarters. After her tiff with Gregor she had returned to live with her aunt. Anikushka conscientiously told her what Stepan had said, but, to give the words greater weight, added on his own responsibility that Stepan had threatened to come to Vieshenska if she did not turn up.

She obeyed the order and began to make preparations. Her aunt hurriedly set dough to rise and baked rusks, and two hours later the dutiful wife Aksinia was riding with Anikushka towards the spot where the Tatarsk company was located.

Stepan greeted his wife with suppressed agitation. He gazed interrogatively into her face, which he saw was much thinner, and cautiously questioned her, but not once did he make the mistake of asking whether she had seen Gregor. Only once during the talk did he ask, his eyes downcast, his head turned aside:

"But why did you go to Vieshenska that way? Why didn't you cross the river opposite Tatarsk?"

She answered dryly that she had had no opportunity of crossing with strangers, and she had not felt inclined to ask the Melekhovs. Immediately she spoke, she realized that her words implied that the Melekhovs were not strangers, but friends. And she was disconcerted at the thought that Stepan also might understand her to mean that. In all probability he did take them in that sense. There was a momentary quiver under his brows, and a shadow seemed to pass over his face.

He raised his eyes interrogatively to her and, understanding that mute question, in her confusion and annoyance with herself she suddenly flushed.

To spare her, Stepan pretended he had not noticed anything and turned to talking of the farm, asking which of their possessions she had managed to conceal before retreating from their home and whether she had hidden them safely.

She mentally noted her husband's magnanimity and answered his questions, but all the time she felt a certain constraint and, to convince him that all that had happened was of no import, and also to hide her own agitation, she deliberately spoke more slowly, with a methodical restraint and precision.

They sat talking in the dug-out. They were continually being interrupted by Cossacks. First one came in, then another. Christonia arrived and at once prepared for sleep. Seeing that he would have no chance of talking except with others present, Stepan reluctantly cut short the conversation.

Delighted, Aksinia got up, hurriedly untied her bundle, regaled her husband with the rusks she had brought, and, taking the dirty linen from his field-pack, went out to wash it in the marshy pond close by.

An early morning silence and a dove-grey mist hung over the forest. Bowed down with the dew, the grass was bent to the earth. Frogs were croaking angrily in the marshes, and somewhere quite close to the dug-out, behind an exuberant bush of maple, a corn-crake was gratingly crying.

Aksinia went past the bush. From its very crown to the bole, hidden in a dense grassy undergrowth, it was entangled with gossamer. The threads were adorned with the finest of dewdrops, which gleamed like pearls. The crake was silent for a moment, but then, before the grass trodden by Aksinia's bare feet had time to rise again, it once more raised its voice, and a peewit winging up beyond the marsh called mournfully in answer.

To give herself more freedom of movement, Aksinia threw off her short jacket and bodice, waded up to her knees in the steamily warm water of the marsh, and began to wash the clothes. Above her, midges swarmed, mosquitoes buzzed. She passed her full, swarthy arm, bent at the elbow, over her face to drive off the mosquitoes. She thought importunately of Gregor and of their latest quarrel before his departure for the Tatarsk company.

"He may be looking for me even now! I'll return to Vieshenska this very night," she decided irrevocably, and smiled as she thought that she would be seeing Gregor and that soon there would be a reconciliation between them.

And strange: of recent days, whenever she thought of Gregor she never pictured him as he was in reality. Before her eyes arose not the present-day Gregor, the manful giant of a Cossack who had lived through and experienced so much, with eyes screwed up wearily, with reddish tips to his black moustache, a premature greyness at the temples, and deep furrows on the forehead—with all the ineradicable traces of deprivations experienced during the years of war—but the old Grishka Melekhov, youthfully rough and clumsy in his caresses, with a youthfully thin, round neck and an unconcerned fold in his continually smiling lips. And because of all this, Aksinia felt even greater love and almost a motherly tenderness towards him.

And so now, as with the utmost clarity she recalled every one of those infinitely precious features, she began to breathe heavily, her face broke into a smile, she straightened up, and, throwing her husband's half-washed shirt underfoot and feeling a burning lump in her throat as the sweet tears suddenly started, she whispered:

"Curse you, you've entered into me for ever!"

The tears were a relief to her, but afterwards the pale-blue morning world around her seemed suddenly to fade in hue. She wiped her cheeks with the back of her hand, threw the hair back from her moist brow, and, with misty eyes, long and unthinkingly watched a tiny grey gull slipping over the water to vanish in the rosy filigree of the mist foaming in the wind.

She finished washing the linen and hung it out on bushes, then went back to the dug-out.

Christonia was awake and was sitting by the entrance, wriggling the angular, contorted toes of his feet, insistently forcing conversation on Stepan, who, lying on his rug, was smoking, saying nothing, and obstinately refusing to answer Christonia's questions.

"So you think the Reds won't cross to this side? You don't answer? Well, don't, then! But what I think they'll do is try to cross by the fords. . . . It'll be by the fords all right. There's nowhere else where they can cross. Or maybe you think they'll send their cavalry to swim the river. Why don't you speak, Stepan? It looks as if the last fight is coming at this spot, and you're lying there like a log!"

Stepan half sat up and answered angrily:

"What are you plaguing me for? A funny lot you all are! Here's my wife come to see me, but there's no getting away from you! You come butting in with your silly talk and won't let a man exchange one word with his woman."

"A good 'un to talk to, you are!" The disgruntled Christonia got up, drew on his patched shoes over his bare feet, and went out, knocking his head painfully against the lintel at the entrance.

"They won't give us a chance of talking here; let's go into the forest," Stepan suggested.

Not waiting for Aksinia's assent, he went towards the entrance. She humbly followed him.

They returned to the dug-out at noon. Cossacks of the second troop were lying in the cool shade of an alder bush, and, noticing Aksinia and Stepan, the men put down their cards and were silent, exchanging knowing winks, laughing and sighing affectedly.

Aksinia walked past them, contemptuously twisting her lips, tidying her crumpled white lace-edged kerchief as she went. She was allowed to pass without comment; but Stepan, walking behind her, was hardly level with the Cossacks when Anikushka rose and stepped out from the group. With assumed respect he bowed low to Stepan and said in a loud voice:

"A good holiday to you . . . now you've broken your fast!"

Stepan smiled readily. He was glad the Cossacks had seen him and his wife returning from the forest. It would help a little to stop the rumours that he and Aksinia got on badly together. He even shrugged his shoulders youthfully, self-satisfiedly exhibiting the back of his shirt with the sweat still not dry on it.

At that, encouraged by Stepan's behaviour, the Cossacks laughed and passed lively remarks.

"But she's hot, boys! You could wring out Stepan's shirt. . . . It's sticking to his shoulders."

"She's ridden him hard, he's foaming all over."

One youngster stared with rapturous, filmy eyes after Aksinia all the way to the dug-out and distractedly let fall:

"In all the wide world you won't find such a beauty, God forgive me!"

To which Anikushka reasonably remarked:

"Why, have you tried to find one, then?"

As she caught the smutty innuendoes the colour ebbed a little from Aksinia's face; she went down into the dug-out, frowning with loathing at the memory of the recent intimacy with her husband and at his comrades' obscene remarks. With one glance Stepan realized what she was feeling and said in a pacifying tone:

"Don't be angry with those stallions, Ksiusha! It's only because they're all eaten up with desire themselves."

"I've got no one to be angry with," she answered numbly as she rummaged in her canvas pack, hurriedly pulling out all the things she had brought for her husband. And still more quietly: "I ought to be angry with myself, but I haven't the heart. . . ."

Somehow they could not find anything to talk about. After ten minutes or so Aksinia rose. "I'll tell him I'm going back to Vieshenska," she thought, but then she remembered that she hadn't brought in his dry linen.

She sat long mending her husband's sweat-eaten shirts and pants, sitting at the entrance to the dug-out, frequently glancing at the sun dropping down from the zenith.

Even so, that day she did not depart. She lacked sufficient resolution. But next morning the sun was hardly risen when she began to get ready. Stepan tried to detain her, asked her to stay with him for just one more short day; but she refused his request so decisively that he did not attempt to argue and only said before they parted:

"Are you thinking of living at Vieshenska?"

"Yes, for the present."

"Maybe you could stay here with me?"

"It's not wise for me to be here . . . with the Cossacks."

"Maybe you're right," Stepan agreed, but his leave-taking was chilly.

A strong south-easterly wind was blowing. It flew over the great expanses, then died away for the night; but towards morning it once more carried the burning heat of the Trans-Caspian deserts to the Don and, falling on the stretches of water-meadow along the left bank, dried up the dew, swept away the mist, and wrapped the chalky spurs of the Donland hills in a rosy, sultry haze.

Aksinia took off her shoes and, catching up the edge of her skirt in her left hand (in the forest the dew was still lying), lightly walked along a rarely used forest road. Her bare feet were pleasantly chilled by the damp earth, while the greedy wind avidly kissed her plump, naked calves and her neck.

In an open glade, close to a flowering bush of eglantine, she sat down to rest. Somewhere close at hand wild ducks were rustling in the reeds of a half-dried pond; a drake hoarsely called to his mate. Beyond the Don machine-guns were rattling, not rapidly, but almost incessantly, and there were rare bursts of gunfire. The explosions of the shells on this side rumbled like echoes.

Then the firing grew intermittent, and the earth revealed itself to Aksinia in all its hidden sounds: the green, white-edged leaves of the ashes and the moulded, figured oak leaves rustled tremulously under the wind; a coalescent, muffled soughing came from a thicket of young aspens; far, far off, a cuckoo indistinctly and mournfully counted out his unspent years; as it flew over the pond a crested lapwing called insistently: "Peewit, peewit"; some tiny grey bird two paces from Aksinia drank water from a road rut, throwing back its little head and pleasurably blinking its eye; the velvety, dusty bumble-bees hummed; swarthy wild bees rocked on the coronas of the meadow flowers. Then they vanished, carrying the aromatic pollen into the shady cool of hollow trunks. Juice dripped from the poplar branches. And from beneath a bush of hawthorn oozed the beery, pungent scent of the rotting last-year's leaves.

Sitting motionless, Aksinia insatiably drank in the varied scents of the forest. Filled with a marvellous and myriad-voiced sonority, the forest lived its mighty, elemental life. Saturated to overflowing with spring moisture, the flood-water soil of the glade was fringed and overgrown with such a rich variety of grasses that her eyes were bewildered by this marvellous entanglement of flowers and herbs.

Smiling, and soundlessly moving her lips, she cautiously touched the stalks of nameless, pale-blue, modest flowers, then bent her swelling waist to smell them and suddenly caught the exhausting and voluptuous perfume of lilies of the valley. Groping with her hands, she found the plant. It was growing right beside her, beneath an impenetrably shady bush. The broad, once green leaves were still jealously protecting from the sun the bent, low-growing stalk, crowned with the snow-white, fugitive little calyces of the flowers. But the leaves, covered with dew and yellow rust, were dying, and the flower itself was already touched by mortal decay: the two lower calyces were wrinkled and blackened, and only the upper one, all dressed in the sparkling tears of dew, suddenly lit up in the sunlight with a dazzling, captivating whiteness.

For some reason, in that brief moment while through her tears Aksinia was looking at the flower and breathing in its mournful scent, she recalled her youth and all her long life so meagre in happiness. Clearly she was growing old. . . . When a woman is young does she pause to weep because her heart is caught by a fortuitous memory?

And so in her tears she fell asleep, hiding her tear-stained face in her hands, pressing her wet and swollen cheek against her crumpled kerchief.

More strongly blew the wind, bending westward the crowns of the poplars and willows. The pallid trunk of the aspen swayed, wrapped in a white, seething whirlwind of tossing leaves. The wind fell, dropped to the full-flowering bush of eglantine under which Aksinia was sleeping; and then, like a startled flock of green birds, the leaves flew up with an anxious rustle, sending the rosy, feathery petals flying. Sprinkled with the fading petals of the eglantine, Aksinia slept and heard neither the sullen noises of the forest nor the renewed firing beyond the Don; nor did she feel the sun in the zenith burning her uncovered head. She awoke when she heard human speech and a horse snorting above her and hurriedly sat up.

Beside her stood a young white-moustached and white-toothed Cossack, holding his saddled, white-nosed horse by the rein. He was smiling broadly, shrugging his shoulders and dancing, and in a rather hoarse but pleasant tenor voice was singing the words of a gay song:

> "I have fallen and I lie
> Looking round me with one eye.
> Look this way,
> Look that way,
> No one to help, ah, well-a-day.
> Then I turned my head to look back,
> And behind me stood a Cossack."

"I can get up without help," Aksinia smiled, and nimbly jumped up, tidying her crumpled skirt.

"You needn't get upset, my dear! Did your legs refuse to serve you or did you just feel lazy?" the merry Cossack greeted her.

"I was tired out with sleep," she answered, a little abashed.

"Going to Vieshenska?"

"Yes."

"Would you like me to take you there?"

"But what on?"

"You get on the horse and I'll go on foot. You'll treat me. . . ." The young Cossack winked with humorous significance.

"No, you ride and God be with you, but I'll get there on my own feet."

But the Cossack displayed some experience in amatory affairs, and obstinacy also. Taking advantage of Aksinia's preoccupation with her kerchief, with a short but strong arm he embraced her, snatched her to himself, and tried to kiss her.

"Don't play the fool!" she shouted, and struck him with her elbow on the bridge of his nose.

"Darling mine, don't struggle! Look how blessed everything is all around. Every creature finds its mate. . . . So let us also have our moment of sin . . ." he whispered, narrowing his laughing eyes, tickling Aksinia's neck with his moustache.

By no means angrily, Aksinia put out her hands, pushing hard with her palms against the Cossack's brown, sweaty face, and tried to free herself. But he held her firmly.

"You fool! I've got a shameful disease. . . . Let me go!" she pleaded, panting, thinking that such simple cunning would save her from his importunity.

"Ah—but whose disease is the oldest?" the Cossack muttered through his teeth, and suddenly, lightly lifted her off her feet.

Abruptly realizing that the time for joking was past and that the affair was taking a serious turn, with all her strength she struck the Cossack's brown, sunburnt nose with her fist and tore herself away from the arms clinging to her.

"I'm the wife of Gregor Melekhov! You dare come near me, you son of a bitch. . . . I'll tell him, and he'll give you such a . . ."

Still not believing that her words could be efficacious, she snatched up a stout dry stick. But the Cossack at once cooled down. Using the sleeve of his khaki shirt to clean his whiskers of the blood which was streaming plentifully from both nostrils, he exclaimed in a chagrined tone:

"You fool! Ah, what a fool of a woman! Why didn't you say so before? Pah, the way the blood's spurting! As if the enemy didn't make us shed enough of it already, here's our own Cossack women beginning to make it flow. . . ."

In that brief moment his face went grey and unfriendly. While he was washing, getting water from a roadside puddle, Aksinia hastily turned off the road and swiftly crossed the glade. The Cossack overtook her some five minutes later. Silently smiling, he glanced sidelong at her, methodically adjusted his rifle-strap across his chest, and rode on at a swift trot.

Chapter 8

That night, close to a small hamlet, a regiment of Red Army men crossed the Don on rafts made of boards and logs.

The Cossack squadron holding the hamlet was taken by surprise, for the majority of them were on a spree. Since early evening their wives had been arriving at the Cossack quarters to visit their husbands. With them they brought victuals, and home-distilled vodka in pitchers and buckets. By midnight everybody was thoroughly drunk. Songs could be heard coming from the dug-outs, and drunken women's squeals, men's laughter and whistling. . . . The twenty Cossacks on picket duty also took part in the drinking bout, leaving two gunners and a bucket of vodka by the machine-gun.

The laden Red Army rafts cast off in complete silence from the right bank of the Don. The men landed on the opposite bank, deployed in line, and silently moved towards the dug-outs, which lay some four hundred feet back from the river.

The military engineers who had built the rafts swiftly rowed back for a new party of Red Army men.

On the left bank, except for the disconnected Cossack singing, not a sound was to be heard for five minutes or so; then hand-grenades began to burst hollowly, a machine-gun started to stutter, disorderly rifle-fire at once broke out, and a quivering "Hurrah! Hurrah! Hurrah!" rolled far through the night.

The squadron was overwhelmed, and escaped total annihilation only because pursuit was impossible in the impenetrable nocturnal darkness.

Suffering only insignificant losses, the Cossacks with their women ran in panicky disorder across the meadows towards Vieshenska. But meantime the rafts had brought fresh parties of Red Army men across from the right bank, and a half-company of the first battalion of the 3rd Regiment, equipped with two hand machine-guns, was already in action on the flank of the Bazki insurgent squadron.

Further reinforcements streamed into the breach thus formed. But their advance was slow, for none of the Red Army men knew the locality, the forces had no guides, and, moving blindly, in the darkness they continually came up against ponds and deep torrents filled with flood water, which could not be forded.

The brigade commander directing the attack decided to cease the pursuit until daybreak, while bringing up reserves and concentrating on the approaches to Vieshenska, and then to order a further advance after artillery preparation.

But at Vieshenska hurried measures were already being taken to close the breach. As soon as a courier galloped up with the news that the Reds had crossed, the officer on duty at staff headquarters sent for Kudynov and Melekhov. The squadrons of the Kargin regiment were summoned from the hamlets of Chorny, Gorokhovka, and Dubrovka. Gregor Melekhov took over the general direction of operations. He threw three hundred sabres against Yerinsk hamlet, with a view to strengthening the left flank and assisting the Tatarsk and Lebyazhy Cossacks to withstand the enemy's pressure, if he tried to invest Vieshenska from the east. Westward, down the Don, he sent the Vieshenska "foreign" volunteers and one of the Chirsk dismounted squadrons to the aid of the Bazki squadron; he posted eight machine-guns in the threatened sector and himself, with a couple of mounted squadrons, about two in the morning took up a position on the fringe of the forest, waiting for the dawn and planning to attack the Reds with cavalry.

The Great Bear had not yet faded when the Vieshenska "foreign" volunteer detachment, which had made its way through the forest to the Bazki loop of the river, ran into the retreating Bazki men and, taking them for the enemy, opened fire for a few moments, then fled. Across the broad lake separating Vieshenska from the meadowland the volunteers waded, in their hurry throwing their boots and clothing down on the edge. The mistake was quickly discovered, but the news that the Reds were approaching Vieshenska spread at an astonishing speed. The refugees who had been sheltering in the cellars fled out of the village northward, carrying everywhere the rumour that the Reds had crossed the Don, had broken the front, and were advancing on Vieshenska.

Daylight was just beginning when Gregor, who had been informed of the flight of the "foreign" volunteers, galloped up to the Don. The volunteers had now realized their mistake and were already returning to the trenches, talking volubly. Gregor rode up to one group and asked sarcastically:

"Were there many drowned when you swam the lake?"

A rifleman, wet through and wringing out his shirt as he walked, answered in a crestfallen tone:

"We swam like pikes. Why should we drown?"

"Everybody makes mistakes," a second, walking in only his pants, spoke up sententiously. "But our troop commander really was all but drowned. He didn't like to pull his boots off, for he thought it would take too long to unroll his puttees, and so he began to swim, thinking he could take off his puttees in the water. They got tangled round his legs. . . . And the way he bawled! He could have been heard a mile off!"

Finding the volunteers' commander, Gregor ordered him to lead his men to the edge of the forest and to dispose them so that if necessary they could take the Red lines from the flank, then rode off to his own squadrons.

On the road he was met by a staff orderly. The man reined in his horse, which, judging by its heaving flanks, he had ridden hard, and sighed in a relieved tone:

"I've had a fine job finding you!"

"Why, what's up?"

"I've been ordered from the staff to inform you that the Tatarsk

company has abandoned its trenches. They're afraid of being surrounded and are retreating towards the desert. Kudynov told me
himself to tell you to hurry there at once."

Collecting half a troop of Cossacks with the freshest horses,
Gregor made his way through the forest on to the road. After some
twenty minutes' gallop he was close to the Goly Ilmen lake. To the
left of him the panic-stricken Tatarsk men were running in disorder
across the meadow. Those who had been at the front, and other,
older Cossacks made their way along unhurriedly, keeping close to
the lake, concealing themselves in the river-side rushes; but the majority, evidently dominated by the one desire to get as quickly as
possible to the forest, were rushing straight ahead, taking no notice
of the occasional bursts of machine-gun fire.

"Catch up with them! Give them the whip!" Gregor shouted, his
eyes squinting with fury. He was the first to send his horse flying in
chase of his own fellow-villagers.

Christonia was jogging along last of all, limping away in a monstrous dancing shamble. While fishing the previous evening he had
cut his heel badly on a reed, so he could not run with all the spirit
peculiar to his long legs. His whip raised high above his head,
Gregor caught up with him. Hearing the sound of horse-hoofs,
Christonia looked round and perceptibly increased his speed.

"Where are you running? Stop! Stop, I tell you!" Gregor vainly
shouted.

But Christonia had no thought of stopping. He put on a still
greater spurt and broke into a queer sort of shambling camel gallop.

Then the infuriated Gregor hoarsely roared a terrible curse,
whooped to his horse, and, drawing level, with a feeling of deep
satisfaction, brought his whip down on Christonia's sweaty back.
Christonia howled under the blow, took one monstrous side leap,
rather like a hare's twist, sat down on the ground, and slowly and
carefully felt his back.

The Cossacks accompanying Gregor galloped ahead of the fleeing
men, halting them, but did not bring their whips into action.

"Flog them! . . . Flog them!" Gregor shouted hoarsely, shaking
his ornamented whip. His horse twisted under him, reared, and refused to go on. Mastering it with difficulty, he galloped up to the
men running in front. As he tore past he momentarily saw Stepan
Astakhov halted by a bush, silently smiling; he saw Anikushka

double up with laughter and fold his hands into a trumpet, to scream in a piercing, womanish voice:

"Brothers! Every man for himself! The Reds! Ah! Seize them!"

Gregor dashed after yet another villager dressed in a padded jerkin, who was running inexhaustibly and nimbly. The man's round-shouldered figure seemed strangely familiar, but Gregor had no time to decide who it was, and he began to bawl when still some distance behind:

"Stop, you son of a bitch! Stop or I'll cut you down!"

Suddenly the man in the padded jerkin slowed down, then halted. As he turned round, with a characteristic gesture which Gregor had known ever since his childhood, expressing the highest degree of indignation, and, even before the astonished Gregor caught sight of the man's features, he guessed that it was his father.

Pantaleimon Prokoffievich's cheeks twitched convulsively.

"So your own father's a son of a bitch, is he? So you're threatening to cut down your father, are you?" he shouted in a high-pitched, broken falsetto.

His eyes blazed with such a familiar uncontrollable frenzy that Gregor's anger at once died away and, forcibly reining in his horse, he shouted:

"I didn't recognize your back! What are you bawling for, Father?"

"What do you mean by 'you didn't recognize me'? Didn't you recognize your own father?"

So absurd and inept was this demonstration of elderly touchiness that Gregor, laughing, drew level with his father and said in a pacifying tone:

"Father, don't be mad! You're wearing a coat I've never seen before, and besides, you were flying along like a racehorse, and you weren't even limping. So how was I to recognize you?"

Once more, as in former days, and as always at home, Pantaleimon quieted down and, still panting violently, but with more control over himself, agreed:

"You're right, the coat's a new one; I exchanged it for the sheepskin—a sheepskin's heavy to carry around. . . . But as for my limp —this is no time for limping! My boy, there's no question of limping here. . . . Death staring us in the eyes, and here you are chattering away about a game leg. . . ."

"Well, death is still a long way off. Turn back, Father! You haven't thrown your cartridges away, have you?"

"But where are we to turn back to?" the old man protested indignantly.

Gregor at once raised his voice. Emphasizing every word, he commanded:

"I order you to return. Do you know what the regulations pre-
scribe for refusing to obey your commander in the field?"

The words had their effect: Pantaleimon Prokoffievich adjusted
the rifle across his shoulder and reluctantly trudged back. As he
drew level with one of the old men who was walking along even
more slowly, he said with a sigh:

"That's what our sons are like these days! Instead of having respect for his parent, or, as you might say, releasing him from fighting,
he tries to get him—to go right into it! Ye-es! Now my dead Piotra,
may the Lord have mercy on him, was far better. He was a quiet
sort, but this daft one, Grishka I mean, though he is a divisional commander, and rightly so, and all the rest of it, he's different. I'm all
over bruises, and I mustn't touch one of them! At my age it'll be like
sitting on red-hot needles when I climb on to the stove."

The Tatarsk Cossacks were made to see reason without any great
difficulty. Gregor quickly assembled the entire company and led
it under cover. Without dismounting he curtly explained:

"The Reds have crossed the river and are trying to occupy
Vieshenska. Fighting has started along the Don. It's no joking matter, and I don't advise you to run for nothing. If you run a second
time I shall order the cavalry at Yerinsk to cut you down as traitors!"
He ran his eyes over the crowd of his fellow-villagers, taking in their
motley attire, and ended with undisguised contempt: "You've got
a lot of scum collected in your company, and they're spreading
panic. Fine fighters you are, running away and making a mess in
your trousers! And you call yourselves Cossacks, too! And you, old
men, you keep your eyes on me! You've said you'll fight, so there's
no point in your hiding your heads between your legs now. At once,
in troop order, double across to those bushes and through them to
the Don! Then along by the Don to the Semionovsky company.
When you link up with them, strike at the Reds, taking them in the
flank. Quick march! And look sharp!"

The Tatarsk villagers listened in silence and as silently made their
way towards the bushes. The old men groaned despondently, look-

ing back at Gregor and his group of Cossacks as they swiftly galloped away. Old Obnizov, who was walking along beside Pantaleimon, remarked in an admiring tone:

"Well, but the Lord has deemed you worthy of a hero for a son. A real eagle! The way he brought his whip down on Christonia's back! He brought every man to heel right away!"

Pantaleimon's fatherly feelings were flattered by Obnizov's remarks, and the old man assented willingly:

"You needn't tell me! You'd have to search hard through all the world to find another son like him! A whole chestful of medals—that's no joke, is it? Now Piotra, God rest his soul, he wasn't like that, though he was my own son, and my firstborn. He was too quiet, not finished somehow, the plague take him! He'd got a woman's spirit under his shirt. But this other, he's just like me! And he's got even more spirit than me!"

With his half troop Gregor stole up to the Kalmyk ford. They thought themselves safe when they reached the forest, but they were seen from an observation post on the farther side of the river. A gun-team opened a raking fire. The first shell flew over the tops of the willows and squelched into some marshy hollow without exploding. But the second fell not far from the road among the bared roots of an old black poplar and spirted with fire, deafening the Cossacks with its roar, smothering them with clumps of rich earth and crumbs of rotten wood.

Deafened, Gregor instinctively raised his arm to shield his eyes and bent over his horse, feeling a heavy, wet smack, apparently on the horse's crupper.

The explosion shook the ground, and the Cossacks' horses fell back on their haunches and then dashed forward as though at a command. But Gregor's horse reared heavily under him, fell back, and began slowly to roll over. Gregor hastily jumped out of the saddle and took the horse by the snaffle. Two more shells flew past, then a welcome silence fell over the fringe of the forest. The smoke of gunpowder settled on the grass; there was a scent of freshly turned earth, of timber chips, of half-rotten wood. Far away in a thicket the magpies chattered anxiously.

Gregor's horse snorted and its quivering hind legs began to sag.

It bared the yellow line of its teeth tormentedly and craned its neck. A rosy foam bubbled on its velvety grey muzzle. A violent trembling shook all its body, and shudders rolled in great ripples under its bay skin.

"Finished, master?" a Cossack who galloped up asked in a loud voice. Gregor gazed into the horse's fading eyes without answering. He did not even look at the wound, and only shifted away a little when the horse uncertainly began to hurry forward, drew itself up, and suddenly dropped to its knees, its head hanging, as though asking its master's forgiveness for something. With a hollow groan it rolled on to its side, then tried to raise its head. But evidently it had lost all strength; the trembling gradually died away, its eyes glazed, a sweat beaded its neck. Only at the fetlocks, close to the hoofs, was there a last faint pulsation. The chafed wing of the saddle gently quivered.

Gregor glanced sidelong at the animal's left groin, noticed a deep open wound with warm black blood gushing like a spring from it, and said, stammering and not wiping away his tears, as the Cossack dismounted:

"Finish him with a single bullet!" He handed the man his own Mauser.

Mounting the Cossack's horse, he galloped to the spot where he had left his squadrons. He found fighting already going on.

The Red Army troops had renewed the attack at dawn. In the streams of mist their lines rose and silently marched in the direction of Vieshenska. On the right flank they were held up for a minute by a flooded hollow, then they waded up to their chests through the water, raising their cartridge wallets and rifles high above their heads. A little later four batteries simultaneously began majestically to thunder from the Donland hills. As soon as the fan-shaped spray of shells swept through the forest, the insurgents opened fire. The Red Army men had now passed from marching to running with their rifles at the trail. The shrapnel dryly burst in the forest, about half a mile ahead of them; the shells splintered trees, sending them crashing to the ground; smoke rose in white clouds. Two Cossack machine-guns rattled away in curt alternation. Men began to fall in the first line of Red troops. More and more frequently the bullets picked off men belted with rolled greatcoats and flung them down on their backs or their chests; but the others made no attempt to lie down, and the distance separating them from the forest grew shorter and shorter.

In front of the second line a tall, bareheaded commander was running easily, with a long stride, his body bent forward a little, the edges of his greatcoat tucked up. The line slowed down for a second in its advance, but as he ran the commander turned and shouted something, and the men again broke into a run; their hoarse, terrible "Hurrah" again rose in a crescendo of fury.

Then all the Cossack machine-guns began to talk at once, while from the fringes of the forest rifle-shots sounded hotly and rapidly, without a break. From somewhere behind Gregor, who was standing with his squadrons on the road leading out of the forest, the heavy machine-gun of the Bazki company opened fire in long stutters. The Red lines wavered, then lay down and returned the fire. For perhaps an hour and a half the struggle continued, but the insurgents' fire was so effective that the second line could not face it, and rose and fled back to mix with the third line, which was coming up in a series of short dashes. Soon the meadows were sprinkled with Red Army men running back in disorder. Then Gregor led his squadrons out of the forest at a trot, drew them up in formation, and flung them into the pursuit. The retreating troops were cut off from their rafts by the Chirsk squadron, which advanced at a gallop, and a hand-to-hand struggle developed outside the forest, right on the river-bank. Only part of the Red Army men managed to fight their way through to the rafts. They crowded every inch of space on them and cast off. Pressed right down to the river edge, the others fought back.

Gregor dismounted his squadrons, ordered the Cossacks detailed to the horses not to come out of the forest, and led the others down to the bank. Running from tree to tree, they drew nearer and nearer the river. Some hundred and fifty Red Army men were repulsing the attacking insurgent infantry with hand-grenades and machine-gun fire. The rafts cast off again for the left bank, but the Bazki Cossacks mowed down almost all the rowers with gunfire. The fate of the men left on the right bank was settled. Their morale broken, they threw down their rifles and tried to swim across. The insurgents lay down at the gaps in the river-bank and picked them off. Too weak to struggle against the swift main channel of the river, many of the men were drowned. Only two got across safely. One, wearing a sailor's striped jersey, and obviously a fine swimmer, dived in off the steep bank, went down under water, and came up again almost in the middle of the river. Taking cover behind a willow with spreading, bared roots, Gregor watched as with great sweeps of his arms the sailor steadily drew nearer to the farther side. One other man also swam across safely. As he stood breast-deep in water he fired all his remaining cartridges, then shouted something, shaking his fist at the Cossacks, and set out to swim on a diagonal course. Around him the bullets sent the water spirting up, but not one hit him. At a former watering-place for cattle he waded out of the water, shook himself, and unhurriedly began to make his way up the bank to the yards of the village beyond.

The Reds left on the other side lay down behind a sandy hillock; their machine-gun stuttered away until the water boiled in the water-jacket.

"Follow me!" Gregor quietly ordered as soon as the gun lapsed into silence. Drawing his sabre, he made towards the hillock.

Behind him tramped the Cossacks, breathing heavily.

Not more than three hundred feet separated them from the Red Army men when, after three volleys, a tall, swarthy-faced, black-whiskered commander rose to his full height from behind the hillock. A woman dressed in a leather jacket held him by the arm. The commander was wounded. Dragging his shattered leg, he stepped out from the mound, took a firm grip of his rifle with its fixed bayonet, and hoarsely commanded:

"Comrades! Forward! Kill the Whites!"

Singing the *Internationale,* the little handful of brave fighters advanced into the counter-attack, advanced to death.

The hundred and sixteen who were the last to fall on the bank of the Don were all Communist members of the International company.

Chapter 9

It was late that night when Gregor returned from the staff to his quarters. Prokhor Zykov was waiting for him at the wicket gate.

"No news of Aksinia?" Gregor asked with forced unconcern in his tones.

"No. She's vanished into thin air," Prokhor answered, yawning, but anxiously thinking: "God forbid that he should force me to go and look for her again! I'm plagued with all the devils!"

"Bring me something to wash with. I'm sweaty all over. Quick, now!" Gregor said irritably.

Prokhor went into the hut for water, and poured it out of a mug drop by drop into Gregor's cupped hands. Gregor obviously enjoyed his wash. He drew off his tunic, which stank of sweat, and asked:

"Pour some down my back."

The cold water scorched his sweaty back and made him grunt and snort; he rubbed his chafed shoulders and hairy chest. Drying himself on a clean horse-cloth, in a more cheerful voice he ordered Prokhor:

"They're bringing me a horse in the morning. Take him over, give him a good currying, and then a feed of grain. Don't wake me up, but leave me to sleep as long as I can. Only disturb me if anyone comes from the staff. Understand?"

He went under the eaves of the shed, lay down in a wagon, and at once dropped off into an untroubled sleep. At dawn he felt cold, tucked up his legs and drew his dew-damp greatcoat around him. But after the sun had risen he again dozed off, and was awakened about seven o'clock by the heavy sound of gunfire. An aeroplane painted a dull silver was circling in the clear blue sky above the village. Gun and machine-gun fire was being directed against it from the farther side of the river.

"Why, they might hit it!" Prokhor muttered as he zealously curried a high-standing bay stallion tied to a post. "Look, Pantalievich, look at the devil they've sent you!"

Gregor ran his eyes over the stallion and asked in a satisfied tone:

"I haven't looked; how old is he? In his sixth year by the look of him."

"Yes, he's six."

"Ah, that's fine! He's got good legs under him, and all four stockinged. A handsome little brute! Well, saddle him, and I'll ride and see who it is that's arrived."

"Yes, he's fine, there's no denying it. He ought to be fast. By all the signs he should have plenty of spirit," Prokhor muttered as he tightened the saddle-girths.

Yet another smoky white little cloud of shrapnel burst close to the aeroplane.

Choosing a suitable spot for landing, the airman dropped sharply to the ground. Gregor rode through the wicket gate and galloped to the village stables, beyond which the aeroplane had descended.

The stables formerly used for the village stallions, a long stone building standing on the outskirts, was packed tightly with over eight hundred Red prisoners. The guard would not allow them out for fresh air and exercise, and there was not one stool in the place. A thick, heavy smell of human excrement hung like a wall all around the building. Stinking streams of urine were crawling under the door; over them swarmed emerald-green flies.

Day and night muffled groans came from this prison of the condemned. Hundreds of prisoners were dying of exhaustion and the typhus and dysentery which were raging among them. Sometimes the dead were not removed for days on end.

Gregor rode round the stables and was about to dismount when a gun again thundered out from the far side of the Don. The scream of the approaching shell grew louder and clashed with the heavy roar of the explosion.

The pilot and the officer who had arrived in the aeroplane were just climbing out of the cockpit; the machine was surrounded by Cossacks. But at that moment all the guns of the battery on the hill spoke at once. The shells began to fall accurately around the stables.

The pilot swiftly climbed back into the cockpit, but the engine refused to start.

"Push it along!" the officer who had travelled with him shouted stentoriously, and was the first to push at one wing. Swaying, the aeroplane moved easily towards a group of pines. The battery accompanied it with a running fire. One of the shells fell right on the crowded stables. One corner crumbled amid clouds of smoke and rising lime dust. The stable shook with the elemental roar of the terror-stricken prisoners. Three of them dashed out through the breach, but were riddled at point-blank range by the Cossacks.

Gregor galloped off to one side.

"They'll get you! Ride to the pines!" a Cossack with terrified face and rolling eyes shouted as he ran past.

"He's right, they might drop one on us in real earnest! They're not joking!" Gregor thought, and he slowly rode back to his quarters.

That day Kudynov called a strictly secret conference at the staff headquarters and did not invite Gregor to be present. The Don Army officer who had arrived in the aeroplane briefly communicated that at any day now the Red front would be broken by the forces of the shock column concentrated around Kamenskaya, and a mounted division of the Don Army, commanded by General Sekretov, would march to link up with the insurgents. The officer proposed that means of crossing the river should be prepared immediately, so that, after linking up with Sekretov's division, insurgent cavalry regiments could be thrown across to the right bank of the Don. He advised moving the reserve troops closer to the river and, right at the end of the conference, after the plan for transferring the troops across the river and their further operations had been worked out, he asked:

"But why have you got prisoners in Vieshenska?"

"We've got nowhere else to keep them; there aren't any suitable buildings in the hamlets outside," one of the staff answered.

The officer carefully wiped his clean-shaven, sweating head with a handkerchief, unbuttoned the collar of his khaki tunic, and said with a sigh:

"Send them to Kazanska."

Kudynov raised his eyebrows in amazement.

"And then?" he asked.

"And from there—back to Vieshenska," the officer condescendingly explained, screwing up his cold blue eyes. Pressing his lips together, he added harshly: "Really, gentlemen, I don't know why you're standing on ceremony with them. I should have thought the times were hardly suitable at the moment. These scum, who are spreading all kinds of diseases, both physical and social, have got to be exterminated. There's no point in playing the nursemaid with them. That's what I'd do if I were in your place."

The following day the first party of prisoners, numbering two hundred men, was marched out into the sands. Emaciated, deathly pale, hardly able to shift their legs, the Red Army men moved like shades. A mounted convoy closely surrounded the irregularly striding crowd. Some seven miles beyond the village the two hundred prisoners were sabred to the very last man. In the early evening a second party was driven out. The convoy was strictly enjoined only to sabre the stragglers, and to fire only in the last resort. Of these one hundred and fifty men not more than seventeen reached Kazanska. One of the prisoners, a gypsy-looking, young Red Army man went out of his mind on the road. All the way he sang, danced, and wept, pressing a bunch of scented thyme to his chest. He fell again and again face downwards in the burning sands, the wind played with the dirty rags of his cotton shirt, and then the convoy could see the tightly drawn skin of his bony back and the cracking soles of his feet. They picked him up, splashed water over him from a flask, and he opened his black, maniacally glittering eyes, laughed quietly, and, swaying, went on again.

At one of the hamlets on the road compassionate women surrounded the prisoners, and one majestic and portly old woman said sternly to the man in charge of the convoy:

"You set that black one free! He's touched, he's drawn nearer to God, and it'll be a great sin for you if you bring such a one to his end."

The head of the convoy, a dashing, red-whiskered ensign, laughed sarcastically:

"We aren't afraid of taking another sin on our souls, old woman. In any case righteous men can't be made out of us!"

"But you set him free, don't refuse me," the old woman insistently asked. "Death is waving its wings over every one of you."

The other women energetically supported her, and the ensign agreed.

"I don't mind; take him. He can't do any harm now. But as we're so good-hearted you can give us a pipkin of fresh milk for each man."

The old woman led the madman away to her own little hut, fed him, and made up a bed for him in the best room. He slept a whole day through, then awoke, stood with his back to the window, and began to sing quietly. The old woman came into the room, rested her cheek on her palm, long and keenly stared at the youngster's emaciated face, then said in a deep voice:

"They say your people aren't far away. . . ."

The madman was silent for a brief second, then fell to singing again, but more quietly.

The old woman said sternly:

"You stop playing about, my lad, and don't get it into your head that you can fool me. I've lived a lifetime, you can't take me in, I'm no fool! You're quite well in your mind, I know that. . . . I heard you talking in your sleep, and you talked good sense."

The Red Army man went on singing, but more and more quietly. The old woman continued:

"Don't be afraid of me, I don't wish you any evil. I lost two sons in the German war, and my youngest died at Cherkass during this war. And yet I had carried them all below my heart. I'd given them milk, given them food, and had no sleep at night when they were young. . . . And so I'm sorry for all the youngsters who serve in the army and fight in the war." She was silent for a few moments.

The Red Army man was silent also. He closed his eyes, and a barely perceptible flush suffused his swarthy cheeks; a blue vein began to pulsate tensely on his thin, scraggy neck.

For a minute he stood maintaining an expectant silence, then half opened his black eyes. Their look was intelligent and they gleamed with such impatient expectation that the old woman smiled slightly.

"Do you know the road to Shumilinska?" she asked.

"No, mother," the man answered, hardly moving his lips.

"Then how will you get there?"

"I don't know. . . ."

"That's just the point! Now what am I to do with you?" She waited a long time for him to answer, then asked:

"But can you walk?"

"I'll manage somehow."

"These are not the times when you can manage somehow. You have to go by night and walk fast, oh, as fast as you can! Stay here another day, and then I'll give you victuals, and my little grandson as guide, to show you the road, and—Godspeed! Your Reds are just outside Shumilinska, I know that for sure. And you go and get to them. But you can't take the highroad, you'll have to strike across the steppe, along the valleys and through the forests, off the roads, or the Cossacks will come upon you and it'll be the worse for you. And that's that, my darling!"

Next day, as soon as dusk fell, the old woman made the sign of the cross over her twelve-year-old grandson and the Red soldier, whom she had fitted out with a Cossack coat, and said harshly:

"Now go, and God be with you! But see you don't fall into the hands of our soldiers. . . . Not on any account, darling, not on any account! Don't bow to me, but to the Lord God. I'm not the only one, we're all good mothers. . . . We're sorry for you poor devils, mortally sorry! Now, now, off with you, and the Lord keep you safe!" She slammed the yellow, clay-daubed, crooked door of her hut.

Chapter 10

Every day Ilinichna awoke at the first gleam of dawn, milked the cow, and started on her housework. She did not light the stove in the house, but made a fire in the outdoor kitchen, prepared dinner, then went back into the house to the children.

Natalia recovered very slowly after her typhus. She first got up from her bed on the second day after Trinity and, worn out with continual itching, went from one room to another, hardly able to use her legs. She spent a long time searching through the children's heads, and even tried to wash their bits of clothes while sitting on a stool.

Her emaciated face was continually lit up with a smile, a flush showed rosy on her sunken cheeks, and her eyes, grown large with illness, shone with such a beaming, tremulous warmth as if she were after childbirth.

"Poliushka, my darling! Mishatka didn't upset you at all while I was ill, did he?" she asked in a feeble voice, drawling every word uncertainly, stroking her daughter's black hair with her hand.

"No, Mummy. Only once Mishka hit me, but we played together a lot," the girl answered in a whisper, and pressed her face hard against her mother's knees.

"And Granny looked after you?" Natalia continued her questioning, a smile on her face.

"An awful lot!"

"And strangers, Red soldiers, didn't touch you?"

"They killed our little calf, curse them!" Mishatka, who was astonishingly like his father, answered in a childish, yet deep tone.

"You mustn't swear, Mishatka. Why, you're talking just like a man! You mustn't ever use bad words about grown-ups," Natalia said monitorily, suppressing a smile.

"That's how Granny spoke of them, you ask Polya!" the youthful Melekhov glumly justified himself.

"It's true, Mummy, and they killed all our chickens, every one of them!"

Polya grew animated; her little black eyes glittering, she began to tell how the Red soldiers had come into the yard, how they had caught the chickens and ducks, how Granny Ilinichna had asked them to spare a yellow cock with a frost-bitten comb for breeding-purposes, and how a merry Red Army man had answered, swinging the cock in his hand: "This cock, old woman, has crowed against the Soviet régime and so we've sentenced him to death! You can ask as much as you like, but we're going to make soup of him, and we'll leave you our old felt boots in exchange."

Throwing out her arms, little Polya added:

"That's how big the felt boots were that they left. Huge ones, just huge, and all full of holes."

Laughing and weeping, Natalia caressed the children and, not removing her rapturous eyes from her daughter, joyously whispered:

"Ah, my Gregor's girl! My Gregor's true daughter. You're exactly like your father, down to the last drop of your blood."

"But am I like him?" Mishatka asked jealously, and timidly leaned against his mother.

"Yes, you're like him too. Only, remember: when you grow up you're not to be such a bad lot as your father."

"But is he a bad lot? How is he a bad lot?" Polya showed signs of interest.

A shade of sorrow fell across Natalia's face. She did not answer, but rose with difficulty from the bench.

Ilinichna, who was in the room, turned away discontentedly. But, no longer listening to the children's talk, Natalia stood at the window and gazed long at the closed shutters of the Astakhovs' hut, sighing and agitatedly fiddling with the strings of her faded bodice.

Next day she awoke at dawn, rose quietly in order not to disturb the children, washed, and took a clean shirt, a short jacket, and a white kerchief out of the chest. She was visibly agitated and, by the way she had dressed, by her preservation of a mournful and forbidding silence, Ilinichna guessed that her daughter-in-law was going to visit the grave of her grandfather Grishaka.

"Where are you off to?" the old woman deliberately asked, in order to be assured that her conjecture was correct.

"I'm going to visit Grand-dad," Natalia defended herself, not raising her head for fear of bursting into tears. She had learned of her grandfather's death, and that Mishka Koshevoi had set fire to their house and farmstead.

"You're too weak, you'll never get there."

"I'll manage it if I take rests. You give the children their food, Mamma, for I may be kept there a long time."

"But what ever for, what will you be kept there a long time for? A fine time to go visiting the dead this is, God forgive me! I wouldn't go if I were you, Natalia dear."

"But I am going!" Natalia's face clouded, and she took hold of the door-handle.

"Wait a bit, what are you going there hungry for? Have a bite of something; shall I put out some sour milk for you?"

"No, Mamma; Christ have mercy, I don't want it. . . . I'll have something when I get back."

Seeing that her daughter-in-law was resolved to go, Ilinichna advised her:

"You'd better take the path above the Don, through the gardens. You won't be seen so easily that way."

A billowing, milky mist was hanging over the Don. The sun had not yet risen, but in the east the edge of sky concealed behind the poplars was blazing with the livid reflection of the dawn, and a chilling early morning breeze was blowing from below the clouds.

Stepping across the fallen wattle fence with its entanglement of bindweed, Natalia passed into her own orchard. Pressing her hands to her heart, she halted by a fresh little mound of earth.

The orchard was luxuriantly overgrown with nettles and scrub.

On the old apple tree, which had been charred and killed by the fire, a starling was huddled. The grave mound was settling down. Here and there among the clods of dry clay the green little spears of upthrusting grass were showing.

Overwhelmed by a rush of memories, Natalia silently dropped to her knees and fell face downward to the ungracious earth, with its immemorial smell of mortal decay.

An hour later she stealthily crept out of the orchard and looked back, her heart constricted with pain, for the last time at the spot where once her youth had blossomed. The neglected yard was a mournful sight with the charred beams of the sheds, the blackened ruins of the stoves, and the house foundations. Then she quietly took her way down a side-turning.

With every day Natalia got better. Her legs grew stronger, her shoulders rounded out, her body was flooded with a healthy fullness. Soon she began to assist her mother-in-law in the housework. As they bustled about the stove, they talked for long stretches at a time. One morning Natalia said with a hint of anger in her voice:

"And when will it all end? I'm sick at heart!"

"You'll see, it won't be long before our people cross the Don again," Ilinichna confidently answered.

"But how do you know, Mother?"

"My heart feels it."

"So long as our Cossacks are safe and sound! God forbid that any of them should be killed, or wounded. . . . Grisha's so reckless. . . ." Natalia sighed.

"I don't think anything will happen to them. God isn't without pity. Our old man promised to try to cross and visit us, but I expect he's got put off by something. If he was to come, you could go back with him to your man. Our villagers are holding positions opposite the village. While you were still lying unconscious I went one morning at dawn down to the Don to fetch water, and I heard Anikushka shouting across the river: 'Greetings, old lady! A greeting from your old man!'"

"But where's Grisha?" Natalia cautiously asked.

"He's in the rear commanding them all," Ilinichna naïvely answered.

"But where is he commanding them from?"

"It must be from Vieshenska. There's nowhere else he could do it from."

Natalia was silent for a moment. Ilinichna looked across at her and asked anxiously:

"But what's the matter? What are you crying for?"

Natalia did not answer, but pressed her dirty apron to her face and quietly sobbed.

"Don't cry, Natalia my dear, tears won't help now. If God wills, we shall see them again alive and well. You look after yourself; don't go out of the yard unnecessarily, or those Antichrists will see you and come back."

It grew darker in the kitchen. Outside, the window was curtained by someone's form. Ilinichna turned to the window and groaned:

"It's them! The Reds! Natalia, darling! Lie down on the bed quick, pretend you're ill. . . . You never know what sin— Cover yourself with the sacking."

Trembling with fear, Natalia had hardly dropped on the bed when the latch clattered and a tall Red Army man bent and entered the kitchen. The children clung to Ilinichna's skirt. The old woman turned pale. And, where she stood by the stove, there she dropped to the bench, sending a pipkin of scalded milk flying.

The Red soldier swiftly looked round the kitchen and said in a loud voice:

"Don't be afraid! I shan't eat you! Good day!"

Natalia, groaning as though she were really ill, drew the sacking over her head; but Mishatka stared at the visitor from under his eyebrows and said in a tone of delight:

"Granny! It's the very same man who killed our cock. Do you remember?"

The soldier took off his khaki cap, clicked his tongue, and smiled.

"The rascal recognizes me! And do you like recalling that cock? All the same, mistress, this is what I've come about: can you bake some bread for us? We've got flour."

"Yes. . . . Of course—I'll bake it . . ." Ilinichna stammeringly replied, not looking at the visitor, as she wiped up the spilt milk from the bench.

The soldier sat down by the door, drew his pouch out of his pocket, and, rolling himself a cigarette, tried to make conversation.

"Can you get it baked by nightfall?"

"Yes, if you're in a hurry."

"In war-time, granny, we're always in a hurry. But don't you be upset because of that cock."

"I'm not upset," Ilinichna replied in alarm. "The child's stupid. He remembers things that are best forgotten."

"All the same, you're mean, my boy," the talkative visitor smiled benevolently, turning to Mishatka. "What are you staring at me like a little wolf for? Come here and we'll talk to our heart's content about your cock."

"Go to him, silly!" Ilinichna said in a whisper, pushing her grandson with her knee.

But Mishatka tore himself away from his grandmother's skirt and tried to slip out of the kitchen, edging sideways towards the door. With a long arm the Red Army man drew him to himself, and asked:

"Are you upset?"

"No," Mishatka answered in a whisper.

"Well, that's fine! Happiness doesn't depend on a cock. Where's your father? Across the Don?"

"Yes."

"So he's fighting us?"

Encouraged by the man's kindly tones, Mishatka readily informed him:

"He commands all the Cossacks."

"Why, you're lying, my boy!"

"You ask Granny, then!"

But his granny only clapped her hands and broke into a groan, completely disconcerted by her grandson's garrulity.

"He's commanding them all?" the puzzled soldier questioned.

"Well, perhaps not all—" Mishatka answered uncertainly, nonplussed by his grandmother's desperate glances.

The Red soldier was silent for a moment, then, glancing at Natalia, asked:

"So the young wife is ill, is she?"

"She's got typhus," Ilinichna answered reluctantly.

Two Red Army men carried a sack of flour into the kitchen, setting it down by the threshold.

"Light your stove, mistress," one of them said. "We'll come for the loaves before evening. But see you bake good bread or it'll be the worse for you."

"I'll bake as well as I know how," Ilinichna answered, delighted beyond measure that the new arrivals had broken into the dangerous conversation and that Mishatka had run out of the room.

Nodding his head at Natalia, one of the men said:

"Typhus?"

"Yes."

They talked among themselves in undertones, then left the kitchen. The last of them had hardly turned the corner when rifleshots rang out from across the Don.

Bending double, the men ran up to the half-ruined stone wall of the enclosure, lay down behind it, and, rattling their rifle-bolts vigorously, began to return the fire.

In a terrible fear Ilinichna ran out into the yard to look for Mishatka. The men behind the wall called to her:

"Hey, granny, go into the house! You'll be killed!"

"Our boy's in the yard. Mishatka! Darling!" the old woman called, with tears in her voice.

She ran into the middle of the yard, and at once the firing from the farther bank of the Don broke off. Evidently the Cossacks had seen and recognized her. Mishatka ran up, and the moment she had seized his hand and entered the kitchen with him, the firing was renewed, continuing until the Red soldiers had left the Melekhovs' yard.

Talking in whispers to Natalia, Ilinichna set the dough to rise. But she was not destined to bake the bread.

Towards noon the Red Army men of the machine-gun outposts in the village hurriedly abandoned the yards, and made their way up the slopes to the hill, dragging their machine-guns after them. The company holding the trenches on the hill fell in and went off towards the Hetman's highway at a swinging march.

At once a profound silence fell and extended over all the Donside lands. The guns and machine-guns were stilled. Along the roads, over the grass-grown summer tracks, from all the hamlets baggage trains and batteries stretched in endless lines to the Hetman's highway; infantry and cavalry marched along in columns.

Gazing through the window, Ilinichna saw the last Red Army men scramble up the chalky spurs to the hill, wiped her hand on the curtain, and feelingly crossed herself.

"The Lord has brought it to pass, Natalia dear. The Reds are retreating."

"Ah, Mother, they're leaving the village to go to the trenches, and they'll be back again before evening."

"Then what are they running for? Our men have driven them back. They're retreating, the devils! The Antichrists are running!
. . ." Ilinichna exulted. But she set to work again to knead the dough.

Natalia went out to the porch, stood on the threshold, and, setting her hand to her eyes, gazed long over the sunlit, chalky hill at the brown, sun-scorched spurs.

In the majestic stillness presaging a thunder-storm the tops of white, rolling clouds rose from beyond the hill. The noonday sun hotly baked the earth. The marmots were whistling on the pastureland, and their quiet, rather mournful noise mingled weirdly with the joyous singing of the skylarks. So dear to Natalia's heart was the silence which had descended after the gunfire that, without stirring, she avidly listened to the artless singing of the larks, and to the creak of the well-crane, and to the rustle of the wormwood-scented wind.

It was pungent and scented, was that winged, easterly steppe wind. It breathed with the heat of the sun-baked black earth, the intoxicating scents of all the grasses lying beneath the sun. But already the approach of rain was to be felt: a fresh humidity was creeping up from the river; almost touching the earth with their double-pointed tails, the swallows were weaving patterns in the air, and far, far off in the azure empyrean a steppe eagle was sailing, retreating from the approaching storm.

Natalia walked through the yard. Beyond the stone wall on the crumpled grass lay golden heaps of cartridge-cases. The windows and whitewashed walls of the hut yawned with machine-gun bulletholes. Seeing Natalia, one of the chickens left alive flew with a squawk on to the roof of the granary.

The gracious silence hung not long over the village. The wind began to blow, wide-open shutters and doors began to slam in the deserted houses. A snowy hail-cloud blotted out the sun and floated onward towards the west.

Holding her hair from fluttering in the wind, Natalia went as far as the summer kitchen, whence she again looked in the direction of the hill. On the horizon, wrapped in a lilac smoke of dust, single soldiers were galloping along, on horses or in two-wheeled army carts.

"So it's true; they're retreating," she decided with a feeling of relief.

Before she reached the porch, somewhere far beyond the hill gunshots began to sound with a rolling, muffled thunder, and, as though exchanging calls with them, the joyous clash of bells from the two Vieshenska churches floated across the river.

On the farther side of the Don the Cossacks began to pour in a dense crowd out of the forest. They dragged barges along the ground or carried them in their hands towards the river, to launch them on the water. Standing at the stern, the rowers vigorously worked their oars. Some three dozen boats chased one another hurriedly towards the village.

"Natalia, darling! Oh, my dear. . . . Our folk are coming!" Ilinichna cried, her eyes streaming with tears, as she ran out of the kitchen.

Natalia seized Mishatka in her arms and raised him high in the air. Her eyes glittered feverishly, but her voice broke as she panted:

"Look, darling, you've got sharp eyes. . . . Maybe your father's among the Cossacks. . . . Can you see him? That isn't him in the first boat, is it? Oh, but you're not looking the right way. . . ."

At the landing-place they met only the emaciated Pantaleimon Prokoffievich. The old man first inquired whether the bullocks, the farm property, the grain were all safe, then burst into tears and embraced his grandchildren. But when, hurrying and limping, he went into his own yard, he turned pale, fell to his knees, crossed himself with great sweeps of his arm, and, bowing low to the east. for a long time did not raise his grey head from the hot, sunburnt earth.

Chapter 11

On June 10 the cavalry group of the Don Army, commanded by General Sekretov and numbering three thousand men, with six horse-drawn guns and eighteen pack machine-guns, delivered an overwhelming blow and broke through the front close to the district centre of Ust-Belokalitvenska. Then the force moved along the railway line in the direction of the district centre of Kazanska.

Early in the morning of the third day an officers' reconnaissance patrol from the 9th Don Regiment made contact with an insurgent field outpost close to the Don. Seeing mounted men, the Cossacks rushed in to the cliffs; but the Cossack captain in charge of the patrol recognized the insurgents by their dress, waved a handkerchief tied to his sabre, and shouted in a resonant voice:

"We're on your side. . . . Don't run, Cossacks. . . ."

Taking no precautions, the patrol rode to the spur of the cliff. The commander of the insurgent outpost, an old, grey-headed sergeant, was the first to come out, buttoning up his dew-sprinkled greatcoat as he went. The eight officers dismounted, and the captain went up to the sergeant, removed his khaki cap with its officer's white cockade showing clearly against the band, smiled, and said:

"Well, greetings, Cossacks! As is the good old Cossack custom, we'll kiss each other." He kissed the insurgent on both cheeks, wiped his lips and moustache with his handkerchief, and, feeling his companions' expectant gaze fixed on him, asked with a drawl and a meaning smile:

"Well, so you've come to your senses? So your friends have proved better than the Bolsheviks?"

"Exactly so, Your Excellency! We've atoned for our sins. Three months we've been fighting; we never hoped to live to see you arrive."

"A good thing you did think better of it, though it was late. It's all past now, and whoever starts to recall the past can clear out. What is your district centre?"

"Kazanska, Your Excellency."

"Is your detachment across the Don?"

"Just so."

"Which way did the Reds go from the Don?"

"Up the river; to the Donietz settlement, probably."

"Haven't your cavalry crossed yet?"

"By no means."

"Why not?"

"I can't say, Your Excellency. We were the first to be sent over this side."

"Did the Reds have any artillery here?"

"Two batteries."

"When were they withdrawn?"

"During the night."

"They ought to have been pursued. . . . Ah, you let the chance slip!" the captain declared reproachfully and, going up to his horse, took a writing-pad and a map out of his wallet.

The sergeant stood at attention, his hands down his seams. Two paces behind him crowded the Cossacks, with mingled feelings of joy and vague anxiety scrutinizing the officers, the saddles, the thoroughbred but thin horses. Dressed in neatly-fitting British tunics with epaulets and broad breeches, the officers shifted from foot to foot, fidgeted around their horses, took sidelong glances at the Cossacks. Not one of them had the home-made epaulets drawn with indelible pencil which had been so common in the autumn of 1918. Their boots, saddles, bandoleers, field-glasses, the carbines clipped to their saddles were all new and all of non-Russian origin. Only the one who, judging by his looks, was the oldest of them all was in a Circassian coat of fine blue cloth, a round Kuban cap of Bukharan karakul wool, and mountaineer's boots without heels. He was the first to approach the Cossacks; stepping quietly forward, drawing a fine packet of cigarettes adorned with the picture of King Albert of the Belgians from his pocket, he suggested:

"Have a smoke, brothers?"

The Cossacks greedily reached out for the cigarettes. The other officers also drew closer.

"Well, how did you find life under the Bolsheviks?" a big-headed and broad-shouldered cornet asked.

"Not too pleasant," a Cossack in an old peasant's coat answered cautiously, as he avidly drew at the cigarette, keeping his eyes fixed on the long gaiters, laced to the knee, which tightly embraced the officer's hefty calves.

The Cossack's broken shoes hardly remained on his feet. His white, well-darned woollen stockings, and the trousers tucked into them, were in ribbons, and so the man could not remove his enraptured gaze from the British-made boots, with their fascinatingly stout soles and brilliantly gleaming brass eyelets. He could not restrain himself and artlessly expressed his admiration·

"But you've got a fine pair of boots!"

The cornet did not feel inclined to enter into friendly conversation. With a sneer and a challenge in his voice he said:

"You wanted to change your foreign equipment for the Moscow bast shoes, so you've got no reason to covet other people's now!"

"We made a mistake. We've admitted it and we've been punished," the Cossack said in a disconcerted tone, looking round at the other Cossacks in search of support.

The cornet went on sneeringly with his lecture:

"You showed you'd got bullocks' brains. A bullock's always like that: he shifts first, and stops to think afterwards. 'Made a mistake!' But when you laid the front bare in the autumn, what were you thinking of then? You wanted to be commissars! Fine defenders of the fatherland you were!"

"Drop it, that's enough!" a youthful-looking company commander quietly whispered into the fuming cornet's ear. The cornet trod on his cigarette, spat, and with a rolling gait went off to the horses.

The captain handed him a note and said something in an undertone. With unexpected ease the heavily built cornet leaped on his horse, turned the animal sharply, and galloped off westward.

The Cossacks maintained a disconcerted silence. The captain came up to them and asked in a ringing, cheery baritone:

"How far is it to the village of Varvarinsky?"

"Nearly twenty-five miles," several of the Cossacks answered in an assortment of voices.

"Good! Well now, Cossacks, go and inform your commander that the cavalry forces are to cross to this side without a moment's delay. One of our officers will go with you to the crossing, and he will lead the cavalry. The infantry can advance on Kazanska, in marching order. Understand? Well, as we say, about turn and quick march!"

The Cossacks went in a crowd down the hill. For perhaps two hundred yards they strode along in silence, as though by agreement, but then a homely-looking Cossack in a peasant's coat, the same man whom the zealous cornet had lectured, shook his head and sighed mournfully:

"Well, so we're united again, brothers. . . ."

A second excitedly added:

"A horse-radish is no sweeter than a radish!" And he swore juicily.

Chapter 12

As soon as the news that the Red forces were in retreat arrived at Vieshenska, Gregor Melekhov and two cavalry regiments swam their horses across the Don, sent out strong patrols, and moved southward.

Fighting was going on beyond the Donside hills. They could hear the blended roar of gunfire thundering muffledly, as though underground.

"You can see the Cadets don't spare the shells! They're putting down a barrage," one of the commanders said in an admiring tone as he rode up to Gregor.

Gregor held his peace. He was riding ahead of the column, gazing about him attentively. For a distance of two miles from the Don to Bazki hamlet thousands of light carts and wagons left behind by the insurgents were strewn along the road. Everywhere in the forest lay scattered possessions: broken chests, tables, clothing, harness, domestic utensils, sewing-machines, sacks of grain, all the things that in a great lust for household property had been snatched up and carried so far in the retreat to the Don. In places the road was littered knee-high with golden wheat. And here and there were the swollen, stinking carcasses of bullocks and horses, horribly distorted with decay.

"There's fine husbandry for you!" Gregor exclaimed, shocked at the sight. Baring his head, trying not to breathe, he cautiously rode round a little mound of fusty grain over which the body of an old man in a Cossack cap and a bloodstained coat was stretched.

"That old man's kept guard to the end over his goods! The devils must have bewitched him into staying here," one of the Cossacks said compassionately.

"He couldn't bring himself to leave the wheat behind. . . ."

"Well, move on at a trot! He stinks like God knows what! Hey, get a move on!" came indignant shouts from the ranks in the rear.

The squadron broke into a trot. The talk died away. Only the clatter of innumerable horse-hoofs and the jingle of tightly strapped Cossack equipment rang in accord through the forest.

There was fighting going on not far from the Listnitskys' estate. The Red Army men were running in a dense crowd along a waterless valley to one side of Yagodnoe. Shrapnel was bursting above their heads, machine-guns were firing at their backs, and a stream of men from a Kalmyk regiment poured over the hill to cut off their retreat.

Gregor arrived with his regiments when the battle was over. The two Red Army companies covering the retreat of the shattered forces and baggage trains of the Fourteenth Mironov Division were smashed by the Kalmyk regiment and completely destroyed. On the heights above the valley Gregor remarked as he handed over the command to Yermakov:

"They've managed here without us. You go and make contact; I'm just going to slip along to that estate for a moment."

"What for?" Yermakov asked in surprise.

"Well, that's difficult to say. I worked here when I was a youngster, and something draws me to take a look at the old spots. . . ."

Calling Prokhor, Gregor turned in the direction of Yagodnoe. They had ridden a quarter of a mile when, looking back, he saw a white sheet, which one of the Cossacks had thoughtfully brought along, fluttering in the wind at the head of the squadrons.

"It looks just as though they were surrendering!" Gregor thought anxiously, and he watched with a vague yearning at his heart as slowly, almost it seemed reluctantly, the column dropped into the valley, towards a mounted group of Sekretov men, who were riding at a trot straight across the grass to meet them.

An air of mournfulness and neglect welcomed Gregor as through the tumbledown gateway he rode into the courtyard. The yard was

overgrown with goosefoot. Yagodnoe was unrecognizable. Everywhere he saw signs of terrible neglect and ruin. The once handsome
house was dingy and almost seemed to have sunk on its foundations.
The long unpainted roof was marked with yellow patches of rust,
broken gutter pipes hung from the eaves, the shutters were hanging
awry, half off their hinges, the wind tore with a whistle through the
shattered windows, while the sour, mouldy smell of a place long
uninhabited came from the rooms.

The eastern corner of the house, together with the porch, had been
demolished by a shell from a three-inch gun. The crown of a maple
bowled over by the shell was thrust into the broken Venetian window of the corridor. So it had been left lying, its butt buried in a
heap of bricks torn up from the foundations. Along its faded
branches a wild hop was already crawling and twining exuberantly;
whimsically overgrowing the panes still left whole, it reached up to
the cornice.

Time and weather had done their work. The yard buildings had
rotted and looked as though solicitous human hands had not touched
them for many a year. The stone wall of the stable had fallen,
washed down by the spring rains; a storm had torn off the roof of
the coach-house, and only here and there were handfuls of half-
rotten straw left on the spectrally bleached rafters and crossbeams.

Three savage borzois were lying on the steps of the servants' quarters. Seeing human beings, they jumped up and, barking hoarsely,
vanished into the porch. Gregor rode up to the wide-open window
of the servants' wing, bent across from his saddle, and called:

"Is there any living soul here?"

There was a long silence, but at last a woman's strained voice
answered:

"Wait a bit, for the love of Christ! I'll be out in a minute."

Shuffling along on bare feet, the aged Lukeria came to the steps.
Screwing up her eyes to keep out the sunlight, she stood gazing long
at Gregor.

"Don't you know me, Aunty Lukeria?" Gregor asked as he dismounted.

Only then did a tremor pass over Lukeria's pockmarked face, and
the look of dull indifference gave place to one of terrible agitation.
She burst into tears, and for a long time could not utter a word.
Gregor tethered his horse, and waited patiently.

"The things I've suffered! God grant that I may never again suffer like it!" Lukeria began to lament, rubbing her cheeks with a dirty canvas apron. "I thought it was them arrived again. . . . Ah, Grisha, the things that have happened here. You'd never believe! Only me is left. . . ."

"Why, where's Grand-dad Sashka? Did he retreat with the masters?"

"If he had, he might have been alive still. . . ."

"Surely he's not dead?"

"They killed him. He's been lying in the cellar these past three days. . . . He ought to be buried, but I fell ill. . . . I had to force myself up to answer you just now. . . . And I'm mortally afraid to go to him, to the dead. . . ."

"What did they do it for?" Gregor asked thickly, not raising his eyes from the ground.

"It was over the mare. . . . The masters left in a hurry. They only took their money, and they left almost all the property with me." Lukeria's voice dropped to a whisper. "I kept everything, down to the last thread. It still lies buried to this day. And they only took three Orlov stallions from the horses and left the others with Grand-dad Sashka. When the rising began, the horses were taken by both Cossacks and Reds. The raven stallion Whirlwind—I expect you remember him?—was taken by the Reds in the spring. They had a struggle to get the saddle on him. You know he'd never been broken in to a saddle. But they were not destined to ride him, to triumph over him. Some Kargin Cossacks arrived here a week later and told us about it. On the hill they ran into the Reds and began to fire at them. The Cossacks had got some silly little mare with them, and just at that moment she began to whinny. And Whirlwind flew like wildfire to the mare, and the man riding him couldn't hold him in at all. He saw he couldn't control the stallion, and so he tried to jump off while in full gallop. He jumped off all right, but he failed to get his foot out of the stirrup. So Whirlwind dragged him right into the hands of the Cossacks."

"Fine!" Prokhor exclaimed enthusiastically.

"Now a Kargin lieutenant's riding the stallion," Lukeria continued measuredly with her story. "He's promised that as soon as Master arrives he'll return Whirlwind to the stable. And so they took away all the horses, and only the trotting-horse Arrow was left. She was

in foal, and so nobody touched her. She only dropped the foal recently, and old Sashka took such great care of that little foal, you
wouldn't believe! He carried it about in his arms and gave it milk
and some herb potion from a horn, to make it stronger on its legs.
And then trouble came on us! Three days ago three men rode up
late in the afternoon. Sashka was mowing grass in the orchard.
They shouted at him: 'Come here, you this and that!' He threw
down his scythe, went over and greeted them; but they wouldn't
look at him, only drank milk and asked him: 'Have you got any
horses?' And he said: 'We've got one, but she's no good for your
military work; she's a mare, and she's suckling a foal!' The most savage of the three shouted: 'That's nothing to do with you! Bring
the mare here, you old devil! My horse has got a chafed back, and
I've got to change her.' Sashka should have submitted and not stood
out over the mare, but you know what a character the old man
was. . . . There were times when the master himself couldn't make
him hold his tongue. I expect you remember."

"And so he didn't hand her over?" Prokhor intervened in the story.

"Why, how could he help handing her over? He only said to
them: 'Before you came we've had I don't know how many horsemen come and take away all the horses, but they all had pity on this
one, so why should you . . .' That made them angry: 'But they say,
you lickspittle, that you're keeping her for your master.' Well, and
they pulled him away. . . . One of them led out the mare and began
to saddle her, and the foal crawled under her to the teat. Old Sasha
began to plead: 'Have pity, don't take her! Where is the foal to go?'
'I'll show you where,' another of them said, and drove the foal away
from its mother, slipped his rifle from his shoulder, and fired at it.
I burst into tears. . . . I ran up and pleaded with them, and I got
hold of Sasha and tried to lead him out of trouble, but as he looked
at the foal his little beard began to shake; he went as white as a wall
and said: 'If that's the case, then shoot me too, you son of a bitch!'
He rushed at them and clung to them and wouldn't let them saddle
the mare. And they went mad and killed him on the spot. I was
near crazed when they fired at him. . . . And now I can't think
what to do about him. He ought to have a coffin made, but is that
woman's work?"

"Bring us two spades and some canvas," Gregor asked.

"Are you thinking of burying him?" Prokhor inquired.

"Yes."

"A fine idea, taking that on yourself, Gregor Pantalievich! Let me go and fetch some Cossacks at once. They'll make a coffin and dig him a proper grave. . . ."

It was obvious that Prokhor had no desire to be bothered with the burial of some unknown old man, but Gregor resolutely rejected his suggestion.

"We'll dig the grave and bury him ourselves. Old Sasha was a good sort. Go into the orchard and wait for me by the lake while I go and have a look at him."

Under the same poplar with its roots spreading over the ground, by the duckweeded pond where Sasha had once buried Gregor's and Aksinia's little daughter, the old man found his own last resting-place. They wrapped his withered body in a clean sheet used for covering leaven and smelling of hops, laid it in the grave, and filled in the earth. Beside the infant's mound rose yet another, neatly trodden down by Cossack boots, gleaming cheerfully with fresh, damp clay.

Numbed with memories, Gregor lay down on the grass not far from this tiny, dearly cherished cemetery and gazed long at the majestic expanse of blue sky above him. Somewhere in the heights of that infinite space winds were wandering, chilly clouds gleaming with sunlight were floating along; but on the earth which had just taken the merry ostler and drunkard Sashka to itself life was still seething as furiously as ever. On the steppe stealing in a flood of green to the very edge of the orchard, and in the tangle of wild flax around the borders of the ancient threshing-floor, he could hear the incessant quiet rattle of struggling quails; marmots were whistling, bumble-bees were humming, the grass was rustling beneath the wind's caresses, the skylarks were singing in the spirting light of the sunset, and, to confirm the grandeur of man's place in nature, somewhere a long way off in the valley a machine-gun stuttered insistently, angrily, and hollowly.

Chapter 13

General Sekretov, who arrived in Vieshenska with his staff officers
and a personal escort of a squadron of Cossacks, was welcomed hospitably, with bread and salt, and with the ringing of church bells.
The bells of both the churches were rung all day by anyone who
cared to go up into the belfries and ring, just as at Easter-time. Cossacks from the lower Don rode through the streets on meagre Don
horses exhausted with long marches. Close to the merchant's house
where the general had taken up his quarters a crowd of orderlies
was standing in the square. Husking sunflower seeds, they made
conversation with the village girls passing by in their Sunday best.

The church bells were rung and vodka drunk in Vieshenska until
dusk fell. But in the evening the insurgent command organized a
banquet for the new arrivals, holding it in the house set aside for the
officers' mess.

The tall, well-built Sekretov, a Cossack of Cossacks, a native of
one of the hamlets in the Krasnokutsk district, was passionately fond
of riding-horses; he was a superb rider, and a dashing cavalry general. But he was no speaker. The speech he made at the banquet
was filled with drunken bragging and included unequivocal reproaches and threats addressed to the upper Don Cossacks.

Gregor, who was present at the banquet, listened tensely and
angrily to Sekretov's words. The general, still not quite sober, stood
resting his fingers on the table, sending the scented vodka sprinkling
from his glass, giving superfluous emphasis to every phrase.

". . . No, it is not we who ought to thank you for help, but you
who ought to thank us. You, and only you—that has got to be said
plainly. Without us the Reds would have annihilated you. You
know very well. But we would have crushed the scum without
you. And we are crushing it, and will crush it, bear that in mind,
until we have cleaned up all Russia. In the autumn you abandoned
the front. You let the Bolsheviks enter the Cossack lands. You
wanted to live at peace with them, but you couldn't! And so you
rose, to save your property, your lives. Putting it bluntly, you were
afraid of your own and your cattle's hides. I recall the past not in

order to reproach you with your sins. I do not say this to you to offend you. But it never does any harm to establish the truth. We have pardoned your betrayal. As brothers, we have come to you at your most difficult moment, we have come to your help. But your shameful past must be redeemed in the future. You understand, gentlemen? You must redeem it with your exploits and with irreproachable service to our gentle river Don, you understand?"

"Well, here's to the redemption!" an elderly Cossack officer sitting opposite Gregor said to nobody in particular, smiling almost imperceptibly. Not waiting for the others, he was the first to drink. He had a manly face a little scarred with smallpox, and humorous deep brown eyes. During Sekretov's speech his lips more than once twisted into an indefinite, lurking smile, and then his eyes darkened and seemed jet black. As he watched this officer, Gregor noticed that he was on familiar terms with Sekretov and behaved very offhandedly towards him, while he was markedly restrained and cold in his relations with the other officers. He alone was wearing khaki epaulets sewn to a khaki tunic, and Kornilov chevrons on his sleeves. "A man with ideals!" Gregor thought. "Probably a volunteer!" The Cossack officer drank like a horse. He did not eat anything, yet he did not get drunk, only let out his broad British belt from time to time.

"Who is that sitting opposite me—the pockmarked fellow?" Gregor whispered to Bogatiriev, who was sitting next to him.

"The devil knows!" Bogatiriev, who was well on the way to getting drunk, evaded the question.

Kudynov did not spare the vodka for his guests. Liquor appeared on the table, and Sekretov, who had difficulty in finishing his speech, threw open his khaki coat and dropped heavily into his armchair. A young company commander with an obviously Mongolian type of face leaned across to him and whispered something.

"Go to the devil!" Sekretov answered, turning livid, and he tossed off the glass of liquor Kudynov had complaisantly poured out.

"And who's that with the slanting eyes? An adjutant?" Gregor asked Bogatiriev.

Covering his mouth with his palm, his companion answered:

"No, that's Sekretov's adopted son. He brought him back as a boy from Manchuria during the Japanese war. He brought him up and sent him to a Junkers' military school. And the boy's made good!

He's a daring devil! Yesterday he captured the Reds' treasury chests close to Makeevka. He grabbed two millions in notes. Look, you can see packets of them sticking out of all his pockets. The devil struck it lucky! An absolute treasure! But drink up, what are you staring about you for?"

Kudynov made a speech in reply, but hardly anyone listened to him. The carousal grew more and more uncontrolled. Throwing off his jacket, Sekretov sat in his waistcoat. His clean-shaven head glittered with sweat, and his irreproachably spotless linen shirt more and more set off his purpled face and almost olive-coloured, sunburnt neck. Kudynov whispered something to him, but Sekretov obstinately repeated without looking at him:

"No, excuse me! But you must excuse me. We trust you, but only in so far as— Your treachery will not quickly be forgotten. Let all those who played about with the Reds in the autumn engrave that on their memories. . . ."

"Well, but we in our turn shall serve you only in so far as . . ." the intoxicated Gregor thought with cold fury. He rose to his feet.

Not putting on his cap, he went out on to the porch and, with a feeling of relief, with all his lungs he breathed in the fresh night air.

Down by the Don the frogs were tumultuous, and the water beetles were grumpily humming, as before rain. On a spit of sand snipe were calling to one another. Somewhere afar off in the waterside reeds a foal which had lost its mother was neighing in thin, long-drawn-out tones. "Bitter need has betrothed you to us, otherwise we wouldn't have wanted so much as a smell of you. The accursed scum! He swells up like a penny piece of gingerbread and reproaches us, and in a week's time he'll start treading on our necks. . . . What is done is done. . . . It's all as I thought. . . . It was bound to be so. But now the Cossacks will turn up their noses! They've got out of the habit of saluting and standing to attention before their Excellencies!" Gregor thought as he went down the steps and groped his way towards the wicket gate.

The liquor had had its effect on him also: his head was swimming, his movements acquired an uncertain heaviness. As he passed through the wicket gate he reeled, clapped his cap on his head, and, dragging his feet, walked down the street.

Close to the little house belonging to Aksinia's aunt he halted for a moment hesitantly, then resolutely strode towards the door. The inner door leading to the porch was not fastened. He walked into the best room without knocking, and directly before him saw Stepan Astakhov sitting at the table. Aksinia's aunt was busy at the stove. The table was covered with a clean tablecloth, and on it stood an unfinished bottle of home-made vodka and some pieces of rosy pink dried fish on a plate.

Stepan had just emptied his glass and evidently was about to have a smoke. But, seeing Gregor, he pushed away his plate and leaned his back against the wall.

Though Gregor was drunk, he noticed Stepan's face turn deathly pale and saw his eyes flame wolfishly. Dumbfounded by the meet‚ing, Gregor yet found strength enough to remark hoarsely:

"You've been doing yourself well!"

"Glory be!" the housewife answered in alarm, undoubtedly fully aware of Gregor's relations with her kinswoman and not expecting any good to come from this chance meeting of husband and lover.

Stepan silently stroked his whiskers with his left hand and kept his burning eyes fixed on Gregor.

But Gregor, standing with feet set wide apart on the threshold, smiled wryly and said:

"Well, I just looked in . . . you must excuse me."

Stepan was silent. The awkward silence lasted until the housewife plucked up courage enough to invite Gregor to stop.

"Come in and sit down," she said.

Now Gregor had nothing to conceal. His arrival at Aksinia's house was explanation enough to Stepan. And he marched straight into the breach:

"But where's your wife?"

"Have you come to see her, then?" Stepan asked quietly but distinctly, and dropped his fluttering eyelashes over his eyes.

"Yes, that's right," Gregor admitted with a sigh.

He was ready for anything at that moment and, growing sober, prepared to defend himself. But Stepan half opened his eyes (their previous fire had faded) and said:

"I've sent her for some vodka; she'll be back in a minute. Sit down and wait."

He went so far as to rise, revealing his tall, well-built figure, and he pushed a chair towards Gregor. Not looking at the housewife, he asked:

"Aunty, bring us a clean glass." And to Gregor: "You'll have a drink, won't you?"

"Just one glass."

"Well, sit down."

Gregor sat down at the table. Stepan shared out the rest of the vodka equally in the glasses and raised his strangely misty eyes to Gregor:

"Here's to everybody."

"And their health!"

They clinked glasses together. They drank. They were silent for some time. The housewife, as nimble as a mouse, handed the guest a plate and a fork with a dented handle.

"Have some fish," she said. "It's mild-cured."

"No, thank you."

"Go on, put some on the plate and enjoy it," the woman, now greatly cheered, urged him. She was pleased beyond expression that all was passing off so well, without a fight, without the smashing of crockery, without shouting. The ominous exchange of remarks had stopped. Now they were eating silently, not looking at each other. The prudent housewife took a clean hand-towel from the chest and in a sense united Gregor with Stepan by laying the two ends across their knees.

"Why aren't you with your company?" Gregor asked, studying the fish.

"I've come on a visit too," Stepan said after a momentary pause, and from his tone it was quite impossible to determine whether he were serious or sarcastic.

"The company's back at home, I suppose?"

"They're all enjoying themselves in the village. Well, shall we finish our drink?"

"All right."

"Your health!"

"Good luck!"

In the porch the door latch rattled. Now quite sober, Gregor glanced from under his brows at Stepan and noticed that a pallor again washed over his face.

Aksinia entered, her head wrapped in an embroidered kerchief. Not noticing Gregor, she approached the table and took a side glance at him. Terror spirted in her black, dilated eyes. She panted, then said with an effort:

"Greetings, Gregor Pantalievich!"

Stepan's great angular hands, which were resting on the table, began to tremble. Gregor silently bowed to Aksinia, not letting fall one word.

Setting two bottles of home-made vodka on the table, she again threw Gregor a glance full of anxiety and secret joy, turned and went into the dark corner of the room, sat down on the chest, and tidied her hair with trembling hands. Mastering his agitation, Stepan unbuttoned his shirt collar, which seemed to be choking him, filled the glasses to the brim, and turned to his wife:

"Take a glass and sit down at the table."

"I don't want any."

"Come and sit down!"

"But I don't drink vodka, Stepan."

"How many times have I got to tell you?" Stepan's voice shook.

"Sit down, neighbour," Gregor smiled encouragingly. She gave him a pleading glance and swiftly went to the cupboard. A dish fell from the shelf and crashed on the floor.

"Ah, what a pity!" The housewife clapped her hands in chagrin. Aksinia silently gathered up the fragments.

Stepan filled her glass also to the brim, and once more his eyes flamed up with yearning and hatred.

"Well, let's drink—" he began, and was silent.

In the silence Aksinia's violent and spasmodic breathing as she sat down at the table was clearly audible.

"We'll drink, wife, to a long parting. Why, don't you want to? Won't you drink?"

"But you know—"

"I know everything now. . . . Well then, not to any parting. Here's to the health of our dear guest Gregor Pantalievich."

"Yes, I'll drink his health!" Aksinia said in a ringing voice, and tossed off her glass at one gulp.

"You've got a stupid headpiece!" the housewife muttered, running out into the kitchen.

She huddled into a corner and pressed her hands to her breast, waiting for the table to go flying with a crash, for a shot to roar deafeningly. . . . But in the best room the silence was as of the grave. The only sound to be heard was that of the flies, disturbed by the light, buzzing below the ceiling, while outside the window the cocks called to one another, welcoming the midnight all over the village.

Dark are the nights of June along the Don. In the oppressive silence the golden summer-lightning flashes over the slaty-black sky, stars fall and are reflected in the flowing swiftness of the river. From the steppe a dry warm wind brings the honeyed perfume of the flowering thyme to the human habitations, and in the low-lying river-side there is a vapid scent of damp grass, of silt, of rawness; the corncrakes cry unceasingly, and the river-side forest is all covered with a silvery brocade of mist, as in a fairy story.

Prokhor awoke at midnight. He asked the master of the house in which they were quartered:

"Hasn't our man arrived?"

"Not yet. He's enjoying himself with the generals."

"I expect they're having a good time with the vodka there." Prokhor sighed enviously and, yawning, began to dress.

"Where are you off to?"

"I'm going to water the horses and give them some grain. Pantalievich said that we were riding to Tatarsk at sunrise. We shall spend the day there, and then we'll have to catch up with our forces."

"It's a long time yet to sunrise. You might wait until the sky begins to lighten."

In a dissatisfied voice Prokhor answered:

"Anyone can see with half an eye that you weren't in the army when you were young, old man. In our service, if we weren't to feed the horses and look after them we might not come through alive. You can't go all out at a gallop on a half-starved little nag, can you? The better the beast under you, the swifter you can get away from the enemy. That's me all over. There's no need for me to overtake them, but if we find ourselves in a tight corner, then I'm the first to show my heels. I've had my face to the bullets for so many years now that I've had enough! Light a light, old man, or I'll never find my leg-rags. Thanks! Ye-es, our Gregor Pantalievich now, he's carried off all the crosses and orders and dived head-first into hell. But I'm not such a fool, I've got no need of them. Well, the devils take charge of him; I expect he's drunk into the bargain."

There was a gentle knock at the door.

"Come in," Prokhor shouted.

A Cossack with the epaulets of a junior non-commissioned officer on his khaki tunic and wearing a peaked cap with a cockade came in.

"I'm an orderly from General Sekretov's staff. Can I see His Excellency Mr. Melekhov?" he asked, saluting and standing at attention at the door.

"He's not here," Prokhor answered, amazed at the well-trained orderly's bearing and manner of address. "But don't stretch your bones like that! When I was a youngster I was just as foolish as you. I'm his orderly. But what do you want him for?"

"I have been commanded by General Sekretov to see Mr. Melekhov. He is requested to present himself at once to the House of the Officers' Mess."

"He went there early in the evening."

"He was there, but later he left and went home."

Prokhor whistled, and winked at the master sitting on the bed:

"Get that, old man? He slipped away, which means he's gone to his darling. . . . Well, you can go, soldier; I'll find him and send him there hot-foot."

Telling the old man to water the horses and give them grain, Prokhor set off for the house of Aksinia's aunt.

The district centre of Vieshenska was sleeping in an impenetrable darkness. On the farther side of the Don the nightingales were whistling, outvying one another in the forest. Unhurryingly Prokhor went up to the well-known little hut, entered the porch, and had just taken hold of the door latch when he heard Stepan's deep voice. "Now I'm in a hole," thought Prokhor. "He'll want to know what I've come for. And I'll have nothing to say. Well, it can't be helped. I'll say I came out to buy vodka, and the neighbours sent me to this house."

Plucking up courage, he entered the best room and, struck dumb with astonishment, stood silent with gaping mouth: there was Gregor sitting at the same table as Astakhov and—as though there never had been any quarrel between them—sipping cloudy green, home-made vodka from a glass.

Stepan, a strained smile on his face, looked at Prokhor and said:

"What are you standing there gaping for and not even saying 'Good evening'? Have you seen a ghost?"

"Something of the sort," Prokhor, still flabbergasted, answered, shifting from foot to foot.

"Well, don't be afraid, come in and sit down," Stepan invited him.

"Time won't allow of my sitting down. I've come for you, Gregor Pantalievich. You're ordered to go to General Sekretov at once."

Even before Prokhor's arrival Gregor had started up several times to go. He had pushed away his glass and risen, but had at once sat down again, afraid Stepan would regard his departure as an open manifestation of cowardice. His pride would not allow him to abandon Aksinia, to yield place to Stepan. He drank, but the vodka no longer had any effect on him. Soberly realizing all the equivocal nature of his position, he waited for the denouement. For one second he had felt sure Stepan would strike Aksinia when she drank his, Gregor's, health. But he was wrong. Stepan raised his hairy hand, wiped his sunburnt forehead, and after a brief silence glanced in admiration at Aksinia and said: "You're a great lass, wife! I like you for your daring."

Then Prokhor had entered.

After a moment's reflection Gregor decided not to go, thinking he would give Stepan an opportunity to say what was in his mind.

"Go and tell them you haven't been able to find me. Understand?" He turned to Prokhor.

"I understand all right. Only it would be better if you went, Pantalievich."

"That's not your business. Off with you!"

Prokhor went towards the door. But at that moment Aksinia unexpectedly intervened. Not looking at Gregor, she said dryly:

"But what does this mean? You go with him, Gregor Pantalievich! Thank you for coming and being our guest, spending some of your time with us. . . . But it's getting late, the second cock has crowed. It'll be dawn soon, and Stepan and I have got to go home at sunrise. . . . And besides, you've had enough drink! No more!"

Stepan did not try to keep him back, and Gregor rose. As they shook hands Stepan held Gregor's in his own cold, rough hand, as though at last he wanted to say something. Yet even then he did not speak, but silently watched Gregor to the door, then unhurriedly reached out for the unfinished bottle.

The moment Gregor found himself in the street a terrible weariness took possession of him. Moving his legs with difficulty, he walked as far as the first crossroads, then asked Prokhor, who was following inseparably in his tracks:

"Go saddle the horses and bring them here. I shan't get there on foot. . . ."

"Shall I go and report that you're on the way?"

"No."

"Well, wait a bit; I'll be back in a moment."

This time the always leisurely Prokhor set off for their quarters at a trot.

Gregor sat down by the fence and lit a cigarette. As he mentally reviewed his meeting with Stepan, he unconcernedly thought: "Well, now he knows. So long as he doesn't beat Aksinia." Then his weariness and the emotional excitement he had experienced forced him to lie down. He dozed off.

Prokhor rode up very soon after.

They crossed by the ferry to the farther side of the Don and put the horses into a swinging trot.

Chapter 14

They rode into Tatarsk at dawn. By the gate of his yard Gregor dismounted, threw the rein to Prokhor, and hurrying, agitated, went towards the house.

Natalia, half dressed, happened to come out to the porch for something. At the sight of Gregor her sleepy eyes blazed up with such a bright, spirting light of joy that his heart beat and his eyes momentarily, unexpectedly, moistened. But Natalia silently embraced her beloved one, pressing all her body against his, and by the way her shoulders quivered Gregor realized that she was weeping.

He went into the hut, kissed the old people and the children sleeping in the best room, and stood in the middle of the kitchen.

"Well, how did you come through? All well?" he asked, breathing heavily with agitation.

"Glory be, my son, we've seen things to put fear into our hearts, but we can't say we've been overmuch troubled," Ilinichna hurriedly answered. Glancing sidelong at the tear-stained Natalia, she harshly shouted at her: "You ought to be glad, and you're crying, you little fool! Now, don't stand there doing nothing! Get some wood, light the stove. . . ."

While she and Natalia were hastily getting breakfast ready, Pantaleimon Prokoffievich brought his son a clean hand-towel and suggested:

"You have a wash, I'll pour water into your hands. It freshens up the head. You stink of vodka. I suppose you were celebrating the joyful event yesterday?"

"We celebrated right enough. Only at the moment it isn't clear whether it's a joyful or a mournful event."

"What's that?" the old man was surprised beyond measure.

"Why, Sekretov's rather angry with us."

"Well, that's no woe. Surely he didn't drink with you too?"

"M'yes, he did."

"You don't say! The honour you've been done, Grishka! Sitting at the same table as a real general! To think of it!" Giving his son a tender look, Pantaleimon clicked his tongue in delight.

Gregor smiled. He did not share his father's naïve exultation in the least.

As he seriously questioned the old man about the cattle and property and asked how much damage had been done to the grain, Gregor noticed that his father was not so interested as formerly in talking about the farm. Something more important was weighing on the old man's mind, something was oppressing him.

Pantaleimon was not slow in giving expression to his fears:

"What's going to happen now, Grisha? Surely we shan't have to serve any more?"

"Who are you referring to?"

"The old men. Me, for instance."

"There's nothing definite at present."

"So we shall have to go?"

"You can stay."

"But really?" Pantaleimon exclaimed in delight, and went limping about the kitchen in his agitation.

"Sit down, you lame devil! Don't carry the dirt on your boots all over the house. You're so overjoyed you're running about like a half-starved whelp," Ilinichna sternly called to him.

But the old man paid no attention to her shout. He hobbled several times from the table to the stove, smiling and rubbing his hands. Then he was seized by doubts:

"But can you give me my discharge?"

"Of course I can."

"You'll write me out a document?"

"Of course."

The old man stammered irresolutely, but at last got out the words:

"What sort of document will it be? . . . Without a seal? Or perhaps you've got a seal with you?"

"It'll do all right without a seal." Gregor smiled.

"Well, then there's no point in talking." The old man again cheered up. "God grant you health! When are you thinking of going off again?"

"Tomorrow."

"Have your forces gone on ahead?"

"Yes. But don't you worry about yourself, Father. In any case all the old men like you will be allowed to go home soon. You've served your time."

"God grant it!" Pantaleimon crossed himself, evidently now completely reassured.

The children woke up. Gregor took them in his arms, seated them on his knees, and, kissing them in turn, a smile on his lips, listened long to their merry chatter.

How the hair of these children was scented! With sun, with grass, with warm pillows, and with something else infinitely near and dear to him. And they—this flesh of his flesh—were like the tiny steppe birds. How clumsy seemed his great black hands as they embraced the two children! And how foreign to this peaceful scene did he seem—this horseman who had slipped from his horse for one day, who was soaked through and through with the pungent scent of soldiering and horse's sweat, the sour smell of campaigning and of leather equipment!

Gregor's eyes were filmed with a mist of tears, his lips quivered beneath his whiskers. Three times he failed to answer his father's questions, and he came to the table only when Natalia touched him on the sleeve of his tunic.

Truly, Gregor was no longer the man he had been! He had never been particularly sensitive and had wept rarely even as a child. But now these tears, these muffled, hurried beats of his heart and the feeling as though a little bell were tolling noiselessly in his throat. . . . For that matter, it may all have been because he had drunk a great deal the previous night and had had no sleep.

Daria returned from driving the cows out to the pasture. And when, after jocularly stroking his whiskers, she put her smiling lips up to Gregor, he brought his face close to hers, and she closed her eyes. He saw her lashes quivering as though under the wind, and for a moment he was conscious of the fusty scent of cream coming from her unfading cheeks.

So Daria was the same as ever. It would seem that no sorrow could ever be strong enough even to bow her to the ground, far less to break her. She lived in the world like a red-barked switch of dogwood: flexible, beautiful, and accessible.

"So you're flourishing?" Gregor asked.

"Like the roadside henbane." Daria smiled dazzlingly, half closing her radiant eyes. She at once went over to the mirror to adjust the hair which had broken free of her kerchief and to smarten herself up.

But she had always been like that, had Daria. There was nothing to be done with such a woman, surely? Piotra's death had had the effect of spurring her on and, as soon as she had recovered from the blow, she had grown still more greedy of life, still more attentive to her outward appearance.

They awoke Dunia, who was sleeping in the granary. After crossing themselves, all the family sat down at the table.

"Oh, but you've grown old, brother!" Dunia said commiseratingly. "You've gone as grey as a wolf."

Gregor gave her a silent, unsmiling look across the table and only then said:

"So I should. It's for me to grow old, and it's for you to come of age, to look for a husband. . . . But I tell you this: from today on you're to forget even to think about Mishka Koshevoi. If from today on I hear that you're pining for him I'll step on one of your feet, and I'll take hold of the other, and I'll rip you in two like a little frog. Understand?"

Dunia flamed up like a carrot and gazed at Gregor through her tears.

He did not turn his angry eyes away from her face, and in all his harsh features, in the teeth bared beneath his moustache, in his narrowed eyes, the innate Melekhov, animal traits emerged still more clearly.

But Dunia also was of the same breed. Recovering from her embarrassment and shame, she quietly but resolutely said:

"Don't you know, brother? You can't command the heart."

"The heart that does not obey you has to be torn out," Gregor advised her coldly.

"It's not for you to talk like that, my son," Ilinichna thought. But at that point Pantaleimon Prokoffievich joined in the conversation. He banged his fist down on the table and roared:

"You daughter of a bitch, hold your tongue in my presence! Or I'll give you such a heart that you won't have a hair left on your head! You hussy! I'll go this minute and get some reins. . . ."

"But, Father, we haven't got one pair of reins left. They've all been taken," Daria interrupted him, a meek look on her face.

Pantaleimon shot a furious glance at her and, not lowering his voice, continued to unburden his soul:

"I'll get a saddle-girth, and I'll drive all the devils out of you. . . ."

"The Reds have taken the saddle-girths too," Daria intervened, this time in a louder voice, but still gazing at her father-in-law with innocent eyes.

But that was too much for Pantaleimon. He stared at his daughter-in-law for a second, turning livid with dumb fury, his mouth silently gaping (at that moment he looked like a pike hauled out of the water), then hoarsely shouted:

"Shut up, damn you; there's a hundred devils in you! They won't let me say a word. What do you call this? But you, Dunia, understand: that sort of thing's unnatural! I speak to you as your father. And Gregor was right: if you go on thinking of such a scoundrel, killing will be too good for you. A fine wooer she's found! A gallowsbird has captured her soul! He set fire to half the village, shot helpless old men—is that what you call a man? Do you think I'd have such a Judas as my son-in-law? If he ever falls into my hands I'll hand him over to death myself. Only give me one more back-answer, and I'll get a willow switch and I'll give you . . ."

"Why, you could look all over our yard with a light in broad daylight and you'd never find a willow switch," Ilinichna said with a sigh. "You can roll like a ball into every corner of the yard and you won't find so much as a twig to light a fire with. That's the state of things we're reduced to!"

Even in this artless remark Pantaleimon detected an evil intent. He looked fixedly at the old woman, then jumped up like a madman and ran out into the yard.

Gregor threw down his spoon, covered his face with his hand-towel, and shook with soundless laughter. His anger had passed, and he laughed as he had laughed in days long past. They all laughed except Dunia. Now a more cheery note reigned at the table. But the moment Pantaleimon was heard stamping up the steps of the porch, all their faces grew serious. The old man burst in like a hurricane, dragging a very long alder bough behind him.

"There you are! It'll be enough for all the lot of you damned long-tongues! You long-tailed vixens! There aren't any switches? Then what's this? And you'll get a taste of it too, you old she-devil! You try giving me . . ."

The branch was too big to be found a place for in the kitchen, and, after tipping a pot over, the old man threw it down with a crash in the porch, then, breathing heavily, sat down at the table.

His good spirits were gone. He wheezed, and ate without speaking. The others were silent also. Daria did not raise her eyes from the table, for fear of bursting into laughter. Ilinichna sighed and whispered almost inaudibly: "O Lord, Lord! Heavy and grievous are our sins!" Only Dunia did not feel like smiling, while Natalia, who while the old man was outside had smiled a queer, laboured smile, again grew abstracted and sorrowful.

"Pass the salt! The bread!" Pantaleimon occasionally bellowed menacingly, sweeping his glittering eyes over his family.

The family quarrel ended in a decidedly unusual fashion. In the general silence Mishatka gave his grandfather fresh cause for offence. He had often heard his grandmother call his grandfather all kinds of nasty things when they were quarrelling, and, childishly upset because his grandfather was talking of thrashing everybody and was bawling all over the kitchen, he suddenly remarked in a ringing voice, his nostrils quivering:

"The way you carry on, you lame devil! You need a stick about your head, to make you stop frightening us and Grandmother."

"Did you say that to me—to your grandfather?"

"Yes, to you!" Mishatka declared valiantly.

"But how dare you use such words to your own grandfather?"

"Well, what are you making all that noise for?"

"What a little devil!" Stroking his beard, Pantaleimon ran his eyes in amazement around the room. "And he's picked up all that talk from you, you old hag! It's you who teaches him!"

"Who teaches him? He's just as uncontrollable as you and his father," Ilinichna angrily defended herself.

Natalia rose and spanked Mishatka, instructing him the while:

"You're not to talk to your grand-dad like that! Do you hear?"

Mishatka began to bellow and buried his face on Gregor's knees. But Pantaleimon, who had not expected such spirit in his grandchild, jumped up from the table and, tears streaming from his eyes, not wiping away the tears running down over his beard, joyously shouted:

"Grishka! My son! Son of your mother! The old woman said truly. It's ours all right! It's the Melekhov blood! That's when the blood shows. No one can pass that by in silence. Little grandson! My darling! Here, beat the old fool with whatever you like. Drag him about by his beard!" Snatching Mishatka away from Gregor, the old man lifted the boy high above his head.

They finished breakfast and rose from the table. The women began to wash up, but Pantaleimon lit a cigarette and said to Gregor:

"It's sort of awkward to ask you, for you're only here on a visit, but what else can I do? Give me a hand with setting up the fence and barring off the threshing-floor, for everything's fallen down, and you can't ask strangers just now. They're all in the same state."

Gregor willingly agreed, and the two of them worked in the yard until dinner-time, putting the fencing in order.

As they drove in a paling, the old man said:

"It's time to mow, but I don't know whether to get in more grass or not. What do you think in regard to the farm? Is it worth the bother? For, after all, in a month's time the Reds may be calling on us again, and everything will go to those devils once more."

"I don't know, Father," Gregor frankly admitted. "I don't know what turn events may take and who's going to win. Carry on so that you've got nothing to spare either in the bins or in the yard. At such times as these it's all for nothing. Take my father-in-law, for instance. All his life he strained his throat, he made money, he sweated the blood out of himself and out of others, and what is left of it all? Only charred stumps in the yard."

"That's just what I was thinking, lad," the old man agreed, suppressing a sigh.

He made no further attempt to talk about the farm. Only, just after noonday, noticing that Gregor was taking extra pains over fixing up the gate to the threshing-floor, he said in a chagrined and openly bitter tone:

"Just do it anyhow! What are you taking all that trouble for? It hasn't got to stand for a lifetime."

Evidently only now was the old man realizing all the futility of his efforts to organize his life along the old lines.

Just before sunset Gregor stopped work and went into the house. Natalia was alone in the best room. She had dressed herself up as though for a holiday. Her blue woollen skirt and dove-blue poplin jacket with embroidery at the breast and with lace cuffs fitted her neatly. Her face was tenderly rosy and shone a little after a recent wash with soap. She was looking for something in the chest, but when she saw Gregor she dropped the lid and straightened up with a smile.

Gregor sat down on the chest and said:

"Sit down for a while, for I'm off tomorrow and we shan't have had any talk together."

She humbly sat down at his side, looking at him sidelong with eyes a little startled. But he unexpectedly took her hand and said in a caressing tone:

"But you're as smooth as if you'd never been ill."

"I've got over it. . . . We women have as many lives as a cat," she said, timidly smiling and bowing her head.

Gregor noticed the tenderly rosy, fluffy lobe of her ear and the yellowish skin at the nape of her neck through the strands of her hair and asked:

"Is your hair falling out?"

"It's almost all out. I'm moulting all over, I shall be bald soon."

"Let me shave your head?" he suggested suddenly.

"What!" she exclaimed in alarm. "But then what will I look like?"

"It's best to shave, or the hair won't grow again."

"Mamma promised to cut my hair with scissors," Natalia said, smiling in her embarrassment, and she dextrously threw a snow-white, heavily blued kerchief over her head.

She, his wife and the mother of Mishatka and Poliushka, was at his side. For him she had decked herself out and had washed her face with soap. Hurriedly flinging on her kerchief, so that he could not see how unsightly her hair had become since her illness, sitting there with her head bent slightly to one side, she looked so pitiful, so uncomely, and yet so beautiful, beaming with some pure, intrinsic beauty. She always wore high-standing collars, to hide from him the scar which disfigured her neck. It was all done for his sake. . . . A tremendous flood of tenderness swept over Gregor's heart. He wanted to say something warm and kindly to her, but he could not find the words and, silently drawing her to himself, he kissed her white, lofty brow and mournful eyes.

Never before had he spoilt her with a caress. All her life Aksinia had stood in her path. Moved by her husband's display of feeling, flaming with agitation, she took his hand and raised it to her lips.

For a minute they sat without speaking. The western sun threw livid rays into the room. The children were playing on the steps. As they sat they heard Daria take the well-baked pipkins out of the oven and say discontentedly to her mother-in-law: "I'm afraid you haven't been milking the cows every day. The old one is yielding less milk, it looks like."

The herd returned from the pasture. The cows lowed, the lads cracked the hairy lashes of their whips. The village bull bellowed hoarsely and spasmodically. His silky chest and steep, moulded back were bitten to blood by gadflies. The bull shook his head angrily; raising the Astakhovs' wattle fencing on his short, wide-set horns as he went along, he flung it down and trampled across it. Natalia looked out of the window and said:

"You know, the bull retreated across the Don as well. Mother said that as soon as firing began in the villages he swam straight across the river from his stall, plunged into the reeds, and hid there the whole time."

Gregor was silent, lost in thought. Why had she got such mournful eyes? And then something secretive, elusive, first appeared, then disappeared again in them. Even in her joy she was sorrowful and somehow incomprehensible. . . . Perhaps she had heard rumours of his visits to Aksinia in Vieshenska? At last he asked:

"Why are you so downcast today? What is lying on your heart, Natasha? You might tell me, won't you?"

He expected tears, reproaches. But Natalia answered in a frightened tone:

"No, no, it only seems so to you. I'm all right, I'm all right. . . . It's true I'm not quite well again yet. My head swims, and if I bend or pick something up everything goes dark before my eyes."

Gregor gazed at her inquisitively and again asked:

"You've been all right here without me? Nobody interfered with you?"

"No; what are you saying? I've been lying ill the whole time." She gazed right into his eyes and even smiled very faintly. After a silence, she asked: "Are you leaving early tomorrow?"

"At dawn."

"But can't you spend another day here?" An uncertain, timid hope sounded in her voice.

He shook his head, and she said with a sigh:

"How will it be now—have you got to wear epaulets?"

"I shall have to."

"Well then, take off your tunic and I'll sew them on while it's still light."

With a groan Gregor drew off his tunic. It was still damp with his sweat. Wherever his military straps had rubbed the cloth, shiny spots showed wet on his back and shoulders. Natalia took a pair of faded khaki epaulets out of the chest and asked:

"Are these the ones?"

"Yes. So you kept them?"

"We buried the chest," Natalia said indistinctly as she pushed the thread through the needle-eye. Stealthily she raised the dusty tunic to her lips and avidly sniffed at the saltish scent of sweat which was so dear to her.

"What did you do that for?" Gregor asked in astonishment.

"It smells of you," she said, her eyes glittering. She bent her head to hide the sudden flush in her cheeks and skilfully began to sew.

Gregor put on his tunic. His face clouded and he shrugged his shoulders.

"You look better with them on!" Natalia said, gazing at her husband in open admiration.

But he squinted round at his left shoulder and sighed:

"I wish I'd never seen them! You don't understand at all!"

They remained sitting a long time on the chest in the best room, holding each other's hand, silently thinking their own thoughts.

When dusk began to fall and the heavy lilac shadows of the buildings extended over the cool earth, they went into the kitchen for the evening.

And so the night passed. Until sunrise the summer lightning flickered in the sky, until the white daybreak the nightingales in the cherry orchard filled the night with tumult. Gregor woke up and lay a long time with closed eyes, listening to the nightingales' melodious and pleasant song; then quietly, without arousing Natalia, he rose, dressed, and went out into the yard.

Pantaleimon Prokoffievich had fed Gregor's horse, and with a soldier's forethought he suggested:

"Shall I get on his back and give him a bathe before you start?"

"He can manage without it," Gregor said, bristling with the early morning rawness.

"Did you sleep well?" his father asked.

"Too well! But the nightingales woke me up! It's the limit the way they carried on all night!"

Pantaleimon took the grain basket from the horse, and smiled.

"They've got nothing else to do, lad. There are times when you feel envious of those divine birds. They know nothing about war or ruin. . . ."

Prokhor rode up to the gate. His face was clean-shaven and, as usual, he was cheerful and talkative. Fastening his horse's leading rein to a post, he came up to Gregor. His sailcloth shirt had been ironed smooth. On his shoulders were new-looking epaulets.

"So you've put epaulets on too, Gregor Pantalievich?" he shouted as he came up. "They've been waiting for us, damn them! Now we may wear them, but we'll never wear them out. They'll last out our time. I said to my wife: 'Don't sew them on so they'll never come off, you fool! Just tack them on so that the wind can't blow them away, and that'll be all right.' You know the state of our affairs. If we get taken prisoner they'll see at once that I may not be an officer, but all the same I'm a senior non-com. And then they'll shout: 'You this and that, you knew how to earn your stripes, now learn how to hold your head for the noose!' Do you see how they're hanging on me? It's just comic!"

Prokhor's epaulets had certainly been sewn on hurriedly, and they hardly remained in position.

Pantaleimon burst into a roar of laughter. Untouched by time, his white teeth gleamed amid his grizzled beard.

"There's a soldier for you! So if there's the least sign of anything happening you'll be pulling off your epaulets?"

"What do you think?" Prokhor laughed.

Smiling, Gregor said to his father:

"You see what a fine orderly I've managed to get hold of? Even if I get into trouble, with him around I shall never get lost!"

"That's all very well, Gregor Pantalievich, but you know—you die today, and I die tomorrow," Prokhor said in extenuation. He tore off his epaulets with the greatest ease and carelessly thrust them into his pocket, remarking: "When we get near the front I can sew them on again."

Gregor ate a hurried breakfast, then took leave of his family.

"May the Queen of Heaven preserve you!" Ilinichna whispered fervently as she kissed her son. "You're the only one we've got left. . . ."

"Now, see me off, and no tears! Good-bye!" Gregor said in a quivering voice, and went across to his horse.

Throwing Ilinichna's black three-cornered kerchief over her head, Natalia went out beyond the gate. The children clung to her skirt. Poliushka sobbed disconsolately. Choking back her tears, she asked her mother:

PART IV

The Shadows Fall

THE SHADOWS FALL

Chapter 1

FIGHTING was going on around the approaches to the district centre of Ust-Miedvieditsa. Gregor first caught the muffled sound of gunfire as he turned off the summer track on to the Hetman's highroad.

All along the highroad the traces of the Reds' hurried retreat were visible. He came across numerous abandoned two-wheeled carts and britskas. In a ravine beyond a hamlet stood a gun with its axle shattered by a shell and with its barrel twisted. The traces to the singletrees of the limber had been slashed obliquely. Half a mile from the ravine, in salt-marshes, on stunted, sunburnt grass, soldiers' bodies in khaki shirts and trousers, with puttees and heavy, iron-shod boots, were lying in swathes. They were Red Army men who had been overtaken and sabred by the Cossack cavalry. As Gregor rode past he could easily tell this from the blood dried copiously on the shrivelled shirts and by the position of the bodies. They lay like scythed grass. The Cossacks had not stripped their clothing off them, probably because they had continued the pursuit.

A Cossack was lying close to a bush of hawthorn. The red stripes showed rustily on his wide-flung legs. A little way off lay

379

a light bay horse, saddled with an ancient type of saddle, the pommels painted with ochre.

Gregor's and Prokhor's horses were growing tired. It was time they had a feed, but Gregor did not feel like halting in a spot where a fight had recently taken place. He rode on nearly a mile farther, dropped down into a ravine, and halted his horse. A little way off he could see a pond with a dam washed away down to the foundations. Prokhor rode towards the crumbling and cracking edges of the pond, but suddenly turned back.

"What's the matter?" Gregor asked.

"Ride closer and look!"

Gregor rode his horse towards the dam. A dead woman was lying in the mud. Her face was covered with the lower edge of her blue skirt. Her full white legs, with sunburnt calves and dimpled at the knees, were straddled shamelessly and horribly. Her left arm was twisted behind her back.

Gregor hurriedly dismounted, took off his cap, stooped, and pulled the dead woman's skirt down over her body. Her youthful, swarthy face was handsome even in death. Under her painfully knitted brows the half-closed eyes gleamed faintly. In the grin of her softly outlined mouth the clenched, close teeth shone like mother-of pearl. A fine strand of hair hung over the cheek pressed to the grass. And over this cheek, which death was already tingeing with fugitive, saffron-yellow shades, fussy ants were crawling.

"The beauty the sons of bitches have destroyed!" Prokhor said in an undertone. He was silent for a good minute, then he spat fiercely. "I'd put such—such clever scum against a wall! Let's get on, for Christ's sake! I can't stand looking at her. It makes my heart turn over."

"Don't you think we might bury her?" Gregor asked.

"Why, have we got to bury all the dead we come across?" Prokhor objected. "We buried some old gaffer at Yagodnoe, and now there's this woman. . . . If we're going to bury them all, we shan't have enough calluses on our hands! And what are we going to dig a grave with? You can't do it with a sabre, brother; the earth's baked hard with the heat for a good two feet down."

He was in such a hurry to get away that he caught the toe of his boot in the stirrup.

Once more they rode up the hill, and then Prokhor, who had

been concentratedly pondering over something, asked Gregor:

"What do you think, Pantalievich? Haven't we poured out enough blood on the earth?"

"Pretty well!"

"But what do you think, will it be finished soon?"

"It'll finish when they've smashed us."

"Well, it's a gay life we've run into, the devil be praised! Perhaps the sooner they smash us, the better. In the German war a man would shoot off his own finger and they'd let him go home. But now you could tear all your hand off and they'd still make you serve. They take the halt, the maimed, the blind; they take the ruptured, they take all sorts of scum, so long as they can toddle on their two legs. Is that the way to bring the war to an end? May they all be damned!" Prokhor said in despair, and, turning off the road, he dismounted, muttering something in an undertone, and began to loosen his horse's saddle-girths.

After nightfall they arrived at a hamlet situated not far from Ust-Miedvieditsa. A picket of the 3rd Regiment, posted on the outskirts of the village, held them up, but, recognizing their divisional commander by his voice, the Cossacks reported that the divisional staff was situated in this very village, and that the chief of staff, Captain Kopylov, was expecting him any minute. The garrulous outpost commander detailed a Cossack to lead Gregor to the staff and added as his final word:

"They've taken up very strong positions, Gregor Pantalievich, and I don't suppose we shall be taking Ust-Miedvieditsa for a long time. And then, of course, who knows? . . . We've got sufficient troops, too. They say British troops are arriving from Morozovsky. Have you heard anything about it?"

"No," Gregor answered as he touched up his horse.

At the house occupied by the staff the shutters were closed and fastened. Gregor thought there was nobody in the house, but as he went into the corridor, he heard muffled, excited talk. After the darkness outside, the light of the large lamp hanging from the ceiling of the best room blinded him; a thick and pungent smell of tobacco-smoke tickled his nostrils.

"So here you are at last!" Kopylov said in delight, appearing unexpectedly out of the blue cloud of smoke billowing above the table. "We've been a long time waiting for you, brother!"

Gregor greeted everybody, took off his cap and greatcoat, and went to the table.

"You've smoked out the place! It's impossible to breathe! Open just one little window!" he said, frowning.

Kharlampy Germakov, who was sitting beside Kopylov, smiled and retorted:

"But our noses have got used to it, and we don't even notice it." Pushing out a window-pane with his elbow, he flung open the shutter.

The fresh night air burst into the room. The lamp flame flared up and went out.

"Well, there's good management for you! What did you push the pane out for?" Kopylov asked discontentedly, rummaging over the table with his hands. "Who's got any matches? Careful, there's a pot of ink right by the map."

They lit the lamp, covered the hole in the window, and Kopylov hurriedly began to explain:

"At the present moment the situation at the front, Comrade Melekhov, is as follows: the Reds are holding Ust-Miedvieditsa, covering it on three sides with forces numbering approximately four thousand bayonets. They have sufficient artillery and machine-guns. They've dug trenches around the monastery and in several other places. They occupy the Donside heights. And as for their positions, well, I won't say they're inaccessible, but they're decidedly difficult to take. On our side, in addition to the divisions commanded by General Fitzhelaurov and two officers' storm detachments, Bogatiriev's 6th Brigade and our First Division have arrived. But the division isn't up to its full strength; the infantry regiment is missing, it's still somewhere near Ust-Khopersk; but the cavalry have all arrived, though the squadrons are far from being up to full strength."

"For instance, in my regiment the third squadron numbers only thirty-eight Cossacks," said the commander of the 4th Regiment, Cornet Dudariev.

"And how many were here originally?" Yermakov asked.

"Ninety-one."

"Why did you allow the squadron to break up? What sort of

commander do you call yourself?" Gregor asked, frowning and drumming on the table.

"Well, who's going to hold them back? They scattered through the villages, rode off to see their folk. But they'll be dribbling back again soon. Three arrived today."

Kopylov pushed the map across to Gregor. Pointing with his index finger, he showed the disposition of forces and went on:

"We haven't made any attack yet. The 2nd Regiment advanced on foot against this sector yesterday, but without success."

"With great losses?"

"According to the regimental commander's report, yesterday he lost twenty-six men killed and wounded. Now for the relative state of the forces. We've got the numerical superiority, but we haven't sufficient machine-guns to support an infantry attack, and the supply of shells is bad. The commander of our supplies commissariat has promised us four hundred shells and a hundred and fifty thousand cartridges as soon as they're brought up. But that's when they're brought up, whereas we've got to attack tomorrow, so General Fitzhelaurov has ordered. He proposes that we should allocate a regiment to support the storm detachments. They went into the attack four times yesterday and suffered enormous losses. I must say they fought like devils! Well, and Fitzhelaurov proposes that we should strengthen the right flank and transfer the attack to this point here. D'you see? Here the terrain makes it possible to approach within seven hundred to a thousand feet of the enemy's lines. And, as it happens, his adjutant has only just ridden off. He brought me and you oral instructions to go to General Fitzhelaurov's staff tomorrow morning at six for a conference on the coordination of operations. He and his staff are in Bolshoi Senin hamlet at present. The task consists in immediately driving the enemy back, before his reinforcements arrive from Serebryakovo station. On the farther side of the Don our forces are not displaying very great activity. . . . The Fourth Division has crossed the Khoper, but the Reds have thrown out strong covering forces and are obstinately holding the roads to the railway. But meantime they've thrown a pontoon bridge across the Don and are removing equipment and reserves from Ust-Miedvieditsa as fast as they can."

"The Cossacks are saying that the Allies are on the way. Is that true?"

"There's a rumour that several English batteries and tanks are on their way from Chernyshevsky. But this is the question: how are these tanks going to cross the Don? In my opinion, it's only talk in regard to the tanks. That sort of talk has been going around for some time. . . ."

There was a long silence in the room.

Kopylov unbuttoned his brown officer's tunic, rested his puffy, scrubby cheeks on his hands, and long and reflectively chewed a dead cigarette. His wide-set, round, dark eyes were half-closed with weariness, his handsome face was marred by the traces of sleepless nights.

At one time this man had been a teacher in a day church school, but on Sundays he had been the guest of merchants in the district and had played cards for small stakes with the merchants and their wives; he had played the guitar well and had been a gay, sociable young man. Then he had married a young woman teacher, and he would have gone on living in the district centre and doubtless would have worked until he retired on a pension, but during the World War he had been called up for service. After training in a Junkers' military college he had been sent with one of the Cossack regiments to the front. The war did not change his character and appearance at all. There was something inoffensive, fundamentally civilian about his full, short figure, his good-natured face, the way he carried his sword, the way he addressed subordinates. His voice lacked the metallic tone of command characteristic of the soldier; he wore his officer's uniform like a sack; despite all his three years at the front he had never acquired a military bearing and trim. All his looks betokened a man who was in the war by accident. He was more like a stout burgher dressed in officer's uniform than a genuine officer, yet the Cossacks had great respect for him and listened to what he said at staff conferences. The insurgent command greatly esteemed his sober mind, his easy-going character and undemonstrative bravery, which he had often proved in battle.

Gregor's previous chief of staff had been the illiterate and ignorant ensign Kruzhilin. Kruzhilin had been killed in one of the battles on the Chira, and when Kopylov took over the staff he carried out his duties intelligently, prudently, and with success. He sat as conscientiously in the staff meetings, planning operations, as he had once sat over the correction of pupils' exercise books. Yet,

when required, at Gregor's first word he left the staff to look after
itself, mounted a horse, and, taking over the command of a regiment, led it into battle.

At first Gregor had been a little prejudiced against his new chief
of staff; but in the course of a couple of months he came to know
him better and one day after a battle told him frankly:

"I thought pretty poorly of you, Kopylov, but now I see I was
wrong; so what I ask you is to overlook it if you can."

Kopylov smiled and made no answer, but he was obviously flattered by this decidedly boorish confession.

He lacked all desire for fame and possessed no fixed political
views, and his attitude to the war was that it was a necessary evil
and he did not expect its speedy end. So now he was not consid-
ering how to develop operations for the capture of Ust-Miedvieditsa, but was recalling his people at home, his native village,
and thinking it would be a good idea to gallop home on leave for
a month or six weeks. . . .

Gregor gazed long at Kopylov, then rose to his feet.

"Well, brothers and atamans, let's go to our quarters and sleep.
There's no point in sitting here racking our brains over the capture
of Ust-Miedvieditsa. The generals will think and decide for us
now. We'll ride off to Fitzhelaurov tomorrow; let him teach us
intelligence and sense, poor wretch! But this is what I think in
regard to the 2nd Regiment: we've still got the authority, and I
think it would be best to degrade Regimental Commander Dudariev, stripping him of his rank and titles."

"And his ration of porridge," Yermakov interrupted.

"No, I'm not joking," Gregor went on. "We must reduce him
this very day to the rank of squadron commander and send Kharlampy as commander of the regiment. You go off at once, Yermakov,
take over the regiment, and wait for our instructions tomorrow
morning. Kopylov will write out the order for Dudariev's degrada-
tion at once, you can take it with you. Dudariev will never manage
a regiment. He's got no sense at all, and I'm afraid he might expose
the Cossacks to a fresh blow. You know what infantry fighting
is. . . . It's easy enough then to risk your men's lives, if the commander doesn't know what he's doing."

"That's true. I'm in favor of degrading Dudariev," Kopylov
supported Gregor.

"Well, Yermakov, are you against?" Gregor asked, noticing a look of dissatisfaction on Yermakov's face.

"Why, no; I didn't say anything. Can't I even raise my eyebrows now?"

"So much the better. Yermakov is not against. Ryabchikov will take over his mounted regiment for the present. Mikhail Gregorich, write out the order, and then get some sleep until dawn comes. And up again at six. We'll go and see this general. I shall take four orderlies with me."

Kopylov raised his eyebrows in astonishment. "What do you want all them for?"

"For show! After all, we're not nobodies either, we command a division." Gregor laughed and shrugged his shoulders, threw his greatcoat around his back, and went to the door.

He lay down under the eaves of a shed, covering himself with a horse-cloth, not removing his boots or his greatcoat. For a long time the orderlies were noisy in the yard; somewhere close at hand horses snorted and chewed measuredly. There was a scent of fresh dung-fuel and of earth not yet cool after the heat of the day. Through his drowsiness Gregor heard the orderlies' voices and laughter and heard one of them, a youngster, judging from his tones, saddle his horse and declare with a sigh:

"Ah, brothers, I'm fed up! Here it is midnight, and off I've got to ride with a packet. Never any sleep for us, or rest. . . . Oh, stand still, you devil! Your hoof, raise your hoof, I tell you!"

And a second man with a muffled, frozen bass voice said in an undertone:

"We're fed up with you, soldiering, you've bored us stiff! You've worn out all our good horses. . . ." His voice passed into a pleading, hurried patter: "Pour us out some baccy for a cigarette. Ah, you're a fine friend! You've forgotten the Red Army boots I gave you when we were at Belyavin, haven't you? You swine! Others would have remembered me forever because of those boots, but I can't even wheedle baccy for a cigarette out of you!"

The bit clattered and rattled against the horse's teeth. The horse breathed long and deeply and trotted off, its shoes clattering dryly over the stonily hard, dry earth. "They're all talking about the same thing. 'We're fed up with you, soldiering, you've bored us stiff!' " Gregor mentally repeated, smiling. And he at once fell off

to sleep. The moment he dozed off he had a dream which he had
dreamed many times before: . . . Over the brown fields, over
high-standing stubble, lines of Red Army men were moving. The
first rank extended as far as the eye could reach. Behind it were six
or seven other ranks. The men drew nearer and nearer in the oppressive silence. The little black figures grew, increased in size, and
now he could see them coming on at a swift, stumbling stride, on,
on, on, coming within firing range, running with their rifles at the
trail, in ear-flapped cloth helmets, with mouths silently gaping.
Gregor was lying in a shallow trench, convulsively rattling the lock
of his rifle, firing again and again; under his fire the Red Army
men fell, throwing themselves down headlong; he thrust in a fresh
clip of cartridges and, glancing for a second to either side, saw the
Cossacks leaping out of the neighbouring trenches. They turned
and ran, their faces distorted with fear. He could hear the terrible
beating of his heart; he shouted: "Fire! You swine! Where are you
going? Stop, don't run!" He shouted at the top of his voice, but
his voice was terrifyingly weak, hardly audible. He was seized
with horror. He, too, jumped up, and as he stood he fired a last
time at a swarthy, elderly Red Army man who was silently running straight towards him. He saw he had missed. The soldier had
a tensely serious, fearless face. He ran lightly, his feet hardly
touching the ground, his brows knitted, his cap on the back of his
head, the edges of his greatcoat tucked up. For one moment Gregor
stared at the approaching enemy, saw his glittering eyes and pale
cheeks overgrown with a youthful, curly little beard, saw the short,
broad legs of his boots, the little black eye of the slightly depressed
rifle-barrel, and above it, swinging rhythmically, the point of the
dark bayonet. An invincible terror took possession of him. He
tugged at the bolt of his rifle, but the bolt would not shift: it had
jammed. In despair he beat the bolt against his knee, with no
result. But the Red Army man was now only five paces away.
Gregor turned and fled. Before him all the bare brown field was
sprinkled with fleeing Cossacks. Behind him he heard his pursuer
breathing heavily, heard the hollow thud of his boots. But he could
not run any faster. He had to make a terrible effort to force his
feebly bending legs to move faster. At last he reached a half-ruined,
gloomy cemetery, jumped across the fallen fence, ran between the
sunken graves, the crooked crosses and little shrines. Yet one more

effort and he would be safe. But now the thunder of feet behind him increased, grew louder. The pursuer's burning breath scorched his neck, and at that moment he felt himself seized by the tail and skirt of his greatcoat. A muffled cry burst from him, and he awoke.

He was lying on his back. His feet, squeezed in the tight boots, had gone numb; there was a cold sweat on his brow, all his body ached as though he had been thrashed. "Oh, hell!" he said hoarsely, listening with satisfaction to his own voice and still unable to believe that what he had just lived through was a dream. Then he turned over on his side, wrapped himself up to his head in his greatcoat, thought: "I ought to have let him come close, parried his blow, struck him down with the bayonet, and then run. . . ."

For a moment he lay reflecting on this dream he had now had several times, experiencing a joyous emotion at the feeling that it was only a bad dream and that in reality there was no danger near at all. "It's extraordinary that in a dream everything's ten times as terrible as in real life. Never in all my life have I known such terror, even in the tightest corners," he thought as he dozed off and gratefully stretched out his numbed feet.

Kopylov aroused him at dawn.

"Get up, it's time to get ready and go. We were ordered to be there at six!"

The chief of staff had only just shaved, cleaned his boots, and put on his creased but clean tunic. He had obviously been in a hurry: his puffy cheeks had two razor cuts. But he had a general air of spruce elegance that he had lacked before.

Gregor ran his eyes critically over him and thought: "Bah, how he's togged himself up! He doesn't want to look anyhow when he presents himself to the general. . . ."

As though he had followed the course of Gregor's thought, Kopylov said:

"It's bad to turn up looking slovenly. I advise you to make yourself presentable, too."

"I'll go as I am!" Gregor muttered, stretching himself. "You say we were ordered to be there at six? So they're already beginning to send you and me orders?"

Kopylov laughed and shrugged his shoulders.

"New times, new manners! As he's senior in rank, we're bound to obey. Fitzhelaurov's a general, it's not for him to come to us."

"You're right; they did come to us, but now we go to them," Gregor said, and went off to the well to wash.

The mistress of the house rushed into her hut, brought out a clean, embroidered hand-towel, and bobbed as she handed it to him. With the end of the towel he furiously rubbed at his face, burnt a brick-red by the cold water, and said to Kopylov:

"You're quite right; but the messieurs the generals should bear in mind this one thing: the people have changed since the Revolution; they've been reborn, as you might say. But the officers still go on measuring with the old measures. I'm afraid their measures are broken now, though. . . . The officers are a little stiff in the joints. They need some axle-grease in their brains, to stop the creaking."

"What are you getting at?" Kopylov abstractedly asked, as he blew a speck of dirt from his sleeve.

"Why, at the fact that they're carrying on just in the same old way. For instance, I've held the rank of officer ever since the German war. I earned it with my blood! But when I'm in officers' company I feel just as if I was going out of a hut into the frost in my pants. They give off such a cold feeling towards me that I feel it all down my back!" Gregor's eyes glittered furiously and, without knowing it, he raised his voice.

Kopylov looked about him displeased, and whispered:

"Don't talk so loud; the orderlies will hear."

"And why is that, you ask?" Gregor went on, lowering his voice. "Why, it's because to them I'm a white blackbird. They've got hands, but, because of my calluses, I've got hoofs! They scrape their feet, but it doesn't matter what I do, I knock into everything. They smell of toilet soap and all sorts of womanish creams and paints, but I smell of horse-piss and sweat. They're all educated, but I had difficulty in getting through a church school. I'm foreign to them from my head to my heels. That's why it's all like that! And when I leave them I always have the feeling that a spider-web has settled on my face: I'm ticklish all over and horribly uncomfortable, and all I want is to get clean." He threw the towel down on the well-frame and combed his hair with a piece of broken comb. Un-touched by sunburn, his forehead showed a brilliant white against his swarthy face.

"They don't want to understand that all the old has broken to pieces and gone to hell!" he went on more quietly. "They think we're made of different dough, that an uneducated man, one of the ordinary folk, is some sort of cattle. They think that in military affairs I, or such as I, understand less than they. But who are the Reds' commanders? Is Budionny an officer? He was a sergeant in pre-war days, but it was he who gave the generals of the staff a good hiding! Is Zhloba an officer? But it was through him that the officers' regiments were smashed. Guselshchikov is the most famous fighter of all the Cossack generals, but he galloped away from Ust-Khopersk in only his pants last winter. And do you know who sent him packing? Some Moscow locksmith, a Red regimental com-mander. The prisoners were all talking about him afterwards. You've got to understand that! And how about us uneducated officers, did we lead the Cossacks so badly during the rising? Did the generals help us to any extent?"

"They helped quite a lot," Kopylov said significantly.

"Well, they may have helped Kudynov, but I've gone without their help, and beaten the Reds without listening to others' coun-sels."

"Well, and what of it; don't you believe in applying science to military matters?"

"Yes, I do. But that's not the main thing in war, brother."

"Well, what is, Pantalievich?"

"The cause you're fighting for."

"Well, that's another thing . . ." Kopylov said, smiling. "That goes without saying. . . . In this war the idea's the main thing. The one who wins is the one who knows what he's fighting for and believes in his cause. That's a truth as old as the world itself, and it's no use your trying to put it forward as a discovery of your own. I'm for the old, for the good old times. If things were going to be different I wouldn't lift a finger to go anywhere or fight for any-thing. All those on our side are men who are defending their old privileges, suppressing the revolting people by force of arms. And you and I are among those suppressors. I've been studying you for a long time, Gregor Pantalievich, and I can't understand you."

"You'll understand later. Let's go," Gregor retorted, and went towards the shed.

Desiring to please him, the mistress of the house, who had been watching his every movement, said to Gregor:

"Would you like a drink of milk?"

"Thank you, mother, but I haven't time to drink milk. I'll have some later."

Near a shed Prokhor Zykov was zealously sipping sour milk from a cup. He did not wink an eye as he watched Gregor untie his horse. He wiped his lips with his sleeve, and asked:

"Going far? And am I coming with you?"

Gregor boiled over and said with cold fury:

"You mange, what the hell are you playing at? Don't you know your duty? What's my horse standing bridled for? Who's supposed to bring me my horse? You devil's glutton! You're always chewing and never ending! Now, drop that spoon! Where's your discipline? You bottomless pit!"

"And what have you flared up for?" Prokhor muttered in an injured tone as he made himself comfortable in the saddle. "You bawl away, but it's all for nothing. You're not so old in the feathers, after all. Can't I have a bite or sup before a journey? What are you shouting about?"

"Because you're enough to drive me mad, you pig's chitterlings! How dare you speak to me like that? We're just off to call on a general, so you keep your eyes skinned! You're too used to being familiar with your superiors! Who am I to you? Ride five paces behind!" Gregor ordered as he rode out of the gate.

Prokhor and the three other orderlies fell back, and Gregor, riding beside Kopylov, continued the conversation. He asked in a jesting tone:

"Well, what is it you don't understand? Perhaps I can explain to you?"

Not noticing the sneer in the tone of Gregor's voice and the form of his question, Kopylov answered:

"Why, I don't understand your position in this business, that's what. On the one hand you're fighting for the old régime, but on the other hand you're something—excuse me if I put it bluntly—

something rather on the lines of a Bolshevik yourself."

"How am I a Bolshevik?" Gregor's face clouded and he sat up sharply in the saddle.

"I don't say you are a Bolshevik, but something rather like a Bolshevik."

"In what way, I ask."

"Well, take your talk about the officers and their attitude to you. What do you want them to do? And what is it you want at all, for that matter?" Kopylov questioned, smiling good-naturedly and playing with his whip. He glanced back at the orderlies, who were animatedly discussing something, and raised his voice: "You're offended because they don't accept you as an equal, because they look down on you. But they're quite right from their point of view, you must realize that. It's true you're an officer, but it's only by chance that you've reached the rank of officer. Even when you wear an officer's uniform you're still—forgive me for saying so—a boorish Cossack. You've got no manners, you express yourself badly and coarsely, you lack all the qualities which are natural to an educated man. For instance, instead of using a handkerchief, as all cultured people do, you blow your nose on your finger and thumb; when you're eating you wipe your hands on the leg of your boot or on your hair; after washing you're not too squeamish to wipe your face on a horse-cloth; you either bite your nails short or cut them with the end of your sword. Or even better: last winter in Kargin I heard you talking to a certain woman of the intelligentsia class, whose husband had been arrested by the Cossacks, and you stood buttoning up your fly in front of her."

"So it would have been better if I'd left it undone?" Gregor asked, smiling morosely.

Their horses were striding along side by side, and Gregor took a sidelong look at Kopylov, at his good-natured face, and listened with a touch of chagrin to his words.

"That's not the point," Kopylov exclaimed, frowning with annoyance. "How can you interview a woman at all when all you're wearing is your trousers and you've got bare feet? You didn't even fling your jacket around your shoulders: I remember that very well. Of course, these are small things, but they sum you up as a man. . . . How shall I put it?"

"Put it as simply as possible!"

"Well, as an extremely boorish sort of man. And the way you speak! It's horrible! Instead of 'quarters,' you say 'quawters'; instead of 'evacuation,' you say 'evakiation'; for 'seemingly' you say 'it looks like as if.' And, like all illiterate people, you have an inexplicable passion for fine-sounding foreign words; you use them in season and out of season, you twist them unbelievably, and when military terminology is used at staff conferences—such words as 'dislocation,' 'dispositions,' 'concentrations,' and so on—you stare at the speaker in admiration and, I venture to say, even with envy."

"Now you're talking bosh!" Gregor exclaimed, and a merry look appeared on his face. Stroking his horse between its ears, scratching its silkily warm skin under the mane, he asked: "Well, carry on; give your commander a good dressing-down!"

"Now, listen: why should I dress you down? It ought to be quite clear to you yourself that you happen to be unfortunate in regard to these things. And then you get upset because the officers don't treat you as an equal. So far as manners and education are concerned you're just a blockhead!" The insulting term fell out almost by accident, and Kopylov took alarm. He knew how uncontrollable was Gregor's anger, and he was afraid of an outburst. But he took a swift glance at Gregor and at once felt reassured: throwing himself back in the saddle, Gregor was laughing silently, and a dazzling grin of teeth gleamed under his whiskers. Kopylov was so surprised at this result of his words, and Gregor's laugh was so infectious, that he also burst into laughter, saying: "There you are! A sensible man would have wept at such a scolding, but you're neighing away. . . . Aren't you queer?"

"So you call me a blockhead? Then damn you!" Gregor remarked when he stopped laughing. "I don't want to learn your manners and customs. They'll be no use to me when I'm driving bullocks. But God grant, if I live so long, I shall have to handle bullocks, and it won't do for me to bow and scrape to them and say: 'Ah, do submit, Baldhead! Pardon me, Speckle! Permit me to adjust the yoke on you! My dear sir, Mr. Bullock, I most humbly request you not to break down the furrows.' You have to talk more curtly to them: 'Gee up!' That's all the bullocks know about 'dishlocation.' "

"Not 'dishlocation,' but 'dislocation,' " Kopylov corrected him.

"Well, as you wish. But there's one thing I don't agree with you on."

"What's that?"

"That I'm a blockhead. I may be a blockhead to you, but **you**
wait a bit! Give me time, and I'll go over to the Reds, and with them
I shall be heavier than lead. And then you well-mannered and educated parasites had better not fall into my hands! I shall wring out
your entrails, and your souls with them!" Gregor said, half in jest,
half serious. He touched up his horse, putting it into a sharp trot.

Over the Donside lands the morning was coming in such a fine-
spun silence that every sound, even the faintest, disturbed it and
awoke the echoes. In the steppe only the skylarks and quails were in
possession, but in the near-by hamlets that incessant, quiet rumbling
could be heard which always accompanies the movement of large
military forces. Gun-carriage wheels and ammunition wagons clattered in the ruts, horses were neighing by the wells, the steps of passing companies of Black Sea infantry Cossacks gave off a soft, muffled
tramp, britskas and lines of civilian wagons carrying stores and ammunition up to the front were thundering along; around the field
kitchens hung a pleasant smell of stewing millet, of tinned meat
garnished with laurel leaves, and of fresh-baked bread.

Below Ust-Miedvieditsa itself a frequent exchange of rifle-fire was
going on, and rare cannon-shots boomed lazily and hollowly. The
battle had just begun.

General Fitzhelaurov was having breakfast when an elderly,
harassed-looking adjutant reported:

"The commander of the First Insurgent Division, Melekhov, and
his divisional chief of staff, Kopylov."

"Ask them to my room." With a large, gnarled hand Fitzhelaurov
pushed away his plate with its litter of egg-shell, unhurriedly drank
a glass of fresh milk, and, neatly folding his serviette, rose from the
table.

Of extraordinary height, agedly massive and puffy, he seemed
incredibly large in that tiny Cossack room with its crooked door
lintels and dim and small windows. Coughing hollowly, adjusting
the high collar of his irreproachably fitting uniform as he went, the
general passed into the next room, curtly bowed to Kopylov and
Gregor as they rose to their feet, and, not offering them his hand,
beckoned them to the table.

Steadying his sword with his hand, Gregor cautiously sat down on the very edge of the stool and glanced sidelong at Kopylov.

Fitzhelaurov heavily lowered himself on to the Viennese chair, making it creak beneath him, bent his shanky legs, laid his great hands on his knees, and said in a thick, low voice:

"I have invited you here, gentlemen, in order to settle certain questions. . . . The insurgent partisan warfare is finished. Your forces will cease to exist as an independent unit, and, for that matter, they never have been a unit in reality. A fiction! They are to be amalgamated with the Don army. We shall pass to a planned offensive. It is time to realize that, and unconditionally to subordinate yourselves to the orders of the higher command. Be so good as to inform me why your infantry regiment did not support the storm battalion's attack yesterday. Why did the regiment refuse to go into the attack, despite my orders? Who is the commander of your so-called division?"

"I am," Gregor answered in a low voice.

"Be so good as to answer the question, then."

"I didn't return to the division till yesterday."

"And where had you been pleased to be before that?"

"I had been home on a visit."

"A divisional commander is pleased to go home on a visit at a time of military operations! The division's a rabble! Sheer arbitrariness! A disgusting state of affairs!" The general's bass voice thundered louder and louder in the confined space of the little room; outside, the adjutants went about on tiptoe, whispering, smiling to one another. Kopylov's cheeks turned whiter and whiter, but as Gregor stared at the general's face, at his swollen, clenched fists, he felt an uncontrollable frenzy awakening in himself also.

Fitzhelaurov jumped up with unexpected agility and, seizing the back of his chair, shouted:

"It's not military forces you command, but Red Guard rabble! They're not Cossacks, they're the dregs of humanity! You, Mr. Melekhov, shouldn't be in command of a division, you should be working as an orderly. You ought to be cleaning boots! Do you hear? Why wasn't the order obeyed? You weren't holding a meeting, were you? You weren't discussing the order by any chance? Beware! We're not 'comrades' here, and we won't allow the introduction of Bolshevik methods. We won't allow it!"

"I must ask you not to shout at me!" Gregor said in a thick voice, and rose, pushing back his stool with his foot.

"What did you say?" Fitzhelaurov cried hoarsely, panting with agitation, leaning across the table.

"I must ask you not to shout at me!" Gregor repeated in a louder tone. "You sent for us in order to decide—" He was silent for a second, lowered his eyes, and, not removing his gaze from Fitzhelaurov's hands, dropped his voice almost to a whisper. "If you, Your Excellency, attempt to lay even your little finger on me, I shall sabre you on the spot!"

The room grew so quiet that Fitzhelaurov's gasping breath could be heard distinctly. The silence lasted a good minute. The door creaked a little. A scared adjutant looked through the chink. The door was as cautiously closed. Gregor stood with his hand gripping his sabre-hilt. Kopylov's knees were trembling, his eyes wandered over the wall. Fitzhelaurov dropped heavily into his chair, groaned in an aged voice, and barked:

"A fine business!" Then, quite quietly, but not looking at Gregor: "Sit down! We got worked up a bit, and now it's past. Now be so good as to listen. I order you immediately to transfer all your mounted forces— But sit down, do!"

Gregor sat down and with his sleeve wiped away the copious sweat which suddenly beaded his face.

"To proceed. All mounted forces are immediately to be transferred to the south-east sector and to open an attack at once. On your right flank you will be in contact with the second battalion of the military commander Chumakov. . . ."

"I shall not take the division there," Gregor said in a weary tone, and groped in his trouser pocket for his handkerchief. With Natalia's lace handkerchief he once more wiped the sweat from his brow, and repeated: "I shall not take the division there."

"And why not?"

"The regrouping of forces will take a lot of time. . . ."

"That's nothing to do with you. I am responsible for the outcome of the operation."

"But it has to do with me, and you're not the only one who will be responsible."

"So you refuse to carry out my command?" Fitzhelaurov asked hoarsely, restraining himself with obvious effort.

"Yes."

"In that case be so good as to hand over the command of the division at once! Now I understand why yesterday's order was not carried out. . . ."

"You can please yourself about that, but I shall not hand over the command of the division."

"And how am I to understand that?"

"Just as I said." Gregor smiled almost imperceptibly.

"I dismiss you from your command!" Fitzhelaurov raised his voice. But Gregor at once rose to his feet.

"I am not subordinate to you, Your Excellency!"

"Then whom are you subordinate to?"

"I am subordinate to the commander of the insurgent forces, Kudynov. But it amazes me to hear all this from you. . . . At the moment, at least, you and I are of equal rank. You command a division, and I command a division. And for the time being you'd better not shout at me. . . . When I'm reduced to the rank of squadron commander, then by all means! But even then—" Gregor raised his dirty forefinger and, smiling even while his eyes blazed furiously, he ended: "Even then I'm not going to be shouted at."

Fitzhelaurov rose, adjusted his tight collar, and said with a slight bow:

"There is nothing more for us to discuss. Do as you wish. I shall immediately report your conduct to the army staff and, I dare to assure you, the results will not be slow in revealing themselves. Our field court martial is at present functioning with the greatest promptitude."

Paying no attention to Kopylov's despairing glances, Gregor clapped on his cap and went to the door. At the threshold he halted and said:

"You can report to where you like, but you can't frighten me. I'm not a nervous sort. . . . And for the present you'd better keep your hands off me. . . ." He stood thinking a moment and added: "For I'm afraid my Cossacks might shake you up a bit. . . ." He kicked open the door and, his sabre clattering, went with a swinging stride into the porch.

The agitated Kopylov overtook him on the steps.

"You're mad, Pantalievich!" he whispered, squeezing his hands in despair.

"The horses!" Gregor shouted in a ringing voice, crushing his whip in his hands.

Prokhor flew up to the steps like a devil.

As Gregor rode out of the gate he looked back: three orderlies were fussing around General Fitzhelaurov, helping him to climb into the handsome saddle of his high-standing horse.

Gregor and Kopylov rode for nearly half a mile in silence. Kopylov held his peace, realizing that Gregor was not inclined for conversation and that at the moment it would be dangerous to argue with him. At last Gregor could no longer restrain himself.

"What are you so silent about?" he asked sharply. "What did you come with me for? To act as a witness? Wanting to make out that you said nothing?"

"Well, brother, but you played a fine game!"

"And didn't he?"

"I grant you he was in the wrong, too. The way he spoke to you was absolutely disgusting."

"I wouldn't say he spoke to us at all! Right from the start he bawled as though someone had stuck a needle in his arse."

"All the same you did a fine thing! Insubordination to a senior officer . . . in field conditions, my friend. . . ."

"That's nothing! The only pity is that he didn't try to attack me! I'd have brought my blade down on his forehead hard enough to splinter his brain-box!"

"As it is, you can't expect any good to come from it!" Kopylov said discontentedly, and slowed his horse into a walk. "By all the signs it's clear they're going to tighten up discipline, so you had better look out!"

Snorting, their horses walked side by side, driving off the gadflies with their tails. Gregor humorously ran his eyes over Kopylov and asked:

"What did you tog yourself up like that for? I suppose you thought he'd give you tea? Would lead you to the table with his own fair hand? Shaved yourself, cleaned your tunic, polished your boots. . . . I saw you spit on your nose-rag and clean spots off your knees!"

"Please drop it!" Kopylov reddened.

"And all your labour was in vain!" Gregor jeered. "Not only was there no tea, but he didn't even offer you his hand."

"With you present that wasn't to be expected," Kopylov muttered hurriedly. Screwing up his eyes, in amazement and delight he ex-claimed: "Look! They're not ours! They're Allies."

A team of six mules was dragging a British gun towards them along the narrow street. At its side a British officer was riding on a dock-tailed, sorrel horse. The rider on the leading mule was also in British uniform, but he had a Russian officer's cockade in the band of his cap, and he was wearing lieutenant's epaulets.

When still several yards away from Gregor, the officer set two fingers to the peak of his cork helmet and, with a movement of his head, requested Gregor to make way. The street was so narrow that it was only possible to pass by edging the saddle-horses right up against the stone wall at the side.

The muscles quivered in Gregor's cheeks. Clenching his teeth, he rode straight at the officer. The man raised his brows in astonish-ment and drew a little aside. They passed with difficulty, and even then the Englishman had to lay his right leg, in its tight leather leg-ging, along his thoroughbred mare's gleaming, beautifully curried croup.

One of the artillery team, apparently a Russian officer, angrily looked Gregor up and down.

"I think you might have drawn aside! Surely you don't have to exhibit your rudeness even here?" he remarked.

"You ride on and shut up, you bitch's udder, or I'll put you aside!" Gregor advised him half aloud.

The officer raised himself on his seat, turned, and shouted: "Gen-tlemen! Hold this rascal!"

Expressively swinging his whip, Gregor made his way at a walk-ing pace along the lane. The weary, dusty artillery-men, all of them young, officers without moustaches, gave him unfriendly glances; but not one attempted to restrain him. The six-gun battery vanished round a bend, and Kopylov, biting his lips, rode up alongside Gregor.

"You're playing the fool, Gregor Pantalievich! You're behaving like a little child!"

"Why, have you been attached to me as my teacher?" Gregor snapped back.

"I can understand your getting angry with Fitzhelaurov," Kopylov said, shrugging his shoulders, "but what had that Englishman done to you? Didn't you like his helmet?"

"I didn't quite like it here, close to Ust-Miedvieditsa—he could have worn it somewhere else. . . . When two dogs are snapping at each other, a third doesn't interfere, you understand?"

"Aha! So you're against foreign intervention? But I think, when you're seized by the throat, you're glad of any help."

"Well, you can be glad, but I wouldn't let them set foot on our soil."

"Have you seen the Chinese fighting with the Reds?"

"Well?"

"Isn't that just the same? They're foreign help, too, you know."

"That's nothing to do with it! The Chinese volunteered to help the Reds."

"And do you think these others have been forced to come here?"

Gregor did not know what to answer, and he rode a long time in silence, tormentedly thinking it over. Then he said, with unconcealed chagrin in his voice:

"You educated people are always like that. You never make any allowances, you're like hares in the snow! I, brother, feel that your argument isn't sound somewhere, but I don't know how to pin you down. Let's drop the subject. Don't lasso me, I'm already muddled enough without your help."

Kopylov offendedly lapsed into silence, and they said no more for the rest of the ride. Except that Prokhor, goaded by curiosity, rode up to them and asked:

"Gregor Pantalievich—Your Excellency—tell me if you will, what is that animal the Cadets had got harnessed to the guns? They'd got ears like asses, but the rest of them was a natural horse. I didn't even like looking at the cattle. What the devil are they? Do tell me, for we've made bets on it. . . ."

For a good five minutes he rode behind them, but got no answer. So he fell back and, when the other orderlies drew level with him, informed them in a whisper:

"They're riding along without saying a word, brothers, and it's clear they're astonished themselves and don't for the life of them know how such filth found its way into daylight."

For the fourth time the Cossack companies rose from their shallow trenches and, under the Reds' murderous machine-gun fire, lay down again. From early dawn the Red Army batteries concealed in the forest on the left bank had been incessantly pounding away at the Cossack positions and the reserves assembled in the ravines.

Milkily white, melting clouds of shrapnel blazed up over the Donside heights. Before and behind the broken line of Cossack trenches the bullets sent the brown dust flying.

Towards noon the fight grew fiercer, and the western wind carried the roar of artillery fire far along the Don.

From an insurgent battery's observation post Gregor watched the course of the battle through field-glasses. He could see that, despite their losses, the officers' companies persistently advanced into the attack with a series of short sprints. When the fire intensified they lay down, digging themselves in, and then with another series of sprints they moved on to a new point. But more to the left, in the direction of the monastery, the insurgent infantry showed no signs of activity at all. Gregor wrote a note for Yermakov and sent it by a courier.

Yermakov rode up in a fury half an hour later. He dismounted by the battery tether-post and, breathing heavily, made his way to the trench of the observation post.

"I can't get the Cossacks to move! They won't move!" he shouted when still some distance off, waving his hands. "We've already lost twenty-three men, gone as though they'd never been. Did you see the way the Reds mowed them down with machine-guns?"

"The officers are advancing, but you tell me you can't get your men on to their feet?" Gregor hissed through his teeth.

"But you look! Every one of their platoons has got a hand machine-gun, and they're stuffed with cartridges to their eyebrows. But what have we got?"

"Now, no excuses! Lead them into the advance at once or we'll have your head off!"

Yermakov cursed terribly and ran down from the rise. Gregor followed him, resolved to lead the 2nd Infantry Regiment into the attack himself.

Close to the flank gun, which was cleverly concealed under branches of hawthorn, he was halted by the battery commander.

"Just come and admire the British handiwork, Gregor Pantalievich! They're about to open fire on the bridge. Let's go up to the top of the rise."

Through field-glasses they could just discern the slender ribbon of the pontoon bridge which Red engineers had thrown across the Don. Wagons were rolling across it in an unbroken stream.

Some ten minutes later the British battery, situated in a hollow beyond a stony ridge, opened fire. With the fourth shell the bridge was smashed almost in its centre. The stream of wagons came to a halt. The Red Army men hurriedly set to work to throw the shattered britskas and dead horses into the river.

Four barges crowded with engineers set out from the right bank. But as soon as they had succeeded in repairing the broken planking of the bridge, the British battery sent over another packet of shells. One of them blew the approach ramp on the left bank high into the air, the second sent up a green column of water right by the bridge, and the stream of wagons once more came to a halt.

"But they can put up an accurate fire, the sons of bitches!" Gregor's battery commander said in admiration. "Now they won't give them a chance to cross till nightfall. That bridge isn't going to be left whole for a minute!"

Without removing his field-glasses from his eyes, Gregor asked:

"But why are your guns silent? You should be supporting your infantry. You can see the Red machine-gun nests plainly enough."

"I'd be glad to, but we haven't got one shell left. It's half an hour since I sent over the last one and began to fast."

"Then what are you stopping here for? Harness up and clear out of the way."

"I've sent to ask the Cadets for shells."

"They won't let you have any," Gregor said decisively.

"They have refused us once, but I've asked again. They may be merciful this time. They might let us have a couple of dozen just to smash those machine-guns. It's no joke, their killing twenty-three of our men. And how many more will they still bowl over? Look at them stitching away!"

Gregor turned his gaze to the Cossack trenches; on the near-by slope the bullets were still kicking up the dry earth. Wherever the line of machine-gun fire was laid, a strip of dust arose, as though someone invisible was running a melting grey line over the trenches. Along their entire length the Cossack trenches seemed to be smoking; the dust hung above them in clouds.

Gregor no longer watched the fire of the British battery. For a minute he listened to the incessant thunder of artillery and machine-

guns, then strode down from the mound and overtook Yermakov.
"Don't go into the attack until you receive orders from me," he
said. "We'll never drive them out without artillery support."

"Didn't I tell you so?" Yermakov said reproachfully, seating himself on his fretting horse.

Gregor watched as Yermakov fearlessly galloped off under fire,
and thought anxiously: "What the devil has he taken the direct road
for? They'll mow him down with a machine-gun. He should have
dropped into the hollow, ridden along the watercourse and made his
way round the hill back to his men." At a furious gallop, Yermakov
rode to the hollow, plunged into it, and did not appear again on the
farther side. "So he's realized! Now he'll get there!" Gregor sighed
with relief and lay down below the rise, unhurriedly rolling a cigarette.

He was possessed by a strange indifference. No, he would not lead
the Cossacks out under that machine-gun fire. There was no point
in it. Let the officers' storm companies make the attack. Let them
capture Ust-Miedvieditsa. There, lying under the rise, for the first
time in his life he evaded directly taking part in a battle. Not cowardice, not fear of death or of useless losses, governed his decision
at that moment. Not long before, he had spared neither his own life
nor the lives of the Cossacks entrusted to his command. But now it
was as though something had snapped. . . . Never before had he
realized so clearly all the senselessness of what was going on all
around him. It may have been the talk with Kopylov, or the clash
with Fitzhelaurov, or perhaps the two incidents together, that had
provoked the mood which had so unexpectedly taken possession of
him. In any case he was determined not to expose himself any more
under fire. He vaguely considered that it was not his job to reconcile
the Cossacks with the Bolsheviks; for that matter, he could not himself be reconciled with them. But he felt that he could not and
would no longer defend all these people who were alien in spirit,
who were hostile to him—all these Fitzhelaurovs, who had a profound contempt for him and whom he condemned no less pro-
foundly. And once more he was faced with the old contradictions in
all their inexorability. "Let them fight! I'll stand and look on! The
moment I'm relieved of the division I shall ask to be sent to the rear.
I've had enough!" he thought and, mentally returning to the argument with Kopylov, he caught himself trying to find justification for

the Reds. "The Chinese march with the Reds with bare hands; they joined up with them and risk their lives every day for miserable soldier's pay. And besides, what's the pay to do with it? What the devil can you buy with it? You can only lose it at cards. . . . So it's not a question of making money, but something else. Yet the Allies are sending officers, tanks, and guns, and they've even sent mules! But afterwards they'll be demanding a handsome pile of rubles for it all! There's the difference! Yes, we'll argue it all out again this evening. As soon as I get back to the staff I shall call him aside and say: 'But there is a difference, Kopylov; and don't try to make a fool of me!' "

But he was not destined to renew the argument. That afternoon Kopylov rode off to the 4th Regiment, which was being held in reserve, and on the way was killed by a stray bullet. Gregor learned of his death only two days later.

Next morning the Fifth Division, commanded by General Fitzhelaurov, took Ust- Miedvieditsa by storm.

Chapter 2

Some three days after Gregor's departure, Mitka Korshunov turned up in Tatarsk. He was not alone, he was accompanied by two fellow-soldiers in his punitive detachment. One of them was an elderly Kalmyk, the second an insignificant little Cossack. Mitka contemptuously called the Kalmyk: "Come here!" but dignified the Cossack tippler and rascal with the title of Silanty Petrovich.

Evidently Mitka had done no small service to the Don army by his activities in the punitive detachment; during the winter he had been raised to the rank of sergeant-major and then to that of ensign, and he arrived in the village in all the glory of his officer's uniform. It must be deduced that he had lived quite well during the retreat beyond the Don: his light khaki tunic still fitted tightly across his broad shoulders, greasy folds of rosy skin lay over his close, standing collar, his blue, striped trousers fitted him so closely that they all but split across the buttocks. With all his superficial virtues

Mitka would have been in the Ataman's lifeguards, he would have lived at the palace and defended the sacred person of His Imperial Majesty, if it had not been for this accursed revolution. But even so, he had no complaint to make of life. He had won his way to officer's rank, and that not like Gregor Melekhov, by risking his head and indulging in reckless heroics. Service in a punitive detachment called for other qualities! Mitka had enough and to spare of such qualities. Having no great trust in the other Cossacks, he himself settled the account of anyone suspected of Bolshevism; he was not too fastidious to deal with deserters with his own hands, wielding a whip or ramrod; and as for cross-examining prisoners, there was no one in the detachment to equal him, and the commander himself shrugged his shoulders and said: "Say what you like, gentlemen, but it's impossible to surpass Korshunov. He's not a man, he's a dragon!" Mitka was distinguished by one other remarkable quality: when it was not advisable to shoot a prisoner, yet it was thought undesirable to let him go free, the man was sentenced to corporal punishment with the birch, and Mitka was entrusted with the execution of the sentence. He carried out his task so well that after the fiftieth stroke the condemned man succumbed to a bloody vomit, and after a hundred the other Cossacks confidently rolled him up in sacking without listening to his heart. Not one man so sentenced had escaped alive from Mitka's hand. He himself had said more than once with a laugh: "If trousers and skirts were made of all the Reds I've flogged to death, I could clothe all the village of Tatarsk."

The cruelty innate in Mitka's nature since childhood not only found fitting application in the punitive detachment but, with nothing to bridle it, developed extraordinarily. By the very nature of his service he came into contact with the dregs of the officer class, with drug addicts, with rapists, with pillagers and other scum, and in his hatred for the Reds he willingly, with all a peasant's assiduity, learned all they could teach him and had no great difficulty in excelling his teachers. Where a neurasthenic officer, worn out with other men's blood and sufferings, could not go on, Mitka only screwed up his yellow, glittering eyes and carried the task through to the end.

When he arrived in the village, carrying himself with great dignity and hardly deigning to answer the bows of the passing women, he rode at a walking pace towards his home. By the half-burnt, smoke-stained gates he dismounted, handed the rein to the Kalmyk, and, straddling his legs, went into the yard. Accompanied by Silanty, he silently walked round the foundations. With the end of his whip he touched a lump of turquoise-coloured window-glass which had melted during the fire, and said in a voice hoarse with emotion:

"They've burnt it down! And it was a wealthy house, the best in the village. One of our own villagers, Mishka Koshevoi, burned it. He killed my grandfather, too. Well, Silanty Petrovich, I've had the experience of visiting my native hearth and home. . . ."

"Are any of the Koshevois left behind?" Silanty asked excitedly.

"There should be. But we'll see them later. . . . Now let's ride to our father-in-law."

On the road to the Melekhovs' hut Mitka asked Bogatiriev's daughter-in-law, whom he happened to meet:

"Has my mother returned from beyond the Don?"

"I don't think she has yet, Mitry Mironich."

"Then is Melekhov at home?"

"The old one?"

"Yes."

"He's at home; the whole family's at home except Gregor. Piotra was killed last winter; have you heard?"

Mitka nodded and put his horse into a trot.

He rode along the deserted street, and his yellow cat's eyes, satiated and cold, revealed no trace of his recent agitation. As he rode up to the Melekhovs' yard he said in a low tone, not addressing himself to either of his companions particularly:

"That's the way your own native village welcomes you! I've even got to go to relations for dinner. . . . Well, we'll pull up again yet."

Pantaleimon Prokoffievich was mending a harvesting machine under a shed. Noticing horsemen, and recognizing Korshunov among them, he went to the gate.

"Come in by all means," he said hospitably, opening the wicket gate. "We're glad to have guests. Welcome back."

"Hello, Father! All alive and well?"

"Glory be, all well so far! But surely you aren't going about in officer's uniform?"

"Why, did you think your sons were the only ones entitled to wear the white epaulets?" Mitka said in a self-satisfied tone, giving the old man his long, venous hand.

"My sons weren't so very anxious to get them!" Pantaleimon Prokoffievich answered with a smile, and went in front, to show the newcomers where to tether their horses.

The hospitable Ilinichna gave the guests dinner, and then they turned to conversation. Mitka asked details of his family, and was taciturn, revealing neither anger nor sorrow. He casually asked whether any of Mishka Koshevoi's family was left in the village and, learning that Mishka's mother and her children were still at home, gave Silanty a swift, surreptitious wink.

The guests soon made ready to go. As he saw them off, Pantaleimon Prokoffievich asked:

"Are you thinking of staying long in the village?"

"Well, yes, two or three days perhaps."

"Will you be seeing your mother?"

"That depends."

"And are you going far now?"

"Hm—just going to see some of the people in the village. We'll be back soon."

Before Mitka and his companions had time to return to the Melekhovs' hut, the rumour was spreading through the village that Korshunov had arrived with Kalmyks and had killed all the Koshevoi family.

Pantaleimon did not hear the rumour. He went to the smithy and back and was preparing to tackle the harvesting machine again when Ilinichna called him in:

"Here, Prokoffich! Hurry up!"

A note of undisguised alarm sounded in the old woman's voice, and the astonished Pantaleimon at once made his way to the hut.

Natalia was standing, tear-stained and pale, at the stove. With her eyes Ilinichna indicated Anikushka's wife and asked in a deeply upset tone:

"Have you heard the news, old man?"

"Oh, something's happened to Gregor! God be merciful and protect him!" The thought scared Pantaleimon. He turned pale and, fearful and furious because nobody spoke, shouted:

"Spit it out at once, curse you! Well, what's happened? Something to do with Gregor?" As though rendered helpless by his shout, he dropped on the bench and stroked his trembling legs.

Dunia was the first to realize that her father was afraid of bad news concerning his son, and she hurriedly said:

"No, Dad, it's not news of Gregor. Mitka's killed the Koshevois."

"What do you mean by 'killed'?" The weight fell at once from Pantaleimon's heart and, still not understanding what Dunia had said, he again queried: "The Koshevois? Mitry?"

Anikushka's wife, who had run to the Melekhovs with the news, began to stammer out her story:

"I was looking for our calf, old man, and I happened to go past the Koshevois' hut, and Mitry and two soldiers with him rode up to the yard and went into the hut. I was thinking: the calf won't go farther than the windmill. It was time the calf—"

"What the devil do I want to hear about your calf for?" Pantaleimon broke in angrily.

"—and they went into the hut," the woman went on, sobbing, "and I stood and waited. And I heard them start shouting inside, and I could hear the sound of blows. I was terrified to death; I wanted to run, but I'd only just stepped away from the fence when I heard footsteps behind me. I looked back, and there was your Mitry had thrown a rope around the old woman's neck and was dragging her along the ground, just as though she was a dog, God forgive me! He dragged her to the shed, and she, poor thing, didn't make a sound; she must have been unconscious already. The Kalmyk that was with him sprang up to a crossbeam. . . . As I watched, Mitry threw the end of the rope up to him and shouted: 'Pull it up and tie it with a knot.' Oh, what I suffered then! In my very sight they strangled the poor old woman, and then they jumped on their horses and rode down the street, to the administration, I expect. I was afraid to go into the hut. . . . But I saw blood flowing from the porch, under the door, on to the steps. God grant I never see such horrors again!"

"Fine guests God's sent us!" Ilinichna said, looking challengingly at her husband.

Pantaleimon listened in a state of terrible agitation to the story and, when Anikushka's wife had finished, went out into the porch without saying a word.

Mitka and his assistants appeared at the gate soon afterwards. Pantaleimon nimbly limped towards them.

"Stop!" he shouted when still some distance away. "Don't bring your horses into this yard!"

"What's the matter, Father-in-law?" Mitka asked in astonishment.

"Turn back!" Pantaleimon went right up to him and, gazing into Mitka's yellow, twinkling eyes, said firmly: "Don't be annoyed, cousin, but I don't wish you to stay in my house. You'd better go your ways."

"A-ah!" Mitka drawled in an understanding tone, and turned pale. "So you're driving me away?"

"I don't want you to soil my house!" the old man said resolutely. "And never put your foot across my threshold again! We Melekhovs have no kinship with executioners, know that!"

"I understand! But you're a little too merciful, cousin!"

"And it seems you don't know what mercy is, seeing that you've begun to execute women and children. Ah, Mitry, it's an unworthy trade you've taken up. . . . Your dead father wouldn't rejoice if he could see you now!"

"You old fool, would you like me to fondle them? They killed my father, they killed my grandfather, but I'm to exchange Christian kisses with them, am I? You can go to—you know where!" Mitka furiously pulled on the rein and rode his horse out of the wicket gate.

"Don't swear, Mitry, you're like my own son to me. And there's nothing between you and me, go in peace!"

Turning more and more pale, shaking his whip threateningly, Mitka shouted thickly:

"Don't cause me to sin, don't force me to! I'm sorry for Natalia, otherwise I'd show you, you merciful one. . . . I know you! I see you through and through, I see the sort of spirit you breathe out! You didn't retreat beyond the Donietz, did you? You went over to the Reds, didn't you? That's just it! You all ought to be treated like the Koshevois, you sons of bitches! Come on, boys! Well, you lame hound, don't you fall into my hands! You'll never escape my fist! And I shall remember your hospitality to me. I've raised my fist even against such kinsmen!"

With trembling hands Pantaleimon shut the wicket gate and bolted it, then limped into the hut.

"I've driven your brother away," he said to Natalia, not looking at her.

She said nothing, although in her heart she agreed with her father-

in-law's step. But Ilinichna swiftly crossed herself and said in a happier tone:

"And glory be! He's gone for good! Forgive me what I'm saying, Natalia dear, but your Mitka has turned out a real scoundrel. He's found himself a fine job! Look at him! Not serving like other Cossacks in the real forces! He's joined a punitive detachment! And is that the Cossacks' task, to be executioners, to hang old women, and to cut down innocent children with their sabres? Are they responsible for Mitka's doings? Why, at that rate the Reds might have sabred me and you, and Mishatka and Poliushka, for Grishka's doings. But they didn't; they had mercy. No, God forbid; I don't agree with such goings on."

"Nor do I defend my brother, Mother," was all Natalia said as she wiped away her tears with the end of her handkerchief.

Mitka rode out of the village that same day. Rumour said that he rejoined his punitive detachment somewhere near Kargin and went off with it to bring order to the Ukrainian settlements of the Donietz region, whose population had been accused of helping to suppress the upper Don rising.

Chapter 3

After Mitka's departure he was the subject of discussion in the village for a whole week. The majority of the people condemned his arbitrary butchery of the Koshevoi family. The bodies were buried out of communal resources; attempts were made to sell the little hut, but no purchaser was to be found. On the order of the village ataman, boards were nailed across the shutters; and for long after, the children were afraid to play around that fearful spot, while as they passed the hut old men and women crossed themselves and prayed for the peace of the murdered ones' souls.

Then the time arrived for the steppe haying, and these recent events were forgotten.

The village was absorbed as before in work and in rumours of the front. Those of the farmers who had managed to save their working animals groaned and cursed as they supplied wagons and animals for communal services. Almost every day bullocks and horses had to be taken from the fields and sent to the district centre. As the old men unharnessed the horses from the mowing machines they frequently cursed the long-drawn-out war. But shells, cartridges, reels of barbed wire, foodstuffs, had to be carted to the front. And they carted them. But now, as though of evil intent, such fine days had set in that all they wanted was to mow and then to harvest the ripe, unusually luscious grass.

Pantaleimon made ready for the mowing and grew furiously angry with Daria. She had driven off with the yoke of bullocks to carry cartridges. She was to have returned from the transhipment point, but a week passed and still there was no news of her. And without the yoke of old, thoroughly reliable bullocks nothing could be done in the steppe.

To tell the truth, he should not have sent Daria. . . . His heart had been filled with foreboding when he had entrusted the bullocks to her, for he knew how fain she was to pass her time merrily, and how negligent she was of the animals. But there was no one else to send. Dunia could not go, for it was no maiden's work to drive with strange Cossacks on a long journey. Natalia had the little children to see to, and surely it wasn't for the old man himself to take those accursed cartridges? But Daria willingly answered the call. She had already driven with the greatest of satisfaction to all kinds of places: to the mill, or on some other task connected with the farm, and all simply because she felt far more free outside the house. Every journey brought her amusement and pleasure. She escaped from her mother-in-law's oversight, she could gossip her fill with other women, and, as she said, could "strike up a love affair" with any dissolute Cossack who happened to glance her way. At home, even after Piotra's death, the strict Ilinichna allowed her no freedom, as though Daria, who had been false to her husband while he was alive, was bound to be true to him now he was dead!

Pantaleimon knew that the bullocks would not be looked after properly, but there was nothing else to be done; he sent his elder daughter-in-law on the journey. But he lived all the ensuing week in the greatest of anxiety and mental unrest. "My old bullocks are done for," he thought more than once, waking up in the middle of the night and sighing deeply.

Daria returned in the morning of the eleventh day after her departure. Pantaleimon had just come home from the fields. He was mowing together with Anikushka's wife, and had left her and Dunia in the steppe to return to the village for water and provisions. The old people and Natalia were having breakfast when the wheels of the britska rattled with their familiar clatter past the window. Natalia nimbly ran to the window and saw Daria, wrapped right to her eyes, leading in the tired, emaciated bullocks.

"Is it she?" the old man asked, choking over a piece of food swallowed too quickly.

"Yes."

"I never expected to see the bullocks again. Well, glory be to God! The accursed draggletail! She's turned up in the yard only because she had to!" the old man muttered, crossing himself and belching with satiation.

Daria unyoked the bullocks and went into the kitchen, laid the folded horse-rug on the threshold, and greeted the others.

"But why so soon, my dear? You could have spent another week on the road!" Pantaleimon said in a grumbling tone, looking at Daria from under his brows and not answering her greeting.

"You should have gone yourself!" she snapped, removing her dusty kerchief from her head.

"Why were you gone so long?" Ilinichna joined in the conversation, in order to take off the chilliness of the reception.

"They wouldn't release me, so I couldn't help it."

Pantaleimon shook his head distrustfully and asked:

"They discharged Christonia's wife at the transhipment point, so why didn't they you?"

"Well, they didn't!" Daria's eyes glittered angrily, and she added: "If you don't believe me, ride and ask the man who was in charge of the wagons."

"I've got no reason to go and ask about you, but the next time you stay at home! Death is the only thing you can be sent for."

"Now you're threatening me! Yes, you are! I won't go in any case. Even if you send me I won't go!"

"Are the bullocks all right?" the old man asked more amicably.

"Yes. Nothing's happened to your bullocks . . ." Daria answered reluctantly, and looked blacker than night.

"She's had to part from some lover of hers on the road, and that's why she's so cross," Natalia thought. She always had a feeling of pity and fastidiousness about Daria and her unclean, amorous adventures.

After breakfast Pantaleimon made ready to drive off; but at that moment the village ataman arrived.

"I'd say 'good journey,' but wait a minute, Pantaleimon Prokoffievich, don't go off!" he said.

"You haven't come for a wagon again, have you?" the old man said in an exaggeratedly submissive tone, though he was well-nigh choking with fury.

"No, it's something else this time. The commander of all the Don army, General Sidorin himself, is coming here today. You understand? I've just received a document by courier from the district ataman, ordering all the old men and the women down to the very last to assemble for a meeting."

"Haven't they got any sense?" Pantaleimon shouted. "Who's going to organize a village assembly at such an urgent time? Is your General Sidorin going to provide me with hay for the winter?"

"He'll provide you with as much as he'll provide me," the ataman replied calmly. "What I'm ordered to do, that I do. Unharness your animals! We must welcome him hospitably. They say, by the way, that Allied generals are travelling with him."

Pantaleimon stood by the wagon for a moment, thinking it over, then began to unharness the bullocks. Seeing his remarks had had effect, the ataman cheered up and asked:

"Is there any chance of borrowing your mare?"

"What do you want her for?"

"They've ordered us, may they sit on a hedgehog, to send two troikas as far as Durnoi Dell to meet them. But where I'm to get the tarantasses and horses I've no idea! I was up and running about before dawn; I've soaked my shirt five times, and still I've only got hold of four horses. Everybody's out at work, and you can shout as much as you like. . . ."

The mollified Pantaleimon agreed to let the ataman have his mare, and even offered his small, springed tarantass. After all, it was the commander-in-chief of the army who was coming, and foreign generals with him, too, and Pantaleimon always had had a feeling of fluttering respect for generals.

The endeavours of the ataman resulted at last in the assembly of two troikas, which were sent off to Durnoi Dell to meet the honoured guests. The people gathered in the square. Many of them left their haying to hurry in from the steppe.

Turning his back on the work, Pantaleimon dressed himself up, put on a clean shirt, striped cloth trousers, and the cap which Gregor had once brought home as a present for him. Then he limped off sedately to the market square, after ordering his old wife to send Daria out with water and food for Dunia.

Soon a heavy dust was whirling up along the track and moving in a cloud towards the village; through the dust something metallic gleamed, and from afar came the monotonous note of a car horn. The guests were riding in two new-looking, gleaming dark-blue cars; driving round the mowers returning home from the steppe, the empty troikas bounced along far behind them, and the postal bells, which the ataman had acquired for this solemn occasion, tinkled dismally beneath the yokes. There was a perceptible stir among the crowd in the square, a hum of talk arose, and children's merry shouts. The distracted ataman wandered through the crowd, collecting the worthy elders who were to be entrusted with the presentation of bread and salt. His eyes fell on Pantaleimon, and he gladly seized on him:

"Help me out, for Christ's sake! You're a man of experience, you know the ways. . . . You know how to hobnob with them and all that sort of thing. . . . And besides, you're a member of the regional administration, and your son's a— Please take the bread and salt, for I've always been a nervous sort, and I'm all trembling at the knees."

Flattered beyond words by this honour, Pantaleimon refused at first, for decency's sake; then, seeming to draw his head down between his shoulders, he swiftly crossed himself and took the dish with its bread and salt covered by an embroidered hand-towel. Pushing the crowd aside with his elbows, he stepped to the front.

Accompanied by a drove of hoarsely barking dogs of all kinds, the cars swiftly approached the square.

"How do you feel? You're not nervous?" the pale-faced ataman inquired of Pantaleimon. It was the first time he had ever seen such big bugs. Pantaleimon flashed a sidelong glance at him and said in a voice husky with agitation:

"Here, hold this while I comb my beard! Take it!"

The ataman submissively took the dish, while Pantaleimon smoothed his moustache and beard and youthfully flung out his chest; then, resting on the tips of the toes of his maimed leg, so that his deformity was not evident, he again took the dish. But it shook so violently in his hands that the ataman anxiously inquired:

"You won't drop it, will you? Oh, look out!"

Pantaleimon shrugged his shoulders with the utmost contempt. He drop it! Could any man talk such nonsense? He, a member of the regional administration, he who had been on handshaking terms with everybody in the Governor's palace, suddenly to be afraid of some general! This wretched little ataman had gone right out of his mind!

"My brother, when I was in the army region, I had tea with sugar in it with the vice-ataman himself . . ." Pantaleimon began. But the words froze on his lips.

The leading car halted about a dozen paces away. A clean-shaven chauffeur in a cap with a large visor and narrow non-Russian epaulets on his tunic nimbly jumped out and opened the door. Two officers dressed in khaki gravely got out and made their way towards the crowd. They walked straight towards Pantaleimon and, as he drew himself up to attention, so he remained transfixed. He guessed that these modestly dressed people must be the generals, and that those who came behind and were dressed more finely were simply members of their suite. Then where were the generals' solid epaulets? Where the shoulder-knots and medals? And what sort of generals were these, if they were quite indistinguishable from ordinary military clerks?

The old man stared without blinking at the approaching guests, and his look revealed more and more open amazement. For one moment he was bitterly disillusioned. He even felt affronted, both because of his solemn preparations for the meeting and also because these generals were a disgrace to the very title of general. Damn it, if he had known this was the kind of general that was going to turn up, he wouldn't have dressed himself so carefully, and wouldn't have waited for them with such a tremor of expectation, and in any case wouldn't have stood like a fool, with a dish in his hands, and on it bread badly baked by some snotty-nosed old woman. No, Pantaleimon Prokoffievich had never been a laughing-stock in the people's eyes, but now that had happened. A moment ago he had heard the children giggling behind his back, and one little devil even shouted at the top of his voice: "Boys, look how old hoppy Melekhov has given himself a pain! He looks as though he'd swallowed a brush!" If only there had been good reason for enduring the jeers and straining his stiffly-held lame leg! All Pantaleimon's entrails were bubbling with indignation. And this accursed coward of an ataman was the cause of it all! He had come and gabbled away, taken the mare and the tarantass, and had run all over the village with his tongue hanging out, looking for bells for the troikas. And in truth the man who has never seen anything worth seeing is glad of a rag! In all his life Pantaleimon had never seen such generals! Take the Imperial review, for instance: you'd see a man marching along with his chest covered with medals, and wearing gold lace. It did your heart good to look at him; he was an ikon, not a general! But these, all in grey, like jackdaws. One of them hadn't even got a proper cap with a visor, as he should have when in dress uniform, but a kind of top-hat under muslin, and his face was shaved quite bare; you couldn't have found one little hair, even if you'd searched with a lantern. . . . Pantaleimon's face clouded and he all but spat with disgust. But someone gave him a hard jog in the back and whispered in a loud voice:

"Go on, take it to them. . . ."

He stepped forward. Looking over his head, General Sidorin ran his eyes around the crowd and uttered in a ringing voice:

"Greetings, worthy elders!"

"We wish you health, Your Excellency!" the villagers shouted in a ragged chorus.

The general graciously accepted the bread and salt from Pantaleimon's hands, said: "Thank you," and passed the dish to his adjutant.

After handing over the bread and salt Pantaleimon fell back to mix with the crowd. He did not stop to listen while some Vieshenska orator welcomed the visitors in the name of the Cossack population of the Vieshenska district, but made his way to the troikas standing a little distance off.

The horses were covered with foam, and their flanks were sunken. The old man went up to his mare, rubbed her nostrils with his sleeve, and sighed. He felt like cursing, unharnessing the mare at once, and leading her home, so great was his disillusionment.

Meantime General Sidorin was making a speech to the inhabitants of Tatarsk. Approvingly referring to their militant activities in the rear of the Reds, he said:

"You have fought valiantly against our common enemies. Your services will not be forgotten by your native land, which is gradually being liberated from the Bolsheviks, from their terrible yoke. I should like to present tokens of our gratitude to those women of your village who, as we know, were especially prominent in the armed struggle against the Reds. I ask our Cossack heroines whose names will be announced in a minute to step forward."

One of the officers read out a short list. The first name was that of Daria Melekhova, the others were widows of Cossacks killed at the beginning of the rising, women who had participated, like Daria, in the massacre of the Communist prisoners driven to Tatarsk after the surrender of the Serdobsky regiment.

Daria had not driven out to the fields, as Pantaleimon had ordered her. She proved to be on the square, among the crowd of village women, and she was attired as though the day were a holiday. The moment she heard her name called out, she pushed the women aside and boldly walked to the front, tidying her white, lace-edged kerchief as she went, half-closing her eyes, and smiling a little with embarrassment. Tired as she was after her journey and amorous adventures, she was still devilishly good to look at. Her pale cheeks, untouched by sunburn, reflected the hot glitter of her questing eyes, and in the wilful curl of her painted eyebrows and in the folds of her smiling lips lurked something challenging and unclean.

Her way was barred by an officer standing with his back to the crowd. She gently pushed him aside, saying:

"Let a soldier's widow pass!"

And she went right up to Sidorin.

He took the medal with its St. George ribbon from the adjutant and, with fumbling fingers, pinned it to the left breast of Daria's jacket, gazing with a smile into her eyes.

"So you're the widow of Ensign Melekhov, who was killed in March?"

"Yes."

"In a moment you will be given a monetary reward, five hundred rubles. This officer will give it to you. The military ataman Africano Petrovich Bogaevsky and the government of the Don express their thanks to you for the great valor you have shown, and ask you to accept their sympathy. . . . They deeply sympathize with you in your sorrow."

Daria did not understand all the general said to her. She thanked him with a nod of her head, took the money from the adjutant's hand, and, smiling silently, gazed straight into the eyes of the still youthful general. They were almost of the same height, and Daria examined the general's gaunt face with no great constraint. "They've valued my Piotra cheap, at no more than the cost of a yoke of bullocks. But he's not bad-looking, this general, quite passable," she was thinking with her native cynicism. Sidorin waited, expecting her to go; but she still lingered. The adjutant and other officers standing behind him raised their eyebrows, drawing one another's attention to the sprightly widow; their eyes twinkled merrily.

"May I go?" Daria asked.

"Why, yes, of course," Sidorin permitted hurriedly.

With an awkward movement Daria thrust the money into the neck opening of her jacket and went back to the crowd. Weary with speeches and ceremonies, the officers closely followed her light, gliding walk.

Martin Shamil's widow approached Sidorin uncertainly. When the medal was pinned to her old jacket she broke into tears, so unceremonious and so femininely bitter that the officers' faces at once lost their amused expressions and grew serious, sympathetically sour.

"So your husband was killed too?" Sidorin asked, his face clouding.

The weeping woman covered her face with her hands and nodded silently.

"She's got so many children, you couldn't get them all into one wagon," a Cossack remarked in a deep voice.

Shortly afterwards the guests departed for the district centre. The people hurriedly began to disperse, hastening to get on with the mowing, and soon after the cars, escorted by a horde of clam-

orous dogs, had disappeared, only three old gaffers were left standing by the church fence.

"Strange days these are!" one of them said, throwing out his arms
expansively. "In the old days when there was a war on they gave
the Cross of St. George or a medal for really big deeds, for heroism.
And the men they gave them to! The most daring, the most desperate! It wasn't for nothing that the people made up the saying:
'Either come back with a cross or remain dead on the field.' But
these days they've started pinning crosses on women. It wouldn't
be so bad if the women had done anything, but—the Cossacks drove
prisoners into the village, and the women killed the prisoners, unarmed men, with stakes. Where's the heroism in that? I don't
understand, God forgive me!"

Another weak-sighted and feeble old man planted one foot aside,
slowly drew a rolled cloth wallet out of his pocket, and said:

"The authorities can see better from Novocherkass. I expect they
reasoned it out this way: the women have got to have something to
attract them as well, so as to raise everybody's spirits, so everybody
should fight better. Here's a medal, and here's five hundred rubles;
what woman could say no to such an honour? Some of the Cossacks
might not want to go to the front, might want to keep safely out of
the war, but could they stay at home now? Their wives would
scorch their ears for them. The night cuckoo always cuckoos the
loudest. And every woman will begin to think: 'Maybe they'll pin
a medal on me.'"

"You're talking nonsense, Cousin Fiodor," the third man objected.
"They deserved to be rewarded, and so they were rewarded. The
women are left widows, the money will be a great help to them on
their farms, and the medals have been given them for their bravery.
Daria Melekhova was the first to condemn Kotliarov to death, and
quite right, too! The Lord is the judge of them all, but you can't
blame the women: their own blood calls loud. . . ."

The old gaffers argued and swore away until the church bell rang
for vespers. The moment the sexton struck the bell, all three rose,
removed their caps, crossed themselves, and decorously entered the
church enclosure.

Chapter 4

It was amazing how life had changed in the Melekhov family. It was not so long since Pantaleimon Prokoffievich had felt himself the all-powerful master of the house, and every member of the family obeyed him unconditionally; the work was carried on by all jointly, they shared their joys and their sorrows, and a strong, abiding agreement was evident in all their existence. The family had been firmly welded together in one. Yet since that last spring everything had changed. Dunia was the first to break away. She did not openly disobey her father, but she did any work that fell to her with obvious reluctance, and as though she were not working for herself, but for hire. Outwardly she grew very reserved, alienated from the others; rarely was her carefree laugh to be heard nowadays.

After Gregor's departure for the front, Natalia also grew less intimate with the old people. She spent almost all her time with the children, talked freely only with them, and occupied herself with them, and it seemed as though she were quietly but deeply grieving over something. But not by a single word did she share her sorrow with any other member of the family; she complained to nobody and kept her burden entirely to herself.

As for Daria, she changed completely after her journey with the wagon and bullocks. She contradicted her father-in-law more and more frequently, paid no attention whatever to Ilinichna, was cross with everybody for no apparent cause, avoided taking part in the haying on the score of sickness, and behaved as though she had only a few more days to spend in the Melekhov house.

Before Pantaleimon's very eyes the family was breaking up. He and his old wife were left alone. The family ties were destroyed swiftly and unexpectedly; the warmth of their relationships was gone; touches of irritation and hostility crept more and more into their conversation. They did not sit down at the common table as in former times, like a single, friendly family, but like people who happened to find themselves together by chance.

The war was the cause of it all; Pantaleimon realized that well enough. Dunia was annoyed with her parents because they had robbed her of the hope of marrying Mishka Koshevoi, the one man whom she loved with all the intensity of her virgin passion. With her native secrecy Natalia was silently and deeply suffering because of Gregor's latest entanglement with Aksinia. Pantaleimon saw it all, but he could do nothing to restore the old order in his family. In very deed, after all that had occurred he could not give his consent to his daughter's marriage with an inveterate Bolshevik; and besides, what use would it be if he did consent, seeing that the devil of a bridegroom was dashing about somewhere at the front, and in the Red Army into the bargain? The same applied to Gregor: if he hadn't been wearing an officer's uniform Pantaleimon would have dealt properly with him! He would have dealt with him so thoroughly that afterwards Gregor would not even have squinted at the Astakhovs' yard. But the war had messed up everything and robbed the old man of the possibility of living and ruling his house as he desired. The war had ruined him, had robbed him of his former zest for work, had taken his elder son from him, had brought discord and disorder into his family. It had passed over his life like a storm over ripened wheat; yet even after a storm the wheat rises again and is beautiful under the sun, but now the old man could not rise. He mentally let everything slide. So be it!

Daria cheered up after receiving her award from the hands of General Sidorin. She returned excited and happy from the square. Her eyes glittering, she showed Natalia the medal.

"What have you got that for?" Natalia asked in amazement.

"That's for my cousin Ivan Alexievich, may he rest in peace, the son of a bitch! And this is for Piotra." With a flourish she unfolded the packet of crackling Don credit notes.

But even then Daria did not go out to the fields. Pantaleimon wanted to send her out with food, but she flatly refused:

"Let me be, Father, I'm worn out after the journey."

The old man's face clouded. To soften her rough refusal, Daria said half-jokingly:

"On such a day it's a sin for you to force me to go out to the fields. Today's a holiday for me."

"I'll take the food myself," the old man agreed. "Well, and what about the money?"

"What about the money?" Daria raised her eyebrows in surprise.

"I ask, what are you intending to do with the money?"

"That's my affair. I'll do what I like with it."

"But that is—what do you mean? Didn't they give you the money for Piotra?"

"They gave it to me, and it's not for you to dispose of it."

"But are you one of the family or what?"

"And what do you want of this one of the family, Father? To take the money for yourself?"

"I don't mean the lot; but was Piotra our son or not, in your view? The old woman and I ought to have a share, shouldn't we?"

The old man's claims were made in an obviously uncertain tone, and Daria resolutely took the upper hand. In a contemptuously calm voice she said:

"I shan't give you anything; I shan't even give you a ruble! You've got no share in this, or he'd have put it in your hand. And why are you kicking up a fuss about your share? No one said anything about shares, and you needn't stretch your hand out for my money, you won't get it!"

Then Pantaleimon made his last attempt.

"You live with us, you eat our bread, and that means that everything ought to be in common. What sort of order will there be if each begins to run his own affairs separately? I won't allow that!" he said.

But Daria repulsed this final attempt to take possession of money which belonged to her. Smiling shamelessly, she announced:

"I'm not married to you, Father. I live with you today, but tomorrow I shall get married, and then you'll be glad to set eyes on me! And I'm not bound to pay you for my food. I've worked ten years for your family, never straightening my back."

"You've worked for yourself, you sinful hussy!" Pantaleimon shouted indignantly. He shouted something else also, but Daria did not stop to listen to him. Sweeping up the edge of her skirt, she swung round right under his nose and went off to the best room. "He tried it on the wrong woman!" she whispered, with a sneering smile.

There the conversation ended. And, truly, Daria was not the one to yield her rights out of fear of the old man's anger.

Pantaleimon made ready to drive off to the fields, but before his departure he had a short talk with Ilinichna.

"You keep an eye on Daria!" he ordered.

"Why, what am I to keep an eye on her for?" Ilinichna asked in astonishment.

"Why, just in case she gets out of hand and leaves home, and takes some of our property with her. It looks to me as if she wasn't spreading her wings for nothing. . . . It's clear she's found a young man for herself, and one of these fine days she'll be getting married."

"You may be right," Ilinichna agreed with a sigh. "She lives like any *Khokhol* on the outskirts of the village; nothing pleases her, everything's all wrong for her. . . . These days she's cut off from the rest of us, and, no matter how much you try, you can't stick a piece of bread back on the loaf again."

"There's no reason why we should try to stick her on again! You old fool, don't think of holding her back if she talks about it. Let her leave the house. I've had enough of having to handle her!" Pantaleimon climbed on to the wagon; as he called to the bullocks he ended: "She saves herself from work like a dog from flies, but she's always trying to get the best piece for herself and to have a good time. Now Piotra's gone, God rest his soul, we don't want to keep the likes of her in the family. She's not a woman, she's a sticky disease!"

The old people's assumptions were mistaken. Daria was not even thinking of getting another husband. She was not thinking of married life, she had another burden on her mind. . . .

All that day she was sociable and gay. Even the dispute over the money had no effect on her spirits. She spent a long time twisting and turning before the mirror, examining the medal from all angles; she dressed and redressed herself five times, to see which jacket the striped St. George ribbon most suited, and joked: "Now I ought to win some more crosses." Then she called Ilinichna into the best room, pushed two twenty-ruble notes into her palm and, pressing the old woman's knotted hand to her breast with her own burning hands, whispered: "That's for prayers for Piotra. Order masses for him, and boil some porridge to take to church for him."[1] She burst into tears. But a minute later, though her eyes were still glittering with tears, she was playing with Mishatka, flinging her silk holiday

[1] It was the custom to boil barley, rice, or other cereals with honey and currants, to take to church when memorial masses were to be said.

shawl over him, and laughing as though she had never wept and never known the salty taste of tears in all her life.

She grew even more gay when Dunia returned from the fields. She told how she had been given the medal and jokingly imitated the solemn tone in which the general had spoken. Then saucily, surreptitiously winking at Natalia, with a serious face she assured Dunia that soon she, Daria, an officer's widow awarded the Cross of St. George, was to be raised to officer's rank and appointed to the command of a company of elderly Cossacks.

Natalia sat mending the children's shirts and listening to Daria, suppressing a smile. But Dunia was completely bewildered, and asked, folding her hands imploringly:

"Daria! Daria dear! Don't tell stories, for Christ's sake! For now I really don't know when you're telling stories and when you're telling the truth. Tell me all about it seriously."

"Don't you believe me? Well, then you must be a stupid girl! I'm telling you the simple truth. The officers are all at the front, and who's going to teach the old men how to march and all the things you have to know when you're a soldier? You wait till they're put under my command, and then I'll handle them, the old devils! This is how I shall command them!" Daria closed the door leading to the kitchen, to make sure her father-in-law did not see her, then swiftly tucked the edge of her skirt between her legs and, seizing it from the back with one hand, her bare, shining calves gleaming, she marched about the best room, halted close to Dunia, and gave orders in a chesty voice:

"Old men, at-tention! Raise your heads higher! March in a circle to the left!"

Dunia could not control herself, and she burst into laughter, hiding her face in her hands. Through her laughter Natalia said:

"Oh, that's enough! No good will come of it!"

"So no good will come of it? And have you ever known any good in your life? If you don't let yourself go, you'll go mouldy in this house!"

But Daria's outburst of gaiety ended as suddenly as it had begun. Half an hour later she retired to her room, angrily tore the ill-boding medal from her breast, and flung it into the chest. Then, resting her cheeks on her hands, she sat a long time by the window. At night she slipped off somewhere or other and returned only after the first cockcrow.

After that she worked hard in the fields for four days.

The haying was in a sad way. There was a shortage of workers. Not more than four acres or so could be mowed in a day. The mown hay was soaked with rain, and that added to the work: the swaths had to be tossed and dried in the sun. Before they could be raked into cocks a heavy rain again fell and continued from nightfall till dawn with autumnal constancy. Then fine weather set in, an eastern wind blew, the mowing machines again began to clatter out in the steppe, a sweetish bitter scent of mildew came from the blackened cocks, the steppe was enveloped in haze, and the indistinct outlines of the guardian mounds, the bluish gaps of the ravines, and the green caps of the willows above the distant ponds emerged vaguely through the azure mist.

On the fourth day Daria made ready to go to the district centre straight from the fields. She announced her intention when she sat down in the field camp for the noonday break.

In a disgruntled, sneering tone Pantaleimon asked:

"Why all this hurry? Can't you wait till Sunday?"

"I've got business to do, and it won't wait."

"Not even one day?"

Through set teeth Daria answered:

"No."

"Well, if it's worrying you so much that you can't be the least bit patient, you go. But all the same, what is this urgent business you've got to see to? May we be informed?"

"If you know everything you'll die before your time."

As always, Daria did not mince her words, and, spitting with annoyance, Pantaleimon cut his questions short.

Next day, on her way back from the district centre, Daria turned aside to call at Tatarsk. Only Ilinichna and the children were at home. Mishatka was about to run up to his aunt, but she coldly pushed him away and asked her mother-in-law:

"Where's Natalia, Mother?"

"She's in the vegetable plot, watering the potatoes. What do you want her for? Has the old man sent for her? He isn't mad, is he? You tell him I said so."

"Nobody's sent for her; I had something I wanted to say to her."

"Did you come in on foot?"

"Yes."

"Will our folk be finished soon?"

"Tomorrow, probably."

"But wait a bit, where are you flying off to? Has the rain spoilt much of the hay?" the old woman questioned with importunity, following Daria as she went down the steps.

"No, not much. Well, I'm going, I haven't got time. . . ."

"Drop in on your way back from the garden, and pick up a shirt for the old man. Do you hear? . . ."

Daria pretended she had not heard and hurriedly made her way to the cattle-yard. By the landing-place at the river edge she halted and, half-closing her eyes, looked at the green expanse of the Don. The freshly humid air above the river struck a chill into her. She slowly made her way along the bank to the gardens.

Over the Don a wind was wandering, seagulls were wheeling. The water crawled lazily up the sloping bank. Enveloped in a transparent lilac haze, the chalky hills gleamed faintly beneath the sun, and the rain-washed forest on the farther bank showed youthfully and freshly green, as in early spring.

Daria removed her shoes from her aching feet, washed her legs, and sat a long time on the bank, on the burning shingle. Shading her eyes from the sun with her palm, she listened to the seagulls' yearning cries, to the measured lap, lap of the water. She was moved to tears at the stillness, at the heart-rending cries of the gulls; and the misfortune which had so unexpectedly come upon her seemed still more burdensome and bitter.

Natalia straightened her back with difficulty, leaned her mattock against the wattle fence, and, noticing Daria, went to meet her.

"Do you want me, Dasha?"

"I've come to you with my trouble. . . ."

They sat down side by side. Natalia took off her kerchief, tidied her hair, and glanced expectantly at Daria. She was amazed at the change which had occurred in Daria's face during the past few days:

her cheeks were sunken and grey, a deep frown knitted her forehead, there was a feverish, anxious glitter in her eyes.

"What's the matter with you? You've gone quite dark in the face," Natalia asked sympathetically.

"You'd go dark in my place." Daria forced a smile, then was silent. "Have you got much more to hoe?"

"I'll be finished by evening. But what has happened to you?"

Daria convulsively swallowed her spittle and answered hurriedly, in a dull voice:

"I'll tell you what. I'm ill. I've got—a filthy disease. . . . I caught it when I went on that last journey. . . . Some accursed officer gave it to me!"

"So you've paid for your pleasure!" Natalia clapped her hands in fear and distress.

"Yes, I've paid for it. . . . And there's nothing to be said, and nobody to complain of. . . . It's just my weakness. . . . The swine made up to me, soft-soaped me. . . . He had white teeth, but he was rotten at heart. . . . And now I'm finished!"

"Poor wretch! But now what? Now what are you going to do?" Natalia stared at Daria with dilated eyes, while Daria, gazing down at her feet, recovered her composure and went on more calmly:

"You see, even on the way back I began to notice things. At first I thought maybe it was just—you know yourself that women have all sorts of troubles. Last spring I lifted a sack of wheat from the ground, and it made me go three weeks over my period. Well, but afterwards I realized that it wasn't quite the same this time. . . . The signs appeared. . . . And yesterday I went to see the doctor at the district centre. I could have died with shame. . . . But it's all over now. . . . The good girl has got her reward!"

"You must get cured of it, only it's such a disgrace. They say that sort of disease can be cured."

"No, girl, you can't cure mine." Daria smiled wryly, and she lifted her burning eyes for the first time during the talk. "I've got syphilis, and there's no cure for that. Your nose drops off with that. . . . Like old Mother Andronokha—have you ever seen her?"

"Now what will you do?" Natalia asked in a weeping voice, and her eyes filled with tears.

Daria sat silent for a long time. She tore a convolvulus flower from the maize stalk around which it had entwined itself, and raised it close to her eyes. The tender, rosy-fringed trumpet of the tiny flower, so translucently light, almost imponderable, gave off a heavy, fleshy perfume of sun-drenched earth. Daria stared at it eagerly and curiously, as though she had never seen a common and insignificant convolvulus before, then carefully laid it on the wind-dried, crumbling earth and said:

"What shall I do, you ask? As I came back from the district centre I was thinking and planning all the way. . . . I'll lay hands on myself; that's what I'll do. It's a pity, but there seems to be no other way out. It doesn't matter if I do try to get cured, everybody in the village will find out; they'll all point their finger at me, they'll all turn their backs and laugh. Who will want me in the state I am now? My beauty will fade, I shall wither completely, I shall rot alive. . . . And I don't want that!" She spoke as though she were discussing the question with herself and paid no heed to Natalia's gesture of protest. "Before I went to Vieshenska I thought that if I had got a filthy disease I'd get cured. And that's why I didn't give Father the money; I thought it would come in useful to pay the doctors. . . . But now I've changed my mind. And I'm fed up with it all. I don't want to get cured."

Daria swore a terrible, masculine oath, spat, and with the back of her hand wiped away a tear hanging on her long eyelashes.

"The things you're saying! You ought to be afraid of God . . ." Natalia said quietly.

"He—God—is no use to me now. As it is, He's got in my way all my life. . . ." Daria smiled; and in that smile, mischievous and crafty, for one second Natalia recognized the old Daria. "You couldn't do this, and you couldn't do that; everybody frightened you from sinning with talk of the Day of Judgment. . . . But you couldn't think of anything more terrible than the judgment I'm going to carry out on myself. I'm fed up with it all, Natalia. Everybody's turned horrible. . . . It'll be easy for me to do away with myself. I've got nobody behind me or before me. And nobody to tear out of my heart. . . . But it's true!"

Natalia argued ardently, pleaded with Daria to think it over and to put the thought of suicide out of her mind. But Daria, who listened abstractedly at first, collected herself and angrily interrupted:

"Drop all that, Natalia! I haven't come here for you to talk me out of it and plead with me. I came to tell you about my trouble and to warn you that from today on, you mustn't let your children come near me. My disease is infectious, so the doctor says, and I've heard say it is myself, and I don't want them to catch it from me. Don't you see, stupid? And you tell the old woman, I haven't got courage enough. . . . But I—I'm not going to put my head in a noose at once, don't think that; there's plenty of time for that. . . . I'll live a little longer and enjoy myself in the world, taking my farewell of it. You know what we're like. So long as there's no tugging at our heart we go on blindly. . . . Look at the life I've lived. I've been sort of blind; but as I was coming back from Vieshenska along by the Don, and as I thought that soon I would have to leave all this, it was as though my eyes had been opened. I looked at the Don, and it was all rippling, and in the sunlight it was pure silver, and dancing so that it made the eyes smart to look at it. I turned all round and looked. . . . Lord, how beautiful it all was! And yet I'd never noticed it before. . . ." Daria smiled shamefacedly and was silent. She clenched her fists and, choking down the sobbing rising in her throat, began to speak again, in a still higher and more strained voice. "Already along the road I'd cried more than once. . . . As I came near the village I looked and saw the tiny children bathing in the river. . . . And as I looked at them my heart suddenly ached, and I burst into a bellow, like a fool. I lay a couple of hours on the sand. It's not easy for me if I stop to think. . . ."

She rose from the ground, shook out her skirt, and with a habitual movement adjusted the kerchief on her head.

"The only joy I get when I think of death is that in the next world I shall see Piotra again. . . . 'Well!' I shall say, 'my old friend, Piotra Pantalievich, take back your wanton wife.'" With her customary cynical facetiousness she added: "But he won't be able to beat me in that world; they don't let quarrelsome ones into heaven, do they? Well, good-bye, Natalia dear! Don't forget to tell Mother about my trouble."

Natalia sat covering her eyes with her slender, dirty palms. Between her fingers tears glittered like resin in splinters of pine. Daria reached the plaited wattle gate, then turned and said in a businesslike tone:

"From today on I shall eat from separate dishes. Tell Mother so. Oh, yes, and one other thing: tell her she's not to say anything to

Father about it, or the old man will go mad and turn me out of the house. And that would be the last straw. I'm going straight out to the mowing now. Good-bye!"

The mowers returned from the steppe next day. Pantaleimon decided to start carting in the hay after dinner. Dunia drove the bullocks down to the Don for water, and Ilinichna and Natalia swiftly laid the table.

Daria came last to the table and sat down at the end. Ilinichna set a small plate of cabbage soup before her, put a spoon and a piece of bread before her, and, as usual, poured the soup for the others into the one large, common bowl.

Pantaleimon stared at his wife in surprise, indicated Daria's plate with his eyes, and asked:

"What's all that? Why have you poured out her soup separate? Isn't she any longer of our faith?"

"What ever do you want? Get on with your food!"

The old man gave Daria a humorous look and smiled. "Aha! I understand! Since she's been given a medal she doesn't want to eat out of the common dish. What's the matter, Daria? Turning up your nose at supping out of the one bowl with us?"

"No, I'm not turning up my nose. I mustn't," Daria huskily answered.

"And why not?"

"My throat hurts."

"Well, and what of it?"

"I went to Vieshenska to see the doctor, and he said I was to eat out of a separate dish."

"I had a sore throat once, but I didn't keep away from everybody else, and, glory be, I didn't give it to anybody else. So what sort of chill have you got?"

Daria turned pale, rubbed her lips with her palm, and laid down her spoon. Angered by her husband's importunity, Ilinichna shouted at him:

"What are you plaguing the woman for? We get no peace from you even at the table! He sticks like a bur, and there's no getting away from him!"

"But what's all the fuss about?" Pantaleimon barked irritably. "For all I care, you can do what you like!"

In his annoyance he poured a spoonful of hot soup into his throat, burned himself, and, spitting out the soup all over his beard, roared madly:

"You don't know how to serve up food properly, curse the lot of you! Who ever serves up soup straight from the fire?"

"If you were to talk less at the table the soup wouldn't burn you," Ilinichna consoled him.

Dunia almost burst into laughter as she watched her father, his face a vivid purple, collect the cabbage and pieces of potato out of his beard. But everybody else was so straight-faced that she refrained and turned her eyes away, for fear of laughing at an awkward moment.

After dinner the old man and both his daughters-in-law drove off to bring in the hay. Pantaleimon passed the hay on a long pitchfork up to the wagon, while Natalia took the fusty-smelling pile and trod it down. She and Daria returned from the fields together. Pantaleimon had driven on far ahead with his old, long-striding bullocks.

The sun was setting behind the mound. The bitter wormwood scent arising from the mowed steppe grew stronger towards evening, yet at the same time it grew milder, more pleasant, and lost the choking pungency it had had during the day. The heat was declining. The bullocks moved willingly and, thrown up by their hoofs, the heavy dust of the summer track rose and settled on the clumps of wayside thistles. The thistle heads with their spreading raspberry crowns flamed brilliantly. Over them the bees were hovering. Lapwings flew off to the distant steppe pond, calling to one another as they went.

Daria lay face downward on the swaying wagon, resting on her elbows, occasionally glancing at Natalia. Lost in thought, Natalia was gazing at the sunset; coppery crimson lights roved over her calm, clear face. "But Natalia's happy; she's got a husband and children, there's nothing more she wants. Everybody in the family loves her. But as for me, I'm finished. When I die nobody will shed a tear." As Daria thought enviously of her sister-in-law she suddenly felt a desire stirring within her to embitter Natalia somehow, to cause her pain. Why had she, Daria, got to be the only one to struggle with attacks of despair, to think incessantly of her ruined life and suffer so cruelly? She took another swift glance at Natalia and said in a tone which she tried to make sound sincere:

"I want to make a confession to you, Natalia."

Natalia did not reply at once. Gazing at the sunset, she was recalling that day long ago when she was still Gregor's betrothed, and he had come to her home to see her. When he left she had gone out to the gate to see him off. That day also the sunset had flamed, a raspberry-coloured afterglow had spread in the west, and the rooks had been calling in the willows. Gregor had ridden away half-turned in his saddle, and she had gazed after him through tears of joyous agitation and, pressing her hands to her pointed, virgin breasts, had felt the violent beating of her heart. . . . She was not pleased when Daria suddenly broke the silence, and she reluctantly asked:

"Why, what have you got to confess?"

"I've committed a sin. . . . Do you remember when Gregor came home from the front on leave? On the evening of that day, I remember, I was milking the cow. As I went to the hut I heard Aksinia calling me. Well, she called me over and gave me this little ring, simply forced it on me"—Daria turned the gold ring on her ring-finger—"and coaxed me into sending Gregor to her. Well, it was none of my business. . . . And I told him. All that night he . . . Do you remember he said Kudynov had come and he had sat talking with him? It was all nonsense! He was with Aksinia."

Natalia sat benumbed, whitefaced, silently breaking a dry piece of clover in her hands.

"Don't be angry with me, Natasha. I'm sorry now that I told you," Daria said humbly, trying to look into Natalia's eyes.

Natalia silently choked back her tears. So unexpected and oppressive was the sorrow which had again come upon her that she had no strength to answer Daria and only turned away to hide her distorted face.

As they drove into the village Daria thought in her vexation with herself: "The devil must have egged me on to peck at her! Now she'll stream with tears for a whole month! I should have let her go on

without knowing. It's better for such cows to live in their blindness."
Desiring to soften the impression her words had made, she said:

"But don't you be too upset. What is that to sigh about? My
trouble is heavier than yours, but I keep my chin up. And the devil
knows—after all, he might not have been with her at all in reality,
but did go to see Kudynov. I didn't follow him. And if you're not
caught you're not a thief."

"I guessed where he'd gone," Natalia said quietly, wiping her
eyes with the corner of her kerchief.

"But if you guessed, why didn't you ask him about it? Ah, you
good-for-nothing! He wouldn't have wriggled away from me! I'd
have got him into such a corner that he'd have felt sick!"

"I was afraid to know the truth. . . . Do you think it's easy to
bear?" Natalia said, stammering with emotion. Her eyes flashed.
"You might have—lived like that with Piotra. . . . But when I remember—when I remember all I've had to—had to go through—it's
terrible to bear even now."

"Well, then, forget it all!" Daria naïvely counselled her.

"That's not the sort of thing you ever forget!" Natalia exclaimed
in a queer, husky voice.

"I'd forget it! A lot of fuss over nothing!"

"You forget your disease!"

Daria burst into a laugh.

"I'd be delighted to, but it won't let me, curse it! Listen, Natasha;
if you like I'll find it all out from Aksinia. She'll tell me. God punish
me! There isn't a woman alive who could keep quiet and not tell
others who loves her and how. I know from my own case."

"I don't want your service! You've already done me one service!"
Natalia dryly answered. "I'm not blind, I know why you told me
all about it. It wasn't because you were sorry for me that you confessed, as you pretended, but because you wanted to see me more
unhappy. . . ."

"You're right," Daria assented with a sigh. "But you judge for
yourself: I'm not the only one who ought to suffer, am I?"

She slipped down from the wagon, took the bullock-rein in her
hand, and led the wearily shambling animals down the hill. At the
entrance to their lane she went up to the wagon and said:

"Natalia dear, there's one thing I want to ask you. . . . Do you
love your man very much?"

"As best I can," Natalia answered indefinitely.

"So you do!" Daria sighed. "But I've never happened to love anyone very much. I've loved as a dog loves, just anyhow, as it came along. . . . If I had to live my life over again, I'd be different, too."

The black night followed the short summer gloaming. They stacked the hay in the yard in the darkness. The women worked without talking, and Daria made no retort even when Pantaleimon shouted at her.

Chapter 5

Vigorously pursuing the enemy as they fell back from Ust-Miedvieditsa, the united forces of the Don army and the upper Don insurgents moved northward. At Shashkin the broken regiments of the Ninth Red Army attempted to hold up the Cossacks, but they were driven out of their positions and again retreated almost to the Tsaritsyn railway, without making any resolute stand.

Gregor with his division took part in the battle and rendered considerable assistance to General Sutulov's brigade, which was attacked from the flank. Yermakov's mounted regiment, which Gregor ordered into the attack, captured some two hundred Red Army men, four machine-guns, and eleven ammunition wagons.

Late in the afternoon Gregor rode into Shashkin with a group of Cossacks belonging to the 1st Regiment. Close to the house occupied by the divisional staff a dense crowd of prisoners, glimmering white in their cotton shirts and pants, were guarded by half a company of Cossacks. The majority of the prisoners had been relieved of their boots and had been undressed down to their underclothing, and only here and there a dirty khaki tunic showed a greenish hue among the general whiteness of the crowd.

"Why, they've gone as white as geese!" Prokhor Zykov exclaimed, pointing to the prisoners.

Gregor pulled on the reins and turned his horse sideways. Seeking out Yermakov in the crowd of Cossacks, he called him across:

"Ride closer; what are you burying yourself behind other men's backs for?"

Coughing into his fist, Yermakov rode up. Blood was caked under his meagre black moustache, on his crushed lips; his right cheek was swollen and going blue with fresh abrasions. During the attack his horse had stumbled and fallen under him in full gallop; flying like a stone a good fifteen feet, Yermakov had slid on his belly over the hummocky ground of a cornfield left fallow for the season. He and the horse jumped to their feet simultaneously. And a minute later Yermakov was in the saddle again. Capless, with blood streaming from him, but with his bared sabre in his hand he flew to overtake the flood of Cossack cavalry streaming down the slope.

"And why should I bury myself?" he asked with apparent surprise as he drew level with Gregor. His eyes were still aflame with the light of battle and suffused with blood. But he averted his gaze in embarrassment.

"The cat knows whose meat she's eaten! What are you riding behind me for?" Gregor asked angrily.

"What meat are you talking about? Don't ask me your riddles now, I shan't guess them in any case. I fell off my horse head-first today. . . ."

"Is that your work?" Gregor pointed at the prisoners with his whip.

Yermakov pretended that he had not noticed them before and assumed a boundless astonishment:

"Well, the sons of bitches! The damned rogues! They've stripped them! But when did they manage to do that? You wouldn't believe it! Why, I only left them a minute ago, after giving strict orders that they were not to be touched. And now look at them! They've stripped the poor devils clean!"

"Don't try to pull the wool over my eyes! What are you acting for? Did you give orders to undress them?"

"God forbid! Are you in your senses, Gregor Pantalievich?"

"Do you remember my command?"

"You mean in regard to—"

"Yes, in regard to that!"

"Why, of course I remember. I remember it by heart. Like the poetry we used to learn at school."

Gregor involuntarily smiled. Leaning across his saddle, he seized

Yermakov by the strap of his sword-belt. He was very fond of this
daring, desperately brave commander.

"Kharlampy, no wriggling! Why did you allow it? The new
colonel they've put in the staff in place of Kopylov will report it,
and you'll have to answer for it. You won't be so glad when you're
facing the music and it's nothing but questions and cross-examina-
tions."

"I couldn't stand it, Pantalievich!" Yermakov answered seriously
and simply. "They were all dressed up like new pins, they'd been
issued new clothing in Ust-Miedvieditsa, while my lads were going
short; they haven't got much even at home. And they'd have been
stripped when they got to the rear in any case. Have we got to
capture them for the rear rats to strip them? No, better that our
men should have the use of the clothing. I shall answer for it, but
they won't get much change out of me! And don't you come down
on me! I know nothing about it and wasn't responsible even in my
sleep!"

They drew level with the crowd of prisoners. The low murmur
of talk died away. The men on the flanks made way for the horsemen, staring at them with sullen fear and anxious expectation. One
Red Army man recognized Gregor as a commander and went right
up to him, touching his stirrup with his hand:

"Comrade commander! Tell your Cossacks to return our greatcoats at any rate. Have that much pity on us! It's cold at night, and
we're absolutely naked, as you can see for yourself."

"I don't suppose you'll get frost-bite in the middle of summer, you
marmot!" Yermakov replied harshly. Pushing the man aside with
his horse, he turned to Gregor: "Don't you worry, I'll give orders
for them to be allowed some of the old clothing. Now stand away,
stand away, warriors! You should be killing the lice in your trousers
and not fighting Cossacks!"

In the staff room the captured company commander was being
examined. The new chief of staff, Colonel Andreyanov, was sitting
behind a table covered with ancient oilcloth. Andreyanov was an
elderly, snub-nosed man, with hair very grey at the temples and
with large, childishly prominent ears. The Red commander stood
in front of the table, a couple of paces away. The prisoner's state-

ments were being taken down by one of the staff officers, Captain Sulin, who had been assigned to the division with Andreyanov.

The Red commander, a tall, fiery-moustached man with lint-white hair cut so short that it bristled, stood with bare feet on the ochre-painted floor, shifting from foot to foot, occasionally giving the colonel a swift glance. The Cossacks had left him only his soldier's shirt of yellow, unbleached cotton, and in exchange for his own trousers had given him ragged and badly patched Cossack trousers with faded stripes. As Gregor went over to the table he saw the prisoner make a swift, awkward attempt to cover his naked body, pulling his trousers, torn at the seat, around him.

"The Orlov Provincial Military Commissariat, you say?" the colonel asked, swiftly glancing at the man over his spectacles. He lowered his eyes again and, half-closing them, turned to examining a document in his hands.

"Yes."

"In the autumn of last year?"

"At the end of the autumn."

"You're lying!"

"I'm telling the truth."

"I repeat that you are lying!"

The man shrugged his shoulders and said nothing. The colonel looked at Gregor and said, nodding contemptuously in the prisoner's direction:

"Here, come and admire! A former officer of the Imperial Army, but now, as you see, a Bolshevik. He's got caught, and now he wants to tell us that he was with the Reds by accident, that he was mobilized. He lies as naïvely and absurdly as a high-school girl and thinks we're going to believe him. But he hasn't got the courage to admit that he's been a traitor to his fatherland. . . . He's afraid, the scoundrel!"

Speaking with difficulty, the man said:

"I gather, colonel, that you've got sufficient courage to insult a prisoner."

"I don't talk to scoundrels!"

"But I've got to speak!"

"Be careful! Don't force me to insult you in a more active fashion!"

"That is easy enough for you in your position, and, most important of all, you run no risk in doing so!"

Gregor, who had not said a word, sat down at the table and looked with a sympathetic smile at the prisoner. The man was white with indignation. "He's made the colonel sit up!" Gregor thought with satisfaction, and felt a touch of malevolent joy as he looked at Andreyanov's fleshy, livid, nervously twitching cheeks.

Gregor had disliked his new chief of staff from the moment of their first meeting. Andreyanov was one of the class of officers who had not seen the front at all during the World War, but had prudently remained in the rear, pulling strings with influential official and family connections, and clinging with all his strength to a safe post. Even during the civil war he had been clever enough to get work in the rear, at Novocherkass, and he was forced to go to the front only after Ataman Krasnov had been removed from power.

During the two nights Gregor and Andreyanov had been quartered together, Gregor had learned from the officer's own lips that he was very devout, that he could not speak of divine worship without tears in his eyes, that he had the most exemplary wife imaginable, that her name was Sofia Alexandrovna and the deputy ataman von Grabbe himself had once unsuccessfully paid court to her. The colonel had added many fond details of the estate his dead father had possessed, of his own struggle to reach the rank of colonel, of the highly-placed personages with whom he had hunted in 1916. He had also informed Gregor that he regarded whist as the finest of all games, cognac distilled from cummin leaves as the most valuable of all drinks, and service in the military commissariat as the most profitable of all appointments.

Colonel Andreyanov shook at every near-by gunshot and would not ride a horse more than he could help, giving liver trouble as the reason. He showed continual anxiety to increase the number of the staff headquarters guard and could hardly conceal his dislike of the Cossacks, who, he said, had all been traitors in 1917. Since then he had hated all the "lower ranks" without discrimination. "Only the nobility can save Russia," he said, casually indicating that he also was of noble birth, and that the Andreyanov line was one of the oldest and most honourable in all the Don province.

Certainly his chief weakness was garrulity—that elderly, uncontrollable, terrible garrulity which afflicts the declining years of a certain class of talkative and unintelligent people who all their lives have been in the habit of passing superficial and facile judgments on everything and anything.

Gregor had met many a man of this kidney and had always disliked them intensely. He tried to avoid Andreyanov as much as possible and succeeded quite well during the day. But as soon as they halted for the night, Andreyanov sought him out, hurriedly asked: "Shall we share quarters for the night?" and, without waiting for a reply, began: "You say, my friend, that the Cossacks can't be relied on in infantry attacks, but when I was an officer attached to His Excellency's— Hey, someone out there bring in my trunk and bedding." Gregor lay on his back, closed his eyes, and listened, clenching his teeth. Then he disrespectfully turned his back on the indefatigable talker, covered his head with his greatcoat, and thought with dumb fury: "As soon as I get the order for my transfer, I'll hit him on the head with something heavy! Perhaps that'll rob him of speech for a week at any rate." "Are you asleep, divisional commander?" Andreyanov asked. "Yes, I'm asleep," Gregor answered in a muffled voice. "Excuse me, but I haven't finished yet." And the story was continued. As Gregor dozed off he thought: "They've sent me this parrot on purpose. Fitzhelaurov must have taken some step. Well, how can anyone serve with such a rotten apple?" And as he dropped off, he still heard the colonel's penetrating tenor voice sounding like a fine patter of rain on an iron roof. ✿

All this explains why Gregor felt such malevolent joy as he heard the captured Red commander ticking off the talkative chief of staff so neatly.

Andreyanov was silent for a good minute, sitting with eyes halfclosed. The long lobes of his protruding ears went a brilliant crimson; his white, puffy hand, with a massive gold ring on the indexfinger, trembled as it rested on the table.

"Listen, you mongrel," he said in a voice hoarse with agitation, "I didn't have you brought in front of me in order to indulge in repartee, don't forget that! Do you realize that, whatever happens, you can't get away with it?"

"I realize that perfectly."

"So much the better for you. In the last resort I don't care a damn whether you joined the Reds voluntarily or were mobilized. That doesn't matter; what does matter is that through a false conception of honour you are refusing to talk."

"Evidently you and I have a different conception of questions of honour. . . ."

"That's because you haven't any honour left, that's all!"

"Judging by the way you are treating me, I doubt whether you ever had any!"

"I take it you want to get to the end quickly!"

"Why should I try to drag it out? Don't try to frighten me; you can't do it!"

With trembling hands Andreyanov opened his cigarette-case, lit a cigarette, took a couple of hurried puffs, and turned again to the prisoner.

"So you refuse to answer the questions?"

"I've told you all about myself."

"Go to the devil! I'm not interested in your lousy personality. Please answer the following question: What reinforcements did you receive from the station of Serebryakovo?"

"I've told you I don't know."

"You do know!"

"Very good! If it pleases you, then I do know, but I shan't tell you!"

"I shall order you to be flogged with ramrods, and then you'll tell!"

"I doubt it!" The prisoner touched his moustache with his left hand and smiled confidently.

"Did the Kamishinsky regiment take part in this battle?"

"No."

"But your left flank was covered by cavalry: what regiment was it?"

"Give it a rest! I tell you once more that I shall not answer such questions."

"Take your choice: either you loosen your tongue this minute, you cur, or in ten minutes you'll be set against a wall! Well?"

In an unexpectedly high-pitched, youthful, ringing voice the prisoner answered:

"I've had enough of you, you old fool! You nitwit! If you'd fallen into my hands I wouldn't have cross-examined you like this. . . ."

Andreyanov turned pale and seized his pistol holster. Gregor unhurriedly rose and warningly raised his hand:

"Well, that's enough! You've had your chat, and that'll do. You're

both quick-tempered, I can see that. . . . You haven't managed to reach an agreement, but it doesn't matter, and there's nothing more to talk about. He's quite right to refuse to betray his own men. By God, he's fine! I never expected him to stand out like that."

"But allow me!" Andreyanov fumed, vainly trying to unbutton his holster.

"No, I won't allow you!" Gregor said cheerfully, going right up to the table and covering the prisoner with his body. "There's no point in killing a prisoner. Aren't you ashamed to go for a man in his position? Unarmed, a prisoner, not even left his clothes, and you're raising your hand—"

"Stand aside! That scoundrel's insulted me!" Andreyanov forcibly pushed Gregor away and pulled out his pistol.

The prisoner swiftly turned to face the window, shrugging his shoulders as though cold. Gregor watched the colonel with a smile as he gripped the rough revolver-butt in his palm, awkwardly flourished the weapon, then lowered the barrel and turned away.

"I don't want to soil my hands . . ." he said hoarsely, gaining his breath and licking his dry lips.

Making no attempt to restrain the laugh which gleamed under his moustache, Gregor said:

"You wouldn't have had to! If you look you'll see your pistol's unloaded. When I got up this morning I picked it up from the table and had a look at it. There wasn't a single bullet in it, and it can't have been cleaned for a couple of months. You don't take very good care of your personal equipment."

Andreyanov lowered his eyes, spun the revolver barrel with his fingers, and smiled:

"Damn it! But you're right. . . ."

Captain Sulin, who had been silently watching, a humorous smile on his lips, rolled up the statement he had been taking down, and said with a pleasant burr:

"I've told you more than once, Semion Polikarpovich, that you treat your weapons disgustingly. Today's example is one more proof that I'm right."

Andreyanov knitted his brows and shouted:

"Hey, anyone there of the lower ranks? Here!"

Two orderlies and the commander of the guard came in from the front room.

"Take him away!" Andreyanov nodded at the prisoner.

The man turned and faced Gregor, silently bowed to him, and went towards the door. Gregor had the impression that his lips parted in a hardly perceptible smile of gratitude under his fiery whiskers.

When the men's steps had died away, Andreyanov removed his spectacles with a weary gesture, carefully cleaned the lenses on a small piece of chamois leather, and said in a jaundiced tone:

"You defended that scum brilliantly, though that's a matter for your own conscience. But what do you mean by mentioning my pistol in his presence, putting me in an awkward position?"

"That isn't such a great misfortune," Gregor answered in a conciliatory tone.

"Maybe not, but all the same you shouldn't have done it. Though it's true I might have killed him. He's a loathsome type! I'd been struggling with him for half an hour before you arrived. It was terrible the way he lied and wriggled, giving obviously false information. And when I caught him at it, he flatly refused to speak at all. He said his officer's honour did not allow him to betray military secrets to the enemy. The son of a bitch didn't think of his officer's honour when he hired himself out to the Bolsheviks. . . . I suggest that we have him and two others of the command quietly shot. So far as getting the information we want is concerned, they're hopeless in any case. They're inveterate and incorrigible scoundrels, and so there's no point in sparing them. What do you think?"

"How did you find out that he was the company commander?" Gregor asked, instead of answering the question.

"One of his own Red Army men betrayed him."

"I suggest that we have that man shot and spare the commanders." Gregor shot a challenging look at Andreyanov.

The colonel shrugged his shoulders and smiled as one smiles at a bad joke.

"No, but seriously, what do you think?"

"Why, exactly what I said."

"Excuse me, but on what grounds?"

"On what grounds? On the grounds of maintaining discipline and order in the Russian Army. When we went to bed yesterday, you, colonel, talked very much to the point about the sort of order that must be introduced into the army when we've shattered the

Bolsheviks, in order to purge the youth of the Red infection. I completely agreed with you, do you remember?" Gregor stroked his moustache, watching the changing expression on the colonel's face, and went on judiciously: "But now what are you suggesting? That way you'll corrupt the men of the army. The soldiers will think they can betray their officers! That's a fine thing to teach them! But suppose we should happen to find ourselves in a similar situation, what then? Excuse me, but I don't agree with the idea."

"As you wish!" Andreyanov said coldly, staring closely at Gregor. He had heard that the insurgent commander had his own standard of morals and was a queer customer, but he had not expected anything like this from him. He only added: "We always have dealt with captured Red commanders like that, especially when they were former officers. Your idea is new to me. . . . And I don't quite understand your attitude in such a seemingly obvious matter."

"We killed them in battles if we had the chance, but we never shot prisoners without good reason," Gregor answered, turning livid.

"Good, then we'll send them to the rear," Andreyanov agreed. "Now here's another problem: some of the prisoners, mobilized peasants of Saratov province, have expressed the desire to fight in our ranks. Our 3rd Infantry Regiment is short by three hundred bayonets. Do you think it possible, after a careful selection, to assign some of the volunteer prisoners to it? We have got definite instructions on the subject from the army staff."

"I shan't take a single peasant into my command. Let the shortage be made up with Cossacks," Gregor flatly declared.

Andreyanov endeavoured to argue with him. "Listen, we won't quarrel," he said. "I understand your desire that the division should consist entirely of Cossacks, but necessity forces us not to turn up our noses even at prisoners. Even in the volunteer army certain regiments have been brought up to strength with prisoners."

"They can do as they like, but I refuse to accept peasants. We won't talk any more about it," Gregor snapped.

A little later he went out to give instructions concerning the dispatch of the prisoners to the rear. Over dinner Andreyanov said in a tone of some agitation:

"It's clear we're not going to work well together. . . ."

"That's just what I was thinking," Gregor answered unconcern-

edly. Ignoring Sulin's smile, he fished a piece of boiled mutton out
of his plate with his fingers and set to work to crunch the hard gristle
with such a wolfish appetite that Sulin frowned as though he had a
pain, and even closed his eyes for a second.

Two days later the pursuit of the retreating Red forces was taken
over by General Salnikov's detachment, and Gregor was urgently
summoned to the headquarters staff. After acquainting him with
the order issued by the commander of the Don army breaking up
and re-allocating the insurgent forces, the chief of staff, a handsome
elderly general, said without further preamble:

"During the partisan war against the Reds you commanded your
division very successfully. But now we cannot entrust you with a
regiment, far less a division. You've had no military education, and
in the present conditions of a widely extended front and with con-
temporary methods of waging war you are not capable of commanding a large military unit. Do you agree?"

"Yes," Gregor answered. "I was myself anxious to resign the command of the division."

"It is very satisfactory that you don't over-estimate your abilities.
That quality is very rarely found in young officers these days. Well,
then, by order of the commander of the front you are appointed
commander of the fourth squadron of the 19th Regiment. The
regiment is now on the march some fifteen miles from here, somewhere near the village of Vyaznikov. Report to the regiment today,
or tomorrow at the latest. I think you have something you want to
say?"

"I wanted to be assigned to the commissariat."

"That's impossible. You'll be needed at the front."

"In two wars I've received fourteen wounds and contusions."

"That is entirely without significance. You are young, you look
fit, and you can still fight. As for your wounds, how many officers
haven't got wounds to show? You can go. Good luck!"

Probably in order to forestall the dissatisfaction which was bound
to arise among the upper Don Cossacks when the insurgent army
as such was disbanded, immediately after the capture of Ust-Mied-

vieditsa many rank-and-file Cossacks who had distinguished themselves in the rising were made non-commissioned officers, the
sergeants were almost all raised to the rank of ensign, while the
officers who had taken part in the rising were also rewarded and
raised in rank. Gregor was not overlooked. He was awarded a
captaincy, and an army order mentioned his outstanding services in
the struggle against the Reds and expressed the gratitude of the
command.

The disbandment of the insurgent regiments was carried through
within a few days. The illiterate commanders of divisions and
regiments were replaced by generals and colonels, experienced
officers were appointed company commanders, the battery and staff
commands were completely changed, while the rank-and-file Cossacks were allocated to the various Don regiments, which had been
reduced far below their full complement during the battles on the
Donietz River.

Late in the afternoon Gregor assembled the Cossacks of his division, announced the disbandment of the insurgent army, and said
in farewell:

"Don't bear any grudge against me, brother Cossacks! We've
served together; necessity forced us to; but from today on we shall
be nursing our sorrows separately. The main thing is to take good
care of your heads and not to let the Reds make holes in them. Our
heads may be stupid, but there's no point in unnecessarily stopping
a bullet with them. We shall yet need them to think with, to do
some hard thinking about the next step. . . ."

The Cossacks listened in dejected silence. When he had finished
they all began to talk at once, in voices thick with agitation.

"So the old days are coming back again?"

"Where are we to go to now?"

"They're forcing the people to do as they wish, the swine!"

"We don't want to be disbanded! What's this new system they're
starting?"

"Well, boys, we've united to tread on our own necks!"

"The Excellencies are going to squeeze us again!"

"Hold on now! They'll be pulling out our joints for all they're
worth. . . ."

Gregor waited until there was silence, and said:

"It's no use your shouting your throats sore. The easy times when we could discuss orders and oppose the commanders are past. Disperse to your quarters and don't let your tongues wag so much or these days you'll find them getting you to field court martials and the punishment companies."

The Cossacks came up to him in troop order, shook hands with him, and said:

"Good-bye, Pantalievich! Don't think evil of us, either."

"It's not going to be easy for us to do our service under strangers."

"You shouldn't have let us go. You shouldn't have agreed to re-sign command of the division."

"We shall miss you, Melekhov. The new commanders may be more educated than you, but that won't make it any the lighter for us. It'll be heavier, that's the trouble."

But one Cossack, the squadron jester and wag, remarked:

"Don't you believe them, Gregor Pantalievich! Whether you serve with your own folk or under strangers it's all the same if your conscience doesn't agree with it."

That night Gregor sat drinking home-made vodka with Yermakov and the other Cossacks, and next morning he rode off with Prokhor Zykov to overtake the 19th Regiment.

Before he had had time to take over the squadron and to get properly acquainted with his men he was summoned to the regimental commander. It was early morning. Gregor inspected the horses, hung about, and reported half an hour later. He expected the strict regimental commander, a martinet to his officers, to pull him up. But the commander gave him a friendly welcome, asked: "Well, what do you think of your squadron? A fine lot, eh?" and, not waiting for an answer, staring past Gregor, went on:

"Well, my friend, I've got to communicate some very mournful news to you. . . . You've had a great misfortune at home. A tele-gram arrived last night from Vieshenska. I'm granting you a month's leave to arrange your family affairs. You can go at once."

"Give me the telegram," Gregor muttered, turning pale.

He took the folded sheet of paper, opened it, read it, crushed it in his suddenly sweating hand. With a little effort he regained his self-control, and he hardly stammered as he said:

"Well, I didn't expect that. I'd better go. Good-bye!"

"Don't forget to take your pass."

"Of course. Thanks, I shan't forget."

He strode into the porch, walking confidently and firmly, holding his sword steady as usual. But as he began to descend from the veranda he suddenly ceased to note the sound of his own steps, and felt as though a sharp pain had struck like a bayonet into his heart.

On the bottom step he stumbled. With his left hand he clutched at the rickety balustrade, while with his right he swiftly unbuttoned the collar of his tunic. For a minute he stood breathing deep and fast, but in that minute he seemed to grow drunk with his suffering, and when he tore his hand away from the balustrade and went to the wicket gate, where his horse was tethered, he walked heavily, swaying as he went.

Chapter 6

For several days after her talk with Daria, Natalia suffered as one does in sleep, when oppressed by a bad dream and helpless to awake. She sought a plausible excuse for visiting Prokhor Zykov's wife and trying to find out from her how Gregor had lived at Vieshenska during the retreat and whether he had seen Aksinia there or not. She wanted to be convinced of her husband's misdoings, for she both believed and disbelieved Daria's story.

It was late in the evening when she made her way to the Zykovs' yard, unconcernedly waving a switch. Her work finished for the day, Prokhor's wife was sitting by the gate.

"Hello, soldier's wife!" Natalia called. "Have you seen our calf?"

"Glory be, my dear! No, I haven't seen it."

"He's such a wanderer, curse him! He won't stay at home at all! I haven't any idea where to look for him."

"Stop and have a rest; he'll turn up. Would you like some sunflower seeds?"

Natalia went and sat down beside her. They fell into women's artless talk.

"Any news of your soldier?" Natalia inquired.

"Not a word. It's just as though the Antichrist had vanished into thin air. Has yours sent any news?"

"No. Grisha promised to write, but so far he hasn't sent one letter. They say our troops have got beyond Ust-Miedvieditsa, but I haven't heard anything else." Natalia shifted the conversation to talk of the recent retreat across the Don and cautiously began to ask how the soldiers had lived in Vieshenska and whether any of the village people had been there. Prokhor's crafty wife guessed what Natalia had come to see her about, and answered warily, curtly.

Her husband had told her all about Gregor, but although her tongue was itching to wag, she was afraid to say anything, remembering Prokhor's admonition: "You mark my words: if you say a word of what I've told you I'll put your head down on the chopping-block, pull your tongue out a yard, and chop it off. If any rumour of this reaches Gregor he'll kill me without thinking twice about it. And I'm fed up with you already, and we've not started to live yet, you understand? You're to be as silent as the grave. . . ."

"Your Prokhor didn't happen to see Aksinia Astakhova in Vieshenska?" Natalia asked outright, losing all patience.

"Why should he have seen her? Do you think he had time for that there? God's truth, I know nothing, Mironovna, and you mustn't even ask me about it. You can't get any sense out of my white-headed devil. The only words he knows are 'give' and 'take.'"

When Natalia left her she was even more vexed and agitated. But she could remain no longer in ignorance, and she was driven on to go and see Aksinia herself.

Living in neighbouring huts, they had met frequently of recent years. On such occasions they silently bowed to each other or sometimes exchanged a few remarks. The days when they had refused to greet each other and had exchanged hateful glances were gone; their mutual hostility had lost its original asperity, and when she went to see Aksinia, Natalia hoped she would not drive her away or talk of indifferent things, but would talk about Gregor. She was not mistaken in her expectation.

Making no attempt to hide her astonishment, Aksinia invited

Natalia into the best room, pulled the curtains, lit the lamp, and
asked:

"What good has brought you here?"

"I have no cause to come with good to you. . . ."

"Your words sound bad. Has anything happened to Gregor Pantalievich?"

Such deep, unconcealed anxiety was there in Aksinia's question
that Natalia realized all. In one phrase Aksinia had revealed all
herself, all she lived for and all her fears. After that there was
essentially no point in asking about her relations with Gregor. Yet
Natalia did not go, and after a momentary hesitation she said:

"No, my husband's alive and well; don't be alarmed!"

"I'm not alarmed; what are you hinting at? It's for you to be
concerned about his health; I've troubles enough of my own."
Aksinia spoke easily, but, feeling the blood rushing to her face, she
swiftly went to the table. Standing with her back to her visitor,
she spent a long time adjusting the lamp wick, although it was
already burning quite well.

"Is there any news of your Stepan?"

"He sent me his greetings recently."

"Is he fit and well?"

"It seems so." Aksinia shrugged her shoulders.

Again she could not be false to herself or dissemble her feelings;
her unconcern for the fate of her husband was so obvious that
Natalia involuntarily smiled.

"I can see you don't worry very much about him. . . . But that's
your business. This is what I've come for: the silly story is going
round the village that Gregor's making up to you again, and that
you see him when he comes home. Is it true?"

"You've come to the right person to ask!" Aksinia said in a jeering
tone. "Suppose I ask you whether it's true?"

"Are you afraid to tell the truth?"

"No, I'm not."

"Then tell me, so that I know and don't go on tormenting myself.
Why should I get upset over nothing?"

Aksinia narrowed her eyes, then raised her brows.

"In any case you won't get any pity from me," she said sharply.
"It's like this between you and me: when I'm miserable, you're

glad; and when you're miserable, I'm glad. . . . For we share the same man, don't we? Well, I'll tell you the truth, so that you may know in good time. It's all true, they're not talking nonsense. I've won Gregor again, and this time I shall do my best not to let him slip out of my hands. And now what are you going to do? Smash the windows of my hut, or stab me with a knife?"

Natalia tied the flexible switch in her hand into a knot, threw it towards the stove, and answered with an unnatural firmness:

"I shall do no wrong to you now. I shall wait until Gregor comes back and have a talk with him. And then we shall see what I'm going to do about the pair of you. I've got two children, and I shall know how to stand up for them and for myself, too!"

Aksinia smiled and answered:

"So for the present I can live without fear of anything?"

Ignoring the sneer, Natalia went up to Aksinia and touched her by the sleeve.

"Aksinia, all my life you've stood in my way, but now I shall not plead as I did once before, you remember? Then I was younger, stupider; I thought: 'I'll plead with her and she'll have pity, she'll soften her heart and give Gregor up.' I shan't this time. One thing I know: you don't love him, you only hanker after him out of habit. Did you ever love him as I do? I doubt it. You played about with Listnitsky, and whom haven't you played about with, you wanton? When a woman loves a man she doesn't do that."

Aksinia turned pale; pushing Natalia away, she rose from the chest.

"He never reproached me with that. But you do! And what business is it of yours? All right! I'm bad and you're good. What then?"

"That's all. Don't be angry. I'm going now. Thank you for telling me the truth."

"Don't bother to thank me; you'd have found out without my help. Wait a bit; I'll come out with you and close the shutters."

In the porch Aksinia halted and said:

"I'm glad we part in peace, without a fight. But I tell you, dear neighbour, that so far as the future is concerned, it's going to be like this. If you've got the strength, take him; but if you haven't, don't be offended. I shan't willingly give him up any more than you will. I'm not so young now, and though you called me a wanton,

I'm not your Daria. In all my life I have never played about where such things are concerned. You have got children, but all the same to me he's—" Aksinia's voice quivered, and went huskier and deeper. "He's all I care for in the whole world. He's my first and my last. But let's not talk about him any more. If he comes through alive, if the Queen of Heaven saves him from death and he comes back, then he'll choose for himself. . . ."

That night Natalia could not sleep. Next morning she went with Ilinichna to weed the melons. She found things easier to bear when she was working. Her mind was not so occupied with the one thought as she steadily brought the hoe down to the clods of sandy, sun-dried, crumbling clay. Occasionally she straightened her back to rest, to wipe the sweat from her face and to take a drink.

White clouds, tousled and torn by the wind, were floating and melting across the blue sky. The rays of sunlight scorched the red-hot earth. Rain was approaching from the east. Without raising her head Natalia could feel when a flying cloud covered the sun. She felt a momentary coolness on her back; a grey shadow impetuously hurried over the brown, hot earth, over the tangle of watermelon tendrils. It covered the melons scattered over the slope, the grasses limp and flattened with the heat, the bushes of hawthorn and bramble with their dismal-looking foliage sprinkled with bird-droppings. The yearning cry of the quails grew louder, the pleasant song of the skylarks came more distinctly to the ear, and even the wind stirring the warm grasses seemed less sultry. But then the sun pierced the dazzling white selvage of the cloud as it floated westward and, freeing itself from its net, once more threw slanting, sparkling golden torrents of light down to the earth. Somewhere a long way off, over the azure spurs of the Donside hills, the shadow advancing with the cloud was still rummaging over and speckling the ground. But the amber-yellow noontide was again reigning in the melon-patches, the fluid haze quivered and danced on the horizon, the earth and its grasses smelled still more parched.

At noon Natalia went to a spring in the cliff and brought back a pitcher of icy water. She and Ilinichna drank their fill, washed their hands, and sat in the sunlight to eat their dinner. Ilinichna spread out a kerchief and neatly cut up bread on it. She took spoons and a cup out of the wallet and drew a narrow-necked ewer of sour milk from under her jacket, where she had hidden it away from the sun.

Natalia ate poorly, and her mother-in-law asked:

"I've noticed for some time that you've changed somehow. . . . Has anything gone wrong between you and Grisha?"

Natalia's weathered lips quivered miserably. "He's going with Aksinia again, Mother."

"What—how do you know?"

"I went to see her yesterday."

"And did she admit it, the hussy?"

"Yes."

Ilinichna was silent, thinking. Her lined face set sternly, the corners of her lips drew down grimly.

"Maybe she's only bragging, curse her."

"No, Mother, it's true. Why should she? . . ."

"You haven't kept your eye on him . . ." the old woman said tentatively. "You mustn't take your eyes off that sort of husband."

"But how can anyone keep her eyes on him? I relied on his conscience. . . . Had I got to tie him to my apron strings?" Natalia smiled bitterly, and added almost inaudibly: "He's not Mishatka, to be kept in check like a child. He's gone grey quite a lot, but he doesn't forget the past. . . ."

Ilinichna washed and wiped the spoons, rinsed out the cup, collected the utensils in the bag, and only then asked:

"Is that all the trouble?"

"You are strange, Mother! That one trouble's enough to make life miserable."

"And what are you thinking of doing?"

"What is there I can do? I'll take the children and go to my own people. I shan't live with him any longer. Let him take her into his home and live with her. . . . I've been tortured enough already."

"I thought like that, too, when I was young," Ilinichna said with a sigh. "My man was a dog, too, there's no gainsaying it. I couldn't tell you all I suffered through him. Only it isn't easy to leave your own husband; and besides, what's the use of it? You think it out a bit more and you'll see that for yourself. And how can you take the children away from their father? No, you're talking nonsense.

You're not even to think of it; I shan't allow it!"

"Well, Mother, I shan't live with him, so don't waste your breath."

"What do you mean by 'don't waste your breath'?" Ilinichna took offence at the remark. "Aren't you my daughter, then, or what? Am I sorry for the accursed pair of you or not? And you can say such things to me, to your mother, to an old woman? I've told you to put it right out of your head, and that's enough! Pah! you think: 'I'll leave home.' But where will you go? Who of your own people wants you? You've got no father, your house is burned down, your own mother is glad to Christ to live in someone else's hut. And yet you're going off to her and drag my grandchildren with you? No, my dear, that won't do! We'll see what to do with Grishka when he comes back; but now you're not even to talk to me about it. I won't have it, and I don't want to hear another word about it!"

All the pain that had been accumulating for so long in Natalia's heart suddenly broke out in a convulsive fit of sobbing. With a groan she tore the kerchief from her head, fell face downward on the dry, ungracious earth, and, pressing her breast to the ground, sobbed on and on without ceasing.

Ilinichna—wise and brave old woman—did not even stir from where she was sitting. After a while she carefully wrapped the ewer with the rest of the milk in it in the jacket, laid it aside in a cool spot, then poured water into the cup and sat down beside Natalia. She knew that words were of no help in such sorrow; she knew, too, that tears were better than dry eyes and firmly pressed lips. She let Natalia weep till she could weep no more, then laid her work-worn hand on her daughter-in-law's head. Stroking the black, lustrous hair, she said harshly:

"Well, that's enough! Don't use up all your tears, leave some for another time. Here, take a drink of water."

Natalia quieted down. Her shoulders still heaved occasionally and a fine trembling possessed her body. Unexpectedly she jumped up, pushed Ilinichna aside, and turning her face eastward, putting her tear-stained palms together in prayer, hurriedly, sobbingly screamed:

"Lord! He's tortured my soul to death! I haven't the strength to go on living like this. Lord, punish him, curse him! Strike him dead! May he live no longer, torture me no longer!"

A black, rolling cloud crawled onward from the east. Thunder rumbled hollowly. Piercing the precipitous cloudy masses, a burning white lightning writhed and slipped over the sky. The wind bent the murmuring grass westward, sent a pungent dust flying up from the track, bowed the sunflower caps with their burden of seeds almost to the ground. It tousled Natalia's dishevelled hair, dried her wet face, wound the edge of her grey workaday skirt around her legs.

Ilinichna stood for several seconds staring at her daughter-in-law in superstitious horror. Against the background of the black thunder-cloud which had climbed to the zenith Natalia seemed a strange and terrible creature.

The rain came upon them impetuously. The calm before the thunder-storm lasted only a moment. Dropping obliquely, a sparrow-hawk began to cry anxiously, a marmot whistled a last time close to its burrow, the violent wind threw a fine sandy dust into Ilinichna's face and went howling over the steppe. The old woman struggled to her feet. Her face was deathly pale as, through the roar of the approaching storm, she shouted:

"What are you saying? God help you! Whose death are you calling for?"

"Lord, punish him! Punish him, Lord!" Natalia screamed, fixing her frenzied eyes on the majestically and wildly gathering clouds, piled into masses by the wind, lit up by blinding flashes of lightning.

The thunder broke with a dry crash over the steppe. Beside herself with fear, Ilinichna crossed herself, went with uncertain steps to Natalia, and seized her shoulder.

"Go down on your knees! Do you hear, Natalia?"

Natalia looked at her mother-in-law with unseeing eyes and helplessly sank to her knees.

"Ask God for His forgiveness!" Ilinichna authoritatively ordered. "Ask Him not to accept your prayer. Whose death are you asking for? The father of your own children? Oh, it's a mortal sin. . . . Cross yourself! Bow yourself down to the ground! Say: 'Lord, forgive me my wickedness, sinful that I am.'"

Natalia crossed herself, whispered something with white lips, and, clenching her teeth, awkwardly fell over on her side.

Washed by the downpour, the steppe turned astonishingly green. A brilliant arching rainbow was flung from the distant pond right to the Don. The thunder was still rumbling hollowly in the west. Muddy hill water was pouring and gurgling along the runnel. Foaming rills streamed down to the Don over the slope, over the melon plots, carrying with them leaves torn away by the rain, grass washed by its roots out of the soil, broken ears of rye. Oily, sandy alluvium crawled over the melon plots, piling against the melon and watermelon tendrils. Along the summer tracks flowed the rejoicing water, washing out deep ruts. A stack of hay, set on fire by lightning, was burning out on a spur of a distant ravine. The lilac column of smoke rose high, almost touching the crest of the rainbow arching over the sky.

Setting their bare feet cautiously on the dirty, slippery road, lifting high their skirts, Ilinichna and Natalia made their way down to the village. As they went, Ilinichna said:

"You're terribly touchy, you youngsters, God's truth! The least thing and you go into a frenzy. If you'd lived as I had to live when I was young, then what would you have done? All his life Grisha hasn't raised a finger against you, and still you're not satisfied, but you must go and carry on like that. You were all ready to throw him over, and you go off into a fit, and I don't know what you didn't do. You even brought God into your dirty business. . . . Well, tell me, my sick child, is that good? But when I was young my game-legged idol used to thrash me almost to death, and that all for nothing, all over nothing. I hadn't done the least thing to deserve it. He himself behaved abominably, but he worked his temper off on me. He used to come home at dawn, and I would scream and cry bitterly, fling reproaches at him, and he would give his fist its sweet will. . . . For a month I'd go about as blue as iron all over, and yet I lived through it and brought up the children, and not once did I try to clear out. I'm not going to crack up Grishka, but you can at least live with a man like that. If it hadn't been for that snake he'd have been the foremost Cossack in the village. She's bewitched him, no less."

Natalia walked along for some time silently turning over something in her mind, then said:

"I don't want to talk about it any more, Mother. When Gregor comes back, then we'll see what I'm to do. Maybe I'll clear out of my own choice, or maybe he'll turn me out. But for the present I shan't leave your house to go anywhere else."

"Now, you should have said that long ago!" Ilinichna rejoiced. "God grant everything will work out for the best. He wouldn't turn you out for anything, and you're not to think of it! He loves both you and the children so much, do you think he'd ever hear of it? Never! He won't forsake you for Aksinia; he can't do that! And there are quarrels even in the best of families! So long as he comes back alive. . . ."

"I don't want him to die. I said that in my temper. Don't throw that up in my face. . . . I can't turn him out of my heart, but all the same, life is heavy enough."

"My dear, my own one! Don't you think I know? Only you never ought to do anything in a rush. Let's drop all the talk about it. And for God's sake don't say anything to the old man about it. It's nothing to do with him."

"There's one thing I must tell you. . . . It isn't clear at the moment whether I shall live with Gregor or not. But I don't want to have any more children by him. Even with the two I've got it's not certain where I may have to go. . . . But I'm already carrying another, Mother. . . ."

"Since when?"

"I'm in my third month."

"But how can you get away from that? You've got to bear the child whether you want to or not."

"I won't!" Natalia said resolutely. "I'm going this very day to see old Mother Kapitonovna. She'll rid me of it. . . . She's done it for other women."

"What, you'll kill the seed? And you can talk like that, you shameless hussy?" The indignant Ilinichna halted in the middle of the road and clapped her hands. She was about to say something more, but behind them there was a rattle of wheels, the sucking noise of horse-hoofs in the mud, and someone's shout to his horse.

Ilinichna and Natalia stepped off the road, letting their tucked-up skirts down as they went. Old Beskhlebnov was driving back from the fields, and as he drew level with them he reined in his spirited little mare.

"Climb in, women, and I'll take you home; you don't want to knead the mud for nothing."

"Thank you, Agievich; we're tired out with slipping about," Ilinichna said contentedly; she was the first to seat herself in the capacious wagon.

After dinner Ilinichna wanted to have a talk with Natalia, to explain to her that there was no reason why she should free herself of her pregnancy. As she washed up the dishes she mentally ran over the arguments which seemed to her to carry the most conviction, and even thought of telling Pantaleimon of Natalia's decision and calling in his aid to dissuade their grief-crazed daughter-in-law from her unwise step. But while she was dealing with domestic matters Natalia quietly got herself ready and left the house.

"Where's Natalia?" Ilinichna asked Dunia a little later.

"She collected a bundle and went out."

"Where to? What did she say? What sort of bundle?"

"Why, how should I know, Mother? She put a clean skirt and something else into a kerchief and went out without saying a word."

"Unhappy child!" To Dunia's amazement, Ilinichna helplessly burst into tears and sat down on the bench.

"What's the matter, Mother? God help you, what are you crying for?"

"Mind your own business, you impudence! It's nothing to do with you! But what did she say? And why didn't you tell me when she was getting ready?"

In a vexed tone Dunia answered:

"You're really quite impossible! Why, how was I to know I'd got to tell you? She hasn't gone for good, has she? She must have gone off to see her mother, and what you're crying for I haven't the least idea."

Ilinichna waited with the greatest anxiety for Natalia's return. Fearing her husband's reproaches and censure, she decided to say nothing to him about it.

At sunset the herd returned from the steppe. The short summer gloaming descended. Rare lights were lit in the village, but Natalia was still missing. The Melekhov family sat down to supper. Pale with agitation, Ilinichna served up the home-made vermicelli with its garnishing of onion fried in vegetable oil. The old man picked up his spoon, crushed crumbs of stale bread in it, poured them into his bearded mouth, and, abstractedly looking around at the others seated at the table, asked:

"Where's Natalia? Why don't you call her to the table?"

"She's out," Ilinichna replied in a low tone.

"Out where?"

"She must have gone to see her mother and decided to stay."

"She's staying a long time. She's old enough to know better . . ." Pantaleimon muttered discontentedly.

As always, he ate diligently, zealously; occasionally he laid his spoon down bottom upward on the table, took a sidelong, approving glance at Mishatka, who was sitting beside him, and said roughly: "Turn round a bit, my boy; let me wipe your lips. Your mother's a wanton, and there's no one to look after you. . . ." He wiped his grandson's tender, rosy little lips with his large, black, horny palm.

They ate their meal in silence and rose from the table. Pantaleimon gave the order:

"Put out the light. We haven't got much oil, and there's no point in wasting it."

"Shall I bolt the door?" Ilinichna asked.

"Yes."

"But how about Natalia?"

"If she turns up, she'll knock. Maybe she'll go roaming till morning. She's gone in for the fashion, too, now! You shouldn't let her talk so much, you old hag! A fine idea, taking it into her head to go visiting at night. . . . I'll tell her so in the morning. She's following Daria's example. . . ."

Ilinichna lay down without undressing. For half an hour she lay sighing, silently turning over. She was about to get up and go to see Kapitonovna when she heard uncertain, shuffling steps under the window. She jumped up with an agility not common to one of her years, hurriedly ran out into the porch, and opened the door.

Natalia, as pale as death, clutching at the hand-rail, slowly came up the steps. The full moon brilliantly lit up her sunken face, her hollow eyes, her painfully knitted brows. As she walked she swayed like a seriously wounded animal, and wherever she set her feet she left a dark bloodstain.

Ilinichna silently put her arms around her and led her into the porch. Natalia leaned her back against the door and hoarsely whispered:

"Is everybody asleep? Mother, wipe up the blood behind me. . . . Look, I've left traces. . . ."

"What have you done to yourself?" Ilinichna half exclaimed, choking back her sobs.

Natalia tried to smile, but a miserable grimace distorted her face.

"Don't shout, Mother, or you'll wake the others up. . . . Well, I've rid myself. . . . Now I've got a quiet heart. . . . Only there's a lot of blood. It's pouring out of me as if I was a slaughtered animal. . . . Give me your hand, Mother. My head's swimming."

Ilinichna bolted the door; then, as though she were in a strange house, she rummaged a long time with a trembling hand and could not find the handle to the inner door in the darkness. Walking on tiptoe, she led Natalia into the large best room. She woke up Dunia and sent her out, called Daria, and lit the lamp.

The door leading to the kitchen was open, and through it came Pantaleimon's measured, mighty snore. Little Poliushka was sweetly smacking her lips and muttering something in her sleep. Deep is a child's untroubled, restful sleep!

While Ilinichna was puffing up the pillow and getting the bed ready, Natalia sat down on a bench and weakly laid her head on the edge of the table. Dunia wanted to come into the room, but Ilinichna harshly told her:

"Go away, you shameless hussy, and don't show yourself here! It's nothing for you to poke your nose into!"

Scowling, Daria took a wet rag and went into the porch. Natalia painfully raised her head and said:

"Take the clean bedding off the bed. . . . Spread a piece of sacking for me. . . . I'm sure to soil it. . . ."

"Hold your tongue!" Ilinichna ordered. "Undress and lie down! Do you feel bad? Shall I bring you some water?"

"I'm feeling terribly weak. . . . Bring me a clean shift and water. . . ."

With an effort Natalia rose and went with uncertain steps to the bed. Only then did Ilinichna notice that her skirt was soaked with blood and hanging heavily around her, clinging to her legs. She stared with horror as Natalia bent down and wrung out the edge of the skirt as though she had been out in the rain, then began to undress.

"But you're bleeding to death!" Ilinichna exclaimed.

Natalia undressed and closed her eyes, breathing spasmodically and quickly. The old woman took one glance at her and then, with a resolute air, marched into the kitchen. After a struggle she managed to arouse Pantaleimon and said:

"Natalia's ill. . . . She's very bad, she may be dying. . . . Harness up horses at once and drive to Vieshenska for the doctor."

"A devilish fine thing! What's happened to her? What's she ill with? She'd do better not to go roving at night. . . ."

The old woman briefly explained what had happened. Pantaleimon jumped out of bed in a frenzy and, buttoning up his trousers as he went, strode towards the best room.

"Ah, you filthy bitch! Ah, you daughter of a bitch! What have you been up to, eh? Necessity forced her to it! Well, I'll teach her. . . ."

"Are you mad, damn you? Where are you going? Don't go in there, she doesn't want you. . . . You'll wake the children up. Go out to the yard and harness the horses quickly!" Ilinichna tried to stop the old man. But, paying no attention to her, he went to the door of the best room and kicked it open.

"You've done a fine thing, you daughter of the devil!" he roared, halting on the threshold.

"You mustn't! Father, don't come in, for Christ's sake don't come in!" Natalia screamed piercingly. She had taken off her shift, and she pressed it to her breast.

Swearing violently, Pantaleimon looked for his coat, his cap, the harness. He was so long over it that Dunia could not control herself. She burst into the kitchen and fell on her father, while the tears started to her eyes:

"Drive off at once! What are you rummaging about like a beetle in dung for? Natalia's dying, and he takes a whole hour to get ready! And he calls himself a father! If you don't want to go, why don't you say so? I'll harness up the horse myself and drive to Vieshenska."

"You're daft! What have you snapped your chain for? Who's going to take orders from you, you sticky scab? Here's another of them shouting at her father, the filth!" Pantaleimon threw his coat edges together defiantly and, muttering curses under his breath, went out into the yard.

After his departure everybody in the house felt less constrained. Daria washed the floor, ruthlessly shifting chairs and benches. Ilinichna allowed Dunia into the best room, and the girl sat at Natalia's head, smoothing the pillow, giving her water. Ilinichna occasionally stole in to the children sleeping in the side room; then, returning to the best room, she gazed at Natalia, resting her cheek on her palm, shaking her head bitterly.

Natalia lay silent; her head with its tangled skeins of dank, sweat-soaked hair rolled about the pillow. Every half-hour Ilinichna gently lifted her, drew away the saturated bedding, and spread clean linen.

With every hour Natalia grew weaker. Some time after midnight she opened her eyes and asked:

"Will it begin to get light soon?"

"No sign as yet," the old woman soothed her, thinking to herself: "That means she isn't going to come through. She's afraid of going without seeing the children. . . ."

As though to confirm her guess, Natalia quietly asked:

"Mother, wake up Mishatka and Poliushka. . . ."

"What for, my dear? What do you want to disturb them in the middle of the night for? They'll be terrified if they see you, and they'll start crying. . . . Why wake them up?"

"I'd like to see them. . . . I'm feeling bad."

"God have mercy. . . . What are you saying? In a minute father will be bringing the doctor, and he'll help you. You ought to try to get some sleep, my dear, don't you think?"

"What sleep can I get?" Natalia answered with a hint of annoyance in her tone. After that she said no more for some time, and her breathing grew more regular.

Ilinichna quietly stole out onto the steps and gave way to her tears. She returned with a red and swollen face to the room when the dawn was beginning to show a faint glimmer in the east. As the door creaked, Natalia opened her eyes and asked again:

"Will it be getting light soon?"

"It's dawning now."

"Cover my feet with a sheepskin."

Dunia threw a sheepskin over her feet and tucked in the warm blanket at the sides. Natalia thanked her with a look, then called Ilinichna closer and said:

"Sit down by me, Mother, and you, Dunia and Daria, go out for a while. I want to talk to Mother alone. . . . Have they gone?" she asked, without opening her eyes.

"Yes."

"Father hasn't come back yet?"

"He'll be back soon. Are you feeling worse, then?"

"No; it doesn't matter. . . . This is what I wanted to say. Mother, I'm going to die soon. I can feel it in my heart. I've lost so much blood, it's terrible! Tell Daria when she lights the stove to put on plenty of water. . . . You wash me yourselves; I don't want strange . . ."

"Natalia! Cross yourself, darling! What are you talking about death for? God is merciful; you'll get better."

With a feeble gesture Natalia asked her mother-in-law to be silent and said:

"Don't interrupt me. It's already hard enough for me to talk, and I want to say— My head's swimming again. . . . Have I told you about the water? But I must be strong. . . . Kapitonovna did it quite early, as soon as I arrived after supper. . . . She was terrified at what happened, poor woman. I lost an awful lot of blood. . . . If only I can live till morning. . . . Put on a lot of water. I want to be clean when I die. . . . Mother, dress me in my green skirt, the one with the embroidery around the edges. Grishka liked me in that one. . . . And my poplin jacket—it's in the chest at the top, in the right-hand corner, just under a shawl. . . . And when I die, they're to carry me to our people. . . . You might send for Mother; let her come at once. . . . I must say good-bye to her. Get the sheet from under me. It's all wet. . . ."

Raising Natalia with one arm behind her back, Ilinichna drew away the sheet and somehow managed to tuck another under her. With an effort Natalia whispered:

"Turn me over—on my side." And she lost consciousness.

The dove-grey dawn peered in at the window. Dunia washed a

bucket and went out into the yard to milk the cows. Ilinichna threw the window wide open, and the best room, heavy with the scent of fresh blood, the smell of burnt paraffin, was freshened with the sharp, cheering chill of the summer morning. The wind swept the teardrops of dew off the cherry leaves lying on the outside window-ledge; the early voices of birds, the lowing of cows, the thick, spasmodic cracks of the shepherd's whip came through the window.

Natalia came to, opened her eyes, licked her dry, bloodless, yellow lips with the end of her tongue, and asked for a drink. She no longer asked after the children or her mother. Everything was slipping away from her, and slipping away for ever.

Ilinichna closed the window and went across to the bed. How terribly Natalia had changed during this one night! The previous day she had been like a young apple tree in blossom—beautiful, healthy, strong; but now her cheeks were whiter than chalk from the Donside hills, her nose was peaked, her lips had lost their recent brilliant freshness, had grown thinner, and seemed to be shrinking back from her parted teeth. Only her eyes retained their former glitter, but their expression had changed. They had a new, strange, alarming look as from time to time, submitting to some inexplicable necessity, she raised her bluish lids and peered around the room, then rested her glance on Ilinichna for a second.

Pantaleimon returned at sunrise. The heavy-eyed doctor, weary with sleepless nights and endless bother with typhus and wounded cases, stretched himself and climbed out of the tarantass, took a bundle from the seat, and went into the hut. On the steps he removed his canvas raincoat, and, leaning over the hand-rail, spent a long time washing his hairy hands, looking up under his eyebrows at Dunia as she poured water from a jug into his palms, and even winking at her. Then he went into the best room and spent a good ten minutes with Natalia, first sending out everybody else.

Pantaleimon and Ilinichna sat down in the kitchen.

"Well, how is she?" the old man asked in a whisper as soon as they left the best room.

"Bad. . . ."

"Did she do it of her own will?"

"It was her own idea," Ilinichna evaded the question.

"Hot water, quick!" the doctor ordered, thrusting his tousled head round the door.

While the water was being heated he came into the kitchen. At the old man's mute question he waved his hand hopelessly:

"She'll be gone by dinner-time. She's lost a terrible quantity of blood. There's nothing to be done! Have you sent word to Gregor Pantalievich?"

Without answering, Pantaleimon hurriedly limped out into the porch. Daria saw the old man go under the eaves of the shed to the mowing machine, lean his head against a pile of old dung-fuel bricks, and weep aloud.

The doctor remained another half-hour and sat a little while on the steps, dozing under the rays of the rising sun. When the samovar began to boil he went back into the best room, gave Natalia a camphor injection, then came out and asked for some milk. Stifling a yawn, he drank two glasses of milk and said:

"Take me back at once. I've got sick and wounded waiting at Vieshenska, and there's nothing I can do here. It's quite hopeless. I'd do anything I could for Gregor Pantalievich, but I tell you frankly I can do nothing. There's little enough we can do at the best of times: we can only heal the sick; we haven't yet learned how to resurrect the dead. And your little woman has been so badly cut about that she's got nothing left to live with. . . . The womb's torn terribly, there's nothing of it left. I expect the old woman used an iron hook. It's our ignorance; you can't ever get away from it!"

Pantaleimon threw hay into the tarantass and told Daria:

"You drive him back. Don't forget to water the mare when you drop down to the Don."

He was about to offer the doctor money, but the man flatly refused it, shaming the old man with:

"You ought to be ashamed even to speak of it, Pantaleimon Prokoffievich! My own people, and you're offering me money! No, don't come near me with it. How can you repay me? You needn't ask. If I could put your daughter-in-law on her feet it would be a different matter."

About six o'clock in the morning Natalia felt considerably better. She asked for a wash, combed her hair before a mirror which Dunia held for her, and, looking around at her dear ones, her eyes glittering, she forced a smile.

"Well, now I'm on the mend! But I was really frightened! I thought I was done for. . . . But why are the children sleeping so late? Dunia, go and see if they're awake yet."

Her mother, Lukinichna, arrived with her younger sister, Aggripina. The old woman burst into tears when she saw her daughter, but Natalia said again and again in an agitated tone:

"What are you crying for, Mother? I'm not so bad now . . . you haven't come to bury me, have you? Oh, do tell me, what are you crying for?"

Aggripina gave her mother a nudge and, guessing the reason, Lukinichna swiftly wiped her eyes and said in a soothing tone:

"Why, what are you thinking, child? I was crying just because I've such a stupid head. My heart ached as I looked at you. You've changed so much. . . ."

A faint flush glowed in Natalia's cheeks when she heard Mishatka's voice and Poliushka's laugh.

"Bring them in here! Call them quick!" she asked. "They can dress after."

Poliushka came in first and halted at the door, rubbing her sleepy eyes with her little fist.

"Your mummy's fallen ill," Natalia said with a smile. "Come over to me, my treasure!"

Poliushka looked in surprise at the grown-ups sitting gravely on the benches and, going over to her mother, said in a vexed tone:

"Why didn't you wake me up? And what have they all come for?"

"They've come to see me. . . . But why should I have woke you up?"

"I'd have brought you some water and sat with you. . . ."

"Well, go and wash, comb your hair and say your prayers, and then you can come and sit with me. . . ."

"But will you be getting up for breakfast?"

"I don't know. I don't think so."

"Well, then I'll bring your breakfast in here. Would you like that, Mummy?"

"She's the very image of her father; only her heart's not like his, hers is softer . . ." Natalia said with a feeble smile, letting her head fall back and pulling the blanket around her legs as though she were cold.

An hour later she took a turn for the worse. She beckoned the children to her, embraced them, signed the cross over them, kissed them, and asked her mother to take them to her. Lukinichna entrusted the children to Aggripina and remained with her daughter.

Natalia closed her eyes and said, as though delirious:

"I can't see him like that. . . ." Then, as though she had remembered something, she sharply raised herself on the bed and asked: "Bring Mishatka back."

The tear-stained Aggripina pushed the boy into the room and remained, quietly moaning, in the kitchen.

Sullen, with the Melekhovs' ungracious look, Mishatka timidly came into the room. The sharp change which had occurred in his mother's face made her almost a stranger, unrecognizable. Natalia drew her son towards her and felt his heart fluttering swiftly, like that of a trapped sparrow.

"Bend down to me, little son! Closer!" she asked.

She whispered something into his ear, then pushed him away, questioningly gazed into his eyes, compressed her quivering lips, and, forcing a miserable, tormented smile, asked him:

"You won't forget? You'll tell him?"

"I shan't forget." Mishatka clutched his mother's forefinger, squeezed it in his hot little fist, held it tightly for a second, then let it go. As he stepped away from the bed, for some reason he walked on tiptoe, balancing himself with his arms.

Natalia watched him to the door, then silently turned to the wall. She died at noon.

Chapter 7

Innumerable were Gregor's thoughts and memories during the two days' journey from the front to his native village. Afraid to remain alone in the steppe with his grief, with his importunate thoughts of Natalia, he took Prokhor Zykov with him. As soon as they were clear of the village in which his squadron was quartered, Gregor turned to talking of the war, recalling how he had served in the 12th Regiment on the Austrian front, how they had marched into Rumania, how they had fought the Germans. He talked on and on without stopping, recalling all kinds of absurd incidents in which their comrades of the regiment had been involved, and laughing. . . .

At first, amazed at Gregor's unusual garrulity, the simple-minded Prokhor took astonished sidelong glances at him. But then he guessed that Gregor was trying to find relief from his oppressive thoughts in these memories of past days, and helped to keep the conversation going with perhaps unnecessary effort. As he was telling of the time he had spent in Chernigov Hospital, Prokhor happened to glance at Gregor and saw the tears streaming down his swarthy cheeks. Prokhor respectfully dropped back a few yards and rode behind for half an hour. Then he again drew level and tried to talk about some casual, insignificant matter. But Gregor did not take up the conversation. So they trotted along until noonday, in silence, side by side, stirrup to stirrup.

Gregor hurried along desperately. Despite the heat he kept his horse at a sharp trot, then broke into a gallop, and only occasionally slowed him down into a walking pace. He did not call a halt until noon, when the vertical rays of the sun began to burn intolerably. Then he stopped in a ravine and unsaddled his horse, turning him loose to graze. He went off into the shade, stretched himself face downward, and lay so until the heat began to abate. They gave the horses a feed of oats, but Gregor did not observe the proper feeding-time. By the end of the first day their horses, accustomed though they were to long marches, had deeply sunken flanks, and they no longer moved with the unwearying spirit of the morning. "It's stupid to spoil the horses," Prokhor thought irritably. "Who ever rides like this? It's all very well for him, the devil! He's forcing his own animal along and he can get himself another at any moment. But where could I get a mount? He'll gallop the horses to death, and then we'll have to go on foot all the rest of the way to Tatarsk, or else drag along on a requisitioned wagon."

Next morning he could keep silent no longer and at last said to Gregor:

"Anyone would think you'd never owned your own horse! Who ever would gallop like this, day and night, without a rest? Look how the horses are worn out! Let's give them a proper feed when evening comes, at any rate."

"Keep up, don't lag behind!" Gregor answered absent-mindedly.

"I can't keep up with you; my horse is dead beat. Couldn't we have a rest?"

Gregor did not answer. For half an hour they trotted along without exchanging a word, then Prokhor resolutely announced:

"Let's give them a breather at least! I'm not going to ride on any farther like this. Do you hear?"

"Whip him up! Whip him up!"

"But how long are we to go on whipping him up? Until he loses his hoofs?"

"Don't argue!"

"Have pity, Gregor Pantalievich! I don't want to flay my horse, but things are coming to such a pass—"

"Well, then, halt, and damn you! Look for a spot with good grass."

The telegram had been wandering in search of Gregor through all the districts of the Khopersk region, and it arrived too late. He reached home on the third day after Natalia was buried. He dismounted at the wicket gate. Dunia ran out of the house and burst into sobs. He put his arm around her as he strode along and asked, knitting his brows:

"Give the horse a good long walk. . . . Now, don't bellow!" Turning to Prokhor, he ordered: "Ride home! If you're wanted I'll let you know."

Holding Mishatka and Poliushka by the hands, Ilinichna came out to the steps to welcome her son.

Gregor snatched up the children in his arms and said in a quivering voice:

"Now, don't cry! Now, no tears! My darlings! So you're left motherless? Now, now. . . . Your mummy's done us an ill turn. . . ."

But he himself had difficulty in choking back his sobs as he went into the hut and greeted his father.

"We couldn't keep—" Pantaleimon said, and at once limped off into the porch.

Ilinichna led Gregor into the best room and told him about Natalia. The old woman did not want to tell all the truth, but Gregor asked:

"Why did she take it into her head not to have the child? Do you know?"

"Yes, I do."

"Well?"

"She had called on your—that . . . the previous day. And Aksinia told her everything."

"Aha! So that's it!" Gregor flushed heavily, and his eyes dropped.

He came out looking older, and pale; soundlessly working his bluish, quivering lips, he sat down at the table, fondled the children for some time, and seated them on his knees. Then he took out a piece of greyish, dusty sugar from his field-pack, broke it on his palm with a knife, and guiltily smiled. "That's all I've been able to bring you. . . . That's the sort of father you've got. . . . Well, run into the yard and call your grand-dad."

"Will you visit the grave?" Ilinichna asked him.

"Later, when I can get the chance. . . . The dead never take offence. . . . How are Mishatka and Poliushka? Are they all right?"

"They cried a lot the first day, especially Poliushka. . . . But now it's just as though they'd come to some agreement, and they never talk about her in front of us. But last night I heard Mishatka quietly crying. He'd put his head under the pillow so as not to be heard. . . . I went to him and asked: 'What's the matter, darling? Would you like to come and lie with me?' But he says: 'It's all right, Granny; I must have been crying in my sleep. . . .' You talk to them, have pity on them. Yesterday morning I heard them talking to each other in the porch. Poliushka was saying: 'She'll come back to us. She's young, and the young don't die.' They're still foolish, but their little hearts ache as though they were grown up. . . . I expect you're hungry. Sit down and I'll get something ready for you; what are you sitting dumb for?"

Gregor went into the best room. He behaved as though he had found his way there for the first time in his life: he looked attentively around the walls and rested his gaze on the bed. It had been made, and its pillows were puffed up. On that bed Natalia had died, from that bed her voice had sounded for the last time. He imagined her saying good-bye to the children, kissing them, and perhaps signing the cross over them. And once more, as at the moment when he had read the telegram telling of her death, he felt a sharp, stabbing pain in his heart, a muffled ringing in his ears.

Every little thing in the house reminded him of Natalia. His memories of her were indestructible and tormenting. For some reason he went from room to room, visiting them all, then hurriedly went out, almost ran on to the steps. The pain in his heart seared more and more. A sweat beaded his brow. Fearfully pressing his palm against his left breast, he went down the steps, thinking: "This old grey nag has galloped up a steep hill or two!"

Dunia was walking his horse about the yard. By the granary the horse resisted the rein and halted to snuff at the earth, stretching out its neck and rolling back its upper lip, laying bare the yellow plates of its teeth. Then it snorted and awkwardly bent its hind legs. Dunia pulled on the rein, but the animal paid no attention and began to lie down.

"Don't let him roll over!" Pantaleimon shouted from the stable. "Can't you see he's saddled? Why didn't you unsaddle him, you devilish little fool?"

Unhurriedly, still listening to the thumping in his chest, Gregor went up to the horse, removed the saddle, and forced a smile as he said to Dunia:

"Father still shouting?"

"As usual!" Dunia said with an answering smile.

"Lead him about a little longer, sister."

"He's quite dry now; but I will if you want me to."

"Let him have a roll if he likes, don't stop him."

"Now, now, brother. . . . Grieving?"

"And why shouldn't I?" Gregor answered with a sigh.

Moved by a feeling of compassion, Dunia kissed him on the shoulder and, upset to the point of tears, she swiftly turned and led the horse to the cattle-yard.

Gregor went across to his father, who was diligently raking dung out of the stable.

"I'm getting the place ready for your charger," the old man said.

"Why didn't you tell me? I'd have cleaned it out myself."

"A fine idea! Why, am I helpless? My boy, I'm like a flint lock; there's no wearing me out! I can still hop around a bit! Tomorrow I'm thinking of going out to sow the rye. Are you staying for long?"

"A month."

"Now, that's fine! Shall we drive out to the fields? You'll find it easier if you're working. . . ."

"I'd already thought of that myself."

The old man threw down the pitchfork, wiped the sweat from his face with his sleeve, and said in a mysterious tone:

"Let's go into the hut, and you have some dinner. You can never get away from it—sorrow, I mean. You can't run away from it and you can't bury yourself from it. That's how it is. . . ."

Ilinichna laid the table and gave Gregor a clean hand-towel. And yet again Gregor recalled: "In the old days Natalia waited on me." To hide his feelings he attacked the food vigorously. He gave his father a grateful look when the old man brought a ewer of home-made vodka, its neck closed by a bunch of hay, from the cellar.

"We'll drink in memory of the dead—may she rest in God!" Pantaleimon said in a firm tone.

They each drank a glass. Without waiting the old man filled the glasses again and sighed:

"Two of the family gone in one year. . . . Death's taken a fancy to our hut."

"Don't let's talk about that, Father!" Gregor asked.

He drank his second glass at one gulp, chewed long at a piece of dried fish, and waited for the drink to go to his head, to stifle his importunate thoughts.

"The rye's fine this year. And our sowings are far better than anybody else's!" Pantaleimon said boastfully. In that very boastfulness, in the very tone of his father's voice, Gregor detected a forced and studied note.

"But how about the wheat?"

"The wheat? It's been nipped a bit with the frost, but it's not too bad, it'll be a middling harvest. But the hard wheat—others have done well with that, but as luck would have it, we didn't happen to sow any. But I don't mind overmuch. With such destruction all around, what can you do with grain? You can't sell it, and you can't keep it in the bins. When the front comes back this way, the comrades will carry it all off, they'll lick it up. But don't you worry; even without this year's harvest we've got grain enough for a couple of years. Praise be, we've got our bins full to the lids, and some more elsewhere. . . ." The old man winked craftily and said: "You ask Daria how much we've buried against a rainy day! The hole's your height deep, and half as wide again as your arms outstretched, and we filled it to the edge! This accursed life has made us poor, but, after all, we've managed to look after ourselves, too. . . ." The old man laughed drunkenly, but after a moment he stroked his beard with dignity and said in a serious, businesslike tone: "Maybe you're thinking about your mother-in-law, so I tell you I haven't forgotten her, and I've helped them in their need. Before she had time to say a word I'd filled a wagon with grain, not stopping to measure it, and took it to her. Your dead Natalia was very pleased; she cried when she heard about it. . . . Shall we put away a third glass, son? You're the only joy left to me now."

"All right, pour it out!" Gregor assented, pushing his glass across the table.

At that moment Mishatka came up timidly, edging his way to the table. He climbed on to his father's knee and, awkwardly putting his left arm around Gregor's neck, gave him a hearty kiss on the lips.

"What's that for, little son?" Gregor asked, deeply moved. He looked into the child's tear-filled eyes and tried to avoid breathing vodka fumes into his son's face.

Mishatka answered in a low voice:

"When Mummy was lying in the best room . . . when she was still alive, she called me to her and told me: 'When your father comes, kiss him for me and tell him to have pity on you.' She said something else, too, but I've forgotten. . . ."

Gregor set down his glass and turned away to the window. There was a long, oppressive silence in the room.

"Shall we drink up?" Pantaleimon asked in a low tone.

"I don't want any more." Gregor lifted his son down from his knee, rose, and hurriedly made for the porch.

"Wait a bit, son; how about your meat? We've got boiled chicken, and pancakes!" Ilinichna rushed to the stove; but Gregor had already slammed the door behind him.

Aimlessly wandering, he looked at the cattle-yard, the stable

s horse, he thought: "I ought to take him for a
t under the eaves of the shed. By the harvester,
dy for mowing, he saw pine chips, shavings, and a
ooked board lying on the ground. "Father made the
Natalia," he decided, and hurriedly strode back to the
the house.

ding to his son's demand, Pantaleimon hastily made ready,
essed the horses into the harvester, and loaded a small keg of
ter on to the platform. He and Gregor drove out to the fields
at night.

Gregor suffered not only because he loved Natalia in his way and
had grown used to her during the six years they had lived together,
but also because he felt responsible for her death. If Natalia had
acted on her threat to take the children and go to live with her
mother, if she had died there, hating her faithless husband and
unreconciled with him, maybe Gregor would not have felt the burden of his loss so deeply, and doubtless he would not have been so
painfully racked with remorse. But his mother told him Natalia
had forgiven him everything, and that she had loved him and
spoken of him until her last moment. And the knowledge added
to his suffering, burdened his conscience with incessant reproach,
forced him to see the past years and all his conduct in a new light.

There had been a time when he felt nothing but cold indifference
and even hostility to his wife. But of recent years he had come to
feel very differently towards her. The children had been chiefly
responsible for changing his attitude to her.

Gregor had not always felt that profound fatherly feeling for
them which developed in later days. When he came home from
the front for short periods of leave, he caressed and fondled them,
almost from a sense of duty and to please their mother, but he could
not even watch Natalia and her violent demonstrations of maternal
feeling without a sense of distrustful amazement. He did not understand how anyone could love those tiny, noisy creatures so self-
forgetfully, and more than once while Natalia was still breast-
feeding them he told her at night with chagrin and a sneer in his
tone: "What makes you jump up like that as though mad? You're
on your feet before they've had time to cry. Let them kick and

shout a bit; I don't suppose they'll cry tears of go
were no less indifferent to him, but as they grew old
ment to their father grew also. Their love aroused
him, and his feeling for them was extended to their mot

After the break with Aksinia, Gregor had never seriousl
of leaving his wife; never, not even when they came togethe
had he thought of Aksinia as taking the place of the mother
children. He was not unready to live with them both, loving
of them in his own way. But now he had lost his wife he abrup
felt alienated from Aksinia and was suddenly filled with mute ange
against her for having betrayed their relations and so driven Natalia
to her death.

Try as he would to forget his sorrow, as he worked in the fields
he inevitably returned to it in thought. He wore himself out with
work, he did not climb out of the harvester seat for hours, yet he
still recalled Natalia; his memory persistently resurrected various
long-past, frequently insignificant incidents of their life together,
their talks together. He had but to remove the bridle from his
willing memory for a moment, and the living, smiling Natalia would
arise before him once more. He recalled her figure, her walk, her
way of tidying her hair, her smile, the intonation of her voice.

On the third day they began to harvest the barley. At midday,
when Pantaleimon halted the horses, Gregor climbed down from
the harvester seat, laid the short pitchfork on the floorboards, and
said:

"I want to go home for an hour or so, Father."

"What for?"

"I just want to see the children. . . ."

"All right, off with you," the old man willingly agreed. "And
meantime we'll be doing some stacking."

Gregor at once unharnessed his horse from the harvester,
mounted it, and rode at a walking pace over the yellow, brushy
stubble towards the highroad. "Tell him to have pity on you!"
Natalia's voice sounded in his ears. He closed his eyes, dropped
the rein, and, lost in memories, let the horse take its own way.

In the deeply azure heaven rare, wind-scattered clouds hung
almost motionless. Rooks were hopping with half-spread wings
over the stubble. They settled in flocks on the stacks; beak to
beak the old ones fed the young newly fledged birds which still

rose uncertainly on the wing. Over the harvested acres the rooks' croaking blended into a steady groan.

Gregor's horse tried to pick its way along the side of the road, occasionally tearing up and chewing clumps of clover as it went. Its bit clattered as it hung loose. Twice, seeing horses in the distance, it came to a halt and neighed; and then Gregor roused himself and urged the animal on, while with unseeing eyes he gazed over the steppe, the dusty road, the yellow sprinkle of stacks, the greenish-brown plots of ripened millet.

As soon as Gregor reached home the glum-looking Christonia put in an appearance. Despite the heat, he was dressed in an English cloth tunic and broad riding-breeches. He walked in, leaning on an enormous, freshly trimmed ash stick, and greeted Gregor:

"I've dropped in to see you. I heard about your trouble. So they've buried Natalia Mironovna?"

"How did you get back from the front?" Gregor asked, pretending not to hear Christonia's question, satisfiedly examining his awkwardly built, slightly bowed figure.

"They sent me home to get better after a wound. I had two bullets at once score me across the belly. And they're still stuck there, by my entrails it looks like, damn them! And that's why I'm using a stick, you see?"

"Where did they make that mess of you?"

"Close to Balashov."

"Did we capture it? And how did you get your packet?"

"We were making an attack. And I think Balashov was taken."

"Well, tell me what regiment you're with, and who else of the village is with you. Sit down; have a smoke?"

Gregor was delighted to see a fresh face, to have an opportunity to talk with someone outside the family who had had nothing to do with his suffering. Christonia revealed some understanding and guessed that Gregor did not want his sympathy. He willingly but slowly began to tell how Balashov was captured and how he got his wound. Smoking an enormous cigarette, he said in his thick deep voice:

"We were advancing on foot through sunflowers. The Reds were firing from machine-guns and guns, and of course from rifles too, that goes without saying. I'm easily picked out, among the others I'm like a goose among chickens; no matter how low I bend, all of me can be seen; well, and they—the bullets I mean—found me. For that matter, it's a good job I was moving at full height, for if I'd been bending they'd have caught me right in the head! It appears they were spent bullets, but the moment they struck me, everything in my belly began to grumble, and they were both so hot, damn them, you'd have said they'd flown straight out of a stove. I clapped my hand to the spot, and I could feel them inside me, rolling about under the skin like a couple of tumours, one close to the other. Well, I felt at them with my fingers and then dropped, it seems. I thought: 'This is a poor joke; to hell with such jokes!' Better keep still or another might come flying, sharper than the others, and go right through me. Well, so I lay there. And I felt them—the bullets I mean. They were still there, one close to the other. I got alarmed, for I thought they might make their way into my belly, and then what? They'd go rolling about among my intestines, and then how would the doctors ever find them? And besides, they wouldn't be any pleasure to me. A man's body, even mine, is fluid; the bullets would go wandering into my bowels, and then I'd go walking about rattling like a post-bell. It would break me up completely. I lay and twisted off a head of sunflower and ate the seeds, but I was frightened all the same. Our line had gone on. Well, and when Balashov was taken, I was ordered there too. Then I lay in the field hospital at Tishanka. The doctor there was as cocky as a sparrow. He kept asking me: 'Shall we cut out the bullets?' But I lay thinking it over. . . . I asked him: 'Your Excellency, can they get lost in my inside?' 'No,' he said; 'they can't.' Well, then I thought, I'm not going to let them be cut out! I know that game! They'd cut them out, and before the wound had had time to heal I'd be sent back to my regiment. 'No,' I said, 'Your Excellency, I won't have them cut out. It's even more interesting for me with them inside. I'd like to carry them home to show my wife, and they're no bother to me, they're not a great weight.' He swore at me good and hard, but he let me go home on sick-leave for a week."

Gregor smiled as he listened to the artless story, and asked:

"What regiment have you got into?"

"The 4th."

"Who else from the village is with you?"

"Quite a lot: Anikushka, Beskhlebnov, Akim Koloveidin, **Semka** Miroshnikov, Tikhon Gorbachov."

"Well, and how are the Cossacks? Not complaining?"

"They're upset with the officers, it looks like. They've put such filthy swine over us there's no living with them. And they're almost all Russian; there isn't a Cossack among them!"

As he spoke, Christonia pulled down the short sleeve of his tunic and examined and stroked the excellent cloth of his English breeches as though he could hardly believe that he was wearing such good material.

"But, you know, I couldn't find boots to fit my feet," he said meditatively. "The people who live in the English country haven't got such healthy legs. . . . We sow and eat wheat, but I expect in England it's like in Russia; they only have rye to eat. Otherwise how could they have such small feet? They've clothed and shod all our company and sent us scented cigarettes; but all the same, things are bad."

"What's bad?" Gregor asked with interest.

"It seems all right outside, but inside it's bad. You know, the Cossacks are again wanting to get out of fighting. So nothing will come of this war. They were saying they wouldn't go farther than the Khopersk region."

When he had said good-bye to Christonia, after a moment's reflection Gregor decided: "I'll stay here a week and then go back to the front. I shall die of misery here." He remained at home until evening. He remembered the days of his childhood and made Mishatka a windmill of reeds, fashioned a sparrow-snare from a horse hair, expertly made his daughter a tiny carriage with wheels that turned and a centre-pole painted in extraordinary colours, and even tried to make a doll out of rags. But nothing came of that; Dunia had to help to finish the doll.

At first the children, to whom Gregor had never been so attentive before, were distrustful of his intentions. But afterwards they would not leave him for a minute, and late in the afternoon, when Gregor was making ready to ride back to the fields, Mishatka declared with tears in his voice:

"You're always like that! No sooner are you here than you leave us again. . . . Take your snare, and the mill, and the rattle with you. Take them all; I don't want them."

Gregor took his son's little hands in his own great fists and said: "If that's how you feel, let's settle it this way. You're a Cossack, and you'll ride out with me to the fields. We'll mow the barley and we'll stack it; you'll sit with Grandfather on the harvester, you'll drive the horses. And the grasshoppers you'll find out there in the grass! The birds you'll see in the ravines! But Poliushka will stay at home with Grandmother. She won't mind. She's a girl, and it's her job to sweep the floors, to bring Grandmother water from the Don in a little pail, and to do all sorts of women's tasks. Agreed?"

"Oh yes!" Mishatka exclaimed rapturously. And his eyes glittered at the prospect.

"Where are you taking him to?" Ilinichna tried to object. "I don't know what you're thinking of! Where's he going to sleep? And who's going to look after him out there? God help us, he'll go too close to the horses and get kicked, or else a snake'll bite him. Don't go with your father, darling; you stay at home!" She turned to her grandson.

But Mishatka's narrowed eyes suddenly blazed ominously (exactly like his grandfather's when the old man was losing his temper), he clenched his little fists, and shouted in a high-pitched, weeping tone:

"Grandmother, shut up! I'm going, whatever happens!"

With a laugh Gregor took his son by the hand, and reassured Ilinichna:

"He'll sleep with me. We'll ride back at a walking pace. I shan't let him fall. Get his clothes ready, Mother, and don't be afraid; I'll see he's safe and sound, and I'll bring him back whole tomorrow evening."

And thus Gregor and Mishatka struck up a friendship.

During the three weeks he spent in Tatarsk, Gregor saw Aksinia only three times, and then he had only glimpses of her. With her native sense and tact she avoided a meeting, realizing that it would be better for her not to come within his sight. Womanlike, she realized his mood, realized that any incautious and untimely demonstration of her feelings for him might set him against her and throw a cloud over their relations. She waited for Gregor himself to speak to her. The moment came a day before his departure for the front. He was driving back late from the fields with a wagon-load of grain, and in the dusk he met Aksinia by the lane nearest to the steppe. She bowed when still some distance away and faintly smiled. Her smile was challenging and anxious. He answered her bow, but could not pass her by in silence.

"How are you getting on?" he asked, imperceptibly pulling on the reins, slowing the horses down from their fast walking pace.

"Quite well, thank you, Gregor Pantalievich."

"How is it we haven't seen anything of you?"

"I've been out in the fields. I'm struggling with the work single-handed."

Mishatka was sitting with Gregor in the wagon. Possibly for that reason Gregor did not halt the horses and did not stop for further conversation. He had driven on several yards when, hearing a call, he turned. Aksinia was standing by the fence.

"Are you staying long in the village?" she asked, agitatedly pluck-ing the petals of a daisy.

"I'm off any day now."

By the way she hesitated for a second, it was evident that she wanted to ask something more. For some reason she did not, but waved her hand and hurriedly walked on into the commonland, not once looking back.

Chapter 8

The sky was overcast with clouds. A rain so fine that it seemed to have been sieved was sprinkling down. The young aftermath, the scrub, and the bushes of wild thorn scattered about the steppe were gleaming with rain.

Highly indignant at his premature departure from the village, Prokhor rode along in silence and hardly spoke to Gregor all the way back to the regiment. Beyond a certain hamlet they fell in with three mounted Cossacks. The men were riding in a row, urging their horses on with their heels, talking energetically among themselves. One of them, elderly and red-haired, dressed in a peasant's grey homespun coat, recognized Gregor and said in a loud voice to his companions: "But that's Melekhov, brothers!" As they drew level with Gregor he reined in his high-standing bay horse.

"Our greetings to you, Gregor Pantalievich," he cried.

"Greetings!" Gregor answered, vainly trying to recall where he had met this red-bearded, sullen-looking Cossack before.

Evidently the man had only recently been raised to the rank of ensign and, in order not to be taken for a rank-and-file Cossack, he had sewn his new epaulets on his greatcoat.

"Don't you know me?" he asked, riding right up to Gregor, stretching out his hand, and breathing the smell of vodka fumes into Gregor's face. An idiotic self-satisfaction beamed on the face of this newly cooked ensign; his small blue eyes sparkled, and his lips twisted into a grin beneath his red moustache. Gregor was amused by the absurd appearance of this officer in a peasant's coat. Not attempting to hide his smile, he answered:

"No, I don't. I must have met you when you were still a rank-and-file Cossack. Have you been made an ensign recently?"

"You've hit the mark! It's just a week since they raised me to my present rank. But we met at one of Kudynov's staff meetings, close to Blagoveshchenie, I think. You saved me from a little bit of trouble then, do you remember? Hey, Trifon! Ride on slowly, and I'll catch up with you!" he shouted to the other Cossacks, who had halted a little way off.

After some difficulty Gregor recalled his previous meeting with the red-haired ensign and Kudynov's comment on him: "He never misses when he fires, he can shoot hares in flight with his rifle, he's a devil in a fight, a good scout, but a babe in intelligence." The man had commanded a company during the rising, and had made some blunder. Kudynov had wanted to deal sternly with him, but Gregor had intervened, and he had been pardoned and left with the rank of company commander.

"Come from the front?" Gregor asked.

"Yes; I'm going on furlough from Novokhopersk. I've ridden a hundred miles out of my way to call on kinsmen of mine. I've got a good memory, Gregor Pantalievich! Don't refuse me the pleasure of treating you. I've got a couple of bottles of hundred-per-cent liquor in my pack. Let's open them on the spot, shall we?"

Gregor flatly refused, but he accepted the bottle the man offered him as a present.

"You should have been there! Cossacks and officers were loaded down with goods!" the ensign boastfully declared. "I was in Balashov too. We captured the place and made straight for the railway, where we found three full train-loads standing; all the tracks were crowded with freight cars. One car was full of sugar, a second full of uniforms, and a third had all sorts of things in it. Some of the Cossacks carried off up to forty sets of clothing. And afterwards, when we went to shake up the Jews, you'd have laughed. In my half-company one clever Jew-catcher collected eighteen watches, ten of them gold. He hung them all over his chest, just as though he was the richest merchant in the land. And the rings and bracelets he'd got—you couldn't have counted them! He had two or three on each finger. . . ."

Gregor pointed to the man's swollen saddlebags and asked:

"And what's that you've got?"

"Why—all sorts of things."

"So you went looting too?"

"Well, call it that if you like. . . . But we didn't loot, we won it legally. Our regimental commander said: 'Take the town and it's at your disposal for two days.' And am I any worse than the others? I took legal stuff, whatever came to my hand. Others did much worse."

"Fine fighters!" Gregor gazed at the ensign in disgust, and added: "The likes of you lurk under the bridges on the highroads, but you don't fight! You've turned the war into a looting expedition. Ah, you scum! You've got a new trade! But don't you think that some day or other you and your commander too will be flayed alive for this?"

"For what?"

"For all that."

"But who's going to do the flaying?"

"A superior officer."

The man smiled sarcastically and said:

"But they're all the same! We only take stuff in our saddlebags or our wagons, but they're sending away whole train-loads of baggage."

"Why, have you seen them?"

"Have I seen them! I myself convoyed one such baggage train to Yarizhenka. There was a whole wagon-load of silver dishes, cups, and spoons. Some of the officers flew at us with: 'What have you got there? Here, show us!' But when I said it was the personal property of General So-and-so they went off empty-handed."

"Who is this general?" Gregor asked, narrowing his eyes and nervously fiddling with the reins.

The man smiled craftily and answered:

"I've forgotten his name. What is it? God help me to remember! No, it's gone; I can't recall it. But there's no point in your swearing, Gregor Pantalievich. God's truth, everybody's doing it. Compared to the others I'm like a lamb to wolves. I took very little, but others stripped people naked in the very middle of the street and raped the Jew girls wherever they came upon them. I didn't go in for such things. I've got my own lawful wife, and what a wife! She's a stallion, not a woman! No, you've got no cause to be angry with me. Wait a bit; where are you off to?"

Gregor coldly nodded in farewell to the man and put his horse into a trot, saying to Prokhor:

"Keep up behind me!"

On the road they met more and more Cossacks riding off on furlough in ones and twos and in groups. Quite often they passed wagons drawn by a pair of horses, with their loads covered by tarpaulins or blankets carefully tied down. Cossacks in new summer tunics and Red Army khaki trousers trotted, standing in their stirrups, behind the wagons. Their dusty, sunburnt faces were animated and cheerful. But when they saw Gregor they hurried past as quickly as possible, riding in silence, raising their hands to the visors of their caps as though at a command, and fell to talking again only when they had put a respectable distance between themselves and Gregor.

"Merchants on the move!" Prokhor jested when in the distance he saw horsemen convoying a wagon loaded with plunder.

But not all the men they met going on furlough were weighed down with loot. Halting to water the horses at a well in one of the villages, Gregor heard singing coming from the next yard. Judging by the youthfully clear, fine voices, it was a group of young Cossacks singing.

"Giving a farewell party to a soldier, I should say," Prokhor said as he drew up a pail of water. The bottle of liquor they had drunk the evening before had put him in the mood for a carousal, and so, hurriedly watering the horses, he suggested with a laugh:

"What do you think, Pantalievich, shall we go and join them? Maybe a stirrup cup will fall to our lot, too. The hut's got a reed thatch, but you can tell they're rich."

Gregor agreed to go and see how the young Cossack was being speeded on his way. Tying the horses to the fence, he and Prokhor went into the yard. Four saddled horses were standing by circular mangers under the eaves of a shed. A lad with an iron measure filled to the brim with oats came out of the granary. He glanced at Gregor and went to the whinnying horses. A song came floating round the corner of the hut. A high, vibrating tenor was singing:

> As along the path they went,
> Not a man on foot. . . .

A thick, smoky bass voice repeated the last words and blended with the tenor, then further voices joined in harmony, and the song flowed on majestically, expansively, and mournfully. Gregor did not want to interrupt the singers, so he touched Prokhor's sleeve and whispered:

"Wait a bit, don't let them see you. Let them finish."

"It isn't a send-off. The Yelanska Cossacks always sing like that. But they can sing, the devils!" Prokhor remarked approvingly and spat with annoyance: it looked as though his expectations of a drink would go unrealized.

The pleasant tenor told to the end the story of the Cossack who made a mistake during a war:

> Nor foot nor horse's trace was to be seen.
> The Cossack regiment marched along the road.
> Behind the regiment ran a spirited horse.
> A Circassian saddle had slipped to his side,
> And the bridle hung over his right ear;
> The silken reins were tangled in his feet.
> Behind him ran a youthful Don Cossack.
> And to his faithful steed he shouted loud:
> "Stop, wait a bit, my spirited, faithful horse,
> Do not abandon me, for without you
> Never shall I escape from the wicked Chechens. . . ."

Entranced by the singing, Gregor stood leaning against the white-washed base of the hut, hearing neither the horses' neighing nor the creak of wagons passing along the street.

When the song ended, one of the singers coughed and said:

"We didn't sing like that when we were taken up. Never mind,

we do our best. But you ought to give the soldiers something more
for the road, women. We've eaten well, Christ be thanked; but we
haven't got a bite or sup to take with us for the road. . . ."

Gregor roused himself from his reverie and walked round the
corner. Four young Cossacks were sitting on the bottom step below
the door; women and children who had come running from the
neighbouring huts surrounded them in a dense crowd. Sobbing and
snuffling, the audience wiped away their tears with the ends of their
kerchiefs. As Gregor went up to the steps one old woman, tall and
black-eyed, with the traces of a stern, ikon-like beauty on her
withered face, was saying in a slow drawl:

"My dears, how beautifully and how sorrowfully you sing! And
I expect every one of you has got a mother, and I expect, when she
thinks of her son and how he's perishing in the war, she streams with
tears." Flashing the yellow whites of her eyes at Gregor as he
greeted the crowd, she suddenly said angrily: "And you, Your Excellency, are you leading such flowers to their death? You're causing
them to perish in the war!"

"We're perishing ourselves, old woman," Gregor answered
moodily.

Discountenanced by the arrival of a strange officer, the Cossacks
nimbly jumped up. With their feet they pushed aside the plates
with remnants of food on the steps and tidied their tunics, rifle-
straps, and belts. They had been singing without even removing
the rifles from their shoulders. The very oldest of them did not appear to be more than twenty-five years.

"Where are you from?" Gregor asked, running his eyes over the
men's fresh, youthful faces.

"From a regiment . . ." a snub-nosed youngster with humorous
eyes answered irresolutely.

"I mean, where were you born, what is your native district?
You're not local men, are you?"

"We're Yelanska men. We're going on furlough, Your Excellency."

Gregor recognized the solo singer by his voice and smiled as he
asked:

"You were the soloist, weren't you?"

"Yes."

"Well, you've got a fine voice. But what were you singing for?
For joy? You don't look to be drunk!"

A tall, fair youngster with a dashing, dusty forelock, a deep flush on his swarthy cheeks, glanced sidelong at the old woman and reluctantly answered with an embarrassed smile:

"What joy do you think we've got? Need is what makes us sing. Life isn't too good in these parts, they don't feed you too well—just a hunk of bread, and that's all. And so we hit upon the idea of singing. As soon as we start, all the women come running to listen; we strike up some sad song, and they're touched and bring a piece of fat, or a pipkin of milk, or something else that's good to eat. . . ."

"We're sort of priests, captain! We sing and collect alms!" said the soloist, winking at his comrades. His humorous eyes narrowed in a smile.

One of the Cossacks took a greasy paper out of his breast pocket and held it out to Gregor, saying:

"Here's our furlough paper."

"What do I want it for?"

"You might think we were deserting."

"You can show it when you fall in with a punitive detachment," Gregor said with some annoyance. But none the less, before leaving he advised them: "Ride at night, and put up somewhere each day. Your paper's useless; see you don't get into trouble with it. Is it stamped?"

"Our squadron hasn't got a stamp."

"Well, you take my advice if you don't want to be thrashed with ramrods by the Kalmyks."

Some three miles outside the village, perhaps three hundred yards from a small wood which reached to the edge of the road, Gregor again saw two horsemen riding towards him. They halted and stood gazing for a moment, then turned sharply into the wood.

"They haven't got any papers," Prokhor opined. "Did you see the way they turned off into the trees? They're deserting even in the daytime now, the devils!"

During the day several other men turned off the road and hurried to hide when they saw Gregor and Prokhor. One elderly Cossack on foot, stealthily making his way homeward, plunged into a field of sunflowers and crouched down like a hare on the edge of the field. As they rode past him Prokhor rose in his stirrups and shouted:

"Hey, countryman, that's not the way to hide! You've hidden your head, but you're showing your arse!" And with a pretence of fury he shouted: "Well, out you come! Let's see your documents!"

The Cossack jumped up and, bending double, ran off through the sunflowers. Prokhor laughed uproariously and was about to touch up his horse to chase the man. But Gregor halted him:

"Don't play the fool! Let him go to the devil; he'll go on running until he's broken-winded. And he'll die of fright. . . ."

"You're all wrong! You couldn't catch that man with borzois! He won't stop galloping for a good ten miles. Did you see the way he tore through the sunflowers? Where does a man get all that energy from at such times, I'd like to know." He expressed some decidedly disapproving opinions about deserters generally, and remarked:

"The way they ride! Just like wolves! How did they get away, tell me. You look out, Pantalievich, or before long you and I will be holding the front by ourselves."

The closer they drew to the front, the more Gregor saw signs of the demoralization of the Don army. That demoralization had set in just at the moment when, reinforced by the insurgents, the army had achieved its greatest successes on the northern front. Already its forces not only were incapable of opening a decisive offensive and smashing enemy resistance, but would be unable to face any serious attack.

In the district centres and villages where the front-line reserves were quartered the officers were carousing incessantly; baggage trains of all kinds were groaning with property looted but not yet dispatched to the rear; not more than sixty per cent of the complement was left in any of the component forces; Cossacks were arbitrarily going on furlough and the Kalmyk punitive detachments scouring the steppe were not strong enough to hold up the flood of mass desertion. In the occupied villages of the Saratov province the Cossacks were behaving like conquerors in foreign territory; they were pillaging the population, raping the women, destroying the grain stocks, slaughtering the cattle. Reinforcements of callow youths and men over fifty were being drafted into the army. In the advancing companies there was open talk of unwillingness to fight, while the Cossacks in the forces moving towards Voroniezh were flatly refusing to obey the officers. Rumour had it that instances of officers being murdered in the front line positions were growing frequent.

As dusk was falling, Gregor halted for the night in a small village not far from Balashov. A fourth reserve company of Cossacks drawn from older conscripts and an engineers' company of the Taganrog regiment had occupied all the living-quarters in the place. Gregor spent a good deal of time searching for quarters. He could have passed the night in the fields, as they usually did; but rain began to fall, Prokhor was shivering in one of his bouts of malaria, and so they had to spend the night somewhere under cover. At the entrance to the village an armoured car which had been put out of action by a shell stood by a large house surrounded with poplars. As Gregor rode past he read the still legible inscription on its green side: "Death to the White scum!" and, below it, the name: "Fury!" Horses were snorting at the tether-posts in the yard, human voices were to be heard; a camp-fire was burning in the garden behind the house, smoke was drifting over the green crowns of the trees. Lit up by the glare, Cossack figures were moving around the fire. The smell of burning straw and burnt hogs' bristles was carried away on the wind.

Gregor dismounted and went into the house.

"Who's the master here?" he asked as he went into a low-ceilinged room filled with people.

"I am. What do you want?" A thickset peasant leaning against the stove looked round at Gregor, but did not change his position.

"Can we spend the night here? There are two of us."

"We're already as crowded as seeds in watermelons," an elderly Cossack lying on a bench barked in a disgruntled tone.

"I wouldn't mind, but we have got rather a lot in here," the master said in a deprecatory voice.

"We'll find room somehow. We can't spend the night in the rain, can we?" Gregor insisted. "I've got a sick orderly with me."

The Cossack lying on the bench groaned, dropped his feet to the floor, and, staring at Gregor, said in a different tone:

"Your Excellency, together with the master's folk there are fourteen of us in two small rooms, and the third is occupied by officers."

"Maybe you could fit yourself up with them somehow," a second

Cossack with a heavy sprinkle of grey in his beard, a non-commissioned officer, judging by his epaulets, said in a friendly tone.

"No, I'd rather be here. I don't need much room, I'll lie on the floor. I shan't crowd you." Gregor removed his greatcoat, brushed his hair with his palm, and sat down at the table. Prokhor went out to see to the horses.

Some time later Gregor went out to the porch. A fine slanting rain lashed into his face. A flash of lightning lit up the spacious yard, and wet fence, the lustrous, gleaming foliage of the trees in the orchard. As he went down the steps he heard voices.

"The officers still drinking?" someone asked, striking a match in the porch.

A muffled, frozen voice answered with restrained menace:

"They'll drink their fill. . . . They'll drink their fill till they get what's coming to them!"

Chapter 9

In twelve months the Melekhov family was reduced to half its number. Pantaleimon was right when he remarked one day that death had taken a fancy to the hut. Hardly had they had time to bury Natalia when once more the scent of incense and cornflowers filled the Melekhovs' spacious best room. Some ten days after Gregor had gone back to the front Daria drowned herself in the Don.

On the Saturday, after returning from the fields she went with Dunia to bathe. Below the kitchen gardens they undressed and sat a long time on the soft, trampled grass. From early morning Daria had been out of spirits, complaining of headache and weakness, and several times she had surreptitiously wept. Before stepping into the water Dunia gathered her hair into a knot, tied it up in a three-cornered kerchief, and, glancing sidelong at Daria, said commiseratingly:

"How thin you've got, Daria! Your bones seem to be all outside your skin."

"I'll soon get better. . . ."

"Has your headache gone?"

"Yes. Well, let's bathe, for it's late already." Daria was the first to enter the water at a run. She plunged in over her head and, coming up, snorting the water out of her nose and mouth, swam to the middle. The swift current caught her up and began to carry her away.

Admiringly watching Daria as she shot forward with great masculine sweeps, Dunia waded in up to her waist, washed, wetted her breast and her sun-warmed, strong, femininely rounded arms. The two daughters-in-law of the Obnizovs were watering cabbages in a neighbouring garden. They heard Dunia laughingly call to Daria:

"Swim back, Dashka, or a sheatfish will carry you off!"

Daria turned back, swam some twenty feet, then momentarily flung herself out of the water up to her waist, folded her arms behind her head, shouted: "Good-bye, women!" and went to the bottom like a stone.

Some fifteen minutes later Dunia, white-faced, dressed in only her underskirt, ran into the Melekhovs' hut.

"Daria's drowned, Mamma!" She could hardly pant the words out.

Not till the following day did they recover Daria's body with fishing tackle. At dawn the oldest and most experienced fisherman in Tatarsk, Arkhip Peskovatkov, set the six ends of his tackle across the current below the spot where Daria had sunk, and later he went with Pantaleimon to check the lines. A crowd of children and women gathered on the bank, Dunia among them. When, hitching up the fourth line with his oar handle, Arkhip had gone some sixty feet from the bank, Dunia distinctly heard him say in an undertone: "This seems like it."

He began to draw in the tackle more carefully, pulling with obvious effort on the line, which ran plumb into the depths. Then over by the right bank there was a glimmer of white, both the old men bent over the water, the boat scooped up water with its gunwales, and the muffled thump of a body hauled into the boat reached the ears of the silent crowd. A sudden shiver ran through them all. One of the women broke into a quiet sobbing. Christonia, who was standing a little way off, roughly shouted at the children: "Now, clear out of here!" Through her tears Dunia saw Arkhip, standing at the stern, expertly and silently row with one oar to the bank. The boat touched ground, crushing through the fine chalky shingle with a jarring scrunch. Daria was lying with her legs tucked up lifelessly, her cheek against the wet bottom. Her white body was just beginning to turn blue, and deep holes, the marks of the hooks, were clearly visible in the flesh. On her lank, swarthy calf, just below the knee, by the linen garter which evidently she had forgotten to remove before bathing, a fresh scratch was showing rosy and bleeding a little. The point of a hook had slipped over her leg and had furrowed a crooked, jagged line. Convulsively crumpling her apron, Dunia was the first to go up to Daria, to cover her with a sack ripped down the seams. With methodical haste Pantaleimon rolled up his trousers and pulled the boat up the bank. A wagon drove up a minute or two later, and Daria was carried to the Melekhovs' hut.

Mastering her fear and feeling of disgust, Dunia helped her mother to wash the cold body, which still retained the iciness of the deep Don current. There was something unfamiliar and stern about Daria's slightly swollen face, the faded gleam of the eyes glazed by immersion in the water. Silver river sand sparkled in her hair, the moist threads of water-weed were vividly green against her cheeks, and in the outflung arms hanging helplessly from the bench was such terrible repose that as Dunia glanced at them she hurriedly fell back, amazed and horrified at the complete lack of resemblance between this dead woman and the jesting, laughing Daria who had been so much in love with life. Afterwards, as she recalled the stony clamminess of Daria's breasts and belly, the springiness of the stiffened limbs, Dunia long shook convulsively and tried her utmost to forget it all. She was afraid the dead woman would visit her in her sleep at night, and for a week she slept in Ilinichna's bed and, before getting in, prayed to God, asking: "Lord, don't let me dream of her! Cover me, Lord!"

If it had not been for the Obnizov women, who had heard Daria shout: "Good-bye, women!" she would have been buried quietly and without fuss. But when he heard of this last shout, which clearly indicated that Daria had intended to take her own life, Father Vissarion resolutely declared that he would not bury the suicide. Pantaleimon was furious.

"What do you mean: you won't bury her? Is she unbaptized, or what?"

"I can't bury suicides; the law won't allow it."

"Then how is she to be buried, in your opinion? Like a dog?"

"In my opinion, how and where you like, except in the cemetery, where honest Christians are buried."

"But please do have some pity!" Pantaleimon tried persuasions. "We've never had such a disgrace in our family."

"I can't. I've got great respect for you, Pantaleimon Prokoffievich, as an exemplary church attendant, but I can't. It will be reported to the archdeacon, and I shan't be able to avoid the consequences." The priest turned obstinate.

It was a disgrace. Pantaleimon tried every means of persuading the pig-headed priest, promised to pay more and to pay in reliable Nicholas rubles, offered a yearling lamb as a gift. But, seeing at last that arguments were of no avail, he resorted to threats:

"I shan't bury her outside the cemetery. She's not some piece of makeweight, but my own daughter-in-law. Her husband fell in the struggle against the Reds and held officer's rank, and you talk nonsense like that to me! No, father, it won't come off; you'll bury her for the sake of my respect. Let her lie in our best room for the time being, and I'll inform the district ataman about it at once. He'll talk to you!"

Pantaleimon went out of the priest's house without a word of farewell, and in his temper even slammed the door. But the threat was effective: half an hour later a messenger came from the priest to say that Father Vissarion would be arriving to say the prayers in a minute.

They buried Daria, as was right, in the cemetery, beside Piotra. When they dug the grave, Pantaleimon took a fancy to the spot for himself. As he worked with the spade he looked about him and reflected that he would not find a better place, nor was it worth while looking for one. Over Piotra's grave a recently planted poplar was rustling its tender branches, the oncoming autumn had already painted the leaves of its crown the yellow, bitter hue of decay. Calves had trampled out a path through the broken fence and between the graves; the road to the windmill ran past the fence; the trees planted by the solicitous hands of the dead's kinsfolk—maples, poplars, acacias, and the wild-growing thorn—stood welcomingly green and fresh; around them the bindweed twined exuberantly, belated rape showed yellow, wild oat and full-grained quitch were in ear. The crosses stood wound from foot to head with friendly, blue convolvulus. The spot was certainly cheerful, and dry. . . .

As the old man dug the grave, he threw down the spade from time to time and seated himself on the damp, clayey earth, to smoke, to think of death. But evidently the times had not yet arrived when old people could once more die quietly in their own huts and rest where their own fathers and grandfathers had found their last shelter.

After Daria was buried, life grew still quieter in the Melekhovs' house. They carted the grain, threshed it, gathered a rich harvest from the melon plot. They expected news from Gregor, but nothing had been heard of him since his departure for the front. Ilinichna said more than once: "The devil doesn't even send greetings to his children! His wife's dead, and now he has no need of any of us. . . ." Then Cossacks on active service began to return more and more often on visits to Tatarsk. The rumours spread that the Cossacks had been beaten on the Balakhov front and were retreating towards the Don, there to take refuge behind the watery defence line and to act on the defensive until winter. But as to what would happen in the winter, all the front-line men talked of that without any attempt at secrecy: "When the Don freezes over, the Reds will drive us right back to the sea."

Pantaleimon, zealously working at the threshing, did not seem to pay any particular attention to the rumours roving around the Don lands. But he could not remain indifferent to what was happening. He shouted even more frequently at Ilinichna and Dunia, grew more and more irritable as he heard that the front was drawing nearer. He not infrequently set to work to fashion something for the farm; but the work had only to go at all wrong in his hands for him to throw it down in a fury, and, spitting and cursing, he would rush to the threshing-floor, to allow his indignation to simmer down. Dunia was more than once the witness of such explosions. One day he set to work to mend a yoke; the job did not go well, and for no reason whatever the furious old man snatched up an axe and chopped at the yoke until only splinters were left. The same thing occurred with a horse-collar he was mending. One evening by the fire he twisted a wax-end and set to work to sew up the burst padding of the collar. Maybe the thread was rotten, or maybe the old man was too fidgety, but the thread broke twice in succession. That was enough; swearing horribly. Pantaleimon jumped up, sent his stool flying, kicked it towards the stove, and, bellowing like a dog, tore at the leather padding of the collar with his teeth. Then he flung the collar to the floor and, hopping like a cock, started to jump on it. Hearing the noise, Ilinichna, who had gone to rest early, jumped out of bed in a fright. But, seeing what was happening, she lost her temper and reproached him:

"Have you gone mad, damn you, in your old age? What's the collar done to you?"

Pantaleimon gazed at his wife with frenzied eyes and roared:

"Shut up, you this and that!" Snatching up a piece of the collar, he threw it at the old woman.

Choking with laughter, Dunia flew like a bullet out into the porch. But after raging for a while, the old man calmed down, asked his wife's forgiveness for the words he had used in his anger, and scratched the nape of his neck for a long time as he stared at the fragments of the unfortunate collar, thinking out what they might be useful for. Such attacks of frenzy were repeated more than once, but, instructed by bitter experience, Ilinichna found a different way of intervening. The moment Pantaleimon began to belch out curses and smash up some domestic article, the old woman humbly but loudly enough remarked:

"Smash it up, Prokoffich! Break it up! You and I will yet make money for more!" And she even attempted to assist in the destruction. Then Pantaleimon at once simmered down, stared for a minute with vacant eyes at his wife, rummaged with trembling hands in his pockets, found his tobacco-pouch, and sat down in bewilderment somewhere out of the way to smoke, to soothe his jangled nerves, inwardly cursing his explosive nature and reckoning up the losses he had sustained by his action.

A three-months-old pig which made its way into the enclosure fell a victim to his elderly, unbridled anger. He broke its back with a stake, and five minutes later, after slaughtering the animal, as he was tearing off the bristles with a nail, he looked guiltily, wheedlingly at Ilinichna and said:

"You know that pig was nothing but trouble. He'd have died in any case. They always get the plague at this time of year, and now we shall at least eat him, and he'd have been lost to us altogether. That's true, isn't it, old lady? Well, what are you looking like a thunder-cloud for? May he be triply damned, that pig! Now, if he'd been a pig, as pigs go; but he was only a gammon! It didn't need a stake to kill him, snot would have done it! And what a one he was for poking his snout into places! He'd rooted up a good forty potatoes."

"If he'd eaten all the potatoes in the garden there wouldn't have been more than thirty all together!" Ilinichna quietly corrected him.

"Maybe; but if there'd been forty he'd have spoilt all the forty. He was like that. And thank God we're saved from him, from the enemy!" Pantaleimon answered without thinking.

The children grew bored after they had seen their father off. Occupied with the house, Ilinichna could not give them sufficient attention and, left to their own devices, they played for hours on end somewhere in the orchard or the threshing-floor. Mishatka vanished one day after dinner and came back only at sunset. When Ilinichna asked where he had been, the boy said he had been playing with other boys down by the Don. But Poliushka at once gave him away:

"He's telling lies, Granny! He's been to see Aunty Aksinia."

"But how do you know?" Ilinichna asked, unpleasantly surprised by the news.

"I saw him climb across the fence from their yard."

"Is that where you've been? Now, speak up, child; what are you going red for?"

Mishatka gazed straight into his grandmother's eyes and answered:

"I was telling you wrong, Granny. It's true I haven't been down by the Don, but with Aunty Aksinia."

"What did you go there for?"

"She called me, and I went."

"Why did you tell me you'd been with the boys?"

Mishatka was dumb for a second, then he raised his eyes and whispered:

"I was afraid you'd be angry."

"Why should I be angry with you? No. . . . But what did she want you for? What did you do there?"

"Nothing. She saw me and shouted: 'Come here!' I went up to her, she led me into the hut, seated me on a chair. . . ."

"Well?" Ilinichna asked impatiently, concealing the agitation which was mastering her.

". . . She gave me cold pancakes to eat, and then she gave me this." Mishatka pulled a piece of sugar out of his pocket, showed it proudly, and hid it in his pocket again.

"But what did she say to you? Did she ask you anything?"

"She said I was to go and visit her, because she was lonely all by herself, and she promised to give me a treat. . . . She said I wasn't to tell anyone I'd been with her. She said you'd be annoyed."

"Did she!" Ilinichna uttered, panting with suppressed indignation. "Well, and did she ask you anything?"

"Yes."

"Then what did she ask? Now, tell me, darling; don't be afraid."

"She asked me whether I missed my daddy. I said I did. She also asked when he would be coming back and what news there was of him, but I said I didn't know, and that he was fighting in the war. Then she seated me on her knee and told me a fairy story." Mishatka's eyes glittered and he smiled. "It was a nice story! About someone called Vania, and how swan-geese carried him on their wings, and about Baba Yaga."

Ilinichna pursed up her lips as she listened to Mishatka's confession. At the end she said sternly:

"You're not to go there any more, grandson, it isn't good. And don't take any presents from her; you'd better not or your grandfather will hear of it and give you a whipping. God grant Grandfather doesn't find out, for he'd flay the skin off you. Don't go again, dear child!"

But, despite the strict prohibition, two days later Mishatka visited the Astakhovs' hut again. Ilinichna found out about it when she saw Mishatka's shirt: the torn sleeve which she had not time to mend in the morning was darned perfectly, and a little new mother-of-pearl button showed white on the collar. Knowing Dunia had been busy with the threshing and could not find time during the day to mend the children's clothes, Ilinichna reproachfully asked:

"Visited the neighbours again?"

"Yes!" Mishatka said in his confusion, and at once added: "I shan't any more, Granny; only don't be upset with me."

Ilinichna decided to have a talk with Aksinia and to tell her flatly that she was to leave Mishatka in peace and not to wheedle herself into his favour either with presents or by telling stories. "She's driven Natalia off this earth, and now the devil's trying to worm her way into the children's good books, so as to entangle Gregor through them. What a snake! Aiming at being my daughter-in-law with her own husband still alive! Only nothing will come of it. And besides, would Gregor ever take her after such a sin?" the old woman thought.

Her penetrating and jealous, motherly eyes had not overlooked the circumstance that when Gregor was at home he had avoided meeting Aksinia. She realized that he had done so not out of fear of people's reproaches, but because he regarded Aksinia as guilty of his wife's death. Secretly Ilinichna hoped that Natalia's death would part Gregor from Aksinia for all time, and that she would never become one of the Melekhov family.

The same evening Ilinichna saw Aksinia at the landing-stage by the Don and called to her:

"Here, come over to me for a minute; I want to have a talk. . . ."

Setting down her bucket, Aksinia calmly walked across and greeted Ilinichna.

"This is the point, my dear," Ilinichna began, gazing interrogatively at her neighbour's beautiful but hated face. "What are you taking other folk's children away for? What are you calling the boy to you and talking to him for? Who asked you to sew up his shirt for him and give him presents? What's in your mind—that there's no one to care for him, now his mother's gone? That we can't manage without you? Haven't you got any conscience, you with your shameless eyes?"

"But what harm have I done? What are you annoyed about, grandmother?" Aksinia asked, flaring up.

"What do you mean: what harm have you done? Have you any right to touch Natalia's child, when you yourself sent her to her grave?"

"How can you say such a thing, grandmother? Come to your senses! Who sent her to her grave? She laid hands on herself."

"And not because of you?"

"I know nothing about that."

"But I do!" Ilinichna cried excitedly.

"Don't shout, old woman; I'm not your daughter-in-law, for you to shout at me. I've got a husband to do that."

"I can see you through and through! I see even what you're hoping for! You're not my daughter-in-law, but you'd like to be! First you want to win over the children, then you'll make up to Grishka. Isn't that it?"

"I've got no intention of becoming your daughter-in-law. Are you going mad, old woman? I've got a husband still alive."

"That's just the point, that you're trying to get away from a living husband in order to fasten yourself on to another!"

Aksinia noticeably turned pale and said:

"I don't know what you're setting about me and abusing me for. I've never fastened myself on to anyone and never intend to, and what I said to your grandson—what harm is there in that? You know full well I've got no children of my own, I'm glad to see others' children, and so I called him. Do you think I loaded him down with presents? I gave him a lump of sugar, if that's what you call presents! And why should I give him presents anyway? You're gabbling God knows what!"

"You never called him into your hut when his mother was alive. But as soon as Natalia's dead you suddenly grow good-natured."

"He used to visit me even when Natalia was alive!" Aksinia said with the least trace of a smile.

"Don't tell lies, you shameless hussy!"

"You ask him, and then call me liar if you like!"

"Well, I don't care how it was; don't you dare to call him into your place any more. And don't take it into your head that you're going to find favour in Gregor's eyes that way. You'll never be his wife, know that!"

Her face distorted with anger, Aksinia said hoarsely:

"Hold your tongue! He won't ask you! And don't poke your nose into other people's affairs!"

Ilinichna was about to make some further retort, but Aksinia silently turned away, went to her buckets, heaved the yoke on to her shoulders, and, splashing water as she went, swiftly strode up the path.

From that time on, if she met any of the Melekhovs she said not a word of greeting to them, but walked past with satanic pride, dilating her nostrils. But whenever she happened to see Mishatka alone, she timidly looked about her and, if there was no one near, ran up to him, bent down, and pressed him to her breast. Laughing and crying, kissing his sunburnt brow and sullen, black little Melekhov eyes, she whispered disconnectedly: "My dear little Gregorievich! My darling! How I've been longing for you! Your Aunty Aksinia's a fool. . . . Ah, what a fool!" Afterwards a tremulous smile long hovered on her lips, and her moistened eyes shone with happiness as brightly as those of a young girl.

PART V

Flight to the Sea

FLIGHT TO THE SEA

Chapter 1

At the end of August, Pantaleimon was mobilized. With him all the Cossacks capable of bearing arms in Tatarsk also went off to the front. Only war-wounded, youngsters, and the decrepit old men were left of the male population in the village. The mobilization affected everybody down to the last man, and only the obviously maimed were exempted by the medical commissions.

When Pantaleimon received the order from the village ataman to present himself at the assembly point, he hurriedly said good-bye to his old woman, his grandchildren, and Dunia and, groaning, went down on his knees. He bowed himself twice to the ground and, crossing himself before the ikons, said:

"Good-bye, my dears. It looks as though we shan't be granted to see each other again; the last hour has come. My command to you is: thresh the grain both day and night, try to get it finished before the rains set in. If necessary, hire a man to help you. If I don't come back by autumn, carry on without me; plough up the autumn fields as much as you've got strength for, and sow rye, at least a couple of acres of it. Watch out, old woman, and carry on the work properly, don't let your hands drop! Whether Gregor and I return or whether we don't, you'll need grain most of all. War is war, but it's a miserable life without bread, too. Well, God preserve you!"

Ilinichna accompanied her husband to the square, watched for the

last time as he limped along at Christonia's side, hurrying after the
wagon, then wiped her swollen eyes with her apron and made her
way home without one look back. A heap of half-threshed wheat
was awaiting her on the threshing-floor, milk was standing on the
stove, the children had not had any food since morning, the old
woman had a great many things to attend to. And she hurried home
without stopping, silently bowing to the few women she passed, not
entering into talk, and only nodding affirmatively when one of her
acquaintances asked her commiserately: "Seen the soldier off, then?"

Several days later Ilinichna milked the cows at dawn, then drove
them out into the lane and was about to return to the yard, when a
muffled, oppressive thunder reached her ears. Looking around, she
could not see even one little cloud in the sky. After a brief interval
the thunder was repeated.

"Do you hear that music, old woman?" the old cowherd as-
sembling the cows asked her.

"What music?"

"Why, all that bass music."

"I can hear it all right, but I don't rightly know what it can be."

"You'll know soon enough. When it starts coming from that direction right over the village, you'll know at once! That's gunfire.
They're shaking the guts out of our old men. . . ."

Ilinichna crossed herself and silently went through the wicket
gate.

The gunfire sounded incessantly for four days. It was especially
loud in the dawns and dusks. But when a north-easterly wind blew,
the thunder of the distant battles could be heard in the middle of the
day also. On the threshing-floors the work came to a halt for a moment, the women crossed themselves and sighed deeply, recalling
their dear ones, whispering prayers. Then the stone rollers again
rumbled muffledly on the threshing-floors, the driver boys urged on
the horses and bullocks, the day of toil entered upon its indefeasible
rights.

The end of August was fine and amazingly dry. The wind carried
the chaff dust through the village, a sweet scent of threshed, rusty

straw hung everywhere, the sun burned mercilessly, but the approach of the imminent autumn made itself felt in everything. The faded, dove-grey wormwood showed dimly white over the pasturage, the crowns of the poplars beyond the Don turned yellow, the scent of the autumn apples in the orchards grew keener, the distant horizons turned autumnally clear, and the first flocks of migrating cranes were seen in the harvested fields.

Baggage trains carrying military stores to the Don crossings rolled along the Hetman's highway from west to east; refugees arrived in the Donside hamlets. They told that the Cossacks were making a fighting retreat; some of them declared that this retreat was being carried out deliberately, in order to lure on the Reds, with the intention of surrounding and annihilating them. Some of the Tatarsk people began quietly to make ready for flight. They fed up their bullocks and horses, buried grain and chests filled with their most precious possessions in pits by night. The gunfire, which had died away on September 5, was renewed with greater intensity and now sounded distinct and menacing. The fighting was taking place some twenty-five miles beyond the Don, north-east from Tatarsk. A day later, gunfire could be heard rolling upstream from the west also. The front was steadily drawing nearer the river.

Hearing that the majority of the villagers were preparing to leave, Ilinichna suggested to Dunia that they also should go. She felt bewildered and perplexed, and did not know what to do about the farm, the house—whether they should abandon it all and drive off with the others or should remain at home. Before his departure for the front Pantaleimon had talked about the threshing, about ploughing, about the cattle; but he had not said one word indicating what they were to do if the front came near Tatarsk. In the end Ilinichna decided to send Dunia and the children together with their most valuable possessions with one of the villagers, and to remain behind herself, even if the Reds occupied the village.

During the night of September 17 Pantaleimon unexpectedly arrived home. He had come on foot from close to Kanzanska district centre and was worn out and ill-tempered. After resting for half an hour, he sat down at the table and began to eat as Ilinichna had never seen him eat before in all their life together. He threw a good half-bucketful of thin cabbage soup down his throat, then fell upon some millet porridge. Ilinichna clapped her hands in astonishment.

"Lord, the way you're eating, Prokoffich! I'd say you'd had nothing to eat for three days!"

"Well, and do you think I have, you old fool? It's exactly three days since I last had a bit between my teeth."

"Why, don't they feed you in the army, then?"

"May the devils feed them like it!" Pantaleimon answered, purring like a cat, his mouth crammed to the lips. "Whatever you can get hold of, you guzzle; but I haven't learned to steal yet. That's all very well for the youngsters, they've got no conscience. Through this accursed war they've got their hands so used to filching that I was aghast; but at last I got over it. They pinch everything they see and drag it off. . . . It's not war, but a scourge of God!"

"You'd better not eat your fill at one go. Something might happen to you. Look how you've swollen up, just like a spider."

"Hold your tongue! Bring me some milk, and some more bread." Ilinichna burst into tears as she watched her famished husband.

"Are you back for good?" she asked when at length he leaned back from his plate.

"We'll see," he answered evasively.

"I suppose they've let you old men go home?"

"They haven't let anybody go home. How can they, when the Reds are pushing towards the Don? I just cleared out."

"But won't you have to answer for it?" Ilinichna asked fearfully.

"If they catch me I may have to."

"Why, are you going to bury yourself, then?"

"And were you thinking I'd go visiting friends or seeing the sights? Pah, you stupid blockhead!" Pantaleimon spat in his annoyance; but the old woman did not stop pestering:

"Oh, what a sin! As if we hadn't enough sorrow, now they'll arrest you. . . ."

"Well, and it may be better to sit in prison than go dragging over the steppe with a rifle," Pantaleimon said wearily. "I'm no youngster to go marching twenty-five miles a day, to dig trenches, to attack at the double, and to crawl along the ground and bury myself away from the bullets. The devil can bury himself from them! A bullet caught a comrade of mine from Krivaya Rechka right under the left shoulder-blade, and he didn't even kick out his legs once. You don't get much pleasure out of such things!"

The old man carried his rifle and wallet of cartridges outside and hid them in the chaff-shed. But when Ilinichna asked where his fur coat was, he answered moodily and reluctantly:

"I've worn it out, or, to be more exact, I threw it away. Beyond Shumilinsk they pressed on us so hard that everybody dropped everything and ran like mad. There was no time to worry about coats then. . . . Some men had sheepskins, and they threw even them off. And what the devil have you thought of the coat for? Now, if it had been a good one—but it wasn't fit for a beggar."

In reality the coat had been a good new one, but anything the old man had had to abandon was always no good at all, so he said. It was the way he had of consoling himself. Ilinichna knew that, and so she did not bother to argue about the quality of the coat.

In a family council that night they decided that Ilinichna and Pantaleimon would remain at home with the children until the last moment, to look after their possessions and to bury the grain that had been threshed, while Dunia would drive off with the yoke of old bullocks and the family chests to relations in the hamlet of Latyshev, on the Chira.

This plan was not destined to be carried out in its entirety. They saw Dunia off next morning, but at noon a punitive detachment of Kalmyk Cossacks rode into Tatarsk. One of the Tatarsk villagers must have seen Pantaleimon making his way home, for an hour after their arrival the Kalmyks galloped up to the Melekhov yard. Catching sight of the horsemen, Pantaleimon scrambled up into the loft with extraordinary speed and agility. Ilinichna went out to meet the guests.

"Where's your old man?" an elderly, well-built Kalmyk with sergeant's stripes asked, dismounting and pushing past Ilinichna through the wicket gate.

"At the front. Where else should he be?" Ilinichna answered roughly.

"Lead us to your house; we are going to search it."

"What for?"

"To look for your old man. Ah, shame on you! An old woman like you, and telling lies!" The youthful-looking sergeant shook his head reproachfully and bared his white, close-set teeth.

"Don't you grin like that, you unchristened one! I said he's not here, and that means he's not here!"

"Drop your joking and lead us to your house. If you don't, we'll go by ourselves," the offended Kalmyk said sternly. He resolutely strode towards the porch, setting his out-turned feet wide apart.

They carefully searched the rooms, talked among themselves in Kalmyk, then two went off to look in the backyard, while one, short and swarthy, almost black, with a pockmarked face and snub nose, pulled up his broad-striped trousers and went into the porch. Through the wide-open door Ilinichna saw the Kalmyk jump, grip the crossbeam with his hands, and dextrously draw himself up. Five minutes later he nimbly jumped down again, and behind him, groaning, smothered with clay, a spider-web entangled in his beard, Pantaleimon carefully clambered down. Looking at the old woman, who was standing with lips tightly pressed together, he said:

"So they've found me, damn them! Someone must have told them. . . ."

He was taken under escort to the district centre of Kargin, where the field courts martial were being held. Ilinichna wept a little and, listening to the renewed gunfire and the clearly audible rattle of machine-guns beyond the Don, went into the granary to hide at least a little of the grain.

Fourteen captured deserters were awaiting trial. The trial was brief and merciless. The elderly captain who was president of the court asked the accused his name, his regiment, and found out how long he had been a deserter. Then he exchanged a few words in an undertone with the other members—a lieutenant who had lost one arm, and a bearded and puffy-faced sergeant out to curry favour— and announced the sentence. The majority of the deserters were sentenced to corporal punishment with the birch, the sentence being carried out by Kalmyks in an uninhabited house set apart specially for this purpose. Desertion had grown too extensive in the militant Don army to allow of open and public birching, as in 1918.

Pantaleimon was the sixth to be called before the court. Agitated and pale, he stood in front of the judges' table, his hands down his trouser seams.

"Your surname?" the captain asked, not looking at the accused.

"Melekhov, Your Excellency."

"Your Christian name, and Patronymic?"

"Pantaleimon Prokoffiev, Your Excellency."

The captain raised his eyes from his papers and looked fixedly at the old man.

"Where are you from?" he asked.

"From Tatarsk village in Vieshenska district, Your Excellency."

"You're not the father of squadron commander Gregor Melekhov, are you?"

"Yes, Your Excellency." Pantaleimon at once recovered his spirits, feeling that, so to speak, the birch was drawing farther away from his aged body.

"Listen! Aren't you ashamed of yourself?" the captain asked, not shifting his prickly eyes from Pantaleimon's sunken face.

At that the old man, breaking all the regulations, laid his left hand on his chest and said in a weeping tone:

"Your Excellency! Captain! Make me say prayers to God for you for the rest of my life! Don't sentence me to be whipped. I had two married sons. The elder one was killed by the Reds. . . . I've got grandchildren, and is it necessary to whip such a broken-down old man as I?"

"We have to teach old men also how to serve. Did you think you'd be awarded crosses for running away from the forces?" the one-armed lieutenant interrupted him. The corners of his mouth twitched nervously.

"What do I want a cross for? . . . Send me to my regiment and I shall serve in faith and truth. . . . I don't myself know how I came to run away; the unclean spirit must have taken hold of me." Pantaleimon went muttering on about the unthreshed grain, about his lameness, the neglected farm. But with a gesture the captain reduced him to silence, then bent over to the lieutenant and whispered into his ear. The lieutenant nodded, and the captain turned to Pantaleimon:

"Good! Have you said all you want to say? I know your son, and I am astonished that he has got such a father. When did you desert from the forces? A week ago? Well, and do you want the Reds to occupy your village and to flay the skin off you? Is that the sort of example you show the young Cossacks? By law we ought to con-

demn you and sentence you to corporal punishment; but out of respect for your son's rank as an officer I spare you that disgrace. Were
you a non-commissioned officer?"

"Yes, Your Excellency."

"What rank?"

"I was a corporal, Your Excellency."

"Reduced to the ranks!" The captain raised his voice and roughly
ordered: "Report to your regiment at once! Inform your company
commander that by decision of the field court martial you are deprived of the rank of corporal. Did you have any awards for this or
previous wars? . . . Off with you!"

Beside himself with joy, Pantaleimon went out, crossed himself
as he faced the church cupola, and, striking across the trackless hills,
made his way home. "Well, this time I shan't bury myself like that!
It'll take devils themselves to find me; they can send three companies of Kalmyks to look for me!" he thought as he limped across
the stubble-field, overgrown with meadow grass.

Out on the steppe he decided that it would be better to go along
the road, in order not to attract the attention of people riding by.
"They'd be bound to think I was a deserter. I might run into soldiers, and they'd lay on the whip without trying me first," he deliberated aloud, turning off the ploughed lands on to a neglected
summer track overgrown with plantain, and already no longer
thinking of himself as a deserter.

The closer he drew to the Don, the more frequently he fell in with
refugees' wagons. The scenes which had occurred in the spring during the insurgents' retreat to the left bank of the river were now being repeated. Wagons and britskas loaded with household treasures,
and droves of bellowing cattle like cavalry on the march, stretched
in all directions over the steppe; flocks of sheep raised clouds of
dust. The creaking of wheels, the neighing of horses, human
shouts, the trample of innumerable hoofs, the bleating of sheep,
children's weeping, filled the tranquil expanses of the steppe with
incessant and disturbing noise.

"Where are you off to, grand-dad? Go back, the Reds are right behind us!" a Cossack with bandaged head shouted from a passing
wagon.

"Fine talk! Where are the Reds?" Pantaleimon halted in consternation.

"On the farther side of the Don. They're getting near Vieshenska. Are you going over to them?"

Reassured on hearing that the river was between him and the Reds, Pantaleimon continued his journey and towards evening drew near to Tatarsk. As he dropped down from the hill he carefully examined the terrain. The village amazed him by its deserted look. Not a soul was to be seen in the streets. Neither human voices were to be heard, nor the lowing of cattle; but down by the river itself people were scurrying about actively. As he drew nearer, Pantaleimon had no difficulty in recognizing that they were armed Cossacks drawing up barges and carrying them into the village. Tatarsk was completely abandoned by its inhabitants, Pantaleimon could see that clearly. Cautiously turning into his side lane, he strode towards the hut. Ilinichna and the grandchildren were sitting in the kitchen.

"Why, here's Grand-dad!" Mishatka cried out in delight, flinging his arms around the old man's neck.

Ilinichna burst into tears of joy and said through her tears:

"I never hoped to see you again! Well, Prokoffich, it's as you wish, but I'm not willing to stay here any longer. Let everything be burned to the ground, but I'm not going to watch over an empty hut. Almost everybody else has left the village; but here am I sitting with the children like a fool. Harness up the mare at once, and let's ride wherever we can. Have they let you go?"

"Yes."

"For good?"

"For good, so long as they don't catch me!"

"Well, you can't hide here. This morning, when the Reds were firing from the opposite bank, it was terrible. I took the children down into the cellar so long as it went on. But now they've been driven off. Some Cossacks came and asked for milk and advised us to clear out of here."

"Cossacks? They're not our villagers, then?" Pantaleimon asked with interest, closely examining a fresh bullet-hole in the window-frame.

"No, they're strangers; from the Khopra, I think."

"Then we've got to go," Pantaleimon said with a sigh.

Late in the afternoon he dug a hole under the dung-fuel heap, rolled seven sacks of wheat into it, carefully filled it up, and piled dung-fuel bricks over it. As soon as dusk fell he harnessed the mare into the wagonette, put two sheepskin coats, a sack of flour, millet, and a bound sheep in it, tied both cows to the back, and, seating Ilinichna and the children on the sacks, said:

"Well, and now God be with us!" He drove out of the yard, handed the reins to his old wife, closed the gates, and as far as the hills strode along beside the wagonette, sniffing and wiping the tears away with his coat sleeve.

Chapter 2

For two and a half weeks Pantaleimon lived safely with his family in the little village of Latyshev. Then he heard that the Reds had fallen back from the Don, and made ready to drive home.

Some three miles outside Tatarsk he climbed down with a resolute air from the wagon and said:

"I can't stand any more of this footpace! And with those damned cows you can't go at a trot! What the devil did we drive them with us for? Dunia, halt your bullocks! Tie the cows to your wagon, and I'll trot off home. Maybe there's only ashes left of our hut."

Urged on by the greatest impatience, he transferred the children from his wagonette to Dunia's spacious wagon, put all the surplus load into it also, and, with a lighter wagonette, rattled over the humpy road at a trot. The mare sweated even during the first two miles; never had her master treated her so mercilessly. He did not let the knout out of his hands, but incessantly whipped her on.

"You'll overdrive the mare! What are you galloping along like an infidel for?" said Ilinichna, clinging to the ribs of the wagonette, painfully knitting her brows as she was violently jolted about.

"In any case she won't come to my grave to weep. . . . Now! You devil! Sweating like that! Maybe there's only stumps left of our hut . . ." Pantaleimon said through clenched teeth.

His fears proved unfounded: the hut stood whole. But almost all its windows were broken out, the door had been torn from its hinges, the walls were pitted with bullets. Everything in the yard had a look of neglect and desolation. One corner of the stable had been carried away by a shell; a second shell had dug a shallow crater close to the well, smashing the frame and breaking the well-crane in two. The war from which Pantaleimon had fled had itself come to his home, leaving behind it the hideous traces of its destruction. But still greater damage had been done to the farm by the Khopersk Cossacks who had been quartered in Tatarsk. In the cattle-yard they had thrown down the fences and had dug trenches to the depth of a man's height. To avoid extra work they had taken a granary wall to pieces and had used the beams as flooring for the trenches; they had scattered stones from the stone wall when making a loop-hole for a machine-gun; they had got rid of half a stack of hay, recklessly feeding it to their horses; they had set fire to the wattle fences and had made a mess of the outdoor kitchen stove.

When he had surveyed the house and the yard buildings Pantaleimon clutched his head. This time his usual habit of depreciating his losses forsook him. Damn it, he couldn't say that all he had lost had cost him nothing and was good only for straw! A granary was not a coat, and it had cost no small sum to build.

"It's just as though it had never been a granary," Ilinichna said with a sigh.

"And it was a granary, too!" Pantaleimon said energetically. But he did not finish his sentence; he waved his hand and went into the threshing-floor.

The pockmarked walls of the house, mutilated with bullets and fragments of shell, looked forbidding and neglected. The wind was whistling through the rooms, dust lay thickly on the tables and benches. It would take much time to put everything in order again.

The very next day Pantaleimon rode on horseback to Vieshenska and after some trouble wheedled out of his medical friend a document certifying that owing to his leg trouble the Cossack Pantaleimon Prokoffievich Melekhov was incapable of walking and needed a course of treatment. This certificate saved the old man from being sent back to the front. He presented it to the ataman, and whenever he went to the village administration, to make his case look more convincing he leaned heavily on his stick, limping on each leg in turn.

Never before had life in Tatarsk involved so much bustle and disorder as after that return from the retreat. People went from yard to yard identifying their possessions, which had been scattered about by the Khopersk Cossacks. They wandered over the steppe and through the ravines in search of cows separated from the herd. The very first day Tatarsk came under artillery fire, a flock of three hundred sheep had vanished altogether from the upper end of the village. According to the shepherd, one of the shells had burst just in front of the grazing flock, and the sheep, waving their thick tails, had torn off into the steppe in terror and had vanished. They were found some twenty-five miles away, a week after the inhabitants had returned to their deserted village. But when they were driven back and were sorted out, it appeared that half the flock were strange sheep, with an unknown clip in their ears, while more than fifty of the Tatarsk sheep were missing. A sewing-machine belonging to the Bogatirievs was found in the Melekhovs' garden, while Pantaleimon discovered the sheet-iron roof of his granary on Anikushka's thresh-ing-floor. The same sort of thing had happened in all the neighbour-ing villages. And for a long time the inhabitants of near and far villages of the Donside area came visiting Tatarsk, and for a long time afterwards the questions were being asked: "You haven't seen a cow, red, with a bald patch on her forehead, the left horn broken short?" "A yearling bull, a dun, hasn't happened to wander into your village, by any chance?"

Without doubt more than one yearling bull had been boiled in the Cossack squadrons' cauldrons and cooked in the field kitchens. But, spurred on by hope, the owners went striding across the steppe until they were convinced that they would never find all they had lost.

Now he was released from service, Pantaleimon energetically put the outbuildings and the fencing in order. Stacks of grain still un-threshed were piled on the threshing-floor, the gluttonous mice went burrowing through them, but the old man did not set his hand to the threshing. How could he, when the farm stood unfenced, there was no sign of a granary, and everything on the farm bore the shameful stigma of disorder? In addition, bad weather set in with the autumn, and there was no chance of getting on with the threshing.

Dunia and Ilinichna replastered and whitewashed the hut and helped Pantaleimon to erect a temporary fencing and to do other jobs. Somehow or other they got hold of glass, reglazed the win-dows, cleaned up the summer kitchen, the well. The old man himself went down the well and evidently caught a cold down there, for he went coughing and sneezing with his shirt wet with sweat for a week. But he had only to drink a couple of bottles of home-made vodka at one sitting, then to lie awhile on the hot stove for his malady to vanish as though suddenly taken from him.

There was still no news from Gregor, and only at the end of October did Pantaleimon learn by chance that he was quite well and with his regiment somewhere in Voroniezh province. He gleaned this information from a wounded Cossack of Gregor's regiment who passed through the village. The old man cheered up mightily, and in his joy drank his last bottle of medicinal vodka distilled from red pepper. Afterwards he was talkative all day and as proud as a young cock. He halted every passer-by to tell them:

"Have you heard the news? Our Gregor's captured Voroniezh. We've had a rumour that he's been raised in rank and is now commanding a division again, or possibly an army corps. You'd go a long way to find such warriors as him! You know yourself. . . ." So the old man spun his yarns, feeling an invincible necessity to share his joy, to brag.

"Your son's a hero," the villagers told him.

Pantaleimon winked happily.

"And how could he help being a hero when you know whose son he is? When I was young I, too—I say it without boasting—I was no worse than him! My leg prevents me or I wouldn't let him better me even now! If there were more of us old men at the front we'd have taken Moscow long ago. But now we're marking time, we can't manage the peasants anyhow. . . ."

The last person to whom Pantaleimon happened to talk that day was old Beskhlebnov. He came past the Melekhovs' yard, and Pantaleimon did not fail to stop him with:

"Hey, wait a bit, Filip Agievich! How are you getting on? Come in for a minute and let's have a chat."

Beskhlebnov came up and greeted Pantaleimon.

"Have you heard what a dance my Grishka's leading me?" Pantaleimon asked.

"Why, what's he been up to?"

"They've put him in command of a division. That's the chaff he's in charge of now!"

"A division?"

"Yes, a division."

"You don't say!"

"But I do! Who else should they put in command of it, tell me."

"Of course."

Pantaleimon exultantly stared at his companion and continued the conversation so dear to his heart:

"I've got a son who's the astonishment of everybody! A chest full of crosses—what do you say to that? And the times he's been wounded and got contusions! Any other man would have given up the ghost long ago, but it's nothing to him, it's like water on a duck's back. No, real Cossacks haven't yet died out altogether in the Don lands."

"You're right, there, but somehow we don't seem to get much benefit from them," old Beskhlebnov, who was never noted for garrulity, repeated thoughtfully.

"How do you make that out? Look how far they've driven the Reds, right beyond Voroniezh now, and they're getting near to Moscow."

"They're taking a long time to get near. . . ."

"It can't be done in a hurry, Filip Agievich. You've got to realize that in war nothing is ever done in a hurry. Hurried work is botched work. You've got to do everything little by little, according to the maps, according to the plans . . . according to all sorts of things. Peasants in Russia are as plentiful as grasshoppers, and how many of us Cossacks are there? A handful?"

"That's all true, but it looks as though our men won't be able to hold out for long. We must expect guests again by winter, so people are saying."

"If they don't take Moscow quickly now, then the Reds will be back here again. You're right so far as that goes."

"But do you think they'll take Moscow?"

"They ought to; but it's as God wills. Surely our men can manage it? The Cossacks have been raised down to the last man, and can't they manage it?"

"The devil knows! And how about you—done with fighting now?"

"I'm a fine warrior! But if it wasn't for this trouble with my leg I'd show them how to fight the enemy! We old men are a sturdy lot!"

"They say the sturdy old men ran so hard from the Reds on the other side of the Don that not one of them was left with a sheepskin. They stripped themselves of everything down to their skin and threw it all away. They say all the steppe was yellow with sheep-skins, and it looked like a carpet of flowers."

Pantaleimon gave Beskhlebnov a sidelong glance and said dryly: "In my view that's all lies! Maybe some of them did throw off their clothing to make things light, but why should people go and make it out a hundred times worse than it is? A great matter—a coat, or even a sheepskin jacket! Life is more precious than that—or isn't it, I ask. And besides, it isn't every old man that can run well in his clothes. In this accursed war you need to have legs like those of a borzoi bitch. And take me, for instance: where am I to get legs like that? And why are you so upset about it, Filip Agievich? God for-give me, but what the devil is the use of them—the sheepskins, I mean—to you? It isn't a question of sheepskins, or even coats, but of smashing the enemy as much as possible. That's so, isn't it? Well, so long; we've got talking, and there's work waiting for me. Did you find your calf, by the way? Still looking for it? And no news of it? Well, I expect the Khopersk men ate it; may it choke them! But don't you worry about the war: our men will get the better of the peasants!" And Pantaleimon limped with an important air towards the steps.

But evidently it was not so easy to "get the better of the peasants." The last Cossack offensive had not been achieved without losses. Only an hour later Pantaleimon's cheerful mood was clouded by un-happy news. As he was adzing a beam for the well-frame he heard a woman crying and lamenting for the dead. The sounds came closer. Pantaleimon sent Dunia to investigate.

"Run and find out who's died," he said, setting his axe into the chopping-block.

Dunia quickly returned with the news that three dead Cossacks had been brought home from the Filonovsk front: Anikushka, Chris-tonia, and another, a seventeen-year-old youngster from the far end of the village. Dumbfounded by the news, Pantaleimon took off his cap and crossed himself.

"May the Lord take them to His kingdom! What a fine Cossack

he was!" he said mournfully, thinking of Christonia and recalling how recently he and Christonia had set off together from Tatarsk to go to the assembly point.

He could work no longer. Anikushka's wife was howling as though she were being slaughtered and lamenting so bitterly that the old man's heart sank. To get away from the heart-rending cry he went into the house and shut the door fast behind him. In the best room Dunia was sobbing as she told Ilinichna:

"I—I looked, dear Mamma, and Anikushka was almost without a head, it was like porridge instead of a head. Oh, it was horrible! And he stank so much you could have smelt him a mile away. And why they brought them home I don't know! But Christonia was lying on his back right along the wagon, his legs were hanging out from under his greatcoat. . . . He was clean and so white, so white as though he'd been boiled. Only under his right eye was a little hole, very small, no bigger than a kopek piece, and behind his ear blood was caked."

Pantaleimon spat furiously, went into the yard, took the axe and an oar, and limped off to the Don. As he went he called to Mishatka, who was playing close to the summer kitchen:

"Tell your granny I've rowed across the river to cut down brush-wood. Do you hear, my dear?"

In the forest beyond the Don a quiet, gracious autumn had settled. The dry leaves were falling with a rustle from the poplars. The bushes of thorn seemed wrapped in flame, and among their scanty leaves the crimson berries flamed like little tongues of fire. The bitter, all-conquering scent of rotting oak bark filled the forest. Bilberries, dense and clinging, entangled the ground; beneath the network of their creeping branches smokily dove-blue, ripe bunches of berries hid artfully from the sun. In the shade dew lay on the dead grass until noonday, a spider-web glittered silver with its beads. Only the methodical tapping of the woodpecker and the twittering of the missel-thrushes violated the silence.

The taciturn, severe beauty of the forest had an appeasing effect on Pantaleimon. He stepped quietly among the bushes, his feet scraping the damp coverlet of the fallen leaves, thinking: "That's life, that is! Only recently they were alive, and today they're robbed of life. What a Cossack's been knocked over! And it seems only the other day that he came and visited us, and stood down by the river when we fished out Daria. Ah, Christan, Christan! An enemy bullet has been found for you, too, now! And Anikushka—! What a cheery sort he was! He loved drinking and laughing, and now he's only a corpse!" Pantaleimon recalled Dunia's description and, with unexpected clarity calling to mind Anikushka's smiling, whiskerless, emasculated face, he simply could not imagine him lifeless, with shattered head. "I did wrong to anger God by boasting about Gregor," he reproached himself, as he recalled his talk with Beskhlebnov. "Maybe Gregor himself is lying somewhere now, pecked to bits by bullets. God forbid and prevent that! What would us old folk have left to live with then?"

A brown woodcock starting up from under a bush made Pantaleimon fall back in alarm. He aimlessly watched the little bird's slanting, impetuous flight, then went on. By a small forest pool he took a fancy to several bushes of brushwood and set to work to cut them down. As he worked he tried not to think of anything. In one year death had struck down so many dear ones and friends that at the very thought he was oppressed, and all the world faded and seemed to be enveloped in a film of black.

"Now I must cut down that bush! It's good brushwood, that! Just right for making wattle fencing," he talked aloud to himself, in order to distract himself from his gloomy thoughts. When he had worked long enough, he removed his jacket, sat down on the pile of cut brushwood, and, avidly drawing in the pungent scent of faded leaves, gazed long at the distant horizon merged into an azure haze, at the copses gilded with autumn, adorned with their last beauty. Not far off stood a maple sapling. It was indescribably beautiful, gleaming under the cold autumnal sun, and its spreading branches, burdened with purple foliage, were unfolded like the wings of some legendary bird about to soar up from the earth. Pantaleimon sat long admiring it, then he happened to glance down at the pool and in the translucent, stagnant water saw the dark backs of great carp floating so close to the surface that he could see their fins and their wriggling purple tails. Occasionally they disappeared under the green shields of water-lilies, then swam out again into clear water, darting at the wet, drowning leaves fallen from a willow. By autumn the pool had almost dried up, and it would not take a great deal of effort to catch those carp. After a little search Pantaleimon found a sack without a bottom to it, abandoned beside a neighbouring pond. He returned to the pool, removed his trousers, and, groaning with the cold, his flesh bristling, waded through the water with the sack, pressing its lower edge against the bottom of the pool. Then he thrust his hand inside, feeling sure a powerful fish would be splashing and bubbling in it. His labours were crowned with success: he managed to catch three carp, each weighing a good eight pounds. But he could not continue his fishing any longer, for owing to the cold his maimed leg began to get cramp. Satisfied with his catch, he wiped his legs dry, dressed, and again set to work to cut down brushwood in order to get warm. All the same, he had done a good day's work. It wasn't everybody's luck to catch three fish nearly thirty pounds in weight like that! The fishing had distracted his thoughts, driven away his gloomy mood. With the intention of returning to catch the remaining fish, he carefully hid the sack and looked about him anxiously, to make sure no one had seen him as he threw the fat, golden, almost piglike carp on to the bank. Then he strung the fish on a switch, lifted his bundle of brushwood, and unhurriedly made his way to the river.

With a satisfied smile he told Ilinichna of his fisherman's luck and once more admired the ruddy copper hue of the carp. But Ilinichna was not ready to share his raptures. She had been to look at the dead men and had come back tear-stained and sorrowful.

"Are you going to see Anikushka?" she asked.

"No, I shan't. Haven't I ever seen dead men before? I've seen enough to last my lifetime."

"You ought to go. Other folk'll think it strange; they'll say you didn't even call to pay your last respects."

"Oh, leave me alone, for Christ's sake! He wasn't godfather to the children, and there's no reason why I should pay my last respects," the old man snapped back furiously.

Nor did he go to the funeral; he rowed across the river early in the morning and spent all day in the forest. While he was in the forest he heard the bell tolling and felt impelled to take off his cap, to cross himself. But then he grew annoyed with the priest: was there any sense in ringing the bell so long? He could have tolled the bell and been done with it; but it went on ringing for a whole hour. And what good came of all that ringing? It only wrenched people's hearts and made them think unnecessarily of death. And as it was, in the autumn everything reminded you of death: the falling leaves, and the geese flying and crying through the azure sky, and the dead-lying grass.

Despite all his attempts to spare himself any kind of painful experience, he was destined to suffer a new blow ere long. One day after dinner Dunia glanced out of the window and said:

"Why, they're bringing back yet another man killed at the front. His saddle charger is walking tied by the leading-rein behind the wagon, and they're driving ever so slowly. . . . One man's driving the horses, and there's a dead man lying under a greatcoat. The man driving is sitting with his back to us, and I can't see whether he's from our village or not. . . ." Dunia gazed fixedly, and her cheeks went whiter than linen. "But it's—it's—" she whispered incoherently, and suddenly gave a piercing scream: "It's Grishka they're bringing! It's his horse!" Crying, she ran out into the porch.

Ilinichna covered her eyes with her palm and remained sitting at the table. Pantaleimon rose heavily from the bench and went towards the door, stretching out his hands before him as though he were blind.

Prokhor Zykov opened the gates, glanced at Dunia as she ran down the steps, and said in a cheerless tone:

"Here's a guest for you. . . . You weren't expecting us, were you?"

"Our darling! My darling brother!" Dunia groaned, wringing her hands.

Only then, as he stared at her face wet with tears, at Pantaleimon standing speechless on the steps, did Prokhor think of saying:

"Don't get alarmed, don't get alarmed! He's alive. He's got typhus."

Pantaleimon weakly leaned his back against the doorpost.

"He's alive!" Dunia shouted to him, laughing and weeping. "Grishka's alive! Do you hear? They've brought him home ill. Go and tell Mother. Well, what are you standing there for?"

"Don't be alarmed, Pantaleimon Prokoffich! I've brought him back alive, but don't ask after his health," Prokhor hurriedly confirmed as he led the horses into the yard.

Pantaleimon took a few uncertain paces, then sank down on one of the steps. Dunia flew like a whirlwind past him into the house to reassure her mother. Prokhor halted the horses by the steps and looked at Pantaleimon.

"What are you sitting there for? Fetch a hurdle and we'll carry him in."

The old man sat without speaking. The tears were streaming from his eyes, but his face was rigid, and not a muscle quivered on it. Twice he raised his hand to cross himself and dropped it, powerless to lift it right to his forehead. Something bubbled and gurgled in his throat.

"I can see you're crazed with fear," Prokhor said commiserately. "Why didn't I think of sending someone on to warn you? I was a fool, a real fool, and no mistake. Well, get up, Prokoffich, the sick man's got to be carried in all the same. Where's a rug? Or shall we carry him in in our arms?"

"Wait a bit . . ." Pantaleimon said hoarsely. "My legs seem to have given way. . . . I thought he was killed. Glory be! . . . I didn't expect . . ." He tore away the button at the neck of his old shirt, threw open the collar, and gulped in air with his gaping mouth.

"Get up, get up, Prokoffich!" Prokhor hurried him. "There's nobody else but us to carry him in, is there?"

With obvious effort Pantaleimon rose, went down the steps, threw back the greatcoat, and bent over the unconscious Gregor. Something again began to gurgle in his throat, but he mastered himself and turned to Prokhor. "Take hold of his legs. We'll carry him."

They carried Gregor into the best room, took off his boots, undressed him, and laid him in the bed. Dunia anxiously called from the kitchen:

"Father! Mother's bad! Come here!"

Ilinichna was lying on the kitchen floor. Dunia was on her knees beside her, sprinkling water on her ashen face.

"Run and fetch old woman Kapitonovna, quick! She knows how to let blood. Tell her your mother must have her blood let, tell her to bring her instruments with her," Pantaleimon ordered.

But Dunia, a girl of marriageable years, could not run through the village with head uncovered; she snatched up a kerchief and said as she hurriedly wrapped her head:

"The children are frightened to death. God, what a blow this is! . . . Look after them, Father, and I'll be off in a moment."

Possibly Dunia might even have stopped to glance into the mirror. But Pantaleimon, who had now recovered, looked at her with such a fierce expression that she fled headlong out of the kitchen.

As she ran out of the wicket gate, she saw Aksinia. There was not a drop of blood in Aksinia's white face. She was standing leaning against the wattle fence, her hands hanging lifelessly. No tears glittered in her filmy black eyes, but in there were so much suffering and dumb entreaty that Dunia halted for a second and said reluctantly, surprising herself:

"He's alive, alive! He's got typhus." She ran off along the side lane at full speed, steadying her supple, dancing breasts with her hands.

From all sides inquisitive women were hurrying to the Melekhovs' yard. They saw Aksinia slowly walk away from the Melekhovs' wicket gate; then she suddenly hastened her steps, bowed her head, and covered her face with her hands.

Chapter 3

Gregor was well again within a month. He first rose from his bed towards the end of October and, tall, as gaunt as a skeleton, uncertainly walked about the room and halted by the window.

A young, thin snow showed a dazzling white on the ground and on the straw-thatched roofs. The tracks of sledge-runners were visible along the side lane. A bluish rime feathered the fences and trees, glittering and giving off rainbow colours under the rays of the setting sun.

He stood gazing long out of the window, smiling thoughtfully, stroking his moustache with his bony hands. One would have thought he had never seen such a glorious winter before. To him everything seemed unusual, imbued with freshness and meaning. After his illness his sight seemed to have grown keener, and he began to discover new objects in his surroundings, to find changes in things which he had known for many years.

He unexpectedly developed a far from characteristic curiosity and interest in everything occurring in the village and on the farm. Everything in his life acquired a new, secret significance, everything attracted his attention. With eyes expressing a slight astonishment he gazed at the new world which had been revealed to him; over his face hovered a simple, childlike smile, in strange contrast to his harsh features, to the expression of his animal-like eyes, and softening the cruel folds at the corners of his lips. Occasionally he picked up and examined some object of domestic use which he had known since childhood, tensely knitting his brows and looking at it as though he were someone recently arrived from a strange, distant land and seeing it all for the first time. Ilinichna was amazed beyond measure one day to find him examining a distaff from all sides. The moment she entered the room he stepped away from the distaff, looking a little sheepish.

Dunia could not look at his bony, lanky figure without laughing. He walked about the room dressed only in his underlinen, holding up his slipping pants with one hand, hunching his back, uncertainly straddling his thin, shanky legs. And when he sat down he was always afraid of falling and clutched at something with his hand. His black hair, grown long during his illness, was falling out; his curly, grizzled forelock was lank.

He got Dunia to help him shave his head, and when he turned his face to his sister she let the razor drop to the floor, clutched at her belly, and, falling on the bed, nearly choked with laughter.

Gregor patiently waited for her to laugh her fill; but at last he could wait no longer and said in a feeble, quivering tenor voice:

"Look out, you're not far from sinning! You'll be ashamed afterwards, you're a woman now, you know!" A hint of injury sounded in his words.

"Oh, my brother! My dear! I'd better go . . . I haven't the strength! Oh, what do you look like? Why, you're an absolute scarecrow!" Dunia could hardly get the words out between her attacks of laughter.

"I'd like to see what you'd look like after typhus! Pick up the razor! Now!"

Ilinichna took up the cudgels on his behalf, saying in a vexed tone:

"And what are you neighing at, after all? You're a fool, Dunia!"

"But see what he looks like, Mother," Dunia said, wiping away her tears. "His head's all bumps, it's as round as a watermelon and just as dark. . . . Oh, I can't any more!"

"Give me a mirror," Gregor asked.

He looked into the tiny scrap of mirror and then himself laughed long and noiselessly.

"What did you shave your head for, son? You'd have done better to have left it as it was," Ilinichna said discontentedly.

"So you think it's better to go completely bald?"

"Well, even as you are it's a terrible disgrace. . . ."

"Oh, you're the limit!" Gregor said angrily, whipping up a soapy foam with his brush.

Unable to go outside the house, he spent much time with the children. He talked with them about everything, but avoided mentioning Natalia. One day, however, Poliushka nestled against him and asked:

"Daddy, won't Mummy be coming back to us?"

"No, dear; you don't come back from there."

"From where? From the cemetery?"

"You see, the dead just don't come back."

"But is she quite dead?"

"Why, what else could she be? Of course she's dead."

"But I thought she might sometimes long for us and come . . ." Poliushka whispered almost inaudibly.

"Don't think about her, my dear; it's better not to," Gregor said huskily.

"How can I help thinking of her? But don't they ever come to see you? Not even for a tiny bit? Never?"

"No. Now go and play with Mishatka." Gregor turned away. Evidently his illness had sapped the strength of his will; tears appeared in his eyes and, to hide them from the children, he stood a long time at the window, his face pressed to the glass.

He did not like talking to the children about the war, but Mishatka was more interested in the war than in anything else in the world. He frequently pestered his father with questions: how did people fight, and what were the Reds like, and what did they kill them with, and what for? Gregor's face clouded, and he answered irritably:

"So you're singing that same old song again? What is it worrying you for—this war? Let's talk of how we'll catch fish with hooks when summer comes. Shall I make you a hook? As soon as I can get out into the yard I'll twist you a line of horsehair."

He felt an inward shame whenever Mishatka began to talk about the war; he could find no answers whatever to the child's artless and simple questions. Who can say why? Maybe it was because he himself had not found answers to these questions. But it was not so easy to shake off Mishatka; he seemed to listen attentively to his father's plans for going fishing, but afterwards asked again:

"Daddy, have you killed anybody in the war?"

"Stop plaguing me, little bur!"

"But is it terrible to kill them? And does the blood run out of them when they're killed? Lots of blood? More than out of a chicken or a sheep?"

"I've told you to stop all this talk!"

Mishatka was silent for a moment, then said thoughtfully:

"I saw Grand-dad slaughter a sheep recently. I wasn't afraid. . . . Just a little teeny bit, perhaps, but not at all really."

"Drive him away!" Ilinichna said angrily. "He'll grow up to be another murderer. A real criminal! All he talks about is the war; he doesn't know anything else to talk about. Is it sensible for you to talk about that—God forgive me—accursed war, child? Come here! Take this pancake and keep quiet for a moment at least."

But every day the war reminded them of its existence. Cossacks returned from the front called to see Gregor, and told how the generals Shkuro and Mamontov had been smashed by Budionny's cavalry, of the unsuccessful battles close to Orlo, and the retreats which had set in on all the fronts. Two more Tatarsk Cossacks had been killed in the fighting at Gribanovska and Kardaila, while Gerasim Akhvatkin had been brought home wounded, and Dmitry Goloshchekov had died of typhus. Gregor recalled all the Cossacks of his village who had been killed in the two wars, and it seemed to him that not one home in Tatarsk was left without its dead.

Gregor was still unable to leave the house when the village ataman brought an instruction he had received from the district ataman, ordering him to inform Squadron Commander Melekhov that he was to present himself immediately before a medical commission for further examination.

"Write back and tell him that as soon as I learn to walk I'll turn up of my own accord, without any reminders," Gregor said angrily.

The front steadily drew nearer the Don. In the village there began to be renewed talk of retreat. A little later an order issued by the regional ataman, commanding all adult Cossacks to take part in the retreat, was read out in the market square.

Pantaleimon came home from the square, told Gregor of the order, and said:

"What shall we do?"

Gregor shrugged his shoulders.

"What can we do? We've got to retreat. Even without the order everybody will go."

"I'm talking about you and me—shall we go together, or how?"

"We can't go together. In a day or two I'll ride to Vieshenska and find out what forces are to pass through there, and I'll join up with one of the regiments. But your job is to flee as a refugee. Or do you want to join up with a military force?"

"God forbid!" Pantaleimon said in affright. "In that case I'll ride with old gaffer Beskhlebnov; the other day he invited me to ride with him for company. He's a peaceable old man, and he's got a good horse, so we'll harness up and gallop along with a pair of horses. My mare's lost all her fat too. She's been driven almost to death, and she kicks so much that she's terrible."

"Well, then you go with him," Gregor willingly supported the idea. "But meantime let's talk over the way you're to go, for maybe I shall have to take the same road."

He took a map of southern Russia out of his wallet and detailed to his father the villages through which the old man would have to drive, then began to write the names down on paper. But the old man, who had been respectfully examining the map, remarked:

"Stop, don't write them down! Of course, you understand these things better than me, and a map's a serious matter. It never lies and it shows you the straight road. But how am I to keep to that road if it isn't suitable for me? You say that first we've got to drive through Kargin. I can see it's a straighter road that way, but all the same I've got to take a roundabout road."

"But why have you?"

"Because I've got a first cousin living in Latyshev, and I can get food for myself and the horses there. But if I put up with strangers I shall have to use my own food. And you say that according to the map I ought to drive through Astakhov village. That's the straighter road, I know, but I shall drive through Malakhov. I've got distant relations there too, and I can save my own hay and use other people's. Remember you can't carry a stack of hay about with you, and in a strange district you may find that you not only can't beg hay, but you won't even be able to buy it."

"But haven't you got any relations on the other side of the Don?" Gregor asked venomously.

"Yes, I have."

"So you'll go that way too, I suppose?"

"Don't put those devilish ideas about!" Pantaleimon flared up. "You speak to the point, and don't try to be funny! A fine time to make jokes! We've got a clever man in the family now!"

"There's no point in your visiting all your relations. A retreat's a retreat, and not a matter of visiting relations. It's not carnival time."

"Well, don't instruct me the way to take, I know it without you."

"If you know, then go whichever way you like."

"It's no good my trying to drive according to your plans. Only a magpie flies straight; you've heard that said, haven't you? I might go driving the devil knows where, in places where maybe there aren't any roads in the winter-time at all. Were you really using your wits when you started talking such nonsense? And you commanded a division, too!"

Gregor and the old man wrangled for a long time, but, after thinking it over, Gregor had to admit that there was a good deal of force in the old man's remarks, and he said in a conciliatory tone:

"Don't be angry, Father; I won't try to make you follow my route. You drive as you wish. I shall try to look for you beyond the Donietz."

"You should have said that long ago," Pantaleimon rejoiced. "You go on suggesting all sorts of plans and routes, but the one thing you don't understand is that a plan's one thing, but horses can't go anywhere without fodder."

The old man made leisurely preparations for departure even while Gregor was still ill: he had fed up his mare with unusual care, had repaired the sledge, had ordered new felt boots to be made for him, and had himself lined them with leather, so that they would not get soaked on wet roads; and he had poured selected oats into sacks. Even for the retreat he made ready like a true master of the house; he prudently prepared everything that might be of some use on the journey. An axe, a hand-saw, a chisel, shoe-repairing tools, threads, spare soles, nails, a hammer, a bunch of straps, two ropes, a lump of pitch—everything down to horseshoes and farriers' nails was carefully wrapped in tarpaulin and could be laid in the sledge in a moment. He even proposed to take a steelyard with him, and when Ilinichna asked what need he would have for a steelyard he reproachfully answered:

"You know, wife, the more you try, the more stupid you get. Do you mean to say you can't answer such a simple question for yourself? Shan't I have to buy chaff or hay by weight while on the retreat? Do they measure hay out by the yard?"

"But won't people have scales of their own?" Ilinichna asked in amazement.

"How do you know what sort of scales they'll have?" Pantaleimon grew indignant. "Maybe all their scales are false, in order to give short weight to the likes of us. That's just it! We know the sort of people who live there! You buy thirty pounds, but you pay enough money for a pood.[1] And if I've got to stand such a loss every time we stop, it would be better for me to take my own steelyard with me. It won't weigh us down! But you can manage here without scales; what the devil would be the good of them to you? If the military forces come they'll take hay without weighing it. All they're concerned about is carting it off. I've seen them, the hornless devils; I know them only too well!"

At first he even thought of taking a wagonette on the sledge, so as not to waste money buying one in the spring. But afterwards he thought better of it and gave up this hopeless idea.

Gregor also began to make ready. He cleaned his Mauser, his rifle, put his faithful sabre in good order. A week after his recovery he went out to see his horse and, looking at its gleaming crupper, was satisfied that the old man had not fed only his own mare. He climbed painfully on the restive horse, gave it a good ride, and, on his return home, saw—or maybe he only imagined he saw—someone

[1] Thirty-six pounds.

wave to him with a tiny white handkerchief through the window of the Astakhovs' hut.

At a village assembly the male inhabitants of Tatarsk decided to leave all on one day. Two days the women spent baking and frying all kinds of provisions for the Cossacks' journey. The departure was fixed for December 12. The previous evening Pantaleimon put hay and oats into the sledge, and next morning, as soon as dawn began to break, he put on his great sheepskin overcoat, belted himself tightly, thrust his capacious leather driving gloves into his belt, said his prayers to God, and took leave of his family.

Soon an enormous baggage train was extending up the hill from the village. The women went out to the common pasturage and long, long waved their handkerchiefs to their departing menfolk. But then a low breeze sprang up in the steppe, and through the seething, snowy mist neither the wagons slowly climbing the hill nor the Cossacks striding beside them were visible.

Before his departure to Vieshenska, Gregor had a meeting with Aksinia. He went to see her in the evening, when lights were already lit in the village. Aksinia was spinning. Beside her Anikushka's widow was sitting knitting socks and telling some story. Seeing the stranger, Gregor curtly said to Aksinia:

"Come outside for a minute; I've got business with you."

In the porch he laid his hand on her shoulder and asked:

"Will you come with me on the retreat?"

She was long silent, thinking over her answer. Then she quietly said:

"But how about the farm? And the horse?"

"You must leave everything in someone's charge. I've got to retreat."

"But when?"

"I'll drive round for you tomorrow."

Smiling in the darkness, Aksinia said:

"You remember I told you a long time ago that I'd go with you to the very edge of the world? And I'm just the same now. My love for you is true. I shall go and not once look back. When shall I be waiting for you?"

"In the evening. Don't bring much with you. Clothes and as much food as possible, that's all. Well, good-bye for now."

"Good-bye. But maybe you'll come in? She's going in a minute.

I haven't seen you for an age! My darling, Grisha! But I was beginning to think you— But no, I won't say it!"

"No, I can't come in. I've got to ride to Vieshenska now. Goodbye. Be waiting for me tomorrow."

Gregor went out and passed through the wicket gate. But Aksinia remained standing in the porch, smiling and rubbing her flaming cheeks with her palms.

In Vieshenska the evacuation of the regional offices and organizations and the commissariat warehouses had already begun. At the regional ataman's office Gregor inquired about the position at the front. A youthful ensign acting as adjutant told him:

"The Reds are close to Alexandrovsk station. We don't know what forces will pass through Vieshenska, or whether any will pass through at all. You can see for yourself that nobody knows anything, everybody's hurrying to get away. . . . I'd advise you not to search for your regiment now, but to ride to Millerovo, where you'll find it easier to ascertain where it is at the moment. In any case your regiment will be retreating along the railway line. Will the enemy be held up at the Don? No, I don't think so. Vieshenska will be yielded without a struggle, that's definite."

Gregor returned home late at night. While Ilinichna was getting his supper ready she said:

"Your Prokhor turned up. He came about an hour after you'd gone and said he'd be coming back. But he hasn't been near us since."

Delighted at the news, Gregor hurriedly ate his supper, then went to see Prokhor. His orderly welcomed him with a cheerless smile and said:

"I was beginning to think you'd dashed off to retreat straight from Vieshenska."

"Where the devil have you sprung from?" Gregor asked, laughing and slapping his faithful orderly on the shoulder.

"That's quite clear: from the front."

"Hopped it?"

"Why, what makes you think that? A desperate soldier like me run away? I came in accordance with the law: I didn't want to go off to the warm countries without you. We've sinned together, and we must ride together to the Last Judgment. Our affairs aren't worth a pinch of tobacco, you know."

"Yes, I know. Tell me how they came to release you from the regiment."

"That's a long story; I'll tell you later," Prokhor said evasively, and grew still more glum.

"Where's the regiment?"

"The devil knows where it is at the moment."

"Then how long have you been away from it?"

"I left some two weeks ago."

"Then where have you been since?"

"What a pest you are, by God!" Prokhor said discontentedly, and gave his wife a sidelong glance. "With your where and how and why. . . . Wherever I've been, I'm there no longer. I said I'd tell you, and that means I'll tell you. Hey, wife! Got any liquor? When I meet my commanding officer I ought to wet my whistle, so have you got anything to drink? No? Well, run along and get something, and see that you're back in a jiffy! You've got unused to military discipline while your husband's been away. You've got out of hand."

"And what are you letting off steam for?" his wife asked with a smile. "Don't you shout at me too much; you're not the real master here, you only spend a couple of days at home in a twelvemonth."

"Everybody shouts at me, and I don't shout at anybody except you. You wait till I've risen to the rank of general, then I'll shout at others. But meantime you grin and bear it; put on your uniform quick, and run!"

When his wife had put on her outdoor clothes and gone, Prokhor gave Gregor a reproachful look and said:

"You know, you haven't got the least understanding, Pantalievich! I can't tell you everything with a woman present, and you go on pressing me with your how and why and what. Well, have you got over your typhus?"

"Yes, I've got over it; now tell me about yourself. You're hiding something, you son of the enemy! Spit it out, what have you got mixed up in? How did you get away?"

"It's worse than just getting away. . . . After I'd brought you home I returned to the regiment. They assigned me to the third troop in your squadron. But I'm terribly keen on fighting! I went twice into an attack, and then I thought: 'I'll have to show a leg here! I've got to find some hole, or you'll be done for, Prokhor, my boy!' And then, as though on purpose, the Reds began to press us so hard and there were such fierce battles that they didn't even give us time to breathe. Wherever the Reds broke through, there they shoved us; wherever there was any unreliability, there they shoved our regiment. Within a week eleven Cossacks in our squadron were as though they'd been licked off the face of the earth by a cow's tongue. Well, and I got such a longing, I went real lousy with longing!" Prokhor lit a cigarette, held out his pouch to Gregor, and unhurriedly went on: "And then it fell to me to go on a reconnaissance close to Liski. There were three of us. We were riding over a rise at a gentle trot, keeping our eyes wide open, when we saw a Red crawl out of a brook and raise his hands above his head. We galloped up to him, but he shouted: 'Cossacks, I'm on your side. Don't cut me down, I'm one of you.' But the devil must have got hold of me, for I got wild for some reason, and I rode up to the man and said: 'You son of a bitch,' I said, 'if you've agreed to fight, then you oughtn't to surrender! You're a dirty swine,' I said. 'Can't you see that as it is we're only holding on by the skin of our teeth? And here you are surrendering, bringing us reinforcements!' And at that I pulled my scabbard from the saddle and stretched it across his back. And the other Cossacks with me also made it clear, and asked him: 'Is it fair to fight like that, to go turning and twisting in all directions? If you'd all come over earlier, the war would have been finished by now.' But how the devil was I to know that this turncoat was an officer? Yet that's what he turned out to be! When I struck him with my scabbard he went pale and said quietly: 'I'm an officer, and you're daring to strike me! I served in the hussars in the old days, and I fell into the Reds' hands during the mobilization. You take me to your commander, and there I'll tell him everything.' We said: 'Hand over your documents.' But he proudly answers: 'I have no wish to talk to you; take me to your commander.'"

"But why didn't you want to talk about this in front of your wife?" Gregor asked in surprise.

"I haven't come to that point yet, and please don't interrupt. We decided to escort him to the squadron, but we were fools. We should have killed him on the spot, and that would have been the end of it. But we drove him in, as we were supposed to do, and a day later we found he was appointed commander of our squadron. That was a fine how-d'you-do! And then the band began to play! A day or two later he sent for me and asked: 'So you're fighting for a single, indivisible Russia, are you, you son of a bitch? What did you say to me when you took me prisoner? Do you remember?' I tried to get out of it, but he wouldn't show me any mercy, and when he recalled that I'd struck him with my scabbard he shook all over. 'Do you know,' he said, 'that I'm a captain of a hussar regiment and a noble, and you, you boor, dared to strike me?' He sent for me once, he sent for me twice, and I never had any mercy from him. He ordered the troop commander to send me on outpost and guard duty out of turn, shook fatigues on me like peas out of a pail, and in a word, he made life a misery, the swine! He did the same to the other two who'd been on reconnaissance with me when we took him prisoner. The boys stood as much as they could, but at last one day they spoke to me and said: 'Let's put him out or our lives won't be worth living.' I thought it over and decided to tell the regimental commander all about it, but my conscience wouldn't allow me to kill him. We could have done it when we took him prisoner, but afterwards I couldn't raise my hand, somehow. I have to screw up my eyes when my wife cuts a chicken's throat, and this was a matter of killing a man."

"But you did kill him?" Gregor again interrupted.

"Wait a bit; you'll know all about it in due course. Well, I told the regimental commander. I got to see him, but he laughed and said: 'It's no good your being upset, Zykov, once you struck him. He's quite right in restoring discipline. He's a good and intelligent officer.' So I left him, but I thought to myself: 'You can hang that good officer round your neck instead of a cross, but I'm not going to serve in his squadron!' I asked for a transfer to another squadron, but nothing came of that either; they wouldn't do it. Then I thought of clearing out altogether. But that's easier said than done. They transferred us to the rear for a week's rest, and then the devil went and got me all messed up again. I decided the only thing to do was to get hold of some poor devil of a woman with the clap, then I'd be put on light sick duty, and then the retreat would start, and things would settle themselves. And—something I'd never done before—I began to run after the women, to see which of them looked the worst. But how can you tell? It isn't written in a woman's forehead that she's got this or that. So what was I to do?" Prokhor spat vigorously and listened to make sure his wife was not coming back.

Gregor covered his mouth with his hand to hide his smile. His eyes glittered with laughter as he asked:

"And did you get the clap?"

Prokhor gazed at him with tearful eyes. His look was sad and calm, like that of an old dog who has had his day. After a brief silence he said:

"Do you think it was so easy to get it? When you don't want it it's blown at you by the wind; but now I couldn't find it anywhere, even if I shouted aloud for it."

Half turning away, Gregor laughed soundlessly, then took his hand from his face and asked in a choking voice:

"Don't torture me, for Christ's sake! Did you get it or not?"

"Of course it seems funny to you!" Prokhor said in an injured tone. "It's only fools who laugh at other people's misfortunes; at least, that's what I think."

"But I'm not laughing. . . . Well, and what happened?"

"Then I began to set my cap at the daughter of the house where we were quartered. She was a maiden some forty years old, or maybe a little younger. Her face was smothered in pimples, and she looked—well, in a word, the Lord defend us from all such! The neighbours hinted that recently she'd been playing about with a doctor. 'Well,' I thought, 'I'm sure to get it from her!' And I hung around her just like a young cockerel; I strutted and puffed up my crop and said all sorts of things to her. . . . And where they all came from I rightly don't know myself." He smiled guiltily and even seemed to cheer up a little at the memory. "I promised to marry her, and talked all sorts of filth. . . . At last I won her over, and the matter came very near to sin. Then she suddenly goes and bursts into tears. I tried to calm her and said: 'Maybe you're ill? But that's nothing, that's all the better.' But I myself got frightened; it was night-time, and supposing someone heard our noise and came creeping into the chaff-shed where we were? 'Don't shout, for Christ's sake!' I said. 'And if you're ill, don't be afraid; I love you so much that I'm ready for anything!' But she says: 'My dear Proshenka, I'm not ill in the least. I'm an honest maid, I fear; and that's why I cried out.' Believe me or not, Gregor Pan-

talievich, but as she said that to me I broke into a cold sweat and
let her have it! 'Lord Jesus!' I thought, 'the mess I've got into!
That's the last straw!' I roared at her: 'But what did you go running to the doctor for? What did you go around taking in the
people for?' 'I went to see him,' she said, 'to get some ointment to
clear my face.' Then I clutched my head and told her: 'Get up and
go away this minute, damn you, you horrible witch! I don't want
you honest, and I shan't marry you!' "

Prokhor spat still more violently, and reluctantly went on: "And
so all my labours were in vain. I went to the hut, collected my
belongings, and transferred to other quarters the very same night.
Then the boys gave me a hint, and I got what I was in need of from
a certain widow. Only this time I went straight to the point. I
asked her: 'Are you ill?' She answered: 'Yes, I am a bit.' 'Well,
I don't want a hundredweight of it.' I gave her a twenty-ruble note
for helping me out, and the next day I boasted about my achieve-
ment and got put on light duty. And from there I came straight
home."

"Did you come without your horse?"

"Of course not! I've come on my horse and in full fighting order.
The boys sent my horse to where I was on sick-leave. But that's
not important; you advise me what I'm to tell the wife. Or maybe
it'd be better to get out of sinning by coming and spending the
night with you?"

"No, by hell! You spend the night at home! Say you're wounded.
Have you got any bandages?"

"I've got my field dressing."

"Well, then use that."

"She won't believe me," Prokhor said despondently. But he got
up none the less. He rummaged in his saddlebag, went into the
best room, and whispered from there: "If she comes back, keep
her talking, and I'll be out in a second."

As Gregor rolled himself a cigarette he thought over his plans for
departure. "We'll harness both the horses to a sledge," he decided.
"We must leave in the evening, so that our people don't see Aksinia
with me. Though they'll find out all the same."

"I didn't finish telling you about the squadron commander."
Prokhor limped out of the best room and sat down at the table.
"Our men killed him off the third day after I went sick."

"Really?"

"God's truth! They shot him in the back in a fight, and that was the end of him. So I got the clap for nothing, that's what riles me."

"Didn't they catch the one who did it?" Gregor, absorbed in thoughts of the forthcoming departure from Tatarsk, asked abstractedly.

"What chance had they got of looking for him? The retreat was so general that there was no time to look for anybody! But where's my wife got to? I badly want a drink! When are you thinking of leaving?"

"Tomorrow."

"Can't we leave it for just one more day?"

"What for?"

"I could shake the lice off me at any rate. It's no fun riding with them!"

"You can shake them off on the road. The situation doesn't advise delay. The Reds are two marches from Vieshenska."

"Are we leaving in the morning?"

"No, at night. We've only got to get to Kargin; we'll spend the night there."

"But won't the Reds catch us?"

"We must be ready to move on at any moment. . . . I was thinking—I thought of taking Aksinia Astakhova with me. You don't mind, I suppose?"

"What's it to do with me? You can take a couple of Aksinias if you like. . . . It'll be rather a lot for the horses."

"She's not very heavy."

"It's awkward travelling with women. . . . And what the cholera is she yielding to you for? As if we wouldn't have enough trouble without her!" Prokhor sighed. With eyes averted, he added: "I knew you'd be dragging her about with you. You're always acting the husband! Ah, Gregor Pantalievich, the knout's long been weeping bitter tears for you!"

"That's nothing to do with you," Gregor said coldly. "Don't go gabbling to your wife about it."

"Have I ever gabbled to her about it? You ought to know me better! But who is she going to leave her house with?"

They heard steps in the porch. Prokhor's wife entered. Snow was sparkling on her fluffy grey kerchief.

"A blizzard?" Prokhor took glasses from the cupboard and only then thought of asking: "But did you bring anything?"

His crimson-cheeked wife took two steaming bottles from her breast and set them on the table.

"Well, now we'll be able to see the road!" Prokhor said cheerfully. He sniffed at the vodka and pronounced: "First rate! And as strong as the devil!"

Gregor drank two small glasses of vodka, then pleaded that he was tired and went home.

Chapter 4

"Well, the war's all over. The Reds are driving us so hard that now we shall go on falling back till we reach the sea and steep our arses in brine," said Prokhor as they drove up the hill.

Below them lay Tatarsk wrapped in a bluish haze. The sun had set behind the snowy, rosy selvage of the horizon. The snow scrunched crisply under the sledge-runners. The horses moved at a fast walking pace. Gregor reclined in the back of the two-horsed sledge, his shoulders against the saddles. Aksinia sat beside him, wrapped in a sheepskin jacket trimmed with fur. Her black eyes glittered and sparkled joyously beneath her white fluffy kerchief. Gregor glanced surreptitiously at her, at her cheek tenderly crimsoned by the frost, at the thick black eyebrows and the gleaming, bluish whites under the arched, rimed eyelashes. Aksinia looked about her with eager curiosity, gazing at the steppe in its pall of drifted snow, at the road worn down to a smooth polish, at the distant misty horizons. Everything was new and unusual to her, who hardly ever left her house; everything attracted her attention. But occasionally, lowering her eyes and feeling the pleasant, nipping cold of the rime on her lashes, she smiled at the thought that the dream which had so long held her captive had so strangely and unexpectedly come true. Now she and Gregor were driving somewhere far away from Tatarsk, far from her native and hated district, where she had suffered so much, where she had spent half her life in torments with an unloved husband, where everything always aroused oppressive memories. She smiled as with all her body she felt Gregor's presence beside her, and she did not think either of the price at which she had gained this happiness or of the future, which was enveloped in as dark a haze as those steppe horizons which were beckoning her into the distance.

Happening to look round, Prokhor noticed the tremulous smile on Aksinia's crimson and frost-swollen lips and asked in an aggrieved tone:

"Well, what are you grinning for? A fine bride you are! Are you glad to get away from home?"

"Do you think I'm not?" Aksinia asked in a ringing voice.

"A fine thing to be glad about! You're a fool, woman. You don't know yet how this little trip will end, so don't be too quick to smirk! You save your teeth!"

"The future won't be any worse than my past has been."

"You make me feel sick to look at you. . . ." Prokhor furiously brought his whip down across the horses.

"You turn round and stuff your fingers in your mouth!" Aksinia advised him with a laugh.

"Now you're showing again what a fool you are! Have I got to drive all the way to the sea with my finger in my mouth? A fine idea!"

"What's making you feel sick?"

"You should keep quiet! Got mixed up with someone else's daddy and riding the devil knows where! But supposing Stepan was to turn up at the village now, what then?"

"Do you know what, Prokhor? You shouldn't get mixed up in our affairs," Aksinia said, "or you may have a spell of bad luck too!"

"I'm not getting mixed up in your affairs. You needn't snap back at me like that! I can say what I think, can't I? Or am I your coachman, and I'm only to talk to the horses? That's another fine idea! You can be annoyed or not, as you like, Aksinia. But you ought to be whipped with a good switch, whipped and ordered not to cry out! But don't try to frighten me about luck! I carry my luck everywhere with me. I've got a special kind; it won't sing, but it won't let me sleep. . . . Now, you devils! Always going at a walking pace, you lop-eared Satans!"

Gregor listened, smiling, and at last said in a pacifying tone:

"Don't start swearing at each other when we're hardly out of the village! We've got a long road before us, you'll have plenty of time for that. What are you plaguing her for, Prokhor?"

"I'll plague her!" Prokhor answered harshly. "She'd better not contradict what I'm going to say! I'm thinking at this moment that there's nothing worse than woman in the whole wide world. They're a lot of . . . You know, brother, women were God's very worst invention! The way I'd deal with them, right down to the last one, there wouldn't be a smell of woman left on the earth! That's how bad I'm feeling about them just now. And what are you laughing at? Only a fool laughs at other people's misfortunes. Hold the reins; I'm getting out for a minute."

Prokhor went on foot for some time, then he made himself comfortable in the sledge and held his peace.

They spent the night in Kargin and set out again after breakfast next morning. By nightfall they had put some forty miles of road between them and Tatarsk.

Endless trains of refugee wagons were dragging southward. Close to Morozovsky they fell in with the first Cossack troops. Some thirty to forty mounted men went past, army baggage trains dragged along. The farther they went, the more difficult they found it to get quarters for the night. By evening all possible quarters in the villages were occupied, and there was not even stabling for the horses, far less room for themselves. In one of the Tauridan districts Gregor drove from door to door in the vain search for a sleeping-place, and in the end they were compelled to pass the night in a shed. Their clothes were wet through with the blizzard, but by morning they were frozen solid, and jarred and cracked with their every movement. They hardly slept a wink all night, and only just before dawn did they manage to get warm by lighting a camp-fire of straw in the yard.

Next morning Aksinia timidly suggested:

"Grisha, don't you think we might spend the day here? We've been suffering torture all night with the cold and we got hardly any sleep, so we ought to take a little rest."

Gregor agreed. After some difficulty he found a free corner. At dawn the other refugees had driven on, but a field hospital carrying over a hundred wounded and typhus cases also remained in the village for the day.

In one tiny room ten Cossacks were sleeping on the dirty earthen floor. Prokhor brought in a horse-cloth and the sack of food, spread some straw right by the door, took a soundly sleeping old Cossack by the feet and dragged him to one side, and said with rough tenderness to Aksinia:

"Lie down here, for you're so worn out that you don't look your old self."

Towards nightfall the village again filled up with people. All night camp-fires flamed in the side lanes, all night the place was noisy with human voices, neighing horses, grating sledge-runners. Dawn was hardly breaking when Gregor aroused Prokhor and whispered:

"Get the horses harnessed up. We've got to get moving."

"Why so early?" Prokhor asked with a yawn.

"Listen!"

Prokhor raised his head from his saddle pommel and heard a distant, muffled rumble of gunfire.

All the northern districts of the Don were pouring southward. Innumerable refugees' baggage trains were streaming across the railway line from Tsaritsyn to Likhaya and converging on Manich. At every stop during their first week of travelling Gregor inquired for his fellow-villagers from Tatarsk, but he found none in any of the villages through which he passed. In all probability his father and the others had borne more to the left and, avoiding the Ukrainian settlements, had driven through the Cossack villages to Oblivskaya. Only on the thirteenth day did he come upon traces of them. On putting up for the night, he happened to learn that a Cossack from the Vieshenska district was lying ill with typhus in the next hut. He went to find out where the man was from and, entering the low-ceilinged, tiny room, saw the old man Obnizov lying on the floor. From him he learned that the Tatarsk refugees had left this same village two days previously; many of them had fallen ill with typhus, two of them had already died on the road, and Obnizov had been left behind by his own request.

"If I get better and the Red comrades have mercy on me and

don't kill me, I'll make my way home somehow. And if not, I'll die here. It's all the same where I die; wherever death comes it's anything but sweet . . ." the old man declared as Gregor said goodbye to him.

Gregor asked the old man about his father, but Obnizov answered that he had no news of him, for he had left Tatarsk on one of the last sledges, and he had not seen Pantaleimon Prokoffievich since they passed through Malakhovsky village.

Gregor had more luck in finding quarters at their next stop. In the first house he entered he came upon Cossack acquaintances from Vierkhne-Chirsk village. They made room for him, and he made his party comfortable by the stove. Fifteen refugees were lying packed like fish in barrels; three of them were ill with typhus, and another was suffering from frost-bite. The Cossacks cooked some millet porridge with bacon-fat for supper and hospitably offered some to Gregor and his companions. Prokhor and Gregor ate heartily, but Aksinia refused to touch the food.

"Why, aren't you hungry?" Prokhor asked. During the past few days he had inexplicably changed in his attitude to Aksinia, and now he spoke to her roughly but sympathetically.

"I'm feeling a little sick. . . ." Aksinia threw her kerchief around her head and went out into the yard.

"She hasn't fallen ill, has she?" Prokhor asked Gregor.

"Who's to know?" Gregor put down his plate of porridge and went out after her. He found her standing by the steps, her hand pressed to her breast. He put his arms around her and anxiously asked:

"What's the matter, Ksenia, dear?"

"I'm feeling sick, and I've got a headache."

"Come into the hut and lie down."

"You go in; I'll follow in a minute."

Her voice was thick and toneless, her movements sluggish. Gregor gazed at her interrogatively as she entered the stiflingly hot room; he noticed the crimson flush on her cheeks, the suspicious glitter in her eyes. His heart sank: she was obviously ill. He remembered that the previous day she had complained of shivering and dizziness, and when he awoke early that morning, he noticed she had been sweating so much that her curly hair was as wet as though she had just washed it. He had lain gazing at her as she slept, and had not dared to rise for fear of disturbing her rest.

She had bravely borne the deprivations of the journey, she had even cheered Prokhor on, when more than once he had said: "What the devil is this war, and who thought of it? You drive on and on all day, and when you arrive at night you've got nowhere to spend the night, and you don't know where you'll be ordered to go before you're finished." But that day she had failed to keep up her spirits. When they lay down to sleep, Gregor had the impression that she was weeping.

"What's the matter?" he asked in a whisper. "Where do you feel ill?"

"I'm ill all right. . . . Now what shall we do? Will you desert me?"

"Well, you are silly! Why should I desert you? Don't cry, perhaps you've only got frozen on the road, and you've got frightened."

"Grisha dear, it's typhus."

"Don't talk nonsense! There's no signs of it; your forehead is quite cool, so why should it be typhus?" Gregor comforted her. But in his heart of hearts he was convinced that she was ill with typhus, and wondered miserably what they could do with her if she had to take to her bed.

"Oh, it's hard to ride like this!" she whispered, huddling close to him. "Look at the lot of people that crowd into the quarters every night. The lice are eating us up, Grisha! And I've not got a chance to look after myself, because of the men. . . . Yesterday I went into a shed and undressed, and I had so many lice on my shirt— Lord, I've never seen such a sight in all my life! I feel sick when I think of it, and I don't want to eat. . . . But did you see how many that old man lying on the bench yesterday had got? They were crawling all outside his coat."

"Don't think about them! You've got yourself interested in a devilishly fine subject! Lice are only lice; you don't count them when you're in the service," Gregor whispered irritably.

"I'm itching all over."

"Everybody's itching all over; what can we do about it now? Keep going! When we get to Yekaterinodar we'll have a good wash."

"But we can't put on clean clothes!" Aksinia said with a sigh "They'll be the death of us, Grisha!"

"You get off to sleep; we shall be setting out early in the morning."

Gregor could not sleep for hours. Nor did Aksinia sleep. She sobbed quietly more than once, covering her head with her great sheepskin coat; then she tossed and turned for a long time, sighed, and dozed off only when Gregor turned to her and put his arms around her. In the middle of the night he was disturbed by a loud knock. Someone was banging on the door and shouting:

"Hi, there, open the door or we'll break it down! You're sleeping soundly, you devils!"

The master of the house, an elderly and inoffensive Cossack, went out into the porch and asked:

"Who's there? What do you want? If you want somewhere to spend the night, it's no good coming here. We're already crowded and haven't even got room to turn over."

"Open the door, I tell you!" came a further shout from outside. The next moment half a dozen armed Cossacks flung the door wide open and poured into the front room.

"Who have you got spending the night here?" asked one of them, a man iron-black with the frost, hardly able to move his frozen lips.

"Refugees. But who are you?"

Without answering him a Cossack strode into the best room and shouted:

"Hey, you! Stretched yourselves out nicely, haven't you? Get out of here at once! Troops are to be quartered here. Get up, get up! And hurry up about it or we'll soon shake you out!"

"Who are you, to shout like that?" Gregor asked hoarsely, and slowly got up.

"I'll show you who I am!" The Cossack strode towards Gregor, and in the dim light of the little paraffin lamp the barrel of a pistol gleamed dully in his hand.

"Why, aren't you smart!" Gregor said in a wheedling tone. "Well, show us your toy!" With a swift movement he seized the Cossack by his wrist and squeezed it with such force that the man groaned and opened his fingers. The pistol dropped with a muffled crash to the horse-cloth. Gregor pushed the Cossack away, swiftly bent, picked up the pistol, put it in his pocket, and said calmly: "And now let's have a talk. What regiment are you from? How many of you smart fellows are there?"

Recovering from his surprise, the Cossack shouted:

"Boys! This way!"

Gregor went to the door. Standing on the threshold, he leaned his back against the doorpost and said:

"I'm a squadron commander of the 19th Don Regiment. Quieter now! Stop shouting! Who's that barking? Well, my dear Cossack comrades, what are you making all this fuss for? Who are you going to shake out? Who gave you such powers? Quick march out of here!"

"And what are you bawling for?" one of the Cossacks half shouted. "We've seen all sorts of squadron commanders! Have we got to spend the night in the yard? Everybody out of the house! We've been given orders to turn all the refugees out, understand? And you're kicking up all this fuss! We've seen people like you before!"

Gregor went right up to the speaker and hissed through clenched teeth:

"You've never seen anyone like me before. Do you want me to make a couple of fools out of the one you are? I'll do it! Don't back away! This isn't my pistol, I took it from your man. Here, give it back to him, and clear out quick, before I start fighting, or I'll flay the skin off you!" He gently turned the Cossack round and pushed him towards the door.

"Shall I let him have it?" a big Cossack with his face enveloped in a camel-hair cowl asked reflectively. He was standing behind Gregor, closely examining him; his enormous, leather-soled felt boots creaked as he shifted from foot to foot.

Gregor turned to him and, losing command of himself, clenched his fists. But the Cossack raised his hand and said in an amicable tone:

"Listen to me, Your Excellency, or whatever you call yourself. Wait a bit, don't raise your fist! We'll avoid any trouble. But in these times don't push the Cossacks too hard! Serious times are coming again now, like those in 1917. You might run up against some desperate characters, and they wouldn't make two, but five of you! We can see you're a brave officer and, judging by your speech, you were born one of us. So you behave a little more sensibly or you'll run into sin. . . ."

The man from whom Gregor had taken the pistol said irritably:

"Don't stand there singing 'Te Deums' to him! Let's go to the

next hut." He was the first to stride to the door. As he passed
Gregor he gave him a sidelong glance and said commiseratingly:
"We don't want to be bothered with you, officer, or we'd christen
you!"

Gregor twisted his lips contemptuously and replied:

"You'd be christening yourself! Get on, get on, before I take your
trousers down! So a Baptist's turned up now! Pity I gave you your
pistol back; such daredevils as you shouldn't wear pistols, but sheep's
fleeces!"

"Come on, boys, let him go to the devil! If you don't stir up muck
it won't stink!" one of the other Cossacks, who had taken no part in
the conversation, remarked with a benevolent chuckle.

The Cossacks went cursing to the door, clattering their frozen
boots. Gregor sternly ordered the master of the house:

"Don't dare open that door again! They can knock and go away.
And if they don't, wake me up!"

The Vierkhne-Chirsk men, who had been aroused by the noise,
lay talking in undertones among themselves.

"The way discipline's gone to pieces!" one of the old men sighed
mournfully. "They talk to an officer as if he was any son of a bitch!
That wouldn't have happened in the old days. They'd have roasted
them in penal servitude!"

"Talk? What's talk? Did you see how they were getting ready
to fight? 'Give him a crack!' said the unhewn poplar in the cowl.
That shows what desperadoes they've become."

"Why did you let them off so lightly, Gregor Pantalievich?" one
of the Cossacks asked.

Gregor listened to the talk with an amiable smile on his lips. As
he wrapped himself in his greatcoat he answered:

"Well, what are you to do with them? They've got clean out of
hand and won't submit to anyone; they go about in bands, with no
command over them. Who's to be their judge and commander?
Their commander is simply anyone who proves himself stronger
than they! I don't suppose they've got one officer left in all their
troops. I've seen whole squadrons like that, absolutely fatherless.
Well, let's get off to sleep."

Aksinia whispered to him:

"But what made you go for them, Grisha? Don't go running up

against men like that, for the live of Christ! Such heathen might kill you."

"You sleep; we've got to be up early tomorrow. How do you feel? Any better?"

"Just the same."

"Your head still aching?"

"Yes. I'm afraid I shan't be getting up again. . . ."

Gregor laid his palm on her brow and sighed:

"You're giving off heat like a stove! Well, all right, don't worry! You're a healthy woman, you'll get over it!"

Aksinia made no answer. She was tormented with thirst. She went out several times into the kitchen, drank some of the unpleasantly warm water, and, mastering her nausea and giddiness, lay down again on the horse-cloth.

During the night four further parties seeking for quarters came to the hut. They banged their rifle-butts on the door, opened the window-shutters, drummed on the windows, and went away only when the master, profiting by Gregor's example, shouted from the porch: "Clear out of here! This is a brigade headquarters."

At dawn Prokhor and Gregor harnessed up the horses. Aksinia struggled into her outdoor clothes and went into the yard. The sun was rising. A thin grey smoke was streaming from the chimneys into the azure sky. A heavy rime lay on the fences, on the roofs of the sheds. Steam was billowing from the horses' bodies.

Gregor helped Aksinia into the sledge and asked:

"Perhaps you could lie down. You'll find it more comfortable."

She nodded, gave him a grateful look when he carefully wrapped her legs, and closed her eyes.

At noon, when they halted to feed the horses in a village some two miles off the main road, Aksinia could not climb out of the sledge. Gregor took her by the arm and led her to the house, and put her in the bed which the mistress hospitably placed at their disposition.

"Are you feeling bad, dearest?" he asked, bending over Aksinia, noticing how white she had gone.

She forced open her eyes, looked at him with filmed pupils, and again dozed off into semi-consciousness. With trembling hands he removed the kerchief from her head. Her cheeks were as cold as ice, but her forehead was burning; little icicles had frozen on the temples, which were beaded with a fine sweat. Towards evening she lost consciousness altogether. A moment earlier she asked for a drink, whispering:

"Only some cold water, some melted snow." She was silent for a moment, then said indistinctly:

"Call Grishka!"

"Here I am. What do you want, Ksenia dear?" Gregor took her hand and stroked it awkwardly and shyly.

"Don't leave me behind, Grisha dear!"

"I shan't leave you behind. What makes you think I shall?"

"Don't leave me behind in a strange place. . . . I shall die here."

Prokhor gave her a drink. She thirstily set her parched lips to the rim of the copper mug, drank a few drops, and with a groan let her head fall back on the pillow. Within five minutes she was talking disconnectedly and unintelligibly. As he sat at her head, Gregor distinguished a few words: "I must wash . . . get some blue . . . early . . ." Her incoherent speech faded into a whisper. Prokhor shook his head and said reproachfully:

"I told you not to bring her on this trip. Now what are we going to do? It's a punishment, that's all it is, God's truth! Shall we spend the night here? Are you gone deaf, or what? I ask: shall we spend the night here or drive on?"

Gregor made no response. He sat huddled up, not taking his eyes off Aksinia's ashen face. The mistress, a hospitable and kind-hearted woman, indicated Aksinia with her eyes and quietly asked Prokhor:

"His wife? Are there any children?"

"Yes. And there are children too; we've got everything except good luck," Prokhor muttered.

Gregor went out into the yard and, seating himself on the sledge, smoked cigarette after cigarette. Aksinia would have to be left behind in the village; to carry her on might be the death of her. He saw that clearly. He went into the house and sat down again by the bed.

"We'll spend the night here, shan't we?" Prokhor asked.

"Yes. And we may stop over tomorrow."

Shortly afterwards the master of the house arrived. He was a stocky and sickly peasant with crafty, shifty eyes, who had lost one leg from the knee. Tapping with his wooden leg, he nimbly limped to the table, took off his outdoor clothes, gave Prokhor a sidelong look, and asked:

"So the Lord's sent us guests? Where are you from?" Without waiting for an answer, he ordered his wife: "Hurry up and give me something to eat. I'm as hungry as a dog."

He ate long and greedily. His shifty eyes frequently rested on Prokhor and on Aksinia's motionless form. Gregor came out of the best room and greeted him. The man nodded his head without speaking and asked:

"Retreating?"

"Yes."

"So you've had enough of fighting, Your Excellency?"

"That's it, more or less."

"Who's that—your wife?" he nodded at Aksinia.

"Yes."

"What did you put her on the bed for? Where are we going to sleep?" He turned discontentedly to his wife.

"She's ill, Vania, and I couldn't help feeling sorry for her."

"Sorry! You can't be sorry for all of them, and look how many there are going past! You're crowding us, Your Excellency!"

A note of entreaty, almost of supplication sounded in Gregor's voice as, turning to the man and his wife, pressing one hand to his chest, he asked:

"Good people, help me in my trouble, for Christ's sake! If we take her on any farther she'll die. Let us leave her with you. I'll pay you for looking after her, as much as you ask. And all my life I shall remember your kindness. . . . Don't say no, do me this favour!"

At first the master flatly refused, saying they had no time to look after a sick woman, and that they had no room for her. But at last, when he had finished his dinner, he said:

"It stands to reason, who's going to look after her for nothing? But how much would you give us to look after her? How much can you afford to offer for our trouble?"

Gregor drew all the money he had out of his pocket and held it out to the man. The peasant irresolutely took the packet of Don government credit notes, spat on his fingers, counted them, and asked:

"But haven't you got any Nicholas money?"

"No."

"Maybe you've got Kerenski rubles? This stuff isn't too safe. . . ."

"I haven't any Kerenskis either. If you like, I'll leave you my horse."

The man reflected for some time, then thoughtfully answered:

"No. Of course, I'd take the horse; for us peasants a horse is more important than anything else. But in such times as these it isn't any use. If the Whites don't take it the Reds will, and we shan't get anything out of it. I've already got a little mare that's no good at all, and yet before you can look round they'll be taking and leading her out of the yard." He was silent, thinking. Then, as though to justify himself, he added: "Don't think I'm so terribly greedy. God forbid! But judge for yourself, Your Excellency! She may lie a month, or even more, and it'll be nothing but giving her this, and taking from her that, and she's got to be fed, with bread and milk, an egg or two, and meat. And all that costs money; that's true, isn't it? And her clothes have got to be washed and she's got to be washed too, and all the other things. . . . My wife's busy with the house and farm, and she'd have to look after her. That's no easy matter. Don't be mean; you add something more. I'm an invalid; you can see I've lost a leg. What good am I as an earner and worker? We live on what God sends us and manage with bread and kvass. . . ."

With numb, simmering irritation Gregor said:

"I'm not being mean, my good man! I've given you all the money I've got. I can manage without money. What else do you want from me?"

"So you've given me all your money?" The man laughed distrustfully. "With your pay you ought to have saddlebags packed with it."

"Tell me straight out," Gregor said, turning pale, "will you keep the sick woman or not?"

"No. If that's the way you're reckoning, there's no reason to leave her with us." The man's voice took on an injured tone. "It's not so simple, you know. . . . An officer's wife, and all that . . . the neighbours will find out. And the comrades are on your heels;

they'll hear about it and come down on us. No, in that case you take her away; maybe one of the neighbours will agree to look after her." With obvious regret he handed Gregor his money, took out his tobacco-pouch, and began to roll a cigarette for himself.

Gregor put on his greatcoat and said to Prokhor:

"You stay by her; I'll go and look for other quarters."

He was lifting the door latch when the master stopped him:

"Wait a bit, Your Excellency. What's the hurry? Do you think I don't feel sorry for the poor woman? I'm very sorry for her, and I've been in the army myself and I respect your position and rank. But couldn't you add something or other to the money?"

Prokhor could not restrain himself any longer; livid with indignation, he roared:

"What else can we add, you legless asp? You ought to have your other leg chopped off, that's what you deserve! Gregor Pantalievich! Let me shake him up a bit, and then we'll put Aksinia into the sledge and drive on. May he be triply cursed, the devil!"

The master heard Prokhor to the end without interruption and then said:

"You've got no reason to insult me, soldiers! This is a question to be settled to mutual satisfaction, and there's no point in swearing and cooling me off. What are you bawling for, Cossack? Do you think it's money I'm talking of? I wasn't thinking of that sort of extra at all. What I meant was that perhaps you'd got some extra equipment, a rifle, say, or a revolver. . . . It's all the same to you whether you have them or not. But in these times it's a whole fortune to us. We've got to have weapons to guard the house with. That's what I was getting at. Give me back the money you offered and add your rifle into the bargain, and we'll shake hands on it. Leave us your sick woman; we'll look after her as though she was one of our own family. I give my oath on it."

Gregor looked at Prokhor and said quietly:

"Give him my rifle and cartridges, then go and harness up. . . . Aksinia will stay. . . . God be my judge, I cannot carry her on to her death."

Chapter 5

The days dragged by grey and joyless. The moment they left
Aksinia behind, Gregor lost all interest in everything. Each morning he climbed into the sledge and drove over the endless, snowy
steppe; and each evening he sought quarters for the night and lay
down to sleep. And so on, day after day. He was not interested
in what was happening at the front. He realized that all genuine,
serious resistance was over, that the majority of the Cossacks had
no intention of defending even their own districts, that, judging by
all the signs, the White armies were ending their last campaign
and, as they had not held up the Red advance at the line of the
Don, they would be unable to hold it up at the Kuban.

The war was coming to an end. The close was coming swiftly
and inevitably. The Kuban Cossacks were abandoning the front
by the thousands, scattering to their homes. The Don Cossacks were
smashed. Anæmic with fighting and typhus, with three quarters
of its complement gone, the volunteer army was unable to resist
the pressure of the Red Army as it advanced on the wings of success.

Among the refugees there were rumours that there was growing
indignation at General Denikin's bestial treatment of the members
of the Kuban Rada. It was said that the Kuban was organizing a
rising against the volunteer army and that apparently negotiations
were already being carried on with representatives of the Red Army
for the Soviet troops to have unhindered passage to the Caucasus.
There was a stubborn rumour that the people of the Kuban and
Terek were extremely hostile to the Don Cossacks and the volunteer army, and that already a big fight had occurred between a Don
division and Kuban Cossack infantry.

At the halts Gregor listened attentively to the talk, and he grew
every day more and more convinced of the final and inevitable
defeat of the Whites. And yet at times he had a mournful hope
that the danger would compel the disintegrated, demoralized, and
mutually hostile White forces to unite, to renew their resistance
and throw back the Red forces in their triumphant advance. But
after the surrender of Rostov he lost that hope, and he did not

believe the story that after fierce battles close to Bataisk the Reds had begun to retreat. Oppressed by his inactivity, he wanted to link up with some military force. But when he suggested this to Prokhor, his orderly resolutely opposed the idea.

"You've gone clean out of your wits, Gregor Pantalievich!" Prokhor declared indignantly. "What the devil should we go poking our noses into that hell for? The question's settled, you can see that for yourself. So why should we throw our lives away? Or do you think that the two of us can do any good? So long as we're not touched and not taken into the army by force, we've got to go on driving as far as possible and as quickly as possible from the sin. No, please let us retreat quietly, as the old men do. You and I already have had fighting enough and to spare during the past five years; let others try their hand now. Is that what I got the clap for, to be maimed again at the front? Thank you! Very kind of you! I'm so fed up with this war that my belly turns over every time I think of it. You can join up if you like, but I'm not going to. In that case I'll go into a hospital; I've had enough!"

After a long silence Gregor said:

"As you wish. We'll drive to the Kuban, and then we'll see."

Prokhor had his own methods: at every place with a large population he sought out the doctor and brought back powders or liquids. But he showed no great desire to get cured of his trouble. When Gregor asked him why he took only one powder and threw away the rest, treading them diligently into the snow, he explained that he did not want to get rid of his disease altogether, but only to keep it from getting worse, as then, if he had to have a medical examination, it would be easier for him to get out of being allocated to a regiment. In one village a worldly-wise Cossack advised him to cure himself with a brew made from ducks' feet. After that, whenever Prokhor drove into a village, he asked the first person he met: "Tell me, do you keep ducks in this village?" When the astonished inhabitant said there was no water in the vicinity and so there was no point in their keeping ducks, Prokhor hissed with devastating contempt: "You don't live like human beings! I suppose you've never heard a duck quack in all your born days. You steppe blockheads!" Turning to Gregor, he would add with bitter contempt: "A priest must have crossed our road. We're out of luck. If they'd got any ducks I'd buy one at once at any price, or I'd steal one, and then my affairs would be on the mend. But now my disease is playing about a bit too much! At first it was amusing, though it wouldn't let me doze on the road. But now, curse it, it's becoming an absolute punishment. I can't stay seated in the sledge."

When he found that Gregor was quite unsympathetic, he lapsed into silence and sometimes, icily incommunicative, drove for hours on end without saying a word.

Exhaustingly long seemed the days spent driving from point to point, but still longer were the endless winter nights. Time to think over the present and to recall the past Gregor had in abundance. He spent hours remembering the swiftly departed years of his strange and incoherent life. Sitting in the sledge, fixing his misty eyes on the snowy expanses of the oppressively silent steppe, or lying at night with closed eyes and clenched teeth in some stifling, overcrowded little room, he thought only of Aksinia, sick, unconscious, left behind in a little unknown village, and of his kinsfolk back in Tatarsk. Back there in the Don region the Soviet régime had been established, and with griping anxiety Gregor continually asked himself: "Surely they won't treat Mother or Dunia roughly because of me?" He at once reassured himself, recalling that again and again on the road he had heard that the Red Army marched in good order and behaved decently to the people of the occupied Cossack districts. His anxiety gradually died away; the idea that his old mother would have to answer for him seemed incredible, monstrous, quite unjustified. When he recalled his children his heart was clenched with sorrow for a moment; he was afraid they would not escape typhus. Yet he felt that, with all his love for them, after Natalia's death no other sorrow could shake him so all-powerfully.

To give the horses a rest, he and Prokhor lived for four days in one of the winter huts of the Salsk steppe. During this time they more than once discussed what they should do next. They had hardly arrived at the hut when Prokhor asked:

"Will our forces hold a front at the Kuban or go on to the Caucasus? What do you think?"

"I don't know. But does it make any difference to you?"

"A fine idea! Of course it makes a difference. At this rate they'll drive us right into some heathen country, somewhere under the Turks, and then it'll be a fine how-d'you-do."

"I'm not Denikin; don't ask me where they'll drive us to," Gregor answered discontentedly.

"I'm only asking because I've heard a rumour that they'll stand on the defensive again at the Kuban River, and set out for home in the spring."

"Who's going to stand on the defensive?" Gregor laughed sneeringly.

"Why, the Cossacks and Cadets. Who else is there?"

"You're talking rot! They've been fooling you; can't you see what's happening all around? Everybody's trying to slip off as quickly as possible, and who's going to put up any resistance?"

"Ah, my lad, I can see for myself that our affairs aren't worth a pinch of snuff, but I still can't believe it," Prokhor sighed. "But supposing it comes to a question of sailing to a foreign land, or crawling there like a crab, what will you do? Go?"

"Well, what will you do?"

"My position is: where you go, I go. I'm not going to be left behind alone if everybody else goes."

"That's just what I was thinking. Once you've got yourself into a sheep's pen, you've got to hang on to the sheep!"

"They—the sheep, I mean—sometimes make you look a fool by taking you the devil knows where. Drop that sort of talk. You stick to the point!"

"Don't keep nagging! We'll see when we get there. Why should we meet our troubles half-way?"

"Well, and Amen! I shan't ask you any more," Prokhor agreed.

But next day, when they went to fetch the horses, he returned to his previous conversation.

"Have you heard anything about the Greens?" he asked tentatively, pretending to examine the handle of a pitchfork.

"Yes; what about them?"

"Well, what are these Greens that have turned up now? Whose side are they on?"

"The Reds'."

"Then why are they called 'Greens'?"

"The devil knows! It seems they hide in the forests, and that's why they're called 'Greens.'"

"What do you say to you and me going Green?" Prokhor hesitantly suggested after prolonged reflection.

"I don't particularly want to."

"But apart from the Greens there isn't any way of getting home quickly, is there? It's all the same to me whether they're green devils or blue or egg-yellow devils, so long as they're against the war and let the soldiers go home. . . ."

"Wait a bit longer, and maybe some like that will turn up," Gregor advised.

At the end of January, one misty and thawing noonday, Gregor and Prokhor arrived at the village of Belaya Glina. Some fifteen thousand refugees were crowded into the village, and a good half of them were ill with typhus. Cossacks in short English overcoats, in short-cut sheepskins, in long Caucasian coats were striding through the streets in search of quarters and food for their horses, and horsemen and sledges were moving in all directions. Dozens of emaciated horses stood around the mangers in every yard, miserably chewing straw; in the streets and side lanes were abandoned sledges, army wagonettes, ammunition chests. As they drove along one of the streets, Prokhor stared at a high-standing bay horse tethered to a fence and said:

"Why, that's Cousin Andriusha's horse! So our Tatarsk people must be here." He nimbly leaped out of the sledge and went into the house to inquire.

A few minutes later Prokhor's cousin and neighbour Andrei Topolskov came out of the hut, with his greatcoat flung around his shoulders. Accompanied by Prokhor, he gravely strode towards the sledge and gave Gregor his black hand, which stank of horses' sweat.

"Are you with our villagers?" Gregor asked.

"We're all suffering together."

"Well, what's the journey been like?"

"Like everybody else's. After each stop for the night we leave people and horses behind. . . ."

"Is my father still alive and well?"

Staring past Gregor, Topolskov sighed:

"I've got bad news, Gregor Pantalievich—very bad. . . . Say

prayers for your father; he yielded his soul to God yesterday evening. He's dead. . . ."

"Is he buried?" Gregor asked, turning pale.

"I can't say. I haven't been round there yet today. I'll show you the house. . . . Keep to the right, cousin; the fourth house on the right from the corner."

Prokhor drove up to a large house with a sheet-iron roof and halted the horses by the fence. But Topolskov advised him to drive into the yard.

"They're crowded a bit here too, with some twenty men. But you'll find room somewhere," he said as he jumped out of the sledge to open the gate.

Gregor was the first to enter the fiercely heated room. Acquaintances from his village were lying and sitting closely packed on the floor. Some were mending boots or harness; three of them, including old Beskhlebnov, with whom Pantaleimon had driven, were eating soup at a table. At the sight of Gregor the Cossacks rose and answered his curt greeting in chorus.

"Where's my father?" he asked, taking off his fur cap and looking around the room.

"I've got bad news. . . . Pantaleimon Prokoffievich is dead," Beskhlebnov quietly answered. He laid down his spoon, wiped his mouth with the sleeve of his coat, and crossed himself. "He went last night; may God take him to Himself!"

"I know. Is he buried yet?"

"Not yet. We were going to bury him today, but he's still here. We carried him into the best room, where it's cold. This way." Beskhlebnov opened the door to the next room and said as though apologizing: "The Cossacks didn't want to spend the night in the same room; it's made them feel a bit down in the mouth, and besides, he's better here. . . . This room isn't heated."

In the spacious best room there was a strong smell of hemp seeds and mice. All one corner was filled with a heap of millet and hemp; barrels of flour and butter were standing on a bench. Pantaleimon Prokoffievich lay on a horse-cloth in the middle of the room. Gregor drew Beskhlebnov aside, went into the room, and halted by his father.

"Two weeks he was ill," Beskhlebnov told him in an undertone. "He was knocked over by typhus away back in Mechetka. And this is where your father found his rest. . . . Such is our life. . . ."

Bending down, Gregor gazed at his father. The features of the well-known face had been changed by illness and had grown strangely unlike, unfamiliar. Pantaleimon's pale, sunken cheeks were overgrown with a grey scrub, his moustache hung low over the mouth, the eyes were half-closed, and the bluish enamel of the whites had already lost their sparkling vitality and gleam. The old man's lower jaw was tied up with a red neckerchief, and against the red material the grey curly hair of the beard seemed still whiter, more silvery.

Gregor dropped to his knees to take one last attentive look and to fix that dear face in his memory and involuntarily shuddered with horror and disgust: over Pantaleimon's grey, waxen face, filling the sockets of the eyes, the furrows of the cheeks, lice were crawling. They covered the face with a living, moving film; they swarmed in the beard, stirred among the eyebrows, and lay in a grey layer over the stiff collar of his blue jacket.

Gregor and two other Cossacks pecked out a grave with crowbars in the frozen, iron-hard, clayey loam. Prokhor knocked a rough coffin together from bits of wood. At the close of the day they carried Pantaleimon Prokoffievich out and buried him in the alien Stavropol earth. And an hour later, as lights were already being lighted in the village, Gregor drove out of Belaya Glina in the direction of Novopokrov.

In Koronovsky village he felt unwell. Prokhor spent half a day looking for a doctor and at last succeeded in finding some half-drunk military surgeon and, after some difficulty, persuading him to come to the hut. Without removing his greatcoat the doctor examined Gregor, felt his pulse, and confidently declared:

"Relapsing typhus. I advise you, captain, to cut short your journey; otherwise you'll die on the road."

"To wait for the Reds?" Gregor smiled wryly.

"Well, we must assume that the Reds are still some distance off."

"But they'll be near."

"I don't doubt that. But it would be better for you to remain. I would choose that as the lesser of the two evils."

"No, I'll go on somehow," Gregor said resolutely, and put on his tunic. "You'll give me some medicine, won't you?"

"Go on if you like; it's your affair. I was bound to give you my advice, but after that you can do as you please. As for medicine, the best of all would be rest and attention. I could give you a prescription, but the druggist has evacuated and I've got nothing but chloroform, iodine, and liquor."

"Well, give me some liquor, then!"

"With pleasure. You'll die on the road in any case, so the liquor won't make any difference. Send your orderly with me, and I'll let you have a thousand grammes; I'm good-natured. . . ." The doctor saluted, and went out with an uncertain stride.

Prokhor brought the liquor, got hold of a two-horse wagonette from somewhere or other, harnessed up the horses, and reported with gloomy irony as he entered the room:

"The carriage waits, Your Excellency!"

And once more the oppressive, dreary days dragged on from one to another.

In the Kuban a hurried southern spring was coming from the foothills of the Caucasus. In the steppe plains the snow suddenly melted, laying bare thawed patches of shining black earth; the streams chattered with silvery voices, the road was speckled with snow-puddles, the far azure distances had a springlike gleam, and the spacious Kuban heaven grew deeper, bluer, warmer.

Within a couple of days the winter wheat lay bare to the sun; a white mist arose over the ploughed lands. The horses squelched along the miry road and sank over their fetlocks in the mud, getting stranded in the ruts, straining their backs, steaming with sweat. Prokhor thoughtfully tied up their tails and often climbed out of the wagonette and walked alongside, forcibly pulling his feet out of the mud and muttering:

"This isn't mud, it's clinging tar, God's truth! The horses don't get a chance of drying from one spot to another."

Gregor was silent, lying in the wagonette, shivering and wrapping himself up. But Prokhor found the journey boring without someone to talk to; he touched Gregor by the foot or sleeve and said:

"This mud here is the limit! Get out and try it! And then you'll be glad to be ill."

"Go to the devil!" Gregor whispered almost inaudibly.

Whenever they fell in with someone, Prokhor asked:

"Is the mud any worse farther on or just the same?"

They answered with a laugh and a joke, and Prokhor, satisfied to exchange a word or two with a living man, walked on for a time in silence, frequently halting the horses and wiping the granular juicy sweat from his brown forehead. From time to time they were overtaken by horsemen, and Prokhor felt that he must halt them to exchange greetings. He always ended by saying:

"You're wasting time by going on. . . . You can't ride at all farther on. Why not? Why, because the mud's so thick there, I'm told by people coming from those parts, that horses have to swim up to their bellies, wagon-wheels won't turn, and short people walking along fall and drown in the mud on the very road. A dock-tailed bitch may lie, but I don't! Why are we going on? We can't do anything else; I'm taking along a sick bishop, and of course he and the Reds couldn't live together. . . ."

The majority of the horsemen cheerfully swore at Prokhor and rode on. But others stopped to stare hard at him and made some insulting remark, such as:

"So the fools are retreating from the Don too? Is everybody in your district like you?"

One Kuban Cossack, who had got separated from his party, grew seriously annoyed with Prokhor for holding him back with such nonsensical talk. He was about to bring his whip down across Prokhor's face, but with extraordinary agility Prokhor jumped on to the wagonette, snatched his carbine from under the horse-cloth, and laid it across his knees. The Kuban Cossack rode off swearing violently, while, roaring with laughter, Prokhor bawled after him:

"This isn't like Tsaritsyn, where you could hide in the maize! You block, you sleeveless ninny! Hey, come back, you hominy porridge! Tuck up your overalls or you'll be dragging them in the mud! Taken to wing, chicken-killer? You female ham! I haven't got a dirty cartridge or I'd send it to you! Drop your whip, do you hear?"

Prokhor was half silly with boredom and inactivity, and he found his own way of amusing himself.

From the first day of his illness Gregor lived as though in a dream. He lost consciousness at times, then came to again. At one such moment, when he had recovered his senses after long oblivion, Prokhor bent over him.

"Are you still alive?" he asked, gazing commiseratively into Gregor's filmy eyes.

The sun was glittering above them. Now crowding together, then stretching out into a broken, velvety black line, flocks of dark-winged barnacle geese flew crying through the deep blue of the sky. The warmed earth, the young grass, gave off a stupefying scent. Breathing rapidly, Gregor avidly drew the invigorating spring air into his lungs. Prokhor's voice only faintly reached his ears, and everything around him seemed unreal, incredibly diminished, distant. Behind them, muffled by distance, gunshots thundered hollowly. Not far away the wheels of an iron wagon chassis rattled harmoniously and measuredly, horses snorted and neighed, human voices were to be heard. He caught a pungent scent of baked bread, of hay, of horses' sweat. All this came to Gregor's consciousness as though from another world. Exerting all his will, he listened to Prokhor's voice, and with the greatest of effort he realized that his orderly was asking him:

"Would you like a drink of milk?"

Hardly moving his tongue, Gregor licked his parched lips, feeling that a thick cold fluid with a familiar fresh taste was being poured into his mouth. After several sips he clenched his teeth. Prokhor stoppered the flask and bent over Gregor again; and by the movement of Prokhor's weather-beaten lips Gregor guessed rather than heard the question he asked:

"Don't you think I ought to leave you at this village? It's hard going for you, isn't it?"

A look of suffering and anxiety appeared on Gregor's face; once more he summoned all his will and whispered:

"Carry me on—until I die. . . ."

From Prokhor's face he realized that he had been heard and, reassured, he closed his eyes, accepting unconsciousness as a relief, sinking into the dense darkness of oblivion, departing from all this tumultuous, noisy world. . . .

Chapter 6

Along all the road as far as the village of Abinskaya Gregor remembered only one thing: one pitch-dark night he was awakened by the
sharp, penetrating cold. Wagons were moving several abreast along
the road. Judging by the voices, by the incessant, muffled chatter
of the wheels, the train of wagons was enormous. The wagon in
which he was riding was somewhere in the middle. The horses were
moving at a walking pace. Prokhor clacked his tongue and occasionally, in a frozen voice, called hoarsely: "Now, children!" and
waved his knout. Gregor heard the thin whistle of the leather knout,
felt the horses pull more strongly on the traces, making the singletrees rattle, and the wagon rolled along more swiftly, sometimes
knocking the end of the centre pole against the back of the britska in
front.

With an effort Gregor pulled the ends of the sheepskin around
himself and lay on his back. Across the inky sky the wind was driving massive, rolling clouds southward. Very rarely a single star
flamed out for a moment in a yellow spark through a tiny gap in the
clouds, then the impenetrable darkness once more enveloped the
steppe, the wind whistled mournfully in the telegraph wires, a rare
and fine, beady rain broke and fell to the ground.

On the right-hand side of the road a column of cavalry was marching. Gregor caught the long-familiar, unisonous, rhythmic clink of
tightly braced Cossack equipment, the muffled and unisonous
squelch of innumerable horse-hoofs in the mud. Not more than two
squadrons had passed, but the thud of horse-hoofs still sounded: a
regiment must be riding by at the roadside. Suddenly, in front, the
coarse, valiant voice of a solo singer flew up like a bird over the silent
steppe:

> "Oi, down by the river, brothers, down by Kamyshinka,
>   On the glorious steppe, the boundless steppe of Saratov...."

Many hundreds of voices took up the ancient Cossack song, and
high above all danced a tenor accompaniment of astonishing power
and beauty. Covering the basses as they died away, the ringing tenor

still fluttered somewhere in the darkness, clutching at the heart. But
the soloist was already beginning the next verse:

> "There the Cossacks lived and spent their lives as men of
> freedom,
> All the Don, the Greben, and the Yaitsk Cossacks. . . ."

Inside Gregor something seemed to snap. A sudden spasm of
tears shook his body; his throat was clutched with convulsive sorrow. Choking back his tears, he greedily waited for the solo singer
to begin and soundlessly whispered after him words he had known
ever since childhood:

> "And their ataman was Yermak, son of Timofei,
> While their captain was Astashka, son of Lavrentei. . . ."

The moment the solo singer struck up the first words of the song
the Cossacks travelling in the wagons ceased talking, the drivers
stopped urging on their horses, and that train of thousands of wagons
moved along in a profound, a sensitive silence. Only the clatter of
the wheels and the squelch of horse-hoofs kneading the mud was to
be heard as the soloist, carefully enunciating the syllables, sang the
first words of each verse. A single ancient song which had outlived
the ages lived and ruled over the sombre steppe. In artless, simple
words it told of the free Cossack ancestors who at one time had fearlessly shattered the czarist troops, who had wandered along the Don
and the Volga in their light piratic barges, pillaging the czarist ships,
"squeezing" the merchants, the nobles, and the governors, humbling
distant Siberia. And the descendants of the free Cossacks, shame-
fully retreating after being broken in an inglorious war against the
people of Russia, listened to the mighty song in a gloomy silence.

The regiment passed on. Overtaking the wagons, the singers rode
far beyond the refugees. But for a long time afterwards the wagons
rolled on in an enchanted silence, and no talk came from them, nor
shout at the weary horses. But out of the darkness the song floated
back from afar and spread spaciously, like the Don in flood:

> ". . . All their thoughts they thought as one.
> And as the summer passed, the warmth of summer,
> And winter came, brothers, the chilly winter,
> How and where, brothers, shall we spend that winter?

> To move on to the Yaik is a long, long march,
> And if we wander along the Volga, all will think us
>   thieves;
> If on to Kazan city we go, there is the Czar;
> Like the menacing Czar, Ivan Vasilievich. . . ."

Now the singers were no longer to be heard, but the accompaniment rang out, died down, and again flew up. All listened to it in the same tense and moody silence.

And also, as though in a dream, Gregor remembered coming to his senses in a warm room. Without opening his eyes, in all his body he felt the pleasant freshness of clean bed-linen; the strong smell of some medicine tickled his nose. At first he thought he was in a hospital; but from the next room came a burst of unrestrainable masculine laughter, the clatter of utensils, and drunken voices. Some familiar bass voice said:

". . . And you're a clever one! You should have found out where our regiment was, and we'd have helped. Well, drink up! What the devil are you hanging fire for?"

Prokhor answered in a tearful, drunken voice:

"By God, how was I to know? Do you think I found it easy nursing him? I fed him with sips, as though he was a little baby, and gave him milk to drink, by the true Christ! I chewed his bread for him and thrust it into his mouth, by God I did! I opened his teeth with the point of my sabre. And one time I began to pour milk into his throat and he choked and all but died. . . . I can't bear to think of it."

"Did you give him a bath yesterday?"

"I gave him a bath and ran the clippers over his hair and spent all I had on milk. . . . Not that I regret it, you can have every bit of it for all I care. But to chew his food and feed him by hand! Do you think that's easy? Don't say it was, or I'll strike you, for all your rank."

Prokhor, Kharlampyi Yermakov, and Piotra Bogatiriev, his grey karakul fur cap thrust on the back of his head, his face as red as a beet, also Platon Ryabchikov, and two other strange Cossacks, came into Gregor's room.

"He's awake!" Yermakov gave a mad shout, making with uncertain steps towards Gregor.

Shaking a bottle and weeping, the dashing and merry Platon Ryabchikov bawled:

"Grisha! Dear old lad! Do you remember how we galloped along the Chira? And how we fought! Where has our glory gone? What are the generals making of us and what have they done with our army? Curse them! Have you come round? Here, drink, you'll feel better at once. It's pure liquor!"

"We found you despite yourself!" Yermakov muttered, his black, oily eyes glittering joyously. He dropped heavily on Gregor's bed, crushing it under his weight.

"Where are we?" Gregor asked faintly, shifting his eyes with difficulty, passing them over the Cossacks' familiar faces.

"We've captured Yekaterinodar! We're retreating farther soon. Drink, Gregor Pantalievich, our old pal! Get up, for God's sake! I can't bear to see you lying there!" Ryabchikov fell on Gregor's feet. But Bogatiriev, who was smiling silently and seemed to be more sober than the others, seized him by his belt, easily lifted him, and carefully laid him down on the floor.

"Take the bottle from him! It'll be wasted!" Yermakov exclaimed in alarm. With a broad, drunken smile, turning to Gregor he said: "Do you know what we're drinking? As the Cossacks have got to live in a foreign land, we looted a wine warehouse, so it wouldn't fall into the Reds' hands. And the stuff we found! You wouldn't believe it! . . . We fired at a cistern with our rifles and made a hole in it, and liquor poured out of it as if out of a tap. We riddled the cistern with bullets, and each man stood by a hole, putting caps, pails, and flasks under them, while others caught it straight in their palms and drank on the spot. We sabred the two volunteers guarding the warehouse and got to the stuff, and then the fun began. I saw one brave little Cossack climb on top of the cistern, evidently intending to draw out liquor through the top with a horse-bucket. But he fell in and was drowned. The floor was a concrete one, the liquor poured all over it up to our knees, and the Cossacks went wading about in it, bending down and drinking like horses in a stream, from right under their feet. And they lay down on the spot. . . . There'll be more than one drink himself to death! And we did ourselves proud there too! We don't need much: we rolled back a barrel hold-

ing a good five bucketfuls, and that's enough for us. Drink your fill,
my soul! In any case our gentle Don is finished. Platon all but got
drowned. They flung him down on the floor and held him by his
feet. He took a couple of mouthfuls and was ready to snuff out. I
pulled him away by sheer force."

All of them smelt strongly of liquor, onion, and tobacco. Gregor
had a slight feeling of nausea, of dizziness. Smiling a weak, exhausted smile, he closed his eyes.

Chapter 7

He lay a week in Yekaterinodar, in a house belonging to an acquaintance of Bogatiriev's, slowly recovering after his illness. Then, as
Prokhor said, "he began to mend," and at the village of Abinskaya
he sat a horse for the first time during all the retreat.

Novorossisk was being evacuated. Steamers were transporting
the Russian money-bags, landowners, generals' families, and influential politicians into Turkey. Ships were being loaded day and
night at all the quays. Junkers were working as gangs of stevedores,
filling the steamers' holds with military property and the trunks and
boxes of the refugee notables.

The forces of the volunteer army outstripped the Don and Kuban
Cossacks in the flight and were the first to arrive at Novorossisk.
They crowded on to the transport vessels. The staff of the volunteer army prudently betook themselves to the British Dreadnought
which had arrived at the port. Fighting was going on close to Ton-
nelnaya. Tens of thousands of refugees thronged the streets of the
town. Military forces continued to arrive. There was an indescrib-
able press of people at the quays. Abandoned horses wandered in
droves of thousands over the lime slopes of the hills surrounding
Novorossisk. The streets around the harbour were piled high with
Cossack saddles, equipment, and military property, all of which was
no longer wanted by anyone. Rumours sped through the town that
only the volunteer army was to be taken on board the vessels, while
the Don and Kuban Cossacks would have to proceed by forced
marches to Georgia.

On the morning of March 25, 1920, Gregor and Platon Ryabchikov went to the quay to find out whether the forces of the Second Don Corps would be embarked. The previous evening the rumour had spread among the Cossacks that General Denikin had issued the order to carry to the Crimea all the Don Cossacks who had retained their equipment and horses.

The quay was a solid mass of Kalmyks from the Salsk region. They had driven droves of horses and camels from Manich and Sal and had carried their wooden dwelling huts as far as the sea. Turning up their noses at the sour scent of sheep-fat given off by this crowd, Gregor and Ryabchikov approached the gangway of a large transport steamer moored alongside the quay. The gangways were guarded by a reinforced guard of officers from the Markov division. Don Cossack artillery-men were crowded close by, awaiting embarkation. The stern of the vessel was littered with guns under khaki tarpaulins. Forcibly pushing his way through the crowd, Gregor asked a youthful-looking, black-moustached sergeant:

"What is this battery, friend?"

The sergeant gave Gregor a sidelong look and reluctantly answered:

"The 36th."

"From Kargin?"

"Yes."

"Who's in charge of the embarkation?"

"Why, there he stands by the rail. Some colonel, he is."

Ryabchikov pulled Gregor's sleeve and angrily said:

"Let's go, and they can go to the devil! Do you think you'll get any sense out of this lot? They needed us when we were fighting, but they've got no use for us now. . . ."

The sergeant smiled, and winked at the artillery-men drawn up in line. "You're lucky, men! They're even turning down the officers!"

The colonel in charge of embarkation operations swiftly came down the gangway; after him hurried a bald-headed official in an expensive, unbuttoned sheepskin. The man imploringly pressed his catskin cap to his chest and made some remark. There was such a beseeching expression on his sweaty face and in his short-sighted eyes that the colonel turned away and shouted roughly:

"I've already told you once! Don't pester me or I'll give orders for you to be taken to the shore. You've lost your wits! Where the devil

can we put your rubbish? Are you blind? You can see what's happening. Oh, go away! For God's sake go and complain to General
Denikin himself if you like! I've said I can't . . . and I can't! Don't
you understand Russian?"

Turning to rid himself of the importunate official, the colonel
started to pass Gregor. Gregor barred his way and, putting his hand
to the visor of his cap, agitatedly asked:

"Can officers count on being embarked?"

"Not on this vessel. There's no room."

"Then on which one?"

"You'll find out at the evacuation point."

"We've been there, but they don't know anything."

"Nor do I know. Let me pass!"

"But you're embarking the 36th battery. Why isn't there room
for us?"

"Let me pass, I tell you! I'm not an information bureau!" The
colonel tried to push Gregor gently aside, but Gregor had planted
his feet firmly apart. Bluish sparks flamed up and died away again
in his eyes.

"So you don't need us now? But you did before, didn't you? Take
your hand away: you won't shift me!"

The colonel gazed into Gregor's eyes and looked round; the
Markov men standing with crossed rifles at the gangway could
hardly restrain the surging crowd. Staring past Gregor, the colonel
asked wearily:

"What is your regiment?"

"I'm from the 19th Don Regiment; the others are from various
regiments."

"How many of you are there all together?"

"Ten."

"I can't. There's no room."

Ryabchikov saw Gregor's nostrils quivering as he said in an undertone:

"What game are you playing, you cur? You rear louse! Let us
pass at once, or . . ."

"Grisha will cut him down in a minute!" Ryabchikov thought with
angry satisfaction. But, seeing two Markov men hurrying to rescue
the colonel, clearing a way through the crowd with their rifle-butts,
he touched Gregor's sleeve:

"Don't get mixed up with him, Gregor. Come on. . . ."

"You're an idiot! And you shall answer for your conduct!" the colonel said, his face going white. Turning to the Markov men, he pointed to Gregor:

"Gentlemen! Arrest this epileptic! You must establish order here! I've got urgent business with the commandant, and here I've got to stand listening to all kinds of pleasantries from all kinds of . . ." He hurriedly slipped past Gregor.

A tall Markov man with neatly trimmed moustaches, wearing captain's epaulets on his blue tunic, went right up to Gregor and demanded:

"What do you want? Why are you violating discipline?"

"A place on the steamer—that's what I want."

"Where is your regiment?"

"I don't know."

"Show me your documents."

The second man, a young, puffy-faced youngster in pince-nez, said in a quavering bass:

"We must take him to the guardroom. Don't waste time, Visotsky."

The captain carefully read Gregor's document, and returned it.

"You must find your regiment. I advise you to clear out of here and not to interfere with the embarkation operations. We have been ordered to arrest all, irrespective of their rank, who violate discipline or interfere with the embarkation." The captain pursed up his lips and, giving Ryabchikov a sidelong glance, bent to Gregor's ear and whispered: "I would advise you to have a talk with the commander of the 36th battery. Stand in their ranks and you'll get on the steamer."

Ryabchikov, who had heard the captain's whisper, said in a cheerful voice:

"You go to the Kargin men, and I'll run and fetch the lads. What else shall I bring besides your saddlebags?"

"We'll go together," Gregor said unconcernedly.

On the way back they met a Cossack acquaintance from Semenovsky village. He was driving a huge wagon-load of baked bread, covered by a tarpaulin, to the quay. Ryabchikov called to the man:

"Hello, Fiodot! What are you carrying there?"

"Ah, Platon, and Gregor Pantalievich! Greetings! I'm supplying
my regiment with bread for the road. We've had it baked in a hurry
or we'd have had oniy porridge to eat all the way."

Gregor went up to the wagon and asked:

"Are your loaves all weighed, or are they counted?"

"Who the devil's counted them? Why, do you want some bread?"

"Yes."

"Take some, then."

"How much can I have?"

"As much as you can carry; there is plenty here."

Ryabchikov watched in amazement as Gregor took loaf after loaf
and, unable to restrain his curiosity, asked at last:

"What the hell are you taking so much for?"

"I need it," Gregor answered curtly.

He asked the driver for two sacks, put the bread into them,
thanked him for his kindness, and, after saying good-bye, ordered
Ryabchikov:

"Pick one up; we'll carry it."

"You aren't intending to spend the winter here, are you?" Ryabchikov asked humorously as he tumbled the sack across his shoulder.

"It isn't for me."

"Then who is it for?"

"My horse."

Ryabchikov neatly swung the sack to the ground and asked in bewilderment:

"Are you joking?"

"No, I'm quite serious."

"So you— What have you got in your mind, Pantalievich? Are
you intending to remain behind? Is that the idea?"

"You've got it. Pick up the sack and let's go on. My horse has got
to be fed; he's already chewed all the manger. A horse may be of
value yet, you can't serve on foot."

As far as their quarters Ryabchikov did not say another word, but
groaned and shifted the sack from shoulder to shoulder. As they
went up to the wicket gate he asked:

"Will you tell the boys?" Without waiting for an answer, in an aggrieved tone he said: "You've got a fine idea into your head! But
how about us?"

"That's for you to decide," Gregor answered with affected uncon-

cern. "If they won't take us, if they can't find room for us, well, they
needn't! What the hell do we want them for, to cling on to? We'll
stay behind. We'll try our luck. Get on; what have you got stuck in
the wicket gate for?"

"A fine way of talking to me! . . . I didn't even see the wicket
gate! Well, it's a funny business. You've given me a fine clout on
the ear, Grisha! Knocked me down with a feather! And there I was
thinking: 'What the devil has he asked for all that bread for?' Now
our lads will find out and get all worked up."

"Well, and how about you? Won't you remain?" Gregor was
curious to know.

"What are you thinking of?" Ryabchikov exclaimed in alarm.

"You think it over!"

"There's nothing to think over. I'll go off without talking about it,
while I've got the chance. I'll attach myself to the Kargin battery
and clear out."

"You'll regret it!"

"Oh, yes, of course! I value my head more than that, brother! I've
got no desire to have the Reds try their executioners on it."

"But do think it over, Platon. The position is . . ."

"Don't talk about it. I'm going off at once."

"Well, as you wish. I won't try to argue with you . . ." Gregor
said irritably, and was the first to stride towards the stone steps leading to the porch.

Yermakov, Prokhor, and Bogatiriev were all out. The mistress of
the house, an elderly, hunchbacked Armenian woman, said the Cossacks had gone off saying they would be back soon. Keeping on his
outdoor clothes, Gregor cut up a loaf of bread into great chunks and
went out to the horses in the stable. He divided the bread into two
portions and gave half to his own and half to Prokhor's horse. He
had just picked up the bucket to bring some water when Ryabchikov
appeared at the stable door. In the folds of his greatcoat Platon was
carefully carrying bread broken into large pieces. Scenting its master, his horse gave a brief snort. Ryabchikov silently passed the
quietly smiling Gregor and, without looking up, said as he rolled
the pieces of bread into the manger:

"Don't bare your teeth like that, please! If you show such an example, then I've got to feed my horse too. Do you think I'd be glad
to go? I'd have to take myself by my own collar and run myself to

that damned steamer! I wouldn't get there any other way. It's living
fear that's driving me on. . . . I've only got one head on my shoulders, haven't I? God grant I don't get this one cut off; a second
wouldn't grow in time for Lady Day!"

Prokhor and the others did not return until late in the afternoon.
Yermakov was carrying a huge bottle of liquor, while Prokhor had
a kitbag full of hermetically sealed flasks containing a thick yellow
liquid.

"We've done a fine day's work! Enough for all night!" Yermakov
boasted as he pointed to the bottle. He went on to explain: "We
came across a military doctor who asked us to help him carry medical goods from a warehouse to the quay. The stevedores had refused
to work, and there were only Junkers dragging things from the
warehouses, so we teamed up with them. The doctor paid us for our
help with liquor, but Prokhor pinched these flasks! By God, I'm not
joking!"

"But what's in them?" Ryabchikov asked inquisitively.

"That's purer than liquor, brother!" Prokhor shook up the flasks
and held them to the light, revealing a thick fluid bubbling inside
the dark glass, and ended in a self-satisfied tone: "That's nothing
but expensive foreign wine. They only give it to the sick—so a
Junker woman who knows English told me. We'll get on board the
steamer, drink in our misery, strike up 'My Dear Beloved Country,'
and drink all the way to the Crimea. And we'll throw the flasks into
the sea."

"Hurry up and embark, or they'll have to hold up the steamer
for you and won't get away. 'Where's Prokhor Zykov, the hero of
heroes? We can't sail without him!' they'll be saying," Ryabchikov
said with a sneer. Pointing a yellow, smoke-stained finger at Gregor,
he added: "He's changed his mind about going. And so have I."

"You don't say!" Prokhor groaned, almost dropping a flask in his
amazement.

"What's all this? What have you got into your head now?" Yermakov asked, frowning and staring fixedly at Gregor.

"We've decided not to go."

"Why?"

"Because there isn't any room for us."

"If there isn't today, there will be tomorrow," Bogatiriev said confidently.

"Have you been to the quay?"

"Well, what about it?"

"Have you seen what's happening there?"

"Well, yes."

"'Well, well'! If you've seen, what is there to explain? They
would only take me and Ryabchikov, and then a volunteer told us
we were to fall in with the Kargin battery, otherwise it wouldn't be
possible."

"It hasn't embarked yet, has it—the battery, I mean?" Bogatiriev
asked swiftly. Learning that the men of the battery were standing
in line awaiting embarkation, he at once made ready to go. He
packed his linen spare trousers and a tunic in his kitbag, added some
bread, and said good-bye.

"Stay with us, Piotra!" Yermakov advised him. "There's no point
in breaking up the party."

Without answering, Bogatiriev held out his hand, bowed once
more at the door, and said: "Keep well! If it's God's will we shall
meet again." Then he ran out.

After his departure there was a long, unpleasant silence in the
room. Yermakov went into the kitchen to see the mistress, brought
back four glasses, silently poured liquor into them, set a great copper tea-pot filled with cold water on the table, cut up bacon-fat and,
still not saying a word, sat down at the table, rested his head on his
elbows, gazed numbly at his feet for several minutes, drank some
water straight from the tea-pot spout, and asked hoarsely:

"Why does the water always stink of paraffin in the Kuban?"

Nobody answered. Ryabchikov wiped the steamy blade of his
sabre with a clean twig, Gregor rummaged in his bag, Prokhor abstractedly gazed out of the window at the bare slopes of the hills
sprinkled with droves of horses.

"Sit down at the table and let's drink." Without waiting for the
others, Yermakov flung half a glass of liquor down his throat and
took a drink of water. Chewing a piece of bacon, looking at Gregor
with more cheerful eyes, he asked:

"I suppose the Red comrades won't make mincemeat of us?"

"They won't kill all of us. More than a thousand men will be left
behind here," Gregor answered.

"I'm not worrying about all of us!" Yermakov laughed. "I'm only concerned with my own skin."

When they had drunk plentifully, the conversation took a more cheerful turn. But a little later Bogatiriev unexpectedly returned, frowning and sullen, his face blue with cold. He flung down a whole bale of new-looking English tunics at the door and silently began to undress.

"Welcome back!" Prokhor said viciously, with a bow.

Bogatiriev shot an angry glance at him and said with a sigh:

"If every one of these Denikin men and other bastards were to plead with me I wouldn't go! I stood in the queue, got frozen stiff, and all for nothing. They stopped short just in front of me. There were two men left in front of me, and they took one and not the other. Half the battery's been left behind. What do you call that?"

"That's the way they deal with the likes of us!" Yermakov burst into a roar of laughter and, splashing the liquid out of the bottle, poured out a full glass for Bogatiriev. "Here, drink to your misery! Or will you wait for them to come and ask you to go? Look out of the window! That's not General Wrangel coming for you, is it?"

Without answering, Bogatiriev sucked the liquor through his teeth. He was in no humour for jokes. But Yermakov and Ryabchikov, both of them half drunk, regaled the old Armenian woman until she could hold no more, then talked of going out to find an accordion-player somewhere or other.

"You'd better go to the station," Bogatiriev advised them. "They're opening up the freight cars. There's a whole trainful of uniforms going begging."

"What the devil do we want your uniforms for?" Yermakov shouted. "The tunics you've brought along will be enough for us. They'll strip us of anything extra in any case. Piotra, you hound, we've decided to go over to the Reds, understand? Are we Cossacks or what? If the Reds allow us to live we'll go and serve them. We're Don Cossacks! Cossacks of the purest blood, without any mixture! Fighting's our job! Do you know how I wield my sabre? Like a cabbage-stump! Stand up and I'll try my hand on you! What, feeling too weak? It's all the same to us whom we sabre, so long as we can sabre someone. That's true, isn't it, Melekhov?"

"Don't worry!" Gregor answered wearily.

His bloodshot eyes squinting, Yermakov tried to get at his sabre, which was lying on a chest. Bogatiriev good-humouredly pushed him away and asked:

"Don't rage too much, Anika the Warrior, or I'll quiet you down at once. Drink in moderation! Remember you're an officer!"

"I'll resign my rank together with the epaulets! At the moment I need it just about as much as a pig needs a trough. Don't remind me of it! Shall I cut your epaulets off for you? Piotra, my sorrow, wait a bit; I'll have them off in a jiffy."

"It's not time for that yet; there's plenty of time yet," Bogatiriev laughed, pushing aside his uncontrollable friend.

They drank till dawn. During the evening other Cossacks turned up, one of them with an accordion. Yermakov danced the "Cossack" dance until he dropped. They dragged him aside, and he at once fell asleep on the bare floor, throwing his legs wide apart, flinging his head back awkwardly. The cheerless carousal lasted until morning. "I'm from Kumshatka," one of the strangers, an elderly Cossack, said, sobbing drunkenly. "We had bullocks so big you couldn't reach their horns from the ground. My horses were like lions. And now what have we got left on the farm? Only one mangy bitch. And she'll die soon, there's nothing for her to feed on." A Kuban Cossack in a ragged Circassian coat ordered the accordion-player to strike up a "Naursk" dance and, picturesquely throwing out his arms, slipped about the room with such astonishing agility that Gregor felt sure the soles of his boots did not touch the scratched, dirty floor at all.

At midnight several of the Cossacks brought two tall, narrow-throated, earthenware pitchers from somewhere or other. Half rotting, faded labels were stuck to their sides, their corks were sealed, and massive leaden seals hung from the cherry-red sealing wax. Prokhor held the huge pitcher, which contained perhaps a bucketful of liquid, in his hands, painfully moving his lips, trying to read the foreign words on the label. Yermakov, who had woke up, took the pitcher from him, set it down on the floor, and drew his sabre. Before Prokhor had time to groan he cut through the neck with a slanting stroke of his sabre and shouted: "Bring your glasses!"

The thick, amazingly aromatic and bitter liqueur was disposed of in a few minutes. Ryabchikov clicked his tongue again and again in ecstasy and muttered: "That's not wine, but the blessed Sacrament That's only to be drunk before your death, and then not by every-

body, but only those who've never played cards, never sniffed tobacco, never touched women. . . . It's a drink for bishops, in a
word!"

Then Prokhor remembered that he had the flasks of medicinal
wine in his kitbag, and cried:

"Wait, Platon! Don't boast too soon! I've got better wine than
that! That's muck, but the stuff I got from the warehouse—now,
that's wine! Incense with honey, and maybe even better! It's not
bishop's wine, brother, but, I tell you straight, it's czar's wine. In the
old days the czars drank it, but now it's fallen to our lot . . ." he
bragged away as he opened one of the flasks.

Ryabchikov, always ready for a drink, swallowed half a glass of
the thick fluid in one gulp. He at once turned pale, and his eyes
bulged.

"That's not wine, it's carbolic!" he shouted hoarsely. In his fury,
spitting the remains from his glass over Prokhor's shirt, he rushed,
staggering, into the passage.

"He's lying, the snake! It's English wine. The finest quality!
Don't believe him, brothers!" Prokhor bawled, trying to outshout the
babel of voices. He tossed off a whole glassful of the liquid and at
once turned even paler than Ryabchikov.

"Well, what's it like?" Yermakov asked, dilating his nostrils and
gazing into Prokhor's bleary eyes. "Like czar's wine? Strong?
Sweet? Speak up now, you devil, or I'll smash this flask over your
head!"

Suffering silently, Prokhor shook his head, hiccuped, nimbly
jumped up and rushed out after Ryabchikov. Choking with laughter, Yermakov winked conspiratorially at Gregor, and went out into
the yard. A minute or so later he came back, laughing so uproariously that he drowned all the other voices in the room.

"What's all that for?" Gregor asked wearily. "What are you neighing for, idiot?"

"Oh, my boy, go and look at the way they're turning their insides
out. Do you know what they drank?"

"Well, what?"

"Some English anti-louse ointment."

"You're lying!"

"It's God's truth! When I was at the warehouse I thought it was
wine too, but then I asked the doctor: 'What's this stuff, doctor?'

'Medicine,' he said. 'It doesn't happen to be the remedy for all sorrows?' I asked. 'It isn't liquor, is it?' 'God forbid!' he said. 'It's some anti-louse ointment the Allies have sent us. It's for external application; it mustn't be taken inside at all.' "

"Then why didn't you tell them, you fool?" Gregor asked in angry reproach.

"Let the devils clean themselves before surrendering! I don't suppose they'll die." Yermakov wiped the tears from his eyes and added not without a touch of malevolence: "And besides, now they'll drink a little more steadily. You couldn't keep up with them before. Such thirsty souls need a lesson. Well, shall you and I have a drink or shall we wait a bit? Let's drink to our end!"

Just before daybreak Gregor went out on the porch, with trembling fingers rolled himself a cigarette, lit it, and stood in the mist with his back against the damp wall.

The house was riotous with drunken shouts, the sobbing tones of the accordion, and furious whistling. The heels of the ardent dancers unwearyingly drummed out a fine tattoo. But the wind carried the thick, low wail of a steamer siren from the bay; on the quays the human voices blended into a solid roar, broken by loud shouts of command, the neighing of horses, the whistles of steamers. Somewhere along the railway line fighting was going on. There was a muffled thunder of guns; in the intervals between the shots the burning rattle of machine-gun fire was faintly audible. Beyond the mountain pass a rocket flew high into the heavens, sprinkling light. For a few seconds the humped summits of the mountains grew visible, lit up by a green translucent light; then the sticky darkness of the southern night covered the hills once more, and the artillery cannonade sounded still more distinctly and frequently, blending into a steady roar of gunfire.

Chapter 8

A cold, salty, heavy wind was blowing from the sea. It carried the scent of strange, unknown lands to the shore. But to the Don Cossacks not only the wind, but all else was strange, unhomelike in that boring, seaside town with its innumerable draughts. They stood on the quay in a solid mass, waiting to be embarked. Green foaming waves seethed along the shore. A chilly sun peered at the earth through the clouds. In the roadstead English and French destroyers were smoking; a Dreadnought hung its grey, menacing bulk above the water. Over it spread a black pall of smoke. An ominous silence hung around the quays. Where the last transport had recently been swinging at her moorings officers' saddles, trunks, clothing, sheep-skin coats, chairs upholstered in crimson plush, and other jumble, hurriedly flung from the gangways, were floating.

Early in the morning Gregor rode down to the quay. Giving Prokhor charge of his horse, he spent a long time in the crowd, look-ing for acquaintances, listening to the disconnected, anxious talk. He saw an elderly retired colonel who had been refused a place on the last steamer shoot himself on the gangway.

A few minutes previously the colonel, a little, fussy man with a grey scrub on his cheeks, with tear-stained, swollen, marsupial eyes, had seized the officer of the guard by the strap of his sword-belt, had miserably whispered something, sniffing and wiping his tobacco-stained moustache, eyes, and trembling lips with a dirty handker-chief. Then he had suddenly appeared to make up his mind. . . . A moment later some swift-fingered Cossack drew the gleaming Browning from the dead man's warm hand and with his feet rolled the body in its light-grey officer's greatcoat to a pile of boxes. Then the crowd seethed still more furiously around the gangway, the fighting in the queues grew still more violent, the hoarse voices of the refugees rose in a harsh howl of rage.

When the last steamer drew away from the quayside there was a crescendo of women's sobs, hysterical cries, curses. Before the curt bass roar of the ship's siren had had time to die away, a young Kal-myk in a fox-skin cap with ear- and neck-flaps jumped into the water and swam after the steamer.

"He couldn't wait!" one of the Cossacks sighed.

"It's clear that whatever happened he couldn't remain behind," said a Cossack standing close to Gregor. "He must have done the Reds too much harm. . . ."

Clenching his teeth, Gregor stared after the swimming Kalmyk. More and more slowly swung the swimmer's arms through the air, lower and lower sank his shoulders. His saturated greatcoat was dragging him down. A wave washed his shabby red fox-skin cap off his head and threw it back.

"The damned heathen will drown!" some old man in a long Caucasian coat said commiseratively.

Gregor turned sharply on his heel and went to his horse. He found Prokhor talking excitedly to Ryabchikov and Bogatiriev, who had just galloped up. Seeing Gregor, Ryabchikov fidgeted in his saddle, impatiently dug his heels into his horse's flanks, and shouted:

"Hurry up, Pantalievich!" Not waiting for Gregor to reach them, he shouted to him: "Let's retreat before it's too late. We've collected a good half-squadron of Cossacks, and we're thinking of making our way to Gelendzhik, and then on to Georgia. How do you stand?"

His hands thrust deep into the pockets of his greatcoat, silently pushing aside the aimlessly gathering Cossacks, Gregor went up to them.

"Will you come with us or not?" Ryabchikov asked insistently, riding right up to him.

"No, I won't!"

"We've got a Cossack military commander to join in with us. He knows every inch of the road and says he could lead us blindfold all the way to Tiflis. Come on, Grisha! And from there we'll go on to the Turks. What do you say? We've got to save ourselves somehow! We're getting near the end now, but you're just like a half-dead fish."

"No, I shan't go!" Gregor took the reins from Prokhor's hand and climbed heavily, like an old man, into the saddle. "I won't go! There's no point in it. And besides, it's rather late now. . . . Look!"

Ryabchikov looked round and in his despair and rage crushed and tore away the sword-knot on his sabre. Lines of Red Army men were streaming down from the mountains. Machine-guns feverishly began to rattle close to a cement works. Armoured trains opened fire with their guns against the lines of men. The first shell burst near a windmill.

"Ride to our quarters, lads, and keep close behind me!" Gregor ordered, suddenly cheering up and drawing himself erect again.

But Ryabchikov seized Gregor's horse by the rein and exclaimed in alarm:

"Don't go! Let's stay here. . . . You know, even death is beautiful when life is peaceful. . . ."

"Ah, you devil, come on! Why talk about death? What are you babbling?" In his annoyance Gregor was about to add something more, but his voice was drowned by a thunderous roar from the sea. The British Dreadnought had swung into position and had sent over a packet of shells from its twelve-inch guns. Covering the steamers sailing out of the bay, it raked the lines of Red and Green Army men streaming down to the outskirts of the town, then transferred its fire to the top of the pass, where the Red batteries had taken up positions. The British shells flew with an oppressive roar and howl over the heads of the Cossacks crowded on the quay.

Pulling tightly on the reins, holding up his horse as it fell back on its haunches, through the roar of the firing Bogatiriev shouted:

"Well, the British cannon use strong language! But they're wasting their fire. It's not doing anything, only making a lot of noise!"

"Let them roar! It's all one to us now." Smiling, Gregor touched up his horse and rode down the street.

Their horses prancing in a furious gallop, six horsemen with drawn sabres rode round a corner to meet him. Across the breast of the leading rider was a strip of blood-red bunting.

PART VI

Home at Last

HOME AT LAST

Chapter 1

For two days a warm wind had been blowing from the south. The last snow had melted off the fields. The foaming spring runnels had ceased their roaring, the gullies and rivulets of the steppe had finished gurgling. At dawn of the third day the wind died away and heavy mists descended over the steppe; the clumps of last-year feather-grass were silvered with moisture; the mounds, ravines, and villages, the spires of the belfries, the arrowing crowns of the pyramidal poplars, were all drowned in an impenetrable milky haze.

That misty morning, for the first time after her recovery, Aksinia went out on the porch and stood long, intoxicated with the heady sweetness of the fresh spring air. Mastering her nausea and dizziness, she walked as far as the well in the orchard, put down the bucket, and seated herself on the parapet.

Altogether different, marvellously fresh and enchanting seemed the world to Aksinia. With glittering eyes she agitatedly gazed about her, fingering the folds of her dress as would a child. The enmisted distance, the apple trees in the orchard swimming with thaw-water, the wet palings, and the road beyond them with its deep, water-filled ruts—all seemed incredibly beautiful to her; everything was blossoming with heavy yet delicate tints, as though irradiated with sunlight.

A scrap of clean sky peering through the haze dazzled her with its chilly azure; the scent of rotting straw and thawed black earth was so familiar and pleasant that she sighed deeply and smiled at the cor-- ners of her lips; the artless snatch of song of a skylark reaching her ears from somewhere in the misty steppe awakened an unconscious sadness within her. And it was that snatch of skylark's song heard in a strange land that sent Aksinia's heart beating more quickly and wrung two meagre little tears from her eyes.

Unthinkingly rejoicing in the life which had returned to her, she experienced a tremendous desire to touch everything with her hands, to look at everything. She wanted to touch the currant bush which stood blackened with moisture, to press her cheek against the branch of an apple tree covered with a velvety pale-pink bloom; she desired to stride across the fallen fencing and to walk through the mire, away from all tracks, to where beyond a broad hollow the fields of winter corn were showing wondrously green, merging with the misty distance.

For several days Aksinia lived in the expectation that at any mo- ment Gregor would turn up. But at last she learned from neigh- bours who called on her host that the war was still going on, and that many Cossacks had sailed from Novorossisk to the Crimea, while those who had stayed behind had joined the Red Army or had been sent to the mines.

By the end of the week she had firmly made up her mind to go home, and a travelling companion was quickly found for her. One evening a little hunchbacked man entered the hut without knock- ing. He bowed, but did not speak, and began to unbutton the muddy English greatcoat, bursting at the seams, which was hanging around him like a sack.

"Why, my good man, what do you mean by not even saying 'Good evening,' but behaving as though you'd come to stay?" the master asked, staring at the uninvited guest in astonishment.

The old man nimbly removed his greatcoat, shook it out on the threshold, and carefully hung it on a hook. Then, stroking his little grey beard, he smiled and said:

"Forgive me, for the love of Christ, my dear man, but I've learned my lesson for these times: first take off your things and then ask if you can stay the night; otherwise you won't be let in. These days the people have grown churlish, they aren't pleased to see guests. . . ."

"But where are we to put you? You can see we're crowded out already," the master said more amicably.

"I don't need more room than a dog. I'll curl myself up here by the door and sleep."

"But who are you, daddy? Did you run from the Soviets?" the mistress asked inquisitively.

"You've hit it: I ran from the Soviets. I ran and ran, and ran all the way to the sea; but now I'm quietly making my way back again. I'm tired of running . . ." the garrulous old fellow answered, squatting down on his heels by the door.

"But who are you, all the same? Where are you from?" the master renewed the examination.

The old man drew a large pair of tailor's scissors out of a pocket, turned them over and over in his hands, and said with the same fixed smile on his lips:

"Here's my document: I've come all the way from Novorossisk under its orders. But my native place is a long way off, the other side of Vieshenska district. And that's where I'm off to now, after having had a taste of the salt water in the sea."

"I'm from Vieshenska too, daddy," Aksinia cried in delight.

"You don't say!" the old man exclaimed. "Well, of all the places to meet a fellow-countrywoman in! Though these days even that isn't surprising; we're like the Jews now, we're scattered over the face of the earth. In the Kuban it was so bad that if you threw a stick at a dog you'd hit a Don Cossack. You came across them everywhere, you couldn't get away from them, and there were even more of them buried in the ground. My dear people, I've seen all sorts of sights during this retreat. You wouldn't believe the misery the people are suffering. Two days ago I was sitting in a station, and beside me was a gentlewoman wearing spectacles, and through her spectacles she was looking for the lice on her. And they were marching over her in regiments. And there she was, picking them off with her fingers, and her face as sour as though she'd bitten a rotten apple. Every time she crushed one poor little louse she frowned still more, as though she was about to double up and be sick, she looked so disgusted. And yet you'll find a stout fellow killing a man and not frowning in the least, nor even turning up his nose. I saw one such daredevil cut down three Kalmyks, and afterwards he wiped his sabre on his horse's mane, took out a cigarette, lit it, rode up to me and asked: 'What are you staring your eyes out for, daddy? Do you want me to cut you down too?' 'What are you saying, my son?' I said. 'God forbid! If you cut off my head how shall I be able to chew my bread?' He laughed and rode off."

"Say what you like, it's easier for a man to kill another man than to crush a louse. Men have grown cheap during the Revolution," the master remarked sententiously.

"That's true!" the guest confirmed. "Men aren't cattle, they get used to anything. And so I asked this woman: 'Who might you be? By your face you don't look to be one of the common sort.' She looked at me, her face swimming in tears, and said: 'I'm the wife of Major-General Grechikhin.' 'Well,' I thought, 'with all your major and with all your general, you're as lousy as a mangy cat!' And I said to her: 'Excuse me, Your Excellency, but if you're going to kill off all your creeping insects at that rate you'll be kept busy till the Feast of the Blessed Virgin. And you'll break all your little nails. Crush them all at one blow.' 'But how can I?' she asked. And so I told her: 'Take off your clothes,' I said, 'spread them out on some hard spot, and hammer them with a bottle.' And I saw my general's wife get up and run behind the water-tower, and I saw her basting away at her clothes with a bottle of green glass, and doing it so well that she might have been used to it all her life! I stood admiring her and thinking: 'God has much to be responsible for; he's turned the insects loose even on people of noble birth; let them suck their sweet blood, so to speak, and not always be drinking their fill of the toilers' blood. God's not a nobody, He knows His job! Sometimes He steals quietly up to people and deals with them so fairly that you couldn't think of anything better. . . .'"

The tailor rattled away incessantly, but, seeing that the master and mistress were listening to him with the utmost attention, he adroitly hinted that he had many more interesting things to tell, but that he was so famished that he felt sleepy.

After supper, as he was making himself comfortable for the night, he asked Aksinia:

"And you, fellow-countrywoman, are you thinking of making a long stay here as guest?"

"I'm getting ready to go home, daddy."

"Well, then you come along with me; it'll be more cheerful for both of us."

Aksinia willingly agreed, and next day, after taking leave of her host and hostess, they left the lonely steppe village of Novo-Mikhailovsky.

They arrived at the village of Miliutinsky after nightfall on the twelfth day of their journey. At a large, prosperous-looking house they asked permission to stay the night. Next morning Aksinia's companion decided to stay for a week in the village, to rest and heal his feet, which were chafed and bleeding. He was unable to walk any farther. Some tailoring work was found for him in the house, and the old man, who was eager to get back to his trade, nimbly made himself comfortable by the window, took out his scissors and a bunch of needles tied with string, and swiftly began to unpick some clothing.

As he said good-bye to Aksinia the old wag crossed himself and unexpectedly watered at the eyes. But he at once brushed away the tears and said with his usual jocularity:

"Need isn't your own mother, but it makes people kin. . . . Here am I feeling sorry at leaving you. . . . Well, there's nothing to be done about it; go on alone, my daughter, your guide has gone lame on all his legs; I expect someone fed him on barley bread somewhere. . . . And besides, for my seventy years I've done a good march with you, and even too much. If you get the chance, tell my old woman that her grey dove is alive and well. He's been pounded in a mortar, but he's still alive, and he's sewing trousers for good people on his way, and he may turn up at home at any time. So you tell her: the old idiot has done retreating and is advancing back homeward; but he doesn't know when he'll be climbing on to the stove again. . . ."

Aksinia spent several more days on the road. At Bokovskoi she found a wagon going her way and rode to Tatarsk. Late in the evening she passed through the wide-open wicket gate of her yard, glanced at the Melekhov hut, and choked with the sob which unexpectedly rose in her throat. In the empty kitchen, which smelt of neglect, she shed all the bitter feminine tears which had been accumulating for many a long day, then went down to the Don for water, lit the stove, and sat down at the table, letting her hands fall to her knees. Lost in thought, she did not hear the door creak, and she was aroused from her reverie only when Ilinichna came in and quietly said:

"Well, greetings, neighbour! You've been away a long time in strange lands without our having any news of you. . . ."

Aksinia gave her a startled look and rose to her feet.

"What are you staring at me for? Why don't you speak? You haven't brought bad news, have you?" Ilinichna came slowly to the table and sat down on the edge of the bench, not shifting her questioning gaze from Aksinia's face.

"Why should I have news? . . . I simply wasn't expecting you. I was sitting thinking and didn't hear you come in," Aksinia said in embarrassment.

"You've got terribly thin, there's hardly enough of you to keep your soul in."

"I've had typhus. . . ."

"And our Gregor—how is he? Where did you leave him? Is he still alive?"

Aksinia briefly told all she knew. Ilinichna listened to the end without saying a word and then asked:

"When he left you he wasn't ill, was he?"

"No, he wasn't ill."

"And you haven't heard anything of him since?"

"No."

Ilinichna sighed with relief.

"Well, thank you for your good news. For here in the village all sorts of things are being said about him."

"What things?" Aksinia asked almost inaudibly.

"Oh, it's all nonsense. You can't listen to all the stories going round. . . . Of all our villagers only Vanka Beskhlebnov has come back. He saw Gregor ill in Katerinodar, and I don't believe any of the other stories."

"But what do they say, granny?"

"We were told a Cossack of Singin village had said that the Reds had killed Gregor at Novorossisk. I walked all the way to Singin—a mother's heart can't remain in suspense—and found the Cossack. He denied every word of it. He said he hadn't seen or heard of

Gregor. Then there was another rumour that he'd been put in prison, and that he'd died there of typhus. . . ." Ilinichna's eyes drooped and she was long silent, examining her gnarled, heavy hands. The old woman's face, her cheeks pendulous with age, were tranquil, her lips were pressed sternly together; but suddenly a cherry-coloured flush flooded her swarthy cheeks, and her eyelids began to flicker. She looked at Aksinia with dry, ecstatically burning eyes and said hoarsely:

"But I don't believe it! It can't be that I've been robbed of my last son. God has no cause to punish me. . . . I've only got a little time left to live now—only a very little time left to live, and my cup of sorrow has been filled to overflowing without that! Grisha's alive! My heart has had no sign, and so my darling's alive!"

Aksinia turned away without speaking.

There was a long silence in the kitchen. Suddenly the wind blew the porch door wide open, and they heard the flood water roaring among the poplars on the farther side of the Don, and the wild geese anxiously calling to one another above the waters.

Aksinia closed the door and went and leaned against the stove.

"Don't grieve over him, granny," she said quietly. "Can illness bowl a man like him over? He's strong, as strong as iron. Such men don't die. In a crackling frost he rode all the way without gloves."

"Did he talk about the children at all?" Ilinichna asked wearily.

"He mentioned both you and the children. Are they well?"

"They're well, what can harm them? But our Pantaleimon Pro-koffich died during the retreat. We're left alone. . . ."

Aksinia silently crossed herself; she was amazed at the calm with which the old woman had told of the death of her husband.

Resting her hands on the table, Ilinichna rose heavily.

"Here I've been sitting with you, and it's already dark in the yard!" she remarked.

"Sit as long as you like, granny."

"Dunia's in the house alone, I ought to go." As she adjusted the kerchief over her head, she looked around the kitchen and knitted her brows. "Your stove's smoking. You should have arranged for someone to come and live here when you went off. Well, good-bye!" As she took hold of the door latch, she said without turning her head: "When you've settled down a bit come over and see us, pay us a visit. And perhaps you'll get news of Gregor and can tell us."

From that day there was a complete change in the relations between the Melekhovs and Aksinia. Their anxiety for Gregor's life
seemed to bring them closer and make them kin.

Next morning Dunia saw Aksinia in the yard, called to her, went
up to the fence, and, putting her arms around Aksinia's thin shoulders, smiled at her pleasantly and simply. "Oh, how thin you've got,
Aksinia! You're nothing but skin and bone!"

"You'd get thin with such a life!" Aksinia smiled in answer, feeling a pang of jealousy as she noted the girl's crimson face, abloom
with mature beauty.

"Did Mother come to see you yesterday?" Dunia asked, for some
reason dropping her voice to a whisper.

"Yes."

"I thought she did. Did she ask about Grisha?"

"Yes."

"And she didn't cry at all?"

"No; she's a stout-hearted old woman."

Giving Aksinia a trustful look, Dunia said:

"It would have been better if she had; things would have been
easier for her. . . . You know, Ksinia, she's grown so wonderful
since this past winter, she's not at all like she used to be. When she
heard about Father I thought her heart would break, I was terribly
frightened. But she didn't let fall a single tear. She only said: 'May
he enter the heavenly kingdom! My man has ended his sufferings.
. . .' And until nightfall she said nothing to anybody. I tried to
talk to her about all sorts of things, but she just waved me off and
was silent. The misery I had over her that day! But in the evening
I collected the cattle, came in from the yard, and asked her: 'Mother,
shall we cook anything for supper?' Then her pain passed and she
began to talk. . . ." Dunia sighed and, thoughtfully gazing across
Aksinia's shoulder, asked:

"Is our Gregor dead? Is it true what people are saying?"

"I don't know, dear."

Dunia gave Aksinia a sidelong, questioning look and sighed still
more deeply.

"Mother's nothing but yearning for him! She never speaks of him
except as 'my youngest.' And she simply won't have it that he may
not be alive still. But you know, Ksinia, if she learns that he's really

dead she'll die of sorrow herself. All life has left her now, the sole hope to which she clings is Gregor. Even to the children she's become unwanted, sort of, and at work everything falls from her hands. You just think: in one year there's been four of our family . . ."

Moved by compassion, Aksinia leaned across the fence, embraced Dunia, and gave her a strong kiss on the cheek.

"Get your mother occupied with something, my dear; don't let her grieve too much."

"What can you occupy her with?" Dunia wiped her eyes with the corner of her kerchief and asked:

"You come and see us sometimes and talk to her; that'll make it easier for her. You've got no reason to shun us."

"I'll drop in sometimes. I will, you see!"

"I ought to be going out to the fields tomorrow. We've harnessed up with Anikushka's widow, we want to sow a little wheat. Are you thinking of sowing anything for yourself?"

"I'm a fine sower!" Aksinia smiled a cheerless smile. "I've got nothing to sow, and besides, what's the good? I don't need much for myself, I'll manage to exist somehow."

"Any news of your Stepan?"

"No, not a word," Aksinia answered unconcernedly, and said, to her own surprise: "I'm not over-anxious about him." The confession slipped from her unexpectedly, and she felt embarrassed. To cover her confusion, she hurriedly added: "Well, good-bye, girl; I must go into the hut to tidy up."

Dunia pretended she had not noticed Aksinia's confusion and looked away as she said:

"Wait a moment; I just wanted to ask you, wouldn't you give us a hand with the work? The earth will be dried out; I'm afraid we shan't be able to manage. And there are only two Cossacks left in all the village, and they're lame!"

Aksinia willingly agreed, and, satisfied, Dunia went off to make her preparations.

All day she methodically made ready for the next morning; with the help of Anikushka's widow she sieved the seed, managed to mend the harrow, greased the wagon-wheels, put the sower in order. In the evening she raked some sieved seed-corn into a kerchief and carried it to the cemetery, sprinkling it over the graves of Piotra,

Natalia, and Daria, so that next day the birds would fly to her relatives' graves. In the simplicity of her heart she believed that the dead would hear the merry twittering of the birds and would rejoice.

•

Only during the hour before dawn did silence descend over the Don lands. Muffledly the water gurgled through the inundated forest, washing the pale-green trunks of the poplars, measuredly swinging the flooded summits of the oak saplings and the young aspens; bowed by the current, in the overflowing lakes the panicles of the bulrushes rustled; over the flooded fields, along the lonely creeks—where the flood water stood motionless as though frozen, reflecting the twilight of the starry heaven—the barnacle geese called very softly, the male teals whistled sleepily, and rarely the silvery trumpet voices of migrant swans sounded. At times a fish growing fat in the flooded expanse splashed in the darkness; a fluid wave went rolling far over the scintillating water, and the warning cackle of a startled bird was heard. Then once more the Donside lands were wrapped in silence. But with the dawn, just as the chalky spurs of the hills were turning rosy, a ground breeze started up. Heavy and strong it blew against the current. Great seven-foot waves piled high along the river, the water seethed furiously in the forest, the trees groaned as they swayed. All day the wind roared, to die away late in the night. And this weather lasted for several days.

A lilac haze curtained the steppe. The earth had dried out, the grasses were halted in their growth, fissures ran across the autumn-ploughed fields. The ground was drying more and more with every hour; but in the fields belonging to Tatarsk hardly anyone was to be seen. In all the village only a few senile greybeards were left, only frost-bitten and sick or disabled Cossacks had returned from the retreat, and only women and youths were at work in the fields. The wind drove the dust about the depopulated village, banged the shutters of the huts, rummaged among the straw on the roofs of the sheds. "This year we shall be without bread," said the old men. "Only women in the fields, and even so only every third house is sowing. And dead earth won't give birth."

Dunia and the other women had been two days sowing when at sunset Aksinia drove the bullocks down to the pond. At the dam, holding a saddled horse by the rein, was the ten-year-old son of the

Obnizovs. The horse was chewing with its lips, sprinkling drops of water from its velvety grey muzzle, but the boy was amusing himself throwing clumps of dry clay into the water and watching the rings rippling wider and wider.

"Where are you off to, Vanka?" Aksinia asked.

"I've brought food out to Mother."

"Well, and what news is there in the village?"

"Oh, nothing. Grand-dad Gerasim caught a fine carp in his net last night. And Fiodor Melnikov has returned from the retreat."

Rising on tiptoe, the lad bridled the horse, took a strand of the mane in his hand, and with impish agility sprang into the saddle. He rode away from the pond as a sedate farmer should, at a walking pace, but when he had got a little way he glanced back at Aksinia and set off at a gallop, and his faded blue shirt blew out like a balloon behind him.

Aksinia stretched herself out on the dam while the bullocks were drinking and there and then decided to go back to the village. Melnikov was a soldier Cossack, and he ought to have some news of Gregor's fate. When she drove the bullocks back to the encampment she said to Dunia:

"I'm going off to the village; I'll be back early in the morning."

"On business?"

"Yes."

She returned next morning. As she went up to Dunia, who was harnessing the bullocks, she was unconcernedly swinging a switch; but her brows were knitted and the corners of her lips were folded bitterly.

"Fiodor Melnikov's come home. I went and asked him about Gregor. He doesn't know anything," she said briefly, and, turning sharply, went to the sower.

After the sowing Aksinia set to work on her own farm; she sowed watermelons in the melon plot, plastered and whitewashed the hut, and, to the best of her ability, covered the roof of the shed with what straw she had left. The days passed by in work, but her anxiety for Gregor did not abate. She was reluctant to think of Stepan, and for some reason she felt sure he would not return; yet when one or another of the Cossacks came home her first question was always:

"You haven't seen my Stepan, have you?" and only then did she try discreetly to ferret out some news of Gregor. Everybody in the village knew of their liaison, and even the scandal-loving women had stopped gossiping about them. But Aksinia was ashamed to disclose her feelings, and only rarely, when some taciturn returned soldier made no mention of Gregor, did she ask, narrowing her eyes and obviously embarrassed: "But you haven't chanced to see our neighbour Gregor Pantalievich, have you? His mother's anxious about him; she's quite pining away. . . ."

None of the village Cossacks had seen either Gregor or Stepan after the Don Army's surrender at Novorossisk. But at the end of June a regimental comrade of Stepan's called to see Aksinia as he was making his way back to his own village. He informed her:

"Stepan's gone to the Crimea—it's the truth I'm telling you. I saw him with my own eyes getting on the boat. I didn't get a chance of having a word with him. There was such a crowd that they were walking on the people's heads!"

When she asked about Gregor he gave her an evasive answer: "I saw him on the quay; he was wearing epaulets. But I haven't seen him since. They've carried off a lot of officers to Moscow, and who's to know where he is now? . . ."

But a week later Prokhor Zykov turned up at Tatarsk. He was wounded and was brought from Millerovo station in a wagon. When she heard the news, Aksinia stopped milking the cow, let the calf go to its mother, and, putting on her kerchief as she went, hurried almost at a run to the Zykovs' yard. "At any rate Prokhor will know. He ought to know!" she thought as she went. "But supposing he says Gregor's dead? What shall I do then?" And at every step she slowed down more and more, pressing her hand to her heart, fearful of hearing black news.

Smiling broadly, hiding the stump of his left arm behind his back, Prokhor welcomed her in the best room:

"Hello, comrade-in-arms! Greetings! I'm glad to see you. And we were thinking you'd given up the ghost in that little village. Ah, you lay there pretty bad. . . . Well, and how beautiful it—typhus, I mean—makes the likes of you! But see how the Poles have carved me up, damn them!" Prokhor showed the knotted sleeve of his khaki tunic. "When my wife saw it she wept and cried, but I told her: 'Don't bellow like that, you fool; others have their heads chopped off and don't complain.' But an arm's nothing at all! They can always make a wooden one for you. And at any rate a wooden arm won't be afraid of the cold, and if it gets cut off it doesn't bleed. The only pity, my girl, is that I haven't learned to manage with one hand. I can't button up my trousers. there's the rub! I've travelled all the way home from Kiev with them unbuttoned. It's shameful! So you must excuse me if you notice I'm untidy. Well, come in and sit down; you'll be our guest, won't you? We'll have a chat while my wife's out. I sent her out for vodka, the Antichrist! Here her husband arrives home with one arm torn off, and she hasn't anything to drink his health in! You women are all the same when your husbands are away. I know you all too well, you wet-tailed devils!"

"You might tell me . . ."

"I know! I'll tell you! He asked me to give you a bow like this." Prokhor jokingly bowed, raised his head, and lifted his eyebrows in amazement. "Well, that's a fine to-do! What are you crying for, you fool? You women are all twisted of the same yarn! If their man is killed, they cry; if he comes home alive, they still cry. Wipe your eyes, wipe your eyes; what are you snivelling like that for? At Novorossisk he and I joined Comrade Budionny's cavalry, the Fourteenth Division. Our Gregor Pantalievich took command of a company—a squadron, I mean. Of course I became his orderly, and we rode to Kiev by forced marches. Well, girl, we gave those Poles a taste! As we went Gregor Pantalievich said: 'I've killed Germans, I've tried my sword on all sorts of Austrians, I don't suppose the Poles' brainboxes are any stronger. I think it'll be easier sabring them than our own Russians, don't you?' And he winked at me and bared his teeth. He changed completely when he joined the Red Army; he grew quite cheerful and as sleek as a gelding. Well, but he and I didn't manage to get along without a family quarrel. . . . One day I rode up to him and said by way of a joke: 'Time we called a halt, Your Excellency, Comrade Melekhov!' He rolled his eyes at me and said: 'You drop that sort of joke or it'll be the worse for you!' That same evening he sent for me about something or other, and the devil himself put it into my head to call him 'Excellency' again. . . . The way he snatched up his Mauser! He went quite white and bared his teeth like a wolf—and he's got a full mouth of teeth, at least a troop of them. I ducked under a horse's belly and got away from him. He all but killed me, the devil! Well, we ar-

rived at the Ukraine and tried out the Poles. They're not bad fight‚
ers, but a little weak in the back. They're as puffed up with pride as
a turkey cock, but they can run well when you press them hard!"

"Maybe he'll come home on leave . . ." Aksinia stammered.

"Don't you think of it!" Prokhor snorted. "He says he's going to
serve until he's atoned for his past sins. And he'll do it: a fool's task
isn't difficult. He led us into the attack close to one small town, and
I myself saw him cut down four of their Uhlans. The devil's been
left-handed ever since he was a child, and so he gave it them from
both sides. After the battle Budionny himself shook hands with
him in front of the regiment, and he and the squadron were thanked.
That's the sort of kettle he's kicking over—your Pantalievich!"

Aksinia listened as though dazed. . . . She recovered from the
daze only at the Melekhovs' gate. Dunia was in the porch sipping
milk; without raising her head she asked:

"Have you come for the leaven? I know I promised to bring it
along, but I forgot." But, glancing at Aksinia's eyes, wet with tears,
beaming with happiness, she understood all without a word.

Pressing her flaming face to Dunia's shoulder, panting with joy,
Aksinia whispered:

"Alive and well. . . . He's sent his greetings. . . . Go now! Go
and tell Mother!"

Chapter 2

Of all the Tatarsk Cossacks who had retreated with the Whites, by
the summer some thirty men had returned. The majority were old
men and elderly Cossack soldiers, and, except for sick and wounded,
the Cossacks in the prime of life were still missing. Some of them
were in the Red Army; others, members of Wrangel regiments, were
biding their time in the Crimea, preparing for a new advance into
the Don area.

A good half of those who had gone would remain for ever in
strange lands: some had perished of typhus, others had found death

during the final struggles against the enemy in the Kuban; a number who had been separated from the main forces were frozen to death in the steppe beyond Manich, two were taken prisoner by guerrillas and had vanished without trace. There were many Cossacks missing from Tatarsk. The women spent their days in tense and anxious expectation, gazing under their palms. Who knows? Perhaps some belated wayfarer might be coming along the highroad in the lilac evening haze.

Some ragged, lousy, and emaciated but long-expected master would come home, and at once there would be a joyous, aimless bustle in his hut; water was heated for the dirt-blackened soldier; the children vied with one another in waiting on their father and watched his every movement; half-crazed with happiness, the housewife ran to lay the table, then rushed to the chest to get out a clean set of her husband's underwear. But, as though of malice, the linen proved to be unmended, and the housewife's trembling fingers simply could not get the thread through the needle eye. At that happy moment even the yard dog, which had recognized its master a long way off and had run behind him as far as the threshold, licking his hand, was allowed to come into the hut; the children escaped scot-free even if they broke a utensil or spilled milk, and all they did went unpunished. Before the master had had time to change into clean clothes after his bath, the hut was crowded with women. They came to learn the fate of their own dear ones and caught fearfully and greedily at every word the Cossack said. A little later a woman would go out into the yard, pressing her palms to her tear-stained face, and would walk along the lane as though blind, not choosing her road. And then in one of the little homes a new widow would lament over her dead, and the thin voices of weeping children would accompany her. So was it in Tatarsk: the joy which came to one house brought implacable woe to another.

Next morning the master, clean-shaven, looking much younger, rose almost before dawn, went round the farm, and noted the jobs which needed to be attended to at once. Immediately after breakfast he set to work. Merrily the plane hissed or the axe tapped somewhere under the eaves of a shed, in the cool, as though announcing that capable, masculine hands, greedy for work, had come home to that yard. But in the house and yard where they had learned of the death of a father and husband, a mute silence reigned. Silent lay the mother, prostrated with grief, and around her crowded the orphan children, grown old in one night.

Whenever Ilinichna heard that another Cossack had returned she said:

"And when will our man come home? Others come back, but there's not a word of ours."

"They're not discharging the young Cossacks; don't you understand, Mother?" Dunia answered her in a vexed tone.

"How aren't they discharging them? What about Tikhon Gerasimov? He's a year younger than Grisha."

"But he's wounded, Mother."

"What sort of wound has he got?" Ilinichna objected. "I saw him outside the smithy yesterday, and he was walking along as though on parade. Wounded men don't go about like that."

"He was wounded, but he's getting better now."

"Well, and hasn't our man been wounded quite a lot? His body is marked all over with scars; don't you think he needs to get better too?"

Dunia did her best to make her mother see that it was no use hoping for Gregor's return yet awhile. But it was no easy task to convince Ilinichna of anything.

"Shut up, fool!" she ordered Dunia. "I know as much as you, and you're still young to teach your mother. I say he ought to come home, and that means he will come home. Go away, go away; I don't want to waste my breath on you."

The old woman waited for her son with the utmost impatience and mentioned him at every possible opportunity. Whenever Mishatka was disobedient to her she threatened him: "You wait till your father comes home, you bristle-haired little devil! I'll tell him and he'll lay it on you!" If she happened to see a wagon with new ribs in its sides as it passed the window, she sighed and invariably remarked: "You can see by its state that the master's at home, but our wagon looks as though someone had ordered the road to come home." All her life Ilinichna had never liked tobacco-smoke, and she had always driven smokers out of the kitchen; but now she changed even in this respect. "Go and ask Prokhor to come along," she often told Dunia. "Let him come and smoke a cigarette, for the place smells of the dead. Now when Grisha comes back from service, then the house will smell as though a Cossack lives in it!" Every day she cooked extra food, and after dinner she always set an iron pot full of cabbage soup on the stove. When Dunia asked her why she did it Ilinichna answered in astonishment: "Why, what else should I do? Our soldier may come home today, and then he can have something hot to eat at once; for while you're heating this and that up he may be going hungry." One day, when Dunia returned home from the melon plot she saw Gregor's old coat and peaked cap with its faded red band hanging on a nail in the kitchen. She looked at her mother interrogatively, and, smiling guiltily and miserably, Ilinichna said: "I got them out of the chest, Dunia. You see them as you come in from the yard and it makes things seem more homelike —as though he was already back. . . ."

Dunia grew tired of this endless talk of Gregor. One day she could stand no more and reproached her mother:

"Mother, don't you ever get tired of always talking about one and the same thing? You've made everybody sick with your conversation. All we hear from you is 'Grisha,' 'Grisha.' "

"Why should I grow tired of talking about my own son? You wait till you bear children, and then you'll know . . ." Ilinichna answered quietly.

After that she took Gregor's cap and coat out of the kitchen into her room, and for several days she said not a word about him. But not long before the haying she said to Dunia:

"You may get angry when I talk about Grisha, but how are we going to live without him? Have you ever stopped to think about that, silly? Here is mowing-time coming on, and we've got nobody to sharpen even the hay-rake. Look how everything's gone to rack and ruin, and you and I can't keep up with it. When the master's absent even the chattels weep."

Dunia said nothing. She realized well enough that it was not by any means the farm problems that were troubling her mother, but they served only as an excuse for talking about Gregor and for unburdening her soul. Ilinichna began to yearn for her son with renewed force, and she could not hide her feelings. That evening she refused her supper, and when Dunia asked if she were feeling ill, she answered reluctantly:

"I've grown old. . . . And my heart is aching after Grisha. . . .

It's aching so much that nothing pleases me, and it's painful even for my eyes to look out on the world."

But it was not Gregor who was destined to act the master in the Melekhov yard. Just before the hay-mowing Mishka Koshevoi arrived home from the front. He spent the night with distant relations and called on the Melekhovs next morning. Ilinichna was cooking when, politely knocking at the door and receiving no answer, he entered the kitchen, took off his old soldier's cap, and smiled at her.

"Hello, Aunty Ilinichna! You weren't expecting me, were you?"

"Good morning. And who are you to me, that I should be expecting you? Are you first-cousin switch to our wattle fence?" Ilinichna answered roughly, staring angrily at Koshevoi's hated face.

Not in the least discountenanced by this reception, Mishka said:

"After all, we were acquaintances."

"And nothing more."

"But that's enough for me to come to see you. I'm not going to live with you."

"That pleasure hasn't come my way yet!" Ilinichna pronounced, and, taking no more notice of the visitor, returned to her cooking.

Paying no attention to her words, Mishka looked around the kitchen and said:

"I've called to see you and to find out how you're getting on. We haven't seen each other for a year or more."

"We haven't missed you overmuch," Ilinichna snorted, furiously shifting the pots about over the coals.

Dunia was dressing in the best room. Hearing Mishka's voice, she turned pale and silently clapped her hands. Seating herself on the bench and not daring to move, she listened to the conversation in the kitchen. A deep flush suddenly flamed in her face, then her cheeks went so pale that little stripes of white emerged down the fine hook of her nose. She heard Mishka striding heavily about the kitchen, sit down on a chair which creaked beneath him, then strike a match. The scent of cigarette-smoke floated into the best room.

"I hear your old man's died."

"Yes."

"And Gregor?"

Ilinichna was long silent; then with obvious reluctance she answered:

"He's serving with the Reds. He's got the same sort of star on his cap as you have."

"He should have put it on long before. . . ."

"That's his business."

There was a distinct note of anxiety in Mishka's voice as he asked:

"And Yevdokia Pantelievna?"

"She's dressing. You're too early a visitor; good folk aren't about so soon."

"You'll have to be bad folk. I wanted to see you and so I came. Why should I pick and choose the time?"

"Oh, Mikhail, don't make me angry with you!"

"How am I making you angry, aunty?"

"Why, by all this."

"I'm sorry, but by all what?"

"Why, by the way you're talking."

Dunia heard Mishka sigh deeply. She could stand no more; she jumped up, pulled down her skirt, and went into the kitchen. Mishka was sitting by the window, finishing a cigarette. His skin was yellow, and he was so emaciated that he was almost unrecognizable. His faded eyes lit up and a hardly perceptible flush appeared on his cheeks when he saw Dunia. Rising hurriedly, he said hoarsely:

"Well, good morning!"

"Good morning," Dunia answered almost inaudibly.

"Go and fetch water," Ilinichna at once ordered, glancing at her daughter.

Mishka patiently waited for Dunia to return. Ilinichna said nothing. He also was silent, but at last he crushed his cigarette end between his fingers and asked:

"Why are you so annoyed with me, aunty? Have I crossed your road, or what?"

Ilinichna swung round from the stove as though stung.

"How does your conscience let you come here, you shameless eyes!" she said. "And yet you dare to ask me that! You murderer!"

"How am I a murderer?"

"A real murderer! Who killed Piotra? Didn't you?"

"Yes."

"Very well, then. After that what are you? And you come and visit us . . . you sit yourself down as though—" Ilinichna choked and was silent; but, recovering, she went on: "Am I his mother, or who? How can you dare to look me in the eyes?"

Mishka turned pale. He had been expecting this talk. Stammering a little in his agitation, he said:

"I've got no reason to shut my eyes. Supposing Piotra had caught me, what would he have done? Do you think he'd have kissed me on my topknot? He'd have killed me too. Did we come together on those hills to play kiss-in-the-ring? That's what war's for!"

"And old Korshunov? Is killing peaceable old men war too?"

"Why, what else?" Mishka said in amazement. "Of course it's war! I know those peaceable old men! Those peaceable old men sit at home holding up their trousers, but they do more harm than others at the front. Even such as old Gaffer Grishaka worked up the Cossacks against us. It was through them that all this war began! Who started the agitation against us? They did—those peaceable old men did! And you call me 'murderer'! You've found a fine 'murderer'! In the old days I couldn't even slaughter a lamb or a pig, and I know I couldn't even now. I can't lay my hand on such creatures. Other men can slaughter animals, but I stop my ears and get well away so as not to hear or see it."

"But, cousin—"

"You and your cousin!" Mishka angrily interrupted. "We got as much good from him as milk from a goat! But he did a lot of harm. I told him to come out of the house, but he didn't; he just went and laid himself down there. I get angry with them—with such old devils! I can't kill an animal, or at any rate only in anger, but such—excuse my expression—filth as your cousin or similar serpents I can kill as many of as you like! I've got a steady hand for them, for such enemies who're of no use in this world."

"You're all dried up with your hardness of heart," Ilinichna said venomously. "I suppose your conscience is troubling you. . . ."

"I doubt it!" Mishka smiled amiably. "My conscience isn't going to trouble me over such rubbish as that old gaffer. I've been racked with fever; it gave me a thorough shaking up or, mother, I'd—"

"Don't call me 'mother'!" Ilinichna flared up. "You call a bitch your mother!"

"Now, don't bitch me!" Mishka said thickly, ominously narrowing his eyes. "There's a limit to what I'm prepared to stand from you. But I tell you straight out, aunty! You're not to be angry with me over Piotra. He asked for what he got."

"You're a murderer! A murderer! Clear out of here, I can't stand the sight of you!" Ilinichna declared obdurately.

Mishka lit another cigarette and calmly asked:

"How about Mitry Korshunov, your cousin; isn't he a murderer? And what is your Gregor? You say nothing about your darling son, but he's a real murderer and no mistake!"

"Don't talk nonsense!"

"I gave up talking nonsense long ago. Well, but tell me, what is he? How many of our men has he put out of the way, do you know? That's the point! If you're going to give that name to everybody who's taken part in the war, then we're all murderers. The whole point is whom we murder and why," Mishka said significantly.

Ilinichna remained silent, but, seeing that her guest had no intention of departing, she said harshly:

"Enough! I haven't got time to talk to you, you can go home."

"I've got as many homes as a hare has bedrooms!" Mishka laughed, and rose.

As if he could be scared away by such talk and such names! He was not so thin-skinned as to pay any attention to the insulting remarks of a furious old woman. He knew Dunia loved him, and he cared nothing for anything else, including Ilinichna.

Next morning he called again, greeted Ilinichna as though nothing had happened, sat down by the window, and watched Dunia's every movement.

"You're seeing us a lot!" Ilinichna flung at him, not returning his greeting.

Dunia flamed up, looked at her mother with burning eyes, and lowered her glance, saying not a word. Mishka answered with a smile:

"I'm not coming to see you, Aunty Ilinichna; you needn't fear."

"It would be better if you forgot the way to our house altogether."

"Why, where am I to go to?" Mishka asked, turning serious. "By the kindness of your cousin Mitry I've been left alone in the world, and you can't sit like a wolf in an empty hut. Whether you like it or not, aunty, I shall keep on visiting you," he ended, and seated himself more comfortably, spreading out his legs.

Ilinichna stared at him fixedly. Truly, such a one couldn't simply be put outside the door! All Mishka's stocky figure, the angle at which he held his head, his firmly expressed lips, expressed a bovine obstinacy.

After he had gone, Ilinichna sent the children out into the yard, then turned to Dunia and said:

"You see he doesn't set foot in here any more! Understand?"

Dunia gazed at her mother without blinking. Something common to all the Melekhovs showed for a moment in the furious narrowing of her eyes as she said as though biting off every word:

"No! He shall come! You shan't forbid him! He'll come!" Unable to control herself, she covered her face with her apron and ran out into the porch.

Breathing heavily, Ilinichna sat down by the window and remained there, silently shaking her head, gazing with unseeing eyes far into the steppe, where, silvery under the sun, a selvage of young wormwood divided the earth from the sky.

Early that evening Dunia and her mother, unreconciled and taciturn, were setting up a fallen fence in the garden down by the Don. Mishka came up. He silently took the spade from Dunia's hands and said:

"You're digging the holes too shallow, the next wind will blow your fence down again." And he began to deepen the holes for the posts, then helped to set up the fence, fastened it to the posts, and went off. Next morning he brought two freshly planed rakes and a pitchfork-handle and stood them on end outside the Melekhovs' porch. After greeting Ilinichna, he asked in a businesslike tone:

"Are you thinking of mowing the meadow grass? Other people have already gone across the Don."

Ilinichna did not answer. Dunia spoke instead.

"We've got nothing to get over the river in. Our boat has been lying under the shed since autumn, and it's all dried out."

"You should have set it down in the water in the spring," Mishka said reproachfully. "Perhaps it can be caulked. You can't manage without a boat."

Dunia looked at her mother humbly and expectantly. Ilinichna went on silently kneading dough and behaved as though the conversation had nothing to do with her.

"Have you got any tow?" Mishka asked, smiling almost imperceptibly.

Dunia went into the storeroom and brought back an armful of hemp ends.

Mishka put the boat in order by dinner-time, then came into the kitchen.

"Well, I've dragged the boat down to the water; now it can soak. Tie it up to a trunk or someone may go off with it." He again asked: "Well, how about the haying, aunty? Perhaps I could give you a hand. I've got nothing to do just now in any case."

"You ask her," Ilinichna nodded at Dunia.

"I'm asking the mistress."

"Anyone can see I'm not the mistress here. . . ."

Dunia burst into tears and went into the best room.

"Then I'll have to give a hand," Mishka said decisively. "Where are your carpenter's tools? I'd like to make you a rake, for I don't suppose the old ones are much use."

He went off under the shed and, whistling, began to sharpen the teeth of a rake. Little Mishatka danced around him, imploringly gazing into his eyes, and asked:

"Uncle Mikhail, make me a small rake, for I've got nobody to make one for me. Granny doesn't know how to, and Aunty doesn't either. You're the only one who knows, you know very well how to make one."

"I'll make you one, namesake, by God I'll make you one. But stand back a bit or a shaving may fly into your eye," Koshevoi told him, laughing and thinking in amazement: "Well, isn't he like, the little devil! The very image of his father! His eyes and his eyebrows and the same way of turning back his upper lip. . . . Now there's workmanship for you!"

He set to work to make a tiny toy rake, but he was unable to finish the job; his lips turned blue, an infuriated yet resigned expression appeared on his yellow face. He stopped whistling, laid down the knife, and wriggled his shoulders as though cold.

"Mikhail Gregorich, namesake, go and fetch me a piece of sacking or something and I'll lie down," he asked Mishatka.

"But what for?" the boy asked inquisitively.

"I want to be ill."

"What for?"

"Oh, the way you stick, just like burs! Why, my time has come to be ill, that's all! Fetch it quick!"

"But how about my rake?"

"I'll finish it later."

A violent shiver racked Mishka's body, and his teeth chattered. He stretched himself out on the sacking Mishatka brought, then took off his cap and covered his face with it.

"Have you fallen ill already?" Mishatka asked bitterly.

"Yes, I'm ill now."

"But what are you shivering for?"

"It's the fever shaking me."

"But what are your teeth chattering for?"

With one eye Mishka glanced from under the cap at his troublesome little namesake, smiled curtly, and ceased to answer his questions. Mishatka stared at him in alarm and ran into the hut.

"Granny, Uncle Mikhail's lain down in the shed and he's shivering and shivering till he's almost dancing."

Ilinichna looked out of the window, went to the table, and was long, long silent, turning something over in her mind.

"Why don't you say something, Granny?" Mishatka asked impatiently, tugging at the sleeve of her bodice.

Ilinichna turned to him and said firmly:

"Little one, take a blanket and carry it out to him, the Antichrist, so that he can cover himself. It's fever that's shaking him, a sort of illness. Can you carry the blanket?" She went across to the window again, gazed out into the yard, and said hurriedly: "Stop, stop! Don't bother, there's no need."

Dunia had covered Koshevoi with her own sheepskin coat and now was bending over him, saying something to him.

After the attack had passed, Mishka spent the rest of the day busily preparing for the mowing. He was obviously much weaker. His movements were sluggish and uncertain, but he finished Mishatka's rake for him.

In the evening Ilinichna prepared the supper, seated the children at the table, and, without looking at Dunia, told her:

"Go and call that—what's his name—to supper."

Mishka sat down at the table without crossing himself, his body huddled wearily. His yellow face, marked with dirty streaks of dried sweat, revealed his exhaustion; his hand trembled a little as he carried the spoon to his lips. He ate little and reluctantly, occasionally unconcernedly looking around him at the others. But Ilinichna was astonished to notice that the "murderer's" faded eyes grew warm and lit up whenever they rested on little Mishatka; tiny sparks of admiration and pleasure momentarily flamed up in them and died away, and a hardly noticeable smile lurked at the corners of his lips. Then he shifted his gaze, and a numb indifference again lay like a shadow over his face.

Ilinichna furtively began to watch Koshevoi. Only then did she realize how terribly thin he had become as the result of his illness. The arches of his collar-bones showed prominently under his dusty grey tunic, his broad shoulders were hunched, and the bones almost protruded through the skin, while his hairy Adam's apple looked absurd on his childishly thin neck. The more Ilinichna observed the "murderer's" bowed figure and waxen face, the more she felt an acute discomfort, as though she were being torn in twain. Suddenly an uninvited pity for this man whom she hated so much—that gripping motherly pity which subdues even strong women—awoke in Ilinichna's heart. Unable to master this new feeling, she pushed a plateful of milk across to Mishka and said:

"Eat up, for God's sake! You're so thin that I feel sick to look at you. . . . A fine bridegroom you'd make!"

The villagers began to talk about Koshevoi and Dunia. Happening to meet Dunia at the landing-stage, one woman asked with an obvious sneer in her voice: "Have you taken on Mikhail as a labourer? He never seems to leave your yard!"

To all her daughter's persuasions Ilinichna stubbornly replied: "You can ask as much as you like, I won't give you away to him. You'll never have my blessing!" And only when Dunia announced that she would go off to live with Koshevoi and at once began to collect her finery did Ilinichna change her decision.

"Come to your senses!" she exclaimed in alarm. "What shall I do alone with the children? Are we to perish?"

"You know best, Mother, but I don't want to be the laughing-stock of the village," Dunia said quietly, continuing to throw her maiden finery out of the chest.

Ilinichna stood silently working her lips, but at last, after a long silence, shifting her feet as though they were heavy, she went to the ikon corner.

"Well, so be it, daughter!" she whispered, taking down the ikon. "If that's what you're thinking, then God help you! Come here. . . ."

With alacrity Dunia dropped to her knees. Ilinichna blessed her and added in a quivering voice:

"My dead mother blessed me with this ikon. . . . Oh, your father ought to see you now. . . . Do you remember what he said about your groom? God knows how hard it is for me. . . ." Silently turning away, she went out into the porch.

No matter how hard Mishka tried, no matter how much he pleaded with Dunia to forgo a church marriage, the stubborn girl would not change her mind. So, grinding his teeth, Mishka had to agree. Mentally cursing everything in the world, he made ready for the ceremony as though preparing for execution. Father Vissarion made them man and wife surreptitiously in the empty church at night. After the ceremony he congratulated the youthful couple and said in an edifying tone:

"Well, young Soviet comrade, you see how life has its turns; last year you set fire to my house with your own hand, delivered it over to the burning so to speak, and today I've had the pleasure of officiating at your marriage. As the proverb says: 'Don't spit into the well, you may need to drink from it.' But all the same I'm glad, heartily glad, that you've come round and found your way to Christ's church."

That was the last straw for Mishka. Ashamed of his weakness of will and angry with himself, he had said not a word in the church. But now he shot a furious look at the spiteful priest and whispered, so that Dunia should not hear:

"Pity you fled from the village, then, for I'd have burned you together with your house, you long-maned devil! You get that clear, do you?"

Dumbfounded by the surprise of this attack, the priest stared with blinking eyes at Mishka. But the bridegroom, tugged at his young wife's sleeve, sternly said: "Come on!" and, his army boots clattering noisily, made for the door.

At this cheerless wedding there was no drinking of vodka nor bawling of songs. Prokhor Zykov, who acted as best man, complained about it to Aksinia next day, spitting with disgust again and again.

"Well, girl, it was a fine wedding, I can tell you! In the church Mikhail muttered something to the priest that made the old man's jaw drop! And at supper, do you know what we had? Roast fowl and sour milk. . . . If the devils had only given us a tiny drop of vodka! Gregor Pantalievich ought to have seen how his sister was married off! He'd have clutched his head! No, girl, I've had enough! I'm not going to any more of these newfangled weddings. A dog's marriage is merrier; the bitches do at least tear one another's hair out, and there is plenty of noise. But here there was neither drinking nor fighting, may the infidels be accursed! You know, I was so upset after the wedding that I couldn't sleep all night. I lay scratching myself as though they'd put a fistful of fleas under my shirt. . . ."

Chapter 3

From the day when Koshevoi installed himself in the Melekhov hut, everything on the farm took a new turn; in a short time he had mended the fence, and carted in the steppe hay and stacked it on the threshing-floor, neatly thatching the top; in preparation for the harvest he fitted a new platform and wings to the harvester, diligently cleaned the floor in readiness for the threshing, repaired the old winnow, and mended the harness. For he was secretly dreaming of exchanging the yoke of bullocks for a horse and said more than once to Dunia: "We ought to provide ourselves with a horse. Driving with these yoked apostles is like going to a funeral." One day in the storeroom he discovered a tin of white lead and ultramarine, and at once decided to paint the house shutters, which were grey with age. The Melekhov hut seemed to grow young again as it looked out on the world with the bright blue frames of its windows.

Mishka proved to be a zealous master. Despite his fever he worked without folding his arms. Dunia helped him in everything.

In the first few days of their married life she grew distinctly better-looking and seemed to spread in the shoulders and hips. She had a new expression in her eyes, in her walk, even in the way she tidied her hair. Her former awkward angularity of movement, her childish assurance and energy, vanished. Always smiling, and grown more sedate, she gazed at her husband with loving eyes and saw nothing of what was happening around her. Young happiness is always undiscerning.

But with every passing day Ilinichna felt more and more keenly the loneliness which had come upon her. She had grown superfluous in the house in which she had spent almost all her life. Dunia and her husband worked as though they were building their own nest in some new spot. They discussed nothing with her and did not ask her consent when they made some innovation on the farm; and they did not even find a kindly word to use when speaking to the old woman. When they sat down at the table they would exchange a few insignificant remarks with her; then once more Ilinichna was left alone with her cheerless thoughts. She gained no joy from her daughter's happiness, and the presence of a strange man in the house—and her son-in-law remained as much a stranger to her as before—oppressed her. Life itself was beginning to be a burden to her. In one year she had lost so many of her dear ones, and she lived on, broken by suffering, grown old and pitiful. Much sorrow had she known in her life, perhaps too much. Now she no longer had the strength to resist it, and she constantly had a superstitious presentiment that death, which had grown so accustomed to visiting her family, would yet cross the threshold of the old Melekhov house more than once. Now she was reconciled to Dunia's marriage she had only one desire: to live to see Gregor's return, to hand the children over to him, and then to close her eyes for ever. During her long and arduous life she had suffered enough to earn her right to repose.

Endlessly the long summer days dragged by. Burning hot shone the sun. But the prickling sunlight no longer warmed Ilinichna. She sat motionless for hours on the porch, in the full sunlight, indifferent to all around her. She was no longer the bustling and zealous housewife she had been. She felt no desire to do anything. It was all for nothing and now seemed unnecessary and unreal; nor did she have the strength to work as in past days. She often examined her hands, marred with many years of labour, and thought: "Well, my hands have done their work now. . . . It's time to rest. . . . I've lived my life, and enough. . . . So long as I live to see my Grisha. . . ."

Only once did she recover her former vitality, and then not for long. One day Prokhor dropped in on his way home from Viesh-enska, shouting when still some distance off:

"How about treating me, Granny Ilinichna? I've brought you a letter from your son."

The old woman turned pale. In her mind a letter was inevitably associated with some new misfortune. But when Prokhor read Gregor's brief letter, a good half of it consisting of greetings to his dear ones, and only at the end indicating that he would try to get home on leave in the autumn, for a long time Ilinichna could not speak for joy. Little tears as tiny as beads rolled over her brown face, over the deep furrows in her cheeks. Hanging her head, she wiped them away with the sleeve of her bodice, with her rough hand. But they went on rolling down her face and, dropping one by one on her apron, speckled it as though they were a warm and heavy rain. Prokhor not merely had no pleasure in women's tears, he could not endure them. So, frowning with annoyance, he said:

"You've worked yourself up into a fine state, Granny! What a lot of moisture the likes of you women have! You ought to be glad, and not start crying. Well, I'm off. Good-bye! I don't get much joy out of watching you."

Ilinichna stopped weeping and halted him. "For such good news, my dear—how could I let myself go like that? Wait a bit, and I'll treat you . . ." she muttered incoherently, taking out a bottle she had kept for many a day in the chest.

Prokhor sat down and stroked his moustache.

"Will you have a drink with me, as you're so happy?" he asked. Though he at once thought anxiously: "Well, now the devil's got hold of my tongue again! She'll go and have her share, and there's only enough vodka in the bottle for a smell. . . ."

But Ilinichna refused. She carefully folded up the letter and laid it on the ikon-shelf; but, evidently thinking better of it, she picked it up again, held it in her hands for a moment, then thrust it into her bosom and pressed it firmly against her heart.

When Dunia returned from the fields she read the letter again and again and at last smiled and sighed:

"Oh, if only he'd come soon! You're no longer your old self, Mother!"

Ilinichna jealously took the letter from her, concealed it again at her breast and, smiling, looking at her daughter with beaming, half-closed eyes, said:

"Not even the dogs bark about me, I'm so useless these days, but my younger son has remembered his mother! The way he writes! He calls me by my full name too! I bow low to you, dear Mother, he writes, and also to the dear children; and he didn't forget you, Dunia. . . . Well, what are you laughing at? You're a fool, a complete fool!"

Why, Mother, can't I smile now? But where are you off to?"

"I'm going to the garden to hoe the potatoes."

"I'll do it myself tomorrow; you should stay at home. You're always complaining of feeling ill, and now you've suddenly found work to do!"

"No, I'll go. . . . I'm so happy, I'd like to be by myself," Ilinichna admitted, and youthfully, swiftly, tied her kerchief around her head.

On the way to the garden she called to see Aksinia. For the sake of decency she talked at first of indifferent matters and then took out the letter.

"Our boy's sent me a letter; he's made his mother happy, he promises to come home on leave. Here, neighbour, read it, and I'll listen to it once more."

After that Aksinia often had to read the letter. Ilinichna would drop in of an evening, and would take out the yellow envelope carefully wrapped in a handkerchief, and ask with a sigh:

"Read it, Aksinia dear. Today there's a weight on my heart, and in my sleep I saw him quite small, just as he was when he went to school."

In the course of time the words, written in pencil, began to blur, and many of them could not be distinguished at all. But that made no difference to Aksinia; she had read the letter so often that she knew it by heart. Later still, when the thin paper was falling to pieces, she unhesitatingly told Ilinichna all the contents of the letter, down to the last line.

A couple of weeks after the arrival of the letter Ilinichna felt ill. Dunia was busy with the threshing, and the old woman did not want to take her off the work, yet she could not manage the cooking herself.

"I shan't get up today. You manage somehow on your own," she asked her daughter.

"Why, where are you feeling bad, Mother?"

Ilinichna examined the tucks on her old bodice and answered without raising her eyes:

"I feel bad all over—just as though everything inside me had been beaten to a pulp. . . . When I was younger your dead father used to go mad and beat me. . . . And he'd got cast-iron fists. . . . I'd lie for a week as though dead. And that's just how I feel now: everything inside me seems to be broken, I'm all thrashed. . . ."

"Shall I send Mikhail for the doctor?"

"What do I need him for? I'll get up somehow."

Next day she did get up and went out into the yard; but towards evening she took to her bed again. Her face swelled a little, and bags of water appeared under her eyes. Several times during the night she raised herself on her arms, lifting her head from the piled pillows, breathing fast, suffering from a shortage of breath. Then the choking sensation left her and she could lie quietly on her back and even get out of bed. She passed several days in a state of quiet renunciation and peace. She wanted to be alone, and when Aksinia came to see her, she gave curt answers to her questions and sighed with relief when she went. She was glad that the children spent most of the day in the open air, and that Dunia rarely came in and did not pester her with questions. She no longer had need of any sympathy or solace. A moment had come when she felt an overwhelming need to be left alone, in order to recall much of her life. Half-closing her eyes, she lay for hours without stirring, except for her swollen fingers gathering the folds of the blanket; and during those hours all her life passed before her.

It was amazing how short and mean that life appeared, and how much of it was oppressive and bitter, how much she had no wish to recall. For some reason, her memories and thoughts turned most of all to Gregor. Maybe because she had not known freedom from anxiety for him during all the years since the beginning of the war, and because he was the only link binding her to life. Or perhaps the yearning for her elder son and her husband had been numbed, had faded with time, for she recalled them more rarely, and she seemed to see them through a grey misty haze. She was reluctant to recall her youth, her married life. That was all simply unnecessary, it had receded so far into the distance, and now brought neither pleasure nor relief. Returning to the past in her memories, she remained stern and unsullied in thought. But she recalled her "younger boy" with extreme, almost tangible clarity. Yet the moment she thought of him her heart began to beat faster. Then the choking sensation returned, her face went grey, and she lay a long time unconscious. But as soon as she recovered she thought of him again. She could not forget her last son. . . .

One day she was lying in the best room. The noonday sun was glittering outside. In the southern edge of the sky white clouds, raised on end by the wind, were floating majestically in the dazzling azure. The oppressive silence was broken only by the monotonous, stupefying grate of the grasshoppers. Outside, right beneath the window, the grass huddling against the house substructure—half-faded goosegrass mingled with bromegrass and quitch—had been left unwithered by the sun, and it was here that the grasshoppers had found shelter. Ilinichna listened to their incessant chirruping, caught the scent of the sun-warmed grass which penetrated into the room, and for a moment she had a vision of the sun-baked August steppe, the golden wheat stubble, the glowing azure sky enveloped in a dove-grey haze.

She distinctly saw the bullocks pasturing on the wormwooded bounds of the fields, the wagon with the canopy stretched over it; she heard the dry grating of the grasshoppers, breathed in the cloyingly bitter scent of the wormwood. . . . And she saw herself—young, well-grown, beautiful. There she went, hastening to the encampment. The stubble rustled under her feet and stung her bare calves, at her back the burning wind dried the sweaty shirt gathered into her skirt, and scorched her neck. Her cheeks were flooded with crimson, the rush of blood to her face caused a fine ringing in her ears. With one bent arm she restrained her heavy, straining, milk-filled breasts and, hearing a childish sobbing cry, quickened her steps, unbuttoning the neck of her shirt as she went.

Her weather-beaten lips quivered and smiled as she took the tiny, swarthy Grishatka from the cradle hanging under the wagon. Holding the sweaty string of her cross away from her neck with her teeth, she hurriedly gave him the breast, whispering through her clenched teeth: "My darling, my little son! My beautiful one! . . . Your mother's famished you with hunger. . . ." Still sobbing offendedly, the little Grishka sucked and bit painfully at the teat with his tiny gums. And beside her stood his young, black-moustached father, whetting a scythe. From under her drooping lashes she saw his smile and the bluish whites of his twinkling eyes. The heat made it difficult for her to breathe, the sweat streamed from her brow and tickled her cheeks, and the light faded, faded before her eyes. . . .

She aroused herself from the dream, passed her hand over her tear-stained face, and then lay still a long time, tormented with a cruel attack of choking, occasionally sinking into a coma.

Late that evening, when Dunia and her husband had gone to sleep, she gathered the rest of her strength, rose, and went into the yard. Aksinia was out late, seeking her cow which had got separated from the herd, and as she returned home she saw Ilinichna walking slowly, swaying as she went into the threshing-floor. "What has she gone in there for, ill as she is?" Aksinia wondered, and, stealing up to the fence which bounded the Melekhov's threshing-floor, looked inside. A full moon was shining. A breeze was blowing from the steppe. The stack of straw cast a dense shadow over the bare, stone-rollered floor. Ilinichna was supporting herself with both hands on the fencing, gazing out into the steppe to where a camp-fire lit by the mowers was glimmering like a distant, inaccessible little star. Aksinia clearly saw the old woman's swollen face lit up by the bluish light of the moon, the grey strand of hair breaking from under her black shawl.

Ilinichna stood long gazing into the darkling steppe, then called quietly, as though he were standing quite close to her:

"Grisha dear! My darling boy!"

She was silent for a moment, then in a different, low and husky voice she said:

"Blood of my blood!"

All Aksinia's body shivered, gripped by an inexplicable feeling of anxiety and fear. Sharply falling back from the fence, she went to her hut.

That night Ilinichna realized that soon she was to die, that death had already come to her bed-head. At dawn she took Gregor's shirt out of the chest, rolled it up, and laid it under her pillow. She also made ready her own grave-clothes and the shirt in which she was to be attired after she had drawn her last breath.

Next morning Dunia went in to see her mother as usual. Ilinichna took Gregor's carefully folded shirt from under the pillow and, without speaking, held it out to Dunia.

"What's this?" Dunia asked in surprise.

"Grisha's shirt. . . . Give it to your husband, let him wear it. His old one must be rotten with sweat," Ilinichna said very faintly.

Dunia noticed her mother's black skirt, shirt, and fabric slippers lying on the bench—the clothes in which the body is attired when it is sent forth on its long journey—saw them and paled.

"What have you been getting those things ready for, Mother? Take them away, for Christ's sake! God, but it's early for you to think of death!"

"No, my time has come . . ." Ilinichna whispered. "My turn. . . . Look after the children, watch over them till Gregor returns. . . . I can see now that I'm not going to live till then. . . . Ah, I'm not going to live till then. . . ."

So that Dunia should not see her tears, Ilinichna turned to the wall and covered her face with her kerchief.

She died three days later. Other women of her own age washed her body, attired her in her burial clothes, and laid her out on the table in the best room. In the evening Aksinia came to say farewell to the dead. She had difficulty in recognizing the features of the former proud and great-hearted Ilinichna in the stern and beautiful face of this little old woman. As she touched the cold yellow brow with her lips, Askinia noticed the familiar insubmissive strand of grey hair breaking from under the white kerchief, and the tiny round shell of the ear, just like a young woman's.

With Dunia's consent Aksinia took the children to her hut. They were speechless and frightened by this new death. She fed them and took them to bed with her. She had a queer feeling as she embraced these children of the man she loved, the little bodies huddling quietly one on each side of her. Softly she began to tell them fairy-tales remembered from her own childhood, in order to distract them a little, to take their thoughts off their dead grandmother. Quietly, in a singsong voice, she told them the story of the poor orphan Vaniushka:

> Swan-geese,
> Carry me
> On your wings so white;
> Carry me far
> To my native,
> To my own dear land. . . .

Before she had finished the story she heard the children breathing regularly and evenly. Mishatka was lying on the outside, his face pressed hard against her shoulder. With a movement of this shoulder Aksinia made his backflung little head more comfortable and suddenly felt such a pitiless, rending yearning in her heart that a spasm clutched her throat. She broke into a violent and bitter weeping, shuddering with the sobs which racked her. But she could not even wipe away her tears: Gregor's children were sleeping in her arms, and she did not want to awaken them.

Chapter 4

After Ilinichna's death Koshevoi was left the sole and undisputed master in the house, and it would have been natural for him to turn with still greater ardour to the restoration of the farm, to its further extension. But actually this was far from the case: with every day Mishka worked more and more reluctantly. He often went out and spent the evenings sitting on the porch far into the night, smoking, pondering something. Dunia could not help noticing the change which had occurred in her husband. More than once she was amazed to see that Mishka, who formerly had worked with total disregard of self, would suddenly, for no apparent reason, drop the axe or plane and sit down to rest. The same thing happened in the fields when they sowed the winter rye; he would take a couple of turns up

and down the field, then would halt the bullocks, roll himself a cigarette, and sit long on the ploughed land, smoking, knitting his brows.

Dunia, who had inherited her father's practical sagacity, thought
anxiously: "He's not lasted long . . . either he's ailing for something, or else he's just lazy. I'll only have trouble with such a husband! You might think he was living with strangers: smoking half
the day, scratching himself the other half, and never any time for
work. . . . I must have a talk with him, quietly, so as not to upset
him, for if he goes on working as hard as this we'll be unable to
shovel need out of the house with a spade. . . ."

So one day Dunia guardedly asked him:

"You're not the man you used to be, Mishka; is your fever getting
the better of you?"

"Why my fever? It's sickening enough here without fever," Mishka
answered irritably, touching up the bullocks and setting off behind
the sower.

Dunia thought it unwise to continue her questions; after all, it
wasn't a woman's place to instruct her husband. And there the matter ended.

She was mistaken in her assumptions. The sole cause hindering
Mishka from working with his former zeal was the conviction, which
grew stronger in him with every day, that he had settled down too
soon in his native village. "I've been a little too quick to turn to
farming, I was in too much of a hurry . . ." he thought angrily when
he read the war reports in the regional newspaper or listened of an
evening to the stories of demobilized Red Cossacks. But he was especially disturbed by the attitude of the villagers: certain of them
were openly saying that the Soviet government would be ended by
winter, that Wrangel had advanced from Tauride and together with
Makhno was already close to Rostov, that the Allies had landed a
great expeditionary force in Novorossisk. Rumours, each more
stupid than its predecessor, spread through the village. The Cossacks who had returned from concentration camps or the mines, who
had managed to grow fat on their household victuals during the
summer, kept themselves to themselves, drank home-made vodka of
nights, had their own talks, and when they met Mishka, asked with
feigned unconcern: "You read the papers, Koshevoi; tell us all about
Wrangel, will they put an end to him soon? And is it true or only talk
that the Allies are pressing us hard again?"

Late one Sunday afternoon Prokhor Zykov dropped in. Mishka had only just returned from the fields and was washing himself, standing close to the porch. Dunia was pouring water out of a pitcher into his hands, gazing with a smile on her lips at her husband's thin, sunburnt neck. Prokhor greeted them and seated himself on the bottom step of the porch, before asking:

"I suppose you haven't had any news of Gregor Pantalievich?"

"No," Dunia answered; "he hasn't written."

"Why, are you so anxious about him?" Mishka wiped his face and hands and looked without a smile into Prokhor's eyes.

Prokhor sighed and arranged the empty sleeve of his shirt.

"Of course I am. We served all our service together."

"And you're thinking of doing some more now, are you?"

"More what?"

"Why, service!"

"My days of service with him are over."

"But I thought you might be waiting for him and living to serve again," Mishka went on, still without a smile. "To fight again against the Soviet government. . . ."

"Well, now you're talking nonsense, Mikhail," Prokhor said in an offended tone.

"Why am I? I hear of all kinds of little talks that are going on in the village."

"Have you heard me talking like that? Where have you heard them?"

"Not you, but people like you and Gregor, who're all waiting for 'their people.'"

"I'm not waiting for 'their people'; they're all the same to me."

"That's just the curse of it, that they are all the same to you. Come into the house; don't take offence, I was joking."

Prokhor reluctantly went up the steps, saying as he crossed the threshold:

"Your jokes, brother, are not very funny. . . . The past has got to be forgotten. I've paid for the past."

"Not all the past can be forgotten," Mishka said dryly as he sat down at the table. "Stop and have supper with us."

"Thank you. Of course the past can't all be forgotten. For instance I've lost an arm, and I'd be very glad to forget it. But it won't be forgotten: it's always reminding me of itself."

Dunia said as she lay the table, not looking at her husband:

"Is it your opinion that anyone who's been with the Whites can never be forgiven?"

"Why, what did you think?"

"Well, I thought that anyone who rakes up the past shall have his eyes put out, so they say."

"You may find that in the Bible," Mishka said coldly. "But in my view a man must always answer for his deeds."

"The government says nothing about that," Dunia remarked quietly. She did not wish to wrangle with her husband in the presence of another Cossack, but inwardly she was annoyed with Mishka for his, as it seemed to her, misplaced joke with Prokhor and for the enmity he had openly shown to her brother.

"The government says nothing to you; it's got nothing to talk about with you. But service with the Whites has to be answered for under Soviet law."

"And have I got to answer for mine too?" Prokhor asked.

"You're only a sheep; you've had a graze, now back into your pen! There'll be no questioning of orderlies, but Gregor will have to face the music when he turns up. We'll question him about the rising."

"And you'll do the questioning, will you?" Dunia's eyes flashed as she set a cup of soured milk down on the table.

"Yes, I'll question him too," Mishka calmly answered.

"It's not your business. . . . There'll be questioners enough without you. He's won his pardon by serving in the Red Army. . . ."

Dunia's voice shook. She sat down at the table, gathering the flounces of her apron in her fingers. As though he had not noticed his wife's agitation, Mishka went on unruffled:

"I'll find it interesting to do some questioning too. . . . But so far as his pardon's concerned we'll have to see. . . . We'll have to reconsider how far he's earned his pardon. He's spilt quite a lot of our blood. We'll have to measure out whose blood weighs the most. . . ."

This was the first squabble Mishka and Dunia had had since their marriage. There was an awkward silence in the kitchen. Mishka silently ate the milk, occasionally wiping his lips with a hand-towel. Prokhor smoked, and gazed at Dunia. Then he began to talk of farming matters. He remained for another half-hour. As he was going he said:

"Kirill Gromov's returned. Have you heard?"

"No. Where's he turned up from?"

"From the Reds. He was in the First Cavalry Brigade too."

"Is he the one that served under Mamontov?"

"That's him."

"He was a fine fighter!" Mishka laughed sneeringly.

"I don't think so! He was always the first where it was a question of looting. He had a ready hand for that sort of thing."

"They say he sabred prisoners without mercy. Killed them for their boots. Killed them simply to get their boots and nothing else."

"So they say," Prokhor confirmed.

"And has he got to be pardoned too?" Mishka asked in a wheedling tone. "God forgave His enemies and commanded us to do the same, or what?"

"That's not easy to answer. . . . But what can you do with him?"

"Well, I'd—" Mishka screwed up his eyes. "I'd give him such a time that he'd give up the ghost! And he won't escape it, either. There's the Don Cheka at Vieshenska, they'll put their loving arms around him."

Prokhor smiled and said:

"It's a true saying that only the grave can straighten the hunchback. He's come back with loot even from the Red Army. His wife was boasting to mine that he'd brought her home a woman's coat, I don't know how many dresses, and other things too. He was in Maslak's brigade and made his way home from there. He must have deserted, I think. He's brought his weapons back with him."

"What weapons?" Mishka asked.

"You know what: a carbine and a pistol and possibly other stuff."

"Has he been to the Soviet to register, do you know?"

Prokhor roared with laughter and waved his hand:

"You couldn't drag him there by a rope! I can't help thinking he's on the run. If not today, then tomorrow he'll be slipping away from home. Now Kirill, by all the signs, is thinking of doing some more fighting; but you're wrong in picking on me. No, brother, I've done my fighting; I'm fed up to the back teeth with that form of amusement."

Prokhor left soon afterwards. A little later Mishka also went outside. Dunia fed the children and was getting ready for bed when Mishka came back. In his hands he held something wrapped in a small sack.

"Where the devil have you been?" Dunia asked ungraciously.

"I've been getting my dowry." Mishka smiled amiably. He un-wrapped a carefully packed rifle, a wallet bulging with cartridges, a pistol, and two hand-grenades. He laid them all on a bench and carefully poured some paraffin into a dish.

"Where's all that come from?" Dunia indicated the weapons with her eyebrows.

"They're mine; I brought them back from the front."

"Then where did you have them buried?"

"No matter where; they've been well looked after."

"Well, you're fond of keeping things to yourself, I must say. . . . You didn't say a word about it. Hiding things even from your wife?"

With a forcedly carefree smile, obviously hesitating, Mishka said:

"And why should I have told you, Dunia? This isn't a woman's business. Let that property lie; it's not in the way in the house, girl."

"But what have you brought it into the house for? You're a law-abiding Cossack now, you know all . . . And won't you have to answer for it to the law?"

Mishka's face set hard, and he said:

"You're a fool! When Kirill Gromov brings back weapons, that's a danger to the Soviet régime; but when I bring them back, it'll only be gain to the Soviet régime. Do you understand? Who will I have to answer to? You're babbling God knows what; go to bed and sleep."

He had made what in his opinion was the only sound deduction: if Whites were coming back with weapons, then he had got to be on his guard. He diligently cleaned the rifle and pistol, and next morn-ing, as soon as it was light, he went off on foot to Vieshenska.

As Dunia put victuals into his haversack she exclaimed bitterly and angrily:

"You're always keeping something from me! Do at least say how long you're going for and why you're going. What the devil do you call this life? He just gets ready to go, and you can't get a word out of him! Are you my husband or a button on my shirt?"

"I'm going to Vieshenska, to the Military Commission. What else do you want me to tell you? You'll know everything when I return."

Holding his haversack against his side, Mishka dropped down to the Don, got into the boat, and swiftly rowed across to the farther bank.

At Vieshenska, after a medical examination the doctor curtly told Mishka:

"My dear comrade, you're no good for service in the ranks of the Red Army. Malaria's made rather a bad mess of you. You'd better take a course of treatment or you'll get worse. The Red Army doesn't need such as you."

"Then what sort does it need? I've served two years, but now I'm no longer necessary, am I?"

"What we need first and foremost is men in good health. You get well, and then you'll do. Take this prescription, you'll get quinine at the chemist's."

"Yes! I see now!" Koshevoi drew on his shirt as though putting a collar on a restive horse; he seemed unable to get his head through the opening. He buttoned up his trousers in the street and made straight for the party regional committee.

He returned to Tatarsk as chairman of the village Revolutionary Committee. Hurriedly greeting his wife, he said:

"Well, now we'll see!"

"What do you mean by that?" Dunia asked in amazement.

"Just the same as before."

"And what was that?"

"I've been appointed chairman. Understand?"

Dunia clapped her hands in her vexation. She was about to make some remark, but Mishka did not stop to listen to her. Standing before the mirror, he adjusted the strap on his faded khaki tunic and strode off to the Soviet.

Old Mikheev had been appointed chairman of the Revolutionary Committee in the winter and had held the office ever since. A little blind and deaf, he was overborne by his responsibilities and was delighted when Koshevoi told him he was to be relieved.

"Here are the papers, my eagle; here's the village stamp; take them, for Christ's sake!" he said with unfeigned pleasure, crossing himself and rubbing his hands. "I'm in my seventies now, and never in all my life have I held any office, but it fell to me in my declining years. . . . It's just the right sort of work for a young man like you, but what use am I? I can't see properly, and I can't hear properly. . . . It's time I was saying my prayers, but they went and appointed me chairman. . . ."

Mishka hurriedly scanned the instructions and orders sent by the district Revolutionary Committee, and asked:

"Where's the secretary?"

"Eh?"

"Damn it, I said where's the secretary?"

"The secretary? He's sowing rye. He only comes here once a week, may he be struck by lightning! Sometimes a paper comes from the district, and it's got to be read, but you couldn't find him with bloodhounds. And so an important paper has to lie for several days unread. For I'm bad at my letters, very bad! I can only just manage to sign my name, and I can't read at all; all I can do is use the stamp. . . ."

Raising his eyebrows, Koshevoi examined the scratched and dingy walls of the Revolutionary Committee's room, which was decorated with a single old and flyblown placard.

Old Mikheev was so delighted at his unexpected dismissal that he even ventured to jest: as he handed Koshevoi the stamp, wrapped in a piece of rag, he said:

"That's the entire village property; there's no money to be handed over, and under the Soviet régime the ataman's insignia aren't regarded with favour. If you like I can give you my old stick." Smiling a toothless smile, he held out his ash stick, its handle well polished by much use.

But Koshevoi did not feel in the mood for joking. Once more he looked around the miserable, neglected room, frowned, and said with a sigh:

"We'll reckon that I've taken everything over from you, daddy. Now hop off out of here to the devil!" With his eyes he expressively indicated the door.

Then he seated himself at the table, sprawling his elbows, and sat there long alone, gritting his teeth, thrusting out his lower jaw. My God, what a son of a bitch he had been all these past days, while he had been rummaging about in the earth, not raising his head or listening properly to all that was going on around him! Annoyed beyond words with himself and everything else, he rose from the table, arranged his tunic, and said through set teeth, gazing into the distance:

"My boys, I'll show you what the Soviet government is!"

He shut the door, fastening it by the chain, and strode homeward across the square. Close to the church he met the youngster Obnizov, nodded to him carelessly, walked past and, suddenly struck by an idea, turned and shouted:

"Hey, Andriushka! Wait a bit; here, I want you!"

The fair-haired, bashful lad came back without speaking. Mishka held out his hand to him as though he were a man and asked:

"Where were you off to? The other end of the village? So you're out for a stroll, are you? This is what I wanted to ask you: you went to the advanced elementary school, didn't you? You did? That's good! Do you know anything about office work?"

"What sort of office work?"

"Oh, just the ordinary sort. You know, the incomings and out-goings, that sort of thing."

"What are you getting at, Comrade Koshevoi?"

"Why, the papers you get in an office. Do you know anything about them? You know, there are papers which have to be sent out, and there are other sorts too." Mishka wriggled his fingers vaguely and, without waiting for an answer, said firmly: "If you don't know, you can soon learn. I'm chairman of the village Revolutionary Committee now, and as you're an educated lad, I appoint you the secretary. Go to the Revolutionary Committee house and watch over things there; you'll find them all lying on the table. And I'll be back soon. Understand?"

"Comrade Koshevoi!"

Mishka waved his hand and said impatiently:

"We can talk it all over later; you go and take up your duties." Slowly, with a measured stride, he went on along the street.

At home he put on new trousers, thrust his pistol into his pocket, and spent some time arranging his cap before the mirror.

"I'm just going somewhere on business," he remarked to Dunia. "If anyone asks where the chairman is, tell them I'll soon be back."

The position of chairman made certain things obligatory. Mishka walked slowly and importantly; his gait was so unusual for him that some of the villagers halted and gazed after him with smiles on their faces. Prokhor Zykov, who met him in the street, fell back to the fence with an air of respect and asked:

"But what's all this for, Mikhail? All dressed up in your best on a

work day and marching along as though on parade? You aren't
going to get married again, are you?"

"Something of the sort," Mishka replied, pressing his lips together
meaningly.

Outside Gromov's gate he thrust his hand into his pocket for his
pouch and gave a keen glance around the spacious yard, the buildings scattered about it, and the windows of the hut.

Kirill Gromov's mother happened to be coming out of the porch
with a dish of pumpkin cut into small pieces for cattle food. Mishka
greeted her respectfully and strode towards the steps.

"Is Kirill at home, aunty?"

"Yes, he's at home, go straight in!" the old woman said, stepping
aside for him to pass.

Mishka went into the dark porch and groped in the semi-darkness
for the door-handle.

Kirill himself opened the door of the best room to him and fell
back a step. Clean-shaven, smiling, and a little tipsy, he gave Mishka
a curt, searching glance and said in an easy tone:

"Yet another soldier! Come in, Koshevoi, and sit down, be our
guest. We were just having a drink, just a little drink. . . ."

"Hospitality makes for tasty victuals!" Mishka shook the master's
hands as he looked at the guests sitting around the table.

His arrival was obviously inopportune. A broad-shouldered
Cossack, a stranger to Mikhail, sprawling at the far corner, gave
Kirill a curt, interrogative glance as he shifted his glass. Semion
Akhvatkin, a distant relative of the Korshunovs, who was sitting on
the opposite side, frowned when he saw Mishka and turned his eyes
away.

Kirill invited Mishka to sit down.

"Thank you for the invitation."

"But do sit down, don't take offence, have a drink with us."

Mishka sat down at the table. Taking the glass of home-made
vodka from the master's hands, he nodded. "Here's to your return
home, Kirill Ivanovich!"

"Thank you. Have you been back from the army long?"

"Very long. I've had time to settle down."

"To settle down and get married too, by all accounts. But what
are you pulling a face for? Drink it up!"

"I don't want any more. I've got some business to talk over with you."

"But that's too much! Don't try that on me! I'm not talking about business today! Today I'm enjoying myself with friends. If you've come on business, call again tomorrow."

Mishka rose from the table. Smiling calmly, he said:

"It's only a little matter, but it won't wait. Come outside for a minute."

Stroking his neatly twisted black moustache, Kirill was silent for a moment, then he rose.

"Perhaps we can talk here. Why break up the company?"

"No, let's go outside," Mishka replied quietly but insistently.

"Go outside with him; what are you chaffering over?" said the strange, broad-shouldered Cossack.

Kirill reluctantly led the way into the kitchen. To his wife, who was busy at the stove, he muttered:

"Clear out of here, Katerina!" Sitting down on the bench, he asked curtly: "Well, what's the business?"

"How many days have you been back?"

"Why, what's the matter?"

"How many days have you been back, I asked."

"This is the fourth, I think."

"And have you been to the Revolutionary Committee yet?"

"Not yet."

"And are you thinking of going to see the Military Commission at Vieshenska?"

"What are you after? If you've come on business, talk about your business."

"I'm talking about my business."

"Then go to the devil! Who the hell do you think you are, that I've got to give you an answer?"

"I'm chairman of the Revolutionary Committee. Show me your regimental papers."

"So that's it!" Kirill drawled, and looked with a keen, suddenly sober glance into Mishka's eyes. "So that's what you're after?"

"Yes, you've got it! Hand over your papers."

"I'll call at the Soviet with them today."

"Show them this minute!"

"I've got them packed away somewhere."

"Then find them!"

"No, I'm not going to look for them now. Go home, Mikhail, don't make a scene here."

"It'll be a short scene I'll make with you!" Mishka put his right hand into his pocket. "Get your coat on!"

"Drop it, Mikhail! You'd better not lay hands on me. . . ."

"Come on, I tell you!"

"Where to?"

"To the Revolutionary Committee."

"I don't particularly want to. . . ." Kirill turned pale, but he spoke with a humorous smile on his face.

Swaying a little to the left, Mishka pulled his pistol out of his pocket and cocked the hammer.

"Are you coming or not?" he quietly asked.

Without a word Kirill strode towards the best room. But Mishka placed himself in his way and with his eyes indicated the door leading to the porch.

"Boys!" Kirill shouted with assumed unconcern, "I've been sort of arrested here. Finish off the vodka without me."

The door of the best room was flung wide open, and Akhvatkin started to cross the threshold. But, seeing the pistol pointed at him, he hurriedly fell back behind the doorpost.

"Come on!" Mishka ordered Kirill.

With an affectedly jaunty stride Kirill went towards the door, lazily took hold of the latch, and suddenly, clearing the porch with one bound, furiously slammed the outer door and leaped down the steps. As, bent double, he ran across the yard towards the orchard, Mishka fired at him twice without hitting him. Standing with his feet wide apart, laying the barrel of his pistol across the elbow of his crooked left arm, Koshevoi took deliberate aim. At the third shot Kirill seemed to stumble, but, recovering, he sprang lightly over the fence. Mishka ran down from the porch. The dry crack of a rifle-shot sounded from the house behind him. In front there was a thud as the bullet picked out the clay in the whitewashed wall of a shed and sent grey fragments of stone scattering over the ground.

Kirill ran swiftly and easily. His stooping figure flashed among the green foliage of the apple trees. Mishka leaped the fence, but fell, and as he lay, fired twice more at the fugitive, then turned to face the house. The outside door was wide open. Kirill's mother was standing on the steps, her palm arched over her eyes, gazing into the orchard. "I should have shot him on the spot without stopping to talk!" Mishka thought numbly. He lay for several minutes under the fence, gazing at the house, and with a measured, mechanical movement cleaned off the mud sticking to his knees. Then he rose, climbed heavily across the fence, and, holding the pistol with its barrel pointed downward, went back to the house.

Chapter 5

In addition to Gromov, Akhvatkin and the strange Cossack whom Mishka had seen in the Gromovs' room also vanished. During the night two other Cossacks disappeared from the village. A small detachment of the Don Cheka arrived at Tatarsk from Vieshenska. They arrested certain of the Cossacks and sent four, who had come home without documents from their regiments, to the penal regiment at Vieshenska.

Koshevoi spent all his days sitting in the Revolutionary Committee room, returning home at dusk. He always put his loaded rifle by the bed, thrust his pistol under the pillow, and lay down to sleep without undressing. The third day after the incident with Kirill he said to Dunia:

"Let's sleep in the porch."

"What on earth for?" Dunia asked in amazement.

"They might fire through the window. The bed's close to the window."

Without a word Dunia shifted the bed into the porch. But that evening she asked:

"Well, and how long are we to go on living like hunted hares? The winter's coming on, and are we to roost in the porch then?"

"The winter's a long way off yet, but meantime that's how we've got to live."

"And how long will this 'meantime' last?"

"Until I've caught Kirill."

"Do you think he's going to put his head into your hands?"

"He will some day," Mishka answered confidently.

But he was wrong: Kirill Gromov and his friends had hidden somewhere on the farther side of the Don. Hearing that the White commander Makhno was getting near the district, they made their way back to the other bank and went off to the village of Krasnokutsk, where, so rumour said, the advance detachments of Makhno's band had already appeared. Kirill spent the night in Tatarsk and, chancing to meet Prokhov Zykov in the street, told him to inform Koshevoi that Gromov sent his respectful greetings and asked Mishka to expect a return visit before long. Next morning Prokhor told Mishka of his meeting and talk with Kirill.

"All right! Let him turn up! He's got away once, but he won't a second time. He's taught me how to treat the likes of him, and I thank him for the lesson," Mishka said when Prokhor had finished.

Makhno and his band had in fact arrived on the confines of the upper Don region. In a short fight close to Konkov he smashed an infantry battalion sent from Vieshenska to meet him. However, he did not advance towards the regional centre, but made in the direction of Millerovo station, crossed the railway to the north of it, and retreated towards Starobelsk. The most active of the White Guard elements among the Cossacks went off to join him, but the majority remained at home, waiting to see what happened.

Koshevoi went on living with ears pricked up, closely watching all that went on in the village. But life in Tatarsk was not particularly cheerful. The Cossacks ardently cursed the Soviet régime for all the shortages which they were having to experience. There was almost nothing in the tiny shop which the local co-operative society had recently opened. Soap, sugar, salt, paraffin, matches, tobacco, axle-grease—all these articles of prime importance were lacking, and the bare shelves exhibited expensive packets of cigarettes and bits of ironware which went unsold for months on end.

In place of paraffin the villagers used melted butter and fat in saucers. Manufactured tobacco was replaced by home-grown or self-sown tobacco. In the absence of matches flints and lighters roughly made by the smiths came into general use. Tinder was boiled in a solution of sunflower ash and water to make it catch alight more quickly, but even so it was difficult to obtain a light. More than once, returning home of an evening from the Revolutionary Committee, Mishka saw smokers gathered in a circle at a corner, engaged in vigorously striking sparks from flints, cursing under their breath: "Soviet government, give us a light!" At last one of them would get a spark to fall on the dry tinder, it flared up, and they all blew violently on the feeble flame. After lighting their cigarettes they silently squatted down on their heels, exchanging the news.

Nor was there any paper with which to make cigarettes. All the registers were carried off from the church vestry, and when the Cossacks had smoked them everything in the huts themselves was used for making cigarettes, including children's old school-books and even the older people's religious books.

Prokhor Zykov, who was a frequent visitor to the Melekhov yard, obtained all the paper he could from Mikhail and said mournfully:

"The lid of my wife's family chest was pasted all over with old newspapers—I tore them off and smoked them. We had a New Testament, a religious book like that! But I've smoked it too. And I've smoked the Old Testament. The holy saints didn't write enough of these testaments. My wife had kept a family record; she'd got all our relations, alive and dead, written down in it. I smoked that book too. And now what—have I got to smoke cabbage leaves or use burdocks for paper? No, Mikhail, say what you like, but give us a newspaper. I can't live without a smoke. When I was at the German front I swapped my ration of bread more than once for an ounce of tobacco."

Far from cheerful was life in Tatarsk that autumn. The ungreased wheels of the wagons squeaked as they rolled along, the leather harness and footwear dried and cracked for lack of grease, but most keenly felt of all was the lack of salt. That accursed salt caused much bitterness to Mikhail. One day a group of the old men came to the Soviet. They sedately greeted the chairman, took off their caps, and seated themselves on the benches.

"There's no salt in the village, mister chairman," said one of them.

"There are no misters now," Mishka corrected him.

"Please excuse me, I always say it out of habit. . . . We can live without the misters, but we can't without salt."

"Well, what is it you want, elders?"

"Chairman, you must do something to get salt brought to the village. It can't be carted all the way from Manich with bullocks."

"I've reported on the matter to the Region. They know all about it. They ought to be sending some soon."

"While the sun's rising the dew rots the seeds," said one of the old men, staring down at the floor.

Mishka flared up and rose from the table. Livid with anger, he turned out his pockets:

"I haven't got any salt. Do you see? I don't carry it about with me and I can't suck it out of my fingers for you. Do you understand, elders?"

"Where on earth has it got to, this salt?" hunchbacked old Chumakov asked after a moment's silence, looking around in astonishment with one eye. "In the old days, under the former government, nobody even had to speak about it; it lay in piles everywhere. But now you can't even get hold of a pinch of it. . . ."

"Our government has got nothing to do with it," Mishka said more calmly. "The only government that's to blame for it is your former Cadet government. It was they who did so much destruction that there's not even anything to cart salt with. All the railroad tracks are smashed, and the freight cars too."

He spent a great deal of time telling the old men how during the retreat the Whites had destroyed the state property, had blown up factories, had burned down warehouses. He had seen some of it himself during the war, he had heard more, and the rest he imaginatively invented with the sole object of turning the discontent away from his own Soviet government. To defend that government from reproaches he lied and wriggled shamelessly, thinking the while: "It will be no great woe if I talk the swine's heads off! They're swine in any case, and they won't lose anything by it, while it'll be to our gain. . . ."

"Do you think that these bourgeoisie aren't clever, or what? They're not fools. They collected all the stocks of sugar and salt, thousands of pounds of it, from all over Russia and carried it off to the Crimea, and there they loaded it on steamers and sent it to other countries to be sold," he said, his eyes glittering.

"And did they cart off all the axle-grease too?" crooked Chumakov asked distrustfully.

"Do you think they were going to leave it behind for you, daddy? A lot of need they have of you, or any of the toiling people. They'll find someone to sell even the grease to! They'd have carted off everything with them if they could, so that the people here would die of hunger."

"That's true, of course," one of the old men agreed. "The rich are all like that, out to get the last grain. From time immemorial it's been well established that the richer you are, the greedier you are. In Vieshenska there was a merchant who piled everything he had on wagons when the first retreat took place. He carried off all his property down to the last spool of thread. And the Reds got quite close, but there he was, still not ready to drive out of his yard, running about dressed in a sheepskin, pulling the nails out of the walls with pincers. 'I'm not going to leave a single nail behind for them, damn them!' he said. So it isn't very surprising that they've carried off the grease with them."

"But all the same, how are we going to manage without salt?" old Maksaev asked benevolently towards the end of the talk.

"Our workers will soon dig up more salt, and meantime you can send wagons to Manich," Mishka advised guardedly.

"The people don't want to drive there. The Kalmyks do us harm, they won't let us have salt at the lakes, and they carry off our bullocks. An acquaintance of mine came back with only his knout. One night three armed Kalmyks rode up and drove off his bullocks and pointed to their throats: 'Keep your mouth shut,' they said, 'or you'll come to a bad end, daddy.' And now you drive there!"

"We'll have to wait a little longer," Chumakov sighed.

Mishka managed to come to some kind of agreement with the elders, but at home he and Dunia had a serious conversation over this very question of salt. Something was going wrong in Mishka's relations with his wife.

It had all begun on that memorable day when he had talked about Gregor in Prokhor's presence. That little squabble had not been forgotten. One evening at supper Mishka said:

"Your soup isn't salted, mistress. Or is there a shortage of salt on the table and too much on your back?"

"Under this government there isn't likely to be too much salt for some time to come. Do you know how much salt we've got left?"

"Well?"

"Two handfuls."

"Things are in a bad way," Mishka sighed.

"Other folk rode off to Manich for salt away back in the summer, but you've never had time to think about it," Dunia said reproachfully.

"What could I have driven with? In our first year of wedded life it doesn't seem right to harness you up, and as for real bullocks . . ."

"You leave your jokes for another time! When you're eating unsalted food, then you can joke!"

"What are you turning on me for? Tell me where I'm to get salt from! What a lot you are, you women! 'Belch it up if you like, but give us salt!' But supposing there isn't any, curse it?"

"Other folk drove to Manich with bullocks. And now they've got salt and everything, but we'll be chewing tasteless stuff. . . ."

"We'll get through it somehow, Dunia. They ought to be sending us salt soon. Have we got so little of that commodity?"

"You've got plenty of everything!"

"Who's 'you'?"

"The Reds."

"And what are you?"

"I'm what you see. You've talked and talked: 'We'll have plenty of everything, and we'll all be living on the same level, and well. . . .' Is this what you call living well? With nothing to salt our soup?"

Mishka stared at his wife in alarm and turned pale.

"What's all this, Dunia? What are you saying? How can you talk like that?"

But Dunia had got the bit between her teeth: she also went pale with anger and indignation and, raising her voice to a shout, went on:

"Well, how can we live like this? What are you staring your eyes out for? Do you know, chairman, that already people's gums are swelling from lack of salt? They're digging up earth in the salt-marshes, people go as far even as Nechaev mound, and they put this earth into their soup. . . . Have you heard about that?"

"Wait a bit, don't shout so much. . . . Well, and what next?"

Dunia clapped her hands. "What else do you want?"

"Have we got to live through it somehow or haven't we?"

"Well, you live through it!"

"I am living through it, but you— All your Melekhov character has come to the surface now."

"What character?"

"Your counter-revolutionary character, that's what!" Mishka said thickly, and rose from the table. He stared down at the floor and would not raise his eyes to his wife. His lips quivered as he said:

"If you talk like that again, you and I shan't be living together, understand that! Your words are the words of an enemy. . . ."

Dunia was about to make some objection, but Mishka looked at her out of the corners of his eyes and raised his fist.

"Hold your tongue!" he said huskily.

Fearlessly, with open curiosity, Dunia gazed at him. After a moment she said calmly and cheerfully:

"Well, all right, the devil knows what we've started to talk about. . . . We'll manage without salt!" She was silent for a second and then added with the quiet smile of which Mishka was so fond: "Don't be angry, Misha! If you're going to be angry with us women over everything, you'll never stop being angry. What else can you expect from a stupid head? Will you have some broth or shall I put out some sour milk for you?"

Despite her youth, Dunia was already rich in worldly wisdom, and she knew when to be obstinate in an argument and when it was necessary to make peace and retreat.

A couple of weeks later a letter arrived from Gregor. He wrote that he had been wounded on the Wrangel front and that, after recovering, in all probability he would be demobilized. Dunia told Mishka the contents of the letter and guardedly asked:

"Misha, when he comes home, how shall we manage?"

"We'll move to my hut. He can live here by himself. We'll share the property."

"We certainly can't live together. By all the signs he'll bring Aksinia here."

"Even if it was possible I'd never live under the same roof as your brother," Mishka declared sharply.

Dunia raised her eyebrows in astonishment. "Why not, Mishka?"

"You know well enough!"

"You mean because he served with the Whites?"

"You've got it."

"How you dislike him! And yet you and he were friends once."

"What the devil have I got to like him for? We were friends, but our friendship came to an end long ago."

Dunia was seated at the spinning-wheel. The wheel hummed rhythmically. Suddenly the thread broke. Dunia held the rim of the wheel with her palm and, as she twisted the two ends together, asked without looking at her husband:

"When he comes back, what will happen about his service with the Cossacks?"

"There'll be a trial—a tribunal."

"But what is he likely to be sentenced to?"

"Well, I'm not to know that; I'm not the judge."

"Can he be shot?"

Mishka stared at the bed where Mishatka and Poliushka were asleep, listened to their steady breathing, and, lowering his voice, answered:

"It's possible."

Dunia asked no more questions. Next morning, after milking the cow she went to see Aksinia.

"Grisha will be back soon, so I dropped in to cheer you with the news," she said.

Aksinia silently set an iron pot of water on the coals and pressed her hands to her breast. Looking at her flaming face, Dunia said:

"But don't cheer up too much! My man says he won't be able to get out of a trial. What they'll sentence him to, God alone knows."

For a second, terror peered out of Aksinia's moist and glittering eyes.

"What for?" she asked jerkily, still unable to drive the belated smile from her lips.

"For the rising . . . for everything."

"Nonsense! They won't try him. Your Mikhail knows nothing about it. A fine know-all he is!"

"Perhaps they won't." Dunia was silent, then said, suppressing a sigh: "He's wild with my brother. And it weighs so heavily on my heart, I can't tell you how much! I'm terribly sorry for Gregor. He's been wounded again. His life's all out of joint, somehow."

"So long as he comes back! We'll take the children and hide somewhere," Aksinia said agitatedly.

For some reason she removed her kerchief, then put it on again and began aimlessly to shift the utensils on the bench, quite unable to master the violent agitation which had taken possession of her. Dunia noticed how her hands were trembling as she sat down on the bench and began to smooth out the folds of her old, worn apron over her knees.

A lump rose in Dunia's throat. She felt like going off somewhere to cry by herself.

"Mother didn't live to see him come back . . ." she said quietly. "Well, I'm going. I've got to light the stove."

In the porch Aksinia hurriedly and awkwardly kissed her on the neck, then snatched up and kissed her hand.

"Are you glad?" Dunia asked in a low, broken tone.

"Yes, just a little, only a very little," Aksinia answered, trying to jest, to hide her tears behind a tremulous smile.

Chapter 6

At Millerovo station Gregor, as a demobilized Red commander, was assigned a wagon and horses. He changed the horses at every Ukrainian settlement he passed through on his way home and reached the bounds of the upper Don region the same day. But at the very first Cossack village he drove into, the chairman of the Revolutionary Committee, a young man only recently returned from the Red Army, told him:

"You'll have to have bullocks, comrade commander. We've only got one horse in all the village, and that hobbles on three legs. All the horses were left behind in the Kuban during the retreat."

"Perhaps I can manage with the one?" Gregor asked, tapping his fingers on the table, looking interrogatively into the genial chairman's merry eyes.

"You'll never get there. You'll be driving a week and still you'll not get there! But don't be alarmed, we've got good bullocks with a long stride, and we've got to send a wagon to Vieshenska in any case, to take some telephone wire which got stranded here after the war. So you won't have to change wagons, it'll put you down right outside your door." The chairman screwed up his left eye and added, smiling and winking impudently: "We'll give you our finest bullocks and a young widow for driver. We've got one here who's so hot you'd never even dream of a hotter! With her for company you won't even notice you're home. I've been in the army myself, I know all a soldier's needs. . . ."

Gregor silently reckoned that to wait for a wagon going his way would be absurd; and it was a long way to go on foot. He would have to agree and accept the bullocks.

The wagon drove up within an hour. It was ancient, the wheels squeaked miserably, at the back the frame was broken and jagged, and carelessly piled hay hung in wisps. "There's your war!" Gregor thought as he looked with repugnance at the miserable turn-out. The driver strode along beside the bullocks, waving her whip. She was certainly a very good-looking woman, and well built. Her massive breasts, out of proportion to her height, rather spoilt her figure, while a slanting scar on her round chin gave her face a look of sinister experience and seemed to age her deeply crimson face, which around the bridge of her nose was sprinkled with golden freckles as fine as millet seed.

As she arranged her kerchief she screwed up her eyes, looked Gregor over, and asked:

"Is it you I've got to take?"

Gregor rose from the step and flung his greatcoat around him.

"Yes. Have you loaded the wire?"

"Have I got to load the accursed stuff?" the Cossack woman cried in a ringing voice. "Every day they want me to drive somewhere and do work for them! Is that what I am to them? Let them load the wire themselves, and if they won't, then I'll drive empty."

Yet she dragged the rolls of wire on to the wagon, noisily but amicably exchanged curses with the chairman and occasionally threw sidelong, scrutinizing glances at Gregor. The chairman laughed continually, and gazed at the young widow with genuine admiration. From time to time he gave Gregor a wink, as though saying: "That's the sort of women we've got! But you wouldn't believe me!"

Beyond the village the brown, faded autumnal steppe stretched away into the distance. A dove-grey ribbon of smoke dragged from the ploughed lands across the road. The ploughmen were burning the weeds: dry, bushy hemp nettle, withered meadow grass. The scent of the smoke awakened mournful memories in Gregor: at one time he too had ploughed up the lands in the lonely autumnal steppe, had gazed at night into the black, star-sprinkled sky, had listened to the cries of the flocks of geese flying in the zenith. He shifted about, fidgeting on the hay, and looked at his driver.

"How old are you, good woman?"

"Close on sixty," she answered coquettishly, smiling with only her eyes.

"No, without joking."

"I'm in my twenty-first year."

"And a widow?"

"Yes."

"Then what happened to your husband?"

"He was killed."

"Recently?"

"Two years ago now."

"During the rising, then?"

"Afterwards, in the autumn."

"And how do you manage?"

"Oh, I manage somehow."

"Do you find life dreary?"

She gazed at him attentively and pulled her kerchief over her lips to hide her smile. Her voice sounded thicker and a new note crept into it when she answered:

"There's no time for dreariness when you're at work."

"But isn't it dreary without your husband?"

"I live with my mother-in-law, and we've got plenty to do on the farm."

"But how do you manage without your husband?"

She turned her face towards Gregor. A flush played on her swarthy cheeks, little ruddy sparks flamed up and faded in her eyes.

"What are you getting at?"

"Just what I said."

She shifted her kerchief away from her lips and said with a drawl:

"Well, there's enough of that blessing in this life! The world isn't entirely lacking in good men!" After a pause she went on: "I didn't get much chance of tasting the joys of woman's life with my husband. We only spent a month together, and then he was taken off into the army. I manage somehow without him. It's easier now young Cossacks have come back to the village, but before that it was hard. Gee up, bald-head! Gee up! So now you know, soldier! That's my life!"

Gregor said no more. He had no desire to carry on the conversation in such a bantering tone. Already he felt rather regretful that he had started it.

The great well-fed bullocks strode along steadily with the same measured, shambling gait. At some time or other one of them had had its right horn broken, and the horn had grown obliquely down over its head. Resting on his elbows, half-closing his eyes, Gregor lay in the wagon. He began to recall the bullocks he had worked with in his childhood and later, when he had grown up. They were all different in colouring, in build, in character; even in their horns each had its distinctive feature. At one time he had handled a bullock with a crumpled horn just like this one. Ill-tempered and cunning, it always looked out of the corners of its eyes, rolling its bloodshot whites; it tried to kick when approached from behind, and always in the field season, when the cattle were turned loose to graze on the steppe at night, it tried to make its way home, or, still worse, hid in the forest or in the distant dells. Gregor had often spent a long day riding on horseback over the steppe and, after giving up hope of ever finding the lost bullock, had suddenly discovered it somewhere in the very bottom of a ravine, in an impenetrable thicket of thorn, or in the shade of an old and spreading crab apple. That crumple-horned devil could slip its head out of the bullock lead, and at night it used to raise the crossbar of the gate to the cattle-yard, would get out and, swimming across the Don, would go wandering through the meadowland. Many an unpleasant and bitter moment had that bullock given Gregor in its time.

"What's that bullock with the crumpled horn like? Quiet?" he asked the woman.

"Yes. Why, what about it?"

"I was only interested."

" 'Only' is a good word, if there's nothing more to say," the woman pronounced with a sneer.

Gregor was silent again. It was pleasant thinking about the past, about those days of peace, about work, about everything that had nothing to do with war. For that seven-year-long war had fed him up beyond words, and at the very recollection of it, of some episode connected with his army service, he felt a griping nausea and numb irritation.

He had done with fighting—had enough of it. He was riding home in order, at last, to betake himself to work, to live with his children, with Aksinia. While still at the front he had firmly resolved to take Aksinia to himself, for her to rear his children and to be always at his side. That story also must be ended, and the sooner the better.

He dreamed with satisfaction of how when he got home he would take off his tunic and boots, would put on broad-fitting shoes, would tuck his trousers Cossack-fashion into his white woollen stockings, and, throwing his home-weave coat around his warm jacket, would drive off into the fields. It would be good to have his hands on the plough-handles and walk along the damp furrow behind the plough, his nostrils greedily drinking in the raw and vapid scent of crumbling earth, the bitter smell of grass cut by the ploughshare. In foreign countries even the earth and the grasses had a different smell. More than once in Poland, in the Ukraine and the Crimea, he had rubbed a grey stalk of wormwood between his palms, had smelt it, and had yearningly thought: "No, it's not the same, it's different. . . ."

But his driver was finding life boring. She felt inclined for conversation. She stopped urging on the bullocks, seated herself comfortably, and, playing with the leather tassel of her knout, long and surreptitiously examined Gregor, his concentrated face, his half-closed eyes. "He's not so very old, though he is grey. And he's a queer fellow, somehow! He looks as though he'd seen some trouble in his time. But he isn't bad-looking really. Only a lot of grey hair, and his moustache is almost grey too. But otherwise he's not bad. What's he thinking so much for? At first it looked as though he was going to be jolly, but then he shut up and for some reason asked about the bullock. Doesn't he know what to talk about? Or perhaps he's shy. He doesn't look like it. He's got hard eyes. No, he's a good Cossack, only queer, somehow. Well then, keep your mouth shut, you hunchbacked devil! A lot of need I've got of you! I can hold my tongue too. If you're riding to your wife, you'll never get there! Well, hold your tongue, and much good may it do you!"

She lolled with her head back against the ribs of the wagon and began to sing quietly.

Gregor raised his head and gazed at the sun. The day was still young. A last-year's thistle which morosely stood guard over the road threw a shadow the length of half a stride; in all probability the time was no more than two in the afternoon.

As though enchanted, the steppe lay in a dead silence. The sun warmed but little. A light breeze noiselessly stirred the reddish-brown, withered grass. Neither bird's call nor marmot's whistle was to be heard at all. In the cold, pale-blue sky neither kites nor eagles were soaring. Only once did a grey shadow slip across the road, and, without raising his head, Gregor heard the heavy sweep of great wings: an ashy-grey great bustard flew past and settled close to a distant mound, where a hollow lying in shadow blended with the lilac glooms of the distance. In pre-war days only late in the autumn had Gregor known such a mournful and profound silence in the steppe, when it would seem to him that he heard the chickweed caught up by the wind go rustling over the sapless grass, traversing the steppe far, far ahead.

It seemed that the road would never end. It wound up over a slope, dropped into a ravine, climbed again to the summit of a rise. And always the same—unbounded to the eye—the desolate pasture-land of the steppe extended all around.

Gregor's eyes were gladdened by a bush of maple growing on the slope of the ravine. Scorched by the first frosts, its leaves were glowing with a duskily livid hue, as though springled with ash from the coals of a dying camp-fire.

"What's your name, daddy?" his driver asked, gently touching his shoulder with her knout.

He started and turned his face to her. She looked away.

"Gregor. And yours?"

"Call me what you like."

"You should keep quiet, 'what you like'!"

"I'm tired of keeping quiet. I've been quiet for half a day, my mouth's quite dry. Why are you so sad, Daddy Grisha?"

"Well, why should I be merry?"

"You're going home, so you ought to be."

"My years of merriment have passed."

"Go on! You're an old man, aren't you! But why have you gone grey so young?"

"You want to know everything. . . . Of course I've gone grey as the result of the good life I've led."

"Are you married, Daddy Grisha?"

"Yes. And you'd do well to find another husband quickly."

"Why?"

"Well, you're a little too wanton. . . ."

"Is that so terrible?"

"It can be. I knew one such wanton woman—she was a widow too —she wantoned and wantoned, but then her nose began to drop off."

"By God, how terrible!" the woman exclaimed in mock terror, and at once added in a businesslike tone: "A widow's life is like that. If you're afraid of the wolf, don't go into the forest!"

Gregor glanced at her. She was laughing soundlessly, her fine white teeth pressed together. Her pouting upper lip twitched, her eyes gleamed mischievously from beneath her drooping lashes. Gregor involuntarily smiled and laid his hand on her warm, rounded knee.

"Poor, unhappy wretch!" he said commiseratingly. "Only twenty short years, and how life has gnawed at you!"

In a flash not a trace was left of her merriment. She roughly pushed his hand away, knitted her brows, and flushed so deeply that the tiny freckles vanished from the bridge of her nose.

"You pity your wife when you get home! I've got enough sympathizers and to spare without you!"

"Don't be annoyed! Wait a bit!"

"Oh, go to the devil!"

"I said what I did because I was really sorry for you."

"You can take your sorrow straight . . ." the masculine oath came fluently and easily to her lips, and her darkened eyes flashed.

Gregor raised his eyebrows and muttered in confusion:

"Well, you can swear all right, there's no denying it! What an uncontrollable woman you are!"

"And what are you? A saint in a lousy greatcoat, that's what! I know you! Get married and all the rest of it! But how long have you been so zealous?"

"Not so very long," Gregor said with a laugh.

"Then what are you laying down the law to me for? I've got a mother-in-law who'll do that."

"Now, that's enough! What are you so angry about, you fool of a woman? I only put it that way," Gregor said in a conciliatory tone.

"Now look! While we've been talking, the bullocks have got right off the road."

Making himself more comfortable in the wagon, Gregor gave a swift glance at the merry widow and noticed tears in her eyes. "Well, that's the last straw! These women are always like that . . ." he thought, feeling awkward and vexed.

Soon afterwards he fell asleep, lying on his back, covering his face with the edge of his greatcoat, and awoke only as dusk was falling. The evening stars were faintly shining in the sky. He caught a fresh and joyous smell of hay.

"The bullocks have got to be fed," his driver said.

"All right, let's stop."

Gregor himself unharnessed the bullocks, then took a tin of meat and bread out of his field-pack; he collected a whole armful of dry scrub and made a fire not far from the wagon.

"Well, sit down and have some supper," he said to the woman. "You've been angry long enough."

She sat down by the fire and without a word shook bread and a piece of bacon-fat rusty with age out of her sack. They talked little and amicably over the supper. Then she climbed into the wagon to sleep, while Gregor threw several clumps of bullock-dung on the fire to keep it going and stretched himself out beside it, soldier-fashion. He lay for some time with his head resting on his field-pack, gazing up at the sky glittering with stars, disconnectedly thinking of his children, of Aksinia, then dozed off, and was awakened by a stealthy feminine voice:

"Are you asleep, soldier? Are you asleep or aren't you?"

He raised his head. Resting on her elbow, his companion was half hanging out of the wagon. Her face, lit up from below by the uncertain light of the dying fire, was rosy and fresh; her teeth and the lacy edging of her head-kerchief gleamed dazzlingly in the darkness. She smiled again, as though there had been no words between them, and said, working her eyebrows:

"I'm afraid you'll freeze down there. The earth's cold. If you're very cold come up with me. I've got a warm, a very warm sheepskin. You'll come, won't you?"

Gregor reflected for a moment and answered with a sigh:

"Thank you, girl, but I don't want to. Now, if it had been a year or two back. . . . I don't think I'll freeze by the fire."

She too sighed and said:

"Well, as you wish." And she drew her sheepskin over her head.

A little later Gregor rose to his feet and gathered his things. He had decided to continue on foot in order to reach Tatarsk by dawn. It was absurd for him—a commander returning from service—to ride home in broad daylight in a bullock-wagon. Such a return would cause so much joking and talk.

He aroused the woman.

"I'm going on on foot. You won't be afraid of being left alone in the steppe?"

"No. I'm not a nervous sort, and there's a village not far off. But what's wrong? Getting impatient?"

"You've guessed it. Well, good-bye; don't think badly of me."

He took to the road and turned up the collar of his greatcoat. A first snowflake fell on his eyelashes. The wind had shifted to the north, and in its cold breath Gregor imagined he could catch the familiar and pleasant scent of snow.

Koshevoi had gone to Vieshenska, and returned in the evening. Through the window Dunia saw him drive up to the gate, and she swiftly threw a shawl around her shoulders and went out into the yard.

"Grisha arrived home this morning," she said at the wicket gate, gazing at her husband anxiously and expectantly.

"A great joy for you!" Mishka answered non-committally and with just a touch of humour.

Firmly pressing his lips together, he went into the kitchen. Below his cheekbones the muscles were quivering. Poliushka had climbed up on Gregor's knee; her aunt had solicitously attired her in a clean dress. Gregor carefully set the child on the floor and went to meet his brother-in-law, smiling and holding out his large, swarthy hand. He was about to embrace Mikhail, but noticed the cold, unfriendly look in his unsmiling eyes and refrained.

"Well, greetings, Misha!"

"Greetings!"

"It's a long time since we saw each other last! It seems like a century."

"Yes, it's a long time. . . . Welcome home."

"Thank you. So we're kinsmen now?"

"Looks like it. . . . What's that blood on your cheek?"

"It's nothing; I cut myself with the razor in my hurry."

They sat down at the table and silently examined each other, experiencing a feeling of awkwardness and estrangement. They would have to have a serious conversation together, but that was impossible at this moment. Mikhail was perfectly self-controlled, and he talked calmly about the farm and the changes which had occurred.

Gregor gazed through the window at the earth covered with a first bluish snow, at the bare boughs of the apple tree. This was not how he had imagined his meeting with Mikhail.

Not long afterwards Misha went out. In the porch he diligently sharpened his knife on a whetstone and said to Dunia:

"I'm going to find someone to slaughter a lamb. After all, the master must be given a fitting welcome. Run and get some vodka. No, wait! Go to Prokhor and tell him he's to get hold of vodka somewhere, even if he has to wear his feet out. He can do it better than you. Invite him along for the evening."

Dunia beamed with joy and gave her husband a look of silent gratitude. "Maybe everything will take a good turn. . . . They've done fighting, what else are they to do now? May God bring them to reason!" she thought hopefully as she made her way to Prokhor's hut.

Less than half an hour later Prokhor came running in, panting.

"Gregor Pantalievich! Old lad . . . I never hoped, I never expected to see this day!" he shouted in a high-pitched, weeping voice and, stumbling over the threshold, all but smashed the great ewer of vodka he was carrying.

He embraced Gregor, sobbing, wiping his eyes with his fist, stroking his moustache, from which tears were dripping. Something quivered in Gregor's throat, but he restrained himself. Deeply moved, he roughly clapped his faithful orderly on the back and said incoherently:

"Well, so we've seen each other again. . . . Well, and I'm glad,

Prokhor, terribly glad! What are you crying for, old lad? Grown weak in the guts? The nuts working loose? How is your arm? So your wife hasn't torn your other off yet?"

Prokhor blew his nose violently and removed his sheepskin.

"The old woman and I live together these days like a couple of doves. You can see my second arm is whole, but the one which the Poles took off is beginning to grow again, God's truth! In a year now you'll be seeing fingers on it," he said with his customary cheeriness, shaking the empty sleeve of his shirt.

War had taught each of them to hide his real feelings behind a smile, to savour both bread and talk with a grain of salt; and so Gregor continued his questioning in the same jesting tone:

"How are you living, you old goat? How are you bucking?"

"Like an old man, not in too great a haste."

"You haven't killed anything else since you left me?"

"What are you getting at?"

"Why, the nightingales you brought me last winter. . . ."

"Pantalievich! God forbid! What use would such a luxury be now? And besides, what sort of marksman am I with only one arm? That's your business, that's a young man's job. . . . But it's high time I gave my affairs to a woman to grease and turned to licking out frying-pans."

They stood gazing at each other, these old trench comrades, laughing and rejoicing in the meeting.

"Home for good?" Prokhor asked.

"For good! Absolutely!"

"What rank did you win your way to?"

"I was vice-commander of the regiment!"

"Then why did they discharge you so soon?"

Gregor's face clouded, and he answered curtly:

"They had no more use for me."

"And why was that?"

"I don't know. Because of my past I expect."

"But you got through that Special Department Commission which sifted out all the officers, so how can they bring up the past now?"

"Who's to say?"

"But where's Mikhail?"

"In the yard. He's slaughtering a lamb."

Prokhor moved closer to Gregor and lowered his voice:

"They shot Platon Ryabchikov a month ago."

"What are you saying?"

"It's God's truth!"

In the porch the door creaked.

"We'll talk later," Prokhor whispered and, in a louder tone. "Well, comrade commander, shall we drink to celebrate this great happiness? Shall I go and call Mikhail?"

"Yes, do."

Dunia laid the table. She did not know how best to please her brother; she laid a clean hand-towel over his knee, pushed across a tray of salted watermelon, polished his glass at least five times. With a smile Gregor mentally noted that Dunia was not addressing him in the second person singular, as her brother, but in the plural.

At the table Mikhail was obstinately silent, attentively listening to Gregor's talk. He drank little, and that reluctantly. But Prokhor threw back a full glass at a time and only turned livid and stroked his lint-white moustache more frequently with his hand.

When she had fed the children and put them to bed Dunia placed a large dish of stewed lamb on the table and whispered to Gregor:

"Brother, I'll run and fetch Aksinia; you won't mind, will you?"

Gregor nodded without speaking. All the evening he had been in a state of tense expectation, yet he had felt sure nobody had noticed it. But Dunia had seen him pricking up his ears at every knock, listening and glancing sidelong at the door. Nothing whatever could escape the attention of that girl's unnecessarily sharp eyes!

"And Tereshchenko the Kuban, is he still in command of a troop?" Prokhor asked, holding his glass tightly in his hand, as though afraid someone would take it from him.

"He was killed at Lvov."

"Well, may he enter the heavenly kingdom! He was a good cavalry man." Prokhor hurriedly crossed himself and, not noticing Koshevoi's venomous smile, took a pull at his glass.

"And how about that one with the queer name? The one that rode on the right flank—damn it, what was his name, Maybeard, wasn't it? A Ukrainian, very stocky and merry, the one who split a Polish officer in two at Broda. Is he alive and well?"

"Like a stallion! He's been transferred to a machine-gun squadron."

"And who did you hand over your horse to?"

"I'd got another by then."

"Then what happened to the one with a star?"

"He was killed by a fragment of shell."

"In battle?"

"We were standing in a small town and were raked with fire. He was killed at the hitching-post."

"Ah, a pity! What a good horse he was!" Prokhor sighed and again set his lips to the glass.

The latch rattled in the porch. Gregor started. Aksinia crossed the threshold, indistinctly said: "Greetings!" and began to take off her kerchief, panting and not removing her dilated, radiant eyes from Gregor. She came to the table and sat down beside Dunia. Tiny snowflakes were melting on her eyebrows and lashes and on her pale cheeks. Screwing up her eyes, she wiped her face with her palm, sighed deeply, and only then, mastering herself, looked at Gregor again with eyes darkened with emotion.

"Fellow-soldier! Ksinia! Together we retreated, together we fed the lice. . . . Even if we did abandon you in the Kuban, what else were we to do?" Prokhor stretched out his glass, splashing the vodka over the table. "Drink to Gregor Pantalievich! Congratulate him on his return. . . . I told you he'd return safe and sound, and there he is; you can have him for twenty rubles! Why, he's sitting like a man who's been cheated!"

"He's already canned, neighbour, don't listen to him!" Gregor laughed, indicating Prokhor with his eyes.

Aksinia bowed to Gregor and Dunia and only raised her glass a little from the table. She was afraid everybody would notice how her hand was trembling.

"Here's to your arrival, Gregor Pantalievich, and to your joy, Dunia!"

"And what about you? To your sorrow?" Prokhor burst into a roar and nudged Mikhail in the side.

Aksinia flushed deeply; even the tiny lobes of her ears went translucently rosy. But looking firmly and angrily at Prokhor, she answered:

"And to my joy! My great joy!"

Prokhor was disarmed and touched by such frankness. He cried:

"Drink it down, for God's sake, all to the last drop! You know how to talk straight, know how to drink straight! It's like a sharp knife in my heart when I see anyone leaving good liquor."

Aksinia did not remain long—only so long as decorum permitted, in her judgment. During all her stay she rarely looked at her beloved, and then only momentarily. She forced herself to look at the others and avoided Gregor's eyes, for she could not pretend to be unconcerned, and she did not wish to reveal her feelings to outsiders. Only one glance did Gregor catch as she stood on the threshold, one direct glance filled with love and devotion. But with it everything was said. He went to see her out. The tipsy Prokhor shouted after them:

"Don't be long! We'll drink it all up!"

In the porch Gregor, without saying a word, kissed Aksinia on the brow and the lips, and asked:

"Well, Aksinia?"

"Oh, I can't tell everything. . . . Will you come tomorrow?"

"I will."

She hastened home, walking swiftly as though some urgent task were awaiting her there. Only by the door of her hut did she slow her pace, going cautiously up the creaking steps. She wanted as quickly as possible to be alone with her thoughts, with the happiness which had come so unexpectedly.

She threw off her jacket and kerchief and, lighting no light, passed into the best room. Through the unshuttered window the deep lilac glimmer of the night stole into the room. Behind the stove a cricket was ringingly chirruping. Out of habit Aksinia glanced at the mirror, and although in the darkness she could not see her reflection, none the less she tidied her hair, smoothed out the frills of her muslin blouse at the breast, then went across to the window and tiredly dropped on the bench.

Many times in her life had her hopes and expectations been unjustified, and that, perhaps, is why her constant anxiety came to take the place of her recent joy. What turn would her life take now? What awaited her in the future? And wasn't woman's bitter happiness smiling on her too late?

Worn out with the agitation she had felt all the evening, she sat with her cheek pressed to the cold, hoar-frosted window-glass, fixing her calm and rather sorrowful gaze on the darkness, which was lightened only very little by the snow.

Gregor sat down at the table, poured himself out a full glass from the ewer, and tossed it off in one gulp.

"Is it good?" Prokhor asked.

"I can't tell. I haven't drunk for ages."

"It's just like czarist vodka, by God!" Prokhor said in a tone of conviction, and, swaying, embraced Mishka. "You're less of a judge of such matters, Mishka, than a calf is of swill. But I know what's what where liquor's concerned. The liquors and wines I've come to drink in my time! There's wine which foams out of the bottle like out of a mad dog almost before you've pulled the cork—God knows I'm not lying. In Poland, when we broke through the front and rode with Budionny to shake up the Poles, we took a certain estate by storm. The house on the estate was a couple or more storeys high, the cattle in the yard were packed horn to horn, there were all sorts of fowl wandering about, there wasn't even room to spit. In a word, that landowner lived like a prince. When our troop dashed into the estate on horseback there were officers feasting with the master— they weren't expecting us. We sabred them all in the orchard and on the stairs, but we took one prisoner. He was an important officer by the look of him, but when we captured him his moustache went limp and he sweated all over with fear. Gregor Pantalievich had been called urgently to the staff, and we were left in charge. We went into the downstairs rooms, and there we saw an enormous table. And the stuff that was on it! We stood admiring, but we were afraid to begin, though we were terribly hungry. 'You never know,' we thought: 'it may all be poisoned.' Our prisoner looked like the devil to us. We ordered him: 'Eat!' and he ate. Not very readily, but he did eat. 'Drink!' And he drank. We made him eat a large helping of every dish, and drink a glass out of every bottle. The devil swelled up before our very eyes with all that food, and there we stood dribbling with spittle. Then we saw that he wasn't dying, and we set to work. We ate and we drank the foaming wine till we were stuffed up to our eyes. Then we noticed that the officer was starting to empty himself at both ends. 'Hell!' we thought; 'we're done for! The serpent has deliberately eaten the poisoned food and taken in the lot of us.' We rushed at him with our sabres drawn, but he waved his legs and arms and shouted: 'I've only eaten too much through your kindness; never you fear, the food's all right.' And so we went

back to the wine. We tugged at a cork and it flew out as though shot
from a gun, and the broth boiled up in a cloud until it was alarming to watch. Through the wine I fell off my horse three times that
night. The moment I climbed into my saddle I was sent flying again
as though blown clean off by the wind. Now if only I could always
drink wine like that, a glass or two on an empty stomach, I'd live to
be a hundred. But as things are, is anyone likely to live out his time?
Do you call this drink, for instance? It's an infection, not a drink!
It's enough to make you turn up your toes before your time!" With a
nod Prokhor indicated the ewer of vodka and poured himself out
another glass full to the brim.

Dunia went off to sleep with the children in the best room, and a
little later Prokhor also rose. Swaying, he flung his sheepskin coat
around his shoulders and said:

"I won't take the ewer. My soul won't allow me to go about with
an empty vessel. . . . When I got home my wife would start laying
it on at once. She's a good one for that! Where does she get such
filthy expressions from? I don't know. I come home after a little
drink, and she rants off at me like this: 'You drunken hound, you armless dog, you this and that and the other!' I very quietly and very
gently try to make her see reason. I tell her: 'You devilish idiot, you
bitch's udder, where did you ever see a drunken hound, and armless
at that? Such things don't exist in this world.' I disprove one shameful statement, and she at once makes another; I disprove the second,
and she insults me with a third, and so it goes on all night until
dawn. . . . Sometimes I get tired of listening to her and go off
under the shed to sleep. But sometimes I come home a little drunk,
and if she's silent and doesn't swear at me I can't get to sleep, God's
truth! It's just as though I was short of something, I get a kind of
itch, I can't sleep, and there's an end of it. And then I touch my
spouse and she starts ranting off at me again, until the sparks fly
from me. She takes it out of me, and I can't get away from it. Let
her carry on, she'll be all the better worker. That's true, isn't it?
Well, I'm going; good-bye! Or shall I spend the night in the stable
and not disturb her tonight?"

"Can you get home all right?" Gregor asked with a laugh.

"Like a crab, but I'll crawl there! Am I not a Cossack, then, Pantalievich? I'm quite upset to hear you ask such a question."

"Well then, God go with you!"

Gregor saw his friend as far as the wicket gate. Then he returned to the kitchen.

"Well, shall we have a talk, Mikhail?"

"All right."

They sat opposite each other, separated by the table, and were silent. At last Gregor said:

"There's something between us. I can see by your face that there's something wrong. Aren't you glad of my arrival? Or am I wrong?"

"No, you've guessed right. I'm not glad."

"Why aren't you?"

"It means unnecessary anxiety."

"I think I can manage to feed myself."

"I'm not thinking of that."

"Then what are you thinking of?"

"You and I are enemies. . . ."

"We were."

"Yes, and it's clear that we shall be."

"I don't understand. Why shall we?"

"You're unreliable."

"You're right off the mark. You're talking right off the mark."

"No, I'm not. Why have you been demobilized at such a time? Will you tell me straight out?"

"I don't know."

"Yes, you do, but you don't want to say. They didn't trust you—isn't that it?"

"If they hadn't trusted me they wouldn't have put me in command of a squadron."

"That was when you first joined. But as they haven't kept you in the army, the position's quite clear, brother!"

"But do you trust me?" Gregor asked, gazing straight at Mishka.

"No! Feed the wolf as much as you like, he's always hankering after the forest."

"You've drunk too much this evening, Mikhail."

"You can drop that! I'm no more drunk than you are. They didn't trust you there, and they won't put any great trust in you here, get that!"

Gregor was silent. He lackadaisically took a piece of salted cucumber from the dish, chewed it, and spat it out.

"Has my wife told you about Kirill Gromov?" Mikhail asked.

"Yes."

"I didn't like his return either. As soon as I heard about it that very same day . . ."

Gregor turned pale, and his eyes dilated with fury:

"What am I to you then: Kirill Gromov?"

"Don't shout! In what way are you any better?"

"Well, you know."

"It's not a question of knowing. We've known everything long since. And supposing Mitka Korshunov turns up—am I to be delighted at that too? No, it would have been better if you hadn't shown yourself in the village."

"Better for you?"

"Better for me and better for the people—quieter."

"Don't compare me with those others."

"I've already told you, Gregor, and there's no point in getting upset about it: you're no better than they are; in fact, you're worse, you're more dangerous."

"How am I? What are you getting at?"

"They're rank-and-file Cossacks, but you started the rising."

"I didn't start it, I was only commander of a division."

"And is that nothing?"

"Little or much, that's not the point. . . . If the Red Army men hadn't planned to kill me that evening, I might not have taken any part in the rising."

"If you hadn't been an officer no one would have touched you."

"If I hadn't been taken for the army I wouldn't have been an officer. . . . That's making a long story of it."

"Both a long and a filthy story."

"In any case it can't be gone over again, now it's past and done!"

They smoked in silence. Knocking the ash off his cigarette with his nail, Koshevoi said:

"I know all about your heroism, I've heard about it. You killed a lot of our men, and that doesn't make it easy for me to have you in my sight. . . . That's not to be forgotten in a hurry!"

Gregor laughed sarcastically.

"You've got a good memory! You killed my brother Piotra. But I don't bother to remind you of that. . . . If we're going to remember everything, we'll have to live like wolves."

"Well, I did kill him, I don't deny it. And if I'd had the luck to catch you that time I'd have stretched you out too like a lover!"

"But I, when they took Ivan Alexievich prisoner at Ust-Khopersk, I hurried home because I was afraid you might be among them; I was afraid the Cossacks would kill you. . . . It looks as if I was in too much of a hurry that time."

"So I've got a protector now? I can imagine how you'd have talked to me if you'd won. You'd have torn my back into ribbons, I expect. It's only now that you're turning so kind. . . ."

"Maybe others would flay you alive, but I wouldn't soil my hands on you."

"Then you and I are made differently. . . . I've never been afraid of soiling my hands on enemies, and I shan't turn a hair now if the need arises. . . ." Mikhail poured the rest of the vodka into the glasses and asked: "Will you drink?"

"All right; we've grown too sober for such talk. . . ."

They clinked glasses in silence and drank. Gregor leaned his chest against the table and, twisting his moustache, stared at Mikhail through half-closed eyes.

"But what is it you're afraid of, Mikhail? That I shall revolt against the Soviet régime again?"

"I'm not afraid of anything, but what I do think is that if anything happens to flare up you'll be slipping across to the other side too."

"I could have done that with the Poles, don't you think? We had a whole regiment go over to them."

"Couldn't you manage it?"

"It wasn't that; I just didn't want to. I've served my time. I don't want to serve anybody any more. I've fought more than enough for my age, and I'm absolutely worn out. I'm fed up with everything, with the Revolution and with the counter-revolution. Let all that— let it all go to hell! I want to live the rest of my life with my children, to return to the farm, that's all. Believe me, Mikhail, I say that from the bottom of my heart!"

For that matter, no assurance whatever could convince Mikhail. Gregor realized that and said no more. He felt a momentary bitter annoyance with himself. What the devil had he tried to justify himself for, tried to prove anything for? What was the point of carrying on this drunken conversation and listening to Mikhail's idiotic sermons? To hell with it all! He rose.

"We won't go on with this useless talk. I've had enough! One thing I want to say to you as my final word: I shan't do anything against the régime so long as it doesn't seize me by the throat. But if it does, I shall defend myself! In any case I'm not going to yield up my head over the rising, as Platon Ryabchikov has."

"What do you mean?"

"What I say. Let them take account of my service in the Red Army and the wounds I got as the result. I'm prepared to go to prison for the rising, but if it's a case of being shot for it, then excuse me! That'll be asking too much!"

Mikhail laughed contemptuously. "You've got a fine idea into your head! The Revolutionary Tribunal or the Cheka won't ask you what you want and what you don't want, and they won't strike any bargain with you. Once you've been found guilty, you receive your ration with make weight! The old debts have got to be paid off in full."

"Well, then we'll see."

"We'll see, sure enough!"

Gregor took off his belt and shirt, then, grunting with the effort, began to pull off his boots.

"Shall we share the farm?" he asked, unnecessarily examining the sole of his boot, which was coming away from the upper.

"The share-out won't take long! I'll put my hut in order and go there to live."

"Yes, we'd better separate in any case. You and I will never get on together."

"You're right!" Mikhail confirmed.

"I didn't think you'd have such an opinion of me. . . . Ah, well—"

"I've spoken straight out. I've said what I thought. When are you going to Vieshenska?"

"Some time or other during the next day or two."

"Not 'some time or other'; you've got to go tomorrow."

"I've come almost twenty-five miles on foot, and I'm tired out. I'll take a rest tomorrow, and go and register the day after."

"The order is that registration must be immediate. Go tomorrow!"

"Don't I need any rest? I shan't run away."

"The devil knows! I don't want to be responsible for you."

"What a swine you've become, Mikhail!" Gregor said, studying the harsh face of his former friend not without astonishment.

"Don't you call me a swine! I'm not used to it. . . ." Mikhail took a breath and raised his voice. "You know, you've got to drop your officer's ways. I say you go to Vieshenska tomorrow, and if you won't go of your own accord I'll send you there under convoy, understand?"

"Now I understand everything." Gregor stared with a look of hatred at his brother-in-law's back as Mikhail went to his room and lay down on the bed without undressing.

Ah, well, everything had happened as it was bound to happen. And why should he be given any different welcome? Why, indeed, had he thought that his brief period of faithful service in the Red Army would atone for all his past sins? And perhaps Mikhail was right in saying that not everything was forgivable and that the old debts had to be paid in full.

In his sleep Gregor saw the spacious steppe, and a regiment deployed for attack. Just as from somewhere in the distance came a long-drawn-out command: "Squad—ron!" he realized that his saddle-girths were not tightened under his horse. He put all the weight of his body on the right stirrup—his saddle slipped away under him. Possessed with a feeling of shame and fear, he leaped from his horse to tighten the saddle-girths and at that very moment heard the momentarily increasing and then tempestuously decreasing thunder of horse-hoofs. The regiment had galloped into the attack without him.

He turned over, and, awakening, caught the sound of his own hoarse groan.

Outside the window day was just beginning to appear. The wind must have opened the shutter during the night, and through the hoar-frosted glass he could see the gleaming green disk of the waning moon. He groped for his pouch and lit a cigarette. His heart was still pounding hollowly and swiftly. He lay on his back and smiled: fancy dreaming such a hellish dream! To be left out of the fight! In that early morning hour it did not occur to him that he would yet go into the attack more than once not only in his dreams but in his waking hours.

Chapter 7

Dunia got up early, she had to milk the cow. Gregor was walking quietly about the kitchen, coughing. Drawing the blanket over the children, Dunia swiftly dressed and went into the kitchen. She found her brother buttoning his greatcoat.

"Where are you off to so early, brother?"

"I'm going for a walk through the village, just to have a look round."

"You should have some breakfast first. . . ."

"I don't want any; I've got a headache."

"Will you be back by breakfast-time? I'm just going to light the stove."

"You needn't wait for me; I shan't be back for some time."

Gregor went out into the street. Towards morning a gentle thaw had set in. The wind blowing from the south was moist and warm. Snow mingled with earth clung to the heels of his boots. As he walked slowly towards the centre of the village he attentively examined the houses and sheds, familiar to him ever since childhood, as though he were in a strange locality. The charred ruins of the merchants' houses and shops burned down by Koshevoi the previous year showed black in the square, the half-demolished church wall yawned with gaps. "The bricks have come in useful for stoves," Gregor thought unconcernedly. The church stood as of old, small, huddling into the ground. Its long unpainted roof was gilded with rust, its walls were variegated with brown stains of dampness, and where the plaster had fallen away the bare brick showed a bright, fresh red.

The streets were deserted. Two or three sleepy-eyed women passed him not far from the well. They bowed silently to him as though he were a stranger, and only when he had passed did they halt and stand staring after him.

He turned back. "I ought to go to the graveyard, to visit mother and Natalia," he thought, and walked along a lane leading in the direction of the cemetery. But after going a little distance he halted. His heart was heavy and sorrowful enough without that. "I'll go some other time," he decided, turning to make his way to Prokhor's hut. "It's all the same to them whether I come or not. They're at peace now. It's all over for them. Their graves are blanketed with snow. But the earth must be cold down inside there. . . . Well, they lived their time, and so quickly, as though in a dream. There they all lie together, side by side: my wife, and Mother, and Piotra and Daria. . . . The entire family has crossed to the other side and lie there side by side. They're well off there, but Father alone is lying in a strange country. He must find it dreary among strangers. . . ." Gregor no longer looked about him, but walked along gazing down at his feet, at the white, slightly damp, thawing snow, which was very soft, so soft that one did not even feel it underfoot and it made hardly any scrunch.

Then his thoughts turned to his children. They had grown strangely reserved, taciturn for their years, not as they had been when their mother was alive. Death had taken too much from them. They were frightened. Why had Poliushka broken into tears yesterday when she saw him? Children don't usually cry when they meet anyone; it was not like them. What had she been thinking about? And why did fear flash into her eyes when he took her hand? Maybe all this time she had been thinking her father was dead and would never come back any more, and then when she saw him she had been afraid? In any case, he had no reason to reproach himself in regard to them. But he must tell Aksinia to have pity on them and to try to take their mother's place as far as she could. . . . Maybe they would grow attached to their stepmother. She was a good, kind woman. In her love for him she would love the children too.

He found this subject also painful and bitter to think about. It was not so simple as all that. Life itself was proving to be not so simple as it had seemed to him only recently. In his stupid, childish naïveté he had assumed that he had only to return home, to change his greatcoat for a peasant's coat, and everything would go according to prescription; no one would say a word to him, nobody would reproach him, everything would settle down of itself, and he would live and end his days as a peaceable grain-grower and a model villager. But no, the reality didn't look quite so simple.

He cautiously opened Zykov's wicket gate, which was hanging by one hinge. Wearing well-patched, huge felt boots and a three-cornered cap drawn right down over his eyes, Prokhor was walking towards the steps, jauntily swinging an empty milk-pail. White drops of milk sprinkled invisibly over the snow.

"Had a good night, comrade commander?" he greeted Gregor.

"Praise be!"

"Getting drunk's good work!"

"But why is the pail empty? Have you been milking the cow yourself?"

With a nod Prokhor shifted his cap to the back of his head, and only then did Gregoi notice that his friend's face was gloomy.

"Well, is the devil going to milk her for me? Yes, I've milked her, the accursed female! I only hope she gets a bellyache as the result!" Prokhor furiously flung away the pail and curtly said: "Let's go into the hut."

"How about your wife?" Gregor asked irresolutely.

"The devils have eaten her with kvass! Before there was any sign of dawn she raked herself together and drove off to Kruzhilinsky for firewood. She set about me as soon as I arrived home after leaving you last night. She lectured me and gave me further orders, and then she jumped up: 'I'm going off to get some firewood. Maksaev's daughters-in-law are going today, and I'll go with them.' 'Go by all means,' I thought, 'go for pears if you like, and a smooth road to you!' I got up, lit the stove, and went to milk the cow. I milked her all right! Do you think a man's capable of doing such things with only one arm?"

"You should have asked some woman to do it for you, you idiot!"

"A sheep's an idiot, it'll suck at its mother until the Feast of the Blessed Virgin; but all my life I've never been an idiot. I thought I'd manage it by myself. Well, and I did. I crawled under that cow on all fours; but, damn her, she wouldn't stand still, but shifted about all the time. I even took my cap off in order not to alarm her, but it made no difference. My shirt got wet through with sweat while I was milking her, and I had hardly stretched out my hand to take the pail from under her when she let fly with her leg. The pail went one way and I the other. And that's how I milked her. She's not a cow, she's a devil with horns! I spat into her face and left her. I can do without milk. Shall we have a drink?"

"Have you got any?"

"One bottle. Extra good."

"Well, it'll be enough."

"Come in, be my guest. Shall I fry you some eggs? I can get them ready in two seconds."

Gregor cut up some fat bacon and helped Prokhor to get the fire going at the front of the stove. They watched without talking as the pieces of rosy fat hissed, melted, and slipped about the frying-pan. Then Prokhor drew out a dusty bottle from behind the ikon cupboard.

"That's where I keep all my secrets from my wife," he explained briefly.

They ate in the small, well-heated best room, drank, and talked in undertones.

With whom could Gregor share his most secret thoughts if not with Prokhor? He sat at the table, his long, muscular legs spread wide apart, and his hoarse deep voice sounded husky:

"While I was in the army and all the way home I thought of how I'd live close to the earth, and rest among my family from all the devilish business of war. It's no joke not to have slipped off your horse for eight years, so to speak. Even in your dreams and almost every night you dream of all that glory: either you're killing someone, or they're killing you. . . . But now I can see, Prokhor, that it's not going to turn out as I thought. . . . I can see that others, not I, are going to plough the land, to take care of it. . . ."

"Did you have a talk with Mikhail yesterday?"

"I had that honeyed pleasure!"

"And what did he say?"

Gregor crossed his fingers.

"That's the state of our friendship. He's throwing my service with the Whites up in my face; he thinks I'm nursing designs against the new régime, hiding a knife against it in my breast. He's afraid there'll be a rising, but what the devil I want it for he himself doesn't know, the fool!"

"He said the same thing to me."

Gregor smiled cheerlessly.

"During our advance on Poland we came across a certain Ukrainian who asked us for arms to defend his village. Bandits had entered the place, plundered them all, and slaughtered their cattle. The commander of our regiment—I was present at the time—said: 'Give you arms and you'll go off to the bandits yourselves!' But the

Ukrainian laughed and said: 'You only arm us, comrade, and then we'll not only keep the bandits out of the village but you too.' And just now I'm thinking rather like that Ukrainian: if only it was possible to have neither Whites nor Reds in Tatarsk, it would be much better. In my view my kinsman Mitka Korshunov, say, and Mikhail Koshevoi are both tarred with the same brush. Mikhail thinks I'm so devoted to the Whites that I can't live without them. The horse-radish! I'm devoted to them all right! Recently, when we were advancing into the Crimea, I happened to run up against a Kornilov officer in a fight—a brisk little colonel, with his moustache trimmed English-fashion, two streaks like snot under his nose. And I tackled him with such fervour that my heart leaped for joy! I left that poor little colonel with half his cap and half his head on his shoulders, and his officer's white cockade went flying. . . . That's how much I'm devoted to them! They too have salted my life more than enough. With my own blood I earned my way to that accursed officer's rank, but among the officers I was like a white crow. The swine, they never regarded me as a man, they scorned giving me their hands; and do you think that after that— They can go to hell! It makes me sick even to talk about it. And to suggest that I should want to restore their régime again! To invite the General Fitzhelaurovs here! I've tried that game once, and I was hiccuping for a whole year after. I've had enough, I've learned my lesson, I've felt it all on my own back."

As he soaked his bread in the hot fat, Prokhor said:

"There isn't going to be any rising. To begin with, there are only a few Cossacks left, and those who've come through have also learned their lesson. They've shed the blood of their brothers to further orders, and they've grown so peaceable and sensible that you couldn't drag them into a rising at the end of a rope. And be-sides, the people have grown hungry for a peaceful life. You should have seen how everybody worked this summer: they piled great stacks of hay, and harvested all the corn down to the last grain. They're groaning with the effort, but they're ploughing and sowing as though, you'd say, every one of them intended to live a hundred years. No, there's no point in talking about a rising. It's stupid talk-ing about it. Though the devil knows what the Cossacks may get into their heads next."

"What can they get into their heads? What are you hinting at?"

"Neighbours of ours have got it into their heads. . . ."

"Well?"

"Call it 'well' if you like! A rising has broken out in Voroniezh province, somewhere beyond Boguchar."

"That's all rot!"

"Why is it? A militia-man I know told me about it yesterday. It seems the authorities are intending to send the militia there."

"But where's 'there'?"

"To Monastirshchizna, Sukhoi Donietz, Paseka, Stara, and Nova Kalitva and elsewhere in that district. They say it's quite a big rising."

"Why didn't you say anything about it yesterday, you plucked goose?"

"I didn't want to in front of Mikhail, and besides, there's no pleasure in talking about such things. I never want to hear another word about that sort of thing."

Gregor grew glum. After long reflection he said:

"That's bad news."

"It's nothing to do with you. Let the *khokhols* worry about it. They'll have their arses beaten into sores, and then they'll learn how to rise. But it's nothing whatever to do with you and me. I don't feel at all sorry for them."

"It'll make things difficult for me, though."

"Why will it?"

"Can't you see? If the regional authorities have the same opinion of me as Koshevoi, then I shan't be able to avoid unpleasantness. A rising in the next province, and I a former officer, and an insurgent into the bargain. . . . Now do you see?"

Prokhor stopped chewing and sat thinking. This aspect had not occurred to him before. His head was fuddled with drink, and he thought slowly and painfully.

"But where do you come in, Pantalievich?" he asked in astonishment.

Gregor knitted his brows in his vexation and did not answer. He was obviously disturbed by the news. Prokhor was about to pass his glass across to him, but he pushed his friend's hand away and said resolutely:

"I'm not having any more."

"But won't you have just one more? Drink till you turn black!

The only way of stifling this joyful life is with vodka."

"Turn black by yourself. Your head's stupid enough already, it'll be the death of you sooner or later. I've got to go to Vieshenska today, to register."

Prokhor gazed fixedly at him. Gregor's sunburnt and weather-beaten face burned with a deep brown flush, his skin was a dull white only at the very roots of the hair combed back off his forehead. He was calm enough, this soldier who had seen so much, with whom war and adversity had made Prokhor kin. His rather prominent eyes had a morose gaze, a look of harsh weariness.

"You aren't afraid they'll—they'll put you in prison?" Prokhor asked.

Gregor warmly answered:

"That's just what I am afraid of, my lad! I never have been in prison, and I fear prisons more than death. But it's clear that I've got to experience that happiness too."

"You shouldn't have come home," Prokhor said commiseratingly.

"But where else was I to go?"

"You should have hidden somewhere in a town and waited till all this business has settled down, and then come home."

Gregor waved his hand and laughed.

"That's not my way. To wait till you're caught is worst of all. And how could I leave the children?"

"A fine idea! Haven't they lived without you already? You could have taken them later, and your darling too. And, by the way, I forgot to tell you: your masters, those you and Aksinia worked for before the war, have both gone."

"The Listnitskys?"

"That's the name. My kinsman Zakhar retreated as orderly to the younger Listnitsky, and he told me the old man died of typhus at Morozovsky, but the younger got as far as Yekaterinodar; and there his wife had an affair with General Pokrovsky, and he couldn't stand it, so he shot himself in his temper."

"Well, they can go to the devil!" Gregor said unconcernedly. "I'm sorry for the good men that have been lost, but nobody's going to be sorry for those two." He rose, put on his greatcoat, and, as he held the door-handle, said reflectively: "Though, damn it, I always felt envious of such men as the younger Listnitsky or Koshevoi. . . . Everything was clear to them from the very beginning, but nothing is clear to me even now. Both of them saw straight roads before them, and saw the ends of them; but ever since 1917 I've been going round and round in a circle, reeling like a drunken man. I broke away from the Whites, but I didn't join up with the Reds, and I float like dung in a hole in the ice. . . . You see, Prokhor, of course I ought to have remained in the Red Army until the end; maybe then everything would have gone well for me. And at first, you know, I served the Soviet régime with all my heart; but afterwards everything went wrong. I was a stranger among the Whites, among their command; they always suspected me. And how could it be otherwise? The son of a farmer, an illiterate Cossack—what kinship had I with them? They just didn't trust me! And afterwards it was just the same with the Reds. After all, I'm not blind, I saw how the commissar and the Communists in the squadron watched me. . . . During a battle they didn't take their eyes off me, they watched my every step, and I suppose they were thinking: 'Ah, that swine, the former White, the Cossack officer, we must see he doesn't betray us!' And when I noticed it my heart ran cold. Towards the end I couldn't stand their distrust any longer. After all, even a stone will split with heat. And it was a good job they did to demobilize me. It brought the end nearer." He cleared his throat huskily, said nothing for a moment, and then, not looking at Prokhor, went on in a changed tone: "Thanks for the treat. I'm off now. Keep well. If I return, I'll drop in towards evening. Clear that bottle away, for if your wife comes home she'll smash a frying-pan over your back."

Prokhor accompanied him to the steps and whispered in the porch:

"Ah, Pantalievich, see they don't fix you there!"

"I will!" Gregor answered in a reserved tone.

He did not go home, but dropped down to the river, untied someone's boat from the landing-stage, bailed the water out with his palms, then pulled a stake out of the fence, broke the ice to make a channel, and rowed to the farther side.

Dark-green, wind-lashed waves were rolling westward along the Don. In the quiet water by the banks they broke away the fragile, transparent thin ice and sent the emerald strands of water-weed swaying. Over the banks hung the crystal tinkle of colliding ice, the river-side shingle softly hissed as it was washed by the water; but in the middle of the river, where the current was swift and steady, Gregor heard only the muffled plash and seething of waves piling against the left side of the boat, and the low, deep, incessant roar of the wind in the Donside forest.

He dragged the boat half out of the water, then squatted down, removed his boots, and carefully rewound his leg-rags, to make walking easier.

He arrived at Vieshenska towards midday.

The regional Military Commissariat was crowded and noisy. Telephone bells were ringing sharply, doors were slammed, armed men went in and out, the dry rattle of typewriters came from various rooms. In the corridor a couple of dozen Red Army men stood surrounding a stocky little man dressed in a flounced sheepskin jacket, talking and interrupting one another excitedly, and roaring with laughter. As Gregor walked along the corridor, two Red Army men wheeled out a machine-gun from a room beyond. Its small wheels clattered softly on the uneven wooden floor. One of the gunners, a beefy, hefty man, jokingly shouted: "Now then, out of the way or I'll crush you!"

"It looks as if they're really going off to suppress a rising," Gregor thought.

He was not detained long over the registration. After hurriedly noting his papers, the secretary of the Military Commissariat said:

"Go to the political department of the Don Cheka. As a former officer you'll have to report to them."

"Very well." Gregor saluted, in no way betraying the agitation which had taken possession of him.

In the square he halted irresolutely. He ought to go to the political department, but all his being was resisting violently. "They'll clap you in prison!" an inward voice told him, and he shivered with fear and loathing. He stood by the school fence, gazing with unseeing eyes at the dunged earth and saw himself with bound arms, descending a dirty ladder into a cellar, and behind him a man firmly clutching the rough butt of a pistol. He clenched his fists and stared at the swollen blue veins of his arms. And they would bind those arms? The blood rushed to his face. No, he would not go there today! Tomorrow, if you liked, but today he would go back to the village, he would spend this day with his children, he would see Aksinia and return to Vieshenska tomorrow. Let his foot ache with so much walking! He would go home for just one day and then return here —of course he would return. Come what may tomorrow, but not today.

"Ah, Melekhov! It's ages, ages. . . ."

Gregor turned. Yakov Fomin, Piotra's regimental comrade, former commander of the insurgent 28th Regiment of the Don army, came up to him.

Fomin was no longer the awkwardly and carelessly dressed Cossack of the ataman regiment whom Gregor had once known. In two years he had changed amazingly: his well-cut cavalry greatcoat neatly fitted his figure, his red moustache was twisted impudently, and all his form, the exaggeratedly swaggering gait, the self-satisfied smile, revealed a consciousness of his superiority and distinction.

"What fate has brought you here?" he asked, shaking Gregor's hand, staring into his eyes with his own wide-set blue eyes.

"I've been demobilized. I've just been to the Military Commissariat."

"Been back some time?"

"I arrived yesterday."

"I often recall your brother Piotra Pantalievich. He was a good Cossack, but his death was a pity. He and I were secret friends. You ought not to have joined the uprising last year, Melekhov. You made a mistake."

Gregor felt bound to say something, and he said:

"Yes. The Cossacks made a mistake. . . ."

"What force were you in?"

"The First Cavalry Brigade."

"What as?"

"Squadron commander."

"You don't say! I'm in command of a squadron too, now. We've got a defensive force here at Vieshenska." He looked about him and, lowering his voice, suggested: "Listen, let's move on. Walk a little way with me. There are too many people here, and we don't get any chance of talking."

They walked along the street. Looking out of the corner of his eye at Gregor, Fomin asked:

"Are you thinking of living at home?"

"Where else should I live? Of course."

"Farming?"

"Yes."

Fomin commiseratively shook his head and sighed. "You've chosen a bad time, Melekhov, very bad. . . . You shouldn't have come back for a year or even two yet."

"Why not?"

Taking Gregor by the elbow and bending slightly towards him, Fomin whispered:

"There's trouble in the region. The Cossacks are very discontented with the food-requisitioning. There's a rising in Boguchar County. You'd be well advised to slip away from here, young man, and quickly! Piotra and I were great friends, that's why I'm advising you to clear out."

"I've got nowhere to clear out to."

"Well, watch out! I'm telling you this because the political department is beginning to arrest the former officers. This very week three ensigns from Dudarevka and one from Reshetovka have been brought in, and they're being brought in in droves from the other side of the Don, and they're even beginning to put the screw on rank-and-file Cossacks. Draw your own conclusions, Gregor Pantalievich."

"Thank you for the advice, but I'm not clearing out all the same," Gregor said stubbornly.

"Well, that's your business."

Fomin turned to talking of the situation in the region, of his relations with the regional authorities and the regional military commissar, Shakhaev. Occupied with his own thoughts, Gregor listened to him inattentively. They walked along for three blocks, then Fomin halted.

"I've got a call to make. So long." Putting his hand to his fur cap, he took a chilly leave of Gregor and went down a side turning, his new shoulder-straps creaking, carrying himself erect and with absurd dignity. Gregor followed him with his eyes, then turned back.

As he went up the stone steps of the political department he thought.

"If it's the end, then the sooner the better. There's no point in dragging it out. You knew how to do harm, Gregor; now know how to answer for it!"

Chapter 8

About eight in the morning Aksinia raked together the coals in the stove and sat down on the bench, wiping her flushed, sweaty face with her apron. She had risen before dawn, in order to be free of cooking as early as possible; she had boiled a chicken with vermicelli, had made pancakes, had poured cream liberally over small dumplings, and had put them on to fry. She knew Gregor was fond of fried dumplings, and she had prepared this festive meal in the hope that her beloved would dine with her.

She felt strongly impelled to go along to the Melekhovs' under some pretext, to spend if only a minute there, to glance at Gregor if only with one eye. It seemed quite impossible that he should be there, next door, and she not see him. Yet she mastered her desire and did not go. After all, she was not a girl. At her age there was no point in behaving indecorously.

She washed her face and hands more carefully than usual, put on a clean shirt and a new embroidered underskirt. She stood a long time irresolutely before the open chest: what should she wear, now she had to decide. It was hardly the thing to dress herself in her best on a work day, yet she did not want to remain in her simple working-clothes. Not knowing what to choose, she knitted her brows and carelessly turned over the ironed skirts. Finally she resolutely picked up a dark-blue skirt and an almost unworn blue bodice trimmed with black lace. It was the best she possessed. In the last resort, did it matter what the neighbours thought? Let today be a work day for them; for her it was a holiday. She hurriedly dressed herself in her finery and went across to the mirror. A faint, astonished smile slipped over her lips; youthful, sparkling eyes gazed at her curiously and merrily. She closely, severely examined her face, then sighed with relief. No, her beauty had not faded. More than one Cossack yet would halt when he met her and would watch with flaming eyes as she went by!

As she adjusted her skirt before the mirror she said aloud: "Well, Gregor Pantalievich, now look out!" Feeling that she was blushing, she broke into a quiet, stifled laugh. Even so she did not fail to find several grey hairs on her temples, and pulled them out. Gregor must not see anything that would remind him of her age. For him she wanted to be as young today as she had been seven years before.

She managed somehow to stay at home until dinner-time, but then could restrain herself no longer and, throwing a shawl of white goat's wool around her shoulders, went along to the Melekhovs'. Dunia was alone in the house. Aksinia greeted her and asked:

"You haven't had dinner yet, have you?"

"Have dinner on time with such stay-at-homes? My husband's at the Soviet, and Gregor's gone off to Vieshenska. I've already fed the children, and now I'm waiting for the grown-ups!"

Outwardly calm, by neither movement nor word betraying the disillusionment she felt, Aksinia said:

"And I thought you'd all be at home. And when will Grisha— Gregor Pantalievich be back? Today?"

Dunia ran a swift glance over her neighbour in her finery and said reluctantly:

"He's gone off to register."

"When did he expect to be back?"

Tears glittered in Dunia's eyes. With reproach in her stammering voice she said:

"You've chosen a fine time—to dress yourself up. . . . But you don't know—that he mayn't come back at all. . . ."

"What do you mean?"

"Mikhail says he'll be arrested at Vieshenska. . . ." Dunia began to weep meagre, angry tears. Wiping her eyes with her sleeve, she cried: "Curse it! Curse this life! When will it all end? He went off, and the children—you'd say they'd gone mad, they wouldn't give me a minute's peace: 'Where's Daddy gone and when is he coming back?' And how am I to know? I sent them out into the yard, but my own heart was aching. . . . What do you call this accursed life? There's never any peace for anyone, though you scream your lungs out for it!"

"If he doesn't get back by the evening I'll go to Vieshenska tomorrow and find out." Aksinia said these words in such an unconcerned tone that she might have been talking of something quite commonplace which did not call for the least agitation.

Amazed at her calm, Dunia sighed:

"It's no good expecting him now, that's clear. He came back to his own misfortune!"

"We don't know anything at all yet. Now do stop shouting, or the children will start thinking things. Good-bye!"

Gregor returned late that evening. He spent a little time in the house, then went to see Aksinia.

The anxiety in which she had lived all that long day somewhat blunted the joy of the meeting. By the evening she felt as though she had been at work all day without once straightening her back. Oppressed and weary with expectation, she had lain down on the bed and was dozing. But, hearing footsteps outside the window, she jumped up with the energy of a girl.

"Why didn't you tell me you were going to Vieshenska?" she asked, putting her arms around Gregor and unbuttoning his great-coat.

"I didn't have a chance to say; I was in a hurry."

"But Dunia and I cried to each other, each in her own way, because we thought you wouldn't be coming back."

Gregor smiled wanly.

"No, it isn't as bad as that." After a pause he added: "Not yet."

He limped to the table and began to eat. Through the open door the best room, the broad wooden bed in one corner, a chest with its copper bindings dully glittering, was visible. Everything was as it had been in those days when as a youngster he had called while Stepan was out. He could see hardly any change; it was as though time had gone past this place and had not glanced inside. Even the old smell remained: the yeasty smell of fresh brewed beer, scrubbed floors, and a very faint, almost imperceptible scent of faded thyme. It was as though he had last left this house at dawn only the other day. Yet in reality how long ago it was! . . .

He suppressed a sigh and deliberately began to roll himself a cigarette. But for some reason his fingers trembled, and he sprinkled the tobacco over his knees.

Aksinia hurriedly laid the table. The cold vermicelli had to be warmed up. She ran to the shed for firewood and, panting and rather pale, began to build up the fire at the front of the stove. She blew on the coals, sending the sparks flying, yet she managed to take a look at the huddled, silently smoking Gregor.

"How did your affairs go? Did you settle everything?"

"Everything went well."

"Why did Dunia get it into her head that they were sure to arrest you? She gave me a fright too."

Gregor frowned and threw his cigarette away with a gesture of irritation.

"Mikhail's been blowing in her ear! It's he who's making it all up and calling down trouble on my head."

Aksinia went to the table. He took her by the hands.

"But you know," he said, looking down into her eyes, "my affairs aren't in too good a way. As I went into the political department I myself thought I wouldn't be coming out again. There's no denying it, I did command a division during the rising, and I was a squadron commander. Such as me are taken up at once."

"But what did they say to you?"

"They gave me a form to fill in, and I had to tell all I had done during my service. But I'm not much of a hand with the pen. I haven't had to do much writing in my time, and I sat there a couple of hours describing all my past. Then two others came into the room and asked all about the rising. They were all right, quite friendly. The older man asked me: 'Would you like some tea? Only you'll have to have saccharine.' 'What do I want tea for,' I thought. 'So long as my legs get me away from you whole!'" He was silent for a moment, then added contemptuously, as though speaking of some outsider: "I proved to be rather watery when it came to settling accounts. I was a bit of a coward."

He was angry with himself for having shown cowardice at Vieshenska and for not having the strength to fight the fear which had possessed him. He was doubly annoyed because his fears had proved groundless. Now all his agitation seemed absurd and shameful. His mind had run on this subject all the way back, and maybe that was why he told Aksinia all about it, laughing at himself and a little exaggerating what he had gone through.

Aksinia listened to him attentively, then gently released her hands and went across to the stove. As she made up the fire she asked:

"But how about the future?"

"I've got to go and report there again in a week's time."

"Do you think they'll take you after all?"

"It seems like it. Sooner or later they'll take me."

"Then what are we to do? How shall we live, Grisha?"

"I don't know. Let's talk about that later. Have you got any water I can wash with?"

They sat down to supper, and once more that fullness of happiness which she had experienced in the morning returned to Aksinia. Gregor was here, at her side; she could look at him without removing her eyes, without having to think that outsiders were catching her glances; with her eyes she could say all without concealment and without embarrassment. Lord, how she had longed for him, how she had worn herself out, how her body had yearned for his great, ungracious hands! She hardly touched the food; leaning a little forward, she watched as Gregor ate hungrily, her misted eyes caressing his face, his swarthy neck tightly gripped by the standing collar of his tunic, his broad shoulders, his hands lying heavily on the table. She avidly breathed in the mingled scent of bitter masculine sweat and tobacco which came from him, the familiar and precious scent peculiar to him. With eyes blindfolded she could have distinguished her Gregor from a thousand other men even by his scent. A deep flush burned on her cheeks, her heart beat fast and heavily. This evening she could not be a really attentive housewife, for she saw nothing but Gregor all around her. But he did not demand attention: he cut his own bread, looked for and found the salt-cellar on the stove, helped himself to a second plate of vermicelli.

"I'm as hungry as a dog," he said with a smile, as though excusing himself. "I've eaten nothing since morning."

Only then did Aksinia recall her domestic duties; she jumped up hurriedly.

"Oh, what a head I've got! I've forgotten the dumplings and the pancakes. Have some chicken, do! Eat lots more, my darling. I'll have everything on the table in a moment."

But how long and methodically he ate! As though he had had no food for a week! It was quite superfluous to make him a feast. She waited patiently, but at last she could wait no longer. She sat down beside him; with her left hand she drew his head to her, with her right she took the clean, embroidered hand-towel and herself wiped her beloved's greasy lips and chin. Then, holding her breath, half-closing her eyes so that tiny orange sparks spirted from them in the darkness, she pressed her lips strongly against his.

In truth, it takes very little to make man happy. At any rate, Aksinia was happy that evening.

Chapter 9

Gregor could not endure meeting Koshevoi. Their relations had been determined on the first day of Gregor's return, and there was nothing more to talk about, nor any point in talking. Probably Mikhail also got no pleasure from seeing Gregor. He hired two carpenters, and they hurriedly repaired his small hut; they renewed the half-rotten rafters of the roof, took to pieces and rebuilt one of the tottering walls, fashioned new lintels, frames, and doors.

After his return from Vieshenska, Gregor went to the village Revolutionary Committee, handed Koshevoi his documents, certified by the Military Commissariat, and left again without a word of farewell. He went to live with Aksinia, taking the children and some of his possessions with him. As Dunia saw him off to his new home, she burst into tears.

"Brother dear, don't be angry with me. I've done you no wrong," she said, gazing imploringly at him.

"Why should I be angry, Dunia? Now, don't be upset," he soothed her. "Come and see us sometimes. I'm the only one of the family left to you, I was always sorry for you and I feel sorry now. . . . But your husband—that's another question. You and I shan't drop our friendship."

"We'll be leaving the house soon. Don't be annoyed."

"Of course you mustn't," Gregor said in a vexed tone. "Stay in the house until spring at any rate. You're no trouble to me, and there's room enough for me and the children with Aksinia."

"Are you going to marry her, Grisha?"

"There's plenty of time for that," Gregor said indefinitely.

"You marry her, brother, she's a good woman," Dunia said decisively. "Our dead mother said she was the only wife for you. She came to love her towards the end and often went to see her before she died."

"It sounds as if you were trying to persuade me!" Gregor said with a smile. "Whom else should I marry, if not her? Not old crone Andronikha, surely?"

Andronikha was the most ancient beldam in Tatarsk. She had

long passed her century. As Dunia recalled her tiny doubled-up figure she burst into a laugh.

"The things you say, brother! I was only asking. Don't tell anyone I asked you."

"Who ever else I ask, I shall invite you to the wedding." Gregor jokingly clapped his sister on her back and left his old home with a light heart.

To tell the truth he was quite unconcerned where he lived, so long as he could live in peace. But peace was the one thing he could not find. He spent several days in an oppressive idleness. He tried to tackle certain pieces of work on Aksinia's farm, but at once felt that he could do nothing. He had no inclination for anything. The repressive uncertainty of his position tormented him, prevented him from living; not for a minute did he forget that he might be arrested and, at best, thrown into prison, and that he might even be shot.

Aksinia would wake up in the middle of the night and find him wide awake. Usually he was lying on his back, his hands behind his head, staring into the darkness; and his eyes were cold and hard. Aksinia knew what he was thinking about. There was no way in which she could help him. She herself suffered as she saw how painful it was for him, and guessed that her hopes of life with him were again receding into the distance. She did not question him about anything. Let him decide it all for himself. Only once, one night, when she awoke and saw the livid glow of a cigarette beside her, did she say:

"Grisha, you never sleep. Perhaps you'd better leave the village for the time being. Or perhaps we could go off somewhere and hide."

He thoughtfully covered her legs with the blanket and answered reluctantly:

"I'll think about it. You sleep."

"And we could return later on, when everything had quieted down here, couldn't we?"

He again replied indefinitely, as though he had made no decision whatever:

"We'll see how things go. You sleep, Ksinia." He cautiously and gently pressed his lips to her bare, silkily cool shoulder.

But in reality he had already made a decision: he would not go to Vieshenska again. The man who had received him last time at the political department would wait for him in vain. He had sat behind his table, his greatcoat flung across his shoulders, stretching himself with a cracking of joints and artificially yawning as he listened to Gregor's story of the rising. Well, he would hear no more. All the story was told.

The day Gregor was due to go to the political department he would clear out of the village. If necessary, for a long time. Where to, he himself did not know, but he had firmly resolved to clear out. He had no desire either to die or to sit in prison. He had made his choice, but he did not want to talk about it prematurely to Aksinia. There was no point in poisoning her last few days with him—as it was, they were not so very cheerful. He must speak about it on the last day, he had decided. But now let her sleep calmly, her face in his armpit. Frequently during those nights she said: "It's good for me to sleep under your wing." Well, let her sleep meantime. Poor wretch, she had no long time left in which to nestle against him.

During the day Gregor played with the children, then went wandering aimlessly through the village. In company he felt more cheerful. One day Prokhor proposed meeting at Nikita Melnikov's, to drink with the other young Cossacks who had been their regimental comrades. Gregor flatly refused. He knew from the villagers' conversation that they were discontented with the grain-requisitioning and that there would inevitably be talk of this over the drinks. He did not wish to draw suspicion down on himself, and even when he chanced to meet acquaintances he avoided talking about politics. He had had enough of politics, they had done him enough harm already.

His caution was all the less superfluous because the grain-requisitioning was yielding poor results, and in consequence three old men were arrested as hostages and sent under escort to Vieshenska.

The following day, close to the co-operative shop, Gregor saw the former artillery-man Zakhar Kramskov, who had recently returned from the Red Army. He was thoroughly drunk and reeled as he walked; but as he came up to Gregor he buttoned up all the buttons of his dirty jacket and said hoarsely:

"I wish you health, Gregor Pantalievich."

"Your health!" Gregor shook the stocky and well-knit artillery-man's hefty fist.

"Do you recognize me?"

"Why, of course!"

"Do you remember how last year our battery saved you close to Bokovskoi? Without us your cavalry would have had a bad time. The Reds we bowled over that day, by hell! I was sighting for number-one gun then." Zakhar beat his fist hollowly against his broad chest.

Gregor looked furtively around—some Cossacks standing a little way off were staring at them, listening to their conversation. The corners of Gregor's lips quivered, and he revealed his white, sturdy teeth in an angry snarl.

"You're drunk!" he said in an undertone, through his clenched teeth. "Go and sleep it off, and don't talk so much!"

"No, I'm not drunk," the fuddled artillery-man shouted. "Or maybe I'm drunk with misery! I've come home, but it's not life you live here, but bloody hell! The Cossacks don't live any more, and there aren't any Cossacks! Half a ton of grain they've requisitioned from me, and what do you call that? Did they sow it, that they have the right to take it away? Do they know what makes the grain grow?"

He stared with senseless, bloodshot eyes and suddenly, swaying, pawed Gregor, breathing heavy vodka fumes into his face.

"Why are you wearing trousers without stripes? Have you signed up as a peasant? We won't let you! My dear old Gregor Pantalievich, we've got to fight again! We'll say, as we did last year: 'Down with the commune, but hurrah for the Soviet régime!'"

Gregor roughly pushed him away and muttered:

"Go home, you drunken swine! Do you know what you're saying?"

Kramskov thrust out one hand, spreading out the tobacco-stained fingers, and mumbled:

"Excuse me if there's something wrong. Excuse me, but I'm speaking sincerely to you, as to my commander. . . . As to my own father commander: we've got to fight!"

Gregor silently turned away and walked home across the square. The impression of this untimely meeting remained with him until evening; he recalled Kramskov's drunken shouts, the Cossacks' sympathetic silence and smiles, and thought: "But I must clear out quickly. No good will come of this. . . ."

He was due to go to Vieshenska on Saturday. Within three days he would have to leave his native village. But that was not to be: on Thursday night—he was already getting ready for sleep—someone knocked violently at the door. Aksinia went out into the porch. He heard her ask: "Who's there?" He did not catch the answer, but, moved by a vague feeling of anxiety, he rose from the bed and went to the window. The latch rattled in the porch. The first to enter was Dunia. Gregor caught sight of her pale face and, even before he asked any questions, picked up his cap and greatcoat from the bench.

"Brother—"

"What is it?" he quietly asked as he thrust his arms into his greatcoat sleeves.

Dunia hurriedly panted:

"Brother, clear out at once! Four horsemen have arrived from Vieshenska. They're sitting in the best room. . . . They talked in whispers, but I heard. I stood close to the door and heard everything. I heard Mikhail say you must be arrested. . . . He's telling them all about you. . . . Clear out!"

Gregor strode swiftly across to her, put his arms around her, and kissed her strongly on the cheek.

"Thank you, sister. Now go back or they'll notice you've come out. Good-bye!" He turned to Aksinia. "Bread! Quick! No, not a whole loaf, only the crust."

So his brief life of peace was at an end. . . . He acted as though in a battle, hurriedly yet confidently; he went into the best room, cautiously kissed the sleeping children, then took Aksinia into his arms.

"Good-bye! I'll let you have news of myself soon. Prokhor will tell you. Look after the children. Fasten the door. If they knock, say I've gone to Vieshenska. Well, good-bye, and don't grieve, Ksinia!" As he kissed her he felt the warm, salty moisture of tears on his lips.

He had no time to comfort her and to listen to her helpless, broken words. He gently unfastened the arms embracing him, strode into the porch, listened, then threw the outside door wide open. The chilly wind blowing up from the Don lashed in his face. For a second he closed his eyes, to get accustomed to the darkness.

Aksinia heard the snow scrunching under Gregor's feet. And

every step drove a sharp pain into her heart. Then the sound of footsteps died away and the wattle fence creaked. Everything grew quite still; only the wind howled in the forest beyond the Don.

She tried to catch some sound through the roar of the wind, but she heard nothing. She suddenly felt cold. She went into the kitchen and put out the lamp.

PART VII

The Fugitive

THE FUGITIVE

Chapter 1

L<small>ATE</small> in the autumn of 1920, when, owing to the poor results
achieved by the grain-requisitioning policy, the Soviet government
found it necessary to organize grain-collection detachments, unrest
broke out among the Cossack population of the Don. Small armed
bands sprang into existence in the upper Don districts of Shumilinsk,
Kazanska, Migulinsk, Mieshkovsky, Vieshenska, Yelanska, and elsewhere. These bands were the response of the richer section of the
Cossackry to the organization of grain-collection detachments and
to the Soviet government's increasingly strict measures to carry out
the grain-requisitioning policy.

The majority of the bands, which consisted of anything from five
to twenty men, were formed from local Cossacks who were former
active White Guards. They included men who during the years
1918 and 1919 had served in punitive detachments, non-commissioned officers, and junior officers of the former Don army who had
evaded the Soviet September mobilization, insurgents who had distinguished themselves by military exploits and the execution of Red
Army prisoners during the previous year's rising in the upper Don
area—in short, men who in no circumstances could settle down under
the Soviet régime.

The bands fell upon the requisitioning detachments in the villages, turned back villagers' wagons carrying grain to the collection-points, killed Communists and non-party Cossacks devoted to the Soviet régime, and struggled to the best of their knowledge and power.

The task of exterminating these bands was entrusted to a garrison battalion for the upper Don region, stationed at Vieshenska. But all the attempts to destroy the bands scattered over the extensive Don territory proved unsuccessful, primarily because the local inhabitants were sympathetic to the rebels, supplied them with food, informed them of the movements of the Red Army forces, and also concealed them from pursuit. But in addition the battalion commander Kaparin, a Social Revolutionary and former staff captain in the Czarist army, was by no means anxious to see the elimination of the counter-revolutionary forces in his area and did all he could to hinder operations against them. Only occasionally, when driven into action by the chairman of the party regional committee, did he make brief expeditions with his troops, quickly returning to Vieshenska on the pretext that he must not disperse his forces or take imprudent risks, leaving Vieshenska and its regional organizations and warehouses without adequate defence. The battalion, which numbered some four hundred bayonets and fourteen machine-guns, performed garrison duties; the men guarded prisoners, brought water, chopped down trees in the forest, and also, as part of their compulsory labour duty, collected gall nuts from oak trees, for the manufacture of ink. The battalion successfully supplied wood and ink to all the numerous regional organizations and offices, but meantime the number of small insurgent bands in the area was growing alarmingly. And not until December, when a considerable rising broke out in the Boguchar County of Voriniezh province, contiguous with the upper Don region, was the timber-cutting and gall-nut collecting perforce brought to an end. By order of the army commander of the Don province the battalion, consisting of three companies and a machine-gun section, was sent, with the garrison cavalry squadron, the first battalion of the 12th grain-collecting Regiment, and two small local defence detachments, to crush the rising.

In a battle which was fought at the approaches to the village of Sukhoi Donietz the Vieshenska squadron, commanded by Yakov Fomin, attacked the lines of insurgents on the flank, swept them away, put them to flight and sabred some hundred and seventy men in the pursuit, while losing only three men. With few exceptions every man in the squadron was a Cossack, a native of the upper Don area. In this fight they were once more faithful to the age-old Cossack traditions: despite the protests of the two Communists in the squadron, after the battle almost half the men exchanged their old greatcoats and padded jackets for good sheepskins taken from the dead insurgents.

A few days after the rising had been suppressed the squadron was recalled to Kazanska. Here Fomin rested from the burdens of military life, amusing himself to the best of his ability. An incorrigible woman-chaser, a merry and sociable Cossack, he disappeared night after night, returning to his quarters only a little before dawn. When his men, with whom their commander was on familiar terms, saw Fomin in the street of an evening with his boots brilliantly polished, they exchanged knowing winks and remarked:

"Well, so our stallion is off to the mares again! Now he won't come out till dawn!"

Unknown to the squadron's commissar and political instructor, Fomin was in the habit of visiting the quarters of certain Cossacks with whom he was on good terms whenever they passed him the word that vodka was plentiful and a carousal was on the way. These visits occurred quite frequently. But soon the dashing commander grew bored and moody and almost entirely forgot his recent ways of finding amusement. He no longer cleaned his elegant leg-boots so diligently of an evening and did not bother to shave every day. He still occasionally dropped in for a drink at the quarters of fellow-villagers in the squadron, but he did not take any great part in the conversation.

The change in Fomin's behaviour coincided with a report which he received from Vieshenska: The political department of the Don Cheka briefly informed him that at Mikhailovka, in the neighbouring Ust-Miedvieditsa area, a garrison battalion with its commander Vakulin had revolted.

Vakulin happened to be a regimental comrade and friend of Fomin's. At one time they had served together in the insurgent Mironov corps, and together they had piled their arms when that force was surrounded by the Budionny cavalry. The friendly relations between Fomin and Vakulin had never been broken off, and only a little time before, at the beginning of September, Vakulin had visited Vieshenska. Even then he had ground his teeth and com-

plained to his old friend about the "domination of the commissars,
who are ruining the farmers with their grain-requisitioning and leading the country to perdition." In his heart Fomin agreed with Vakulin's views, but he conducted himself discreetly, with a cunning
which frequently served him in place of mother wit. Fomin was
naturally cautious, never in a hurry, and never committing himself
immediately one way or another. But soon after he had learned of
the revolt of Vakulin's battalion his habitual caution forsook him.
One evening, immediately prior to the squadron's departure for
Vieshenska, a number of the Cossacks gathered in the quarters of
the troop commander Alferov. A great horse-bucket stood filled with
vodka. An excited conversation went on around the table. Fomin,
who was present at this drinking-bout, listened in silence to the talk
and as silently bailed out vodka from the bucket. But when one of
the Cossacks began to recall how they had gone into the attack close
to Sukhoi Donietz, Fomin, thoughtfully twisting his moustache,
interrupted him:

"We cut down the Ukrainians pretty well, boys, but let's hope we
ourselves shan't be grieving before long. Supposing when we get
back to Vieshenska we find the grain-collection detachments have
pumped all the grain out of our homes? The Kazanska people are
thoroughly angry with the grain detachments. They sweep the bottoms of the corn-bins clean with brooms. . . ."

A hush fell over the room. Fomin looked at his men and said with
a forced smile:

"I was only joking. . . . Watch out, and don't let your tongues
wag, for the devil knows what a joke can sound like to others."

On his return to Vieshenska, Fomin, accompanied by half a troop
of his cavalry, rode home to Rubiezhin village. He did not ride right
into his yard, but dismounted at the gate, flung the rein to one of his
men, and strode into the hut.

He nodded coldly to his wife, made a low bow to his mother and
respectfully shook her hand, then embraced his children.

"But where's Father?" he asked, as he sat down on a stool and
placed his sabre between his knees.

"Gone to the mill," his mother answered. Glancing at her son, she
sternly ordered him: "Take off your cap, you heathen! Who ever sits

under the ikon with his cap on? Ah, Yakov, your head will be the
death of you!"

Fomin smiled forcedly and removed his cap, but made no attempt
to take off his outdoor clothes.

"Why aren't you taking off your coat?" his mother demanded.

"I've only ridden home for a minute or two on a visit. I never get
time when on service. . . ."

"We know your service!" the old woman said harshly, hinting at
her son's dissolute behaviour and his associations with women at
Vieshenska. The rumours of his conduct had long been going the
rounds of Rubiezhin.

Fomin's wife, a prematurely aged, pale-faced, and downtrodden
woman, glanced in alarm at her mother-in-law and went off to the
stove. To do something to please her husband, to ingratiate herself
with him, and to win at least one gracious look, she took a rag from
under the stove, went down on her knees, and, bent double, set to
work to clean off the thick mud clinging to his boots.

"What fine boots you've got, Yasha! But they're very muddy. I'll
get them clean for you, I'll clean them till they shine," she whispered
almost inaudibly, not raising her head, crawling on her knees round
her husband's feet.

He had not lived with her for years, and for years he had not had
any feeling except a faint, contemptuous pity for this woman whom
in his youth he had loved. But she had gone on loving him and forgave him everything, secretly hoping that he would come back to
her sooner or later. For many long years she had carried on the farm,
brought up the children, and done all she could to please her capri-
cious mother-in-law. All the burden of the field labour fell on her
meagre shoulders. Excessive labour and an ailment which had
afflicted her after the birth of their second child had sapped her
strength more and more as the years passed. She had grown very
thin. Her face had lost its bloom. Premature old age had thrown a
spider-web of furrows over her cheeks. The expression of terrified
humility which is found in the eyes of intelligent sick animals appeared in her eyes. She herself did not realize how swiftly she was
ageing, how her health was declining with every day, and she still
clung to hope, and on the rare occasions when they met she gazed at
her handsome husband with a timid love and admiration.

Fomin stared down at his wife's miserably bowed back and the gaunt, sharply outlined shoulder-blades beneath her blouse, at her large, trembling hands diligently cleaning the mud from his boots, and thought:

"She's a beauty, and no mistake! And that's what I slept with at one time! But she's aged terribly. How she has aged!"

"That's enough! I'll only get them muddy again," he said in a tone of annoyance, freeing his foot from his wife's hands.

She painfully straightened her back and rose to her feet. A faint flush appeared on her yellow cheeks. There was such an expression of love and doglike devotion in her humid eyes as she looked at Fomin that he turned away and asked his mother:

"Well, and how are you all getting on?"

"Just the same," the old woman replied morosely.

"Has a grain-collecting detachment been in the village?"

"It rode off to Nizhnii-Krivska only yesterday."

"Did they take any grain from us?"

"Yes. How much did they take, Davidka?"

"Grand-dad saw them, he knows. I think it was ten sacks."

"A—ah!" Fomin rose, glanced curtly at his son, and adjusted his sword-belt. His face turned pale as he asked: "Did you tell them whose grain they were taking?"

The old woman waved her hand and smiled, not without a hint of malevolence:

"They don't take much note of you! Their commander said: 'Everybody without distinction has got to hand over their surplus grain. Even if he is Fomin, even if he's the regional chairman himself, all the same we're going to take the surplus grain.' And with that they began to rummage in the corn-bins."

"I'll deal with them, Mother! I'll deal with them!" Fomin said thickly, and took a hurried leave of his family.

After this visit to his home he began discreetly to ascertain the feeling of the men in his squadron and was easily enough convinced that the majority of them were dissatisfied with the grain-requisitioning policy. Their wives and near and distant relations from the various villages and districts came on visits to them and told of how the grain-collecting detachments were carrying out searches and were collecting all the grain, leaving only enough for seed and food. As a result, at a garrison meeting held in Bazki at the end of January, men of the squadron openly interrupted a speech by the regional military commissar, Shakhaev. Shouts came from their ranks:

"Call off the requisitioning detachments!"

"It's time to finish taking our grain!"

"Down with the requisitioning commissars!"

In reply the Red Army men of the garrison company shouted:

"Counter-revolutionaries!"

"Break up those swine and send them to different regiments!"

The meeting was long and stormy. One of the few Communists in the garrison said anxiously to Fomin:

"You must say something, Comrade Fomin! Look at the game your squadron men are playing!"

Fomin smiled beneath his moustache: "But I'm a non-party man. Do you think they'll pay any attention to me?"

He did not break his silence and left the meeting long before it ended. He went out together with the battalion commander Kaparin. On the way to Vieshenska they fell to talking about the situation which had arisen and very quickly found a common language. A week later, during a talk in Fomin's quarters, Kaparin told him frankly:

"Either we act now, or we shall never act, get that clear, Yakov Yefimovich! We must take advantage of the opportunity. It's a very suitable moment. The Cossacks will support us. You have great authority throughout the region. The people will never be in a more favourable mood. Why are you silent? Make up your mind."

"What have I got to make up my mind about?" Fomin slowly pronounced, drawling his words and looking from under his brows. "The question's already decided. Only we must work out a plan, to be sure everything goes smoothly, so that there won't be any mess-up. Let's talk about that."

The suspicious friendship between Fomin and Kaparin did not go unnoticed. Several Communists in the battalion organized a watch over them and communicated their suspicions to Artemiev, the head of the political department, and to Shakhaev, the military commissar.

"A startled raven's afraid of a bush!" Artemiev said with a laugh. "Kaparin's a coward; do you think he's likely to take any decisive step? We'll watch Fomin, we've had our eye on him for a long time now, only it's doubtful whether Fomin himself will dare to do anything. It's all your imagination," he concluded decisively.

But it was now rather late to watch Fomin, for the conspirators had already come to an understanding. The rising was fixed to begin on March 12 at eight in the morning. It was agreed that on that day Fomin was to lead the squadron out for morning exercises, in full fighting array. Then they would make a sudden attack on the machine-gun section stationed on the outskirts of Vieshenska, capture the guns, and afterwards assist the garrison company to carry out a "purge" of the regional organizations.

Kaparin was uncertain whether all the battalion would support him and mentioned his doubts to Fomin. Fomin listened carefully and said:

"So long as we can capture the machine-guns we'll suppress your battalion in two seconds."

The close watch kept on Fomin and Kaparin yielded no results. They met very rarely, and then only in connection with service matters, and not till the end of February did a patrol see them together in the street one night. Fomin was leading his saddled horse by the rein, Kaparin was walking beside him. When challenged, Kaparin answered: "Friend!" They turned into Kaparin's quarters. Fomin tied his horse to the balustrade of the porch. They did not light a light in Kaparin's room. Fomin left at four in the morning, mounted his horse, and rode to his quarters. That was all the patrol was able to establish.

The regional military commander, Shakhaev, reported his suspicions of Fomin and Kaparin in a code telegram to the army commander of the Don province. A few days later he received an answer from the commander, sanctioning the removal of Fomin and Kaparin from their posts, and their arrest.

At a conference of the bureau of the Regional Party Committee it was decided to inform Fomin that by an order of the regional military commissariat he had been recalled to Novocherkass and placed at the disposition of the army commander, and that he was to hand over command of the squadron to his assistant, Ovchinnikov. The squadron was to be sent the same day to Kazanska, on the pretext that an armed band had arrived there, while the conspirators were to be arrested the next night. The decision to shift the squadron from Vieshenska was reached out of fear that it might revolt when it learned of Fomin's arrest. The commander of the second company of the garrison battalion, a Communist named Tkachenko, was instructed to warn the Communist members of the battalion and the platoon commanders of the possibility of a rising and to hold the company and the machine-gun section in fighting order.

Fomin was informed of the order for his recall next morning.

"All right, you take over the squadron, Ovchinnikov. I'm going to Novocherkass," he said calmly. "Do you want to go through the accounts?"

Ovchinnikov, a non-party troop commander, who had received no warning and had no suspicions, buried himself in the papers.

Fomin took the opportunity to write a note to Kaparin: "We act today. I've been recalled. Get ready!" In the porch he handed the note to his orderly, and whispered:

"Put it in your cheek. Ride at a walking pace. Understand? Ride to Kaparin at a walking pace. Hand the note to him and return here at once. If anyone stops you on the road, swallow it."

On receiving the order to lead the squadron to Kazanska district centre Ovchinnikov paraded the Cossacks in the church square in readiness for the march. Fomin rode up to him.

"May I say good-bye to the squadron?"

"By all means! Only get it over quickly, don't hold us up."

Placing himself before the squadron, reining in his prancing horse, Fomin turned to the men:

"You all know me, comrades. You know what I've always fought for. I've always been with you. But today I can't accept a state of things in which the Cossacks are being pillaged, when the men who grow the grain are being pillaged. And that is why I have been released from my command. And I know well what they intend to do to me. That is why I want to say good-bye to you. . . ."

For a second Fomin's speech was interrupted by cries and uproar among the squadron. He stood in his stirrups and sharply raised his voice:

"If you want to free yourselves of this pillaging, drive out the requisitioning detachments, kill the commissars like Shakhaev. They've come to the Don . . ."

His last words were drowned in the tumult. Waiting a moment, he sonorously gave the order:

"By right in threes—right wheel—quick march!"

The squadron obediently carried out the command. Dumb-founded by this turn, Ovchinnikov rode up to Fomin and demanded:

"Where are you going, Comrade Fomin?"

Without turning his head, Fomin jestingly answered:

"Just for a ride round the church."

Only then did Ovchinnikov take in the significance of all that had been occurring during those last few minutes. He rode his horse out of the file, being followed by the political instructor, the vice-commissar, and one man. Fomin noticed that they were missing only when they had gone a couple of hundred paces. Turning his horse, he shouted:

"Ovchinnikov, halt!"

The four riders spurred their mounts out of their easy trot into a gallop. Clumps of half-melting snow went flying in all directions from the horses' hoofs. Fomin gave the command:

"Weapons at the ready! Capture Ovchinnikov! First troop, after them!"

A ragged volley of shots rang out. The sixteen men of the first troop dashed off in pursuit. Meantime Fomin split the rest of the squadron into two groups; he sent one group, under Chumakov, the commander of the third troop, to disarm the machine-gun section, and himself led the rest towards the spot where the garrison company was stationed on the northern outskirts of the village, in large stables.

Firing in the air and waving their sabres, the first insurgent group galloped along the main street. They sabred four Communists as they went, hurriedly formed up on the outskirts, and silently, without a cheer, charged into the attack against the Red Army men of the machine-gun section as they came running out of their quarters.

The house in which the machine-gun section was quartered stood a little apart from the rest of the village. But only some two hundred paces separated it from the last houses. The Cossacks were met by machine-gun fire at point-blank range and at once turned back. Three of them were hit and bowled out of their saddles before they could reach the nearest lane.

The attempt to take the machine-gunners by surprise had failed. The insurgents did not try again. The commander of the group led his men under cover; without dismounting he warily peered round the corner of a stone-built shed and said:

"They've rolled out a couple more Maxims." He wiped his sweaty brow with his fur cap and turned to the others:

"We'll ride back, boys. Let Fomin capture the machine-gunners himself. How many have we left lying on the snow—three? Well, let him try his hand himself."

As soon as firing broke out in the eastern outskirts of the village the company commander Tkachenko dashed out of his quarters, dressing as he went, and ran to the barracks. Some thirty Red Army men were already drawn up in rank outside. They greeted him with a rain of questions:

"Who's shooting?"

"What's up?"

Without answering, he ordered the Red Army men who came pouring out of the barracks to fall in also. Several Communists, workers in the regional organizations, who had run to the barracks also stood in the rank. Scattered rifle-shots sounded in the village. Somewhere on the western outskirts there was the dull thud of a hand-grenade. Seeing some fifty horsemen galloping with bared sabres towards the barracks, Tkachenko unhurriedly drew his pistol out of its holster. In the ranks all talk died away and the men brought their rifles to the ready before he had time to give the order.

"But they're our men coming! Look, there's our battalion commander, Comrade Kaparin!" one Red Army man shouted.

Tearing along the street, the horsemen suddenly, as though by command, bent over the necks of their horses and galloped furiously towards the barracks.

"Don't let them come near!" Tkachenko shouted sharply.

The volley which rang out drowned his voice. When the riders were still a hundred paces away from the serried rank of Red Army men, four flew out of their saddles, and the others scattered in disorder and turned back. A rattle of shots cracked after them. One of the riders, evidently lightly wounded, fell from his saddle, but held on to the rein. For twenty yards or so he was dragged by his galloping horse; then he jumped to his feet, clutched at a stirrup and the rear pommel of the saddle, and the next moment he was back in his seat. Pulling furiously on the reins, he turned his horse sharply as it galloped and vanished down the nearest lane.

The men of the first troop vainly pursued Ovchinnikov and returned to the village. A search for the commissar Shakhaev was also fruitless. He was neither in the deserted military commissariat nor in his quarters. The moment he heard the sound of firing he rushed down to the Don, crossed over on the ice into the forest, thence to the village of Bazki, and the next day he was in the Ust-Khopersk district, a good forty miles from Vieshenska.

The majority of the leading regional officials managed to get away in time. Nor was it safe to search for them, as the Red Army men of the machine-gun section had advanced with hand machine-guns to the centre of Vieshenska and had covered all the streets leading to the main square.

The men of the squadron abandoned the search, dropped down to the Don, and rode to the church square, where they had been taken over by Fomin. Soon all the men were assembled. They again fell in. Fomin gave orders for guards to be set and for the others to go to their quarters, but to keep their horses saddled.

Fomin, Kaparin, and the troop commanders took counsel together in one of the houses on the outskirts.

"Everything's lost!" Kaparin exclaimed in despair, dropping impotently on a bench.

"Yes. We haven't captured the district centre, so we shan't be able to hold out here," Fomin said quietly.

"We must ride round the region, Yakov Yefimovich. What's the point of our getting frightened now? In any case we shan't die before we're dead. We'll raise the Cossacks, and then the district centre will be ours," Chumakov proposed.

Fomin stared at him without speaking and turned to Kaparin.

"Feeling down in the mouth, Your Excellency? Stop snivelling! You may as well be hanged for a sheep as a lamb! We've begun together, now let's carry on together. What do you think? Should we withdraw from Vieshenska or try again?"

Chumakov said sharply:

"Let others try! I'm not going to face a machine-gun. That's a hopeless game."

"I'm not asking you! You shut up!" Fomin glanced at Chumakov, who turned his eyes away.

After a moment Kaparin said:

"Yes, of course, it's senseless to try a second time now. They've got the superiority in weapons. They've got fourteen machine-guns, and we haven't one. And they've got more men. . . . We must retire and organize the Cossacks in a rising. While the Reds are being sent reinforcements the whole region will be in the grip of the revolt. That's our only hope. There's no other."

After a long silence Fomin said:

"Well, we'll have to decide on that. Troop commanders, immediately check up on the equipment and find out how many cartridges each man has. Give the strict order that not a single cartridge is to be wasted. The first man who disobeys I'll sabre myself. Tell the men that." He was silent for a moment, then angrily banged his enormous fist down on the table. "Ah, those damned machine-guns! And it's all your fault, Chumakov! If we'd managed to capture even four of them. . . . Now, of course, they'll drive us out of the place. Well, dismiss! We'll spend the night in Vieshenska, if we're not driven out, and at dawn we'll advance into the region. . . ."

The night passed quietly. At one end of Vieshenska were the men of the insurgent squadron, at the other the garrison battalion, with the Communists and Young Communists who had joined it. Only two blocks of houses separated the enemies, but neither side dared to make a night attack.

Next morning the squadron abandoned the village without a fight and made off in a south-easterly direction.

Chapter 2

For three weeks after Gregor had left home he lived in the village of Vierkhne Krivoi in Yelanska district, staying with a Cossack acquaintance who had been his regimental comrade. Then he moved on to the village of Gorbatovsky, where he lived for more than a month with a distant relative of Aksinia's.

For days on end he remained in the best room, going out into the yard only at night. But this life was as bad as being in prison. He was downcast, oppressed by his inactivity. He was almost irresistibly drawn homeward, to his children, to Aksinia. Frequently during his sleepless nights he put on his greatcoat, firmly resolved to go back to Tatarsk. But each time he changed his mind and took off his coat again, throwing himself with a groan face downward on the bed. This existence was trying him beyond endurance. The master, his host, who was Aksinia's great-uncle, sympathized with him, but he could not keep such a lodger for ever. One evening after supper Gregor, who had gone to his room, overheard the mistress asking in a voice thin with hatred:

"And when is all this to end?"

"All what? What are you talking about?" the master answered in his deep voice.

"When are we going to get rid of this idle guzzler?"

"Hold your tongue!"

"I won't! We've got so little grain left that it would make a cat weep, and yet you're keeping and feeding this hunchbacked devil day after day. How long is this going on, I ask you. And supposing the Soviet finds out? They'll take off our heads, and our children will be left orphans."

"Hold your tongue, Avdotia!"

"I won't! We've got children to think of. We haven't got more than about seven hundred pounds of grain left, and you've been feeding this drone! What is he to you? Your own brother? Your son-in-law's father? A cousin? He's not any near relation to you. So far as you're concerned, he's first-cousin jelly to second-cousin water, and yet you're keeping him, giving him food and drink. Ah, you bald-headed devil! Hold your tongue, don't bark at me, or I'll go to the Soviet myself tomorrow and tell them the sort of flower you're in love with in this house!"

Next day the master came into Gregor's room and said, staring down at the floor:

"Gregor Pantalievich, think what you like, but you can't stay here any longer. I respect you, and I knew your dead father and respected him. But it's difficult for me to go on keeping you eating our victuals. And besides, I'm afraid the government might find out about you. I don't want to lose my head through you. Forgive me, for Christ's sake, but free us of yourself. . . ."

"Good!" Gregor said curtly. "Thank you for giving me food and shelter. Thank you for everything. I can see for myself that I'm a burden to you, but where am I to go? All my paths are closed."

"Go wherever you like."

"All right! I'll leave today. Thank you for everything, Artamon Vasilievich."

"There's nothing to thank me for."

"I shan't forget your kindness. Maybe I shall be able to do you a service some day."

Deeply moved, the master clapped Gregor on the back.

"Why talk about it? So far as I'm concerned, you could stay here for another couple of months. But the wife won't allow it, she carries on at me every day, damn her! I'm a Cossack and you're a Cossack, Gregor Pantalievich! You and I are both against the Soviet régime, and I'll help you. You go today to the village of Yagodny; my son's father-in-law lives there, he'll take you in. Tell him Artamon says he's to take you in as if you were his own son, to feed you and keep you as long as he can. And he and I will settle accounts later. Only you leave us this very day! I mustn't keep you here any longer; the wife's the master in this house, and besides, I'm afraid the Soviet may find out. You've been able to stay here, Gregor Pantalievich, and we'll call it enough. I've got some regard for my own head."

Gregor left the house late that night. But he had not reached the windmill standing on the hill above the village when three horsemen seemed to spring out of the earth and stopped him:

"Halt, you son of a bitch! Who are you?"

Gregor's heart beat violently. Without saying a word, he stopped. To run would have been madness. There was neither hole nor bush anywhere near the road, only the bare, empty steppe. He could not have gone two yards.

"A Communist? Get back, damn you! Now, quick!"

Riding his horse at Gregor, a second man ordered him:

"Hands up! Take them out of your pockets! Out with them or I'll slash your head off!"

Gregor silently took his hands out of his greatcoat pockets and, still not understanding what had happened and who these men were, he asked:

"Where am I to go?"

"To the village. Turn back!"

A single horseman escorted him to the village; the two others left them at the pasturage and rode off to the highroad. Gregor walked along without speaking. When he came to the road he slowed down his steps, and asked:

"Listen! Who are you?"

"Get on, get on! No talking! Put your hands behind you, do you hear?"

Gregor silently obeyed. But a little later he asked again:

"All the same, who are you?"

"Greek Orthodox!"

"I'm not an Old Believer myself!"

"Well, you can be glad you're not!"

"Where are you taking me to?"

"To the commander. Get on, get on, you reptile, or I'll—"

The man gently pricked Gregor with the point of his sabre. The keen, cold steel stung his bare neck just between his greatcoat collar and his fur cap, and for a moment a feeling of terror flared up like a spark within him, to be followed by impotent anger. Turning up his collar, half swinging round to glance at his convoy, he said through his teeth:

"Don't play the fool, do you hear? Otherwise I may get that thing away from you. . . ."

"Move on, you scum, and don't talk! I'll get you away! Hands behind you!"

Gregor went on for a few paces in silence, then said:

"I'll be quiet without your swearing at me. What a swine you are!"

"Don't look back!"

"I'm not looking back."

"Hold your tongue and move quicker."

"Perhaps you'd like me to run?" Gregor asked, brushing the clinging snowflakes from his eyelashes.

Without answering, the escort touched up his horse. The animal's chest, wet with sweat and the dampness of the night, jolted Gregor in the back; a hoof squelched into the thawing snow by his feet.

"Not so much of that!" Gregor shouted, pushing his hand against the animal's chest.

The escort raised his sword to the level of his head and said in a quiet tone:

"You get on, you bitch's bastard, and no talking, or I shan't take you all the way! I'm rather quick at that sort of thing! Shut up, and not a word more!"

They went in silence as far as the village. By the first yard the escort reined in his horse and said:

"Go through that gate!"

Gregor passed through a gate which was standing wide open. In the heart of the yard he saw a spacious, sheet-iron roofed house. Under the eaves of a shed horses were snorting and juicily chewing. Six or more armed men were hanging around the porch. The escort sheathed his sabre and said as he dismounted:

"Go into the house, straight along the passage, and the first door on the left. Get on and no looking round! How many times have I got to tell you?"

Gregor slowly went up the steps of the porch. By the balustrade a man dressed in a long cavalry greatcoat and a Red Army cap was standing. He asked:

"Caught someone, then?"

"Yes," the familiar, hoarse voice of Gregor's convoy answered reluctantly. "Caught him close to the windmill."

"Who is he: the secretary of the party group?"

"The devil knows! Some swine; but we'll soon find out who he is!"

"Either this is a White band, or the Vieshenska Cheka men are trying to be clever and are pretending to be Whites. I'm caught, like any mug!" Gregor thought, deliberately hanging back in the porch, trying to collect his thoughts.

The first man he saw when he opened the door was Fomin. He was sitting at a table, surrounded by a number of men dressed in military uniforms, all of them strangers to Gregor. Greatcoats and sheepskins were flung in a disorderly heap on the bed, carbines were piled by the bench, and on the bench itself was a mixed array of sabres, bandoleers, saddlebags, and wallets. The men, the greatcoats, the equipment all gave off the strong scent of horses' sweat.

Gregor removed his fur cap and quietly said:

"Hello!"

"Melekhov! Well, in very truth the steppe is broad, but the road is narrow. So fate has brought us together again! Where have you turned up from? Take your coat off, come in and sit down." Fomin rose from the table and went across to Gregor, holding out his hand. "What were you doing hanging around here?"

"I'd come to the village on business."

"What business? It's rather a long way for you to come." Fomin stared at Gregor inquisitively. "Tell the truth! You were in hiding here, weren't you?"

"That's the whole truth," Gregor answered, smiling forcedly.

"But where did my lads get hold of you?"

"Outside the village."

"Where were you going?"

"I was following my nose."

Fomin again stared closely into Gregor's eyes and smiled.

"I can see you're thinking we've caught you to carry you off to Vieshenska! No, brother, that road is blocked to us. Don't be afraid! We've finished serving the Soviet régime. We couldn't settle down to live with it."

"We've had a divorce," an elderly Cossack smoking by the stove said in a deep voice.

One of the men sitting at the table burst into a loud laugh.

"Haven't you heard anything about me?" Fomin asked Gregor.

"No."

"Well, sit down at the table and we'll talk. Cabbage soup and meat for our guest!"

Gregor did not believe a word Fomin had said. Pale and restrained, he took off his coat and sat down. He wanted a smoke, but he remembered that he had not had any tobacco for the last two days.

"Have you got anything to smoke?" he asked Fomin.

Fomin complaisantly held out his leather cigarette-case. It did not escape his notice that as Gregor took the cigarette his hands trembled, and Fomin smiled again in his curling, ruddy moustache.

"We've risen against the Soviet régime. We're for the people and against grain-requisitioning and the commissars. They've made fools of us for a long time, but now we'll make fools of them. Do you understand, Melekhov?"

Gregor said nothing. He smoked, taking hurried draws at his cigarette. His head began to swim, and a feeling of nausea rose in his throat. He had been living on poor food during the past month, and only now did he feel how weak he had grown. Putting out his cigarette, he greedily set to work on the food. Fomin briefly told him about the rising and the first days of their wanderings about the region, magniloquently calling these wanderings a "raid." Gregor listened in silence and swallowed down bread and the greasy, badly cooked lamb stew almost without chewing.

"But you've grown thin while you've been enjoying other people's hospitality!" Fomin said with a benevolent laugh.

Hiccuping in his satiation, Gregor snorted:

"I haven't been living with my mother-in-law!"

"I can see that. Eat up, stuff as much as you can into yourself. We're not niggardly masters!"

"Thank you. Now I'd like a smoke." Gregor took the cigarette offered him, went to a pot standing on a bench, and, taking the wooden mug, bailed up some water. It was icy cold and slightly salt to the taste. Fuddled by his heavy meal, he greedily drank two large mugfuls of water, then began to enjoy his cigarette.

"The Cossacks aren't making us too welcome!" Fomin continued his story, seating himself beside Gregor. "They were badly shaken up during the rising last year. . . . Still, we've got some volunteers. About forty men have joined us. But that isn't what we're after. What we're after is to raise the whole region, and for the neighbouring regions, Khopersk and Ust-Miedvieditsa, to help too. And then we'll have a heart-to-heart talk with the Soviet régime!"

A noisy conversation was going on at the table. While Gregor listened to Fomin, he furtively examined his companions. Not one familiar face! He still did not believe Fomin, but thought he was being cunning; and he discreetly held his peace. But he could not remain silent all the time.

"If you're serious in what you say, Comrade Fomin, what is it you want? To start a new war?" he asked, trying to resist the drowsiness which was overcoming him.

"I've already told you about that."

"You want to change the government?"

"Yes."

"And what sort do you want to put in its place?"

"Our own Cossack government."

"A government of atamans?"

"Well, we'll wait a bit before we talk about the atamans! The government the people choose is the one we'll set up. But that isn't

an urgent question; my job is to destroy the commissars and Communists, and Kaparin, my chief of staff, will tell you all about the
government. He's my brains where that question's concerned. He's
a brainy man and educated." Fomin bent towards Gregor and whispered: "He's a former staff captain of the Czarist army! A clever
fellow! He's asleep in the other room at the moment; he's not too
well, probably through not being used to this sort of life. We've been
making some long marches."

In the porch there was a sudden uproar, the stamping of feet, a
groan, a quiet scuffling, and a muffled shout: "Give it to him!" The
talk at the table immediately died away. Fomin looked expectantly
at the door. It was flung open. A billowing white cloud of vapour
poured into the room. Driven forward by a resounding blow on the
back, a tall, bareheaded man in a quilted khaki jacket and grey felt
boots took several impetuous, stumbling paces and struck his shoulder hard against the ledge of the stove. From the porch came a
cheerful shout before the door was slammed:

"Here's one more for you!"

Fomin rose and adjusted the belt around his tunic.

"Who are you?" he asked authoritatively.

Panting, the man in the quilted jacket passed his hand over his
hair, tried to wriggle his shoulders, and frowned with pain. He had
been struck on the spine with something heavy, probably a rifle-butt.

"Can't you speak? Have you lost your tongue? Who are you, I
asked."

"A Red Army soldier."

"From what force?"

"The 12th grain-requisitioning Regiment."

"Aha, this is a find!" one of the men sitting at the table declared
with a smile.

Fomin continued the examination:

"What were you doing here?"

"We were trying to hold . . . we were sent . . ."

"Of course! How many of you were there in the village?"

"Fourteen."

"Where are the others?"

The Red Army man did not answer; he had difficulty in opening
his lips. A bubbling noise came from his throat, a thin stream of
blood flowed out of the left corner of his mouth and over his chin.

He wiped his lips with his hands, looked at his palm, and wiped it on his trousers.

"That's your swine . . ." he said in a gurgling voice, swallowing his blood. "They've injured my lungs. . . ."

"Never you fear! We'll get you well!" a stocky Cossack said jestingly, rising from the table and winking at the others.

"Where are the rest of you?" Fomin asked again.

"Gone to Yelanska with the baggage train."

"And where are you from? In what district were you born?"

The man looked at Fomin with feverishly glittering blue eyes, spat out a clot of blood on to the floor, and answered in a clear, resonant bass:

"Pskov province."

"We've heard of that place!" Fomin said with a sneer. "You've come a long way for other people's grain, my lad! Well, no more talk! What are we to do with you, eh?"

"You must release me."

"You're a simple sort, my lad! But maybe we will release you. What do you say, boys?" Laughing in his moustache, Fomin turned to the men sitting at the table.

Gregor, who had been watching closely, saw quiet, understanding smiles on the brown, weather-beaten faces.

"He can serve with us for a couple of months, and then we'll let him go home to his wife," one of the men said.

"Maybe you will serve with us?" Fomin asked, vainly trying to hide his smile. "We'll give you a horse and saddle, and instead of your felt boots you shall have new leg-boots with shaped calves. . . . Your commanders don't fit you out very well. Do you call that footwear? There's a thaw outside, and you're going about in felt boots! Will you join us?"

"He's a peasant; he's never ridden horseback in his life!" one of the Cossacks lisped in a falsetto voice, pretending to be a halfwit.

The Red Army man was silent. He leaned his back against the stove, looking about him with eyes that had grown clear and bright. From time to time he frowned with pain, gaping when he found it difficult to get his breath.

"Will you join us, or what?" Fomin asked again.

"But who are you?"

"Who are we?" Fomin raised his eyebrows and stroked his whiskers with his palm. "We're fighters for the toiling people. We're against the oppression of the commissars and Communists, that's who we are."

Then Gregor suddenly saw a smile on the man's face.

"So that's who you are. . . . I was wondering who you could be." The prisoner smiled, revealing teeth stained with blood, and he spoke as though he were pleasantly surprised by the news he had heard. But in his voice there was also a note which caused everybody in the room to prick up his ears. "So you call yourselves fighters for the people? M'yes! But in our language you're just bandits. And you want me to serve you? You're joking, simply joking."

"You're a bit of a wag too, I can see that!" Fomin screwed up his eyes and curtly asked:

"A Communist?"

"No, of course not. I'm non-party."

"You don't sound like it."

"On my word I'm non-party."

Fomin cleared his throat and turned to the table:

"Chumakov, put him out!"

"It's not worth while killing me. Not at all," the man said quietly.

The only answer was silence. Chumakov, a well-built, handsome Cossack in an English leather jerkin, unwillingly rose from the table, smoothing his already sleek blond hair.

"I'm fed up with this duty," he said boldly, taking his sabre from the heap flung down on the bench and trying the blade with his thumb.

"You haven't got to do it yourself. Tell the boys in the yard," Fomin counselled him.

Chumakov coldly ran his eyes over the prisoner from head to foot and said:

"Go in front, my boy!"

The Red Army man staggered away from the stove, huddled into himself, and slowly went towards the door, leaving the damp traces of his wet felt boots on the floor.

"He might have wiped his boots when he came in! You turn up, leave the marks of your feet all over the place, and make the floor muddy . . . what a dirty beast you are, brother!" Chumakov said with feigned annoyance as he followed the prisoner.

"Tell them to take him into the lane or into the threshing-floor.

It mustn't be done close to the house or the masters will be upset!"
Fomin shouted after him.

He went across to Gregor, sat down beside him, and asked:

"We give them a short trial, don't we?"

"Yes," Gregor answered, avoiding his eyes.

Fomin sighed.

"It can't be helped. That's how it's got to be now." He was about
to say something more, but there was a noisy tramping of feet in
the porch, someone shouted, and a single shot cracked resonantly.

"May the devil torment them out there!" Fomin exclaimed in an
angry tone.

One of the men sitting at the table jumped up and kicked the door
open. "What's happening out there?" he shouted into the darkness.

Chumakov came in and excitedly reported:

"He proved to be quite smart! What a devil for you! He jumped
from the top step and ran. I had to waste a cartridge on him. The
boys outside are finishing him off. . . ."

"Tell them to drag him out of the yard into the lane."

"I've told them already, Yakov Yefimich."

The room was quiet for a moment. Then someone asked, stifling
a yawn:

"What's the weather like, Chumakov? Is it clearing up?"

"It's cloudy."

"If it rains it'll wash the last snow away."

"But what do you want it to rain for?"

"I don't want it to. I've no desire to go squelching through mire."

Gregor went to the bed and picked up his cap.

"Where are you going?" Fomin asked.

"To get a breath of air."

He went out on the porch. The moon was shining dimly through
clouds. The spacious yard, the roofs of the sheds, the summits of
the poplars, the horses standing covered with horse-cloths at the
hitching-posts, were all illumined with the translucent, dove-blue
light of midnight. Several yards from the porch lay the Red Army
man, his head in a faintly gleaming puddle of thaw-water. Three
Cossacks were bent over him, talking quietly as they did something
to him.

"He's still breathing, by God!" one of them said in a vexed tone.
"What did you kill him like that for, you clumsy devil? I told you

to aim at his head. Ah, you unsalted soup!"

A hoarse-voice Cossack, the same man who had brought in Gregor, answered:

"He'll peg out! He'll give one belch and peg out! But lift his head up! I can't get the coat off anyhow. Lift him by the hair. That's right! And now hold him."

Gregor heard the splash of water. One of the men standing over the prisoner straightened up. The hoarse-voiced Cossack, who was squatting down, grunted as he pulled the quilted jacket off the body. A moment or two later he said:

"I've got a light hand, and that's why he didn't snuff out at once. When I was at home if we happened to be slaughtering a boar— Hold him up, don't let him drop! Oh, damn it! As I was saying, I'd start to slaughter the boar, and I'd slash him right across the throat, I'd drive the knife right into his neck, and even then the damned animal would get up and walk about the yard. And he'd go on walking for quite a long time after! Streaming with blood he'd be, but he'd still go on living. So I must have a light hand. Well, drop him. . . . Is he still breathing? You don't say! Yet my sabre split his skull almost to his brain!"

The third man spread out the dead man's jacket over his outstretched arm and said:

"We've stained the left side with blood. . . . It's sticking to my hands! Pah, the filth!"

"It'll wipe off. It isn't grease," the hoarse-voiced man said, and squatted down again. "It'll wipe off, or wash off at any rate. It isn't serious."

"Now what are you going to do: thinking of taking his trousers off too?" the first Cossack asked discontentedly.

The hoarse-voiced man sharply answered:

"If you're in a hurry or want to go to the horses we'll manage here without you. We can't let good things go begging."

Gregor turned on his heel and went back into the house.

Fomin welcomed him with a swift, appraising glance and rose.

"Let's go into the other room and talk; there's too much of a row going on here," he proposed.

The spacious, warmly heated room stank of mice and hemp-seed. A small man in a khaki tunic was sleeping stretched out on the bed. His thin hair was dishevelled, and sprinkled with fluff and tiny feathers. He lay with his cheek pressed against the ticking of a dirty pillow. The lamp hanging from the ceiling lit up his pale, long unshaven face.

Fomin awakened him and said:

"Get up, Kaparin! We've got a guest. This is Gregor Melekhov, a friend and a former company commander."

Kaparin hung his legs over the edge of the bed, wiped his face with his sleeve, and got up. He shook Gregor's hand, making a slight bow.

"Very pleased to meet you. I'm Staff Captain Kaparin."

Fomin affably pushed a chair across to Gregor, and seated himself on a chest. He must have realized from Gregor's face that the murder of the prisoner had had a depressing effect on him, for he said:

"You mustn't think we treat all our prisoners so sternly. That fellow was a member of a grain-collecting detachment. And we're not going to let such men go, or commissars either. . . . But we spare others. Yesterday we captured three militia-men. We took their horses, saddles, and equipment and set them free. There's no point in killing them."

Gregor was silent. His hands resting on his knees, he was thinking his own thoughts, and he heard Fomin's voice as though in his sleep.

". . . and so we're fighting, as you can see," Fomin went on. "But we think we'll raise the Cossacks all the same. The Soviet régime must die. By all the signs there's war going on everywhere. Everywhere there are risings: in Siberia and in the Ukraine and even at Petrograd. The whole of the fleet has revolted in that fortress—what's it called?"

"Kronstadt," Kaparin prompted him.

Gregor raised his head, looked at Fomin with vacant, apparently unseeing eyes, and shifted his gaze to Kaparin.

"Have a smoke." Fomin held out his cigarette-case. "Well, and so Petrograd has been captured and they're getting near Moscow. There's the same tune being played everywhere. And there's no reason why we should be dozing! We'll raise the Cossacks, sweep away the Soviet régime, and if the Cadets give us any support, then our affairs will go well. Let their educated people set up a government and we'll help them." He was silent for a moment, then asked: "What do you think, Melekhov? If the Cadets drive hard from the Black Sea and we unite with them, they'll give us credit for the fact that we were the first to rise in the rear of the Reds, won't they? Kaparin says of course they will. For instance, surely they won't hold it against me that I led the 28th Regiment away from the front in 1918 and served the Soviet government for a couple of years?"

"So that's what you're aiming at! You're a fool, but a cunning one!" thought Gregor, involuntarily smiling. Fomin awaited his answer. Evidently he was seriously concerned with this problem. Gregor reluctantly said:

"That's a long story."

"Of course, of course," Fomin willingly agreed. "We shall see better later. But now we must act, we must smash the Communists in their rear. In any case we shan't allow them to live! They've put their infantry in wagons and are thinking of chasing after us. Let them try. While cavalry is being sent to their aid we'll turn the entire region upside down."

Gregor again gazed down at his feet, thinking. Kaparin excused himself and lay down on the bed.

"I get very tired. We make such mad marches and get little sleep," he said, smiling faintly.

"It's time we went to bed too." Fomin rose and dropped his heavy hand on Gregor's shoulder. "You were wise, Meleknov, to listen to my advice that day in Vieshenska. If you hadn't hidden they'd have been on your tail! You'd have been lying now in Vieshenska, and your nails would have been rotting. I can see that as plain as a pike-staff. Well, what have you decided? Speak up, and then let's get to bed."

"What am I to speak about?"

"Will you join us, or what? You can't spend all your life hiding in other people's houses."

Gregor had been expecting this question. Now he must make his choice: to go on wandering from village to village, living a hungry, homeless life and succumbing to a numb longing until the master betrayed him to the authorities; or to go to the political department and submit; or to join Fomin. And he made his choice. For the first time that evening he looked straight into Fomin's face and said, twisting his lips into a smile:

"I've got as much choice as the hero has in the fairy-story: ride to the left and you'll lose your horse, ride to the right and you'll be killed. I've got three roads, and not one of them goes my way. . . ."

"You make your choice without any telling of fairy-stories. We'll tell the fairy-stories after."

"I've got nowhere to go to, so I've chosen already."

"Well?"

"I'll join your band."

Fomin knitted his brow discontentedly and bit his moustache.

"You drop that word! Why call it a band? That's what the Communists call us, but it's not for you to use the word. We're simply men who have revolted against the régime. Short and clear!"

His dissatisfaction was only momentary. He was obviously delighted with Gregor's decision and could not conceal the fact. Animatedly rubbing his hands, he said:

"That's one more for our regiment! Do you hear, staff captain? We'll give you a troop, Melekhov, or if you don't want to command a troop you can be on the staff with Kaparin. I'll let you have my own horse. I've got a spare mount."

Chapter 3

Towards dawn a light frost set in. The puddles were filmed with dove-blue ice. The snow turned rough and crunched resonantly. The horses' hoofs left uncertain, crumbling round imprints on the granular snowy pall, and where the previous day's thaw had eaten at the snow, the bare earth with the dead last-year's grass nestling against it was only slightly marked by the hoofs and gave way with a faint crack.

Fomin's band drew up in a column outside the village. Far off along the road the six horsemen of the advance reconnaissance patrol were occasionally to be seen.

"There's my army!" Fomin said with a smile, riding up to Gregor. "We could smash the devil himself with such lads!"

Gregor ran his eyes over the column and mournfully thought: "If you and your army were to run up against my Budionny squadron we'd turn you into a heap of bones in half an hour!"

Fomin pointed with his whip and asked:

"What do you think of them?"

"Not bad for killing prisoners and not bad for stripping the dead, but I don't know what they'd be like in a fight," Gregor answered dryly.

Turning in his saddle with his back to the wind, Fomin lit a cigarette and said:

"You'll get a chance of seeing them in a fight too. Most of my men are regular soldiers, and they don't let you down."

Six two-horse wagons loaded with ammunition and supplies were placed in the middle of the column. Fomin galloped to the front and gave the order to advance. On the rise he rode up to Gregor again and asked:

"Well, how's my horse? To your liking?"

"He's a good horse."

They rode along for some time in silence, stirrup to stirrup, then Gregor asked:

"Are you thinking of going through Tatarsk?"

"Wanting to see your people?"

"I'd like to visit them."

"We may. At the moment I'm thinking of turning towards the Chira, to jolt and shake up the Cossacks a bit."

But the Cossacks were not very willing to be "shaken up." Gregor became convinced of that in his first few days with the band. When they occupied a village or district centre Fomin gave orders for a citizens' meeting to be held. Usually he himself did the speaking, but sometimes Kaparin took his place. They ordered the Cossacks to arms, talked of the "burdens" which had been laid on grain-growers by the Soviet régime, of the "final ruin which will inevitably result if the Soviet government isn't overthrown." Fomin spoke not so grammatically and coherently as Kaparin, but more expansively and in a language which the Cossacks understood. He usually ended his speech with set, memorized phrases: "From today on we free you from grain-requisitioning. Don't cart any more grain to the collection points. It's time to stop feeding the Communist drones. They've grown fat on your grain, but that foreign domination has ended. You are free people. Arm yourselves and support our régime. Hurrah, Cossacks!"

The Cossacks stared down at the ground and were morosely

silent; but the women gave rein to their tongues. Venomous questions and shouts came from their massed ranks:

"Your régime sounds all right, but have you brought us any soap?"

"Where do you keep your government, in your saddlebags?"

"But whose grain are you living on?"

"I suppose you'll be going from yard to yard to beg in a minute?"

"They've got swords! They'll start cutting off the chickens' heads without asking permission!"

"It's all very well telling us not to cart our grain. But you're here today, and tomorrow there'll be no finding you even with hounds, while we'll have to answer for it."

"We won't let you have our husbands. You do your own fighting!"

And much else did the women shout in their great obduracy, for during the years of war they had grown fanatical in all their behaviour, were afraid of a new war, and clung to their husbands with the obstinacy of despair.

Fomin listened unconcernedly to their incoherent shouts. He knew their value. He waited until there was silence and turned to the Cossacks. And then they answered briefly and soberly:

"Don't oppress us, Comrade Fomin; we've had enough of fighting."

"We've tried it, we rose in 1919."

"We haven't got anything to revolt with, and there's no point in it. We haven't any need for it at the moment."

"It's getting near time for sowing, and not fighting."

One day someone shouted from the back of the crowd:

"You're talking sweetly enough now! But where were you in 1919, when we did rise? You've thought better of it rather late, Fomin!"

Gregor saw Fomin's face change, but the commander retained control of himself and made no answer.

During the first week Fomin generally listened quite calmly to the Cossacks' objections at the meetings and to their curt refusal to support his actions; even the women's shouts and curses did not upset his equanimity. "All right, we'll get them!" he said arrogantly, smiling in his moustache. But when he became convinced that the great mass of the Cossack population was not friendly towards him, he completely changed in his attitude to those who spoke at the meetings. And now he talked without dismounting from his horse and did not so much argue as threaten. But the result was the same:

the Cossacks on whom he had counted for support listened to him in silence and as silently began to disperse.

At one of the villages, after Fomin had spoken, a Cossack widow made a speech in answer. A big woman, corpulent and large-boned, she spoke in an almost masculine voice and swung her arms violently, like a man. Her broad, heavily pockmarked face was expressive of angry determination, her large, thick, pouting lips were continually twisted in a contemptuous sneer. Pointing her swollen red hand in the direction of Fomin, who was sitting stonily in his saddle, she seemed almost to spit out the venomous words:

"What are you causing trouble here for? Where do you want to drive our Cossacks to, into what hole? Hasn't this accursed war widowed enough of our women? Hasn't it orphaned enough of our children? Are you calling down new woes on our heads? And who is this czar-liberator that's turned up from the village of Rubiezhin? You should put your own house in order and make an end to your own ruin, and then you could teach us how to live and what régime to accept and what not. For in your own home your own wife can't get free of the collar, we know that very well! But you've fluffed up your moustache and are riding about on a horse, upsetting the people. Yet on your own farm, if the wind didn't hold your hut up, it would have fallen down long ago. A fine teacher you are! What are you silent for, you nob? Is it lies I'm telling?"

A quiet laugh ran through the crowd. It rustled like a wind and died away. Fomin's left hand, lying on the saddle-bow, slowly fingered the reins; his face darkened with restrained anger. But he remained silent, trying to think of a dignified way out of his awkward position.

"And what is this government of yours, that you call on us to support it?" the widow continued energetically, working herself up into a rage.

She put her arms akimbo and slowly made towards Fomin, swinging her broad haunches. The crowd opened a way for her, hiding their smiles, drooping their laughing eyes. They cleared a ring as though for a dance, jostling one another.

"Your régime won't remain one moment on the earth after you've gone," the widow said in her low, deep voice. "It drags after you and never lives more than an hour in any one spot. 'Today on your horse, and tomorrow on your belly in the mud,' that's who you are, and your régime's the same."

Fomin violently kicked his heels into his horse's sides and rode the animal into the crowd. The people fell back in all directions. Only the widow was left in the middle of a great ring. She had seen many things in her time, and so she stared calmly at the snarling teeth of Fomin's horse, at Fomin's white, infuriated face.

Riding his horse at her, he raised his whip high above her head.

"Hold your mouth, you speckled carrion! What are you carrying on agitation here for?"

Held high by the rein, the horse's muzzle with its bared teeth hung right above the fearless woman's head. A pale-green clot of foam flew from the bit and fell on her kerchief and from it to her cheek. She swept it away with her hand and fell back a step.

"So you can speak, and we mustn't?" she shouted, gazing at Fomin with dilated, furiously glittering eyes.

Fomin did not strike her. Shaking his whip, he roared:

"You Bolshevik infection! I'll thrash all the stupidity out of you! I'll give orders for your skirt to be pulled up over your head and for you to be beaten with ramrods. Then you'll grow wise in less than no time!"

The widow fell back another couple of steps and, unexpectedly turning her back on Fomin, stooped to the ground and threw up the back edge of her skirt.

"Haven't you ever seen anything like that before, Anika the warrior?" she shouted and, straightening up with amazing agility, she again turned to face Fomin. "Me? Whip me? You haven't got a ring in your snout!"

Fomin spat furiously and drew on the reins, holding in his back-stepping horse.

"Shut your mouth, you foalless mare! Are you so glad you've got so much meat to your carcass?" he said in a loud voice, and turned his horse round, vainly trying to look stern.

A muffled, stifled laughter ran through the crowd. To save his commander's insulted honour one of Fomin's men ran up to the widow, swinging the butt of his carbine. But a healthy-looking Cossack a couple of heads taller than he shielded the woman with his own broad shoulders and quietly but promisingly said:

"None of that!"

Three other villagers also swiftly came up and pushed the widow back. One of them, a youngster with bristling hair, whispered to the Fomin man:

"What are you swinging your rifle for, eh? It's easy enough to kill a woman! You go and show your pluck out in the fields, we can all be brave in the back yards!"

Fomin rode off at a walking pace to the fence, then stood in his stirrups.

"Cossacks, think it over well!" he cried, addressing the slowly dispersing crowd. "We're asking you decently enough now, but we'll be back in a week, and then we'll talk in a different language!"

For some reason his mood had changed to one of merriment and, laughing, holding in his prancing horse, he shouted:

"We're not cowards! You can't frighten us with women's—arses! We've seen them pockmarked, and with all sorts of other marks. We'll come back, and if none of you joins our detachments voluntarily, we shall mobilize all the young Cossacks by force. Understand that! We haven't got time to cuddle you and gaze into your eyes!"

Laughter and animated conversation arose among the crowd, which had halted for a moment. Still smiling, Fomin gave the order:

"To horse!"

Livid with suppressed laughter, Gregor rode off to his troop.

Extended along the miry road, the Fomin detachment rode over the top of the rise, and the inhospitable village was concealed from sight. But Gregor still smiled from time to time as he thought: "It's a good thing we Cossacks like our fun. Jokes are more frequent guests with us than sorrow, and God grant that it may always be so, for if life were all serious I'd have hanged myself long ago." His cheerful mood remained with him for a long time, and only at the halt did he think anxiously and bitterly that they were not going to succeed in raising the Cossacks, and that all Fomin's schemes were doomed to inevitable disaster.

Chapter 4

Spring came on. The sunlight now had more warmth to it. The snow melted on the southern slopes of the hills, and at noonday the earth, rusty with last year's grass, gave off a translucent lilac mist. In the warm patches, on the mounds, half buried under the quartz boulders showed the first brilliantly green, slender growths of honey-grass. The ploughed lands were bared. From the abandoned winter roads the rooks migrated to the threshing-floors, to the winter-corn fields flooded with thaw-water. In the ravines and dells the snow lay blue, soaked to the surface with moisture; from these spots a harsh cold still breathed. But in the gullies the spring brooklets, invisible to the eye, were already thinly and melodiously gurgling under the snow, and in the glades the branches of the poplars were beginning to display an almost imperceptible, tender vernal green.

The season for field labour was approaching, and Fomin's band melted away more and more with every day. The morning after a halt for the night two or three men would be missing, and one day almost half a troop vanished: eight men with their horses and equipment went off to Vieshenska to surrender. It was time to plough and sow. The earth was calling, drawing the Cossacks to work, and, convinced that the struggle was useless, many of Fomin's men secretly deserted from the band and rode off to their homes. There remained only the wild men who could not return in any case, men whose crimes against the Soviet régime were too great for them to hope for pardon.

By the first days of April, Fomin had not more than eighty-six sabres under his command. Gregor still remained with the band. He lacked the courage to go home. He was firmly convinced that Fomin's cause was lost, and that sooner or later the band would be broken up. He knew that at the first serious clash with any regular Red Army cavalry they would be smashed to the last man. Yet he remained under Fomin, secretly hoping to hang on somehow until the summer and then seize a couple of the best horses in the detachment, gallop at night to Tatarsk, and thence, with Aksinia, to the south. The Don steppe was broad, spacious; there were many lonely tracks and expanses in it; in summer-time all the roads were open, and shelter could be found everywhere. He thought to abandon the horses somewhere, to make his way with Aksinia on foot to the Kuban, to the Caucasian foothills, far from their native spots, and live there through the troublous times. There was no other way out, it seemed to him.

On Kaparin's advice Fomin decided to cross to the left bank of the Don before the ice broke up. On the confines of the Khopersk region, where there were many forests, he hoped to lie concealed from pursuit if necessary.

The band crossed the Don above the village of Ribny. In places where the current ran swiftly, the ice had already been carried away. Under the bright April sun the water glittered as though covered with silvery scales; but where the winter track had been built up, rising a couple of feet above the level of the ice, the Don stood immovable. They laid down wattles over the broken edge, led the horses across one by one, fell in on the farther side, and, sending a reconnaissance patrol on ahead, moved in the direction of Yelanska district.

The following day Gregor chanced to see a fellow-villager from Tatarsk. The one-eyed old man was on his way to relatives at Gryaznovsky and ran into the band not far from the village. Gregor led the old man aside and asked:

"Are my children alive and well, grand-dad?"

"God preserve them, Gregor Pantalievich, they're alive and well."

"I've got a big thing to ask of you, grand-dad. Give them and my sister, Yevdokia Pantalievna, a warm greeting from me, and a greeting to Prokhor Zykov, and say to Aksinia Astakhova that she is to expect me soon. Only don't tell anybody else you've seen me, will you?"

"I'll do it, master; I'll do it. Never fear, I'll tell them all just as you ask."

"What news is there in the village?"

"Nothing at all; everything's as it was."

"Is Koshevoi still chairman?"

"Yes, he's the chairman."

"He isn't doing any harm to my family, is he?"

"I haven't heard anything about it, so he can't have touched them. And why should he? They're not responsible for you."

"What are people saying about me in the village?"

The old man blew his nose, spent a long time wiping his moustache and beard with his red neckerchief, then answered evasively:

"The Lord knows. . . . They say all sorts of things, whatever comes into their heads. Will you be making your peace with the Soviet government soon?"

What could Gregor answer? Holding in his horse, which was straining to follow the detachment, he smiled and said:

"I don't know, grand-dad. So far there's nothing I can say."

"How's that? We fought the Circassians, and we fought the Turks, but peace came of it. But you, you're all our own people, and yet you can't come to any agreement with one another. . . . It isn't well, Gregor Pantalievich; on my word it isn't well! God the all-merciful, He sees all, He won't forgive you all this, you mark my words. I ask you, is it sensible that Russians, true believers, should fight among themselves, and that without end? Well, if you'd done a little fighting—but this is the fourth year you've been at one another's throats. As my old mind sees it, it's time to end it!"

Gregor said good-bye to the old man and swiftly galloped off to overtake his troop. The man stood long, resting on his stick, rubbing his rheumy eye-socket with his sleeve. With his one youthfully keen eye he gazed after Gregor, admiring his brave bearing, and quietly whispered:

"He's a fine Cossack! He's got everything, bearing and everything else; and yet he's a wastrel. He's lost his road. By all the signs he ought to be fighting the Circassians, but look what he's thought of! And what plaguy use is this government to him? And what is it they're thinking, these young Cossacks? It's no good asking Grisha; all their tribe were always wastrels. His dead father, Pantaleimon, was twisted of the same yarn, and I mind his grandfather Prokoffey. . . . He was another crab apple, and not a man. But what other Cossacks are thinking . . . God forgive me, I don't understand."

Now, when Fomin occupied a village, he no longer summoned a meeting of citizens. He had been convinced that propaganda methods were fruitless. He had enough to do to keep his own men, without enrolling new ones. He began to find consolation in vodka. Whenever he happened to spend a night in a village, there were drinking-bouts. Following their ataman's example, his men drank also. Discipline was breaking down. Looting grew more frequent. The houses of the Soviet employees, who went into hiding whenever the band approached, were stripped of everything that could be carried on horseback. Many of the men had their saddlebags crammed almost to bursting. One day Gregor noticed that a man in his troop was carrying a hand sewing-machine. He had hung the reins over his saddle-bow and was holding the machine under his left arm. Only by using his whip did Gregor succeed in forcing the Cossack to give up his prize. That evening Gregor had a sharp altercation with Fomin. They were alone together in the room. His face and body puffy with his drunken bouts, Fomin sat at the table, while Gregor took great strides up and down the room.

"Sit down, don't go flickering about before my eyes," Fomin said angrily.

Paying no attention to him, Gregor paced restlessly a long time about the tiny room and said at last:

"I've had enough of this, Fomin! Put a stop to this looting and drinking."

"Did you have a bad dream last night?"

"More jokes. . . . But the people are beginning to talk badly of you."

"You know as well as I do that I can't do anything with the boys," Fomin said reluctantly.

"But you're not trying to do anything with them!"

"Well, you're not my teacher! And the people aren't worth bothering about, anyway. We're suffering for them, the swine, but they —I'm thinking of myself, and that's enough."

"You've got a poor opinion even of yourself! You've never got any time to think because of your drunken orgies. You haven't been sober for four days now, and everybody else is drinking too. They're even drinking when on outpost duty, and at night into the bargain. What are you after? Do you want us to be caught while we're drunk and be massacred in some village?"

"And do you think we shall avoid it?" Fomin sneered. "We've got to die some time. The pot got used to fetching water, but it was broken in the end. Do you know that?"

"Then let us ride to Vieshenska tomorrow and put our hands up: 'Take us, we surrender!' "

"No, we'll go on enjoying life awhile longer. . . ."

Gregor halted opposite the table with his legs wide apart.

"If you don't introduce order into the ranks, if you don't put an end to the pillaging and drinking, I'll clear out and take half the men with me," he said quietly.

"Try it!" Fomin menacingly answered.

"It'll come off without any trying!"

"You—you stop threatening me!" Fomin laid his hand on his pistol-butt.

"Don't paw your pistol, I can reach you quicker across the table!" Gregor said swiftly, turning pale and half unsheathing his sabre.

Fomin laid his hands on the table and smiled. "What are you nagging at me for? My head's splitting already as it is, and then you come along with your idiotic talk! Put your sabre back in its scabbard. Can't I even joke with you, then? Aren't you strict! Just like a sixteen-year-old girl. . . ."

"I've already told you what I want, and you look out for yourself! Not all of us are of the same mind as you."

"I know that!"

"Know it and remember it! You're to give orders tomorrow that the packs are to be emptied! We've got a cavalry force and not a pack-horse train. Cut it out of them as though with a knife! And they call themselves fighters for the people! They've loaded themselves down with looted goods and go trading in the villages just like the pedlars used to do! I'm ashamed to my very eyes! What the devil did I join up with you for?" Pale with anger and indignation, Gregor spat and turned away to the window.

Fomin burst into a laugh and said:

"We haven't once been hard pressed by cavalry yet. When a well-fed wolf is hunted by horsemen it belches up all it has eaten as it runs. And my rogues would get rid of everything if we were hunted in earnest. All right, Melekhov, don't get worked up, I'll see to it. It's like this: I'd got a little down in the mouth and had loosened the reins a bit. But I'll pull them up! We can't split up the detachment, we must drink our cup of sorrow together."

They were unable to finish the conversation: the mistress entered the room with a smoking dish of cabbage soup, and then Chumakov and a crowd of Cossacks poured in.

But the talk had its effect. Next morning Fomin gave the order for all packs to be emptied, and himself saw that it was carried out. During the examination of the packs one of the most inveterate looters made some resistance and did not want to part with his booty, and Fomin shot him where he stood in the ranks.

"Take away this carrion!" he said calmly, thrusting the body away with his boot. Looking around the men, he raised his voice. "We've had enough of this crawling into chests, you sons of bitches! That's not what I raised you against the Soviet régime for. You can strip a dead enemy of everything, even his dirty pants, if you're not burying him. But you're not to touch their families. We're not fighting the women. And anyone who resists will get the treatment this scum has got!"

A quiet murmur rose and died away in the ranks.

Order seemed to have been restored. For two or three days the band roamed along the left bank of the Don, clashing with and destroying small groups of local defence detachments.

When they reached Shumilinsky district Kaparin suggested that they should ride on into the territory of Voroniezh province. He argued that there they would undoubtedly have extensive support from the population, which had recently revolted against the Soviet régime. But when Fomin announced this plan to the Cossacks they all declared with one accord: "We won't go out of our own region." Meetings were held in the band. The decision had to be rescinded. For four days in succession they retreated continually eastward, avoiding a fight with the cavalry force which had pressed on their heels all the way from Kazanska district.

It was not easy to move without leaving any traces of themselves, for everywhere the spring field labour was in progress, and people were at work even in the most remote parts of the steppe. The band retreated during the dark spring nights, but hardly had it halted in the morning to feed the horses when a hostile mounted reconnaissance patrol appeared not far away, a hand machine-gun began to rattle, and the Fomin men hurriedly bridled their horses. Beyond the village of Melnikov in Vieshenska district Fomin succeeded in tricking the enemy by a clever manœuvre and got clear away from the pursuit. From the reports of his own reconnaissance patrols he knew that a persistent and intelligent Cossack from Bukanovsky district was in command of the Red cavalry; he also knew that this force was numerically almost twice as large as his own band, had six light machine-guns, and fresh horses which had not been exhausted by long marches. All these circumstances rendered it necessary to avoid a battle, so that his men and horses could rest. Then, when the opportunity presented itself, he must break up the Red cavalry not in open fight, but by a sudden onslaught, and so shake off the incessant pursuit. In this way he might also be able to obtain machine-guns and rifle bullets at the expense of the enemy.

But his calculations proved to be mistaken. Gregor's fears for the band were completely confirmed on April 18. The previous evening Fomin and the majority of the rank and file had drunk heavily. At dawn they left the village where they had halted. During the night hardly a man had had any sleep, and now many of them dozed in their saddles. Towards nine o'clock in the morning they made a halt on the outskirts of a wood not far from the village of Ozhogin. Fomin posted guards and gave orders for the horses to be fed with oats.

A strong, gusty wind was blowing from the east. A brown cloud of sandy dust concealed the horizon. A heavy mist hung high above the steppe. The sun hardly pierced the veil of the mist. The wind snatched at the edges of the men's greatcoats, at the horses' manes and tails. The animals turned their backs to it and sought shelter close to the bushes of hawthorn scattered about the fringe of the forest. The men's eyes streamed with the prickling, sandy dust, and it was difficult to see anything even at a short distance.

Gregor carefully wiped his horse's muzzle, hung the oat-basket round its neck, and went to Kaparin, who was feeding his horse on oats poured into the fold of his greatcoat.

"A fine spot you've chosen for the halt!" Gregor remarked, pointing to the forest with his whip.

Kaparin shrugged his shoulders.

"So I told that fool, but you can't convince him of anything."

"We should have halted out in the steppe or on the outskirts of a village."

"Do you think we can expect an attack from the forest?"

"Yes, I do."

"The enemy is a long way off."

"The enemy can be quite close; they're not infantry."

"The forest is bare; we shall see them if they come."

"There's nobody to see them; almost everybody's asleep. I'm afraid the guards may be asleep too!"

"They're not in a fit state to stand up after last night's bout, you won't rouse them now!" Kaparin frowned as though he were in pain and said in an undertone: "We shall be lost with such a leader. He's as empty as a bottle, and stupid, quite incredibly stupid. Why don't you want to take over the command? The Cossacks respect you. They'd follow you willingly."

"I don't want to; I'm only a passing guest here," Gregor dryly answered. He went off to his horse, regretting the indiscreet confession which had fallen from his lips.

Kaparin poured the rest of the oats out of his greatcoat on to the ground and hastened after Gregor.

"You know, Melekhov," he said as he walked along, breaking off a twig of thorn and pinching the tight, swollen buds, "I don't think we shall be able to hold out for long if we don't join up with some large anti-Soviet force—with Maslak's brigade, for instance. He's wandering somewhere in the south of the province. We must break through to him or we'll be massacred here one fine day."

"It's flood-time now. We can't get across the Don."

"Not now. But when the water falls we must retreat. Don't you agree?"

After some reflection Gregor answered:

"You're right. We must clear out of this area. There's nothing to be done around here."

Kaparin grew enthusiastic in his argument. He began to expatiate on the theme that their expectations of support had not been justified, and that now they must somehow or other persuade Fomin not to go on roaming aimlessly about the region, but to decide to link up with a stronger force.

Gregor grew tired of listening to his chatter. He kept his eyes fixed on his horse. As soon as the basket was empty he took it off, bridled the animal, and tightened the saddle-girths.

"We shan't be moving on for a long time yet; there's no need for all that hurry," Kaparin said.

"You'd do better to go and get your horse ready, for there won't be time to saddle it!" Gregor answered.

Kaparin stared hard at him, then went to his mount, which was standing close to the line of wagons.

Leading his horse by the rein, Gregor went across to Fomin. The commander was lying on his cloak with his legs spread wide, lazily gnawing the wing of a boiled chicken. He shifted, and beckoned to Gregor to sit down beside him.

"Sit down here and have a rest."

"We must get away, now's not the time for rest," Gregor said.

"We'll finish feeding the horses and then we'll move on."

"We can finish feeding them later."

"What are you in such a hurry for?" Fomin threw away the picked bone and wiped his hands on his cloak.

"They'll get us here. It's just the right spot for it."

"How the devil can they? The patrol's only just returned and reported that there's not a soul to be seen on the hill. It's clear they've lost track of us or they'd be on our tail now. We needn't expect any attack from Bukanovsky district. The military commissar there is a good fighting lad, but he hasn't got much of a force at his command, and he's hardly likely to come out and face us. We'll have a proper rest, stay here till evening, then set off again. Sit down and have some chicken; what are you standing over me like that for? It seems to me you've turned coward, Melekhov. Soon you'll be riding round every bush and going right out of your way, like this." He swept his hand round in a great semicircle and laughed heartily.

Inwardly cursing, Gregor went off, tied his horse to a bush, and lay down beside it, protecting his face from the wind with the edge of his greatcoat. He dozed off to the whistle of the wind, to the fine, monotonous rustle of the high dry grass bowed above him.

He was brought to his feet by the long-drawn-out rattle of a machine-gun. Before the first burst of fire was finished he had his horse untethered. Above all the other voices rose Fomin's shout: "To horse!" Now two or three more machine-guns began to stutter from the forest on the right. Mounting his horse, with a glance Gregor took stock of the situation. To the right, on the edge of the forest, hardly visible through the dust-clouds, some fifty Red Army men were advancing into the attack, cutting off the line of retreat to the hills. Above their heads their swords glittered coldly and very familiarly, showing a bluish hue in the dim light of the sun. From

the forest, from bushy hillocks, the machine-guns were firing, empty-
ing disk after disk with feverish haste. To the left also about half a
squadron of Red Army men were galloping along without a shout,
waving their sabres, rushing to complete the encirclement. There
was only one way of escape: to break through the thin line of men
attacking from the left and to retreat towards the Don. Gregor
shouted to Fomin: "Keep up behind me!" and put his horse into a
gallop, simultaneously baring his sabre.

When he had covered some forty yards he looked back. Fomin,
Kaparin, Chumakov, and several other men were following at a
furious gallop some twenty yards behind him. The machine-guns
in the forest had stopped firing; only the one on the extreme right
was rattling away with short, angry bursts at the Fomin men scram-
bling around the baggage-wagons. But that last machine-gun also
suddenly stopped, and Gregor realized that the attackers were now
right on top of the camp, and that the men left behind were being
sabred. So he guessed from the desperate shouts, from the rare shots
fired in defence. But he had no time to look back. As his horse
carried him impetuously towards the stream of men advancing
against him, he chose his man. A soldier in a short, pleated sheepskin was galloping towards him on a grey, not very fresh horse. As
though by the light of a flash of lightning, for one elusive moment
Gregor saw the horse with a white star on its foam-flecked chest, the
rider with his crimson, excited, youthful face, and behind him the
broad, sombre expanse of the steppe stretching away to the Don.
The next moment he would have to avoid a blow and wield his
sabre. When some ten yards from the rider, Gregor swung his body
sharply over to the left. He heard the cutting whistle of a sabre
above his head and, jerking himself upright in the saddle, touched
the man on the head with the very point of his sabre as he passed.
His hand hardly felt the force of the blow, but, looking back, he saw
the man sag and slowly slip out of the saddle and saw a thick stream
of blood on the back of his yellow sheepskin coat. The grey horse
slackened down into a fast trot, running sideways as though afraid
of its own shadow, its head carried wildly high in the air.

Gregor dropped over his horse's neck and instinctively lowered
his sabre. The bullets whistled thinly and sharply over his head.
The animal's ears quivered as they lay flat against its head, and at
the ends of them the sweat hung in beads. Gregor heard only the

fierce whistle of a bullet fired after him and the sharp, panting breath of his horse. He looked back again and saw Fomin and Chumakov; Kaparin was a good hundred yards behind them and, still farther off, only one man of the second troop, the lame Sterladnikov, had fought and galloped his way past the two soldiers who rode to attack him. All the other eight or nine men who had fled after Fomin had been sabred. Their tails waving in the wind, the riderless horses were fleeing in all directions, to be followed and caught by Red Army men. Only one high-standing bay belonging to a Fomin man was galloping along at Kaparin's side, snorting and dragging its dead master, who had not been able to free his boot from the stirrup as he fell.

Beyond the sandy rise Gregor halted his horse, jumped out of the saddle, and thrust his sabre into its scabbard. It took him only a few seconds to persuade his horse to lie down. From behind this cover he fired all his clip of cartridges; as his aim was hurried and agitated, however, only with his last bullet did he send a horse down beneath a Red Army man. But it enabled the fifth Fomin man to draw away from the pursuit.

"Mount! You'll be lost!" Fomin shouted as he drew level with Gregor.

The massacre was complete. Of the entire band only five men escaped. They were pursued as far as the village of Antonovsky, and the chase did not end till the fugitives hid in the forest surrounding the village.

In all that mad gallop not one of the five said a word.

Close to a little river Kaparin's horse fell, and they could not get it on to its legs again. Under the others the hard-driven horses were staggering, hardly able to move their legs, dropping thick white clots of foam to the ground.

"You shouldn't be the commander of a detachment, but a shepherd of sheep!" Gregor said, dismounting and not looking at Fomin.

Without speaking Fomin slipped from his horse and began to unsaddle it. But he went off without removing the saddle and sat down on a hummock overgrown with bracken.

"Well, we'll have to abandon the horses," he said, looking fearfully all about him.

"And then?" Chumakov asked.

"And then we must make our way on foot to the other side of the Don."

"Where to?"

"We'll stop in the forest till nightfall, then we'll get across the Don and bury ourselves for the time being in Rubiezhin. I've got lots of relations there."

"Another idiotic idea!" Kaparin exclaimed furiously. "Don't you think they'll look for you there? That's just where they're going to expect you now. What do you use for thinking with?"

"Well, where else are we to go to?" Fomin asked in a distracted tone.

Gregor took the bullets and a piece of bread out of his saddlebags and said:

"Are you thinking of spending much time over your talk? Come on! Tie up the horses, unsaddle them, and get going, or the Reds will get us even here."

Chumakov threw his whip on the ground, trod it into the mire and said in a quivering tone:

"And so we're on foot now! And all our boys have gone under! Mother of God, how they shook us up! I didn't think I was going to come through today alive. . . . Death looked me in the eyes."

Without speaking they unsaddled their horses, tied all the four to one alder bush, and, in single file, one in the tracks of another, like wolves, they made their way down to the Don, carrying their saddles in their arms, keeping wherever possible to the denser thicket of undergrowth.

Chapter 5

In springtime, when the Don overflows its banks and the flood water covers all the low-lying water-meadows, opposite the village of Rubiezhin a small section of the lofty left bank remains high and dry above the inundation.

From the Donside hills this island, densely covered with young willows, oaks, and the dove-blue, spreading bushes of osiers, is visible for a long distance.

In the summer the trees are entwined with wild hops to their very crowns, the ground below is spread with impenetrable, prickly dewberry bushes, pale-blue convolvuluses crawl and twine over the bushes, and in the rare glades the high, thick grass, munificently nourished by rich soil, rises above the height of a man.

In the summer even at noonday it is quiet, twilit, and cool in the forest. Only the orioles disturb the silence, and the cuckoos vie with one another in counting out the unspent years. But in winter-time the woods stand completely deserted, bare, fettered in a deathly silence. The serrated edges of the treetops show a sombre black against the pallid, wintry sky. Only the wolves' litters find a safe shelter in the thickets year after year, spending their days lying in the snow-laden scrub.

On this island Fomin, Gregor Melekhov, and the others who had escaped from the massacre of the band set up their quarters. They lived as best they could, eating the miserable victuals which Fomin's cousin brought them by boat at night. They were half starved, but they could sleep their fill, with their saddle pommels under their heads. They took turns at keeping guard during the night. They lit no fire, for fear that someone would discover their hiding-place.

Washing round the island, impetuously the flood water poured southward. It roared menacingly as it broke through the barrier of old poplars which stood in its path, then murmured on in a lulled, singing tone, setting the tops of the inundated bushes swaying.

Gregor quickly grew accustomed to the never ceasing sound of the water near by. He lay for long hours by the steeply cut bank and gazed at the broad watery expanse, at the chalky spurs of the Donside hills enveloped in a sunny lilac haze. There, beyond that haze, was his native village . . . Aksinia . . . his children. And thither flew his cheerless thoughts. Momentarily a longing blazed up and consumed him as he recalled his dear ones, an impotent hatred for Mikhail seethed within him. But he suppressed these feelings and tried not to look at the Donside hills, to avoid thinking of these things. There was no point in giving the rein to unhappy memories. Life was oppressive enough as it was. Already he had such a pain in his breast that sometimes it seemed to him that his heart had been pierced and was no longer beating, but was streaming with blood.

Evidently his wounds, and the hardships of war, and typhus had
done their work: he began to listen continually to the importunate
thumping of his heart. Sometimes the lacerating pain in his chest,
under the left nipple, grew so unbearably sharp that momentarily his
lips went dry and he had difficulty in choking back a cry. But he
found a sure method of freeing himself from the pain: he lay down
with his left side against the damp earth, or wet his shirt with cold
water; and then it slowly, almost, it seemed, reluctantly, left his body.

The days turned pleasant and still. Only occasionally did little
white clouds tousled by a wind in the height go floating across the
clear sky, and their reflections slipped like a flight of swans over the
flood water, to vanish as they touched the distant shore.

It was good to gaze at the swift current furiously seething along
by the bank, to listen to the myriad sounds of the water and not to
think of anything, to try not to think of anything which caused him
suffering. He gazed for hours at the whimsical and endlessly changing swirl of the current. The ripples altered their forms continually;
where the previous moment a smooth stream had been flowing, bearing on its surface stalks of reeds, crumpled leaves, and clumps of
grass torn away by the roots, a moment after a fantastically curving
funnel appeared which greedily sucked down all that floated within
reach of it; again a little later the funnel had disappeared, and in its
place the water was boiling and swirling in turbid tangles, throwing
to the surface now the blackened root of a sedge, then an outspread
oak leaf, then a bunch of straw carried down from one knew not
where.

Of an evening the cherry-red afterglow burned in the west. The
moon rose from behind a lofty poplar. Its light extended over the
Don in a chilly white flame, broken into reflections and black modu-
lations where the wind tousled the water into a light speckle of froth.
At night, blended with the sound of the water, the voices of innumerable flocks of northward-flying geese sounded as incessantly
over the island. The birds, with no one to disturb them, often settled
on the eastern side of the island. Over the backwater, through the
inundated forest the male teal called challengingly, ducks quacked,
the barnacles and geese quietly cackled and answered one another.
One day, noiselessly making his way to the bank, Gregor saw a large
flock of swans not far from the island. The sun had not yet risen.
The morning glow was flickering brilliantly beyond the barrier of

the forest. Reflecting its light, the water seemed rosy, and the great, majestic birds, with their heads turned to the sunrise, seemed rose-coloured also. Hearing a rustle on the bank, they flew up with a sonorous trumpet-call, and when they rose above the forest the astonishing gleam of their snowy plumage almost dazzled Gregor.

Fomin and the others killed time each in his own fashion. Making his lame leg comfortable, the industrious Sterladnikov worked from morn till night mending clothes and boots. Kaparin, whose health was not improved by sleeping on the damp ground at night, lay for days on end in the sun, coughing hollowly, covered up to his head by his sheepskin. Fomin and Chumakov played endlessly with home-made cards cut out of paper. Gregor wandered about the island and squatted for hours beside the water. They talked but little to one another—all they had to say had been said long since—and they came together only at meal-times and of an evening, while waiting for Fomin's cousin to arrive. They were overcome by boredom, and during all their stay on the island only once did Gregor see Chumakov and Sterladnikov, for some reason suddenly feeling light-hearted, begin to wrestle. They stamped about for a long time on one spot, grunting and exchanging curt jesting remarks. Their feet sank to their ankles in the white, granular sand. The lame Sterladnikov was obviously the stronger, but Chumakov was the more agile. They wrestled with their arms around each other's waist, their shoulders thrust forward, each keenly watching the other's legs. Their faces grew set and pale with the strain, their breathing spasmodic and violent. Gregor watched the struggle with interest. Choosing a fitting moment, Chumakov suddenly threw himself down on his back, dragging his opponent with him, and with a movement of his bent legs threw Sterladnikov across his head. A second later, as supple and nimble as a polecat, Chumakov was lying on top of Sterladnikov, pressing his shoulder-blades into the sand, while the other bellowed, panting and laughing: "But you're cheating. We didn't agree—that we could throw each other over our heads."

"You went for each other like young fighting-cocks; and that's enough for now, or you'll be fighting in earnest," Fomin said.

But they had no intention of fighting. Amicably, with arms interlocked, they sat down on the sand, and Chumakov, in a thick but pleasant bass, broke into a song. Sterladnikov took it up in his thin tenor voice, and they sang in unison and unexpectedly well.

But suddenly Sterladnikov could not restrain himself any more: he jumped up and, snapping his fingers, kicking the sand about with his lame leg, began to dance. Without stopping his singing Chumakov took his sword, dug a shallow hole in the sand, and said:

"Wait a bit, you lame devil! One of your legs is shorter than the other, you can't dance properly on a level spot. . . . You must either dance on a slope or else have your longer leg in a hole and the other outside. Put your sound leg in this hole, and then dance, you see how well it works. Now, off we go!"

Sterladnikov wiped the sweat from his brow and obediently set his good leg into the hole Chumakov had dug.

"But you're right, it does make it easier," he said.

Panting with laughter, Chumakov clapped his hands and began to sing very fast. And Sterladnikov, his face set in the serious expression common to all dancers, began agilely to dance and even attempted to squat down on his haunches and kick out one leg.

The days passed on, each exactly like those that had gone. With the oncoming of darkness they waited impatiently for Fomin's cousin to arrive. All five of them gathered on the bank, talking in undertones, smoking, concealing the lighted ends of their cigarettes under the edges of their greatcoats. They had decided to stay for another week on the island and then to cross at night to the right bank of the Don, to seize horses, and to set out for the south. By all the rumours Maslak's brigade was still roaming somewhere in the south of the region.

Fomin charged his relations to discover where he could get horses suitable for riding, and also told them to report each day all that occurred in the area. The news they brought in was reassuring: Fomin was being searched for on the left bank of the Don, and although Red Army men had visited Rubiezhin, after searching his house they had at once ridden off again.

"We must clear out of here quickly! What the hell is the good of sticking here? Let's clear out tomorrow," Chumakov proposed one day at breakfast.

"We must find out about horses first," Fomin said. "What's the hurry? If only they fed us better I wouldn't give up this comfortable life until winter. Look how beautiful it is all around! We'll have a good rest, and then we'll set to work again. Let them fish for us, we won't let ourselves be caught so easily! They smashed us owing to my stupidity, I know, and of course it's a disgrace, but it isn't everything. We'll collect more men again. As soon as we mount horses we'll ride through the nearest villages, and in a week we'll have half a company around us, and possibly a full company. We'll be overwhelmed with men; by God we will!"

"Nonsense! Overweening arrogance!" Kaparin said irritably. "The Cossacks have let us down. They haven't followed us, and they won't. We must have the courage to look the truth in the eyes and not delude ourselves with idiotic hopes."

"Why won't they follow us?"

"Well, they didn't at first and so they won't now."

"We shall see!" Fomin retorted in a challenging tone. "I won't lay down my arms!"

"That's all empty talk!" Kaparin said wearily.

"You devil's head!" the infuriated Fomin exclaimed. "What are you spreading panic here for? You've fed me up with your tears worse than a bitter radish would! What did we rise at all for, then? Why did you come in, if your guts are so weak? It was you who urged me on to start the rising, but now you want to crawl out of it. Haven't you got anything to say?"

"I've got nothing to say to you, you can go to the devil, you fool!" Kaparin exclaimed hysterically, and went off, wrapping himself chillily in his sheepskin and turning up the collar.

"These well-born people are always thin-skinned! As soon as anything happens they've had enough, they're done," Fomin said with a sigh.

They sat silent for some time, listening to the steady, powerful roar of the water. A duck pursued by two drakes flew over their heads with a grating croak. An excitedly chattering flock of starlings dropped down over the glade, but, seeing human beings, swept up again, turning like a black braid as they went.

A little later Kaparin came back.

"I want to go to the village tonight," he said, looking at Fomin and blinking hard.

"What for?"

"A strange question! Can't you see I've got a bad chill and can hardly keep on my feet?"

"Well, and what of it? Will you lose your chill in the village, do you think?" Fomin asked with imperturbable calm.

"I must have at least a few nights in a warm place."

"You're not going anywhere!" Fomin said firmly.

"What, am I to perish here?"

"Please yourself."

"But why can't I go? These nights sleeping out in the cold will finish me off."

"And supposing you're caught in the village? Have you thought of that? Then they'll finish us all off. Do you think I don't know you? At the first examination you'll betray us. And you'll do it even before that, on the road to Vieshenska."

Chumakov burst into a laugh and nodded approvingly. He completely agreed with Fomin. But Kaparin said obstinately:

"I must go. Your quick-witted arguments haven't made me change my mind."

"But I've told you to sit still and don't fidget."

"But don't you understand, Yakov Yefimovich, that I can't go on living this animal life any longer? I've got pleurisy, and possibly even inflammation of the lungs."

"You'll get over it. You'll lie about in the sun and get well."

"In any case I'm going today," Kaparin declared sharply. "You have no right to restrain me. I'll go whatever happens."

Fomin gazed at him, suspiciously screwed up his eyes, and, winking at Chumakov, rose to his feet.

"It looks to me, Kaparin, as though you really have fallen ill. . . . You must have a high temperature. . . . Let me see whether your head's hot!" He took several steps towards Kaparin, stretching out one hand.

Evidently Kaparin noticed the unpleasant look on Fomin's face, for he fell back and sharply exclaimed:

"Get away!"

"Don't make that noise! What are you making that noise for? I'm only going to find out. What are you up to?" Fomin strode to Kaparin and seized him by the throat. "Intending to give yourself up, you swine?" he muttered thickly and, straining all his body, tried to throw Kaparin to the ground.

Gregor had difficulty in separating them and had to exert all his strength.

After dinner Kaparin went up to Gregor as he was hanging some washing on a bush and said:

"I'd like to talk to you alone. . . . Let's sit down." They sat down on a fallen, rotting poplar trunk.

Coughing hollowly, Kaparin said:

"What do you think of that idiot's behaviour? I'm sincerely grateful to you for your intervention. You acted nobly, as an officer should. But this is terrible! I can't stand any more. We're living like animals. . . . How many days is it now since we ate hot food? And then this sleeping on the damp earth. . . . I've caught a chill, and my side is hurting me terribly. I must have developed inflammation of the lungs. I badly want to sit by a fire, to sleep in a warm room, to change my underclothes. I dream of fresh clean shirts, of sheets. . . . No, I can't go on!"

Gregor smiled and asked:

"Did you think you were going to fight with every comfort?"

"But listen, what sort of war is this?" Kaparin answered energetically. "This isn't war, but endless wandering, murdering individual Soviet workers, and then fleeing. It would be war if the people supported us, if a rising were to break out. But to call this war—no, this isn't war!"

"There's nothing else we can do. You don't want us to surrender, do you?"

"You're right, but what are we to do?"

Gregor shrugged his shoulders. He gave voice to the thought which had frequently entered his mind as he lay about on the island:

"Even a miserable liberty is better than a good prison. You know what the proverb says: 'A strong prison, but it only pleases the devil'!"

Kaparin drew designs on the sand with a twig. After a long silence he said:

"We haven't necessarily got to surrender, but we've got to find new forms of struggle against the Bolsheviks. We must separate from this disgusting scum. You're an intelligent man. . . ."

"Why do you think so?" Gregor laughed. "Why, I can hardly even pronounce that word."

"You're an officer."

"By accident."

"No, joking apart, you are an officer, you've grafted yourself into

officers' society, you've seen real men, you're not a Soviet upstart like
Fomin, and you must realize that it's senseless for us to remain here.
It's equivalent to suicide. He was the cause of our being smashed up
at the forest, and if we continue to link our fates with him he'll do
the same again more than once. He's simply a cad, and an obstreperous fool into the bargain! We shall be lost if we stay with him."

"So you don't suggest surrendering, but leaving Fomin? Where
are we to go to? To Maslak?" Gregor asked.

"No. He's only another adventurer, only on a larger scale. I take
a different view of all this now. We must go not to Maslak—"

"Then where?"

"To Vieshenska."

Gregor shrugged his shoulders irritably.

"I call that throwing good money after bad. It's not to my liking."

Kaparin looked at him sharply with glittering eyes.

"You haven't understood, Melekhov. Can I trust you?"

"Completely."

"On the word of honour of an officer?"

"On the word of honour of a Cossack."

Kaparin glanced in the direction of Fomin and Chumakov, and,
although they were a considerable distance away and could not have
overheard the conversation, he lowered his voice:

"I know your relations with Fomin and the others. You're just as
much a foreign body among them as I am. I'm not interested in the
reasons which have led you to fight against the Soviet régime. If I
understand aright, it's because of your past and your fear of arrest,
isn't it?"

"You've just said you're not interested in the reasons."

"Yes, yes, that was only by the way. Now for a few words about
myself. Formerly I was an officer and a member of the Social Revolutionary Party, but later I completely revised my political convictions. . . . Only the monarchy can save Russia. Only the monarchy! Providence itself points this road for our native country. The
emblem of the Soviet government is a hammer and sickle, a *'serp'*
and a *'molot,'* isn't it?" With the twig Kaparin drew the words *"serp"*
and *"molot"* on the sand, then fixed his feverishly burning eyes on
Gregor's face. "Now read each of those words backward. You have?
Do you understand? Only 'prestolom,' only 'through the throne,'

will the Revolution and the Bolshevik régime be ended. Do you know, I was possessed with mystical horror when I discovered that. I trembled, for, if you like to put it so, it is God's finger pointing to the end of our troubles."

Kaparin was silent, panting with agitation. His keen eyes had a hint of madness in them as he gazed at Gregor. But Gregor did not tremble at all and did not feel any mystical horror as he heard Kaparin's revelation. He had a more sober and matter-of-fact view of things, and so he said in answer:

"That's not anybody's finger. Were you at the front during the German war?"

Perplexed by the question, Kaparin did not answer at once.

"To be frank, why do you ask? No, I was not actually at the front."

"Then where did you go through the war? At the rear?"

"Yes."

"All the time?"

"Yes. I mean, not all the time, but almost all. But why do you ask?"

"Well, I've been at the front continually from 1914 down to the present day, with only a few breaks. And in regard to your finger— How can it be God's finger, when God Himself doesn't exist? I've long since given up believing that nonsense. Ever since 1915, when I got my first sight of war, I've been thinking that God doesn't exist. Not at all! If He did, He would have no right to allow people to do such things as they do! We front-line men have got rid of God, we've left Him to the old men and the women. Let them take comfort in Him. And there isn't any finger, and there can't be any monarchy. The people have put an end to that once for all. And this game you're playing, this twisting letters about—that, if you don't mind my saying so, is a kid's trick and nothing more. And I don't understand what you're telling me all this for. You must speak more simply and plainly. I've never studied in a Junkers' academy and I'm not too well educated, even though I have been an officer. If I'd been better educated perhaps I wouldn't be sitting with you here on this island, like a wolf cut off by a flood," he ended with an obvious note of regret in his voice.

"That doesn't matter," Kaparin said hurriedly. "It doesn't matter whether you believe in God or not. That's a question for your own conviction, your conscience. Nor does it matter in the least whether you're a monarchist or a supporter of the Constitutional Assembly, or just a Cossack fighting for self-government. What does matter is that we're united by a single attitude to the Soviet régime. Do you agree?"

"Go on."

"We put our hopes in a general rising of the Cossacks, didn't we? That hope has proved unjustified. Now we've got to extricate ourselves from this situation. We can fight the Bolsheviks later, but not under Fomin's leadership! The important thing now is to save our own lives, and that is why I'm proposing an alliance with you."

"What sort of alliance? Against whom?"

"Against Fomin."

"I don't understand."

"It's all very simple. I invite you to be my accomplice." Kaparin grew obviously agitated and panted violently as he went on: "You and I will kill these three and go to Vieshenska, understand? That will save us. That service to the Soviet government will save us from punishment. We shall live. You understand? We shall live. We shall save our lives. It goes without saying that when the opportunity occurs we shall fight against the Bolsheviks again. But that will be when it's a serious business, and not some adventure like the present with this wretched Fomin. Do you agree? Bear in mind that this is the only way out of our present desperate situation, and a brilliant one at that."

"But how is it to be done?" Gregor asked. Inwardly he was quivering with indignation, but with all his strength he attempted to hide the feeling which was mastering him.

"I've thought it all out: we'll do it at night, with cold steel. Then the next night the Cossack who supplies us with food will come across, we'll cross the Don, and that's all. It's marvelously simple, and no cunning called for at all!"

Smiling, Gregor said with feigned affability:

"Now, that's really clever! But tell me, Kaparin, when you wanted to go to the village to get warm this morning—were you intending to go to Vieshenska? Did Fomin hit the mark?"

Kaparin stared closely at Gregor's amiably smiling face and smiled also, wanly and a little embarrassed.

"I'll tell you frankly, I was. You know, when it's a question of your own skin you don't show any particular regard about the choice of method."

"So you'd have betrayed us?"

"Yes," Kaparin openly admitted. "But I'd have tried to spare you personally any unpleasantness if they'd caught you here on the island."

"But why didn't you kill us all yourself? That would have been easy enough to do at night."

"There was the risk. While I was dealing with one, the others . . ."

"Lay down your arms!" Gregor said in a repressed tone, snatching out his pistol. "Lay them down or I'll shoot you on the spot! I'm getting up now, and I'll cover you so that Fomin can't see, and then you'll throw your pistol down at my feet. Well? Don't even think of shooting! I'll put you out at the first sign."

Kaparin sat still, turning deathly pale. "Don't kill me!" he whispered, hardly moving his white lips.

"I shan't. But I'll take your weapons."

"You'll betray me. . . ."

Tears rolled down Kaparin's hairy cheeks. Gregor frowned with loathing and pity and raised his voice:

"Throw down your pistol! I won't betray you, though I ought to. Why, what a cur you've proved yourself to be! A dirty cur!"

Kaparin threw his pistol at Gregor's feet.

"How about your Browning? Hand over your Browning. It's in the breast pocket of your tunic."

Kaparin pulled out and threw down the gleaming, nickelled Browning and covered his face with his hands. He shook with the sobs which convulsed him.

"Stop it, you scum!" Gregor said sharply, with difficulty controlling his desire to strike Kaparin.

"You'll betray me! I'm lost. . . ."

"I've told you I won't. But as soon as we leave the island you can make yourself scarce! Such as you aren't wanted by anybody. You can find your own shelter."

Kaparin removed his hands from his face. His wet, livid cheeks, swollen eyes, and shaking lower jaw were horrible to look at.

"Then why did you—why did you disarm me?" he stuttered.

Gregor reluctantly said:

"So that you don't shoot me in the back. Anything is to be expected from men like you—educated men! And there you sat talking about a finger, about the Czar, about God. . . . What a slimy creature you are!"

Without another look at Kaparin, spitting out the copious spittle which filled his mouth again and again, Gregor slowly went back to the others.

Sterladnikov was quietly whistling as he sewed up a slit in his saddle with a waxed-end thread. Fomin and Chumakov were lying on a horse-cloth, playing cards as usual.

Fomin gave Gregor a swift glance and asked:

"What was he saying to you? What were you talking about?"

"He was complaining about the life. . . . He talked as though . . ."

Gregor kept his promise not to betray Kaparin. But that evening he took a quiet opportunity to remove the bolt from Kaparin's rifle and hid it. "The devil knows what he might try at night," he thought as he lay down to sleep.

Next morning Gregor was awakened by Fomin. Bending over him, Fomin quietly asked:

"Did you take Kaparin's weapons from him?"

"What? What weapons?" Gregor raised himself on his elbow, painfully straightening his shoulders. His greatcoat, fur cap, and boots were all wet with the mist which had descended at sunrise, and he was chilled to the bone.

"We can't find his weapons. Did you take them? Do wake up, Melekhov!"

"Why, yes, I took them. But what's up?"

Fomin went off without speaking. Gregor rose and shook out his greatcoat. Some distance away Chumakov was preparing breakfast: he washed the only dish they possessed, then, pressing a loaf of bread to his chest, cut off four equal hunks, poured milk out of a jug into the dish, and, crumbling a solidly boiled piece of millet porridge, looked at Gregor.

"You've slept late this morning, Melekhov! See where the sun's got to."

"The man with a clear conscience always sleeps well," Sterladnikov said as he wiped the wooden spoons on the edge of his greatcoat after washing them. "But Kaparin didn't sleep a wink all night, he tossed and turned. . . ."

Fomin smiled as he looked at Gregor.

"Sit down and have breakfast, brigands," Chumakov proposed. Without waiting for the others he began to spoon up his milk, then bit off a good half of his hunk of bread. Gregor picked up his spoon and, staring hard at the others, asked:

"Where's Kaparin?"

Fomin and Sterladnikov went on eating in silence. Chumakov gazed fixedly at Gregor, but he too said nothing.

"Where's Kaparin got to?" Gregor asked again, though he had a mournful suspicion of what had happened during the night.

"Kaparin's a long way away now," Chumakov answered, smiling imperturbably. "He's floating down to Rostov. I expect he's rocking somewhere about Ust-Khopersk. There's his sheepskin hanging, look. . . ."

"Have you really killed him?" Gregor asked, glancing swiftly at Kaparin's sheepskin coat.

There was no point in asking. Everything was quite clear already, but for some reason he did ask. At first nobody answered, and he repeated the question.

"Why, of course we've killed him," Chumakov said, and covered his grey, femininely beautiful eyes with his lashes. "I killed him. That's my job these days, to kill people. . . ."

Gregor looked at him closely. Chumakov's clean, deep red face was tranquil and even cheerful. His blond whiskers with their golden fringe showed up strongly against his sunburnt face, setting off the darker hue of his eyebrows and sleekly combed hair. He was genuinely handsome and of modest appearance, was this honorary executioner to Fomin's band. He laid his spoon down on the tarpaulin, wiped his moustache with the back of his hand, and said:

"You can be grateful to Yakov Yefimich, Melekhov! It was he who saved your soul, or you'd have been floating down the Don with Kaparin at this moment. . . ."

"What for?"

Spacing out his words, Chumakov slowly said:

"It's clear Kaparin intended to surrender, and he talked a long time with you yesterday. Well, we and Yakov Yefimich thought we'd save him from his sin. May I tell him everything?" He looked interrogatively at Fomin.

Fomin nodded, and Chumakov, his teeth crunching the grains of the insufficiently cooked millet porridge, went on with his story:

"I got an oak cudgel ready yesterday evening, and I said to Yakov Yefimich: 'I'll settle them both, Kaparin and Melekhov, during the night.' But he said: 'Finish off Kaparin, but don't touch Melekhov.' And that's what we agreed on. I watched until Kaparin went off to sleep, and I heard you sleeping, snoring away. Well, I crawled up to him and brought the cudgel down on his head. And our staff captain didn't even kick out his legs. He just stretched himself out so sweetly and gave up the ghost. We quietly searched him, then we picked him up by the arms and legs, carried him to the bank, took off his boots, tunic, and sheepskin, and dropped him into the water. But you were still fast asleep and didn't know anything about it. Death stood very close to you last night, Melekhov! At your head it stood. Even though Yakov Yefimich had said you weren't to be touched, I thought: 'What could they have been talking about yesterday? It's a bad business when out of five two begin to keep themselves apart from the others and talk secrets.' I stole up to you and wanted to land you one, but then I thought: 'If I hit him with the cudgel, he's a healthy devil! Supposing he jumps up and starts blazing away if I don't lay him out with the first blow?' Well, Fomin once more stopped the whole business. He crawled up to me and whispered: 'Don't touch him, he's one of us, we can trust him.' Well, we talked it over, and then we couldn't make out what had happened to Kaparin's weapons. And so I left you. But you slept well; you didn't have any idea what was hanging over you!"

Gregor said calmly:

"And you'd have killed me for nothing, you fool! I wasn't in any plot with Kaparin."

"But how is it you've got his weapons?"

Gregor smiled.

"I took his pistols from him yesterday, and removed the bolt from his rifle in the evening and hid it under a saddle-cloth." He went on to tell of his conversation with Kaparin and the captain's proposals.

Fomin discontentedly asked him:

"But why didn't you say anything about this yesterday?"

"I felt sorry for him, the snivelling devil!" Gregor confessed frankly.

"Ah, Melekhov, Melekhov!" Chumakov exclaimed, genuinely amazed. "You put your pity where you laid the bolt of Kaparin's rifle; you bury it under a saddle-cloth, for it won't do you any good!"

"Don't you teach me! I know my own business!" Gregor replied coldly.

"Why should I teach you? But supposing as the result of your pity I'd sent you off to the next world for no reason at all last night? Then what?"

"I would find my road there too," Gregor quietly answered after a moment's thought. And, more to himself than to the others, he added: "In broad daylight it's terrible for a man to face his death; but while he's asleep it ought to be easy enough. . . ."

Chapter 6

One night at the end of April they crossed the Don in a boat. On the bank outside Rubiezhin a young Cossack named Aleksandr Kosheliov, from Nizhnii-Krivsky village, was waiting for them.

"I'm coming with you, Yakov Yefimich," he said as he greeted Fomin. "I'm fed up with spending my time at home."

Fomin nudged Gregor with his elbow and whispered:

"Do you see? I told you so. We've hardly had time to get away from the island, but already the people are . . . Here they come! He's an acquaintance of mine, a fighting little Cossack! This is a good sign. Our business will get moving now!"

Judging by his voice, Fomin was smiling satisfiedly. He was obviously delighted by the arrival of a new comrade. The successful crossing of the river and the circumstance that one more man had immediately joined him cheered him up and gave wings to new hopes.

"So besides a rifle and a pistol you've got a sabre and a pair of field-glasses?" he said in a contented tone, examining and feeling Kosheliov's equipment in the darkness. "There's a Cossack for you! You can see at once he's a true Cossack and no mongrel!"

Fomin's cousin drove up to the bank in a wagon drawn by a very small horse.

"Put the saddles in the wagon," he said in an undertone. "But hurry up, for Christ's sake, for the night's getting on, and we've got a long road."

He was agitated, and hurried Fomin. But, now he had got away from the island and felt the firm earth of his native village beneath his feet, Fomin would have been by no means averse to dropping in at his home for an hour or so and visiting village acquaintances.

Just before dawn they selected the best horses from a drove close to the village of Yagodny and saddled them. To the old man minding the drove Chumakov said:

"Don't be too upset about the horses, daddy. They're not worth worrying about, and we'll only ride a little way on them. As soon as we find better mounts we'll return these to their owners. If anyone asks who took the horses, say militia from Krasnokutsk had them. Let the owners go there. We're chasing a band, you can tell them."

When they reached the main road they said good-bye to Fomin's cousin, then turned off to the left, and all five rode in a south-westerly direction at a fast trot. There were rumours that the Maslak band had appeared not far from Mieshkovsky district centre within the past day or two. And in that direction Fomin went, resolved to join up with Maslak.

In search of the Maslak band they roamed for three days over the steppe tracks of the Don right-hand bank, avoiding all large villages and district centres. In the Ukrainian villages bounding the lands of Kargin district they exchanged their sorry little nags for well-fed and swift Ukrainian horses.

During the morning of the fourth day, not far from a village, Gregor was the first to notice a cavalry column riding across a distant gap between the hills. Not less than two squadrons were coming along the road, while ahead and to either side of them were small reconnaissance detachments.

"Either Maslak, or—" Fomin put his field-glasses to his eyes.

"Either rain or snow; either it is or it isn't," Chumakov said with a sneer. "You take a better look, Yakov Yefimich, for if it's the Reds, we ought to turn back, and quick!"

"But how the devil can you tell from here?" Fomin said irritably.

"Look! They've seen us. There's a patrol coming this way," Sterladnikov exclaimed.

He was right, they had been seen. The patrol riding on the right-hand side of the column turned sharply and trotted towards them. Fomin hurriedly thrust his glasses into their case; but Gregor, smiling, bent across from his saddle and took Fomin's horse by the bridle.

"Don't be in a hurry! Let them get closer. There are only twelve of them. We'll take a good look at them, and then we can gallop off if necessary. We've got fresh horses, what are you afraid of? Have a look through your glasses."

The twelve horsemen grew steadily nearer, growing larger and larger with every moment. Their forms were now distinctly outlined against the green background of the high-growing grass of the hill.

Gregor and the others gazed at Fomin impatiently. His hands trembled a little as they held the field-glasses. He stared so hard that a tear ran down the cheek turned to the sun.

"They're Reds! I can see the stars on their caps!" he shouted thickly at last, and turned his horse.

They set off at a gallop. Behind them infrequent shots rang out. For two miles or so Gregor galloped at Fomin's side, occasionally looking back.

"Well, we've joined up with them!" he said with a sneering laugh.

Fomin was silent and depressed. Reining in his horse a little, Chumakov shouted:

"We must avoid the villages. We'll make for the Vieshenska steppe, it's more lonely there."

A few more miles of furious galloping, and the horses would be played out. A foamy sweat covered their outstretched necks, the latitudinal folds of flesh lay deep.

"We must take it easier! Slow up!" Gregor commanded.

Of the twelve riders behind them, only nine were left; the others had dropped out of the chase. With his eyes Gregor measured the distance separating them and shouted:

"Halt! Let's give them a round or two!"

All five slowed their horses into a trot, dismounted as they went, and unslung their rifles.

"Hold your reins! Aim at the man on the extreme left. Fire!"

They each fired a clip of cartridges, killed a horse under one of the Red Army men, and again began to retire from the pursuit. They were followed only reluctantly. From time to time shots were fired at them from a considerable distance, then at last the soldiers abandoned the chase completely.

"We must water the horses; there's a pond over there," Sterladnikov said, pointing with his whip to the blue surface of a steppe pond in the distance.

Now they were riding at a fast walking pace, closely examining every ravine and hollow they came to, trying to take cover in the uneven folds of the steppe.

They watered their horses and set off again, at first at a walking pace, then at a trot. At noon they halted to feed the horses on the slope of a deep ravine which cut right across the steppe. Fomin ordered Kosheliov to climb a near-by mound on foot, to lie down there and keep watch. In the event of horsemen appearing anywhere on the steppe he was to give warning and run immediately to the horses.

Gregor hobbled his mount, turned it loose to graze, and lay down not far off, choosing a dry spot on the slope of the ravine.

Here, on the sunny side of the ravine, the young grass was taller and thicker. The vapid exhalation of the black, sun-warmed earth could not stifle the finer perfume of the fading steppe violets. They were growing on a piece of abandoned fallow, making their way between the dry stalks of hart's-clover, spreading in a colourful pattern over the edges of the former field bounds; and even on the flintily hard virgin soil their blue, childishly clean eyes looked out on the world from the withered last-year's grass. The violets had lived their appointed time in this lonely and spacious steppe, and in their place, on the slope of the ravine, marvellously brilliant tulips were already rising, lifting their crimson, white, and yellow chalices to the sun, while the wind blended the varied perfumes of the flowers and carried them far over the steppe.

Over the steep rubble of the northern slope, shadowed by cliffs, still lay coalesced strata of snow, streaming with moisture. A chill arose from the snow, but this chill still further accentuated the perfume of the fading violets, faint and mournful as the memory of something precious and long since past.

Gregor lay with his legs flung out, resting on his elbows, and with avid eyes drank in the sun-hazed steppe, the guardian mounds showing azure along a distant ridge, the flowing opalescent mirage on the bounds of the slope. For a moment he closed his eyes and heard the near and distant songs of the skylarks, the light tread and snorting of the grazing horses, the clanking of bits, and the whisper of the wind in the young grass. He had a strange feeling of resignation and peace as he pressed all his body to the rough earth. It was a long familiar feeling. It always came after he had experienced anxiety, and at such times he seemed to be seeing everything around him with fresh vision. It was as though his sight and hearing had grown keener, and after such a time of agitation all that previously would have passed unnoticed now attracted his attention. With equal interest he watched the whistling, slanting flight of a sparrowhawk pursuing some tiny bird, and the deliberate crawl of a black beetle which struggled over the distance between Gregor's two elbows, and the gentle swaying of a blood-red tulip rocked by the wind, gleaming with a brilliant virgin beauty. The tulip was growing quite close to him, on the edge of a crumbled marmot-hole. He had only to stretch out his hand to pluck it; but he lay without moving, with silent rapture admiring the flower and the stiff leaves, which jealously preserved drops of the morning dew within their folds. Then he shifted his gaze and long, unthinkingly watched an eagle hovering above the horizon, over the dead city of marmot warrens.

A couple of hours later they again mounted their horses, intending to reach the familiar villages of the Yelanska district by nightfall.

Evidently the Red Army patrol had communicated their movements by telephone. As they rode into Kamenka settlement shots rang out to welcome them from across a stream. The singsong whistle of the bullets made Fomin turn aside. Under fire they galloped round the outskirts of the settlement and swiftly made their way into the horse-grazing lands of Vieshenska district. Beyond another settlement a small force of militia attempted to intercept them.

"We'll ride round them on the left," Fomin proposed.

"We'll attack them," Gregor said resolutely. "There are nine of them and five of us. We'll break through!"

He was supported by Chumakov and Sterladnikov.

Baring their sabres, they put their horses into a canter. Without dismounting, the militia-men opened a rapid fire, then galloped aside, avoiding the attack.

"They're a poor lot! They'll write out a long and glowing report, but they're not prepared for a serious fight!" Kosheliov said jokingly.

Returning the fire whenever the militia-men began to press on them, Fomin and the others retreated eastward, fleeing like wolves pursued by borzois, occasionally snapping back and hardly stopping at all. During one of the exchanges of fire Sterladnikov was wounded. The bullet pierced the muscle of his left leg, grazing the bone. He groaned with the pain shooting through his leg and said, turning pale:

"They've hit me in the calf. . . . And it's the same leg—my lame one. . . . There's swine for you!"

Throwing himself back in his saddle, Chumakov laughed at the top of his voice. He laughed so much that the tears started to his eyes. Helping Sterladnikov to seat himself on his horse, he rocked with laughter as he said:

"Well, how did they come to pick on that one? They must have aimed at it deliberately. They saw some lame fellow hopping about and thought they'd get you if they shot at that leg. Oh, Sterladnikov! Oh, you'll be the death of me! Your leg will be shorter by another quarter. And now how will you dance? I shall have to dig a hole a couple of feet deeper for your leg."

"Shut up, you idiot! I haven't got time for you now! Shut up, for Christ's sake!" Sterladnikov said, wincing with the pain.

Perhaps half an hour later, as they rode along the bottom of one of the innumerable ravines, he asked:

"Let's make a halt and rest a bit. . . . I must stop up my wound, for I've lost a whole bootful of blood."

They halted. Gregor held the horses. From time to time Fomin and Kosheliov fired at the militia-men hovering in the distance. Chumakov helped Sterladnikov to remove his boot.

"But you have lost a lot of blood, and no mistake," Chumakov said, knitting his brows as he poured the crimson fluid out of the boot on to the ground. He was about to rip up the leg of Sterladnikov's trousers, which were wet and streaming with blood. But Sterladnikov would not allow him.

"They're good trousers, there's no point in spoiling them," he said, and, resting with his palms on the earth, he raised his wounded leg. "Pull them off, only do it gently."

"Have you got any bandage?" Chumakov asked, rummaging through his pockets.

"What the devil do I want bandages for? I'll manage without."

He closely examined the exit hole of the wound, then with his teeth pulled a bullet out of its cartridge-case, poured the gunpowder on his palm, and thoroughly mixed it with earth, first moistening the earth with spittle. He plentifully plastered both the holes of the wound with this ointment and said in a satisfied tone:

"That's a well-tried remedy. The wound will dry, and it'll heal up in a couple of days."

They did not halt again until they reached the river Chira. The militia-men kept at a respectable distance behind them, and only occasionally did they fire a single shot. Fomin frequently looked back, and remarked:

"They're keeping us in sight all the time—or are they expecting re-inforcements? They're not keeping that distance off without good reason."

They crossed the Chira at a ford near a village and went at a walking pace up the slope of a hill. The horses were tired out. They managed somehow or other to trot downhill, but they had to be led by the rein uphill, and the men combed the quivering flecks of foam from the animals' sides and croups.

Fomin's anxiety was justified: some three miles or so outside a village the pursuit was taken up by seven men mounted on fresh, briskly moving horses.

"If they go on passing us from hand to hand like that, we're done for," Kosheliov said gloomily.

They rode across the steppe, ignoring the tracks, taking turns at firing back. Two of them lay down in the grass and fired at their pursuers, and the others rode on some five hundred yards, dismounted, and kept the enemy under fire while the other two rode on ahead a thousand yards, lay down, and prepared to fire. They killed or seriously wounded one militia-man and shot the horse under a second. Soon afterwards Chumakov had his horse shot under him. He ran on at Kosheliov's side, holding to the stirrup.

The shadows lengthened. The sun sank towards the west. Gregor advised that they should not separate, and they rode on together at a walking pace. Chumakov strode along at their side. A little later they saw a two-horsed wagon on the ridge of a hill and made for the road. The elderly, bearded Cossack driver whipped his horses into a gallop, but shots brought him to a halt.

"I'll sabre the scum! He'll learn what to run for!" Kosheliov muttered through his teeth, bursting ahead, lashing his horse furiously with his whip.

"Don't touch him, Sasha, I forbid it!" Fomin warned him, and shouted to the man when still some distance off: "Unharness your horses, daddy, do you hear? Unharness them while you're still alive!"

Paying no attention to the old man's tearful entreaties, they themselves unhitched the traces, removed the reins and collars from the horses, and quickly saddled them.

"Leave one of yours at least in exchange," the old man asked, weeping.

"Mind you don't get your teeth knocked out, you old devil!" Kosheliov said. "We need the horses ourselves. You thank the Lord God that your life has been spared."

Fomin and Chumakov mounted the fresh horses. But soon afterwards the six riders following in their tracks were joined by three others.

"We must drive our horses hard! Come on, boys!" Fomin said. "If we can reach the Krivsky ravines by nightfall, we shall be saved."

He lashed his horse with his whip and galloped on ahead. On his left hand he led a second horse on a short rein. Under the animals' hoofs the crimson heads of the tulips went flying in all directions like great drops of blood. Gregor, who was riding behind Fomin, looked at these sprinkles of crimson and closed his eyes. For some reason his head swam, and a familiar, severe pain clutched at his heart.

Their horses galloped along with their last strength. The men also were worn out with the incessant riding and with hunger. Sterladnikov was swaying in the saddle, and was as white as linen. He had lost a lot of blood and was tormented by thirst and nausea. He ate a little dry bread, but at once threw it up.

In the dusk, not far from the village of Krivsky they rode into the midst of a drove of horses returning from the steppe, fired a last few shots at their pursuers, and with gladness saw that the chase had been dropped. In the distance the nine horsemen rode together, evidently to discuss the situation, and then turned back.

They spent two days in Krivsky village, staying with an acquaintance of Fomin's. The master was well off and gave them a warm welcome. The horses were kept in a dark shed, had more oats than they could eat, and by the end of the second day had completely recovered from the mad ride. The men took turns guarding the horses, slept on the floor of a cool chaff-shed festooned with spider-webs, and ate their fill to make up for all the days of semi-starvation they had known on the island.

They could have left the village next day, but Sterladnikov held them up: his wound grew worse, a fiery red appeared around its edges, and by evening his leg had swollen and he lost consciousness. He was racked with thirst. All through the night, immediately consciousness returned to him, he asked for water and drank greedily, a little at a time. During the night he drank almost a bucketful of water, but he could not rise even with help, every movement caused him terrible pain. He made water without getting up and groaned incessantly. To muffle his groans the others carried him to a far corner of the shed, but it made no difference. Sometimes his groans were very loud, and when he lost consciousness he shouted incoherently in his delirium.

They had to keep watch over him also. They gave him water, moistened his burning forehead, and covered his mouth with their hands or a cap when he began to groan or talk too noisily.

Towards the close of the second day he came round and said he felt better.

"When are you leaving here?" he asked Chumakov, beckoning him with his finger.

"Tonight."

"I'm going too. Don't leave me here, for Christ's sake!"

"What good are you for going anywhere?" Fomin said in an undertone. "You can't even stir."

"How can't I? You watch!" With a great effort Sterladnikov half raised himself, and at once fell back. His face burned, the sweat stood out in tiny drops on his brow.

"We'll take you," Chumakov said resolutely. "We'll take you, please don't be afraid! And wipe your tears, you're not a woman!"

"It's sweat." Sterladnikov whispered quietly, and pulled his cap down over his eyes.

"We'd be glad to leave you behind, but the master won't agree.

Don't get downhearted, Vassily. Your leg will heal up, and you and I will yet wrestle again and dance the Cossack dance. What are you so down in the mouth for? Now, if the wound were serious . . . but it's nothing!"

Chumakov, always harsh and brutish in his dealings with others, said these words so quietly and in such a touchingly gentle and sincere tone that Gregor stared at him in amazement.

They rode out of the village a little before dawn. They managed with a struggle to get Sterladnikov into the saddle, but he could not keep his seat and fell first to one side, then to the other. So Chumakov rode beside him, with his right arm around the wounded man's waist.

"There's a drag on us! We'll have to leave him behind somewhere," Fomin whispered, drawing level with Gregor and regretfully shaking his head.

"Kill him, do you mean?"

"Well, what else? Look into his eyes? What can we do with him on our hands?"

They rode for some time at a walking pace, not speaking. Gregor relieved Chumakov, then Kosheliov relieved Gregor.

The sun rose. Below them the mist was still rolling above the Don, but on the hills the steppe distances were very clear and bright, and with every minute the vault of heaven turned more blue, with feathery little clouds frozen motionless in the zenith. A heavy dew lay in a silvery brocade on the grass, but where the horses had passed, a dark flowing track was left. Only the skylarks were enriching the great and blessed silence which extended over the steppe.

Sterladnikov, his head tossing helplessly to the movement of the horse's stride, quietly said:

"Oh, it's hard!"

"Shut up!" Fomin roughly interrupted him. "It's no easier for us having to nurse you."

Not far from the Hetman's highway a bustard shot up from under their horses' hoofs. The fine, jarring whistle of its wings aroused Sterladnikov from his oblivion.

"Brothers, get me off my horse," he asked.

Kosheliov and Chumakov carefully lifted him out of the saddle and laid him on the wet grass.

"Let's have a look at your leg. Now, unbutton your trousers!"

Chumakov said, squatting down beside him.

Sterladnikov's leg was monstrously swollen, the skin was stretched tightly without a single wrinkle, and it filled all his ample trouser leg. Right up to his hip the skin had gone a shiny dark-violet hue and was covered with spots velvety to the touch. Similar spots, only of a lighter tinge, had made their appearance on his swarthy, deeply sunken belly. A foul, putrescent stench came from the wound and from the brown blood dried on his trousers, and Chumakov held his nose, knitted his brows, and could hardly restrain the nausea which rose in his throat as he examined his friend's leg. Then he gazed closely at Sterladnikov's drooping blue eyelids, exchanged glances with Fomin, and said:

"It looks as though gangrene's set in. . . . M'yes! You're in a bad way, Vassily Sterladnikov! A quite hopeless case! Ah, Vassia, Vassia, what on earth did you do it for?"

Sterladnikov was breathing in hurried gasps and did not say a word. Fomin and Gregor dismounted as though at a command and approached the wounded man from the windward side. He lay still for a time, then, supporting himself on his hands, sat up and looked at them all with filmy eyes stern in their resignation.

"Brothers, give me over to death. . . . I'm no longer a living soul in this world. . . . I'm completely worn out, I haven't got any more strength. . . ."

He again lay down on his back and closed his eyes. Fomin and the others all knew that such a request must be granted, and they had been awaiting it. Winking briefly at Kosheliov, Fomin turned away. Kosheliov made no protest and snatched the rifle from his shoulder. "Shoot!" he rather guessed than heard the words as he looked at the lips of Chumakov, who had stepped away. But Sterladnikov again opened his eyes, and said firmly:

"Shoot here!" He raised his hand and pointed with his finger to the bridge of his nose. "So that the light goes out at once. . . . If you happen to be in my village, tell the wife how it occurred. . . . Tell her she's not to wait for me."

Kosheliov seemed to fidget a suspiciously long time with the bolt of his rifle, and, drooping his eyelids, Sterladnikov had time to add:

"I've only got the wife—no children. She bore one to me, but it was born dead. . . . And there was nobody else."

Twice Kosheliov threw the rifle up and let it fall again, turning more and more pale. Chumakov furiously pushed him away with his shoulder and tore the weapon from his hands.

"If you can't do it, then don't take on the job, you whelp's blood!" he shouted hoarsely, and took off his cap and stroked his hair.

"Hurry!" Fomin demanded, putting one foot into the stirrup.

Groping for the words he needed, Chumakov said slowly and quietly:

"Vassily, good-bye, and forgive me and all of us, for the love of Christ! We'll meet again in the next world, and there they'll judge us. . . . We'll tell your wife what you asked us." Chumakov waited for an answer; but Sterladnikov was silent, and his face paled as he awaited his death. Only his eyelashes, bleached by the sun, quivered as though fluttered by the wind, and the fingers of his left hand quietly stirred as for some reason he attempted to button up a broken button on his tunic.

Many deaths had Gregor seen in his time, but he did not stop to watch the death of Sterladnikov. He hurriedly walked on, forcibly pulling on the reins, dragging his horse behind him. He waited for the shot with the same feeling that he would have had if the bullet were intended for his own back. He waited for the shot, and his heart counted out every second. But when behind him there was a sharp, sudden crack his knees sagged under him, and he was hardly able to restrain his rearing horse.

For a couple of hours they rode without speaking. When they halted, Chumakov was the first to break the silence. Covering his eyes with his palm, he said huskily:

"What the devil did I shoot him for? We ought to have left him behind in the steppe and not put an unnecessary sin on my soul. I can see him now before my eyes. . . ."

"Can't you ever get used to it?" Fomin asked. "With all the men you've killed, you still can't get used to it? You haven't got a heart, you've got rusty iron. . . ."

Chumakov paled, and stared furiously at Fomin.

"Don't you get across me just now, Yakov Yefimich!" he said quietly. "Don't you peck at me, for I can put even you out. And very easily too!"

"What the devil do I need to get across you for? I've got enough worry without you!" Fomin said in a conciliatory tone, and lay on his back, screwing up his eyes against the sunlight, contentedly stretching himself.

Chapter 7

Contrary to Gregor's expectations, during the next ten days over forty Cossacks joined up with Fomin. They were the remnants of various small bands which had been broken up by Soviet forces. They had lost their leaders and were wandering aimlessly about the region, and they gladly served under Fomin. They were completely unconcerned as to whom they served and whom they killed, so long as they were able to live their free, nomad life and plunder all who fell into their hand. They were a lot of desperadoes, and Fomin remarked contemptuously to Gregor as he looked at them: "Well, Melekhov, it's the riffraff that has joined us, not men. Gallowsbirds, they look as though specially picked for the rope!" In his heart of hearts Fomin still regarded himself as a "fighter for the toiling people," and, though not so frequently as in the past, he would still say: "We're the liberators of the Cossackry." He stubbornly refused to abandon the most absurd of hopes. He again began to wink at the pillaging committed by his companions-in-arms, taking the view that it was all a necessary evil to which he must be reconciled, that as time passed he would free himself of the looters, and that sooner or later he would be a genuine commander of insurgent forces and not the ataman of a miserable little band of brigands.

But Chumakov did not hesitate to call all the Fomin men "brigands," and argued until he was hoarse, trying to convince Fomin that he also was nothing but a brigand on a large scale. When they were alone, furious arguments frequently broke out between them.

"I'm an idealistic fighter against the Soviet régime!" Fomin would shout, turning livid with anger. "And you call me the devil knows what! Do you understand, you fool, that I'm fighting for an ideal?"

"Don't try to pull my leg!" Chumakov objected. "Don't try to pull

the wool over my eyes! I'm not a child! A fine idealist you are!
You're a born brigand, and nothing more. And why are you so
afraid of the word? I don't understand that at all."

"Why do you insult me like that? You foul-mouthed scum! I rose
against the government and I'm fighting against it with weapons, so
how am I a brigand?"

"That's exactly why you are a brigand, because you're fighting
against the government. Brigands have always been against the
government ever since the beginning of time. No matter what the
Soviet government may be, it's the government, it's held on ever
since 1917, and anyone who works against it is a brigand."

"You empty-pate! And how about General Krasnov, or Denikin?
Were they brigands too?"

"Well, what else were they? They were brigands, only they wore
epaulets. And the epaulets don't matter much. You and I can put
them on. . . ."

Fomin banged his fist, spat, and, unable to think of any convincing
arguments, cut short the useless dispute. It was impossible to persuade Chumakov of anything.

The majority of those who joined the band were excellently armed
and dressed. Almost all of them had good horses accustomed to endless marches and easily covering sixty miles a day. Some of them
even had two horses: one to ride and the other to lead at the side.
When necessary, by changing from horse to horse, allowing each to
rest in turn, a rider with two mounts could cover some hundred and
twenty miles a day.

One day Fomin remarked to Gregor:

"If we'd each had two horses at the beginning, no devils on earth
could have caught us. The militia and Red Army forces mustn't
take horses from the people, and they're not willing to do it. But we
can do what we like. We must provide every man with a spare
mount, and then they'll never catch us. Old folk used to say that in
former days that's how the Tatars made their raids, each with two
horses, and sometimes even with three. Who could catch such
riders? And we must do the same. That Tatar wisdom is greatly to
my fancy."

They quickly got hold of more horses, and for a time they did in fact become uncatchable. The mounted militia which had been newly organized in Vieshenska vainly tried to overtake them. The spare horses made it possible for Fomin's numerically small force to throw off the enemy without difficulty and to get several marches ahead of him, so avoiding any dangerous clash.

None the less, in the middle of May a force almost four times as large as the band succeeded in pinning it down against the Don not far from Bobrovsky in Ust-Khopersk district. But after a brief fight the band broke through and retired along the bank of the river, losing eight men killed and wounded. Shortly after this engagement Fomin asked Gregor to take over the position of chief of staff.

"We need someone educated, so that we can move according to a plan, by a map, or some day they'll squeeze us and shake us up again. You take over the job, Gregor Pantalievich."

"You don't need a staff to catch militia-men and cut their heads off," Gregor said moodily.

"Every detachment ought to have its staff; don't talk nonsense!"

"Give Chumakov the post if you can't live without a staff."

"But why don't you want to take it on?"

"I've got no idea of what it means."

"And has Chumakov?"

"No, Chumakov hasn't either."

"Then what the hell are you suggesting him for? You're an officer and you ought to have some idea of it. You ought to know all about tactics and that sort of thing."

"I was about as good an officer as you are a detachment commander! And there is only one tactic for us: to roam about the steppe and keep our eyes skinned," Gregor said sarcastically.

Fomin winked at Gregor and threatened him with his forefinger.

"I can see right through you! Always keeping yourself in the shade? You want to keep out of the light? That won't save you, brother! It's all the same whether you're a troop commander or chief of staff. Do you think they'll give you any discount if they catch you? You wait and see!"

"I'm not thinking of that at all; you're on the wrong track!" Gregor said, fixedly examining the sword-knot on his sabre-hilt. "But I don't want to take on a task I know nothing about."

"Well, if you don't want to, you needn't. We'll manage somehow without you," the incensed Fomin agreed.

The situation was completely changing in the region; the gates of the prosperous Cossacks, who formerly had welcomed Fomin with great hospitality, were now bolted against him, and when the band arrived in a village the masters hurriedly scattered and hid in the orchards and gardens. The itinerant session of the Revolutionary Tribunal, which had arrived at Vieshenska, sternly punished many Cossacks who in the past had made Fomin welcome. The news of the sentences sped through the districts and had corresponding influence on the minds of those who had openly expressed their friendliness towards the bandits.

In the course of a fortnight Fomin made an extensive ride through all the districts of the upper Don. The band now numbered some hundred and thirty sabres, and it was being pursued, not by a hurriedly mustered mounted group, but by several squadrons of the 13th Cavalry Regiment, which had been transferred from the southern front.

Many of those who had recently attached themselves to Fomin were natives of distant parts. They had found their way to the Don by devious roads. Some of them had escaped singly from prison gangs, from prisons and prison camps; but the majority consisted of a group of several dozen horsemen who had broken away from Maslak, and also remnants of the shattered Kurochkin band. The Maslak men willingly allowed themselves to be separated and dispersed into the various troops, but the Kurochkin men did not wish to be broken up. They formed an entire separate troop, strongly welded together and holding themselves somewhat apart from the other members of the band. In battle or in bivouac they acted as a single group, they hung about together, and when they had pillaged some co-operative shop or warehouse, they poured everything into the common troop cauldron and shared out the loot equally, strictly observing the principle of equality.

Several Terek and Kuban Cossacks in ragged Circassian coats, two Kalmyks, a Latvian in hunting boots reaching to his thighs, and five sailor anarchists in striped jerseys and faded sailors' kit still more varied the already motley, heterogeneous composition of the Fomin band.

"Well, you still argue that you aren't in command of brigands, but what do you call these? Fighters for ideals?" Chumakov asked Fo-

min one day, indicating the extended marching column with his eyes.
"We only want an unfrocked priest and a few swine in trousers, and
then we'd have a complete collection of the blessed saints."

Fomin ignored the remark. His sole anxiety was to gather around
him as many men as possible. He took nothing into account when
he accepted volunteers. He himself questioned every man who expressed a wish to serve under his command, and said curtly:

"You're good for service. I'll take you. Go to my chief of staff,
Chumakov; he'll assign you to a troop and give you weapons."

In one of the villages of Migulinsk district a well-dressed, curly-
headed, swarthy youngster was brought to Fomin. He announced
his desire to join the band. On questioning him Fomin learned that
he was a native of Rostov and had recently been sentenced for armed
robbery, but had escaped from the Rostov prison and, hearing of
Fomin, had made his way to the upper Don area.

"What are you by race? An Armenian or Bulgarian?" Fomin asked
him.

"I'm a Jew," the lad answered in some embarrassment.

Fomin was dumbfounded at this surprising avowal and was silent
for some time. He did not know what to do in such an unexpected
situation.

After racking his brains, he sighed deeply and said:

"Well, if you're a Jew you're a Jew. We don't look down our
noses even at such. It means one more man. But can you ride
a horse? No? You'll learn! We'll give you some quiet little mare to
start with, and then you'll learn. Go to Chumakov, he'll assign you
to your troop."

A few minutes later the infuriated Chumakov galloped up to
Fomin.

"Are you mad or are you joking?" he shouted, reining his horse on
to its hind legs. "What the devil have you sent me a Jew for? I
won't accept him! Let him go to the four corners of the earth!"

"Take him, take him, it'll make one more!" Fomin said calmly.

But Chumakov foamed at the mouth and roared:

"I won't! I'll kill him, but I won't take him! The Cossacks are
kicking up a row about it; you go and talk to them yourself."

While they were arguing and cursing each other the Cossacks had
got hold of the young Jew by one of the baggage-wagons and were

stripping him of his embroidered shirt and cloth trousers. As he tried the shirt against himself one of the Cossacks said:

"Do you see that old bush out there beyond the village? Run to it at a trot and lie down. You'll lie there until we leave here, and when we've gone you can get up and go wherever you like. Don't come near us any more or we'll kill you. You'd better go back to Rostov, to your mammy. It isn't your Jewish job to fight. The Lord God taught you to trade, not to fight. We can manage and tackle that job without you."

The Jew was not accepted, but on the other hand that very same day the Cossacks caught the halfwit Pasha, known in all the villages of the Vieshenska district, and, roaring with laughter, assigned him to the second troop. He was captured in the steppe, brought to the village, and solemnly arrayed in a uniform taken from a dead Red Army man. The Cossacks showed him how to handle a rifle and spent much time teaching him how to wield a sabre.

Gregor was on his way to his horse at the hitching-post, but, seeing a dense crowd, he turned aside to find out what was happening. A roar of laughter caused him to hasten his steps, and then in the abrupt silence he heard someone's sober, monitorial voice:

"No, not like that, Pasha! Who ever uses his sabre like that? You can chop wood that way, but not a man. You must do it like this, do you see? When you catch him, order him at once to go down on his knees, for you'll find it awkward to sabre him when he's standing up. He goes down on his knees, and you come up like this, behind him, and slash at his neck. . . . Try not to cut him straight down, but so the blade makes a slanting cut. . . ."

Surrounded by bandits, the halfwit stood at attention, firmly clutching the hilt of his bared sabre. Smiling and beatifically screwing up his grey eyes, he listened to the instructions being given him by one of the Cossacks. The corners of his mouth were dribbling like a horse's with frothy bits of food, spittle was flowing copiously over his coppery red beard on to his chest. He licked his dirty lips and said in a tongue-tied lisp:

"I get it all, my boy. . . . Is this right? I make the slave of God go down on his knees and I cut through his neck—right through. You've given me trousers and a shirt and boots. Only I haven't got a coat. You might give me one little coat, and then I'll please you! I'll try with all my might!"

"You kill some commissar, and then you'll have a coat. But you might tell us how you got married last year," one of the Cossacks suggested.

A look of elemental fear flickered through the halfwit's dilated, filmy eyes. He uttered a string of curses and, to the accompaniment of a roar of laughter, began to tell some story. So loathsome was the scene that Gregor shuddered and hurriedly turned away. "And it's with these men that I've linked my fate!" he thought, possessed by feelings of bitterness and anger with himself, with all this hateful life.

He lay down by the hitching-posts, trying to close his ears to the idiot's shouts and the Cossacks' thunderous laughter. "I'll clear out tomorrow! It's about time!" he decided, looking at his well-fed horses and noting their splendid condition. He had taken documents in the name of Ushakov off a dead militia-man and had sewn them in the lining of his greatcoat. For some two weeks he had been preparing his horses for a short but swift gallop. He watered them at regular times, curried them more diligently than he had ever curried his army mounts, by all legal and illegal means obtained grain for them at night; and his horses looked in better condition than any of the others. Especially his Ukrainian dapple-grey horse. Its coat shone all over, and its hair glittered in the sun like Caucasian niello silver.

With such horses he could be sure of drawing away from any pursuit. He rose and went to a near-by hut. He respectfully asked an old woman who was sitting on the threshold of the granary:

"Have you got a scythe, granny?"

"We did have one somewhere, but the Lord knows where it is. What do you want it for?"

"I wanted to cut some green feed in your garden for my horses. May I?"

The old woman reflected and said:

"When will you get off our necks? It's nothing but give me this and give me that. One lot comes and demands grain, another lot arrives and drags and carts off all they set their eyes on. I won't give you the scythe! Please yourself, but I won't give you it!"

"Why, can't you spare the grass, godly old woman?"

"Do you think more grass is going to grow on the bare spots? What am I to feed the cow on?"

"Isn't there any grass in the steppe?"

"Well then, go out into the steppe and cut it, my eagle. There's plenty out in the steppe."

Gregor said irritably:

"You'd better let me have the scythe, granny. I'll cut a little grass and you'll have the rest. But if we turn our horses into your garden we'll have the lot."

The old woman looked harshly at Gregor and turned away.

"Go and get it yourself," she said. "It ought to be hanging in the shed."

Gregor found an old broken scythe in the shed. As he passed the old woman he distinctly heard her declare: "There's no salvation from you, damn you!"

That was something to which he would never get accustomed. He had long known the Cossacks' attitude towards the band. "And they're right, too," he thought as he carefully swung the scythe, trying to mow the grass cleanly, leaving no edges standing. "What the devil do they want us for? Nobody needs us; we're preventing everybody from living and working in peace. A stop must be put to this, and about time too!"

Occupied with his thoughts, he stood by his horses, watching them avidly seizing tufts of the tender young grass between their black, velvety lips. He was aroused from his meditation by a deep, youthful voice which was obviously on the point of breaking:

"But what a fine horse! He's a real swan!"

Gregor looked in the direction of the speaker. A young Cossack who had only recently joined the band was staring at Gregor's grey horse and rapturously shaking his head. With his fascinated gaze fixed on the animal he walked round it more than once, clicking his tongue.

"Is he your horse?" he asked.

"Why, what do you want to know for?" Gregor answered ungraciously.

"Let's swap! I've got a bay of pure Don blood; he can take any obstacle, and he's spirited: you wouldn't believe how spirited he is! He's like lightning."

"Go to the devil!" Gregor said coldly.

The youngster was silent for a moment or two, then sighed bit terly and sat down not far off. He stared at the grey for a long time, then remarked:

"You know he's got the heaves!"

Gregor silently picked at his teeth with a straw. He was beginning to like this artless youngster.

"Won't you swap, daddy?" the lad asked quietly, looking at Gregor with pleading eyes.

"No, I won't! I wouldn't even if you threw yourself in with your horse."

"But where did you get it?"

"I invented it myself."

"Oh, come on, tell me the truth!"

"It came through the usual gates: a mare dropped it."

"It's no use talking to such a fool!" the lad said in an offended tone, and went off.

Empty, as though dead, the village lay before Gregor. Except for Fomin's men, there was not a soul in sight. A wagon abandoned in a lane, a chopping-block in a yard with an axe hastily driven into it and a half-planed board near by, haltered bullocks lazily cropping the stunted grass in the middle of the street, an overturned bucket by the well-shaft—all these things testified that the peaceful life of the village had been unexpectedly violated, and that the villagers had left their tasks unfinished and had gone into hiding.

Gregor had seen a similar desolation and similar signs of hurried flight when the Cossack regiments had ridden through East Prussia. Now he had lived to see these things in his own country. With the same morose and hateful glances had he been welcomed then by the Germans, and now by the Cossacks of the upper Don. He recalled his talk with the old woman and mournfully looked about him, unbuttoning the collar of his shirt. That accursed pain was again attacking his heart.

The sun was burning the earth. About the lane hung the vapid scent of dust, of goosegrass and horse-sweat. In the orchards, on the lofty willows with their sprinkling of ragged nests, the rooks were croaking. A little steppe stream, fed by springs somewhere at the top of a ravine, slowly flowed through the village, dividing it into two parts. On both sides the spacious Cossack yards crawled down to the water, smothered in a dense growth of gardens, with cherry trees spreading over the windows of the huts, apple trees with stout branches stretching their green foliage and young bunches of fruit to the sun.

With misty eyes Gregor looked at the yard overgrown with ragged plantain, at the hut with yellow shutters and roofed with straw thatch, at the lofty well-crane. By the threshing-floor, on one of the posts of the old wattle fence hung a horse's skull bleached with rains; the holes of its empty eye-sockets were yawning black. A green pumpkin plant entwined the same post, winding in a spiral, reaching up to the light. It had climbed to the top of the post and was clinging with its little tendrils to the teeth and the protuberances of the horse's skull. Its free end, in search of support, was already extending to a branch of a guelder-rosebush standing not far off.

Had he seen all this before in a dream, or in his distant childhood? Gripped by a sudden attack of passionate yearning, he lay chest downward under the fence, covered his face with his palms, and got up only when the distant, long-drawn-out shout "To horse!" reached his ears.

That night during the march he rode out of the ranks, halted as though to change saddles from one horse to the other, and stood listening to the slowly distancing, dying clatter of horse-hoofs. Then, springing into the saddle, he galloped off at right angles to the road.

For three miles he urged on his horses without pause, then slowed down to a walking pace and listened: was there any sound of pursuit behind him? All was quiet in the steppe. Only snipe were calling one to another on sandy spits, and somewhere very, very far off a dog's baying was faintly to be heard.

In the sombre sky was a golden sprinkle of twinkling stars. Over the steppe was silence and a breeze laden with the native and bitter scent of wormwood. Gregor rose in his saddle and with all his lungs drew in a deep breath of relief.

Chapter 8

Long before dawn he galloped into the meadow which stretches before Tatarsk. Below the village, where the Don was shallower, he stripped, tied his clothes, boots, and weapons to his horses' heads, and, holding his wallet of cartridges in his teeth, set out with the animals to swim the river. The water scorched him with its unbearable cold. In the attempt to keep warm he paddled swiftly with his right arm, holding the reins tied together in his left hand, quietly encouraging the grunting and snorting horses.

On the bank he hurriedly dressed, tightened the saddle-girths, and, to warm the horses, galloped swiftly towards the village. His wet greatcoat, the wet flaps of the saddle, his moist shirt, all chilled his body. His teeth chattered, a shiver ran down his back, and he trembled all over. But soon the swift ride warmed him, and not far from the village he dropped into a walk, looking around him and listening intently. He decided to leave the horses in a gully. He dropped down to the bottom of the gully over the loose, stony rubble of the slope. The stones clattered dryly under the horses' hoofs, and fiery sparks were struck out by their shoes.

He tied the animals to a withered elm he had known ever since his childhood and walked to the village.

And there was the old Melekhov hut, the dark cluster of apple trees, the well-crane pointing to the Great Bear. Panting with agitation, he dropped down to the river, cautiously crawled through the wattle fence of the Astakhovs' yard, and went up to the unshuttered window. He could hear only the hurried beating of his heart and the muffled roaring of the blood in his head. He knocked quietly on the window-frame—so quietly that he himself hardly heard the sound. Aksinia silently came to the window and looked out. He saw her press her hands to her breast and heard a faint groan burst from her lips. He signed to her to open the window and removed his rifle from his shoulder. She threw the window wide open.

"Quieter! How are you? Don't open the door, I'll come through the window," he whispered.

He stood on the ledge of the house wall. Her bare arms caught him around the neck. They trembled and quivered against his shoul-

ders so much, did those dear, precious arms, that their trembling
was communicated to him.

"Ksinia—wait—take the rifle," he stammered, whispering almost
inaudibly.

He wanted to embrace her; but she dropped heavily on her knees
before him, put her arms around his legs, and pressed her face to his
wet greatcoat. All her body shook with suppressed sobs. He lifted
her, seated her on the bench. Leaning against him, hiding her face
on his chest, she was silent, shuddering again and again, and with
her teeth biting the lapel of his greatcoat to stifle her sobbing and to
avoid awakening the children.

Evidently she also, strong as she was, had been broken with suffering. Evidently her life also had been bitter during these past
months. He stroked the hair fallen about her back, stroked her
burning brow, wet with sweat. He let her weep her fill, then asked:

"Are the children alive and well?"

"Yes."

"And Dunia?"

"Dunia too. Alive—and well. . . ."

"Is Mikhail at home? But wait a bit! Do stop crying, my shirt's
all wet with your tears. . . . Ksinia! My darling, that's enough.
There's no time for tears, time's short. . . . Is Mikhail at home?"

Aksinia wiped her face and pressed Gregor's cheeks with her wet
palms. Smiling through her tears, not removing her eyes from her
beloved, she said quietly:

"I won't any more. . . . I shan't cry any more. . . . Mikhail's
not in Tatarsk; he's been at Vieshenska for the past two months,
serving in some military force. Come and look at the children. Oh,
we weren't expecting you and we never hoped . . ."

Mishatka and Poliushka were sleeping on the bed, their arms and
legs flung out. Gregor bent over them, stood thus for a moment or
two, then tiptoed away and sat down silently beside Aksinia.

"How about you?" she asked in a burning whisper. "How did you
get here? And where have you been all this time? But supposing
they catch you?"

"I've come to fetch you. I don't think they'll catch me. Will you
come?"

"Where to?"

"With me. I've left the band. I was with Fomin, did you hear?"

"Yes. But where can I go with you?"

"To the south. To the Kuban or farther. We'll manage to live and get our food somehow or other. I shan't be ashamed to do any work. My hands are in need of work and not of fighting. My soul has fallen sick during these past months. . . . But we'll talk about that after."

"How about the children?"

"We'll leave them with Dunia. Then we'll see later on. Later we'll take them too. Well? Will you come?"

"Grisha—my dearest Grisha—"

"None of that! No tears! That's enough! We can cry later, there'll be plenty of time for that. . . . Get yourself ready; I've got horses waiting in a gully. Well, will you come?"

"Why, what did you think?" she suddenly said aloud, and fearfully pressed her hand to her lips and glanced at the children. "What did you think?" she asked again in a whisper. "Is my life so sweet alone by myself? I'll go, Grisha, my darling. I'll go on foot, I'll crawl after you, but I won't stay here alone any longer. I can't live without you. . . . Kill me, but don't leave me again."

She pressed herself passionately against him. He kissed her and glanced covertly at the window. Summer nights are short. They must hurry.

"Perhaps you'd like to lie down for a while?" Aksinia asked.

"What are you thinking of?" he exclaimed in alarm. "It'll be dawn soon, we must be getting off. Dress and go and call Dunia. We'll talk it over with her. We must get to Sukhoi dell in the dark. We'll spend the day in the wood and move on at night. Can you ride a horse?"

"Lord, I'd manage anyhow, and gladly on horseback! All the time I'm wondering whether I'm dreaming it all. I often see you in my dreams . . . and every time different." She hurriedly combed her hair, holding the hairpins in her teeth, and spoke so quietly as to be unintelligible. She swiftly dressed and went to the door.

"Shall I wake the children up?" she asked. "You could take a look at them."

"No, don't bother!" Gregor said resolutely.

He took his pouch out of his cap and began to roll a cigarette; but as soon as Aksinia had gone he hurriedly went across to the bed and kissed the children with long kisses. Then he remembered Natalia and much else in his ill-starred life and burst into tears.

As she crossed the threshold, Dunia said:

"Well, greetings, brother! So you've come home? No matter how much you roam about the steppe . . ." And she broke into lamentations: "The children have lived to see their father. . . . They've been made orphans with their father still alive."

Gregor embraced her and said sternly:

"Quieter! You'll wake the children up. Drop all that, sister! I've heard it all before. I've got enough tears and sorrow of my own. I didn't send for you to hear this. Will you take the children and look after them?"

"But where are you going?"

"I'm clearing out and taking Aksinia with me. Will you look after the children? I'll get work, and then I'll have them."

"Why, what else should I do? If you're both going, of course I'll take them. They can't be left in the street, and you can't throw them on the mercy of strangers."

Gregor silently kissed her and said:

"My great thanks to you, sister. I knew you wouldn't refuse."

She sat down on the chest and asked:

"When are you going? At once?"

"Yes."

"But how about the house? And the farm?"

Aksinia answered irresolutely:

"You do what you like. Let someone live in it or do whatever you can. What is left of the clothing and property you have for yourself."

"What shall I tell people? They'll ask where you've gone, and what shall I tell them?" Dunia asked.

"Say you don't know anything, that's all," Gregor said, and turned to Aksinia. "Ksinia, hurry! Don't take much with you. Just a warm jacket, two or three skirts, whatever linen you can, and food for immediate needs, that's all."

The dawn was just beginning to spirt when, after saying good-bye to Dunia and kissing the still sleeping children, Gregor and Aksinia went out on the porch. They dropped down to the Don and made their way along the bank to the gully.

"You and I once went off to Yagodnoe just like this," Gregor said. "Only you had a larger bundle that time, and we ourselves were younger. . . ."

Rapturous with joy, Aksinia glanced sidelong at him and answered:

"But all the time I'm afraid I shall find I've been dreaming. Give me your hand, let me touch it, or I shan't believe it." She laughed quietly, pressing against his shoulder as she went.

He saw her eyes swollen with tears and shining with happiness, her cheeks, pale in the gloom of the early morning. He smiled indulgently and thought: "She got herself ready and came as though going on a visit. . . . Nothing frightens her; she's a great lass!"

As though in answer to his thoughts, she said:

"You see the sort of woman I am. . . . You whistled, as though to a dog, and I ran after you. My love and yearning for you, Grisha, have bound me so firmly. . . . I'm only sorry for the children, but I wouldn't say one 'Oh' over myself. I'll follow you everywhere, even to death."

Hearing their footsteps, the horses quietly whinnied. Dawn was coming on impetuously. Already a narrow strip of heaven in the eastern confines was perceptibly rosy. A mist was rising above the waters of the Don.

Gregor untied the horses and helped Aksinia into the saddle. The stirrup-straps were rather long for her legs. Angry at his own lack of foresight, he shortened the straps, then mounted the second horse.

"Keep up behind me, Ksinia. When we get out of the gully we'll ride at a gallop. That won't shake you up so much. Don't slacken the reins, the horse you're riding doesn't like it. And mind your knees! He's playful at times and tries to snap at your knees with his teeth. Well, off we go!"

It was some five miles to Sukhoi dell. They had soon covered the distance and were close to the woods by sunrise. On the fringe Gregor dismounted and helped Aksinia off her horse.

"Well, how did you find it? Riding horseback is hard when you're not used to it," he said with a smile.

Crimson with the gallop, Aksinia flashed her black eyes at him.

"It's fine! Better than going on foot. Only my legs—" She smiled with embarrassment. "You turn round, Grisha, and I'll have a look. Something's pinching the skin—it must have got chafed."

"That's nothing, that'll pass off," he reassured her. "Walk about a bit, for your legs are trembling a little." He screwed up his eyes and said in a bantering tone, "Ah, you Cossack lass!"

At the very head of the dell he found a small glade and said: "This'll be our camp; make yourself at home, Ksinia."

He unsaddled the horses, hobbled them, and laid the saddles and his weapons under a bush. A copious, heavy dew lay on the grass, and beneath the dew the grass seemed dove-grey; but on the slope, where an early morning gloom still lurked, it gleamed a dull azure. Orange bumble-bees were dozing in the half-opened chalices of the flowers. Skylarks were ringing above the steppe; in the grain, in the aromatic steppe grasses, the quails were calling: "Time for bed! Time for bed!" Close to an oak sapling Gregor crushed down the grass and stretched himself out with his head on a saddle. The thunderous tattoo of the quails' struggles, the stupefying song of the skylarks, and the warm wind, floating from beyond the Don, from sands which had burned with heat all night, all disposed him to sleep. Others could do as they liked, but for Gregor, who had not slept for several nights in succession, it was time for sleep. The quails convinced him and, overcome with sleep, he closed his eyes. Aksinia sat down beside him and was silent, thoughtfully plucking the violet petals of a flower with her lips.

"Grisha, you don't think anyone will catch us here?" she quietly asked, touching Gregor's scrubby cheeks with the flower stalk.

He aroused himself with difficulty from his drowsy oblivion and said hoarsely:

"There's nobody out in the steppe. It's the slack season now. I'll have a sleep, Ksinia, and you watch the horses. Then you can sleep. I'm worn out with lack of sleep. It's four days since . . . We'll talk afterwards."

"Sleep, my darling; sleep well!

She bent over him, gently brushed a strand of hair from his brow, and quietly touched his cheek with her lips.

"My dear, Grisha darling, the grey hairs you've got!" she whispered. "So you're growing old? And yet it's not so long ago that you were a boy. . . . " She looked with a faint, mournful smile into his face.

He slept, his mouth open a little, breathing regularly. His black lashes, with ends bleached by sunlight, quivered very gently; his upper lip stirred, laying bare his firmly clenched white teeth. She looked at him more closely and only then noticed how much he had changed during the past few months of their separation. There was a harsh, almost cruel expression in the deep vertical furrows between her beloved's brows, in the folds of his mouth, in the prominent cheekbones. And for the first time it occurred to her that he must be terrible in a battle, on a horse, with bared sabre. Lowering her eyes, she glanced at his large angular hands and sighed for some reason.

After a while she quietly rose and crossed the glade, holding her skirt high above the dewy grass to keep it from getting wet. Somewhere not far off, a little stream was purling and tinkling over stones. She dropped down to the watercourse, which was lined with flat, pale-green mossy stones, drank of the cold spring water, washed, and rubbed her crimson face dry with her kerchief. On her lips was an unfading, quiet smile; her eyes glittered joyously. Gregor was with her again! Once more the unknown was beckoning her to a transparent happiness. Many tears had Aksinia shed during sleepless nights, many sorrows had she borne during the past few months. Only yesterday she had been in the garden, and women hoeing potatoes in neighbouring patches had begun to sing a mournful song. Her heart had constricted painfully, and involuntarily she had listened:

> "Teega, teega, grey geese, home you fly!
> Surely it's time you came and had a swim?
> Surely it's time you came and had a swim,
> While I, a woman, sit down and have a cry?"

So a woman's soprano voice sang, complaining of her accursed lot, and Aksinia lost her self-control; the tears spirted from her eyes. She tried to find oblivion in work, to stifle the longing which stirred about her heart. But her tears misted her eyes, dropped on the green leaves of the potato plants, on her helpless hands, and she saw nothing and could not work. She threw down the hoe and lay on the ground, hiding her face in her hands, giving rein to her tears.

Only yesterday she had been cursing her life, and everything around her had seemed as grey and joyless as a cloudy day. But today the world seemed exultant and bright, as though after a plentiful summer downpour. "We too will find our life," she thought, abstractedly looking at the fretted oak leaves flaming beneath the slanting rays of the rising sun.

Scented, varicoloured flowers were growing close to the bushes and in the patches of sunlight. Aksinia picked a great armful of them, carefully seated herself not far from Gregor, and, remembering her youth, began to fashion a garland. The result proved to be decorative and beautiful. She sat admiring it, then thrust several rosy flowers of eglantine into it and laid it at Gregor's head.

About nine o'clock Gregor was awakened by the neighing of the horses and sat up in alarm, groping around him for his weapons.

"There's nobody here," Aksinia said quietly. "What are you afraid of?"

He rubbed his eyes and smiled sleepily.

"I've learned to live like a hare. You sleep, and even in your sleep you peep with one eye and tremble at every sound. . . . It takes a long time to get out of that habit, girl. Have I been asleep long?"

"No. Would you like to sleep longer?"

"I ought to sleep the clock round in order to get all the rest I need. We'd better have breakfast. I've got bread and a knife in my saddlebags; you get them, and I'll go and water the horses."

He rose, took off his greatcoat, and wriggled his shoulders. The sun was scorching now. A wind rustled the leaves of the trees, and through their rustling the singing chatter of the stream was no longer audible.

He went down to the water, made a little dam of stones and twigs, then with his sabre dug up earth and packed it into the openings between the stones. When the water gathered behind his dam, he led the horses down and let them drink, then removed their bits and turned them loose to graze again.

At breakfast Aksinia said:

"Where shall we be going from here?"

"To Morozovsky. We'll ride as far as Platov, and then we'll go on on foot."

"How about the horses?"

"We'll leave them somewhere."

"That's a pity, Gregor. They're such good horses; you simply couldn't get tired of looking at that grey. And we've got to leave him behind? Where did you get hold of him?"

"Get hold of him—" Gregor smiled cheerlessly. "I looted him from a Ukrainian."

After a brief silence he said:

"Pity or not, we've got to leave them behind. It's not for us to trade in horses."

"But what are you riding with a rifle for? What good is it to you? God grant nobody sees it, for it'll bring woe upon us."

"Who's going to see us at night? I kept it just in case. I feel lost without it. When we leave the horses I'll leave the rifle behind too. It won't be needed after that."

After breakfast they lay down on his greatcoat. He vainly fought against his sleepiness, while Aksinia, resting on one elbow, told him the life she had lived without him and how much she had suffered during the past months. He heard her level voice through his invincible doze and had no strength to open his heavy eyelids. At times he completely ceased to hear her. Her voice receded into the distance, sounded fainter, and died away entirely. He shuddered and awoke, but in a few minutes he again closed his eyes. His weariness was greater than his desire and will.

" . . . they used to long for you, and ask: 'Where's Father?' I did what I could with them, and almost always I was kind to them. They got used to me and quite attached to me and didn't visit Dunia so often. Poliushka's quiet and gentle. I made her dolls out of scraps of material, and she sat with them under the table, busying herself with them. But once Mishatka ran in from the street trembling all over. 'What's the matter?' I asked him. He burst into tears, and such bitter tears! 'The other boys won't play with me, they say my daddy's a bandit. Mummy, is it true he's a bandit? What are bandits?' I told him: 'Your daddy isn't a bandit at all. He's just—unfortunate.' But he pestered me with his questions: 'Why is he unfortunate, and what does "unfortunate" mean?' I simply couldn't explain it to him. They themselves started to call me 'Mother,' Grisha; you mustn't think I taught them to. But Mikhail was quite good to them—quite kind. He would never speak to me, he turned his back or walked past; but more than once he brought sugar for them from Vieshenska. Prokhor was always grieving about you. 'There's a good man lost,' he used to say. Last week he came and talked about you until his eyes streamed with tears. . . . They made a search of my hut, looking for weapons under the eaves, in the cellar, everywhere. . . ."

He fell asleep without hearing her story to the end. Above his head the leaves of a young elm rustled in the wind. Yellow gleams of light slipped across his face. Aksinia long kissed his closed eyes, then she too fell asleep, her cheek pressed against Gregor's arm, smiling even in her sleep.

They left Sukhoi dell late at night, when the moon had risen. After two hours' riding they dropped from a rise down to the Chira River. Corncrakes were calling in the meadowland, frogs were straining their throats in the reedy backwaters of the river, and somewhere in the distance a bittern boomed hollowly.

Along the river-side extended a mass of orchards, forbiddingly sombre in the mist.

Not far from a little bridge, Gregor halted. A midnight silence wrapped the village. He touched up his horse with his heels and turned aside. He did not like riding across the bridge. He did not trust this silence and was afraid of it. On the outskirts of the village they forded the stream and had just turned into a narrow lane when a man rose from a ditch, three more behind him.

"Halt! Who goes there?"

Gregor started at the shout as though before a blow and pulled on the reins. At once mastering himself, he cried: "Friends!" and, sharply turning his horse, managed to whisper to Aksinia: "Back! Follow me!"

The four men of the outpost set for the night by a grain-requisitioning detachment silently and unhurriedly came towards them. One halted to light a cigarette, striking a match. Gregor brought his whip hard down on Aksinia's horse. The animal reared and at once tore away in a gallop. Bending over his horse's neck, Gregor galloped after it. There was a silence which lasted for several oppressive seconds, then an irregular, rolling volley rang out and spirts of fire pierced the darkness. Gregor heard the burning whistle of the bullets and a long-drawn-out shout:

"To arms!"

When some two hundred yards from the river, Gregor overtook the grey horse, which was moving at a long, sweeping gallop, and shouted to Aksinia as he drew level:

"Bend lower, Ksinia! Bend lower!"

But she pulled on the reins and, throwing herself back, toppled sideways. Gregor managed to hold her or she would have fallen.

"Are you wounded? Where have they hit you? Speak!" he asked hoarsely.

She was silent and hung more and more heavily on his arm. Pressing her to himself as they galloped, he gasped and whispered:

"For God's sake! Just a word! What's the matter with you?"

But neither word nor groan did he hear from the speechless Aksinia.

Some two miles outside the village he turned sharply off the road, made towards a ravine, dismounted, and lifted Aksinia off the horse, gently laying her on the ground.

He removed her warm jacket, tore the thin cotton blouse and shirt at her breast, and groped for the wound. The bullet had entered her body through the left shoulder-blade, shattering the bone and emerging obliquely below the right collar-bone. With blood-stained, trembling hands he took his field dressing and a clean undershirt from his saddlebag. He raised Aksinia, put his knee behind her back, and began to bandage the wound, trying to stanch the blood spirting out below the collar-bone. The pieces of shirt and bandage were swiftly darkened and soaked. Blood was even flowing from her half-open mouth, and it bubbled and gurgled in her throat. And, going numb with horror, he realized that it was all over, that the most terrible thing that could happen in his life had already happened.

Down the steep slope, down a little path trodden out in the grass and sprinkled with meadow saxifrage, he cautiously made his way into the ravine, carrying Aksinia in his arms. Her helplessly hanging head lay on his shoulder. He heard her whistling, sobbing breath and felt the warm blood leaving her body and flowing out of her mouth on to his chest. The two horses followed him down into the ravine. Snorting, clanking their bits, they began to chew the juicy grass.

She died in his arms a little before dawn. She did not recover consciousness. He silently kissed her on her lips, which were cold and salty with blood, carefully lowered her to the grass, and rose. Some unknown force struck him on the chest, and he fell, dropping on his back; but he at once jumped to his feet in terror. He fell yet again, painfully striking his bare head on a stone. Then, without rising from his knees, he drew his sabre from its scabbard and began

to dig a grave. The earth was damp and soft. He worked with great
haste, but a choking feeling clutched his throat, and to breathe more
easily he tore open the shirt at his neck. The early morning freshness
chilled his sweaty breast, and then he found it not so hard to work.
He dug out the earth with his hands and his sabre, not resting a moment; but while he was digging a grave to the depth of his waist,
much time passed.

Gregor buried his Aksinia by the brilliant morning light. As she
lay in the grave he folded her deathly pale, yet swarthy arms across
her chest and covered her face with her kerchief, so that the earth
should not fill her glazing, half-open eyes as they gazed immovably
at the sky. Then he took his farewell of her, firmly believing that
they would not be separated for long.

With his palms he diligently pressed down the damp yellow clay
over the mound and remained long on his knees beside the grave,
his head bowed, his body swaying a little.

Now he had nothing to hurry for. Everything was finished.

The sun rose above the ravine through the smoky haze of the
burning wind from the east. Its rays silvered the mass of grey hair
on Gregor's head and slipped over his pale and terribly immobile
face. As though awaking from an oppressive sleep, he raised his
head and saw above him the black sky and the blindingly glittering,
black disk of the sun.

a complete end for Gregor

Chapter 9

In the early spring, when the snow vanishes and the grass which had
been buried under it during the winter begins to dry, fires break out
in the steppe. Flames driven by the wind fly along in streams,
greedily consuming the dry foxtail grass, leaping over the lofty stalks
of the thistle-grass, slipping across the brown heads of the mugwort,
spreading out in the hollows. And afterwards the acrid, burning
smell of charred and cracked earth hangs about the steppe. All
around, the young grass is showing merrily green, innumerable sky-

larks are fluttering in the azure heaven above, migrant geese are feeding on the nourishing herbage, and the bustards are settling for the summer and building their nests. But wherever the steppe fires have passed, the dead, charred earth blackens ominously. No birds nest on it, the animals pass round it, and only the wind, winged and swift, flies across it, carrying the dove-grey ash and the dark, pungent dust far over the steppe.

Like the steppe scorched with fires, Gregor's life also turned black. He had been deprived of everything which was dear to his heart. Pitiless death had taken everything from him, had destroyed everything. Only the children were left. But he himself still clung convulsively to the earth, as though his broken life was in very deed of some value to himself and others.

After burying Aksinia he wandered aimlessly about the steppe for three days; but he rode neither home nor to Vieshenska to make his act of submission. On the fourth day, abandoning the horses in one of the villages of the Ust-Khopersk district, he crossed the Don and made his way on foot to the Slashchevsky oak forest, on the fringe of which the Fomin band had first been shattered in the previous April. Even then, in April, he had heard that deserters had settled in the forest. And to them he went, for he had no desire to return to Fomin.

For several days he wandered about the enormous forest. He was tortured with hunger, but he could not bring himself to go to any human habitation. With the death of Aksinia he had lost his native wit and his former daring. The snap of a breaking twig, a rustle in the dense forest, the cry of a night bird, all reduced him to terror and dismay. He lived on the unripe fruits of wild strawberries, tiny wild mushrooms, the leaves of hazel bushes, and grew terribly emaciated. At the close of the fifth day deserters found him in the forest and took him to their dug-out.

There were seven of them. They were all inhabitants of local villages and had settled in the forest in the autumn of the previous year, to avoid being mobilized. In their spacious dug-out they lived as comfortably as at home, and had need of hardly anything. At night they often went off to visit their families, bringing back rusks, millet, bread, flour, and potatoes. And they had no difficulty in obtaining meat for stewing from villages where they were not known, by occasionally stealing a sheep.

One of the deserters, who had served in the 12th Cossack Regiment, recognized Gregor, and they accepted him in their midst without any great wrangling.

He lost count of the tormentingly endless days. He lived somehow or other in the forest until October, but when the autumn rains set in, and then the cold weather, a longing for his children, for his native village, awoke with new and unexpected strength within him.

To kill time he sat for days on end on his plank bed, carving spoons out of wood, hollowing out dishes, dexterously fashioning toy figures of people and animals from soft stone. He tried not to think of anything and not to let the venomous longing find its way to his heart. During the daytime he succeeded, but through the long winter nights the yearning engendered of his memories overwhelmed him. He tossed long and long on the pallet and could not get to sleep. In the daytime none of the other inhabitants of the dug-out heard a word of complaint from him; but at night he frequently awoke trembling and, passing his hand over his face, found his cheeks and his dense six months' growth of beard wet with tears.

He often dreamed of the children, of Aksinia, his mother, and all his other dear ones who were no longer among the living. All his life lay in the past; but the past seemed a brief and fretful sleep. "Just to see the old spots once more, to feast my eyes on the children; and then I can die," he often thought.

One day in the early spring Chumakov unexpectedly turned up. He was wet to the waist, and as cheery and fidgety as ever. After drying his clothes by the fire and getting warm, he sat down on the pallet beside Gregor.

"We've done a bit of wandering, Melekhov, since you left us. We've been almost to Astrakhan, and in the Kalmyk steppe. . . . We've travelled over the wide world! And the blood we've shed— there's no reckoning it! The Reds took Yakov Yefimovich's wife as a hostage and confiscated his property, but he went mad and gave orders that everybody who served the Soviet régime was to be killed. And we began to kill them all off: teachers and doctors and agricultural instructors. . . . The devil knows whom we didn't kill!

But now they've finished us, and completely," he said, sighing and bristling still more with cold. "We were shattered close to Tishanska the first time, and then again near Solony a week ago. We were hemmed in on three sides at night; they left us only one way out up a hill, and there the snow was lying up to the horses' bellies. They opened fire with machine-guns at dawn, and that was the beginning of the end. They mowed us all down with machine-guns. Fomin's young son and I are the only two who escaped. He—Fomin I mean—had taken his son Davidka about with him ever since autumn. Yakov Yefimovich himself was killed. . . . I saw him killed with my own eyes. The first bullet hit him in the leg and smashed his kneecap, the second struck him a glancing blow on the head. Three times he fell from his horse. We stopped and picked him up and seated him in his saddle, but he would ride on a little way and then fall again. The third bullet got him; it hit him in the side. And then we had to leave him. When I had galloped a little way I looked back, and two horsemen were already slashing him with their sabres as he lay. . . ."

"Well, and that's how it was bound to be," Gregor said unconcernedly.

Chumakov spent the night in the dug-out, and in the morning said good-bye.

"Where are you off to?" Gregor asked.

Smiling, Chumakov answered:

"To look for an easy life. Perhaps you'll come with me?"

"No, you go off by yourself."

"You're right, I couldn't live with you. Your craft is carving cups and spoons, and that's not in my line," Chumakov said derisively. He took off his cap and bowed: "God save you, peaceable brigands, for your hospitality and shelter. May God grant you a merry life, for you're having a boring time here! You live in the forest, and d'you call that life?"

After Chumakov's departure Gregor lived another week in the forest, then made ready to depart.

"Going home?" one of the deserters asked him.

And, for the first time during all his stay in the dug-out, Gregor smiled, very faintly. "Yes, going home."

"You should wait till spring. They'll give us an amnesty for May Day, and then we'll all go home."

"No, I can't wait," Gregor answered, and he said good-bye.

Next morning he drew near to the Don opposite Tatarsk. He stood gazing at his native yard, turning pale with the excitement of his joy. Then he slipped off his rifle, took out the shreds of hemp he used for cleaning it, and his little bottle of machine-oil, and for some reason counted his cartridges. He had twelve clips and twenty-six loose bullets.

Below the cliff the ice had retreated from the edge. The translucent green water was splashing and breaking away the needly ice along the bank. Gregor threw his rifle and pistol into the Don, then poured his cartridges after them and wiped his hands thoroughly on the edge of his greatcoat.

Below the village he crossed the Don over the blue, half-thawed, and pitted March ice and went with long strides towards his hut. When he was still some distance away he saw Mishatka on the slope leading down to the landing-stage and could hardly keep himself from running to the lad.

Mishatka was breaking off the icicles hanging from a stone, throwing them down the slope, and watching fixedly as the blue fragments went rolling.

Gregor went along to the slope and, panting, hoarsely called his son:

"Mishenka! Little son!"

Mishatka glanced at him in terror and dropped his eyes. He guessed that this bearded and terrible-looking man was his father.

All the gentle and tender words which Gregor had whispered, as night after night in the oak forest he recalled his children, now fled from his memory. Dropping down on his knees, kissing his son's rosy, cold little hands, in a choking voice he uttered only the words:

"Little son. . . . Little son. . . ."

Then he took his son by the hand. Gazing greedily with dry, ecstatically burning eyes into the boy's face, he asked:

"How are you all? How's Aunty, Poliushka—are they alive and well?"

Still not looking at his father, Mishatka quietly answered:

"Aunty Dunia's well, but Poliushka died in the autumn—of diphtheria. And Uncle Mikhail's a soldier. . . ."

And now that little thing of which Gregor had dreamed during so many sleepless nights had come to pass. He stood at the gate of his own home, holding his son by the hands.

This was all life had left to him, all that for a little longer gave him kinship with the earth and with the spacious world which lay glittering under the chilly sun.

ABOUT THE AUTHOR

MIKHAIL SHOLOKHOV was born in 1905 in a village in the Don region, of a family that had been living there for many generations. Despite poverty, he was able to attend school in Moscow. At the age of fifteen he returned to his native village to become a schoolteacher, then a statistician, a food inspector, and held various other jobs.

He began writing when he was eighteen years old. Today he is the Soviet Union's most famous and widely honored living novelist. *The Don Flows Home to the Sea* was not finished until 1939. It appeared in the United States in 1940. Although complete in itself, it carries to conclusion the story begun in *And Quiet Flows the Don* (available in Vintage Books), which appeared in the Soviet Union in 1928 and in the United States in 1934. Together the two books are often referred to under the title *The Silent Don*. Other volumes by Sholokhov that have been translated into English are *Harvest on the Don*, *Seeds of Tomorrow*, and *Tales of the Don*.

In 1965 Mr. Sholokhov was awarded the Nobel Prize for Literature.

VINTAGE POLITICAL SCIENCE
AND SOCIAL CRITICISM

VINTAGE HISTORY AND CRITICISM OF
LITERATURE, MUSIC, AND ART

A SELECT LIST OF
VINTAGE RUSSIAN LIBRARY

VINTAGE WORKS OF SCIENCE
AND PSYCHOLOGY